17 avril 1847.—

of December, one
—ed and forty five

LOUIS

Par la Grâce de Dieu, Roi de France
de Navarre, à tous présents et à venir Salut

Faisons Savoir que

Pardevant M⁰. pierre Jean Bapt
Cocque, notaire Royal pour le Cantone d
Bacqueville, à la résidence de Bacqueville
Fut Présent, la Dame
Nora Stevenson, demeurant —

Bucquet, comma or animal matter, vegetable or—
and which to whatever depth is contaminated by faecal or animal matter, refuse or insanitary, fill
sheds or by animal refuse of any kind or by anything liable to be, or to become in time, offensive or insani—
in with clean, sound earth the cavities thus formed, ramming down and levelling it until it will bear without
sinking further such weights as are shown in the drawings to be placed upon it during the course of erection,

3. Provide the sum of £20£ for digging trial holes where directed by the Engineer, protect them by rails so as to prevent
accident, and finally fill them with lime concrete.
— — — as in all cases to go down to a solid stratum approved by the Engineer (whether such stratum is to
— that shown by the drawings for foundations, and any variation in the depth of
— — require shall be measured and valued

Sheet 4

Britannia Bridge :- Complete Specification

15 The Contractor will not be at liberty to dig on the site for sand and gravel, or other materials. But if any which, in the
Engineer's opinion, are suitable for the purpose of this contract should occur in the necessary excavations, the contractor will be
allowed to use them for the purposes of this contract as far as they may go.

CONCRETE

1. The Portland cement used in the structural concrete (viz: foundations, walls, and floors) is to be highly burnt and of best quality
approved by the Engineer, and free from lime, slag, dust, or other foreign materials. The cement, when neat, must not set in less
than thirty minutes, and is to be ground so fine that the residue on a sieve of seventy-six meshes each way to the linear inc
shall not exceed one tenth part of the whole by weight. The cement is not to weigh less than 110 lb. avoirdupois per strike—
bushel, unless herein permitted.
2. Cement concrete is to be deposited as soon as it is mixed.
3. Where the concrete is not in excess of 12ft in depth, the entire depth is to be deposited at one operation.

Messrs N. Chambers & C⁰., Dowgate
London

Please pay Yorkshire Banking C⁰ at 9 Westbar, Leeds (on Williams, Deacon, & C⁰.) at sight
the sum of 5000l (five thousand pounds) and debit my acct with the same.

John Stevenson

dated this Tuesday, 11 May, 1847

The RICH ARE WITH YOU ALWAYS

The
ARE WITH

Malcolm Macdonald

RICH
YOU ALWAYS

Alfred A. Knopf   *New York*   *1976*

This is a Borzoi Book
published by Alfred A. Knopf, Inc.

Copyright © 1976 by Malcolm Macdonald
All rights reserved under International and Pan-American Copyright Conventions.
Published in the United States by Alfred A. Knopf, Inc., New York, and
simultaneously in Canada by Random House of Canada Limited, Toronto.
Distributed by Random House, Inc., New York.

LIBRARY OF CONGRESS CATALOGING IN PUBLICATION DATA
Macdonald, Malcolm, [date] The rich are with you always.
I. Title.
PZ4.M13485Ri   [PR6063.A1692]   823'.9'14   76–13702
ISBN 0–394–49850–X

Manufactured in the United States of America
First American Edition

For Ingrid
True Wealth

PART ONE

Thorpe Old Manor, 1845

Chapter 1

Beador was desperate for money. That ought to have made negotiations simple. Sir George Beador wanted money; and John Stevenson wanted land. Specifically, he wanted twenty acres near Stockton on the river Tees, the best place in the whole country, he decided, for a small iron foundry and smelting works. Sir George Beador had land in Stockton, and John had money in the bank. Yet the negotiations were not proving at all simple.

You're a liar, John thought. *And not even a good liar.*

The young baronet's frank, blue, uncaring eyes wavered as if he read John's thoughts.

"See here, Stevenson," he blustered. "I'm putting land into this partnership." He was shivering, as if his sincerity had already been challenged. "Land!" He repeated the word, making it sound like "blood." John could see him trying to say "good land" but the words stuck in his throat.

"And therefore?" John prompted.

"Well . . . I mean to say. Just as land conveys certain privileges in life—privileges that mere money can never purchase—don't ye think it should convey the same sort of privilege in business, too?"

John pretended to consider this nonsense while he wondered what lay behind it. Sir George was trying to distract his attention from something. But from what? Nasty, uncharitable suspicions were already forming in his mind. He hoped he was wrong. In a curious way, he almost liked Sir George—an amateur swindler who had not even practised how to lie convincingly. It touched some reserve of sympathy within him.

One end of a burning log fell onto the hearth. Sir George rose and pulled the bell chain; then he stood looking directly down at the burning wood. The smoke rising from it made him cough. Even his coughing lacked conviction. It sounded like a smothered laugh.

Wheezing, Sir George crossed to the tall French window. His water-filled eyes trembled. The sky beyond was a uniform leaden gray, and from it fell a steady rain, warm for early February. While his breath returned, he looked morosely out. "They'll find nothing today. We had the best of it this morning."

Fleetingly John thought of Nora, still out there somewhere amid the weather; if they had found, she'd be up among the leaders, no matter how strange the country or how cunning the fox. Yet how she'd love to be here, too. She'd soon run Sir George Beador to a standstill. And she'd stay to see him broken.

A footman came in and, without a word, rebuilt the fire. He did not look at Sir George, and Sir George did not even notice him.

"But you've said you're willing to pay me ten thousand pounds for the land," Sir George wheedled. "Surely you'd not go back on your word!"

John, counting silently to retain his patience, looked around the room at the books of polished leather and soft suede, warm by the firelight in their tall glass cases. The man was not the fool he seemed. It would pay to remember that. "I will offer ten thousand to secure the land *and* your partnership. You know the value of your name around Stockton. And elsewhere. Subtract that from ten thousand and you have the price of your land."

Sir George turned toward him at last. John could not read his face against the brightness of the window, but the voice was cold and morose. "Money! Even one's name is negotiable nowadays."

"Be thankful for that," John said.

Sir George laughed. "Aye," he agreed. "I'll not deny it." He came and sat by the fire, cheerful again. The mud that had earlier fallen from his boots crunched on the polished floor. "Should get out of these wet things. I'll regret it."

John smiled. Sir George looked at him and chuckled, an echo of his earlier laugh. "That's a smug sort of a smile, Stevenson," he said. "You've no cause for it, I may say. You may be dry but you stink of that wretched mackintosh stuff."

Sir George would not risk such warmth unless he felt he had somehow mastered this discussion. It was the moment of overconfidence for which John had been waiting.

"Not *railway* shares, is it, Beador?" he asked, his voice suddenly crisp and brutal. "Not been speculating there?"

Sir George's immature cunning could not withstand such an assault. His eyes registered shock, fear, guilt, confusion, and finally anger at having registered anything at all.

"Dammit, Stevenson!" he said.

"What have you applied for?" John did not relent.

"I've been allotted nothing." Sir George Beador regained some of his composure. But it was too late. The mask had slipped, and all the truculence and all the cold blue blood he could muster would never divert John Stevenson from pursuing this particular inquiry to its end, however many weeks or months it might take.

"But you have applied?"

Sir George looked sharply at him, offended.

"As a partner, I'd have to know," John said. "I'd be liable for any debt of yours."

Sir George lowered his eyes; his shoulders slumped. "Damn complicated," he said to the palms of his hands.

"I must know. Before we engage in any deed."

"I'll draw up a list," Sir George said. His interest in his hands was now intense, making it difficult for John to persist.

The distant clatter of hooves on sodden gravel announced the return of the rest of the party. It annoyed John; his whole purpose in leaving the field early had been to settle this partnership once and for all. If only Sir George would behave rationally, like a man needing money, instead of with this boyish mixture of dumb cunning and frosty indifference.

Sir George looked up the avenue and rubbed his hands gladly; for him the returning riders were a rescue party. John kicked a dead ember back into the grate and left the room. A more open show of his annoyance would achieve nothing.

His way out lay through the gun room, then down the passage to the north wing, which flanked the stable yard. This wing was, in fact, the remains of an H-shaped Tudor manor—or I-shaped, to keep the convention that puts north at the top. The passage was the crossbar, but where the southern wing had once stood there was now a large square block built in Georgian stone. Its full three stories laid a permanent shadow over the two humbler floors of the old red-brick manor, now called the north wing.

A large weeping ash dominated the stable yard. Through its tired branches, gleaming in the rain, he saw the riders, some still mounted. The grooms stood waiting to take their charges. He knew at once that they had broken up a fox; why else would people soaked to the skin, weary from a day's hard riding over drenched fields through Hertfordshire gravel and clay, slip so jauntily down, pat their horses' flanks and necks so heartily, and laugh and chatter with such gusto? Vapour from the horses hung above the group, rising with their laughter.

The last to dismount was Nora, savouring the chase to its uttermost moment. In that brief supremacy her eyes raked around the yard until they fell on John, still sheltering from the rain under the canopy of the

Tudor door. The radiance of her smile banished all trace of his annoyance; for a moment their eyes dwelled, each in the other's. He smiled reassuringly, conveying no more than a welcome. Already he could imagine the questions lining up in that part of her mind closest to speech—Had Sir George agreed? What were the terms? What was the extent of his debt? She would put them into words soon enough. And what would he tell her? That Sir George Beador had gone to earth—to a very foul-smelling earth? She hitched up her habit and ran to him through the pendant branches of the ash, reaching the nearer cobbles in a star-burst of rain droplets shaken from its glistening twigs. "We saw blood. There were only six on terms at the end," she said. Rivers of rain gleamed on her skin. An intoxicant steam curled from her sodden clothing.

He grasped her outstretched arms and turned her gently in a half circle, as in a stately dance. "And you among them, I know," he said.

She grinned, breathed happily in, and nodded. The rest of the party now began walking more slowly toward them.

"Missed a slashing good trot, Stevenson," Dalgliesh called; he was a captain in the Greys, a friend of Sir George's younger brother. The others, knowing how shallow was John's love of the chase, laughed.

"I was well represented, I think," he answered.

*   *   *

Sir George, despite the protests of Mrs. Lambourne, his housekeeper, had put the Stevensons in the main guest suite, over the ballroom on the south of the house. All the other guests were of higher rank—indeed, as John had been no more than a railway navvy only six or seven years earlier, it would be hard *not* to be. It was Sir George's none-too-subtle way of stressing how important Stevenson was to him at this moment; it was also, John was sure, Sir George's highly subtle way of blackmailing him—saying, in effect: See how many friends I will slight for the sake of John Stevenson.

Nora had not needed to have all this explained to her. As soon as Mrs. Lambourne had left them alone, having pointedly announced that this was the principal suite, Nora had laughed, with more pity than humour, at the transparency of it. "We'll plug that gun for him," she said. "Behave as if it was no less than our due."

Only Mrs. Lambourne had seemed disappointed at their cool acceptance of the honour.

Now John left Nora to change from her soaking habit and take a bath, while he did his daily correspondence with his deputies, partners, and subcontractors. In railways alone he was laying about 600 miles of road that year, including Berwick–Edinburgh, York–Scarborough, Faversham–Margate, and, for Brunel, a stretch of the new atmospheric railway from Exeter to beyond Teignmouth. He had many other contracts, too: a foundry and some back-to-back housing at Holbeck, just south of Leeds; some harbour works at Newcastle and more at Stockton; some wharfs at Teignmouth; and about fifteen acres of mills and housing in Warrington.

Often he thought back with something close to nostalgia to the days when he had had just one or two contracts to oversee—when sometimes an entire week would pass without a single important problem or setback. Now not a day went by without news through the mails of at least one headache. A quaking bog in the Vale of York. An uncharted subterranean river in Warrington. Nondelivery of the atmospheric tube at Exeter. A scarcity of brick at Stockton, where frost and floods were making the local clay beds unworkable. One needed good partners and smart deputies to work so many contracts at once. Yet he would rather cope with a hundred such troubles, even by mail, than with a single George Beador or his grubby kind.

"I sh'll go back to Yorkshire tomorrow," he called through the open door to the dressing room, where one of the maids was helping Nora to dress. To his surprise the door was slowly closed against him, making further talk impossible. He shrugged and returned to his letters.

Now and then he heard Nora and the maid giggling, and when, at last, she came into the room, he saw her eyes gleaming with the promise of a secret to unfold. The heady, damp smell of her was gone.

"That Kitty," she said when the maid left the room, "has been here more than ten years."

"Oh?"

"She has. That's before Sir George bought this place from—you'll never guess who from."

John thought hard; the vaguest memory of some useless information stirred. "He was a merchant in the Russian trade. Someone on the Baltic Exchange?"

"But his name. His name was Thornton."

John frowned in disbelief. "Not—no, surely not—not connected with *our* Thornton! Dear Walter?"

"His uncle!"

"I don't believe it!"

"It's true. She's just told me it all. . . ."

"The uncle who brought him up! When he was made an orphan?"
The story, as Walter had told it to them—it must have been five years
since, sometime in 1840—began to come back to him.

"That's the one," Nora said. "They took a plunge in forty-three.
This place changed hands then. Kitty stayed on."

Her slow, salacious grin infected him. He took her hand and led
her to the sofa in the bay window. "So she knew our Walter when he
was a lad," he prompted.

"In the most biblical sense!" Nora laughed.

"She told you that?" He was astonished.

"I had to get it out of her. But she wasn't that unwilling, not once
she'd started to talk. He was even worse here, I think, than when we
knew him."

They both laughed again—a little longer and more heartily than
the situation might seem to warrant. Walter Thornton was a subject of
some delicacy between them. Almost six years ago, Nora, then destitute
and tramping from Manchester to Leeds, had sold herself to this Walter
for a few shillings—though, as it turned out, he had eventually given
her a sovereign. A casual suggestion of Walter's had led to her meeting with John, who was then at the very start of his astonishing rise
from being a navvy to becoming one of the foremost contractors in
England—indeed, in the world. John had always known of that transaction between Nora and Walter, yet, though he had never reproached
her, she was never easy in Walter's presence, and she was always a little
too brazen, too cool, when the talk turned to what they politely called
Walter's "Irish toothache"—for Thornton, as the navvies bluntly said,
always carried four spare pricks in his purse.

"I had to tell her a thing or two about his goings on since we
knew him. To get her talking."

"Not . . . ?" he asked.

"Of course not!" She was annoyed he could even think it. "Just
him and that halfwit wench on the canal bank. And the goings on with
that skinny servant girl up in Carlisle—things like that."

She was smiling again. "Go on," he said. "What did Kitty say?"

She looked around, as if for eavesdroppers, before she began, in a
low voice full of gossipy complicity. "He used to . . ." She got no
further, but covered her face and laughed. "It's awful," she said. "I
shouldn't be telling you, really."

He did not reward her with any display of his impatience.

"She says he never left the servant girls alone. He was always hanging about the rooms, trying to lift their skirts while they worked. He

was fierce to get it always, she said. Mind you, I think she was more than half willing, was Kitty. I fancy she's a right little cleaver."

"Why?"

"She said he used to *catch* her in the garden room, which is at the far end of the north wing from here. Well, you couldn't be taken by surprise there, could you? Just imagine it. No matter what direction anyone came from, you'd get good warning. I think she has her heels lightened all right."

"How old was he then?"

"Once he came about her *five* times in one day, she said. He let out he was sick, when the family went away out calling and left him, which they usually did. He often used to say he was sick then, and go to bed, and get cordials brought up."

"By Kitty?"

"Well, she wouldn't volunteer, would she? Not if she wasn't willing. She tried to talk like she hated it and only did it for fear of dismissal."

"I should think he *was* sick after that. Five times!"

Nora laughed again. "Aye! She said it didn't take much pretence when the rest came back. He looked like a second helping of death. But next day he was harder than ever for it. She said from the time he was sixteen he had every below-stairs and every above-stairs unmarried female. As often as they'd let him. Also a retired cook above sixty who came back to see the family and had just been widowed."

"A good chance," John said judiciously. "Thornton would know that."

"She was only here the one afternoon, but he followed her out, up the road, and took her into a field. Over sixty!" She shook her head.

He reached his arm around her. "Thou'll be over sixty one day, see thee." He put his lips to her ear. "And I sh'll still crave after thee."

She grazed her ear on his moustache and shivered, serious now. "Nay," she said softly, dropping back into dialect, too. "Leave off with thee!" But despite this verbal rejection, she did not repel his caresses. The Walter Thornton catharsis was over—until the next time.

Far out over the park the sun slipped below the pall of raincloud, moments before it set. In that brief interval it suffused the canopy of unrelieved grey with a raw, burning red.

"Look at that," John said. "Promises fair tomorrow."

"Talking of promises fair," Nora said, her eyes baleful with the borrowed fire, "what of our host?"

John sighed. "You are sure we need to go into ironfounding?" he asked. He did not want to tell her yet how inconclusive his talk with Sir George had been. Nor did he want to confess that he felt threatened in some obscure way by the very idea of partnership with the man.

She bit her lip. "You speak as though it was me forcing us to it."

He did not answer. She pulled away from him then and grasped his arms, compelling him to face her. "It's our business," she said. "Not me."

He nodded, still unhappy.

"I'm not often wrong in these things," she said.

He smiled then. "That's the annoying part. You're never wrong." He touched her forehead gently. "I trust that instinct. Never fear I don't."

"Yet you hesitate."

He pulled down the corners of his mouth, ruefully. "I think you and Chambers with your ledgers and balances don't see the half of it."

"What half?" She was not belligerent or challenging. She knew too well that the financial insight which had grown during the years she had spent in managing their books was only one small element in their business.

"Trouble like Sir George Beador, for a start," he said. If only he could put his disquiet into words!

"Drop him! We only took him up to get land and influence cheap. But we don't *need* either. Not cheap. It's only our greed."

He shook his head. "We must build in Stockton. We both agree it's the best place in the whole kingdom. And we can't build there without Beador. Not now we've taken him up. We can't afford to make an enemy of him. But"—he waved Sir George away to a distant horizon— "that's not the real worry. It's the *permanence* of a foundry, d'ye see? Till now we've had nothing that's permanent. Not even the depots. It's what I'm used to. I'm a travelling man. But with a foundry we'll have static plant, a fixed gang of workers. . . ." He laid his fist heavily on the sill at each item. "Offices. Staff. Fixed deliveries. Orders. Supply troubles. Labour troubles. It's not—my skill, *my* instinct, it doesn't run that way."

"You've never been one to turn from troubles. Not profitable ones."

"Aye." He laughed. "I'm as keen on profit as the next man." He pinched her cheek lightly. "And as the next woman, too, belike. So I sh'll do it. I shall build. All I'm saying is, don't think that because your books say it's one-tenth of our assets, this new foundry's going to be only one-tenth of our troubles."

His answer pleased her. He had never committed himself so fully to the idea of going into ironfounding; until now he had always called his talks with Beador mere "soundings." She did not again raise her unanswered question about Sir Geoige.

"By the way," he called to her as he was dressing. "I'll likely see Thornton next week. Down in Exeter. I've heard Brunel's asked him to take over daily charge down there."

"Well," she said. "I don't expect we shall ever escape him." But she barely thought of Walter Thornton; instead she wondered what dismal things John had discovered about Sir George—things that had made him lay such an elaborate false trail for her as his own alleged fear of possessing one small factory.

Chapter 2

When the ladies killed that day's fox for the fourth time since dinner, Nora thought it a good occasion to leave them. On her way to the door Hetty Beador, Sir George's sister, beckoned to her.

"If you really are intending to leave tomorrow, Mrs. Stevenson," she said, barely above a whisper, so that Nora had to lean close, "Madame Rodet is in the library. I know she has something particular to say to you."

Nora thanked her and looked uncertainly at the two doors she might use, one leading through the hall, the other through the ball-room. "Take the candle on the bureau," Miss Beador said. "That will light you through the ballroom."

Nora stepped tentatively into the great, dark chamber, where every-thing was kept shrouded except at the big festivities. *Now, if this were my room*, she thought, beginning a favourite game. But a roar of laugh-ter from the gentlemen, still at their port, interrupted her. She did two solemn steps from a waltz, being careful with the candle flame, and then began to wonder what Madame Rodet could want.

Rodet was the ironfounder who had supplied rail for part of the Paris–Rouen line, which John had partnered the great Thomas Brassey in building back in 1841. Since the coming of the railways to France, Rodet had prospered. Beginning as a small, well-established *patron* of the third or fourth generation, he had in less than ten years become one of his country's foremost ironmasters. How he had come to know Sir George Beador, she had not yet learned; but she knew it was Rodet who had put Sir George up to this notion of investing in ironfounding as a way of making more money than his rents and bonds could fetch in. And it was Rodet, too, who had suggested John Stevenson as a likely partner. He had even been here on their arrival at Maran Hill to introduce John and herself to the Beadors; but he had left for France within the hour.

"He doesn't want to get caught between us until things are settled," John said.

Nora could not see that that was a complete explanation.

Madame Rodet had stayed on to enjoy a fortnight with the Hertfordshire and the Puckeridge, for Sir George hunted with both packs. She was the sort of follower Nora had little time for. She rode well enough, very correctly, but she didn't *go*. She was content to drop behind the field early in a chase and was delighted at every check, when she would mill around with the At Home crowd and lose all interest in the hunt itself. In short, she hunted merely in order to ride. Nora, thinking they had little in common, looked forward to their meeting with no very special interest.

At first she did not see Madame Rodet. But when the door latch sprang softly back into its mortice, part of what she had taken to be the upholstery of the high-back sofa moved. It was Madame's lace cap.

"Mrs. Stevenson," she called. "I hoped you would come." Her welcome was very warm; that and the charm of her accent made it hard for Nora to persist in her indifference.

"How do you see to embroider, just by the firelight!" Nora wondered aloud.

"Oh!" It was a Gallic laugh. "I can do it when I am sleeping even, you know." She patted the sofa beside her, next to the fire. "Please."

Nora put the candle on the table before them and sat. She shivered at the heat. "I didn't know how chill it had got."

"Tskoh!" Madame Rodet looked intensely at her, with a curious angry sympathy. She had a face like an eagle. "You must drink whisky. Yes. It's good."

Oh dear, Nora thought, realizing that the other had believed her to say she'd got a chill. Her heart sank at the prospect of the misunderstandings to come. "What are you making?" she asked.

Madame Rodet stabbed two more deft stitches in to complete one small leaf in a formal arrangement of peacocks and vines; the embroidery was barely begun, most of the design was still just pencilled in.

The more Nora looked at it, the more she marvelled at its intricacy. "Did you make all that up?" she asked.

"Oh no!" Madame Rodet laughed. "It's a copy. Of course. From the *moyen age*. The middle times." She pierced the twist of silk on to the edge of the design with the needle and put the frame aside. "Are they still killing the fox?" she asked, inclining her head back toward the drawing room.

Nora smiled. "Better each time. Each telling."

Madame Rodet looked sharply at her. "Strange isn't it, this word 'telling.' It was your name of—*demoiselle*. Your—"

"My maiden name," Nora said, surprised.

"Oh!" Madame Rodet was relieved. "You understand French!"

"No." Nora laughed. "But I do remember my maiden name. I was born Nora Telling. How did you know, Madame?"

"Mr. Stevenson, he told us. '*Racontant*'—oh, it's such a funnay name. For us it's quite strange. But for you not? *Racontant*. We cannot imagine it, you know."

"I wouldn't say it's very common."

"We have some neighbour, Tallien. He has much country. Oh, many farms. And when Mr. Stevenson was by us at Trouville, he heard this man, and the name Tallien, and it reminds him of you, Mrs. Stevenson. Tallien, Telling. You see."

"That's how you knew," Nora said. She grew dizzy trying to think back over the chain of nonsensicals that had led to this most trivial conclusion.

Madame Rodet was looking happily at the fire. "He has told you of La Gracieuse, M'sieu Jean?" she asked. Then, seeing Nora's bewilderment, she laughed, clutched at Nora's arm, and added: "Oh, I must tell you. We call him M'sieu Jean in Normandie. All his men, they call him Lord John. But he's not a lord. That's funnay. Did he tell you of La Gracieuse?"

"Your house in Normandy!" Nora said, understanding at last.

Madame Rodet looked at her uncertainly. "Our home," she corrected. "You say house? We have a house at St. Cloud, but La Gracieuse is our home."

"He said it was very beautiful."

They both looked at the fire for a while; Madame Rodet still clutched Nora's arm in her dry, cool fingers. "And very welcoming," Nora added. "I know he enjoyed his stay with you."

"You shall see," she said, as if to herself. Then she turned and added urgently, "Soon."

Nora did not know what to make of it. Madame Rodet's intonation was so un-English as to turn perfectly ordinary remarks into oracular pronouncements. "He's often spoken of France," Nora said. "Now we've got the Rouen–Havre contract, he'll be going back there quite often."

"You will come too this time. You will stay at La Gracieuse and you will see Normandie. La Basse Normandie—the Pays d'Auge, you know, it's very typical for us. And you can even speak a little French perhaps. *Peut-être.* You will see. *Peut-être.*"

Five years of careful observation and tireless rehearsal had left Nora able to cope with every social occasion she was likely to meet. But this casual invitation, delivered in the manner of a fortune teller, was beyond that competence. In her bewilderment, all she could do was to ask a question that had occurred to her earlier when she had mentioned the Rouen–Havre contract: "Are you supplying the rail? For this new work?"

But Madame Rodet seemed not to hear. Eagerly she searched Nora's eyes for an acceptance. "Oh, it will be such fun!" she said. "Spring in Normandie, you know, is very beautiful. I don't know about the rail; that's Rodet's affairs. Also you can invite your brother, M'sieu Samuel."

At once Nora was alert and attentive. Sam was supposed to be a secret. "You know of Sam, Madame?"

For a moment only, Madame Rodet looked uncomfortable. "Oh, it's so fun*nay*. For us. So English."

"You know that Sam is in service?"

"In France it does not matter. We have *égalité*. All are *égales*. I call my cook 'Madame.' In England it is so . . . you are all . . ." She craned her neck like a giraffe and waved her hands dismissively at the world beneath her chin: "Oh, don't show me all that. Pfff! I don't wish to see."

Her enthusiasm to make her point had led her unwittingly to slight Nora, who now said, quietly, "I make no secret, Madame Rodet, of the fact that circumstance once left me destitute. I was barefoot when I first met Mr. Stevenson. And he was then a navvy ganger."

Madame Rodet quickly realized where she had trodden and, parodying horror and remorse to the point of comedy, interrupted before Nora could encourage herself to become pompous. "Oh, of course. Of course. That's so right. For you, you must be proud. And these English—it's so sill*ay*. But"—she looked crafty—"for them to know that your brother is in service—it's bad for business. Yes?"

"Yes," Nora agreed, smiling despite herself.

"So then! You are right. It's right to keep it secret!" She spoke with a sort of wounded triumph, as if she had just proved that Nora had agreed with her all along—making Nora's quiet reprimand now seem petulant. "But in France it does not matter. M'sieu Sam will be an English milord."

The thought intrigued Nora. It had been very hard to meet Sam—increasingly hard as the years and the Stevensons' success widened the social gulf between them.

"You understand, Madame, that Sam is still in service at his own wish. Stevenson has offered him . . ."

Madame Rodet waved away the explanation and smiled.

Nora thought of Sam. How he would love to play the milord; he would do it well, too. The idea began to take root.

Her amusement must have shown in her face for Madame Rodet pushed her arm lightly and said: "You see. It's good. We will have much fun."

Nora laughed then. "I think we shall," she said. "I've never had such an invitation."

Chapter 3

The train slowed almost to a halt before it coasted under the great Gothic arch that had recently been cut through the city wall. Night had already fallen but the arch intensified the dark still further. Nora pressed herself into John's arms and said, "Home!"

"Give or take an hour." He folded his arms around her. All the muscle his years of navvying had put upon him was still there.

"York," she said. "York is Yorkshire, and Yorkshire's home."

"Home is where the contract is," he said with mock severity.

She butted him sharply in the chest with the back of her head. He pretended lethargically to be hurt and then yawned. "We need exercise," he said. "Being cooped in all day."

"I'm not walking to Thorpe!"

"We could walk the last mile or so. Send the coach on. In fact, I think I will."

"With all our baggage we'll probably have to walk up Garraby Hill anyway."

Folds, the stationmaster, was waiting for them on the platform, an old acquaintance by now. He never failed to greet their arrival when he knew they were travelling. As soon as they had moved to Thorpe, in 1842, George Hudson, the Railway King as they called him, had insisted on giving John all the privileges of a director, and in York, Hudson's word was railway law. It meant, among other things, that they travelled in a private rail carriage and, at their destination, could command the service of the company's coach and horses if any were free.

"I have the big coach with three ready for you, Mr. Stevenson, sir," Folds said. "I fancied you might have more bags than usual."

The coachman's imitation of sobriety was so laborious that they had to bundle quickly aboard for fear he would see their laughter and take offence.

"Er . . ." Folds stuck his head through the door. "He's a good lad is Ironside, drunk or sober. But I'll put another on, if ye wish."

"Nay," John said. "He's taken me that many times drunk, I've forgotten what he's like sober. He'll sleep in our stables tonight. We'll top him up for breakfast and see he sets off westward."

Nora laughed and Folds patted John's thigh. Then Ironside's gruff *haaa!* to the team almost dashed him to the ground. Nora was still laughing as they turned from Tanner Row into Hudson Street. At the corner north of the station and in the shade of the wall, a large vacant lot came into view.

"Know what that ground is?" John asked. "I only learned the other week."

"What?"

"The cholera burial ground from the 1832 outbreak."

Nora held her breath as she looked out.

"There's talk now of new sewers," John said. "Lots of towns. That's something we should look at. Sewerage contracts. Brassey thinks there could be a lot in it."

"Do sewers use iron pipe?" Nora asked, turning away from the window.

Now it was he who laughed. "Top o' the class for persistence," he said wearily.

She wished he would either say yes or no about the ironworks. Since meeting Beador he seemed to have gone back on his commitment.

Out in Micklegate she looked back at all the fine town houses of the last century.

"First time we came here I envied them," she said. "Now—less and less, each time. I fancy we've something ten times better in our rambling, ramshackle old house at Thorpe."

He took her hand and squeezed it. "Not be too long now," he said.

Over the Foss and out of the city they passed the malt kiln. The air was laden with its sugary reek.

"That'll put fresh heart into Ironside," John said.

Nora grinned back, her face red in the glow from the glassworks next door to the malting; it was a wayward grin, too. And sure enough when the light had died she began to worm her hand into his trousers. He gripped her wrist and said firmly, "No."

"You always say no, anywhere except in bed, and you always end up doing it."

"You will make noises when you get excited. And Ironside will hear."

"Any minute now Ironside will start to sing. The dark frightens him and he sings."

"Anyway, I don't always say no."

"Often enough." She helped him not to burst his buttons.

"I'm not going to take them off," he said. "Suppose the coach upset and we were knocked senseless."

As well as her voluminous skirts would allow, she leaped across him, straddling him with open thighs. She put her nose to his as he began to caress her. "So practical," she whispered. "That's why I love you. Practical man. For being such a practical contractor and getting company coaches just for you and me."

She could feel his excitement growing. "These new hoops are more practical than the old walls of Jericho—or calico—or whatever it was," he said. He tried to be light and nonchalant but could not keep the shiver from his voice.

She inched her knees forward, close to contact. His hands strayed over her cheeks, around her waist, and forward to her navel. With his thumbs he pressed gently; there was an answering pressure from the baby inside. She breathed sharply inward. "No denying it now, is there," he said.

"You know how"—she shivered—"superannuated that makes me feel. When they squirm like that. Oourgh!" And she shuddered again at the memory.

His hands slipped away to encircle her waist.

"Shan't hunt anymore," she said. "Just ride."

He chuckled. "With Winifred you gave up riding soon as you knew. It gets later each time."

"Aye. If we have ten, the last will be born in the saddle. A birth at a death." She giggled at the thought.

He patted her bare hips and pushed her lightly away. "I thought you weren't really inter—"

Her warm lips smothered his and, moments later, her fingers eased him into her. The motion of the carriage, over long, luxurious minutes, while they kissed and caressed and amplified its rhythm, carried them up. Ironside did not sing, but Nora did cry out in her ecstasy. The coach went relentlessly on. Only John went limp with the fear that they were overheard. Nora, when she was calm again, chuckled as she felt him shrivel within.

"Sorry!" she whispered into his neck; it was at least half true.

*   *   *

Thorpe Manor, or Thorpe Old Manor as it had now to be called, was begun in the fourteenth century. It had lost its manorial rights some fifty years back when the Creswold family moved to their new Hall, a large Palladian mansion on the higher ground to the northwest of the village of Fangthorpe. On a smiling day in spring or summer, when the warm Yorkshire stone was crisp and sunlit and when the shade of the young cedars dappled the sweeping lawns, it was easy enough to approve the change. But when the northeast winds came howling down out of Scandinavia and thick blankets of snow turned the whole Yorkshire wold into a continent of its own, to which there was no access and from which there was no escape, then the villagers would look up at the new manor and shiver. And they would remember all that their parents and grandparents had said of the folly of building on yon 'ights. Then even the proudest Creswold must have wished to be back at the old place, nestling on sheltered southern slopes overlooking the deep dale of Painslack Dikes. Didn't legends say the Romans had once built a great town there? Well, they had understood the sun and the south, all right.

Even when the night was merely drizzly and uncomfortable as now, it felt somehow milder off the browtop. John and Nora, who had opened the carriage window for a better view, sensed the difference as soon as they lurched off the stony, rutted highway and on to the superbly levelled drive that John had given one of his best gangs a whole month and a hundred pounds to lay.

He relaxed at once, no longer needing to correct the random lurches of the carriage. "Home is where the road runs smooth," he said contentedly.

"That's a definition I prefer," she told him.

They heard Ironside vainly trying to blow a blast on the horn he kept in his pocket. John leaned out of the window, took it from him, and, wiping it well, blew the sweet, piercing note he had learned as a shotfirer years before.

Nora, in a voice deliberately girlish and vapid, said, "Say—is there anything you can't do, Mr. Stevenson?"

"Aye," he said. "*You* proved it." In the dark he felt for her breasts; and though he found only her shoulder blades, she knew what he meant.

"Sorry," she said again, hugging him.

"We'll make up for it later," he said.

She thought, but did not say, *peut-être*; the ambiguities were too rich.

Willet, their groom, came strolling up the lane to meet them. The turn into the stable yard was too sharp for a broad coach with three up so they had to stop outside and unhitch the leader. Tip, the King Charles dog, and Puck, the small Dane dog, yapped and fretted at the perpetual iron cataract of the carriage wheel, impatient to be noticed.

As John and Nora dismounted from the coach, Todd, the younger of the two upstairs maids, came hurrying over the lawn bearing a lantern to light them in. Nora was surprised. "Where's Mrs. Jarrett?" she asked, pushing down the leaping dogs.

"It's her music night at the asylum, m'm," the girl said. And what dull weather! And had the journey been tedious? And please to mind the paving stone that had been put back wrong. Pleasure and nervousness kept her babbling the whole way in.

Tip, the loyalist, stayed by them, sniffing and fussing. Puck, long-suffering egotist, left to claim pride of place at the hearth.

"What's for supper?" John asked.

"The children and Mrs. Jarrett and nurse had collared calf's head. Cold."

They stamped the mud from their feet and John bolted the lobby door. "And the servants?" he asked.

"Shepherd's pie, sir."

"If there's any left, we'll have the shepherd's pie." And when the girl was gone, he added: "The woman's mad. Both of them. She and the nurse. I hope they keep her at the asylum."

"John!" Nora pinched his arm.

"Who else but her would give a cold meal on such a night?"

"It's her way. And we've always said we didn't want them brought up to luxury."

The argument cut not the thinnest ice. "You've been poor, too," he said. "Even if you had only one potato, or a half a turnip, you'd never have served them cold on a night like this. And I'll wager it was cold baths, too. Eay!" His eyes rolled in exasperation. "Cold supper, cold baths, cold nursery."

She caught his arm as he turned to the foot of the stairs. "Well, don't wake them now. They'll get all excited, and it'll be impossible to get them back to sleep. When are you off tomorrow?"

Resigned, he crossed to the fireplace and poked the logs to life. "Early," he said. "I'll ride over to Malton. See to this trouble on the Scarborough line, this quaking bog. I'll come back by York, so I'll be early."

"You'll see the children then."

"I've not seen them for a fortnight," he sighed. "Still . . ." He picked up two letters waiting for him on the mantel. "France," he said, looking at them. "And Exeter."

"What are your plans for the week?" Nora asked; with half an ear she was listening to Willet carrying a trunk upstairs, preparing herself to run out and shout at him if he grazed the woodwork.

"I'll go on to Stockton, Thursday; see how they're coping with the brick troubles. On to Warrington, Friday. And Exeter, Saturday."

She relaxed as Willet reached the landing and put down the trunk.

"I'll revise that," John said, having read the letter from France. "They want me in Rouen next week."

"Not trouble?"

"They mention none. I'll come back here from Warrington and go on to Exeter to arrive Monday." He stretched and yawned. "I can sail to Havre from Plymouth." He pulled a face for he hated sea travel.

"Never mind," she comforted him. "One day they'll build a bridge to France, and then you can ride all the way on horseback."

"Oh, thank you," he said glumly and read the second letter. "From Thornton," he said, passing it to her when he had finished.

She did not at once read it. "What do you think of my coming to France?" she asked. "This strange invitation from the Rodets. The more I think of it, the more certain I am that he put her up to it."

"You don't think she's genuine?"

"Oh, she is genuine. But he knows how to use her."

John smiled to himself.

"What's that grin supposed to convey?" she asked.

He shook his head. "Well, it'd do no harm to learn a word or two of French," he said. "And you'd enjoy meeting Sam at proper leisure."

She nodded and turned to the letter from Thornton:

Dear Stevenson,

I hear from your man Tucker that you and Mrs. S. have been spending some days at Sir George Beador's place. Did you know that it used to belong to my uncle before he sold up and went to France, where you can play the gentleman on £120 a year? He was the uncle who brought me up after my people died. I can just imagine Beador there; he and Uncle Claude George Thornton are two cast from the same mould. How long, I wonder, will *he* last.

I wonder, too, if you met anyone who remembered me? Curious, is it not, that I dislike the place so intensely and desire no memory of it to linger, yet am vain enough to wish to *be* remembered! And who would remember me? Servants and outdoor staff! Heigh ho!! Believe nothing they say, of course. You know how credulous country people are and how they cannot live without making a nine-years' wonder of every petty event.

However, my real purpose in writing was merely to say how glad I was to be appointed down here where I am certain to meet you again, and right soon. Our jaws will ache with talk of old times I'm sure. And you will *marvel* at the atmospheric railway! Have you seen the one near Dublin, from Kingstown to Dalkey? This is to work on the same principle. I may tell you privately that I have grave technical doubts, but I shall not commit them to paper. Do you think Brunel is *really* as confident as he always gives out? I frequently wonder. How the great engineer, who built two trans-Atlantic steamers and designed the whole of the Great Western Railway, can even consider this atmospheric system, baffles me. Still, I suppose that, if Homer is permitted to nod, our own geniuses may be allowed their failures, too. But rather expensive, what?

Mrs. Thornton continues in indifferent health, sometimes blossoming, but always languishing again. She has never been *entirely* healthy since Letty was born a year ago. Perhaps we are to have no more than four children, God be praised that three of them are boys and all are so well. They *adore* their baby sister, who is a pickle and a joy. Nicholas constantly asks after his big godfather and nice godmother. I hope their mother may be well enough this year to accept your kind invitation to Thorpe Manor; I am sure your splendid upland air would benefit her. . . .

Nora skipped the closing pleasantries. "He still wears his heart well hung out," she said.

Chapter 4

A watery moon shone in the dawn sky when John set off next morning on Hermes, his favourite horse. Hermes had been with him since his earliest days as a contractor over in the West Riding. Just before John mounted, Willet put a finger to his lips and beckoned him over to the tack-room door. There in the dark lay Ironside, stuporifically asleep in the sodden greatcoat he had worn through last night's drizzle. He was gently steaming. The air was pungent with him.

They shut the top half of the door quietly. "An amazing machine, the human frame," John said. "When you think of all the punishment it can tolerate."

"Aye," agreed Willet, who did *nothing* to excess.

The light northeasterly breeze grew stronger as John neared the highway. The skies must have cleared in the small hours for the ground and air were close to freezing. There was no shelter from the cold for several miles either; the Malton road led north along a high ridge of the wold. But the views were compensation enough—eastward over the rolling hills to the German Ocean and the sunrise; westward over the deeply shaded Vale of York and down into the dying night.

He blinked to shake the windwater from his eyes and drew his lungs full of the morning air. It was almost worth a quaking bog to have the excuse to ride this way on such a day. The only folk he met were shepherds and field labourers starting their day's work; their greetings were cheerful enough but their pinched faces and starved bodies spoke of poverty and neglect. John noticed it more than most, being used to his navvies, who could outwork half a dozen of these farm labourers. He had always thought starvation wages were bad business. Even on his first contract, when the shopkeepers in the villages beside the line had tried selling rotten goods to his lads, he had set up his own tommy shop to sell cheap wholesome staples like beef and bread and beer and potatoes.

No, he thought, to be fair, their tommy shop had been Nora's idea. She had meant it as a way of making more money; but it had paid both ways—financially and in well-fed gangs. Now, on every contract where

there were more than three hundred lads, there was at least one Stevenson tommy man on commission, buying staples of wholesome quality
and selling at small margins. For the privilege, they paid Stevenson's
thirty pounds a year for each hundred men, and if they weren't altogether too clever, each tommy man could make a little more than that
for himself. If they were too clever and cut the quality or swelled the
price, the gangs could vote them off the site.

The whole system was Nora's, really. She always claimed that she
had hated their first shop, which she herself had managed for several
months. Her dislike was odd, because in fact she had a great gift for the
business. She knew how customers' minds worked. She understood
avarice and cupidity—and how even the poorest customer, who bought,
say, just a pound of udder fat to cook for her man, needed nonetheless
to feel it was *almost* as good as sirloin. Often he had seen her pass over
the counter a poor piece of lean beef without a trace of good fat on it—
and even in the way Nora handled it, even if she said nothing, there was
a suggestion that it was quality meat. And *that* instinct for a customer's
feelings was what she had somehow passed on to the tommy men. At
present the system was earning them three thousand pounds a year; that,
too, was characteristic of Nora.

She was quality, he thought. There were few like her in the whole
kingdom. He had known as much from the day they first met. Without
her, he might well have gone under, like dozens of other ambitious
navvies these last few years. And yet . . . and yet he could not feel entirely easy nor deal quite plainly with her, especially of late. There was
a sense in him that she was manipulating their affairs, pushing him in
directions he would rather not go, while making it seem that each step
was dictated by some outside logic, unconnected with her own will or
preference. Or was that being unfair to her?

For some time he had been aware of a pack of hounds giving tongue
as they approached the road along one of the lanes to the west. He
reached the corner as the leaders, sterns waving, poured on to the highway. It was a bitch pack out for exercise with a whipper-in and some
kennel servants. He nodded curtly to the whipper-in and got a cool nod
in return. This was York Union country, where they would no more
let in the likes of John Stevenson than the King of the Hottentots. He
subscribed—and heavily, too—to the York and Ainsty, and Nora went
down there to hunt. She said that the wold was poor country, but he
knew that was not so and that the exclusiveness of the York Union
hurt her.

"Never mind," he had once said. "They're on the way out, we're on the way in. They have to cling on to something."

"Then I could wish they'd chosen something unimportant for their raft," she said.

The dull red globe of the sun was looming above the far-off mist as he went down over Birdsall Brow and made for Burythorpe. George Hudson's place at Howsham was only a few miles distant, and he toyed with the idea of making a detour that way. He wondered whether Hudson had heard of the trouble on the line, which Hudson had himself surveyed some years earlier. Also he had an idea that the Railway King could help him in the question of Beador's involvement in railway shares.

In fact, John had turned off and was already on the lane to Leavening when he saw coming toward him a mounted figure who could only be George Hudson himself, pink in the rising sun.

"Stevenson!" he called before either could make out the other's features. His tone was filled with relief. "Hoped I might cross your path. I owe you an apology."

"Oh?" John was wary. The great autocrat did not often speak like that, except when he wanted a favour of you.

They shook hands. John looked steadily into those deceptively soft grey eyes, searching for clues that had not been in the voice. They were not in the eyes, either. "Yes," Hudson said. "This wet ground. I'll be damned if it was like that when our party went through."

"Ah!" John was tolerantly laconic. "These summer surveys!"

Their horses sniffed at each other and then stood aloof, breathing steam.

"I hope you won't lose by it," Hudson said, still playing at penitence.

"That's what you employ a big contractor for. You know we'll not come whimpering at every little setback, grumbling about the survey. Anyway, it can't be bad. My engineer missed it, too, and I'd back him against any man." As a deliberate afterthought he added: "Except yourself, of course."

Hudson, knowing full well he was being buttered, laughed hugely. As always, John warmed to his charm and magnetism. The man was a rogue, no doubt of it. A rogue, a genius, a loyal friend, a terrible adversary, a quietly ruthless competitor. But the world was warmer and the air somehow more vibrant when he was near. "If only all the world's rogues were such men as Hudson!" he often said to Nora. The "business side of business" might become more enjoyable to him then.

"Were you coming up to look at it?" John asked, jerking his head toward Portobello, where the trouble lay. He heeled and pulled Hermes around on the spot.

"No," Hudson said. "Not now I have your assurance. But I'll go with ye as far as Burythorpe." They spurred forward into a trot, to get their horses' blood moving again. "Does Mrs. Stevenson keep well? And the children?"

"Indeed. And your people?"

"I think there's only one person in England can rival me at figures-in-the-head, and that's Mrs. Stevenson."

"Oh, you're safe there."

But Hudson shook his head. "If all shareholders were chalkheads like her"—his mouth fell to a dour, inverted U—"railway business would become impossible." He sniffed at the air and repeated: "Impossible."

Why did he come out to meet me? John wondered. Hudson fell back, casually, a foot or two. And just as casually he said: "I'll wager she wishes you had your ironworks already."

"Already?" John asked in surprise, before he realized that the question should have been: *Ironworks?* "Did you say iron or ironworks?" he added to repair the blunder.

Hudson was carefully not smiling, carefully neutral. "I know I wish I had bought a works last year. Trade was so bad I had the chance."

"You'd be comforted now, that's certain," John said. He wondered whether Hudson, despite this disclaimer, had not in fact bought an ironworks.

"I did well enough," Hudson said coolly. "As chairman of the Newcastle & Berwick, I advised them to buy ten thousand tons of iron rail when it was down to six pound ten a ton. They refused, so I bought on my own account."

John whistled. "It's thirteen pound now. Cent per cent!"

Hudson nodded, gratified. "They shall have it for twelve pound—and wish they had let me do them the bigger favour."

John was glad of a large standing puddle to negotiate at that point. What Hudson proposed was certainly illegal; he wished the great man would guard his tongue more carefully.

"I suppose *you* bought then?" Hudson asked. "Iron in plenty. You're too astute not to."

Does he want rail from me? John wondered. *Or to sell at arm's length through me?* He began to worry. "Plenty of iron," he answered, assuming a smugness to match Hudson's. "Aye. But little rail, of course."

"Of course," Hudson echoed. His eyes scanned the horizon in rapid jerks. He was trying to work around to something. "I met Mrs. Stevenson at the station," he continued, and then lapsed into thought.

"Recently?" John prompted.

"Uh? No, no." He frowned. "Last year. December. When the price was still down. I advised her then: Tell you to buy iron. You have no notion." He came alive again. His eyes shone and he spoke rapidly and with emphatic conviction. "No notion. Even I have no notion. The railways that will be built these next five years. I tell you, Stevenson, we shall double the track miles. More! We shall double the *route* miles. Think of that!"

It was fool's bait, John decided; all this golden talk. He felt the first impulse to confess his plans to Hudson, to flatter him, to ask his advice. He laughed. "Oh, I think of it, Hudson. A great deal. And if you go into any foundry business, I'd be happy to take shares in it."

Hudson, watching him like a fox, pretended to chuckle.

"For one thing," John continued, "if there was ever a glut of rail, you'd conjure railroads out of marsh, mountain, and desert to sop it up."

Hudson loved that. He threw back his head and roared with laughter, making a pheasant, a hundred yards ahead, dart early for the hedgerow. "And then I'd amalgamate them," he said. He looked impishly at John. "Talking of which—ye still have the GNE shares?"

John nodded warily. Hudson had given him 200 fifty-pound shares in the Great North of England Railway on condition that Stevenson's kept the tender on this Scarborough line down to Hudson's miserly estimate of less than six thousand pounds per mile. "Aye," he said.

Hudson reined in and took out his watch. "I'll leave you here," he said, though they were still short of Burythorpe. "I was ever too ambitious where time is concerned. Hang on to those shares. They're about to do a great deal better. Just as I promised they would." He leaned forward, speaking as if every yard of the hedge concealed an eavesdropper. "I've formed six companies into the Newcastle & Darlington. We're going to lease the GNE and then amalgamate with it."

John, who had heard the news from his own informers over a week ago, hoped he looked sufficiently surprised and impressed. "What terms?" he asked.

"The ones you're interested in: Two years from now you can be paid off at two hundred and fifty a share!"

John whistled.

"Aye," Hudson said. "That'll be fifty thousand pounds clear to you. Nothing to sneeze at." He always wanted people to know the precise value of his largesse.

"Think you can do it?" John asked.

Hudson frowned at that. "Why?"

"You know damned well it's not legal. You're not going to tell me that—just by the happiest coincidence—all seven companies happen to be already vested with powers to amalgamate with the other six."

Hudson laughed again.

"You think the Railway Board will wink?" John pressed.

"The Board!" Hudson was a master of scorn. "The Board will nudge Parliament and Parliament will jog the Judiciary Committee of the Lords and their lordships will say that it's illegal but that no one has powers to stop it."

At that John laughed and shook his head. "You're the man all right, Hudson," he said. "That's really so, is it?"

Hudson nodded smugly.

"Illegal but none can stop it!" John savoured the thought.

"Then," Hudson concluded, "I'll tell them it's in the public interest. Which is also true. And then they'll yawn and all go back to sleep. Leaving us to look after the public and"—he leaned forward to pat John's arm—"*and* our shareholders."

The word *shareholders* must have stirred something within him for, just as he reined around to go, his visionary, public face came over him —the face John had seen him wear at many shareholders' meetings. "Amalgamations are the *thing*, Stevenson. Look what I did." He counted them off dramatically with jack-in-the-box fingers. "Midland Counties. North Midland. Birmingham & Derby. Bristol & Birmingham. One system now, thanks to *me*. Four hundred miles. Hundred and twenty-six stations. York to Bristol. All on a common timetable. Man—it used to be hell on earth, just trying to get from Sheffield to Derby. Aye!" He tested the wind with an orator's finger. "Amalgamation." Then he chuckled, and public Hudson was swiftly replaced once more by good-friend Hudson as he reached his hand across to shake farewell. "Stevenson! I wish you all the very best! My dear fellow! And every success!"

"Ye need no reciprocation from me," John said. "But ye have it none the less."

Hudson set off at a fast trot that quickly broke to a canter. John watched him fondly until he passed from sight. *Hell on earth*, he thought. *That's rich.* The one man who had made it hell on earth, in order to weary or frighten the others into amalgamation and force the acquiescence of Parliament, was George Hudson.

He still did not know why the man had come out deliberately to meet him. The puzzle, or rather his inability to solve it, nagged at him on and off all day.

At Portobello he reined in at the hilltop and dismounted. The new railroad came winding up the valley of the Derwent, Yorkshire's extraordinary wrong-way river, which rises on the North Moors a few miles from the sea and then flows steadily west and then south, for sixty miles, ever farther from the coast, until it joins the Yorkshire Ouse, where at last it sweeps seaward into the Humber.

Just south of Portobello, the line crossed the river, coming over to its east bank, above which John now stood. Beneath the line, and swelling either side of it in a long lens shape, he saw the telltale darkening of the marshy land. They had built the line continuously over it, for it was strong enough to take the light construction traffic, and the main party had now pressed beyond Malton. Five men had stayed behind to keep this section open. Today, because of John's visit, Ferris, his deputy for this working, had come back to join them.

It was Ferris who saw him first. But he stayed by the line while the rest cheered and hastened uphill to meet John. Three ran all the way. He led Hermes down, smiling as he went until his cheeks ached. Of all men, his navvies were still closest to his affection; there were none whose company he would rather share.

"Eay Lord John, 'ere's a do!" one said.

In his days among them his nickname had been Lord Muck, for he had once loaded as much muck in a day as two champions together. Now he suffered no one but navvies to call him Lord John.

"I know thee," John said. "Tar Wash. On the Paisley & Cathcart, 1841."

The man called Tar Wash was delighted to be remembered, as were two of the others, Plug Billy and Cider Dan, whom he also remembered from earlier contracts. He shook hands with the remaining two, Fussy Peters and Smoked Trout, who had not worked for him before. He asked where they had been.

"Lancaster & Carlisle," Peters said. "Both on us."

"Wild country," Trout added.

"For Mr. Brassey," John said. "What was the rate there?"

"Ah, 't was good, except the land was hard and bad. The rate had to be good."

They wouldn't be exact. John guessed it would be close to three shillings a day. "Any bog?" he asked. "Any trouble like this?"

"Worse," Trout said. "Though it was better—bein' worse, like. The bog 'ud swallow what ye fed it. Brushwood faggots. Everythin'. Ye could soon make a bottomin' for the road."

"And this won't?" John asked generally. They began walking back to the site, where Ferris waited still.

"Take a week, like, to swallow one faggot," Tar Wash said.

"But it does swallow?" John persisted.

"It's more claggy nor a bog," Dan said. "More of a claggy ooze."

"It stands like clay yet sucks like a bog," Billy said, having thought longest.

Thus, before John shook Ferris by the hand, he knew exactly what sort of land he had to deal with.

The five navvies manhandled a wagon laden with several tons of muck back and forth over the twenty offending yards while John and Ferris watched the ties, bedded on brushwood faggots, sink fraction by fraction of an inch into the clay.

"How many faggots sunk already?" John asked.

"Only two," Ferris said. "We could be 'ere a blue month before we touch bedrock. We should of dug it out. I would of, but for the river bein' so nigh and floods threatened."

"Nay," John said. "Thou did right." He watched several more passages of the wagon without comment.

Something was nudging his memory. Somewhere before he had met this problem; but the memory was more that of a dream than of history. Had he read it? Or had someone told him of it? "It's a primeval clay cistern," he said, not quite knowing where the words came from.

Then he heard the words repeated in his mind in Walter Thornton's accents, and suddenly he knew exactly where this problem had occurred before and why his memory was so remote. It had happened at the summit tunnel of the Manchester & Leeds, his first contract; but it had happened while he had still been only a navvy ganger on the site. There they had struck a big silt basin. He remembered Thornton describing it. And how they had made it as good as living rock by sinking tar barrels and piles.

"Tar barrels," he said, and held up a hand for the navvies to rest.

"What about tar barrels?" Ferris asked.

"Something of this nature happened at Deanroyd on the Manchester & Leeds. I was workin at t'other end o' the tunnel so I never saw the way of it. But they cured it with piles and tar barrels. We'll not need piles here. But tar barrels, now. And there's a man here on this contract, too, was there. At Deanroyd. His name'll come to me in a minute." He fidgeted, jogging his memory.

"Tar," Ferris said and looked at the clay.

"Ye'll get all ye want at York gasworks, I daresay. See Mr. Clayton and mention Mr. Hudson. Oh, he was a short tyke. Like a gorilla."

"Mr. Clayton?" Ferris asked in surprise.

"No! Him who was at Deanroyd and is now here. Has a hole in his cheek. Sups gin through it for a farthing."

"Oh!" Ferris said. "I 'ave 'im. Brandy, Barry, Ba . . . begins with a *B*."

"Bacca!" John said, triumphant. "Bacca Barra. He'll tell thee just how it was done. Fetch him back here."

"Tar barrels," Ferris said, speculatively. " 'Appen it's worth a go."

John grinned, liking a skeptical mind. He gave Hermes to Tar Wash to ride to the Cross Keys at Malton; he and Ferris set out to walk the track, through Malton and out as far as Scagglethorpe, where the permanent way ended at present. Though only five miles or so, it took the best part of three hours, for John would tap every fifth or sixth oaken rail key to see it was secure in its chair; he checked cambers and ballasting, stopping in several places to dig down a foot or so; he checked for telltale oozes from embankments that would show where top soil had been wrongly incorporated; and every now and then he would put his ear to the rail while Ferris walked on, tapping it with a hammer to reveal flaws in the metal.

He found no fault in the line, nor did he expect to. Ferris had worked for him long enough to know the Stevenson standard and how John set it and kept it. He wouldn't sack a deputy whose work was below expectation; he wouldn't even demote him. Somehow he would bring the man to feel that he had let down not just John Stevenson, not just the navvies and the tradesmen who looked to him for an example, but, worst of all, *himself*. And thereafter he had to redeem himself in his *own* estimation. In that way John made each man feel that the Stevenson standard was the property of every Stevenson man, not something imposed from on high. A sigh and a reproachful shake of the head from John was more feared than the most ferocious reprimand of lesser contractors or even their blows and curses.

Wherever he saw men he would stop for a talk, renewing fellowship or asking their names, discussing where they had been and what sort of work it was. Each scrap of information was like a mosaic in an ever-changing picture of works now in progress or recently completed

in England and Europe—and in America, too. There were several
navvies who regularly went across the Atlantic each summer for the
higher wages where their kind of labour was short. He wished the world
of business and finance was as easy to investigate and to picture.

Then he and Ferris had a midday dinner at the Cross Keys. He told
Ferris of all the other Stevenson contracts then in progress and described
some of their problems, asking if Ferris had had similar experiences and
canvassing his advice. John liked all his senior staff to have as full a picture as possible of all the firm's workings. Every contract had its peck
of trouble; to share troubles helped each deputy see his own in perspec-
tive. John also used the opportunity to encourage or discourage an
agent, as might be appropriate. To a timid man who tended to send for
him at the first sign of each setback he would tell of another deputy who
overcame far severer problems on his own, ending with some such remark as, "I give Wilf Tenby top marks for that. I was in France at the
time, explaining to a lot of nervous Froggies as how I'd built this business in such a way as I didn't have to be dashing everywhere all the
time. It wouldn't have done to be called off to Sunderland in the middle
of that!" But for a rash deputy, too apt to forge ahead with a half-
thought-out solution to a problem, the story would be different; some
other deputy would get his top marks for having the sense to call in the
master: "Takes a big man, a very experienced man, to recognize the
value of a second opinion and not think twice to call it!" Thus, with a
nudge, a pat, a hint, and a wink, he kept his firm well shaped and
orderly.

Dinner over, he abandoned his intention to go to York and rode
due south for home, relishing the thought of a rare early day with Nora
and the children. These last few hours among iron and oak, stone and
clay, had refreshed him wonderfully.

*   *   *

Winifred saw him first. While she and Young John were straddling the
stile, playing at horses and waiting for Cox, carrying baby Caspar, to
catch up, she looked across the field and saw her father moving among
the bare trees on the skyline. Tip and Puck, aware of him at that same
moment, scampered up the lane, barking all the way.

"Papaaaa!" She called and waved, startling a flock of crows that had
settled in the bare fallow. He waved back and broke into a trot.

Young John, facing his sister, craned back to see and almost fell;
he hitched his skirts higher to get a better grip with his knees but, by

the time he turned, his father had passed from sight at the head of the lane.

Cox tugged a cloth from her sleeve and wiped long strings of snot from Caspar's face. "Good afternoon, sir." She curtseyed when John drew near.

"That's a raw, red face," he said with a frown.

"Aye, it is," Cox agreed. "The wee mite has taken a chill. This cold air might just draw it from him."

John nodded, unconvinced; but it was not his business to interfere. He looked at the girl's big-boned face, plain, pleasant, and unrelenting, polished smooth by the sharp afternoon wind. No tear would soften those steady hazel eyes, no winning smile catch her unawares. Her implacable calm often made him shudder.

"Papa!" Winifred called again and stood on the topmost timber of the stile to reach for him.

No word came from Cox. No tender "Winifred!" or peremptory "Sit down, miss!" John knew well enough what she was thinking: *If the child falls and hurts itself, it will learn.* It.

He spurred forward over the half-dozen yards to the stile and swept Winifred onto the pommel of his saddle. Her lips were cold on his neck, her nose like ice below his ear; but her breath and the hug she gave him were warmth itself.

Young John, solemnly ignoring him, making him be the first to speak, spurred the stile to a final charge homeward. Even when John pulled Hermes back, so that the boy could reach up and be lifted behind him, only a stubborn and distant smile showed his recognition.

John winked at Winifred. "D'ye know," he said, "I was set to swear that was our Young John. It must be"—his voice sank to a horrified whisper—". . . a changeling! Let's hie us hence and right fast!"

The boy could hold out no longer. With a protesting bleat he stood, on the next-to-top rail, feet well locked, and reached up to be hauled aboard. He sat on the cantle, behind his father, hugging as much of him as he could in his tiny embrace.

"King of the castle?" Winifred suggested.

Young John began to jog excitedly. "Kingacastle, Kingacastle!" he said again and again.

John looked westward, where the sun was just dipping down to set. Why not! There'd be a good half hour yet. "Yes," he said. "King o' the castle. Why not!"

Sauntering, Willet just made it to the gate in time to let them through. He helped the children down and then, when John dismounted, took Hermes off to the stable. John opened and shut the gate for Cox and baby Caspar, who stared listlessly around through swollen eyelids and would not be coaxed to either laugh or whimper.

"Best get him to bed," John said.

Cox nodded calm agreement. "Aye," she said.

The dogs looked wistfully after John and the children but, sniffing at the frost, followed Cox indoors, quarrelling over a hearthrug that was still two hundred yards away.

*   *   *

The garden had once been fortified, and a straggling wall, part stone, part brick, still encompassed it on most of three sides. Downhill, to the east of the house and at a sharp angle of the wall, stood the remains of a medieval tower. A stone stair without a balustrade ran steeply up one side to a sharp turn, where it continued up a short tunnel into a small chamber, now roofless; at most it could have held a watch of three in comfort. On its far side a much narrower stair spiralled up three-quarters of a turn to a ruined turret, made slightly less hazardous by a low railing of deeply corroded iron. This was their castle, and the turret the seat of their king.

It was really a game for high summer days when little breezes could be found at that height long after they had died between the baking ramparts down below. Today, in raw February, with a cloudless sky darkening above and frosty evening mists rising silently in the vale below, even the mildest breeze seemed to push icicles through the thickest cloak and down inside the tightest collar.

"We mustn't stop long," John said. "What do my courtiers see?"

"I see beggars three," Winifred said even before he had finished the question.

He looked for three objects. The three pine trees? Could be, but if he guessed wrong he would cease to be king. He looked farther afield. Then nearer at hand. He had to ask soon or he'd be dethroned for silence. Three crows. It could be them. Chance it. "Is their raiment black?"

She wrinkled her face in good-natured disappointment. "Their raiment is black."

"What do we do with beggars three?" he asked, knowing the answer.

"Beat them black and beat them blue! Beat them till they're only two!" she shouted and laughed.

"Beat them. Beat. Bam! Pchhhh!" Young John said with a sudden, astonishing savagery.

Beggars were always beaten. "Why?" John asked, still kingly and judicial.

"Because they steal the farmer's corn. I see angels four," she gabbled.

But Young John did not wait for her to finish; he stole in ahead with "I see football."

He always saw a football and it was always the sun.

"Does it burn the players' feet?" John asked.

Young John punched him and burst into tears. His father squeezed his arm but otherwise ignored him.

"I see a kingly orb," Winifred said. She spoke so reverently it might have been a line of poetry rather than a new step in their game. For a four-year-old she could be very solemn.

"Does it outshine mine?" he asked.

The boy, so easily distracted, stopped crying; leaning into his father, he slipped a cold thumb inside his mouth and listened with rapt attention.

"It does," Winifred said, the game three-quarters forgotten.

They were all looking straight at the setting sun, huge and oval, swathed in mist. Above it, far off, a swan or some other large bird flapped wearily southward.

Mists pinched out the sun before the horizon could mask it. The colour vanished from the sky soon after, leaving the world silver and black, damp and very chill.

He shivered, stirring them. "Come on," he said. "Before we stumble in the dark."

The shadows were uniting and the grass already bore the first thin lining of frost as they stole back over the lawns to the house. The smoke curling from its chimneys and the oil light reaching out through its small leaded panes had never seemed so welcoming.

"Pray for all the poor children sleeping out tonight," John told them as they edged through the rose beds to the garden door.

Nora met them in the passage. "Eay, I don't know!" she sighed, running her warm hands over the two children, feeling their ears and fingers. "You're a fine one," she said to John, "talking about cold baths. It's a good thing they've a hot tea coming."

He smiled. "A very good thing," he said, unperturbed.

Cox was waiting for the children at the foot of the nursery stairs. She turned them as a sheepdog turns sheep—with a Look.

"If Cox says you're good, I'll tell you a story later," John promised. He and Nora went to the winter parlour.

The previous week's accounts had come from the London office— summaries of the ledger entries at each contract. Nora had been doing her regular weekly check.

All the firm's business—that endless battle with rock and mud, mountain and marsh (and good men and rogues)—was eventually rendered down to neat rows and columns of figures and passed across Nora's desk. In the earliest days she had kept every account and made every entry herself, in a schoolchild's penny copybook. Now they came in a dozen hands: loose-leaf copies of ledger pages from the workings, and fat duplicate account books with gold lettering on their leather spines, sent up weekly by William Jackson, the chief clerk in their London office.

Over the years Nora had developed "the sharpest eye in the City," as Jackson said. She noted with amusement the way he would often try to anticipate her by pencilling little notes beside certain entries: *I question this . . . too low? . . . twice last week's figure . . .* and so on. In this way he placed himself on her side of the table in her relentless weekly inquisition.

At first Jackson had not liked his situation one bit—to work for a man and yet to take most of the orders from his wife! And in matters of finance, too, where women were supposed to be most supremely ignorant. It went hard. But now she had no greater champion. She needed only to indicate the slightest preference for something and Jackson would turn it into an iron rule. For instance, she had once said she thought it might make accounts easier to follow if debits and liabilities were in red ink, and credits and assets were in blue. The younger clerks made jokes about working in Mrs. Stevenson's Drawing Academy . . . and would she like the accounts on lace-edged paper . . . and much more in that vein; but from that day onward Jackson insisted on Nora's red-blue system. And now everyone agreed it made the pages much easier to read at a glance.

She wished it were as simple to overcome all other opposition to her central role in the business. Their banker, Nathan Chambers of Dowgate, was a particular antagonist. Five years earlier (a lifetime, it seemed), she had intercepted a few letters to him and used them in applying some gentle pressure. Chambers had laughed at the time and, since no actual harm had been done, she had thought herself forgiven. And she had to admit that he never flatly opposed her, never was rude or even short with her; indeed, he treated her with great deference, was always chivalrous and attentive and always praised her financial . . . what did he call it? *Intuition!*

That was the trouble. In a thousand subtle ways he gave out that her brilliance was intuitive. Unreliable. Not based on logic or analysis. At heart it was (that most damning of all City judgements) "not sound."

He never said it openly. He never failed to imply it.

The judgement was doubly galling to her since all the facts spoke the other way. At John's instructions Chambers took a tenth of all the firm's profit and put it into a trust fund for her and the children. No one but Chambers could touch it; certainly it was beyond John's control. Thus if the inconceivable happened and Stevenson's failed, Nora and the children would be safe. They would have (at the moment) ninety thousand pounds to fall back on. That was all that Chambers, safe, stolid, *sound* Chambers, had made out of the eighty-odd thousand he had been given to invest. Yet she, intuitive, unreliable, *unsound* Nora, had taken a mere nineteen thousand pounds—the entire profit of the victualling licences over the last five years—and turned them into investments worth all of sixty thousand.

It began after their first year in business, at Summit Tunnel over near Manchester. When they got their profit on that, John had given her a thousand pounds. Earlier the same year, on her first visit to London, she had seen the power of the railways to promote the outward growth of cities into regions people thought would always be mere farmland. She longed then for some spare cash to put into land. Suddenly she had it.

Within a week she had driven out along the course of the new line south of Manchester, looking for land. Clever people had already bought up around Cheadle Hulme and Handforth. Some adventurous souls had even gone as far as Wilmslow. Only Nora had had the courage to go on, beyond the valley, up to Alderley Edge. There she had taken one look at the view, one sniff at the air, and had snapped up a hundred acres for her money.

Already more than half her land was built over with new houses— and such grand houses! There seemed to be a competition among the Manchester merchants to move far out along the line; the richer you were, the farther you went. The richest came to Alderley Edge. And there, on Nora's land, which was to be had only on ninety-nine years' lease, they built their fine mansions, country houses with miniature

estates of one, two, at most five, acres. They seemed glad to pay ground
rents of ten or even fifteen pounds an acre; it kept out the poor. So in
five years the land had become worth around twenty thousand and when
the remaining seventy acres were leased it would rise to some thirty-five
thousand. Already it brought in substantial rents.

Alderley Edge had been the first of a number of similar purchases.
Not all had worked, of course. She had been too clever over judging the
line to Nelson and was now stuck with forty acres of worthless land
near the Forest of Pendle. But that, and another fifty near Ayr in Scotland, were exceptions. Apart from Alderley Edge, she now had nearly
twelve hundred acres in small estates near Blackpool, Warrington, St.
Alban's, Henley, Plymouth, and Bromley. When they were all developed, their value would be at least a hundred and seventy-five thousand.
So what could she not do with the money Chambers kept tucking away
at a mere two and a half per cent! She seethed every time she ruled
the double line under the accounts for each contract as it finished and
totted up the profit, one-tenth part of which went at once to Chambers.

John himself had no idea that she had done so well. In a foolish
moment, when she had first bought the land at Alderley Edge, the scorn
of those who thought she had thrown her money away had goaded her
to boast aloud to John that she would see the money back tenfold in as
many years. From time to time now he reminded her of the promise, but
she was always vague and furtive, giving out the impression that she
wished she'd never said such a thing. Of course, he knew that she had
made *some* profit, on that and her other transactions, but she hoped
he had no idea of its size. For John had an obsession that if he died,
leaving Nora a rich widow and the money loose, she'd fall victim to
the first fortune hunter who left his card. She had tried everything—
laughter, petulance, ridicule, and anger—to rid him of this absurd notion. But all he ever said was "a grieving woman's easy game." So their
finances were a maze of trusts—trusts for her and the children now, in
case the firm went bankrupt, and *everything* into trust if he died. As
Chambers said, it made fund raising as easy as raising a gale in a shuttered room with a blocked chimney and no door.

Still, through all their first five years the market in money had been
easy, especially for railways. Even the fools had been able to turn in respectable profits, while a blood professional like John had done well
beyond even his own dreams. His specialty was to take the hazardous
parts of a contract, the cutting, tunnelling, embanking, and viaduct
building, where both the risk and the potential profit were high. Then,

by good management, careful planning, and the use of seasoned navvies
all versed in his ways, he would bring the risks as low as those on a
level, open-skies working. Their profit usually fell between thirty and
forty per cent of the tender.

The Penmanshiel Tunnel contract, which they had finished last December and whose accounts she had just closed while John had been
playing with the children on the "castle," was a case in point. The tender
had been taken at £42,800, no trouble being expected. But halfway
through they had met a section where the slaty-black Lingula flagstone
of the lower Silurian beds was badly fragmented. It would have bank-
rupted a less experienced contractor. But John knew just where to lay
his hands on some hydraulic presses, which his engineer, an impatient
little Irishman called Flynn, had quickly adapted to hold the overburden
while iron stanchions were placed. Then, entirely on his own initiative,
Flynn had further modified the hydraulic devices so that they could be
used for forcing a slurry of cement deep into the rock fissures and thus
bind the fragments together, the way you might grout a crumbling
stone wall. The fact that Flynn had wrecked all six hydraulic cylinders,
giving John an awkward day with the friend who had lent them, was
neither here nor there in the long run. The point was that John knew a
thousand dodges for getting around the thousand and one troubles you
could meet on any sort of working, and he'd pick the right men to invent the other eleven, so that Stevenson's could always go ten better
than anything the firm of Nature, Fate & Co. might pit against them.
The proof had come in that day's mail, in the final accounts for the
Penmanshiel tunnel.

"There," she said proudly. "The profit on Penmanshiel was thirty-
seven per cent."

He nodded, trying to look nonchalant. "It'd be more if we'd known
the geology. We are the first to tunnel through that lower Silurian."

"It would have been a loss if any other firm had tried it."

He picked up the summary of the heads of account and looked at
them.

"Were you long with the children?" she asked. "They were freezing."

"Not long," he said. "I'll tell you who I met today. Came riding out
a-purpose to see me. George Hudson." He laid down the account and
crossed the room to draw the curtain. Far away to the west the last
glimmer of twilight was settling on the horizon. "He says he met you
on York platform and you talked about iron."

He saw a confusion behind her eyes. "I'd forgotten that," she said. "It must have been last back end. November, sometime."

"So why, this front end, does he go out of his way, early one cold morning, to see if Stevenson's has gone into ironfounding?"

He watched her closely. This time there was no confusion; her astonishment was genuine. "He never did!"

"Four miles. And rode on with me to Burythorpe, near enough."

"What did he say?"

He snorted. "You know Hudson. His mind clicks like a compound engine. He'd get three bites at any cherry."

"But his exact words?"

John turned and went back to the fire, speaking as he went. "He just said he'd wager I wished I had my ironworks already."

"Already!" Nora said, falling into the selfsame trap.

John spun around, pointing at her and grinning. He did not need to tell her that was just what he had said. "Did he mention ironworks to you?" he asked. "In December. He says it was December, not November."

She stood up then, very firm and erect, and she looked at him steadily. "I first mentioned ironworks to you last August. Because it was during the Reverend Woods' sermon for St. Bartholomew that the notion came to me. You talked to Brassey about it in September. And to Rodet. And again to Rodet in November. There's a dozen ways it could have gotten to Hudson."

John nodded, still restless. "Rodet!" he said. "The little frog is never there—yet never too far away."

"I don't honestly know about Rodet. But this meeting with Hudson means nothing," she assured him, truly believing it. "He sniffs about him like a champion hound. He's forgotten it already. George Hudson can take pound shares and sell them at twenty-pound premium any day of the week. So why should he want to get into anything so dull and safe as simple ironfounding!"

At last John seemed reassured. And her mention of Hudson's freelance stock-jobbing prompted the memory of the GNE shares and the promise of fifty thousand clear. "Beats me," he said, when he had told her that bit of good news, "where the money all comes from."

She had to peer at him in the firelight and the glimmer of her distant oil lamp to see if he was serious. "D'you really not know?" she asked.

"Obviously some of it comes from fools—like Beador if he's applying for shares at big premiums. But that can't be the whole of it." He had not meant to use Beador as an example; the name had slipped out. But now he was glad. Now perhaps they could talk about it.

She appeared not to hear him, her eyes fixed on the dancing flames. And then she continued: "There was a thing you said to me once. It must have been right back early on when we first got married. You said we'd got gold 'not buried in a bloody tropic island, but gold buried in the future. Waiting while we grow toward it.' I've never forgotten that."

"I said that to you the very first night we met. The twenty-sixth of August, 1839." His eye was on her but his mind's eye was back there, relishing the precision of his memory. "On the banks over the south portal of Summit Tunnel. That's when I said that."

"Well, George Hudson's gone one better than you. He's found a way of digging a tunnel to the future. And he's bringing that gold back here by the Troy ton!"

He laughed, delighted at the thought. But Nora was adamant. "It's the shareholders of the eighteen fifties and sixties—and beyond—who are paying that profit to us. What! Capitalize at fourteen million and call up four. Amalgamate with three others and keep the cash switching around so fast that half of it melts and everyone's blinded! I tell you, George Hudson may be the wax on the colonel's moustache for this generation of shareholders, but their sons will curse him—and their grandsons, too—if he continues much longer."

Her vehemence made him smile. "A tunnel in time!" he said, and then fell silent.

"Is *that* your worry about Beador?" she asked suddenly. "Did he say he's been speculating in shares?"

"As good as," John admitted.

"Is he badly stretched?"

"He wouldn't say. I told him we would need to know the full extent of his liability before we made any further move together."

"Not that we'd trust him," she said.

"Of course not. We must make our own inquiry."

"Yes."

"Or perhaps not. I'm coming round to your view. Let's drop Sir George and look for land elsewhere."

"No!" She was emphatic. John's admission excited her. The air carried upon it the distant smell of blood. "No. We can find out. Let's not be hasty. I imagine, then, you didn't ask Hudson about Beador?"

He shook his head. "Certainly not."

"Did you think we might ask Reverend Prendergast? Time we put him to work again."

The Reverend Doctor Prendergast had once tried to blackmail John and Nora. But since they had turned the tables on him, he had earned himself a respectable and far from trifling commission for help rendered; he had the back door password to most of the railway boardrooms in Britain—certainly to all in the north of the country. If Beador was on any applicants' list, the Reverend Doctor Prendergast could soon find out.

"Fancy not thinking of him," John said.

"You live hand-to-mouth, love," she told him. "You only thought of Hudson because he lives so close by."

He smiled, grudgingly, at the truth of it.

But Nora did not smile back. A memory had just come to her. The day she met George Hudson on York station was, in fact, the day she had seen John off to Stockton, the proposed site for the foundry. At the time she had dismissed it as coincidence. But now it had to be something more than that.

What was behind it? Hudson was obviously saying, "I know your game." But why? Was he also saying, "Don't think you can do anything in this world without my getting to hear of it"? In other words, was he just gently joking with them? Or was he laying the ground to walk off with their prize and then turn around and say, "I did my best to warn you; fair's fair and all's fair in business."

It was cat and mouse; but was the cat just playful—or hungry?

She hid these thoughts and fears from John until they had settled in her mind. Much later that night, when they lay in bed reading, she told him why she was sure that Hudson knew.

He took it as calmly as he always did, not pausing long for thought. "So," he said. "Let's assume the worst. Hudson is going to Beador and will magnetize and mesmerize the arrangements out of him and will then offer Beador something better—which is only too easy for Hudson. His signature on a soap bubble would seem worth more to Beador than anything we're justified in offering."

Nora let the silence, and the worry, grow until she judged it right to suggest: "If he's not going to snatch Beador from us, we risk nothing. If he is, then only a desperate remedy will cure him."

"Aye?" John asked, doubting. He trusted only her financial judgement.

"If you told him straight out about Beador, about what we fear he's done with his share applications, and why we need to know . . ."

"If I did that," John interrupted, impatient and disappointed, "he'd snatch the lot. We've already gone over—"

"Aye!" Nora said with redoubled conviction. "If *you* did that. But what if *I* did it? All simple and trusting? Ladylike, you know."

At least John considered the idea.

"You have to remember," she pressed on, "Hudson's carrying two hundred years of gentility on his back."

He still said nothing.

"It'd go against his grain to use intelligence given him by a gentle-woman asking for his help."

John smiled at that. Nora's whole claim to gentility derived from the fact that her great-grandfather had been squire of Normanton. His neglect of that small estate in favour of hunting had been the first step in the family's long slide into poverty and, finally, with the death of Nora's father, to destitution. Paradoxically, the squire-ancestor in the background enabled her to confess frankly to everyone the degree of poverty she had known. She was not the jumped-up servant she might seem, but a true gentlewoman reduced by the folly of others and rescued by her own innate qualities. Not an interloper but a heroine.

"You have a certain instinct in these matters," John conceded.

"Aye." She settled complacently and blew out her candle.

"And it's nearly always wrong," he said with no change of tone. He blew out his candle.

In the dark she smiled. "Never fret, dearest. *You'll* find a way, I'm sure."

But he did not; and next morning after breakfast he reluctantly agreed to try her suggestion.

Chapter 5

The snow began to fall when they were halfway to York. It was a light flurry that looked like a shower; but the land was cold and the flakes stuck to the ground from the very start. By the time they reached the station there was no doubt that the fall was going to be prolonged and no melt was in prospect.

"I hope you get through to Darlington," she said as their carriage halted. "If it's like this here, it's bound to be worse at Northallerton."

"I'm thinking of you," he said. "Forget Hudson and get straight home. At this rate there could be four foot on the tops by evening."

"Aye," she said. "I sh'll just see you off, then head for home."

He knew she was lying, but, as there were no means to insist on his way, he tacitly let her have hers.

When he was in the director's carriage he opened the window and leaned out. She reached up and squeezed his hand, the greatest intimacy they dared in public. He squeezed back and smiled, looking at her grey-brown eyes, eager in her smiling face, framed in dark ringlets that strayed from the edge of her bonnet; he had to remember that face over the next fortnight. "Throw away any bad pennies," he said.

She smiled and blinked.

The train backed out of the station, switched to the down rails, and set off northward. As the last carriage slid from view beyond the broad arch she turned and made at once for Hudson's office.

Hudson had two styles of greeting. The one for insiders was warm and almost conspiratorial; the one for strangers, outsiders, gulls, sheep for shearing, was majestic. It struck at the pit of the stomach; it awed important stockholders and silenced querulous directors. His greeting to Nora was an odd mixture of the two. "Hide the books!" he said in a stage whisper to Noakes, his clerk, while he came around to help Nora into her seat. "Give us a conundrum, lad," he added just before Noakes left.

"Uh . . . eleven per cent of one thousand two hundred and forty-seven pounds," Noakes said as he closed the door; it was a long-established ritual.

Nora and Hudson faced each other, smiling grimly, cat-and-cat. It was Nora's day to be Distressed Lady Seeks Help so she let Hudson say "One three seven pounds three and fivepence," a little ahead of her. Then lamely, with all the pedantry of a born loser, she added, "Three shillings and four and four-fifths pence, if you want a base figure."

He laughed magnanimously, pretending to accept second place. Good. He was slipping into the right mood.

"It was pleasant to see Mr. Stevenson again," Hudson began.

Nora displayed confusion. "This morning?" she asked, unbelieving.

Hudson frowned. "No, no. Yesterday." His grey eyes watched her. "We met near Leavening. I out for a trot. He on his way to repair my great blunder." He pulled a sudden wry, naughty-boy face.

"Great blunder!" Nora rose to his challenge. "Indeed. A chain's length of wet ground, Stevenson says." Then, as an unimportant afterthought, she added: "Odd he never told me you met."

Hudson wet his lips, uncertain of her.

"But then," she added brightly, burying the topic, "I fancy you spoke nothing of moment."

He's uncertain whether to believe me, she thought. It would take an indiscretion to prick his ears and drop that guard. "Stevenson and I were a little out of sorts," she confided, laughing to show it wasn't important. "I want a hand in the management of my trust fund. He and Chambers are *that* cautious. It saddens me to think of so many tens of thousands . . ." She halted, made herself blush, and stammered. "Well . . . thousands anyway—all lying as good as dead in Treasury stock."

Hudson smiled, a touch greedily. "I don't know how he resists the idea," he said.

She composed herself again. "Oh, I shall win," she told him. "I shall have the control of part of it at least."

And that's a notion, she thought, *will come back to him over the months. And no harm to me.*

"It won't please your banker, that," Hudson said, pretending this was all idle chatter.

"I'm out of concert with him, and all," she answered glumly, and then, as if appealing to his judgement, added: "I feel as we've a right to a great deal more intelligence than he ferrets out for us. We've put contracts for over two million pounds through him these five years past. I think we're very poorly served in that department."

Oblique though the appeal was, she made it plain enough to be irresistible to Hudson. "If it's railway intelligence, and ye think I could help . . ."

Nora showed the right mixture of dwindling caution and mounting relief. "You're quick, Mr. Hudson. Quick and kindly. For you know full well I came here of express purpose to ask. But I wanted to avoid a direct request you might have been embarrassed to refuse and loth to grant." She smiled her gratitude. "I'd not have pressed it."

"I'm certain you'd ask nothing dishonourable," Hudson warned.

"Indeed," she said. "I'm very sensible of your honour, which I know would prevent you from taking advantage of anything you might hear from me."

For the first time he saw where he had been manoeuvred. He looked steadily at her until, apparently struck by a sudden thought, he smiled. "Oh, I can't promise that," he said.

She pressed her lips together and waited.

"The day after you get control of that fund I shall be knocking at your door."

She joined his laughter. "Better come on the day before," she warned. "Day after may be too late."

His laughter quickly died. "I believe *that*," he said.

The time for chatting and joking was over. She gathered herself together and, sitting upright, said: "We are turning over the idea of going into foundry work on our own account." He showed only a polite and casual interest. "Nothing as yet is settled, but Rodet, whom I'm sure you know . . ." Hudson nodded. "Rodet has put a friend of his, Sir George Beador, in touch with us. There's a possible partnership in the venture. The interests are mutual."

"Stockton!" Hudson interrupted. "Of course. *That* Beador." A satisfied look came over him. "Stockton, eh?"

"Aye." Nora confirmed his pleasure. "Every scrap of iron we send inland will go over your metals. North out or south out." He rubbed his hands in pantomime. "So you've a further reason to wish us well."

He pouted at that. "My own friendship would ensure my every assistance."

Nora placated him. "I'm sure, Mr. Hudson. But a sound business reason always helps."

He smiled again. "Why iron?" he asked.

There were a dozen and one reasons for going into ironworks, but the one closest to Nora's heart was one that only another financial adept would understand. She had often wanted to put it to John, but he would have known at once that she was showing off, giving the most abstruse reason of all when the dozen simpler ones were compelling enough. Chambers, too, would understand, but he would also find some way to turn it against her. Now was her chance. Hudson would surely see it at once, and admire her shrewdness.

Casually, as if it were really too obvious, she said: "If we can hold our present stocks as a liability, balanced against such assets as unpaid debt on invoiced goods, we're in a much better position than if we just hold the same stock as a depreciating asset."

He coughed and cleared his throat. "Yes," he said. "How true."

To Nora it was barely credible that he did not grasp the point; yet he clearly did not. She pressed on at once, pushing this extraordinary discovery deeper. "Manufacturer's stock-in-trade does not automatically depreciate," she added.

"That's clever," he said at length. His admiration was so quietly genuine that she knew beyond certainty this was the first time in his life the point had struck him.

For her it was a discovery of cardinal importance. On several oc-

casions recently she had been on the point of taking shares in a number
of Hudson's lines; soon her mere intuitive distrust of him would have
been unable to withstand the strong commercial arguments for investing in such huge success as Hudson had shown. But now it was clear
that he was no genius at all. Just a clever lad who had found a tin
whistle and had taught himself to play four or five tunes to perfection.
He did not *understand* accounts; he merely knew a handful of impressive
tricks. God be praised she had discovered the fact in time.

Quickly, to prevent his becoming embarrassed, she said: "Stevenson
tells me not to talk such French. He says if we take up foundry work,
it'll be for the profit, not for tricks with the ledgers." She chuckled. "I
daresay he's right. He usually is."

"So it's not certain?" Hudson was relieved to be back on familiar
ground.

"It is in *my* mind." She grew conspiratorial. "Stevenson resists it
because it takes us out of itinerant trade into manufacture—fixed trade."

Hudson nodded sagely. "Not a loud argument when money is given
a voice," he said.

"My doubt," she said, becoming Distressed Lady once again, "is
Beador. He's on the rack for cash, and well stretched. Yet we fear he's
applied for shares in projected railways. Several of them."

"Ah! Hoping, no doubt, that by the time there was a call he would
have some income from your foundry to meet it. He wants to eat the
calf in the cow's belly."

"Worse than that," Nora said. "The cow isn't even his. It's ours."

Hudson stood and began to pace in front of the tall sash windows
that lit his palatial office; in the deep pile of the carpet his boots made
no more sound than the snow which fell relentlessly outside.

"What may I do?" he asked at length. "Give him his subscription at
par, and tip you the wink when you should tell him to sell?"

Nora did not even smile. "I think," she said, "that honest Yorkshire
folk the likes of you and me were not put upon this world in order to
line the pockets of the ne'er-do-well southern gentility. If apples are
falling from the trees, I'll eat them. Not stick them back on the bough.
It's against Nature."

The pitiless cast of her eyes brought him to a standstill; he glimpsed
an implacable hardness there beyond the melting reach of love or
charity.

"No," she went on. "You can tell us how deep he's dug his grave.
And then I'll tell you how bad we want him burned."

Hudson breathed out sharply, unable to take his eyes from her; unable to reply.

She smiled then. "You think that's hard?" she asked. "You think *me* hard." It was not a question. "Aye, well so I am. And if we are to take a partner, I want one who learned his business sense the hard way. Soft things crumble."

Chapter 6

If she had gone straight home from the station, as she had promised John she would, Nora might have made it without trouble. But the half hour she spent with Hudson had put six more inches of snow on the highway. She and Willet had to abandon the coach—among several others—at the foot of Garraby Hill, unhitch the two horses, and stumble rather than ride the remaining few miles, with Willet leading the horses, forcing them to plunge and tread a path through waist-deep snow, and Nora, dressed in billowing crinolines for a carriage ride, forging behind them like a cork in a tight tube. Just to negotiate the drive, where the snow lay deepest, took over half an hour.

There were times, as she battled through the drifts, when she felt they might not make it to the house, even though its lights were fitfully in view between the flurries of snow. Despite her exertions, and all those layers of clothing, she was cold to the very marrow. It made her realize, in the most immediate and physical way, her vulnerability. All their money, all their power, all their influence—these were of less use out there in that snow-clogged lane than the warmth of a single lucifer!

Yet, in a way, it was merely a physical restatement of how she felt most of the time. Not once had their increasing wealth and position brought her any true ease. Each step up the ladder made the prospect of a fall that much more giddy—without bringing any very tangible reward. John often said he wished they were back at a single contract, so that he could deal at first hand with the men and the rock and the elements. She often wished it too, so that they could feel the poverty at their heels again and feel the reward of each penny of profit. Without those two, the stick and the carrot, what was their struggle all about?

She was glad, when they finally reached the house, that she was too exhausted to pursue such questions.

Next day Willet said "No rest for the wicked" so often that Mrs. Jordan, the cook, almost ran a knife through him. It was certainly one of the most strenuous days of his life. With the help of two field men hired from the farmer below, who naturally had no work for them, he had to dig out the driveway up to the brow of the hill. Then Nora made them clear a trotting circle around the paddock, where she could see it from her bedroom window (and where Willet could never be certain if she were watching or no), and finish the day with a two-hour trot with all four horses and Winifred's pony, Pendle. He brought them in cool and rubbed them down. Before he was finished, another heavy fall of snow began.

Young John and Winifred were delighted. It put another three feet on the previous fall and completely blanked out the windows on the ground floor, so that, even when the sun came out at noon, they walked from room to room in a frosty, opalescent twilight.

Because of the cold, Nora let them stay in the winter parlour and paste in their scrapbooks or play with the acorns, chestnuts, and bits of wood that Young John called "my sojers." Cox and the servants were kept busy digging away the snow before the windows. Every hour they carried pans of boiling water up to the loft to pour into the two big slate cisterns and prevent them from icing over. It was all the water they had, for the pipe from the well had frozen and the handpump would not even turn.

Having less snow to dig, Willet and Co. finished soon after midday dinner, thinking themselves set for a less strenuous afternoon. But Nora sent him up to the ridge of the roof with a rope yoked to a broomhead. One farmhand stood either side of the house, each with a hold on the rope, and together they swept the snow down, before it could melt and freeze and pry apart the tiles. Indoors the children followed their progress from room to room and cheered as each sunlit avalanche fell upon the men below. Nora, looking up and down the vale, saw with pride that the Old Manor was the first to clear its roof. That night another eighteen inches fell.

By noon the following day, the roads were cleared enough for letter mails at least to come through, and Nora heard from John that he would go straight from Warrington to Exeter and then to France. This bland announcement annoyed her, though it was plainly foolish for him even to think of returning to Yorkshire in such weather. She envied him the itinerant freedom of his work; and then she disliked herself for that envy.

The trouble was that John had exactly the sort of freedom she was denied: to do precisely those things he was good at. Her skill, she knew—she *knew*—was to handle money with a flair that few others could equal. In fact, to be quite honest, no one could equal it.

Once, at a dinner of the York & Ainsty hunt, she had overheard a retired general talking about a new book on Caesar's wars in which, he maintained, some of the diagrams were wrong. What had impressed Nora was the general's claim that as soon as he had cut the pages, before he read any of the text and even before he looked to see which particular campaign or battle was being described, he *knew* they were wrong. The wrongness of the supposed dispositions of legions and co-horts leaped at him from the page. There was no conceivable set of circumstances that could have led a commander of Caesar's stature to put men in such-and-such order. Nora could see that the general's listen-ers were politely skeptical, thinking that anything so complex could never be so immediately apparent as to "spring off the page," and she had longed to join in and say "Yes, yes, it *is* so; it can be so; I know it." For that was precisely how she could now "see" anything to do with money.

But it remained no more than a party trick. Like the game Hudson played with her of figures-in-the-head. If she had been born a man, she would have parlayed that skill into a fortune. If she were allowed to own property, even, or to have money that was inalienably her own, she could have gone some way in that direction. But all the money that John called "hers" and all the land she had bought were actually and legally his. If the firm was stretched, every penny of it would go into the melting pot, too. She could lose everything her skill had created, not through any fault of John's but merely because times were slack or through uninsurable geological disaster.

Yet in a way it *would* be John's fault, for it was he who insisted not merely on keeping all the eggs in one basket but on actually having just the one giant egg. There, if anywhere, was the real source of her envy: that he was free to pursue his incautious way while she could achieve all that she knew to be right only through him—and only by making him deviate from what he felt to be right. And her envy shamed her because she knew how tolerant he was of her, how much attention he paid her ideas, how he relied on her judgement—all to a quite extraordinary degree when one thought how other husbands treated their wives, both in the circles that she and John had sprung from and in those where they now moved.

And so, dissatisfied with life, and at odds with herself because of that dissatisfaction, she turned to the railway papers. Usually they brought the welcome tidings of new surveys, new routes, new companies inviting subscription, others beginning parliamentary work, others gaining their charters and actually asking for tenders—work, work, work. Today there were announcements for twenty-five new companies. It did not please her. For a month and more now, such announcements had failed to please her.

As a matter of course she kept in her head a running total of the capital invited for new railway work. It was, after all, from that seemingly inexhaustible well that the Stevenson buckets were filled. For some years past, the annual new capital put into railways had been about six million pounds. But this year people seemed to have gone mad. New lines projected since December, two months ago, would, if sanctioned and completed, call for capital of over a hundred million— £106,724,000 to the nearest thousand. That represented a hundred and four new lines to add to the forty completed and the hundred-odd now under way. It was obvious to her that not one-tenth of that number could be built; vast sums were going to be wasted on surveys, lawyers, parliamentary bribes, prospectuses; vast numbers of people were going to subscribe their deposits for companies that would never exist; and vast fortunes were going to be made by the unscrupulous. Hudson's name was down on twenty of today's twenty-five lists.

How could a country that found it difficult to raise six million a year possibly find nearly twenty times that amount?

John would not be made to worry. And neither would Chambers. "The governors of the Bank of England have great experience in these things," he said. "There will be no repeat of the panic of 1836."

The governors of the Bank of England, Nora thought to herself, were so deep in hot water themselves that they dared not raise the lending rate above two and a half per cent for fear their own private companies would start falling to bits.

She alone seemed to find anything alarming in this ridiculous railway bubble, but that was not what irked her. There was nothing of the journalist or missionary in Nora—no wish to parade her vision before the world or set it to rights. She would rather use private insight for private advantage. Let fools hang.

But here she could not do that. For her private insight amounted to this: A money crisis unparallelled in history was now brewing. Nothing could prevent it. And unless John could be persuaded to share her anxiety, Stevenson's would do nothing to prepare to meet it.

For the first time she began to regret her role in suggesting the Beador partnership; it added one more unknown to a landscape already cluttered with too many uncertainties.

Chapter 7

Ten days later, when John was due to return from France, the snow still lay deep over most of the country. It obliterated hedgerows, filled lanes and cuttings, and smoothed out the wrinkles of the landscape like a flat-iron over linen. Only the mail coach routes were cleared. Villages, hamlets, and farms more than about a half mile off such routes preferred to sink back into ancient self-sufficiency rather than expend the energy needed to put them back in touch with the nation. Shepherds would go after lost sheep, people would run for doctors, creditors would come for their money . . . among them they would beat some sort of usable path. Even the heaviest snow in memory was not eternal.

The worst to suffer were the birds, who could find not an inch of ground to peck at, nor a trickle of water to drink. They huddled fever-ishly in farmyards and at back doors, scratching through the hen runs and barnyards, mobbing the pig swill pails in the hands of the pigmen, and flocking at every thawed-out pump. The sight of them so upset Winifred that she spent a whole morning, part aided and part hindered by Young John, rubbing together the fat skimmed from the lights boiled for the dogs with the sweepings of the hayloft and the winnow-ings from the horses' oats. Her hands felt raw with scratches by the time she and Young John had finished, but they had made a good three pounds of birdfood between them. After lunch they penned the dogs in the harness room and scattered the food over the stable yard; Nora, caught up in their enthusiasm, put out several shallow trays of melted snow water.

Normally there were perhaps a hundred birds, at most, overwinter-ing in the Old Manor grounds. But by some telepathy the mere presence of so much food seemed to become common knowledge among all the birds of the vale, so that several hundred descended on the yard, screech-ing, squawking, chirping, and cawing. They fought, darting shrilly at

one another, rising in alarmed flurries of wind and feathers, while preda-
tory bands wheeled above and fell on the groundlings like clamouring
angels of death. Winifred and Young John were at first delighted at the
wealth their offerings of fat and cereal had conjured up; but as the mob
grew thicker and the noise more menacing, their excitement became
hectic and took on a bright-eyed tinge of fear.

The noise completely masked all sounds of John's approaching
horse. Mrs. Jarrett, who had been upstairs to move the newspapers that
kept the sun off the carpets, saw him from one of the bedroom windows
and just had time to get below and tell Nora before John came trotting
into the yard, scattering the melee of crows, blackbirds, thrushes, and
robins. He reined in, amazed, while birds of every size and winter colour
wheeled and darted around him and then by that same strange telepathy,
rose and scattered to their everyday territory.

"What's this?" he asked as he swung from the saddle. "Robin Red-
breast's workhouse?"

"Papa!" Winifred and Young John ran forward to clutch at his
thighs and try to hug him off the ground.

"Dearest!" Nora, just behind them, held out her arms for him to
grasp in his. Her skirts swept the scanty remains of fatty gleanings into
the hollows of the cobblestone floor.

Willet let out the dogs and came to take the horse, which was railway property. "Sh'll I ride'm back in now, master?" he asked hopefully.
He could just tolerate a good evening in York. Puck and Tip yapped
and fussed around John.

"Nay," John said. "He can follow the mail tomorrow. Unless we go
in ourselves."

Dejectedly Willet took the horse indoors for a rubdown.

"When you've done that," Nora shouted after him, "you can trot
our four to the foot of Garraby Hill and back. And," she turned to
Winifred, "do you want to go, too?"

Winifred looked at her father, not wanting to leave him, yet longing to ride Pendle after so many inactive days. John smiled. "Go on," he
said. "Your mother and I have much to talk about."

"Birds," Young John said, flailing at the walls and gutters and roof
ridges where the remnants of the horde still sat, chattering with impatience.

"Yes," John said. "Who's been feeding birds, eh?"

"Me!" the children shouted.

"They spent all morning, and it went in about two minutes." Nora
laughed.

"Only it wasn't our birds. It was birds from Painslack Farm, and Deepdike, and all around."

"Just like humans," John said.

And though he was joking, there was an edge in his voice that made Nora realize that part of him was not so much displeased as shocked at what she and the children had done. Even Winifred must have felt it for she said quickly: "We used the fat off the dogs' pail and the sweepings from the hayloft. And look at my hands!" She displayed their redness like an honourable scar.

John bent and kissed them before he folded them and pulled her sleeves back straight. "It does your heart credit," he said.

But Nora could sense that there was still something in him that grudged what they had done, so she squeezed his arm and said: "Come on. What is it?"

"If it's waste fat and sweepings, well enough. But soon it'll be drippings from the kitchen and chimpings from the table and oats from the horses." He looked from one to the other, smiling, wondering if the incident was worth the lesson. He decided it was. "This snow . . . this hard weather . . . is sent from God. It's part of God's purpose."

"Why?" Winifred asked.

"We cannot know that," he told her. "Perhaps it is a testing for the birds. Most of them *may* die. But not all. And the ones who live will be the quickest, smartest, and strongest, and cleverest. And all the slow, stupid, lazy ones won't lay eggs because they are dead. So perhaps it's God's way of improving the birds. But how can He do that if"—he pointed at the remnants of the feast—"if we go feeding the five thousand?"

He saw that Winifred was going to cry so he quickly stooped and, taking her hands again, spoke directly to her. "But we mustn't forget God's other purpose, must we. When you feel kindly and wish to feed the birds, *He* put that gentleness in you. So what do we do, eh? There's a puzzle." Curiosity overcame her chagrin. "I'll tell you. We devote our charity to one or two special birds. Make a friend of a pair of robins and look after them. We can't feed the whole world, but we can do our bit for one or two."

Winifred, remembering the frightening dark clamour of the rapacious hordes of birds, was charmed by this new idea.·

"Willet shall make a little table and we can hang it from the old sundial arm over the nursery window and you may put a small measure of oats there every day," John said, straightening again, with a cracking of joints. "Eee!" he added. "Hades' flames are crackling today!"

"We could still put water down for them," Nora said. "That costs nothing."

"Oh, aye," he agreed. "Put down water by all means." They began to stroll back indoors.

"I put down that," she said, pointing to the pans and trays.

He laughed and chucked her under the chin. "I'd never have guessed it," he said, "from your manner of speaking."

She pouted. "Have you eaten?" she asked.

"I could put myself around a slice of cold pie. Hudson is coming at about six and will stop for dinner before going on to Bessingby Hall."

"But that's twenty, nearly twenty-five miles. You go up and look at the children's scrapbook and Winifred's stitching, and I'll see about a bite for you. Hudson'd do better to stop the night."

"Oh, he probably will," John said, lifting a child under each arm to go upstairs; he spoke over their struggling laughter. "But you know him —never promises anyone more than an hour."

"I'll get a fire lit in the rose room and pans in the sheets."

*   *   *

"That wasn't like you, John," she said later, after he had romped with the children and eaten and come back downstairs to go through correspondence and accounts.

"I thought there'd be a crop of problems with the freeze-up," he said. "But it seems to have solved more than it's posed. I don't understand it." He put the pile of letters down.

"John?"

"What's not like me?" he asked, knowing the answer.

"All they did was feed the birds. You made a regular sermon out there. I'd say that's not like you."

"Aye," he laughed, embarrassed. "I thought I was going it to start with. Then . . . I don't know." He sighed. "Winifred is so—she feels everything so. Takes it all so much to heart. She'll have a lot of money one day. It's bad enough running the gauntlet of all that 'sell what thou hast and give it to the poor' and rich men and camels in the eye of a needle or whatever it is. I can see her taking it all seriously and giving every penny away."

"John! She's but four." Nora laughed.

He would not be cajoled into seeing the comic side of it. "She was just the same at two. Always giving things away. We've got to make her understand that that sort of generosity isn't—well, it isn't a kindness in the end. Not to her. Not to the objects of her generosity—certainly not to them. It frustrates God's will, in my view. You'll never make a man better by doing for him what he could and should do for himself."

"I think the birds frightened her. She thought it would be like scattering crumbs after a picnic. It was more like free-beer day at elections. I know I was frightened."

"Well, maybe that's God's way of saying the same thing to her. And to you."

"Aye," she said, slipping facetiously back into dialect. " 'Appen. Belike. Mayhap." She disliked the implied rebuke and grew tired of the subject.

He grinned and looked sharply at her through narrowed eyes. "If I ask you for a kiss," he said, "one kiss, and if you grant it, will you promise not to try any of your mucky tricks."

She breathed out sharply, pretending astonishment, as if he had hit her in the stomach. "You may sing for it," she said and then made him chase her twice around the room before he got his kiss. "Just one," she said, and she kept her hands folded behind her back.

"There must be a happy mean," he said as they settled again.

"You be happy, and I'll be mean," she said.

He gave a hollow laugh and pretended to fall asleep. She sighed and leaned back into the sofa. There were always these trivial failures of mood and understanding when he came back from a journey; like dog and bitch, circling each other warily, wanting a depth of companionship that could not be instantly had—a depth that had to be plumbed anew each time.

"Lucky Thornton," she said. "Came out on top, as ever." In his letter from Exeter he had told her of one of Walter's adulteries.

"Came *in* on top, if I know him," John said.

It was her turn not to laugh, and she wondered why; if he had said it tomorrow, or at any time except in this hour of returning, she'd have laughed.

"Candidly I'd forgotten him," John said. "There's one thing hammering in here." He tapped his skull. "Iron. Ironworks. I tell thee, love, there's no need to goad me on now. I'm red hot to start. The things I've seen."

She sat up, delighted. "In France?"

"Aye. And here, in Manchester. I came back through Manchester."

"Ooh. Tell us!"

"Have ye heard of Schneider-Creusot, the French ironworks?"

"Of course," she said. "They did a lot of rail for the Paris–Versailles. And others."

"Well, they sold a big forging hammer to Rodet. And Schneider himself came up with it. I had a long talk with him. Broken French and mangled English but we got through; now there's a man. At the end of 1839, as near as he can remember it, he happened to be at Nasmyth's works in Patricroft, and Nasmyth was away. One of his assistants skimmed through the pages of Nasmyth's scheme book, thinking it was his book of appointments. Well, while he's doing that, Schneider's eye happens to fall on a sketch. 'What's that?' he asks. 'Oh,' says the assistant, 'that's something Mr. Nasmyth sketched for Humphreys before he died—a steam-powered hammer. For the old paddle shafts of the *Great Britain.* They're not going to build it, though; now they're going over to a propellor instead of paddles. No one else has got any use for a hammer that big.' Ha haaa! When Nasmyth called on Schneider at Creusot next year—'What's that?' he says. 'Why, *your* steam-powered hammer, Mr. Nasmyth!' says Schneider."

Nora was shocked. "And he didn't pay for it?"

"Of course not. Nasmyth hadn't bothered to take out a patent. Why should he pay? Schneider was quite open. Eay—but you never saw such an engine. That's why I came back through Manchester, to see the works at Patricroft."

"What's Nasmyth like?" Nora asked.

John thought a while. "You remember that dancing bear at Kipling Cotes Derby?"

Nora nodded.

"Something about him put me in mind of that bear. Same puzzled eyes, head on one side, tight little mouth. Must be near forty now. He's built a steam hammer there where he can lift it and lower it with steam under ever such fine control. This'll show you—he put an egg under it and brought the hammer down with such force you'd think not a smattering'd survive. And then in the last instant he halted it so that the hard shell was cracked but the soft shell was left intact!" His eyes shone as he spoke. "What do you say to that?"

"It's hard to imagine such power."

"I said at once, 'That's just what we need for driving piles.' Think— it can deliver a blow a second." He began to pound the back of the sofa with his fist in time with the tall clock between the windows. "Ten tons falling like that every second. It solves the problem of wet ground;

we could bridge the Wash with a dozen of those. Anyway, he's promised to get out sketches for a transportable engine for pile driving."

Nora laughed and put her hands to her cheeks. "Think!" she said. "Your Mr. Nasmyth makes a sketch of an engine to forge a paddle wheel and, without knowing it, he quadruples the value of every bit of marshland at present impeding the progress of every city in the kingdom!"

"I also told him when our foundry was built I'd take a pair. Schneider says he's made more wrought iron at less cost with that hammer than with five helve hammers. It's the ability to control them, you see. Schneider said a good operator can crack a nutshell without harming the kernel. I thought it was just Frenchman's talk until I saw Nasmyth."

"So," Nora said, leaning back and grinning at him. "Having procrastinated for eight months, we now want our foundry built yesterday."

He smiled and sighed his agreement.

"Let's hope Mr. Hudson has brought some good news of your friend and mine, Sir George Beador."

*   *   *

When Hudson's coach came crunching over fresh snow into the courtyard, nearer to seven than the promised six, Nora was certain he'd stay the night. He came in by the garden door, being closer to the stables, and stamped the snow off his boots. "Sticky," he said in disgust. "It keeps heaping and crunching under the tyres. Very discomforting."

"You'll surely stay the night, Mr. Hudson," Nora urged.

"Yes, do, Hudson," John said. "You could get halfway to Flamborough and spend the night in a drift."

Hudson patted a bulge at his breast pocket. "Important papers," he said.

"Ah well, do what suits your business best," John agreed.

"Perhaps I will stop," Hudson said quickly. "If it's no great inconvenience." He looked at Nora, who merely smiled as John said, "Madame Clairvoyante there has had a room heated three hours or more."

Hudson rubbed his hands briskly. "Fate then," he said. "I'll give it no argument. Profound thanks, rather."

John had put a poker in the fire to heat while they were seeing Hudson in. As soon as they returned to the winter parlour he withdrew it and plunged it, spitting and fuming, into a punchbowl. "Here's a navvy's drink for you, Hudson," he said. "Rum and rough cider—civilized by Mesdames Stevenson and Jarrett with raisins and cinnebar."

"Cinnamon!" Nora corrected.

"Whichever it is," Hudson said, "it's the most welcoming aroma ever to greet me."

Its fragrance filled the room like an incense.

He took his glass, waited for Nora, and then supped noisily through his teeth; breathing out fiery satisfaction he leaned back and shut his eyes, a careful picture of happy exhaustion.

"Hard times, Hudson?" John asked.

"Capital times," Hudson said.

"It's the obtuseness of his codirectors vexes him," Nora said.

He chuckled scornfully, still with his eyes shut—*a good orator's trick, that,* Nora thought. "Directors! One of them said the other day to me—to me! At a board meeting, too. To me!—'We'd like some account, Mr. Hudson, of the decisions being taken in our name.' " Eyes still shut, he chuckled. Then, quite suddenly he sat up and looked straight at Nora with his blue-grey eyes wide open, as if surprised at himself. " 'Do you, sir!' said I. 'Do you indeed! Then you shall not have it!' " He burst into loud, infectious laughter, compelling them to join him.

"I'll wager you wish you could silence Denison as easily," John said.

Hudson waved him away as if he were a beggar. "Denison will sink without trace, and his great London & York railway with him. I didn't make all my amalgamations to have Mr. Edmund Denison come and take the prize from me. There's only one way to York, and that's over my metals."

"There's a lot of interests against you," Nora said. "The Lincolnshire people have a big voice."

"They shall have a big line, too. My own Nottingham, Newark, & Lincoln. Next year. The man I blame is Locke; I believe Locke to have been a disaster to railway progress. This nonsense at Shap, now. Four miles up a gradient of one in seventy-five. Think of the unnecessary coals that will consume this next fifty years. He says hang the running costs; I say hang the capital cost. I know who the shareholders will bless, fifty years from now."

John and Nora fought the temptation to look at each other and smile.

"He's good for such as us," John said. "Brunel likes a confusion of big and small contractors. But Locke is happy to hand over a hundred miles and more to me or Brassey or Peto."

Hudson supped his drink with relish, cupping the tankard in his hands. "You like him, then. And the coal miners must like him. There's an epitaph—and the sooner, the better." He laughed, and then, changing mood, said: "By the by, there is a basket of eggs outside your kitchen door. I almost fell over them on my way round to the garden."

John and Nora both looked heavenward. "Mrs. Jordan," Nora said wearily. "The cook. Will not bring eggs indoors after sunset. She will also not sweep dirt from the house, because the luck goes with it." Nora began to tally Mrs. Jordan's oddities on her fingers. "She will not cut a child's nails till its first birthday, for fear of making it a thief. She will not count her own teeth, for what reason she will not say. She will not put a lantern on a table; what was it she said about *that?*"

John prompted: " 'A lantern on the table, a death in the stable.' Once when I set a lantern down on her table she came in very triumphant next day—at breakfast, no less—with a dead rat she'd just found in the stable!"

"It had been dead already for weeks," Nora said. "But that didn't worry her. And what was it about hair? When she gets the girl to cut her hair she throws the bits on the fire. And if they flare up, she's going to live a long time. But if they oh, what was the word? A lovely word."

"Crozzil?" Hudson suggested. "If it crozzils up, she'll soon be dead."

"Yes!" Nora said. "That was it."

"That's an old saying hereabouts. What does she say about cutting a loaf at both ends?"

"Yes!" Nora laughed. "The devil will fly over the house. And if you put the loaf on its side, the breadwinner will fall ill. Really! If anyone wanted a book of superstitions they'd only need to follow her around for a week and they'd have a library."

"She wouldn't come to us on Friday," John said. "Remember? We engaged her on a Thursday and she wouldn't come until Saturday. They do it to provoke us, you know. I'm sure of it."

"And she gets the others at it," Nora said. "Even Cox, who is the most sensible of them."

"Yes, I thought that the other day, when I met her out in that cold wind with Caspar, whose nose was *streaming*. She said she thought the chill air might just 'draw the cold from the wee mite.' "

"Aye! That's Mrs. Jordan. And Cox went in and out of the house by different doors, I'll be bound," Nora said. "That's another of hers."

Hudson, who had nodded as to an old friend at each superstition, now wagged his finger. "Power, you see." He turned to John. "You say they do it to provoke us. And you're right. It gives them power of a kind—for we tolerate as superstition what we would otherwise certainly call an outright insubordination. Have you ever known a man who would start to sink a shaft on the thirteenth of any month? Even for triple pay?"

John shook his head. "I had a man once who brought his dinner wrapped in a clout made from one of his wife's old shifts. Took it underground. You never heard such a fuss. I had to dismiss the man, and it almost took bell, book, and candle to get the others back below."

"I'm sure it's to do with power," Hudson said firmly. "And I don't think *we* are so very superior. We smile at Mrs. Jordan and her cross of 'wiggin'—"

"What's that?" Nora asked. "That's a new one to me."

Hudson chuckled. "Somewhere about her, you may be sure, in the hem of a skirt or somewhere, she'll have a rough wooden cross made of wiggin twigs—wiggin is mountain ash, rowan—tied together, to bring fortune and keep off witches and werewolves. We smile at it, yet"—he fished in an inside pocket and drew forth a sheet of paper—"yet what's that? A piece of paper. A share certificate. What, pray, does *that* signify?"

John volunteered the obvious feed: "It's supposed to be a share in an enterprise or an adventure. But?"

"Quite so. A piece of paper, to bring fortune and keep the wolf, if not the werewolf, from the door." He looked at the share. "St. Kilda Railway Company," he read and burst into laughter. "Someone sent me that today, happy and hopeful. St. Kilda! Forty miles beyond the Hebrides, fifty inhabitants, sixty furlongs end to end!"

"Any advance on sixty?" John asked.

"Any advance on sixty and the next stop's New York," Hudson answered. "Yet"—he waved the paper—"people are buying. These will sell."

"They will if George Hudson's put his name on the scrip list," Nora said. "It's a name we see subscribed to many lists."

John looked sharply at her, thinking her tone a bit smart; but she kept her eyes steadily on Hudson. And Hudson looked unblinkingly at her. "That is self-protection," he said, trying to win her with a smile. "If *I* don't, someone else will. And that means some other railway will." He sighed, drained his tankard, and stretched his boots toward the fire. "For five very lean years—not lean for you or me, I know, but lean on the Exchange—people have been straining at the leash for loose capital to invest in railways. And now that money is beginning to float again, there are bound to be"—he crumpled the share certificate and threw it on the hearth—"nonsensicals. Bits of paper like that are going to scour the purses of a lot of fools, including, I regret to say, your Sir George Beador." At once the tension became almost palpable; John and Nora scarcely breathed, watching Hudson intently. "The question is: Who is to get the scourings? Some overnight moneybags who will put it all into land? That's no good to progressive people like yourselves and me. Or will it go to Mr. Edmund Denison, Mr. Glyn, Mr. Labouchere, Mr. McGregor? That's no good to progressive people like my shareholders —and me. Now tell me what I am to do, since this lunatic floating capital must be fixed *somewhere?*"

"Why not tell us about Sir George Beador, instead," John said quietly.

Hudson smiled, taking this as a concession of his point. From another inside pocket he drew a single folded quarto sheet. He was on the point of opening it when he paused and looked up, first at John, then at Nora. "Is it your impression," he asked, "that Beador has mortgaged Maran Hill?"

"He as good as said so," John answered. "I know he's mortgaged Framwell, his place in Durham."

"Interesting." Hudson opened the paper. "I've had my best ferret on this. A man called Croucher. I'd say if he can't find it, it doesn't exist. And he can find no such mortgage on Maran Hill."

Nora was at once alert. If Maran Hill was still free of charge, and if its value was enough to cover the debt, Beador might be one of those problems that turned into blessings.

"Oh, that's hopeful surely," John said.

Hudson, with compassion, merely handed over the paper he had opened. John began to study it.

"Aloud," Nora said.

John, who had already seen enough to raise his eyebrows and sink his guts, sighed and read: "Pilbrow's Atmospheric Railway and Canal Propulsion Company, 40 shares; London and Dublin Direct, 35; Railway Guarantee Company, 10; Great Welch Junction Railway, 10; Railway Banking Company, 15—or is it 13?—no, 15; Atmospheric Rapid Mail Conveyance Co., 20; Prosser's Patent Wooden Railway Guide-wheel Co., 43—*no!*" He let the paper fall. "I can't continue."

Nora, calm—indeed, frigid—took the paper up and scanned it rapidly. "Everything except Cooke's National Extravaganza," she said.

"One or two will pay," Hudson offered, as a bystander might offer cheer in a condemned cell. "But it will stand him a good eighteen thousand, in my view."

John took the paper back. They watched him read it, with more composure. "I could turn a profit on these," he said carefully.

Nora drew in breath to speak but it was Hudson who voiced the thought. "All three of us could. But we'd look to Sir George and the rest of the Foolish Tribe to furnish us those profits. Is that"—he darted Nora a swift, amused glance—"what honest Yorkshire folk the likes of us were put upon this world to achieve?"

"But he's a partner," John protested.

"Then he has an odd way of expressing his idea of a partner's obligation. Half those were subscribed since December last." Hudson looked from John to Nora; neither replied. "Mrs. Stevenson?" he prompted.

Nora, looking steadily at John, laid a finger on the paper and said: "It's the nearest I've seen to an autographed death warrant."

John winced at her hardness but offered no argument. Instead he sat up, thanked Hudson, handsomely and briskly, for his help, and suggested they go in to dinner. The subject was not raised again until after they had retired to bed.

John's lovemaking was brusque and perfunctory, as unrewarding to himself as to her. His warmest act was to kiss her, with a gentleness that was in itself an apology, before he composed himself to sleep.

"Nay," she fretted. "Don't brood now."

He sighed. " 'Death warrant,' " he quoted. "Is it really that simple to you?"

"There's only one reprieve I can see," she said.

"What's that?"

"If Sir George furnishes us a list identical to the one Hudson brought."

John gave a neutral grunt. "It would solve the moral problem."

"But the money problem. No."

She felt John shake his head. "It's not really a money problem. It's a *man* problem, a problem of George Beador."

There was a long, thoughtful silence before Nora said: "What would you say Maran Hill is worth?"

"Every bit of twenty-five thousand; he'd be well covered if eighteen's the limit of his debt."

"Aye," Nora said. "It's not a bad house. And not a bad situation."

She felt John rocking with silent laughter. "Have ye counted the windows?" he asked at length.

"They'll abolish window tax this year. Or next."

"But have ye counted?"

"Eighty-four," she said.

He stopped laughing and sat upright. "You are in earnest!"

"I don't know," she said, truthfully. "But it's a thought."

"A big thought. It would take a lot of thinking."

"It's plain to me we're going to need a house in the south. If you start in Germany, Italy, Spain—never mind France. Living in Thorpe adds two days to every voyage."

"Aye," he said. "That's true, right enough."

He was not going to discuss it further, his tone implied. He sucked a tooth and scratched in his sidewhiskers. "It's strange," he said. "How little freedom we really have!"

"Why d'you say that?"

"If we take a house in the south, it'll not be that we wish to live there, or that it suits our station, or that we find it congenial—but that our business demands it."

"Surely a very good reason." She tugged his sleeve. "Hold me. Lie down and hold me. It frightens me when you talk as if it was all turning to dust and ashes. Why do you so often sneer when you say 'business'?"

He lay down and pulled her firmly to him. "It's not in *me*," he said. "The discontent is not in me. It's in the work. We're big enough now to take on any line, any length, over any terrain; but what's left? Cornwall . . . Wales . . . the Scotch Highlands . . ."

"London–York direct," Nora added.

"If Hudson doesn't squash it. It's not much when it's shared out. The average length of lines recently authorized is about ten miles. It's all little feeder and junction lines."

"They pay as well per mile."

"I learned my trade on the London–Birmingham . . . Liverpool . . . Preston . . . Manchester. All trunk lines. And where am I applying it? On the Piddlehinton–Sopping Wetbury single branch! Where's the glory in that!"

"Oh, I see. It's glory we take to the bank, is it!"

He squeezed her shoulders gently, giving them a little shake as he spoke. "You're right, love. Of course you're right. There's no glory in making a loss, however noble the venture. But why not both, eh? Why not? And the time to start thinking is now. We must think to the Empire. To India, Canada, Australia. And to Europe. They'll all come to us now. Brassey told me the Belgian company couldn't raise the capital until they had guaranteed an English engineer and an English contractor."

Nora relaxed and hugged him, reassured. "We'll amaze them all. Or you will," she said.

"I can do naught without thee."

"And if the profit on the Piddlehinton–Soaking Wetmarsh helps us strike farther afield, we'll build a hundred single branches."

He laughed then. "Aye. Seen in that light, it's endurable. Tolerable."

Much later she said: "I wonder if Beador will turn out honest."

John was so close to sleep that all he did was to grunt.

Before she, too, fell deep into slumber, Nora had rearranged the shrouded ballroom at Maran Hill many times.

One half of her—the cautious half—wanted to be rid of Sir George Beador and all the uncertainty he represented. The other half—the huntress—wanted to part him gently and cleanly from Maran Hill; and Hudson's news seemed to offer a way of doing exactly that.

Chapter 8

The snows of 1845 were the worst anyone could remember. For ten weeks the temperature did not once rise to a thaw. The poor got out-relief cutting timber, clearing snow—even along lanes that none wanted clear—and building needless walls and extensions to kennels and stables; even so, the times dealt hard with them. Eight cords of oak and elm went to keep Thorpe Old Manor warm, and there was no nonsense about cold nurseries; tepid baths were allowed.

John built a snowman, but he rolled the head too long on one axis so that, by chance, it turned into an amazingly lifelike bear. It squatted on its haunches and fixed the house with a daylong, nightlong stare. Winifred scratched a peephole in Jack Frost's patterns on her window and watched to see if Bruin moved at night, as Mrs. Jordan said he did. But there he stood, blue in the glacial moonlight, frozen in the frozen garden; Mrs. Jordan said it was cruel to torment the creature so, for he'd not stretch if he knew folk were looking.

Each day they trotted the horses and the pony, sometimes in the paddock, sometimes up on the highway. On one of her rides Winifred found a broken tin whistle sticking out of a snowdrift. Cox and Todd made a second effigy of snow, to play tin-whistle music to the bear in his loneliness. One night the breeze lay in just the right direction to moan through the pipes as through an aeolian harp. Winifred awoke briefly, heard it, and went smiling back to sleep; magic was abroad.

Next morning she opened her eyes to an indoor fairyland, for overnight the nursery had been transformed into an ice grotto. Folds of ice festooned the wall and long stalactites hung from the ceiling—milky green and grey and white and blue, all scintillating in the early sun. Her first thought was that she had been bewitched and transported to the Halls of the Ice Faeries. She lay rigid, taking stock, and fearing that every movement of her eyes would bring the hordes of her captors around her. But as one and then another familiar nursery feature claimed her attention she realized she was still at home—though a very changed and beautiful home.

Whoever had done it had worked a miracle. The little framed picture of a girl on a pony stared out through a wavy inch of ice upon the wall. The washstand was bound in gnarled roots of ice that grew in columns up the corner. She woke up Young John and together they danced and clapped hands and laughed at the wonder of it all.

Then Cox came in and said "Dear God!" And shortly after their mother appeared and wrung her hands and said that the cistern had cracked. "Just when your father's away, too." After breakfast Willet and the new stable lad, Myles, apprenticed from the orphanage, spent the morning with spades, trowels, hammers, chisels, and crowbars demolishing fairyland and throwing the sherds out the window.

The plumber came and said the cistern hadn't cracked, one side of it had merely been pried slightly apart. He showed Nora how the lead in the screw sockets had shrunk and split and allowed the ice to thrust one side of the cistern away—the screws pulling out of the lead and coming away with the side as it went. He said he could melt fresh lead into the sockets but it might only happen again. The sockets ought to have been skewed, not straight.

That evening John came back wearied by a three-day journey from Havre, through a black-and-white world all the way home. He wanted only to thaw out, eat, love, and sleep. But when he heard why the children were sleeping in the rose bedroom, the problem intrigued him, and after dinner he made Nora take him up to the attic and show him the cistern as the plumber had explained it.

"He's right about one thing: The sockets should've been skewed. But since they weren't, we'll drill diagonal holes, blind, upward and downward from the socket. Make a bird's-foot socket. That's what we are going to do."

Nora took the lantern from him. "*We*," she said, backing down the stairs, "are going to bed. And we are going to leave plumbers' troubles to plumbers because engineering contractors have troubles enough of their own."

"Oh?" He followed her.

"Sometimes I think you're still at heart a ganger, you know," she said. "You'd rather drill that slate than—"

"What troubles?"

"Income tax, for one. Our return is near due."

"Is it bad?"

"A few pence short of ninety pounds."

John winced.

"You shouldn't pull faces," Nora said. "Lady Henshaw, God rest her, always used to say you could tell people of quality from parvenus by their willingness to pay taxes; only parvenus grumble."

He ducked the beam at the foot of the attic steps. "That's because the quality have had time enough to reach certain accommodations with the Revenue."

"We've not done too badly on that score, ourselves."

They went downstairs again to the winter parlour. On the way they passed Mrs. Jarrett, taking a glass of port to her room. "I've poured you a glass each," she said, "and locked the tantalus. Will you have the key?"

John said that one glass would do for them, and they bade her good night.

"There's still no letter from Beador," Nora said.

"I've been to see him," John told her, and then shook his head at the hope that came into her eyes. "Our problem there has simply moved one station down the line."

"How?"

He handed her port over and sipped his own, relishing it on his tongue. "Let's see the tax return first. I suppose, as usual, you've left me nothing to do but to sign."

Smugly she put the forms in front of him. "The solicitors have seen it. The chief clerk has seen the relevant parts. Chambers has seen it."

The summary, after the usual preambles and cautions, read:

PROPERTY TAX

Four wheel carriage (42″ wheels)	£ 4–10–0	
Three horses (riding and carriage)	5– 6–3	
One other mount	10–6	
Twenty-three windows, taxable	12– 7–6	
Two house dogs	16–0	
One groom	1– 4–0	
One stable lad (imposed by parish)	–	
Other servants	1– 0–0	
	£ 25–14–3	£ 25–14–3

INCOME TAX

Schedule A: lands, tenements, mines @ 7d in the £	40–16–8	
B: occupancies, tenancies @ 3½d in the £	11–13–4	
C: shares, annuities, dividends @ 7d in the £	5–16–8	
D: profits and gains in professions and callings @ 7d in the £	58– 6–8	
E: public offices of profit, pensions @ 7d in the £	–	
	£116–13–4	£116–13–4
	Total due	£142– 7–7

Before John could speak she passed him a bill of exchange drawn up by Charles Stoddart, her lawyer, for £52–10–0. "My contribution," she said. "Schedules A and B are mine."

He made an appreciative face. "Doing well," he said. But because he was used to once-for-all profits of thirty to forty per cent, he failed, once again, to realize quite *how* well; for Nora's contribution represented a steady gross income of more than £2,200, year in, year out.

She turned down the corners of her mouth and smiled—courageously, she hoped. "Not—as well as I'd hoped. But," she sighed, "well enough. Yes, well enough. Better"—and you would have thought the comparison had just occurred to her—"better than Chambers and our trust, anyway."

He patted the small of her back. "Ye never give up," he said.

"Never," she agreed. "Anyway. The tax on Schedules C and D represents the two thousand-odd guineas we drew to live on. You moved

£45,000 to France, which has to be spent by the end of June, or we'll face some inquiry on the residue."

"No trouble," he said.

She let a small silence grow before she spoke again. "What about Beador, then?" she asked. "By the way, we've heard from the Reverend Prendergast. He politely declines to help."

He finished his port and tossed the last drop at the fire; it landed on an unburned log and evaporated without catching fire. Glumly he turned to her. "Prendergast is in for a bishopric, so he may be having serious attacks of virtue. As to Sir George, I never met a man more difficult to assess. At one point I really caught myself wondering if he's got all his buttons."

"Oh, he's sane. Did he give us this wretched list?"

John went across to his travelling case and returned with a sheet of paper, which he passed to Nora.

"No tearstains," she said as soon as she looked at it. Then, after closer study: "Mr. Hudson did well; there's only two here he missed—Marine Glue Co. and The Patriot Association. What's that?"

"Beador can't remember."

"Can't remember? Where did he buy them?"

John made a hopeless gesture. "In Bartholomew Lane and Capel Court!"

"From alley men!" Nora was scandalized.

"They were 'so cheap,' he said!"

"Well, at least he can tear those up and burn them. Where did the rest come from?"

"He either wrote away or got them through his bank—through the Stock Exchange."

"So he'll have to pay deposit and calls on them all."

"Or sell out quickly and leave the country."

"John, we cannot let such a man get his feet in our trough."

"He bought them all within the space of one week. He says he has no notion what possessed him, except that he felt utterly convinced of his rightness and virtue. He had a vision of saving his estates and founding a new fortune."

"A brainstorm."

"Now, of course, he's sick with worry. He wants us to buy the foundry land. I told him, it's not worth two thousand. No help at all."

"But a partnership would be far too risky."

"He feels he's let us down. His sister, his tenants, his staff—everyone. He's lacerating himself now."

"I wish to God we'd never heard of George Beador. Did you commit us to help?"

"No. Of course not. I said we'd have a think and see if any sort of rescue were possible. But I doubt it will be."

It was the note of pessimism for which Nora had been waiting. "Very difficult," she agreed. "I see only one possible answer." It caught his interest. "Instead of a partnership, let us form a company under this new, simplified Board of Trade system."

She watched the idea sink in and take hold of him. He smiled. "I hadn't thought of these new companies."

"They're better than a partnership—in this instance, anyway. It would limit our liability to aid Beador. And he could raise money on his share."

He took her hand and pressed it. "I think you've hit it," he said.

She smiled and leaned on his shoulder. "Bed?" she suggested.

"Of course, Beador could try selling these useless shares."

She laughed, a full rich laugh. "Beador couldn't sell free pardons on a gallows morning," she said.

It was working out well. Now Beador could breathe easy all summer, while she was in France. And then, come the autumn, Beador would reach the end of the lifeline—and find the noose that was tied there.

Chapter 9

The French language gave Nora far more trouble than she expected. She had a parrot's gift for mimicry—witness the ease with which she had lost her native Leeds dialect as soon as she and John began to move up in the world. But that was of little use in Thorpe, for Miss Woods' French sounded as English as the bells of York Minister. However, the idea of these lessons was not so much for Nora to gain a good pronunciation as to lay the elementary groundwork on which she could build during her months in France. The impediment, surprisingly enough, lay in the fact that everything in French was artificially endowed with sex. Carpets, for instance, were male. Doors were female. Moreover, there was no logic to any of it. For example, one could hardly think of anything more quintessentially feminine than eggs, or more masculine than beards; yet the French perversely called a beard "she" and an egg "he."

This perversity affronted something too deep in Nora for her to name. But when she pointed out the illogicality of it, Miss Woods warned: "You mustn't say that when you are in France. The French take great pride in being the most logical people in the world. They think *we* are very muddleheaded."

To Nora, whose blood ran imperial red, it was enough to damn the French forever. Only her realization that the language was going to be important to their business kept her at it. And in her pedantic, humourless way Miss Woods was an able teacher, who fully earned her five shillings an hour each weekday. So that when April came, bringing with it the long, slow thaw, Nora could talk about the weather, ask directions, inquire about health, and manage the etiquette of a family meal—all at a very elementary level. *Il fait beau*; *où est la plage*; *je vais bien, merci*; *non, merci, madame, je suis très contente* came out as in the guidebooks: eel fay bow, oo ay lah plahje . . . and so on. She had no idea what French sounded like, but she knew that she sounded very English. That, plus the uncertainty about the sex of everything, was very inhibiting. Nor was John much help. He had picked up a smattering of French on his many visits to the railway workings he'd undertaken with Brassey and on his own. Normally he was very good at accents. He could imitate any navvy, from Cornwall or Scotland or Lincolnshire or Ireland—or anywhere. But he refused to imitate a Frenchman, except in gross parody in which he shrugged, spread his hands, lolled on one side, stuck out his lips, and made Gallic coughs and nonsense syllables.

"It's no self-respecting tongue for an Englishman," he would say. "I swear at their navvies: '*Vous avez workez damn slow—'pechez, 'pechez!*' And they work harder. That's all the French I need."

She wondered how he would respond when she became fluent at it; for it was her firm resolve to come back able to speak and read well enough to continue on her own—or with the help of the real French masters in York.

She was in York quite often that April, mainly to get her new costumes fitted perfectly. Her pregnancy was the problem. The baby was due at the end of July. She would be in France in May and June, the months when she would be swelling the most; so the costumes had to be made with plenty of ribbons and tucks for letting out.

Winifred, who was to come over with John and Cox for the last fortnight in June, had a young version of one of Nora's dresses. She was

not nearly as delighted as Nora had expected. And when she found
some careless sewing at the fringe of the right sleeve of her coat, she
passed it back with such cold asperity that Nora, though angry herself
at the carelessness, was hard put not to laugh.

"Don't you want to come to see me in France, popsie?" she asked
in the carriage on their way home.

"Yes," Winifred said without the slightest conviction.

"What is it?" Nora persisted.

"Can I take my robins?"

"The ones you've been feeding? But they will be able to fend for
themselves now the thaw's come."

"I don't want them to," she said. And she spoke with such lack of
emotion that Nora did not know how to reply.

"They'll soon leave you of their own accord," was all she said.

Winifred's dignified, almost adult sense of assurance was unnerving
at times; Cox, Nora knew, could not abide it and had no way of coping
with it. Was it real? Or was it a bodily trick inherited from John, who
had exactly the same calm way of stating intentions and wishes as if
they were already copper-bottom certainties?

Nora worried for Winifred. Precocious dignity might be amusing
in a child, but if it translated into imperiousness in the adult, it would
be a great drawback to her. Men might admire John Stevenson's sense
of command, but they would flee a thousand miles from the same
quality in Winifred Stevenson. She herself had learned very hard that
as a woman she had to get her way by stealth and secrecy—even with
John. It was extraordinary how both he and Chambers could agree,
with no flattery whatever, that she had a mind for money which would
"knock most men into a cocked hat"—yet the very next minute they'd
ignore her counsel if it cut across their particular wishes. And it was no
good raging or sulking. She simply had to wait and hope that when
events proved her right, the manner of proof would not be too cata-
strophic, and that *next* time they would listen. A wise woman's horizons
always reached as far as next time; "do as I say" was reserved for
servants and subordinates. Somehow they would have to break that
spirit in Winifred.

*   *   *

When her new costumes were ready, and her old ones had been modified and prettified and afternoonified, it took thirteen large trunks to
contain all her things. Even to pack took almost four days. It was only

when they saw the extent of the preparations, and the mountain of boxes which grew in the old manor barn, that the children began to appreciate how long their mother was to leave them. Then Winifred would encourage Young John to cry, so that his tears would make her cry in turn, and they could both go to Nora for a delicious and tender orgy of parting—a form of blackmail at which Nora willingly connived.

And then, finally, the real moment of parting came. The children, perversely, were calmness itself—or, rather, Winifred was calm and Young John took his cue from her. In the very last minute, Sam had written from Newcastle to say that Mr. Nelson, his master, was ill, and the holiday in France, for his part anyway, would have to wait at least a week. Nora sent him a draft for twenty guineas, which she had been going to give him to support his role as gentleman, and left him to make his own way there.

This setback meant that John had to accompany Nora over to France and take her to the Rodets' at Trouville. And so at seven o'clock in the morning, on Tuesday 29 April, while Tip and Puck flirted with death beneath the iron tyres and Winifred and Young John, still warm from their final hugging, ran a losing race with the carriage, John and Nora set off for York and London and France.

"Oh see," Nora said, looking back. "A daffodil."

It would be the first year since they had taken the Old Manor that she would not see the daffodils.

PART TWO

La Gracieuse, 1845

Chapter 10

"What I like about train journeys is that you know, for the next nine hours, no one can upset the arrangements. God willing," Nora said as soon as their coach was locked.

"Not now Hudson's got his amalgamation."

"And the director's coach goes right through?"

"All the coaches are through now. We change engines at Normanton and Rugby, that's all. Let Hudson have his way and there's a sudden epidemic of civilization—from York to Euston Square."

Now that they were private, Nora slipped out of her shoes and pushed her stockinged feet into the maw of the footwarmer, snatching them out when the heat became unbearable.

"You'll get chilblains," John warned.

"Oh, worth it!" She luxuriated in the warmth.

But before they reached Copmanthorpe, a few miles down the line, the heat was no longer enough to scald, and Nora, lost to the world, stood beside a proud young Gascon youth named d'Artagnan as he hastened through Paris with his father's letter to Monsieur de Tréville, captain of the king's musketeers—a company whose name was then beginning to thrill the English-speaking, or English-reading, world.

John drafted letters to those deputies his visit to France would now prevent him from visiting. He looked at her book and raised his eyebrows.

"It's about France," she said defensively. "French history."

He nodded and grinned.

"Anyway, it's like the start of a holiday. There's no harm in historical romances on a holiday."

He turned solemn. "That's no ordinary historical romance," he warned. "It's a revolutionary document—a bugle call to the genius of Europe."

She was wary of him. "What do you know about it? You've never read it."

"On the train back from Newcastle last Friday, there was a young lady told the entire story to her husband—from the duels to the moment they kill the cardinal, roast him, and serve him up at the king's banquet."

"Don't give it all away!" Nora shouted over him.

"But the *real* message," he went on, unshakeable, "is that men of vigour and enterprise can run circles around the state, however great the odds."

"Ah, how very true," she intoned and began again to read.

"So don't think that sort of romance can't be serious."

"Yes, husband dear," she murmured, not looking up.

"A cleverly disguised historical romance could do more than Mr. Cobden or a dozen petitions of redress."

"Mmmm."

When it was clear that nothing could shake her from reading he smiled and returned to his letters.

When his pen was scratching busily she looked carefully up, not catching his attention, and smiled, half in fondness, half in triumph.

By Normanton, where the Midland engine was coupled and new footwarmers handed in, d'Artagnan and the three musketeers had routed the cardinal's guard and were walking back arm in arm to their quarters.

At Syston, John's nudge brought her back from the siege of La Rochelle. He pointed out of the window. "Here's where I'd be getting off if it weren't for going to France. Syston."

She fished in her mental railway cyclopedia. "Syston? Ah yes. The line to Peterborough. Pitched battles with Lord Harcourt's men. Forty-six miles. That would be nice."

"Easy country all the way."

"Earl Ferrers, the Quorn, the Belvoir, the Cottesmore—the best country in the world," she said. La Rochelle was a distant memory as her mind's eyes filled the empty fallows and the pastures with hounds on a burning scent and a hunt in full chase. "Let's move down here all next year."

He laughed. "We haven't even tendered yet. The first thing I'll do when I get back is walk the ground."

The baby within her decided it had had enough of railway banging and thumping; it began to struggle like a landed fish. She pressed hard on her stomach. "If you don't lie still," she shouted, "I'll lace in another inch." The sound of her voice must have been soothing, for the baby ceased its struggles. Taking no chances, she rocked back and forth, humming an irresolute tune, and returned to her book.

"Some pie?" he suggested.

"I'll wait till Rugby."

They reached Rugby at half past two, where ten minutes' wait was allowed while the London & Birmingham engine coupled up.

"I must plant a sweet pea," Nora said.

Being a seasoned traveller, John took a silver brandy canteen and a small funnel into the refreshment room. He made no attempt to drink the scalding hot coffee that was served but poured both cups through the funnel into the canteen. Other regulars were doing the same—carrying their coffee out in china flasks and glass bottles, to the envy of the novices, who desperately tried to fan and blow their cups cool enough to drink before the train pulled out. Few managed it, and three-fourths of the coffee served was tipped straight back into the urns immediately the train departed. One who succeeded was a stout woman who, having purloined an extra cup, stood on the platform pouring the steaming drink from one cup to the other, where the chill wind would cool it. Before she returned to her coach, John and Nora, back in their seats, watched her drink the unspilled remnant with triumph. The two empty cups she left upside down, capping the handles of an upturned porter's barrow.

"We're an orderly people at heart," John said. "If the government owned the railways and behaved like that—serving scalding coffee to stop folk drinking it and then tipping it all back to swell the profit—we'd hold public protests and send petitions to Westminster. But because it's a private company, we say 'smart fellows!' and think of ways to outwit them."

"Swindon is worse," Nora said. "You can't even ask for milk now, to cool the coffee, because they even serve *that* boiling. Hot milk in coffee! Yeurk!"

"I don't even think it's coffee at Swindon. Brunel calls it badly roasted corn, and he's not far out. I won't touch it."

A few miles south of Rugby, the engine whistled and Nora just had time to say "Kilsby," before they were plunged into the dark. Kilsby Tunnel had a special meaning to Nora. It was the last tunnel on which John had been a mere navvy. On his next tunnel, Summit on the Manchester & Leeds, he had started as ganger and ended as main contractor. "I always remember the first time we rode through here together," she said. "All those terrible stories you told me about the navvies."

A dim light rose to a peak and then receded again as they passed under the first ventilation shaft. "God rest them," John said when they were directly under the opening and the smoke and steam coiled around and up. "That's where three of them died, playing follow-my-leader over the hole at the top."

She could just see him faintly, in the satanic light from the engine firebox reflected off the tunnel walls and the billowing steam.

"They were bad days," he said.

"I'd not say Woodhead is any better," Nora argued. "Not for drunkenness, debauchery, cholera . . ."

"Woodhead," John said, as if the word itself were unpalatable, "is what happens when know-it-all engineers think they can be contractors. Folk say 'poor old Vignoles, gone bankrupt'; I say poor navvies, who suffer his folly. Nay, we've come a long way since thirty-eight, the days of the tramp navvy. And *we* can take credit for it, along of Brassey and Peto and Tom Jackson. We're making a science of railroad building and we're making a mechanic out of the navvy. Future's with us, see thou. Not with the old petty barons and smart engineers." She did not reply. To fill the silence he added: "There's naught but bad behind and naught but good before us."

They emerged into the sunlight and it was a short while before they could reopen their eyes.

John laughed. "Just when your sight gets used to the dark, they relight the sun."

Nora stared out of the window. Pytchley country, she thought. There'd be good chases here. Then Waddon Chase, then the Old Berkeley. Her geography of England was hazy about counties but needle-sharp on railway-company and hunting territories.

"You're quiet," John prompted.

"They weren't bad times for us," she said, reluctantly coming back to their conversation. "In their own way they were more exciting than now—when we had one contract and one goal and no . . . experience— no way of knowing how it would come out. Now . . ."

"I don't agree," he said almost crossly. The sun bothered him and he came to sit beside her. "That's better. I don't agree," he repeated calmly. "Thornton was trying to make me admit the same thing the other week, down in Devon. But I wouldn't exchange one of these days for *ten* of those."

She stared at him with a mixture of pity and accusation. "And who was grizzling on about branch lines! And how often have you said you'd like to have just one contract and see it through from first sod to celebration run!"

He sucked a tooth. "I was in a valley then. You see nothing in a valley but your own feet. Now I'm on a hilltop, and I can see it all. And as I say, there's naught but good ahead."

Nora looked out of the window again. "Do you realize," she said, "that not once in these six weeks past has George Hudson sung his own private hymn of praise to the iron road?"

"Of course he has!" John said without even thinking.

"You tell me the last occasion you can actually remember! It's my belief that even mighty King Hudson is beginning to get nervous at the volume of proposals now flooding Parliament."

"Oh, faint heart!" John scoffed. "He only wants them to come more slowly so he can have time to kill off some and amalgamate with others. He was like Horatio on the bridge—until he saw the enemy was quietly building another bridge beside him."

Nora, who had hoped that sometime on this journey the opportunity might have arisen for a serious talk about Stevenson's and the future, realized from the briskness of John's tone that he was in no mood for such an examination. She hid her annoyance and packed the arguments away for another day. She stretched and yawned. "How marvellous," she said. "For two months railways and capital and iron will all take second place."

He put his lips to her ear and whispered: "Thou flamin' bloody liar." He laughed at her shock. "A *day* I might believe. But two whole months! And anyway, who was it arranged for five leading railway journals to be sent to Trouville—each issue?"

She put out her tongue at him and returned to her book, where Richelieu was just about to denounce the queen, using the diamonds Milady had got from the Duke of Buckingham.

"It's a good thing we found each other," John said. "There's no other man I know would fathom thee—and no woman whom I'd not long since have driven to strong drink."

It was several seconds before Nora realized that this was, in effect, an admission that he had known her intentions and had deliberately sidestepped them. She knew he had intended the remark to be placatory but its effect was to anger her. Why should she be ever ready to discuss their affairs, to have a whole line of suggestions for improvement kept at the point of utterance, waiting his nod or the lift of his eyebrow— while he could go as long as he liked, telling her nothing! She did not reply, nor did she look up again until the engine was decoupled at Camden Town. Her annoyance with John was too familiar to possess her for long; by then it had quite evaporated.

Since the previous July, outgoing trains had come up the gradient under their own steam instead of being hauled up by cable; but trains going into Euston Square still coasted down under the control of a brakeman.

"This is the part I like," Nora said. "The smooth part."

They arrived at the terminus ten minutes later, at twenty past five. The porter from the Adelaide, the station hotel, recognized them and came forward to take their bags.

"Don't forget the time, Mr. Stevenson, sir," he said.

John put his watch forward five minutes, from York time to London time.

"It's not changed much then," Nora said, looking around. "D'you realize it's five years almost to the week since we first stood here wondering if we were walking into a fortune or into jail?"

He looked at her a while, oddly indecisive. "Not us," he said. "Two green hands, wet behind the ears. If we had known how thin the ice was . . . !" He looked heavenward.

It's no thicker now, did you but realize, she thought.

"Anyway," he said, taking her arm and strolling with her to the head of the platform, "it won't stay this way long. They're at it again with another grandiosity. This time with Hardwick's son."

"Oh?" Nora asked; it had the sound of money.

"First that pompous Doric arch, now a Great Hall, a furlong by ten poles." He shook his head at the folly of it.

"Why?" she asked, puzzled. "It's become an important terminus. That bedraggled collection of offices . . ."

"It's about to become an impossible terminus. Look. There's the arch there." He pointed to it, towering between the two hotels. "And there's Wriothesley Bridge." He pointed in the opposite direction. "A total of seven hundred and sixty-odd feet. Or forty-six poles. And into that they have to fit *everything*—offices, waiting rooms, wagon sheds, platforms. And right in the middle of that they're going to dump this Great Hall. Seven acres of it. I really think a station was never so bungled as this. The Hardwicks and the London & Birmingham cannot put their heads together without engendering a monster."

"What's the midwife's fee?" Nora asked.

"It's to stand here," John said, pointing out its dimensions. "You see. Not even central with that Doric monstrosity, but skewed off to the west."

"But what's it worth?"

He chuckled. "Don't you care?"

"Of course I care. And then I wonder what's in it for us. I'd say we should build thieves' kitchens and houses of assignation if the price was right." How typical of John—to go on about plans and architecture before he even mentioned profit.

They walked out, through the great Doric portico (which Nora still thought very grand and imposing, despite John's sneers), and turned left toward their hotel.

"I'm guessing a hundred and forty thousand," John said. "But this is one that Prendergast *can* help with, bishop or no, if he wants to stay on terms with us."

Just before they went inside, a pungent draught of foul air engulfed them, making them hold their noses and run through the doorway; the odour of old cheese and bad eggs still hung faintly within.

"What's happened?" Nora asked the porter.

"They think as an ole sewer is busted. But can they find it? They looked 'igh and low. We 'ad a great inwasion o' rats yesterday, so it's most likely a sewer." He had a round face and small black eyes that almost vanished when he laughed.

He assured them that the smell never came round their side of the building. All they need worry about was the last trains of the evening, which made a lot of smoke getting up steam for the steep climb to Camden Town. Still laughing he took his twopence gratuity and left.

"Are you going to the office?" Nora asked.

"I fancy I'll go at once. Let Jackson get off home. He'll wait for me, knowing I'm come to town."

Nora was delighted. "Then I can finish this book before you come back," she said.

"I've told you how it ends. It's the best description of cannibalism in the whole of French literature."

"Yes," Nora said seriously. "They *are* barbaric. D'you know, four of them, four fine French gentlemen, played police, judge, jury, and executioner to this poor woman, Milady, and cut her head off by the river. An English gentleman would never do that. Yet these four go on about honour for pages."

"Honour!" John laughed. "Honour and offer—have you heard that one?"

"No?" She was interested.

He kissed her and turned to leave. "No," he said. "On second thoughts, it would only inflame you. Don't go to sleep before I get back." He was in the doorway now.

"Oh?" she said, with a different interest.

"Yes. There may be some estimates to look at." He bared his teeth and left.

She rang for the maid to come and unpack. "Honour and offer!" she said, and, smiling fondly, picked up her book and settled to read it to the end.

Chapter 11

When they had held the train five minutes at the London Bridge terminus and there was still no sign of John, Nora really did begin to worry. The guard had already stopped saying: "Never fret, Mrs. Stevenson, we'll hold it for *him*." He, too, kept looking at the time. Nine thirty-five. It crept on toward nine forty. Nora was just about to order their things to be unloaded when a clerk came trotting down the platform with a piece of paper, which he handed to the guard. The guard ruffed out his sidewhiskers as he read. He turned to Nora, all smiles again. "A message upon the electric telegraph, Mrs. Stevenson. Mr. Stevenson is now upon the way here."

"Telegraph?" Nora said. "How can that be? Where is it from?"

The guard held the paper to one side and looked at it aslant, making Nora wonder how he'd got the job with such eyesight. "From our Bricklayers Arms station, ma'am. He must have gone there in error. Hundreds do."

Only moments later John came hurrying through the crowd; he sprinted down the platform to ironic cheers from the third-class coaches on the Greenwich line and cries of "Don't shoot up the straight!" and "Yer shop door's open!"

"Bricklayers Arms!" Nora scoffed when he sprawled, breathless and sweating, opposite her. The train began to move at once.

"Damn!" he panted. "I wagered I'd get here before the telegraph. The last time I came to London Bridge . . ." He stopped to catch his breath again. "Last time they said all the Croydon trains and all the South Eastern trains now go from Bricklayers Arms. I wish they'd just stop fighting."

"At least they held the train. I do like travelling with you," she said.

"Oh, if you think this is regal, wait until we get to France. We really *are* kings there." He peered through the window, down the line. "There they are," he said. "The third-class carriages for this train. The third-class, nota bene, *does* go from Bricklayers Arms and it joins up with us here in Deptford—and all because the Greenwich railway charges the Croydon and the South Eastern fourpence halfpenny a passenger between here and London Bridge. And the parliamentary rate for the third-class won't stand it. Madness."

The train halted and there was a brief interval of banging and shuttling while the third-class coaches were coupled up. The baby did not like it and began shunting and shuttling on its own account. "We should have stopped at the Tabard," she said, hoping the sound of her voice would work its usual balm within. "Then you could have just walked to the station and found out. I don't like the Adelaide. I don't like water closets. Give me a good earth closet any day of the week."

"I don't think we'll ever stop at the Tabard again," John said. "I forgot to tell you. Tom Cornelius has sold. Sometime last month. Gone to buy a tavern down in the West Country, they say."

"Oh? I wonder if Sarah Nevill has gone with him! She was sweet on Cornelius, I'm sure."

"Sarah Nevill?" he asked, puzzled.

"Go on!" she chided. "I've seen your eyes on her."

"Me?" he protested. "I'm the butcher's dog, you know that."

"Well, she was the tall, well-spoken upstairs maid. With the room above the Pilgrims' Hall."

"Oh, yes. Quite plain. I didn't see her there last time."

"Perhaps she pined away." Nora lost interest. "Anyway, how was your sewer?"

John had risen at five thirty that morning to go and see the new work on the Fleet Street sewer, which was then being enlarged, section by section, the entire length of the street. "Ah!" he said with relish. "It's our sort of thing. No doubt of it. It's like a twelve-foot-wide cutting with sheer sides, almost forty foot deep. And the sewer is like a tunnel of brick about ten foot high, with a section like an egg, narrow at the foot. Or at what would be the invert if it was a tunnel."

He needed the whole compartment to gesticulate his description. "That means you get a good flow even with low volumes of water, ye see?" She nodded, caught up in his enthusiasm. "That's at the foot of the cutting, of course. And overhead there's a *forest*, a horizontal forest, of struts and walings and poling boards. And there's water pipes, and drains, and gas pipes, and your-guess-is-as-good-as-mine pipes. All supported on struts and chains and ropes and props. It's *our* work. It's skilled work."

"And is it paying work?"

"*I* could make it pay. And I've met the man to keep in with."

"Today!"

He nodded. "Thirty-six foot under Fleet Street, at six of the morning. An enthusiast, ye see. Who else would be in such a place at such an hour? Funny name, too. Bazalgette. Joseph Bazalgette."

"A contractor?" she asked.

John screwed up his face. "Not sure. Difficult to say. He's an engineer in his way of thinking, though. He's like Brunel. This Fleet Street thing is just a single sewer. But Mr. B. has a notion of putting—listen: *hundreds of miles* of sewers under London."

Nora sat up straight and listened with rapt attention.

"You say you don't like water closets," he went on. "Well, I tell you: Use them whenever and wherever you can. They'll be the making of us." She laughed. "I'm serious," he told her. "They fill the cess pits faster than the night men can empty them. That's why they had this burst sewer at Euston Square. The night men don't go out to the farms anymore. They just tip it all down the sewers. All over London people are emptying water closets into sewers, despite the laws against it. And"—his voice dropped—"night soil plus water equals cholera."

Nora's mouth and eyes opened wide. "That's terrible, John." She could just remember the cholera in Manchester and Leeds in her childhood. The drained, limp bodies and faces of its victims had haunted many of her bad dreams.

John nodded. "As Bazalgette said. Don't pray for cholera. But since it must come, pray for it in Westminster and at Guildhall. Then perhaps we'll get a drainage system fit for modern times. Never drink water in Chelsea, by the way. Their intake is right next to the sewer outfall. Eee! I've learned *that* much," he said. "I must get to Hamburg sometime this summer. They have a new system washed through with river water twice a week."

"Hundreds of miles!" Nora gloated.

"Aye." He grinned. "And I'm guessing three to three and a half thousand quid a mile. For a ten or fifteen per cent netto profit. Fault that!"

"It'll do," she said.

"And think," he added. "To walk around a city without middens. And no bubbling lakes of cess. And no stink. And no pigs running loose on the scavenge. We'd be remembered as the firm that made London fit to inhabit."

*   *   *

They got off the train at Folkestone at two, so the South Eastern had lost even more time than John had cost them. The paddle steamer, having missed the tide, now lay at anchor and fast to a buoy beyond the basin. The seas were running high.

"How do you feel?" John asked when they were in the horse coach that plied between station and jetty; the rail line to the harbour carried only goods traffic as yet. "It's not going to be an easy passage."

"Oh," Nora said lightly, "let's be done with it. We could wait a month for a calm sea." Nevertheless she peered nervously down; the steamer looked so very small among those huge waves.

"Sure?" John pressed.

"How long will it be?"

"Oh, quite quick with this wind behind us. Two and a half hours at most."

"Let's go then," she said, her resolve completely recovered.

She regretted it as soon as the rowing boat cleared the harbour mouth. It rose, struggling like a beetle, across huge shivering swells of translucent green water. At the peak, where the oarsmen caught crabs and the salt spray stung like spikes, they could see glimpses of the deck of the oh-so-distant steamer. Then down the side they skittered to the trough, where all the world was a wall of water and where three feet of hard-won headway seemed swallowed in a dozen yards of enforced lee-way. Yet as each towering peak bore them up, the steamer inched miraculously closer and within twenty minutes they were in the relative calm of its lee, rising and falling only slightly faster than its great bulk. At each peak, two or three passengers managed to gain the ladder and shin up it to the deck, helped all the way by the sailors. Nora and John were among the last to get off. And theirs was the last rowing boat to have left the jetty.

"Oh, thank God for something firm underfoot," she said when they were up on the heaving deck at last.

There was a sudden commotion up forward where a sailor, waiting to weigh anchor, had his shirt set on fire by a spark from the funnel. He leaped into the sea like a human torch and then, without pause, climbed on deck by the anchor rope and resumed his place at the capstan as if it had all been a part of his daily routine. Some passengers cheered and he took a bow, grinning.

They weighed anchor and, because of the seas, lashed it inboard before they cast off from the buoy. This brought the ship's bow round so that both paddles turned in unison as she began to make way. The drive was direct, without intermediate gearing, and the two big cylinders seemed to sigh alternately as they filled and emptied. Their maximum turning force was between one-third and two-thirds of the stroke, making the crankshaft sprint and labour by turns, in time with the sighing. On calm days this gave the steamer a lurching motion not unlike a slow train. Today, however, the storm completely masked such irregularities and imposed far severer ones of its own.

Once they were clear of the soaring white cliffs, the swell came at them from the stern and it ran at a slight diagonal to the ship. As a result the two paddle wheels never drew the same amount of water at the same time. And since the deeper draught gave the better purchase, the vessel would always slew toward the shallow quarter, making the bow seek from side to side as it yawed. This motion was superimposed on the random buffeting she took from the waves and the squalls of wind that soughed in her shortened sails and shrieked through her rigging. Smoke and steam and sparks ran before them in a dirty, tangled plume.

Nora watched the white cliffs vanish into the storm and spray. *I'm going to France*, she kept thinking. *Goodbye, England!* She had determined beforehand that this would be an exciting moment; but the weather made it difficult for the reality to match her expectations. Her imagination had passed this way with John too many times since he had first gone over to build the line from Boulogne to Amiens. "I think I'll change my mind and go below," she said. He took her arm and steadied her as they walked.

The Ladies' Cabin was full and they went back up on deck to the General Cabin. Gentlemen and ladies were stretched head to toe, head to toe, on all the divans around the walls; and more gentlemen lay on cushions on the floor. Most of the recumbent men kept their eyes shut, pretending not to see her; but at last one stood and offered her his divan.

She thanked him and, helped by John, lay down full length while he put a rug over her feet and skirt hems.

She had not lain there ten minutes when a vast wave, cutting across the general direction, spun them hard to starboard. A universal shriek and groan went up in the cabin and at least four of them vomited at once. The illness spread among them like a chain letter. Stewards busied themselves throwing sand and passing eau-de-cologne around.

If I stay, I'll lay a carpet, too, Nora thought, and sat up resolutely. One of the floorbound gentry eyed her divan with hope.

"I'm going on deck," she said sweetly to him. "I must offer this back to the gentleman who relinquished it. Will you see no one else occupies it?"

Grudgingly the man agreed and helped her to her feet. He sat on the divan, half claiming it. A delicate-looking lady by the door was being genteelly sick into a handkerchief, a teaspoonful at a time. Only the bracing gale as she pushed open the door brought Nora back from the grip of that same predicament.

All around the outside of the cabin was a thick mahogany rail. Nora used its support to work her way over to the slightly less windward quarter, to starboard, where John and the polite gentleman sat in shouting conversation on a crate with two frightened goats inside it. Both men were wearing thick grey oilskins. They did not notice her until she was almost upon them.

"You may have your divan back, kind sir," she shouted over the roar of sea and wind.

The man smiled and shook his head. "Better here," he said.

John took off his oilskin and wrapped it around her.

The other, unbidden, went to get John a replacement from the crew's quarters.

"Interesting man," John shouted while he was gone. "Name's Addison. Has great knowledge of the iron trade. Knows Nasmyth. Comes from Sheffield."

Addison came back with the oilskin. Nora sat on the goat crate, huddled in the lee of the two men, watching the waves speed ahead of them toward France, and catching one word in ten of the men's impossible dialogue. Inside the oilskin was a warm, still world.

By mid-channel the waves had become truly mountainous—huge, rolling greenbacks of wind-lashed water that thundered toward the ship as if created to destroy her; yet they lifted her and careened onward as if she did not exist. Looking crosswind, Nora could see that any ripple or wavelet which reared more than a few inches was at once peeled from the face of the ocean, turned to black-and-silver grapeshot, and hurled far over the waters by the gale. She could not look upwind for long because that same broadside would lash her face and sting her eyes.

At least she no longer felt nauseous.

Six miles or so from the French coast the storm began to blow itself out. The sea still ran hugely but the lash of the spray and the roar of the wind dropped to a spatter and a moan. For the first time since they had left Folkestone the smoke did not fall seaward near the bow. The cabin folk began to venture out on deck. Looking at the green pallor of their skin Nora felt decidedly superior.

"Your first crossing, Mrs. Stevenson?" Addison asked.

She nodded and smiled.

"Well, you're quite the sailor."

She beamed at him; there was something instantly likeable about Mr. Addison. He was in his early forties, much the same age as John, with curly, pale brown hair, greying and thinning at the temples. Thickets of hair sprouted from his ears and cantilevered over his eyes, blue-green in their shade. It was a reserved, care-worn face, the face of a working gentleman. His hands were gnarled, and flecked with many white scars from the spatterings of slag and molten iron.

"Is this a holiday for you, Mr. Addison?" she asked.

"A working holiday." He nodded. "I am about to go in business on my own account and it occurred to me I might never again have so unfettered an opportunity to see what our French and German rivals are doing."

"He's about to become a competitor," John said.

"Nay," Addison laughed scornfully. "There's room for hundreds more. I'd say the new iron age hasn't even begun. Ye couldn't have picked a better time to go into iron production. I'd swear that. Bible."

"And where shall ye set up shop?" Nora asked, all casual and innocent.

"Not Sheffield, that's certain. It's plagued by the old styles. Ye could pick a dozen places. There's . . . er . . . Doncaster now"—he looked sharply at Nora—"I know it's only a village but if ye look at the railroads, it's bound to grow. Or"—again he looked at Nora, who by now realized she was being fished for her reaction—"there's good land going cheap south of Leeds."

Nora decided to play him out then. "Leeds," she said, nervously looking at John. "Good gracious!" John suppressed a smile.

"Oh?" Addison, thinking he was on the scent, looked even harder at her.

"How extraordinary!" John said heavily. "You were born there, were you not, my dear?"

She looked at him ever so grateful for his rescue. "Yes, that's it!" she said.

"I see." Addison smiled. "And ye could even"—he laughed dismissively, to show how ridiculous the idea was—"you could even build in Cumberland! Good harbours. Good railway soon enough."

They laughed, too. "Build there and you could build anywhere," John said.

"That's a fact!" Addison was seized with a paroxysm of laughter. "Aye. That's a fact."

They docked in the lee of the jetty, where it was calm enough for John to get out his writing case and dash off a letter of introduction to Rodet on Addison's behalf. He thanked them hugely and left, well pleased.

"Cumberland," Nora said thoughtfully. "So he's going to build at Furness."

They went on as far as the fish market and the English churches, opposite the railway station. John pointed to it: "A bit of genuine Stevenson."

"Aye," she agreed. "It has that solid, dependable look. Is that the Napoleon column?" She pointed to a tall monument on a hill over the town. She had been reading her *Murray*.

John chuckled. "This town's full of monuments to futile hopes of invading England. Did ye see a little brick ruin on the cliff north of the harbour? That was built by Caligula while he waited in vain to cross our channel."

"And I must see the château," she said, "where they locked up Napoleon III when he tried to land."

They turned up the hill, toward the old town. "The moral of it seems to be: If you want to get anywhere, don't start from Boulogne."

His words were prophetic, for they never reached the château.

At the corner of the Rue de la Lampe, where it opens into the marketplace, Nora suddenly turned back and pushed John to face into a shop window.

"Earthenware pots?" he asked.

"No," she said quietly. "But look across at the nearest vegetable stall and you'll see a man. In a tall hat. With check trousers."

John looked. "Well, talk of the devil!" he said.

"And the girl with him?"

"Oh, yes! Or is it her?"

"I'd swear it. The point is: Do we acknowledge them?"

He was astonished. "Why ever not?"

"Well," she said, not liking to be pressed. "An English innkeeper arm in arm with one of his female servants in a French seaport."

He parodied a shock far greater than hers. "I hadn't thought of that. You are *right*, my dear. Come, let us hence."

Her arm straightened like an anchor cable, pulling him back. "Don't be hasty," she said.

He abandoned his posture and looked fondly at her. "Have you forgotten, love, what you said when I asked you to marry me? The very minute I asked?"

She coloured.

"You said," he went on, "that I hadn't tried you and you might be barren. And you said: 'Shall us not live together a while?' "

"That was before I knew better," she replied crossly.

"Not in my book." His eyes would not let her escape. "I loved the lass as said them words; and I love her still, see thee."

In the end she had to smile, and her smile was unstinted. "Thou art soft as a suckin' duck," she told him.

"Mebbe," he agreed. Then he straightened himself and dropped the dialect. "So we'll cross this road and we'll greet them and chat with them and maybe we'll have a little glass of something in a café and we'll go our ways. And we'll do naught but give out that what's their business is their business."

She was already pulling him across the road, following a large cart piled with seaweed.

How to attract the attention of two people so rapt in each other's company and in the living moment that the world might catch fire around them? John and Nora stood at right angles to them, at the edge of the stall, smiling, waiting to be noticed and then recognized. "Good news," John said out the corner of his mouth. "There's a wedding ring in it."

After what seemed an age the man looked up. He looked harder, he looked astonished, he looked delighted. "Mr. Stevenson!" he called. "And Mrs. Stevenson, too." He snatched off his hat and shook hands with her and then with John. "My dear, you remember Mr. and Mrs. Stevenson, our favourite guests at the Tabard? Allow me"—he turned back to them—"to present Mrs. Cornelius. Mrs. Sarah Cornelius. Sarah Nevill as was. As I'm sure you'll remember! What? Forget Sarah?" He rattled on as they, smiling under his barrage, reached over the stall and shook hands. "The treasure of the Tabard? The finest jewel—"

"Tom!" Sarah laid a finger on his lip and shook her head.

"Too much, eh? Too much?" He sighed. "Yes, too much. Yes."

Sarah laughed and clung to his arm.

"How marvellous," Nora said. "We were wondering about you only this morning, when we caught the train at London Bridge."

"They all say you've gone to the West Country," John told him. "We heard you'd sold out. But when did you marry?"

"Oh, recently, recently," Cornelius said.

"It's such a whirl." Sarah laughed and clung to his arm even tighter.

"Well, we must congratulate you," John said. "Though it's too late to wish you happiness, for I've never seen it shine so clear."

"We can wish its continuity," Nora said.

"More than that," Cornelius held out an arm to scoop them back into the road, "we can drink to it."

"Or eat," John said. "If London's best tavern keeper can't find Boulogne's best eating house, he *deserves* the West Country."

The stallholder shrieked something abusive at them as they left—

the table and chairs were of rough, scrubbed oak, only a little cleaner than the floor? Or that the plates and cutlery slid greasily between the fingers? The food was a sybarite's dream.

"*Au poile, Madame,*" Cornelius said judiciously, holding thumb and index finger pinched to a nicety and shaking them at her. He teased her about everything except the food; with that he was like a young priest with the ritual—still reverent. He ate as at a devotion, passing the food carefully around his mouth, provoking Madame's anxiety, chewing, breathing, chewing-and-breathing, smacking his tongue, and then closing his eyes and surrendering to the taste like a voluptuary—while Madame breathed again and beamed at him and clucked her delight at his.

It had never occurred to Nora that food could be so—more-than-serious. Sacrosanct. A religion. "Eee, ye're partial to a good bite, Mr. Cornelius, I can see," she said.

"To be sure," he agreed solemnly. "You find me another appetite you may indulge five times daily though ye live to be a hundred, and you may enlist me there, too."

"Where in the West Country are you going, Mr. Cornelius?" John asked.

Cornelius and Sarah exchanged a knowing smile. "Whose West Country?" he asked. "Normandy's West Country. That's where. South of the Cherbourg thumb."

"Are you serious?"

"Never more so. We're buying—have bought—an inn at Coutances, near the sea." He took Sarah's hand.

"You can look right across to Jersey and Brittany," she said. "It's heavenly."

"But why?" John asked. "You're a legend in south London. You've *made* the Tabard. And now you go and give it up."

Cornelius shook his head. "The writing's on the wall, dear fellow. For them as reads. And it's writ in railway iron. London? It's doomed. Finished. In our lifetime—and we're still young men." He clenched his fists and looked around like a pugilist seeking a challenge. "In our lifetime London will become insufferable. When I was a lad, before I went to France, a good stiff trot would get any of us out into green fields. There! From Thames bank at London Bridge to green fields. And where's it get you now? I'll tell you. It gets you down the Old Kent Road to Bricklayers Arms, where you can take a train back home for sixpence. Well, I'm going to spend *my* sixpences on Normandy cider, me. What? I should think so."

"You were in France as a boy?" Nora asked. "That's why you speak it so well."

"My father was an inspector of posts in Brittany. Then he quarrelled —with everyone. He was a very quarrelsome man. I daren't go back *there*. And he came back to England as a teacher. His name was Corneille, Yves Corneille. So—you see!"

"We'll be so much happier here," Sarah said. "Look. Where in England could we walk in off the street and find a place like this? And . . ." —she sought for the words—"and . . . freedom. Relaxation . . . the *ambiance* like this. In England we have liberty and no passports, and we work, and we cooperate with the government, and we are orderly and punctual. And it's very nice to live there. But we don't know how to enjoy ourselves. How to relax. Liberty, but no freedom."

"When I was building the line from here to Amiens, the French people would drive out to watch my lads work. They'd never seen anyone work that hard," John said.

"And your lads," Sarah asked with a teasing smile, "did they flock into the town squares and little cafés to see how the French enjoyed themselves?"

"Did they!" John laughed. "With brandy at two bob a gallon! They took to it like lambs on short pasture."

"Oh, the bounty of this land!" Cornelius was off again. "The yield of it. The wines. The cider. The cheeses. The fruits. I was here last September, with the blackberries ripening. It was like walking through one endless black-and-red mosaic. Also the taxes are more sensible here. The English income tax is going to drive all the most alert and enterprising people abroad, very soon. Mark my word. What! Two shillings in the pound? I should say so."

"I beg leave to differ from you there, Mr. Cornelius," John said. He spoke quietly, without challenge. "England has more talent and skill than she knows how to use. You have only to look at the four of us. What was I? A navvy, humping prodigies of earth for three bob a day. And Mrs. Stevenson? She tended two looms in hell for ten bob a week. And Mrs. Cornelius? An upstairs maid. No sinecure. And yourself? Son of an immigrant teacher in lodgings. Often no more than two farthings to rub together, I'll wager. And look at us now. We've all been lucky. I give regular work to ten thousand men. It'll be fifty thousand before I'm done. Mrs. Stevenson—I'd back her commercial judgement against the governor of the Bank of England. Yourself—you've built the biggest tavern trade south of the Thames. And ye've picked a wife there with a

"What are we talking about?" Nora asked. "Hundreds? Or thousands? Or tens of thousands?"

"Well—" Cornelius was cautious. "Let's say thousands."

"Then it's not worth a great deal of effort," she said, enjoying his mildly offended reaction. "All you do is find a firm—as it may be Stevenson's"—she licked her lips and grinned—"with money to repatriate and you draw a bill on them in France and they draw one on you in London and we can give you a letter to arrange it all with our clerk in London tomorrow if it please you, sir!" she gabbled.

They all laughed. "It sounds like good sense," Cornelius agreed. "Supposing it had been tens of thousands?"

"Ah," Nora said, enjoying the attention. "Then it gets a bit more interesting." She looked at John. "May I?"

John, as proud of her as a hen with one chick—and enjoying Cornelius' amazement—nodded. Cornelius kept looking at him to see if this wasn't all some joke.

"There's dozens of exchanges in Europe, all with paper to sell. But for big sums you needn't look beyond Amsterdam, Hamburg, Frankfort, and Genoa—and, to be sure, Paris and London. All you need remember is that wherever there's a surplus of paper, you can get it cheap; wherever there's a shortage, you can sell it dear. Naturally. What you're trying to do, in moving the money to France, is to buy where the rate is cheap relative to London and dear relative to Paris."

"Oh yes," Cornelius laughed dubiously. "It sounds easy."

"But it *is* easy," Nora said earnestly. "For instance, we've just bought bills drawn on Frankfort. We bought them in London (where they are plentiful just now) at 121 German florins per £10 sterling. Now we've sold those same bills in Paris (where they happen to be scarce) at 212 francs per 100 florins. Indirectly, you see, we get 25 francs 42 centimes to the pound. That's 12 centimes better than a direct draft in Paris on London."

Cornelius rolled his eyes.

"On every ten thousand pounds it makes a saving of—?" John said and pointed at Nora as a conductor to a soloist.

"Forty-eight pounds," she said. "It sounds much less when you say nine shillings and sevenpence in a hundred pounds. Pocket money. But it soon mounts."

John rubbed his hands, delighted at Nora's grasp of the explanation. Cornelius and Sarah looked at her as if seeing her for the first time.

"You really understand all that?" he asked.

"And call it *easy*!" Sarah added.

"But that is the easy part. The difficult part—which people like you and me should never meddle in—is . . ." and she went on to explain how you could buy surplus paper cheap now to sell elsewhere when it became scarce and expensive, financing the deal by drawing three-month bills and selling them short. "You lose one per cent by selling short, but you may make twenty or thirty per cent if you guessed the future of the market right. That's where it stops being pocket money and turns into fortunes."

Cornelius made a pantomime of expiring as she finished; and Sarah stared at her, open-mouthed.

"Don't confuse things," John said, still delighted. She remembered how she had once had to fight to get these simple precepts adopted in their office. "Fuss, fuss, fuss!" John had said.

"How do you keep it all in your mind?" Sarah asked.

"I'm doing it every week," Nora explained. "It's second nature now."

"Well!" Cornelius seemed winded. "You do amaze me. I would never have thought a woman capable of mastering it. What?"

"Yet," Nora said, "if I told you we have two clerks at forty pounds a year who spend part of their time grappling with these differences—for naturally I don't do it all, I merely supervise, from afar—you would find that not the least remarkable?"

Cornelius evaded the point. "I would have thought it a banker's job, in any case."

John laughed. "No man got rich on a banker's advice. *Use* a banker by all means; but *rely* on him and you're as good as dished. Did you go to the parson and ask whom you should marry?"

Cornelius grinned and Sarah blushed.

"A parson's a service. And a banker's a service. It's the same thing."

"Are you sure you didn't muddle the two when you got married?" Cornelius asked. They all laughed at that.

Cornelius paid for their meal; at six francs a head it came to twenty-four francs. "What's that in sterling?" he asked idly.

"Nineteen and twopence halfpenny," Nora said.

Cornelius then extemporized a great pantomime of whether he should pay in bills on Paris or by direct remittance or perhaps he could find some Italian paper that was going to be scarce tomorrow.

"Come on!" the others shouted.

"Oh no!" he said. "It's important to Madame Thierry. She is one of the richest ladies in the world." Madame began a giggling protest but Cornelius insisted. An ancestor in Venice, also a Thierry, had left over four hundred million pounds sterling, all in gold. And under Venetian

John's plan was to go from Abbeville direct to Rouen via Neuf-châtel. At Rouen they could take a train to Havre, from where it was a short sailing across the estuary of the Seine to Honfleur or Trouville, either of which was convenient to La Gracieuse. The diligence, however, was going on beyond Rouen, meandering across country, through Lisieux and the pays d'Auge to Caen. And the conductor refused to sell them the coupé seats as far as Rouen only—even though, as they pointed out and as he admitted, he would almost certainly sell them onward in Rouen. "Almost certainly is not *exactly* certainly," he said.

Another passenger, a short, genial, self-important man went back into the inn and came out with the list of diligence tariffs, which clearly showed that the stretch from Abbeville to Rouen was separately charge-able. But it made no difference. The conductor was adamant, and the diligence would not depart until the coupé seats were paid for all the way to Caen. "It's only because they are English," the helpful man shouted at the conductor. He, staring fixedly ahead, merely grinned. The other turned to them. "It's only because you are English," he repeated, in English this time.

John thanked him and grudgingly paid the 49.50 francs for the three seats all the way. "And three francs for the trunk," the conductor added. John put his money away and stared the man out. In the end the conductor shrugged his shoulders and put their trunk aboard without demanding more.

Nora was seething. Two things she hated—to cut a string that could as easily be untied, and to be forced to buy more of anything than she actually wanted. Drapers who insisted on selling a yard, when all she wanted was twenty-nine inches were a particular loathing. "We have twelve inches to the foot and twelve pence to the shilling, as a special and particular assistance to the feebleminded," she would shout at them. "Yet even that is beyond you!" Here at Abbeville she could not shout a single word the man would grasp. And that doubled her fury.

It was several miles before the peace and charm of the countryside began to soothe her. Though they were into Normandy as soon as they crossed the Somme, the landscape was still reminiscent of Picardy, with its small fields, rolling hills, and lush pasture—a well-watered land, thick with copses and game covert. Through the hilly country toward Blangis every little valley had its own surprises—a small red-brick châ-teau, an elegant hunting lodge, all stucco pillars and rococo plasterwork, or a half-timbered woodframe farmhouse bent dangerously by its years. At two places they saw builders actually putting up new barns or cow sheds, using timber cannibalized from ancient structures, and building in a way that had not changed since the time of William of Normandy.

Every farm had its low-walled orchard, whose grass was kept smooth by a mare and her foal. And almost every tree was in blossom—apples and cherries, plums and pears together. The orchards were heavy with their white and pink boughs. In the fields and hedges, too, everything seemed to have flowered at once—cowslips, wild roses, acacias, lilacs, wallflowers—while cattle and sheep stood half buried in the lush, deep green grasses of the meadows.

"Look," John said. "Elders in flower."

In Yorkshire, elder was a midsummer blossom.

"You'd never think moving a few hundred miles south would make such a difference," Nora said. "We've travelled half a season these three days past."

"How will our Yorkshire farmers compete when it's as easy to send from Normandy to London as it is from the North?" he asked glumly.

"Even the sun is different. Gold. Not pale like English spring sunshine. And what's that lovely smell? It's like something you've *almost* smelled before but not quite."

He sniffed. "Aye. I know what you mean. I can't put a name to it either."

They passed a farm where a woman in a dazzling white apron and cap was spreading a good six weeks' laundry over the bushes to dry.

"It's a rich country," she said, puzzled. "You can see that with half an eye. Yet they don't act rich or dress rich. They don't paint their houses. Do they not understand the importance of appearances?"

"Different habits," John answered. "Different revolution, maybe."

"No, but look at that food we ate last night. That was as good as the best hotel or eating house in London, if not better. Yet you'd have to seek in the worst parts of Leeds or Birmingham to match the *appearance* of that house. Think of the custom that woman could have, and the money she'd make, in a proper place."

"But would she be happier? That woman? That particular woman, could she be happier?"

"Well, *happiness* isn't everything," Nora said, lightly offended; then, seeing his playfully solemn look, she dug him in the ribs and said: "Come on now!"

He looked away, shook his head, and smiled.

"Anyway," she said, "that's where Cornelius and Sarah are going to come topside. Best of everything. Food and standards."

ful bow and passed by; it was the odour of hot, rotting leather mingled with the gluepot stink of debauchery.

Oooh! she mimed to John when the man had passed. He smiled grimly and looked at the ungloved hand Jacques had shaken. "*You* buy some bread and cheese and cider," he said.

"Aye. Lend us your French!" she taunted.

John nodded at Jacques. "His wife—" he began.

"I caught that," she said. "Cholera."

He looked at her with surprised respect. "You'll do," he said. "Trouble is he got drunk and went wild."

"*So* unlike a navvy," she said.

"On our working." John did not share her amusement. "At Yvetot. Broke two trucks, lamed a horse, and hit Hogan. We could overlook the other two, but you can't have a man hit the boss. I'll have to talk to Hogan, see how bad it was."

"What's he at?" Nora asked.

The man had stripped to his waist and was folding his leather jerkin to make a shoulder pad. He stood against the diligence while the conductor and another lowered Nora's trunk down onto him.

"He'll never carry that!" she said.

John looked pityingly at her. "Go on, it's not two hundredweight and the station's less than a mile. I've seen that man carry four hundredweight up forty foot of ladderwork without pause. He could dance all the way."

She watched the man's muscles work and tighten as he accepted the load; and, like others around, she gave a semiwhistling gasp of admiration when he strode off as if it were no more than a sack of potatoes he carried. They followed at sufficient distance to attenuate the smell of him.

Halfway over the square she looked back and saw the conductor helping two gentlemen and a lady up into the coupé. She itched to go back and demand their refund.

Once or twice on their way to the station she heard the words "Lord Jean," as folk recognized him and pointed him out to one another. On the way they bought some cheese from Camembert, some butter, some dense grey bread, and a bottle of cider corked like champagne. Everything was weighed in pounds instead of in the new Buonaparte kilogrammes.

"Forty centimes," Nora said—the lowest John had been able to reduce the butter woman to. "That's threepence three farthings. Butter's a farthing cheaper than Yorkshire."

"Eay, thou knows where to handle for meat in the future then," he said.

*   *   *

The Stevenson office at Rouen was a wooden shed between the passenger section and the goods yard. Hogan, knowing John was coming, had stayed in; normally he would have been up the line somewhere. His greeting froze as his eye took in the huge bulk of Jacques Duquesne, silhouetted thirty yards back on the platform. "Niver," he said at once, taking a step back. "God, no. Not if you're thinkin' what I'm thinkin' you're thinkin'. Niver."

"Was it bad then?" John asked. "Were you hurt?"

"Hurt is it," said Hogan. "I was kilt on the spot." He craned his head forward to the point of imbalance, daring his feet to follow. "Look at it."

There was a nasty bruise lurking in his sidewhiskers. "Seven days of soup, that is," Hogan complained. "Soup and blancmange. And mustn't I sup both without a chew in it." The bruise did not seem to interfere with his talking.

"Did many see it happen?"

"The ones he hadn't blinded. Sure there was eight men and two horses knocked to a pulp. And a good horse is hard got."

"He's a good man. Or was. And I fancy could be again." John smiled. "Still, Hogan, it's your decision. Ye know me, soft as Poor Will. I felt right sorry for him down there. And losing his wife like that. And remembering how he can do the work of three. Still, I'll not interfere like." Another smile. "Eay, I forgot. I've a souvenir for thee." He turned and made for the platform, where the trunk now stood.

Hogan gave a single, wry snort, smiled reproachfully at the heavens, and turned to Nora. "You're lookin' grand, ma'am," he said. "And ye'll soon make your man there even prouder, I see."

"So I hope, Mr. Hogan. And you?"

"Ah, we're ahead of ye still, God be praised, with a darlin' wee girl not six weeks old."

Nora was delighted. "So that's Mary, Dermot, Sean, and what'll you call the girl?"

Hogan swelled with pride that she should remember, not knowing that Nora kept a book for John in which every such detail was recorded for all his senior people. "Isn't that the memory!" he marvelled. "The girl's baptized Kathleen." He watched John returning, cradling some-

"We'd have men at the circumference digging and throwing in to the centre, and men at the centre shovelling the spoil up over their shoulders into a six-foot bucket. They've got eight men there, we'd have twelve or fourteen."

Nora thought briefly. "Difference in wages would never make up the cost and daily expense of that great lump of iron. I'll wager there's some local French Brunel saying 'Hang the cost, I've got this grand idea.'"

He chuckled and squeezed her arm, guiding her back to the fly. "Probably," he said. "But it gives *me* an idea. And one that will pay a bit more than that." He craned forward to look into her face as if he expected a negative response.

"I'm in favour of that," she said. "Never be first. Let others run on the rocks. It makes the safe course easier to chart."

They climbed back into the fly. "We need them, though," he said seriously. "The folk who want to be first."

"Who would you rather be," she asked. "Admiral Lord Franklin in his tomb of ice or plain Mr. Can't-quite-remember-his-name who brought the first paying cargo through the Northwest Passage that Franklin will die in seeking?"

"Who says he's going to die?"

"Suppose."

The question troubled John. He pulled his moustache. He took off his gloves and scratched his knuckles. "I don't know," he said at last. "What I really want to do is find the Northwest Passage *and* bring a paying cargo through, at one and the same time."

*   *   *

The wind was westerly and the tide was flowing against the river, so, after a short reach to starboard, they almost ran before the wind all the way across the estuary to Honfleur. The sun was well down in the sky when they nosed into the slack waters between the sandbars of the harbour mouth. A team of ducks flew overhead and settled noisily in the reeds to the west of the port.

"I saw some spoonbills there in April," John said.

A chill was forming on the air.

"I could just fancy a nice fire, a cup of tea, and a plate of muffins," Nora said.

The carriage waiting for them had a platform at the back, like an

ancient britzka. A coachman, a groom, and a stable lad from La
Gracieuse leaned against it, waiting. The coachman recognized John
first and nudged the others into life. The lad sprang onto a horse and
cantered off on the Trouville road to warn the house of John and Nora's
arrival. Moments later, with their trunk more or less secure upon the
platform, they set off westward into the sunset. They rode through a
world of deepening shadows, where tree-shaded blackness gave way to
sudden grand vistas of the sea, luminous in the twilight. It was dark by
the time they arrived at the gates of La Gracieuse. A faint band of deep
purple light settled upon the horizon, and a crescent moon, only two
hours off its own time of setting, hung in a haze, lighting the waves that
distance moved as slowly as the clouds. Their breaking on the shore,
somewhere below the cliff on which La Gracieuse stood, was a mere
whisper.

"Oh, it *is* beautiful," Nora said, as if that were a concession.

*   *   *

La Gracieuse had been recently built, though it sought to appear quite
venerable, part red-brick château, part baroque palace—all on a domestic scale. Its public face looked northward to the sea and was built
around three sides of a square cobbled yard. The fourth side consisted
of two small, identical gatehouse cottages with blind dormer windows
let into the roof above the ground-floor windows. The wrought iron
gates were in a modern baroque from the Rodet factories, uncomfortable and mannered. The left-hand post had settled a few inches, so the
gate was usually left open until dark, when the mismatch was not
noticeable.

On the wall of the house immediately facing, across the yard from
the gate, was a shallow projecting bay with a two-arched entrance and
three sets of twin-arched windows rising above, being finished at the
top with baroque achievements, almost Dutch in flavour. Thus the first
impression was that the house rose four storeys. But away to the left was
a further bay, with a mere three storeys of windows; only from the inside
was it clear that the "four storeys" of the entrance bay were really lights
for the stairwell. To the right of the yard was a circular stucco turret
with a steep conical roof. The main roof of the house was steep, too,
soaring above the building, as high above the gutter as the gutter was
above the ground. The two northward wings, completely overshadowed
by trees on both sides of the house, were for the servants, of whom the

roses. Then there were two by Corot, a view of Dijon, and an unidenti-
fied landscape. In this room and this company their colour seemed dull
and heavy.

Madame pointed to a tree in one of them. "*Le chêne,*" she said.

"Ah, oak," Nora said and looked toward the window. "Of course.
It's the smell of oak."

"The smell of Normandie in spring."

Finally there was a Millet. "He is very good," Madame Rodet said.
"A friend from Rodet, only it's not right, 'ere. Not this room." It was
a study of a peasant girl. "*Une rose de Picardie.* Oh, and one more!"
Laughing, she pulled Nora two paces sideways until they stood before
an oval rococo mirror, wide enough for each woman to see herself and
the other reflected. "It's the most nicest," she said. "It's called *Les deux
roses.* You understand?"

Nora laughed.

"*La rose de Normandie, et, alors, la rose de Yakshire.*"

"Yorkshire," Nora said.

"Oh! English! It's impossible. Yokeshire!"

They both laughed.

"*Eh bien,*" she challenged. "*La rose de Normandie.*" She waited for
Nora's repetition.

Nora almost managed to get her tongue around the sounds. It was
halfway between Miss Woods and perfection. Madame Rodet, not
realizing what progress that marked, laughed again and waved a hand
as if Nora's failure proved some point. "We manage," she said. "You
will see."

*   *   *

An hour or so later, while Honorine the maid was helping her to dress
after her bath, she heard John taking his bath in the dressing room.
Shortly after, when she was almost ready, he joined her.

"Did they tip your bathwater out the window, too?" she asked.

"Aye," he said. "There's a little, lead-roofed awning runs along
under the balcony. It makes a sort of gutter. I've been talking with
Rodet, who's very worried about our mutual friend Sir G.B. It seems
he's been over here on a visit and is showing an unnatural interest in
properties in Normandy."

Nora said at once, "Before or after we gave him ten per cent of the
company stock?"

"Oh, before."

She smiled then. "Still," she said, "he did *begin* to twitch. So he has some instinct for self-preservation. I wouldn't call his interest in property here at all unnatural."

Chapter 14

Impressions of those first weeks in Normandy soon merged in Nora's mind, making it impossible later to separate one day from the next.

Standing on the balcony one morning she discovered that not only the bathwater was emptied into the gutter formed by the awning and the southern wall of the house, the water closet on the floor above discharged there too. And the force of its water did not always carry the solids as far as the downpipe; they lay stranded on the lead roof, seething with blue-black flies, and making it difficult to enjoy standing on the balcony—or to sit at total ease on the terrace below. Later, when Madame Rodet came into her boudoir, Nora walked casually out onto the balcony and pretended to discover in passing the imperfections below their feet, while ostensibly admiring the garden. Madame smiled proudly. "We have the English water *civilisation* now," she said. "Even when I was young—oh! Terrible. But in my grandmother's time. We must have many houses. To move, you understand?" She drew horizontal circular itineraries in the air. "*Affreux*! And now—*la civilisation*." She gestured at the drainage and the gardens with a grandiloquent sweep of her arm, as if both were part of the same great plan.

The gardens, which sloped away from the terrace, were laid out in absolute symmetry. The gardeners, Nora thought, must spend most of the winter indoors playing with rulers, compasses, and squared paper. The effect was incomplete though, because no one had first tried to level or to balance out the wrinkles of the natural landscape. A formal bed on a small eminence was thus "balanced" by another in a hollow, which then meandered on, more or less diagonally, across a large octagonal lawn. It did not even look like an idea half-achieved, Nora thought—more like one three-quarters obliterated.

Sam wrote to say that he would, at Nora's suggestion, take the diligence from Abbeville all the way to Lisieux and that he would ride up in the banquette "like most solitary Englishmen." He would then take a fly up the valley of the Tocques to Trouville, arriving at about

Rodet turned to Nora and, picking up the thread again, added: "Their theology is contemptible, of course."

*   *   *

Madame had given Rodet five children; Arsène, aged ten, François, César, Héraclide, and Gervaise, nearly four. "And it's enough," she said with sardonic determination. "The harvest is in." She played fiercely with her children, taking the most intense pleasure in their company. In ten minutes she heard from each boy what he had learned and said and done that day; and little Gervaise, ensconced firmly on her lap, sat as solemn as a judge and drank it all in, too. Nora learned more French in those "hours of the children" than she would have in days with her lesson books and Miss Woods.

Church was another good place to learn French—not the meanings but the sounds. The Protestant service lasted almost ninety minutes, and each half hour was taken up by a three-hour sermon, with a lot of praying and very little singing in between. One of the few words she understood was *Amen*, which was spoken with a grateful fervour that Nora found entirely comprehensible. After Evensong she went early to bed and dreamed she had the gift of tongues. And all the tongues were French.

Very soon she felt she had known Madame Rodet for months, if not years. And Madame must have felt the same, too, for on the way back from a shopping visit to Rouen she suggested that they stop all the Madame and Mrs. "You shall call me Rodie," she said. "And I make you Stevie. It's nice, yes? Rodie and Stevie."

Nora was delighted—and half ashamed to admit to herself that she almost regretted Sam's impending arrival, so intriguing did she find her new friendship with Rodie.

And Rodie, for her part, was intrigued at the daily flood of railway papers and accounts that came for Nora, just as they did when she was in Yorkshire. A good part of every morning, and one or two evening hours as well, went in keeping up with these arrivals.

"You know all of Monsieur Jean's business?" she marvelled once as she watched Nora make notes on some estimates she was to return the following morning. By now she usually spoke in French and translated only the parts that Nora obviously failed to understand.

"To the last sou," Nora said. "Better than Stevenson. He relies on it."

Rodie shook her head and sucked her teeth in amazement. "Me, I have no idea what Rodet does. I am not extravagant, and he does not complain. But when I watch you, Stevie, I feel guilty."

"Guilty! Why? Good heavens, why?"

"For me"—she gave that wonderfully expressive shrug—"my house, children, friends, books, furniture . . . it's enough. Paris, *l'opéra,* dancing . . . it's enough. But for you—you have some—" She moved a pointing finger forward, like a slow-motion arrow, until her arm was fully extended. She dropped the arm with a sigh of exasperation. "It's marvellous."

Nora did not share her smile.

"Don't you think?" Rodie prompted.

"Sometimes," Nora said, not really wanting to confess it, but thinking it too important for evasion. "Sometimes it frightens me."

Rodie looked puzzled. Nora realized that she could never explain it without giving the background. "When we started, there was no one but me to do it. I've always been good with figures and calculation ever since I was a child. And when we began, Stevenson worked on the railroad eighteen hours a day and I kept the accounts. Then, because I am good at bargaining"—Rodie, who had seen Nora in action in the shops at Rouen, nodded fervent agreement—"I did all our purchasing, too— iron, timber, stone, tools, powder, fuzes—everything. Then I managed a foodshop, too, for the workmen."

"Because you had not enough to do," Rodie teased solemnly.

Nora laughed. "No. For the money," she said. "We made fifteen hundred pounds—that's about three thousand seven fifty francs—in one year, the first year." Rodie whistled. "So, you see, I became—have become—a prisoner of these beginnings. Because, when we took on the next contracts, we had to go to a bank for capital. And, of course, the banker wants to talk about our accounts and our income and our prospects. Who can he talk with? Only me. And very soon Stevenson discovers that I understand finance better than him."

"And he's *angry!*" Rodie prompted eagerly, thinking of the fight she was about to hear confessed.

"No! Delighted! Stevenson *understands* money, capital, finance, of course. But here." She tapped her forehead. "It is intellectual work for him. But I *live* it." She pressed her breastbone, at its very foot. "Oh, Rodie, I have never confessed this to any living soul, not even to him. But when I am thinking about capital, about moving it, using it, making it *work*, then I am more truly alive than at any other time. Now Stevenson cannot feel any of that; he has to think it. It is a discipline for him. What he feels is *people*. He is most alive with his navvies, and with

two figures tumbled and echoed in her mind: The number of projected railways had risen to 314, and the capital they sought now totalled £287,869,240. And each day more than two new companies announced themselves; each day the quantity of fresh capital sought was augmented by over £1,969,000.

Why did no one in authority cry out that this was sheer madness? Why did even John smile when *she* had the temerity to say it aloud? He above all ought to be worried. If the railway companies fell all of a heap, Stevenson's, too, would very quickly go down with them.

*   *   *

Rodet unwittingly harped on these fears the following morning after breakfast. She thought he had gone back to Rouen and so was surprised to be ambushed by him on a lower terrace well away from the house. They exchanged a few pleasantries and then, apropos nothing in particular, he said, "Yes, it's funnay in England now."

"In what way, m'sieu?"

"Soon, no workers, no servants. All are rich by the railways." His smile was gently sardonic—but turned inward, as if the only important audience for his humour were himself.

Nora laughed perfunctorily. "I hope we may still joke about it when the storm breaks," she said.

He took the cue and became serious himself. "*Alors. Some* railroad building must come out of it. For you, it's not necessarily bad."

"It will disarrange the City." She chose English words that were close to the French. "That will be bad for us."

"But Monsieur Jean, he is 'appy?"

"I believe so."

"Oh yes. He is. I know it." He produced a silver manicure scissors and snipped a rose. Nora thought he was going to offer it to her, but he tugged it firmly through his own buttonhole. "Is it much building in the south of England?"

Some slight alteration in his tone alerted Nora; this question was important to Rodet. "By the end of the year I would think Parliament might have sanctioned—might have permitted—three hundred or so miles."

Rodet whistled, drawing breath. "Much rail!" he said.

"It won't all get built. Probably only a third of it will actually get built."

"Even so." He shrugged. "We are 'appy here for ten miles."

"Then you should sell rails in England, Monsieur Rodet." She meant
the remark lightly, but even as she spoke it she realized that the idea
made great sense. All the rails for southern England were made in the
midlands and over in Wales. Rodet could probably ship from Havre
to Southampton and still quote very keenly. She told him as much and
saw again that reserved—or was it arrogant?—inward grin.

"No, madame. *You* should," he said. "Stevenson's."

"From Stockton!"

"From Le Havre." He waited to see the effect. "I put your name,
Stevenson, on the rails, and you sell them. Hein? We sell much more."

"Have you made this suggestion to Stevenson?"

"I think you, Madame Stevie, are more interested for the iron
foundry in this moment than Monsieur Jean."

"And that is why I am here at La Gracieuse, I suppose." By this
bluntness she wanted him to understand that if they were to talk business, he could not rely on the social constraints.

"Of course," he said, his twisted grin making a joking half-truth
of it.

She began to like Monsieur Rodet, and she knew he could sense it.
"Good," she said. She took his arm. "Good," she said again, and she
patted his arm.

They walked in silence for so long that the conversation almost
seemed to have foundered. But all the while her mind was racing. She
paused near a rosebush festooned with large white blooms, each with a
faint blush at its heart. "I would love one of these," she said.

He snipped half a dozen, saying, "Its name is called Souvenir de la
Malmaison. It's new." He handed them to her.

Choosing this moment, when he would expect her thanks, she said,
"We might do it for a fixed price."

"Ah! You are interested."

"For a fixed price. You leave us to find what profit we can—if any."

He smiled patronizingly. "I can discuse this with Monsieur Jean."

"Then be advised by me, Monsieur Rodet. Stevenson is the best railway contractor in the world for one reason. He understands absolutely
the things that are permanent. From mountains and rivers to masonry
and ironwork. He will like the fixed price."

This time his smile carried no hint of patronage.

Later she began to wonder whether she had done the right thing.
Even more, she wondered whether John would agree that it was right.

Chapter 15

Sam's arrival helped put such fears temporarily to the back of her mind. He came early, left his bags at the inn, and walked up from Trouville. It was a hot summer's day, with the afternoon breeze just beginning to move onshore. Nora was standing in the shade of the gateway, waiting for the britzka to be brought around, when she looked down the road and saw him—that unmistakable walk could only mean Sam.

Wishing she could run she stepped into the road and held her arms as high as her dress allowed, making a shallow **V**, and then, when he waved in response, she reached them toward him. He sauntered slightly faster; his jacket was hitched on one finger over his shoulder and he was fanning his head with his cap. He grinned and shook his head, meaning he could go no quicker.

She dropped her aching arms and waited. Rodie came to her side with a parasol when Sam was still fifty yards away. *"Un vrai* Milor'," she said. Nora felt very proud; sauntering at his ease, Sam indeed looked every stitch the young gentleman.

He made a token trot over eight of the last ten yards and hugged her, speechless with joy. When she presented him to Madame Rodet he kissed her hand as if he kissed twenty hands a day.

The britzka came at last, crunching and rumbling over the gravel and cobbles; its coarse leather hood had gone, being replaced by a light canvas awning with a silk fringe. Rodie waved at it. "You two go," she said. "Collect Mr. Telling's baggages."

"And you, Rodie? Don't let us deprive you of your drive. You know how much you enjoy it."

"Not today." She spoke with great conviction. "It's too hot." And she smiled and returned to the house.

Sam helped Nora aboard. "She's a grand woman," he said.

"One of the nicest and most interesting people I've ever met. But, oh Sam, it's good to see *you*! Isn't this a grand notion of hers!" She gripped his arm and shook it. They started to move.

"She really doesn't mind?" he asked. "She knows I'm in service and she doesn't mind? What does her husband say?"

"Oh, that! In France we look differently upon these things."

"I see!" He grinned. "*We*, eh?"

"*Mais oui!*" Nora laughed.

He looked at her with amused pity. "Another good Yorkshire soul lost."

She clung to his arm and giggled, thinking how like Sarah with Mr. Cornelius. "Oh, Sam," she said, "you're going to be good for me. I was beginning to miss England and home and family."

"That's a deal better," he said, lounging back in the seat and looking born to it.

Sam had been given a splendid room on the top floor to the left of the stairwell—about as far from the entrance as it was possible to get. When Nora asked Rodie why he hadn't been put on the floor below, on the opposite side of the stairwell from her, Rodie laughed and said it was impossible and Sam would not like it. "The decor is ancient and there are no paintings on the walls. But upstairs he have Courbet, Vernet, Boudin, Capronnier, Regnault—he will prefer."

*   *   *

The next day, and the next, Rodie found reasons not to go out driving with them, letting them catch up on all their news and acquaintance. They went to Honfleur, where they sat at a table under the trees, overlooking the inner harbour, and drank cold cordials. Moored crab and lobster boats swayed at their anchorage, nudged by a gentle breeze; the waves were no more than restless ripples that broke the bright reflections of sails and masts and houses into a writhing tableau of colour.

"You could watch it for hours," Sam said.

"D'you recall the wool our dad used to weave in Hunslet?" she asked.

He had to say yes, though he'd only been four when they left and went to Manchester.

"If you looked at it long enough, it used to shiver on the loom like that water. Especially by candlelight."

He nodded. "I wonder what it's like now, that part. And who's living in our place."

"Guess who owns it," she said.

Her smile alerted him. "You?"

She nodded. "I bought back our five acres. And ten more beside. You know that lawyer Hicks who swindled us and stole the land? He never had the benefit of it. They built a foundry and some mills on the Leeds side of the land, and it turned that little stream, Dow Beck, where you lost a shoe and got put through a small sieve by our dad, remember?"

"Aye!" He remembered that well enough.

"Well. The land got all flooded. Hicks never saw the benefit. So there's fairings in the world. He spent a tidy sum seeking compensation at law, which he never got. And then, when he was over a barrel for cash, I took back our five acres, and ten on top, for the same price we agreed for the five when we parted with them."

Sam giggled with delight. The lawyer, Samuel Hicks of Nelson's Yard, had taken the land as his agreed fee for defending Daniel Telling, Nora and Sam's eldest brother, on a charge of conspiracy when he formed a trade union. But at the trial Hicks had put in a plea of guilty and had kept the land.

"Did he know who you were?" Sam asked.

She intoned, "Samuel Hicks, Nelson's Yard, 46 Briggate." And there was such soft malevolence in her voice and such cold delight gleamed in her eye that for a moment Sam was in fear of her.

"Eay, I'd give a lot to have seen that," he said uneasily. "What'll you do with the land?"

She came back as if she'd almost forgotten he was there. She smiled and looked away toward the sea. "It's your inheritance," she said. "You may have it. I'll give it you the day you marry. I've had it drained. There'll be factories on it soon. You'll get a tidy ground rent."

He laughed, not thinking her serious. "It's our Daniel's by rights. He's the eldest."

Again that hardness, even fiercer this time, as she turned upon him. For an instant, as their eyes met, he felt he was staring into the very soul of hate. But her voice was calm and chill. "Daniel is none of my family. He made his choice when his demands were granted. And yet he chose to prolong the strike until they recognized his Union as well. He knew they'd arrest him. He knew he'd be transported. He knew he'd be leaving me to look after you and Wilfrid and Dorrie. In that hovel. Without even a proper door. His last night of freedom he spent organizing his own useless petition instead of mending that door. If that door had been mended——"

She could not finish.

Sam held his breath. "I still get nightmares," he said. "Coming back and finding young Wilfrid's arm like that."

Wilfrid had been eaten alive by a straying boar, all but one arm. Dorrie had died of gangrene following rat bites.

"He wanted it to happen, of course," Nora added.

It struck Sam as such a shocking thing to say that, even when he cleared his throat to speak, the sound had a note of protest.

"He wanted it," Nora insisted. "I almost sent him those paragraphs in the newspaper, about Dorrie and Wilfrid. But I thought, no. That's what he wants. He wants to know that England is a land of oppression and misery, and that it must be torn apart in revolution before he can build the new Jerusalem."

"So he doesn't know yet? About the bairns?"

"Not from me."

"They got up a subscription for his appeal. Did you hear that?"

"Aye. I sent a clipped farthing—and a letter to say it was two thousand guineas more than he was worth."

Sam's laugh had no humour in it. "I gave three pounds," he said. "It took me a year to save."

Nora made a mental note that when she conveyed the land there would be one or two restrictive covenants attached.

"I was fond of him," Sam went on. "He was always kindly to me."

"And to me," Nora said. "That's what made his betrayal worse."

"Mr. Nelson keeps himself informed on the petition. For my sake. He says it's close to being granted. This session of Parliament there may be a pardon."

"I'll have a raspberry drink this time," she said.

*   *   *

It amazed Nora that she could find Sam such good company, for they agreed on almost nothing. Maybe it was that their contentions were so mild and gentle-natured—being really a warm agreement to differ. But Rodie, perhaps sensing that some deeper aggression lay beneath the surface and fearing that a week's confinement and repetition of the same daily pattern might bring it out, suggested that Nora and her brother should take the coach, and a groom and the maid Honorine, and go on a little journey. "Go to Avranches," she suggested. "You can see Mont St. Michel. And your friends who have bought the inn at Coutances—that is very near. It would be pleasant for you."

It was this last suggestion that swayed Nora; the thought of seeing Sarah and Cornelius again—and of introducing Sam to them—was too tempting to refuse.

"What about your baby?" Sam asked.

"Listen," she told him. "When I had Winifred I behaved as if I were carrying a bar of pure gold. And I made my life and John's a martyrdom to it. After that I determined I'd not sacrifice the best ten years of my life and marriage on the altar of motherhood. Babies? Let them blow where they list. I delivered Arabella Thornton's first in a cemetery in Lancashire. And no fuss. I'll do meself the same honour here. If necessary—which it will *not* be. It's not due this seven weeks." She poked him in the ribs. "Doan't fratch so."

"I'm mindful of thy John," he said.

"I'll write to him this day and absolve thee there."

And so, on Sunday, the first in June, having survived three more endless sermons that Matins, they set off westward down the roads Nora had come to know so well. They headed first for Caen and then on to Vire, where they had decided to spend their first night, despite *Murray's* rating of "not good" for the inn there.

The country they drove through was even prettier than on the other side of the Seine—a succession of woods, orchards, and pastures, with increasing stretches of wilderness where rocky outcrops sprang from a sea of heather. Nora could believe Cornelius' description of the land as one mosaic of ripe and unripe blackberries, for here they were in prolific flower all around—vast spreading bushes laden with blossom.

She repeated the description to Sam.

"I'll wager no one picks them," he said. "Not even the children."

"Why?"

"Oh, they're a degenerate, indolent, selfish, arrogant lot, these folk."

"Apart from that," she said, "you quite like them."

He laughed. "There's no quality here. That's the trouble. Even our hosts, they're not *quality*."

"How can you say that, Sam?" She did not show her annoyance.

"They're nice enough folk. Very nice. Nicer than a lot of folk of quality. I grant that. But they've the instincts of peasants. They put equality before quality, if you ask me. Everyone here does."

"I don't understand that."

"All this 'monsieur and madame' to anyone over the age of twenty-five or so. Did you see her on the way to church this morning, saying 'madame' to that beggar woman! And not a smile."

She stifled all the arguments that clamoured to be expressed and laughed instead. "Oh, Sam!"

"Look how all the big houses are shuttered," he went on, undeterred. "Just one or two beginning to open. It's obvious all the great families are away. But could you guess that from the villages? Now, you go into an English village and you can tell at once whether the quality families are away or in residence. The whole atmosphere is dry and dead when they're gone. Here, it makes no difference."

She followed him with great, amused, pitying eyes. "What does that tell you?"

"It tells me that the English can recognize quality and respond to it. Here they are rich peasants, middling peasants, and poor peasants. And" —he quelled an interruption from her—"and it tells me that in England, despite the upheavals of these years, we shall never have revolution. But here, however good the conditions of life, they will never free themselves from the terror of it. You laugh at the English road sweeper in his tall hat and Chesterfield coat cast out by a duke ten years back; I tell you there's enough cold ambition in that to douse any revolutionary heat. But here, where everyone is citizen—" He shook his head. "It's folly."

She smiled, determined not to get drawn. "I miss the smell of the oaks," she said. "A month ago they were stupendous."

He nudged her, gently. "Don't give out you don't know what I mean. You move among the quality yourself now. You hunt with them. You know what—"

"Hah!" Her single scornful cry cut him short. He had touched the open-sesame nerve at last. "Hunt! I'll tell you about hunting, Sam. And quality. In any field of sixty, taken at haphazard, you'll find no more than half a dozen who really understand what they're there for. Three of them'll be hunt servants, one of them a farmer, and two, *two*, out of fifty-odd, two will be folk of quality. The rest are there to enjoy 'a slashin' good trot' or to gossip or to cut a dash or to kill time or because they lack the brains to think up anything better. They have no notion of the true business of a hunt; they'd be happier on a drag scent if they were honest."

Sam tried to pacify her, banking her down with his hands. "I oughtn't to have said about hunting," he said. "I forgot. It was a bad example."

"To the contrary, it was a very good example. You talk about the English country being dead until the big families come down, and you are *right*. Where do they come down from? From London society, from German spas, from Alpine walks and Italian museums. And they're back in the saddle and after Charley James Fox five days a week. And they bring the villages to life with an ideal of leisure and sport. *That's* what your crossing sweeper puts on with the duke's castoffs—the notion that the ideal life is sport and leisure. Just give that belief a good century to soak into the bones of the English workingman and you can kiss England farewell. She'll drown in a *flood* of quality."

He looked at her in astonishment. "It is Nora Stevenson, isn't it? Born Telling? The lass as once told me she could never get through 'Rule Britannia' for the lump it brought to her throat?"

She blushed. "You're right," she said. "I don't mean to attack England. But," she rallied, "I don't think it right to criticize France for being different."

"Not different," he said smugly. "Just inferior."

His condescension rankled with her and, after willing herself not to say it for several furlongs, she taunted him with the words: "You have the heart of a servant, Sam."

He laughed at once, good-naturedly. "Aye," he said. "And a good one. Don't leave me money, Nora love. Nor give me any. You'd ruin me." And later he said, "I'm happier at what I do than any man I know. Many rich folk stop with the Nelsons. There's naught would make me change stations with any on 'em."

She squeezed his arm. "I'm happy for you," she said. "To have an untroubled mind and sleep easy—it's a champion gift."

"And you?" he asked.

She sighed. "I'm not troubled by conscience," she said. "But there's responsibility. Stevenson gives work to nine thousand. That's a lot of men, and wives and bairns, to depend on the wisdom or folly of two people."

It sobered Sam. "Eay, I'd never thought," he said.

"Still"—she sat up and rearranged herself with determination— "I'm free of it for a day or two. Look at this wonderful scenery."

They looked around over a sea of heather, and down into twisting wooded dells where waters dashed and complained unseen, and up along rocky escarpments where trees and shrubs clung perilously to sheer faces of granite.

"I'll tell you what it's like," she said. "It's like Killiecrankie. Have you ever been there?"

He shook his head.

"Well, that part of the Scotch Highlands is very like this."

It was late afternoon and the slanting sun fell across the valleys, modelling them starkly and throwing the hot green of the sunstruck woods against the deep, rich turquoises and blues of the shaded hollows. The trees and the heath were alive with the shrill of birdsong, though

the only birds they could see were the harriers, sitting complacently on
the craggy summits, and the kestrels, teetering on the updraughts overhead.

"These folk don't deserve it," he said.

She pinched his arm until he withdrew it in protest, laughing. "We
must be there soon," she said.

He looked around, remembering something. "The valleys of Vire,"
he said. "What's 'valleys' in French?"

"*Vaux*. I think."

He tugged at the coachman's shirt. "*Les vaux de Vire*, m'sieu?" he
asked.

"*Mais oui, m'sieu. Les vaux de Vire.*" He swung his whip all around,
demonstrating.

"Why?" Nora asked.

"D'you hear any singing?"

"No. Why? Only birds."

"It's something your Monsieur Rodet told me last night. There used
to be some right jolly singing in these parts and that's where we get the
word vaudeville from. Vaudeville—*vaux de Vire*. He *says*. I don't suppose it's true. He also said they make all the shirts for the French army
here."

"What a lot we learn when we travel," she said.

*   *   *

Murray's "not good" had been, if anything, kindly. The rooms were so
filthy Nora had to lift her skirts as she walked. She made the innkeeper's wife sweep the floor and then tried to order her to scrub it, but the
woman refused, saying something of which the only intelligible word
was *anglaise*. Sam saw the horses well stabled and looked at the rooms
and beds for Honorine and the coachman before he went to his own.

"Mr. Nelson always does that," he said. "A master relies on his
horses and his servants."

"He and Stevenson are of a pair," Nora replied. "When John surveys a line he always looks at the lodgings and victuallers beside the
way."

The food was good, though they had to drink everything—wine and
café au lait—from bowls. Cups and glasses seemed to be unheard of.

The beds were alive with fleas and lice, but they were well prepared
for that. As soon as they arrived they had sprinkled spirits of naphtha
(nearly a shilling's worth, as Nora said) into every corner and fold of

the linen and mattresses; by bedtime, half an hour's assiduous hunting was enough to rid both beds of a small pile of dead or twitching livestock.

Sam poked a particularly large louse. "Grey badgers, we used to call them. Remember?"

She looked to see if he was joking.

"Didn't we?" he asked uncertainly.

"Grey badgers," she said, "were those dried peas we ate on mid-Lent Sunday. I'll never be able to eat them again now—thank *you*."

"No, that was Carling peas."

"In Manchester, when we moved there. But in Leeds they were always called grey badgers."

"Take your word for it." He shook his head and sighed. "How soon we forget."

"Speak for yourself," she said. "To me it's like yesterday still."

*   *   *

After breakfast it was a quick run down through Avranches to the coast. The view as they came down out of the hills, with the plains of Brittany beyond, was the most splendid they had yet seen. In the centre, rising out of its vast desert of sand, with the sea sparkling miles beyond, giving dramatic point to the whole, was the fairy-castle abbey of Mont St. Michel. They were so keen to reach it that they drove through Avranches without stopping. Beyond, driving through dunes of salt scrub and tamarisk, they seemed to have come to a world a thousand miles from the green and granite uplands near Vire.

And then they were out onto the sand, as smooth as a table and as firm as the driveway at Thorpe.

"It's like a castle in a legend," she said excitedly, looking at the intricate ranks of turrets, ramparts, battlements, and spires that crowned the little island.

"It's like a toy," he said. "You feel you could just pluck it up like a toy."

"Good thing the tide is out."

The inn was as clean and as pleasant as the one at Vire had been "not good." They had a light lunch of meat loaf, cold herring salad, and blancmange, washed down with cider and a sort of apple brandy from the Calvados hills they had driven through yesterday. It was stronger than it tasted, and Nora felt a little lightheaded as they walked up the twisting cobbled street to the abbey.

Inside it was not nearly as impressive as it had promised to be from a distance. Its fifty years of service as a political and criminal prison had not dealt kindly with the building. Most of the great chambers had been cut up into floors and workshops for the five hundred common-law prisoners who now worked there as weavers, hatters, and bootmakers. Nora and Sam, and their guide, were constantly having to press against walls and into doorways as files of soldiers and rank-smelling convicts were marched by. The Salle des Chevaliers with its massive pillars and soaring groined vaults was entirely filled with looms. The clack of the shuttles, the beating of the heddles, the clatter of the sheds, and the choking, lint-laden air—it was all too strongly reminiscent for Nora and Sam of their days of poverty in the mills at Stockport. The wonderful romanesque church, the crowning of the island, was a cockroach-infested eating hall for the prisoners. Rancid fat, slopped gruel, and rotting scraps lay everywhere. Earlier in the century the nave had been a two-floor straw-hat factory, but that had burned out eleven years ago. The whole upper part was still black with soot.

Outside, on the terrace created by the demolition in 1780 of the last three bays of the nave, the guide pointed to the ruins of the Women's Prison; formerly a hostelry, built in the twelfth century, it had collapsed in 1817. He gave a revoltingly vivid account of the event—the only occasion on which he came alive during their whole tour. "The view of Tombelaine and the Channel Islands," he said, turning to the sea and relapsing into his professional torpor, "is especially magnificent."

But he was right. The smooth sands and the warm salt breeze beckoned them irresistibly.

"Oh, Sam," Nora said, "let's walk to the edge of the sea. When is high water?" She turned to the guide. "High tide? *La marée haute?*"

He pulled out a watch. "Now," he said. "Half an hour ago. It's falling again."

"But it's miles away. Does it not surround this island?"

The man smiled and pointed to the ghost of a half moon in the eastern sky. "Only at full moon and new moon," he said.

"What superstitious nonsense!" Nora sneered when they were walking out over the sands, northward from the Mount.

"It's not superstition," Sam told her. And he explained the whole business of neap tides and spring tides.

The sea was going out faster than they could walk so that, when they were a mile from the island, the waters, which had been only two or at most three miles away and plainly visible, had moved almost out of sight. They turned then and began to stroll back.

Almost at once one of those hot sand winds that seem to blow up out of nowhere began. And with nothing to halt it, it blew with melancholy force. They made a detour to put the island between them and the wind but had to withdraw when they came upon the brown, stinking rivulets that drained the abbey and the surrounding houses, choked with fish offal and street sweepings.

Nora had a good long sleep before their late dinner, and almost immediately went back to bed.

"Tomorrow," she told Sam as he kissed her good night, "you'll meet Mr. and Mrs. Cornelius."

Before she went to sleep she thought of the Corneliuses, leaving the most thriving tavern in the whole of south London and taking a little country place in Normandy, and then of Sam, so contented with his lot and station. And of dear Rodie, happy to take her little pocket money in return for an easily kept bargain and, during the week to be sure, *un peu de tolérance*. Why, she wondered, was she not like them? Had she always been different? The only folk who could tell her had long since gone.

Chapter 16

They made an early start after breakfast, stopping at Avranches only to see if any mail had been sent on and to leave forwarding instructions to Coutances.

"We'll go through Granville," she told the coachman. "Not up through Gavray."

When they were moving again she explained to Sam: "Granville's where he wants to start a bathing beach if he can. We'll have a look at it."

The road took them back through sandy hills and out onto dry flats of salt scrub whose only feature was the occasional tamarisk tree. A few miles northward, though, the shore began to rise; and by the time they reached the little coastal village of Granville, they were at the top of fifty-foot cliffs down which broad pathways had been hewn to the sands and rocks below.

She thought it the drabbest place she had ever seen, so drab its air was almost menacing. Every window was either shuttered or had its curtains drawn. The beach was pockmarked with footprints; at its centre was a large, shimmering patch where the sand was still wet, though the tide was well down.

"They've been busy down there," Sam said.

"It looks like quicksand. You'd think it swallowed the whole village."

They did not stop but pressed on for Coutances, arriving in the early afternoon. They would have been there sooner, she explained to Sarah, if they had not been held up on a bad, narrow stretch of the road by a coach travelling much slower than it had any need to.

"The French can be inconsiderate that way," Sarah conceded.

The inn was very gaily decorated with flowers in all the public rooms and corridors. In the dining room stood a large pyramid of things like doughnuts, held together by a cataract of honey and whipped cream. Sarah showed them through the place with an air of suppressed amusement, like one withholding a happy secret.

"You haven't gone to all this trouble just for us I hope," Nora said.

"In a way." Sarah smiled. "You see, Tom and I are to be married today."

Shocked, Nora turned upon her. "Married?"

Sarah laughed. "You will see. I hope he won't be too long now. His aunt and uncle are already here."

She was very excited, like someone who had spent a long time preparing a magnificent treat for a party of children and was now seeing it unfold, exactly as planned.

Nora's room overlooked the cobbled yard at the back of the inn, so she must have been one of the first to see the coach pull through the arched entrance from the street. It was the coach that had delayed them on the road from Granville. The look upon the driver's face, a solemnity curiously mingled with terror, warned her that something awful was about to unfold in this house.

A maid ran out from the kitchen, intent on opening the carriage door. The driver came suddenly to life, leaped nimbly down, and stayed her hand.

He said something to her.

She put a fist up to her mouth. She seemed to be trying to cram it between her teeth. Then she turned and ran back into the kitchen. Her wild call, "M'sieu Gaston! M'sieu Gaston!" sounded in the passages beneath Nora's feet.

A man, presumably Monsieur Gaston, strode quickly across the yard and held a brief, low-voiced conference with the driver. Before they finished, Sarah came out as if to join them. She stopped when she saw the look upon their faces. Behind her, unseen by anyone save Nora, the servant girl mutely stood, hopelessly clutching at the air as if she could thereby draw Sarah back.

Or perhaps it was a more cosmic gesture than that. Perhaps, in the way that affects us all at such terrible moments, she sought to roll back time itself. Certainly Nora, watching this momentarily frozen group, and remembering what she had seen at Granville and upon the way here, had never more urgently wished that time could be so unravelled.

Without pausing to put on her bonnet and gloves, she went swiftly down to the courtyard.

The carriage door was open. Sarah was nowhere in sight. The two men stood nervously where she had last seen them. The girl clutched one of the wooden pillars that supported the overhanging upper floor, sobbing.

Nora went straight to the men.

"Monsieur Cornelius?" she asked, as if her questioning tone might itself sustain a hope that had already died.

Until then she had not known that *noyé* was the French word for "drowned." From that day she never forgot it; and she never heard it spoken nor saw it in print without remembering the monstrous finality with which Gaston spoke it then. She looked at his eyes. They fell. So did the coachman's. So did hers. What possible comfort could they offer one another?

There was a small noise, not quite a sob, from inside the coach. Nora pushed her head gingerly into its darkness, seeing nothing at first. Then she spied Sarah sitting, calmly rigid, on the forward seat. On the rear seat, also rigid, lay the drowned body of Tom Cornelius.

Nora would not have got into the coach had Gaston not gripped her arm to help her up; her response was then automatic.

"My dear?" she said. "Oh, my dear!"

She did not know whether to call her Sarah or Mrs. Cornelius.

Sarah made no move. She seemed even to have stopped breathing. Nora stood uncertainly just inside the door. In the light that fell over her shoulder she saw a dull gleam in the paler dab that marked the position, but no feature, of Tom's face; in horror she realized that one of his eyes was open. Without thought she leaned forward to close it. Sarah still made no move, no sound.

But the eye had been open so long it had dried. The lid merely rolled down upon itself without breaking the adhesion of its margin.

By the most grisly contrast his skin felt damp, even slimy, to her ungloved touch. She swiftly withdrew her hand; the dull, dry eye gazed up
again, clouded. Blind.

For some obscure reason this failure to achieve any purpose, either
to comfort Sarah or to set Tom properly to rest, left her feeling de-
filed. There was a sudden, almost overwhelming urge to hit Tom
Cornelius, as a kind of punishment. Afterward she explained it to herself as a memory of a newspaper report in which a bystander was said
to have slapped a dead man back to life. At the time she was over-
powered by the sudden and savage intensity of the impulse, and she
took the easy—the only—way out by bursting into tears.

She wanted to collapse onto her knees but was too pregnant for
that. Instead she leaned awkwardly over the seat on which Tom lay
half-stretched, her head buried in the upholstery, sobbing stupidly. The
sudden access of light, as she moved out of the door frame, at last galvanized Sarah into movement.

"There!" she said, her voice wavering, her arms settling on Nora's
neck, bearing her back to the opposite seat. "There now!" Her grip was
firm, almost painful.

That, and the ludicrous reversal of their expected roles, calmed
Nora quite suddenly. She snorted a single half-laugh as she said, "I came
to console *you!*"

As she spoke she felt the first twinge of labour. *God send it's a false
alarm*, she prayed.

Sarah stood. The wavering voice was barely recognizable as hers.
"There is much to do now," she said. "Please help me. All you can."

She thrust past Nora, almost fell from the coach, and ran across
the yard, slamming the kitchen door behind her.

Nora let the silence return before she, too, rose and stepped carefully outside. Gaston, who appeared to be the senior among the inn
servants, looked to her for instructions.

"Please arrange for Mr. Cornelius' body to be carried indoors and
to be properly prepared for burial. Is there an English doctor nearby?"

"*Oui*, Madame. Dr. Grimble, very near."

"Please send for him, too."

She found Sam waiting for her just beyond the kitchen door. His
face told her he had heard. "Eay, love!" he said and took her hands.

"We've much to do, Sam." She echoed Sarah's words. In every corner, flowers danced discordantly. "Have you seen this uncle and aunt
Sarah mentioned?"

Sam nodded and tilted his head toward the stairs. "They are awful!" he said. "Or she is."

It was the unheeding, all-or-nothing judgement of a servant; but it was accurate. They must have come down by the front stairs for Nora found them in the dining room, the room with the doughnut pile. She let the uncle, a Monsieur Corneille, introduce himself and his wife.

Anyone who had known Cornelius would have known the uncle at once; he was the same man thirty years on—with the same smile and the same observant eye, never still. His English was poor, yet he communicated all he needed.

Madame Corneille was very much younger, not yet thirty. Nora found her brassy and unfeminine. She was eating one of the doughnuts.

They had both heard of Tom's death. Monsieur Corneille, though he could hardly have known Cornelius well, was obviously distressed. But with his wife the emotion went no deeper than the rouge on her cheeks. Her eyes traversed the room like cannon swivels, assessing and valuing everything within range.

Nora had time for no more than the conventional expressions of grief and condolence before the maid returned with the English doctor. Grimble was a small man, very fat, and so short of breath he came down the passage like a train huffing and puffing its way through a tunnel. Nora went out to him at once.

They met at the foot of the stair, two figures from a geometry book, she a rhomboid, he a sphere.

"Need me too, eh?" he asked, looking at the advanced state of her pregnancy.

"Not so far," she said.

Gaston appeared and took him, wheezing even harder, up the stairs to the room where Cornelius' body had been laid. Nora followed, not wanting to go back and face the Corneilles. She waited in the passage, wondering where Sarah had gone.

After an eternity Dr. Grimble reappeared. He merely nodded, as if to confirm in some formal way what was too obvious to put into actual words.

"Inquests?" Nora asked. "What about that sort of thing?"

"No need," the doctor said. "He didn't drown, that's certain."

"But . . ."

"Oh, they pulled him out of the water all right, but there's none of it in his lungs. He was certainly dead when he went into, or fell into, the water."

"You're not suggesting foul play?"

"By no means. An apoplexy, in my view. Of the heart, or of the head."

"A stroke?"

"A stroke." He looked over her shoulder and translated, "*Une attaque massive de paralysie,*" for the benefit of the Corneilles, who were coming up the stairs. He then expanded on the explanation for their benefit.

While he was thus distracted, Nora drew Gaston to the far end of the corridor. The move, she saw, did not escape Madame Corneille's notice. She took Gaston into her room, leaving the door open.

"Now tell me about this 'marriage' business," she said. "Were they not actually married?"

"In England, yes. But Monsieur Cornelius 'e is not sure it work in France." Gaston shrugged. " 'E is joke, of course. 'E is fun for everybody."

"It wasn't to be a real wedding then."

"But yes, of course. Even with Monsieur le Maire, the 'mayor' of the ville you say. But for Monsieur Cornelius all is fun. Fun for all! And all for fun, 'e say."

"But there's no question they were already married?"

"I *think*." For the first time he looked dubious.

How could she find out? She could hardly ask! And what had Cornelius done with the money he had mentioned? She must write to John at once.

It was ridiculous—no sooner had she framed the resolve than, through her window, she saw John himself walk into the inn yard accompanied by Sam.

She went quickly to the casement and threw it wide. "John!"

He looked up and smiled thinly. "Don't come down," he said. "I'll join you."

The relief she felt was immense. Now he could take charge of everything; he would know exactly what to do. But how strange—his suddenly appearing like that. Was it also part of the surprise that Sarah's smile had promised?

"What of this inn now?" Gaston asked.

"You must wait and see if Mrs. Cornelius intends to stay. Or if she will sell it."

"It is not yet buyed."

She shrugged and stored the fact away. She could understand Gaston's anxiety, but there was nothing she could do.

When John came into the room her first thought was that he was ill. She had never seen him so ashen grey. He was trembling. He could hardly look at her. She did not recognize these as symptoms of fear.

Gaston, unbidden, went out and returned shortly with a stiff glass of cognac. She took it and helped John to the bed. Then they were alone.

"Is it a fever?" she asked, holding the glass to his lips. "Shall I get the doctor to come in and look at you?"

He snorted glumly. "We're finished, Nora love," he said. "We're ruined." He took no more than a sip of the brandy. "Fucking Beador!"

That more than anything shocked her into the seriousness of it all. John was not a swearing man. Suddenly Tom Cornelius' death and Sarah's tragedy dwindled to nothing.

"How?" she asked, surprised at the calm of her voice. "What has happened?"

His eyes almost met hers, wavered, and lowered again. That struck the fear deep into her. He could not even look her in the eye!

"He's in . . ." John faltered, then shook his head. "Way over. Way . . . deep."

"Beador? Debt, you mean?"

He shut his eyes and nodded.

"Then thank God we're in a Company of Limited Liability instead of a partnership!"

John did not move. His eyes stayed firmly closed.

She knew then that he had gone against her suggestion. Stevenson's had, indeed, gone into partnership with Beador. And Beador must now have dragged them into some very deep water for John to be so broken up.

It astonished her then that she felt no anger. Perhaps whatever emotion she had to spare that day had already been exhausted. She even managed to put herself in John's shoes—to imagine how it must have been for him to travel, maybe all the way from Beador's place up near Stockton, to here, three or four days, knowing what he had to confess at the end of it.

What could she now possibly say to compare with the self-laceration he must already have inflicted!

"You'd better tell me the size of it," she said. "And then we'll sit down and see how best to tackle it." She sat beside him on the bed.

To her intense embarrassment as soon as she was within reach he began to sob. He grasped her tightly, buried his head on her neck and shoulder, and wept. She could smell several days of fear upon him.

"Nora!" he said through his tears. "Thou art a bloody rock! A bloody rock!"

"An ocean rock if you go on at this rate," she said. She hated the exhibition he was giving. The last thing she felt like was a rock.

He regained a little calm and even managed a tight smile. "For the first time in . . . oh, days," he said, "I feel a little hope."

"There!"

He was dour again. "But not much."

"It's bad?"

"Over a hundred thousand pounds." Now that he had finally named the figure his voice was calm. He looked at her, so intently that she immediately wondered how much protective charade there had been in his earlier behaviour.

No sooner had the thought struck her than she began to feel a sort of backlash of self-disgust at her own detachment. But she thrust the feeling aside; for the moment her lack of emotion was too valuable to squander in *self*-examination.

"How?" she asked. "Hudson couldn't possibly have missed anything that size. Is he behind this? Surely not!"

"It's since Hudson. Even since Beador furnished us with his list."

"You'd better explain why it is we're in partnership. It's news to me."

He took her hand. "Where you sit, surrounded by your ledgers, things must often look very simple. But for me, out there in the thick of things . . ."

"I'm not criticizing you, love." She gripped back more firmly to show that she meant it.

"If you were, you couldn't outdo me. Oh, I blame myself right enough." He let go of her, as if to stress his unworthiness.

She folded her hands below the mountain of her belly. A further twinge told her that her labour had definitely begun. Well, she would suppress all outward sign of it as long as possible. Too much was at stake over these next few hours.

"How has it come about, then?" she pressed.

"How does anything come about between the gentry and the aristocracy? It was a wager. I sometimes think they even get married only as the result of wagers."

Relief welled up within her: a wager! She even laughed. "But no wager is legally enforceable . . ." she began, before she saw John's face. "Why not?" she ended.

"You listen! Sir George Beador had a wager with Lord Wyatt—on a horse in some local steeplechase. They were both drunk, of course. Lord Wyatt has speculated in railway shares to the tune of two hundred thousand pounds—which he can probably well afford. In fact, to prove he *can* afford it, he bets our friend Beador another two hundred thou'— only *his* stake is his shares."

"I don't follow that. Surely Beador at last understands . . ."

"I mean that when Beador lost, as of course he did, he didn't pay Wyatt two hundred thousand, he simply accepted Wyatt's liability of worthless shares."

For a moment Nora was too shocked even to breathe. "I don't think Wyatt was drunk at all," she said at last. "Two . . . hundred . . . thousand!" she repeated. She spaced the words out as if that might diminish the sum.

"I'm assuming we can get rid of half—even more—before the bubble breaks. But I think it would be foolish to bank on doing better than that."

"But why did you say *more than* a hundred thousand, then?"

"Call it pessimism—I mean, that's what we ought to prepare to face. D'you think we can do it?"

"If we can use the trust fund."

"No!" He was suddenly vehement, assertive, more like his true self—as she had intended when she made the suggestion. "That fund is for you and the children if . . ." He had finished the sentence many times in the past, but now that the firm's ruin was inevitable, he could only let the ending hang. "It is never to be used, never, not for the rescue of our firm."

"If I'd had the management of it," she said, "it would pay Beador's debt *and* leave over as much as Chambers has now."

He nodded, not in agreement but to avoid a dispute.

"I'm sorry to have to press the point, John, but I'd still like to know why we are in partnership with that man."

He screwed up his face. "These new-fangled Companies of Limited Liability," he said. "The law isn't a year old yet. Too uncertain, you see? There's no case law to guide us."

"That sounds more like Chambers talking than you."

John only nodded.

She got down from the bed and crossed to the window. The courtyard was empty. "Sound, dependable Chambers," she murmured.

"To change the subject," he said, "how about Sarah? How has she taken it? Pretty hard, I imagine."

"Pretty hard."

A cat stalked warily into the yard and sniffed at some fish offal lying on the cobbles.

"An extraordinary thing happened, you know. About a fortnight ago." John's voice was very level. "Tom Cornelius walked into our London office and put near enough to forty thousand pounds in Bank of England notes on Jackson's desk and said, 'This is for Mr. Stevenson. He knows all about it.' Poor Jackson nearly threw a fit."

For a long minute, long enough for the cat to take up the offal and slink back beneath the archway, Nora kept silent. "We must see that Sarah gets it," she said at last.

"No doubt of it."

"Were those his exact words: *This is for Mr. Stevenson?*" She looked hard at John.

"Jackson has already sworn an affidavit to it." He smiled. "Thank God I took that precaution—just in case there was ever any dispute."

"Did we pay Cornelius the equivalent in francs?"

"I have brought the draft with me, ready to give to him."

"Well," she said. "There's no immediate hurry."

They avoided each other's eyes. The temptation was too great, its arrival too providential, for either of them to disavow it out of hand. "Perhaps . . ." Nora began, but she did not finish the sentence.

"We'll see," John said.

"Yes. And I must have another word with Gaston. Sarah will probably not want to stay on here."

They went downstairs.

Gaston told them that the owner of the inn, a Monsieur Colbert, had allowed the Corneliuses to move in on a caretaker lease after paying a deposit. He had already called several times for the balance but Mr. Cornelius had always managed to postpone the payment. But now . . . ?

No wonder Gaston was worried.

A possibility occurred to Nora: If Sarah did not complete the purchase, then she herself could probably get the inn a little cheaper from the worried Monsieur Colbert. A safe bolthole in Normandy for herself and John might not come amiss in the near future.

Before she could begin to work the conversation around to these ideas, the two Corneilles, aunt and uncle, came in. After Nora had presented them to John, Madame announced that they were intending to stay indefinitely.

"Until after the funeral," Corneille explained.

"Indefinitely!" his wife contradicted.

"Ah," Nora said, smiling warmly. "To help poor Sarah. How kind of you, Madame. But I"—she patted the bulge of her dress—"am unlikely to be leaving soon, as you may see. So if you have urgent business at home in Montauban, I would be very . . ."

Madame Corneille's smile was almost an open sneer. "That is *more* than kind, Mrs. Stevenson. But it may not fall to Sarah, or to you, to see to Thomas' affairs."

Everyone looked at her in silence. Her enthusiasm had led her to make the point in a truculent way. She tried now to recover. "I mean—" She coughed a single, placatory laugh and smiled invitingly. "It may not be possible. It is a matter for the law." She looked at each again, smiling still. "The law, you see."

"But *how*, my dear?" Corneille pressed. "What law?"

Now his wife was embarrassed. "Well," she said unwillingly, "if—I say if, only *if* you see—if it should happen that in French law, you see, you understand, that the marriage is not complete, then you, dearest, are next of kin."

She used the phrase *le plus proche parent*, which John had to translate to Nora.

"*Eh bien? Alors?*" Corneille shrugged, still not grasping her conclusion. She made an exasperated noise.

"What Madame means," Nora said, "is that you, Monsieur Corneille, must then administer affairs."

Madame Corneille, not welcoming help from this suspect quarter, stared coldly at Nora, so that she only half-heard John's blunt: "She means, m'sieu, that you will inherit the estate."

Corneille's anger brought her back from her inspection of Nora. He was outraged. It was intolerable. It was monstrous. Had they not enough already? Was he not one of the richest men in Montauban? Had they come here to steal from his nephew, his dear brother's son? What law could force him to do such a thing? The law! The law! He ranted on, blaming the law, while his eyes murdered his wife.

It was the wrong response. *He does not know how to manage her,* John thought. If he had tried to ease her from her embarrassment, or abruptly and firmly changed the subject, or even scolded her openly, it might have served. But to scold her obliquely, in the guise of the law, merely gave her the chance to press her point without, ostensibly, attacking her hubsand's authority.

"The law, *chéri*, is the law. We may have our own opinion of its stupidity, but we must obey its command. Things must be done through regulation or they may later be challenged and upset. . . ." And so on.

She was in triumphant spate when Corneille's face dropped and he rose to his feet. His eyes were fixed on something behind her. She turned and halted in mid-sentence.

There at the bottom of the staircase stood Sarah, one hand still on the kingpost, as if to say that part of her would rather not enter this room and its company. Nora was glad to see she was angry.

"Madame!" Corneille started toward her but she withdrew a pace onto the first step, which stopped him halfway across the room.

"I will save you all such trouble," she said. "Tomorrow I shall sign a paper renouncing all claim to Thomas' estate. It shall be yours."

She turned at once and went back upstairs, leaving them silent. John, seeing Nora's face screwed-up against another twinge, misinterpreted it as the anger he expected to discover. Corneille turned on his wife. "There!" he shouted in fury. "There! You see! Her husband not cold and you—"

"No!" She cut him short. "It is a trick." She turned to Nora, including her in the charge. "It's a trick! If we accept the offer, we recognize her right to make it. So we would accept her marriage. And then, *alors*, pfft!"

Corneille turned to John and Nora and shrugged an apology.

"I think," Nora said, taking John's arm, "I shall retire." At the foot of the stairs she said to John: "The baby is coming. I'm sure of it. Perhaps you should get Gaston to call back the doctor."

His response was immediate. He lifted her in his arms and carried her effortlessly to the stairhead. "Are you sure?" he said. "Yes, you must be. Will you be all right? Of course, yes, of course you will be. Is it bad?"

She laughed. "Just think," she teased. "In a week or two we can take our greens without contortion!"

"How *can* you!" He pretended disgust. "At such a time."

"You have a puritan heart," she began, before the sight of Sarah, in the doorway of Cornelius' room, stopped her.

"Dr. Grimble was sending a woman," she said. "I thought— Are you all right?"

"The baby is coming," Nora said.

It was a second or two before the idea took hold. "Baby? *Your* baby! Ah!" She looked around, lost.

"May we send Gaston for Dr. Grimble?" John asked.

"I'll see he sets off at once," Sarah said.

Moments later the Corneilles passed on their way to their room.

"She's nothing but his mistress," Madame Corneille was saying in a hoarse, compelling whisper. "I don't trust that one at all."

*   *   *

"A proper piece of custom-house goods!" John said.

"What's that mean?"

"I mean Madame Corneille—fairly entered and paid for! Many times, I'd say."

"Of course!" The truth of it struck Nora suddenly. "That's what it is. I thought there was something about her. A harlot—well, well!"

"And I'd say she flew her flag in London. That's pure Titchbourne Street cockney she speaks. After all, that's how a lot of French girls get their dowries abroad and preserve their reputations at home."

Nora, undressed now to her chemise, let him help her into bed. "She wants to get their hands on this place—and on Tom Cornelius' money, if she can."

The worry, never far away, began to claim him again. "I suppose they *were* married, Tom and Sarah?"

"It's not absolutely certain. In any case—French legal proceedings!" She threw her hands up in theatrical horror. "They might even require the actual money to be produced!"

"We must try to . . ." he began.

"We must spare Sarah that at all costs," she said firmly. "Ask Gaston to come here."

"Gaston?"

"Yes. I have an idea."

When Gaston came she asked him his opinion of Madame Corneille. He gave an evasive answer, so she asked him directly whether he would prefer to work for "that woman" or for herself, Mrs. Stevenson.

The question merely puzzled him.

She explained further: "I think I may buy this place instead of Mrs. Cornelius. I believe she will wish to return to England. If I do buy the place, I will leave you here as my manager."

Gaston smiled. "And how may I be of assistance, Madame la Patronne?"

"You will arrange for Monsieur Colbert to call once again to collect his money. You will arrange that he sees Monsieur and Madame

Corneille—especially her. Do this early tomorrow morning when her
wits are at their slowest—that sort of creature. Does Colbert know of
this so-called wedding?"

" 'E knows it is only fun."

"You will suggest that it was perhaps not fun. You will suggest
that if he wants his money, he must now press very hard for it from the
Corneilles—who will probably inherit."

When Gaston had gone, John, smiling broadly for the first time
since his arrival, said, "Thank God you're on our side!"

"It will drive Madame Custom-house Goods to distraction," Nora
said. "She will not turn to her husband for advice; she clearly considers
him a fool. Perhaps . . . if *you* were nearby?"

*   *   *

"How long a fuze do you usually burn?" the doctor asked Nora.

"Very quick. If it's like the three previous, it'll be before dawn."

They brought in a day bed for the doctor. He took off his shoes,
wrapped his feet in a towel, drank a small glass of brandy, and fell almost at once into a wheezy, bronchitic slumber. Nora, dropped into a
fitful state, neither truly awake nor truly asleep.

A further twinge awoke her just before the midwife came. Honorine, the maid from La Gracieuse, was with her.

Nora sat up, determined not to sleep again until after the birth,
thinking that sleep, or even a succession of fitful dozings, might only
prolong the labour. She reread part of *The Three Musketeers*, paragraph
by paragraph, first in French from Rodie's copy, then in English from
her own. It absorbed but did not tire her mind.

Fun for all, and all for fun! she thought. There would be no more
"fun" for years.

*   *   *

In the small hours John tore up his tenth letter and came back upstairs.
He put his ear to her door and heard only the snores of the doctor and
midwife and the crisp rustle of a turning page. He went on to the door
of the Corneliuses' room.

"Would I intrude?" he asked.

Sarah smiled wanly and pointed to the chair on the opposite side
of the bed, nearest the door. He went to it and sat down.

It was not death but the immobility of death that struck him as so
incongruous in Tom's face and body. He had never seen them still for
above a quarter of a second in life.

Sarah cleared her throat. The noise prompted him to speak. "There was many a delightful hour he brought me. Aye. And to how many hundred others? Aye, a rare man. You'll be proud to carry his name."

She nodded.

Some minutes later he asked. "Will you stay? Or sell up and go back to England?"

She frowned.

"I'm sorry," he said. "Perhaps you'd not want to talk of it yet a while."

"No." She sighed. "It must be faced. The inn, this inn, is not in fact paid for. So there'll be no selling up. Yes, I think I will go back to England. Start again somehow."

"You will forfeit the deposit you paid."

There was another long silence before he spoke again. "I have a large sum of money from Mr. Cornelius." And he explained how Tom had brought the money to Stevenson's London office. He did not say how much it was, though.

"It's so like him," she said. "He leaves everything—*left* everything of that sort for another day. If it was for the comfort of a guest or for the smooth running of the Tabard, nothing could be done too speedily. But if it was accounts, or lawyers' work, or—"

"Or getting wed," John fished.

She smiled, not taking the bait. "He'd put it off, and put it off."

"I hope there is a will."

"I doubt it," she said.

He was silent again, but not restful this time. If there was no will, all the rules would change. The church courts would handle the estate, and the Stevensons would be obliged to explain their involvement in what must seem very strange business.

"Why?" she asked, sensing the tension in him.

"If he *is* intestate, you have no power—" He stopped. "Let's talk about it later."

"No. There has already been too much putting off."

"Very well. If he's intestate, the ecclesiastical courts will decide what to do with the estate. Not you."

She sat up at once, white and rigid. "I'd sooner burn every banknote with my own hands than let them touch one pound of it."

"Ah," he said, astonished at her anger. He gave an embarrassed laugh and shrugged, not knowing what to say.

"I'm sorry," she said, looking not the least apologetic. "Tell me. I want to know now. You are sure you're .right?"

"Very sure." He was fascinated at the sudden intensity of her interest. "Well, the church courts appoint an administrator, usually the intestate's closest friend. He takes all reasonable steps to alert creditors, who are allowed a year to press any claim. At the end of the year, he divides the remaining estate according to a formula. Real estate goes to an heir, or, failing an heir, is forfeited to the crown. Possessions and money go half to the widow, the remainder among the children or other kinsmen. If there be none, half goes to the widow, the rest to the crown."

"But he has died in France," she said. "His home is here."

"French law cannot extend to property in England."

"The ecclesiastical courts!" she said bitterly. "There is no other—way?"

"None. I will do anything lawful or that can be made to appear lawful. Anything you wish," he said. "But only because I conceive the money to be morally yours in any case."

She sat like a carving, smiling, her eyes on Tom's face once more.

"And," John went on, "because if, when he handed over the money, your Tom had said 'Should anything befall me until all our business is legally settled . . .' I feel no doubt as to how he would have ended that sentence." There was more passion in his voice than he intended—not than he *felt*, but than he intended. He went on: "And if you had thrown it all away, you'd have done his life, his work, his memory, the biggest insult you could."

It was her turn to stare at him in silence and astonishment.

"I may say it now, I suppose. Now that you've come to sense." His smile brought back the warmth between them. She smiled too, as he had not seen her smile since that evening in Boulogne. A secret smile.

There was a noise from Nora's room. He strained his ears for more. They heard the midwife's voice, then Dr. Grimble's. "I think it's starting," John said.

"Is it worse for you or for her?"

"Oh, it's not bad for her. She usually has an easy time. She rides to hounds so much. It gives her the muscle to stay in control."

"Ah!" Sarah said, embarrassed. "How—how—" She could not think of a suitable adjective.

But he did not even notice. Every fibre of him waited on each sound from across the corridor. She watched him withdraw in all but body from her room. Suddenly she wanted to help, to do anything to reduce or shorten his anxiety. She could not share it—not as *he* felt it; and she could not bear to see him shoulder it alone.

"Shall I go and see?" she asked. "I'll come back and tell you." The intensity of her need to help him astounded her. It was more than a need, it was a compulsion. She stood up.

The move brought him back to his surroundings. He looked at her, dazed, as he collected himself. "No, no," he said. "It's early yet." With a great act of will he cut himself off from all preoccupation with Nora's room. "So you will go back to England," he said affably, picking up the first bit of their conversation he could remember. "You know you are welcome to stay with us in Yorkshire for as long as you wish. Mrs. Stevenson would be delighted, I'm certain. We both would, but she especially."

To his—and her—utter dismay she began to cry. He stood up, bewildered. "Come!" he said, trying to be jocular. "Would it be as bad as that!" He moved toward her.

She laughed through her tears but did not stop crying. "You are so good," she stammered. "Both of you."

Tentatively he put a hand on her bowed shoulder and squeezed. "You wouldn't be alone," he said.

Still hiding her face she stood and leaned into him. "There," he said. "If it's grief, don't stint it. Let it go. It will pass." He put an arm around her, hating himself for the erotic urges the move awakened.

She cried a long time while he stroked her back and spoke trivial comfort. Then, when she had almost wound down, he said, "What do the ecclesiastical courts mean to you?"

*   *   *

The predawn birds had sung to silence and a band of dark green was eating up into the black of the eastern skyline when the baby gave its first cry. It was neither loud nor startled and it soon ceased.

John, now standing at the window, grasped the curtain in his fist and held it to his mouth. His lips moved in prayer. There was only silence.

Sarah stood, shakily, and went across the corridor. In moments she was back, smiling hugely. "All's well," she said. He did not turn until the words were out. "A boy," she added. "All present and correct."

He took her hands in his and shook them, and shook them again, unable to speak his joy and relief. "A boy!" he said. "That's three in a row."

Sarah giggled. "He has a little crease in the palm of his hand, in the shape of an anchor. The midwife says you must call him Clément."

"Clement," John said experimentally, giving it the English pronunciation. "Clement Stevenson. It will do."

Ten minutes later he was allowed in to see Nora and the boy.

"You've done it again, love!" he said, his joy once more at a peak.

She was exhausted but happy; very close to sleep. "I always feel so sorry for you," she told him, barely above a whisper. "Nothing to do but wait. You've done a lot of waiting lately."

He grinned and patted her hand. "I've done aught more this while," he said. "I had a long jaw with Mrs. Cornelius, who I fancy now sees sense—your way. I fancy, too, she'll be stopping with us at Thorpe while she finds her feet."

Nora, too tired to speak her pleasure at this news, gripped his hand, closed her eyes, and smiled. "Do you remember," she asked, "how I joked about 'a birth at a death'? How grim!"

"He's a grand little fellow," John said, looking at the baby for the first time—a damp, shrivelled, unprepossessing bundle of self-will, he thought. Only his conscious mind, saying *yours—your flesh*, enabled him to handle the boy with the outward demeanour of a proud parent; but all his love was for Nora.

"Was it bad?" he asked.

"Never easier," she said. "He's littler than the other three were."

"About three weeks early, I'd say," the doctor added. "But he's breathing all right. Bit of glue in his nose but that'll come away."

A harder, more everyday glint came into her eyes. "Well?" she said, her tone suggesting that he might have raised the subject without her prompting. "How's the old firm of Nature, Fate, and Company?"

"I've spent the night with Mrs. Cornelius."

She raised her eyebrows, accepting it as a joke.

"Yes, I think she'll be coming to stop with us—'indefinitely,' as someone once said."

"It would solve many problems," she said delicately. "And how is the 'indefinitely' respectable lady?" She did not want to use the name in front of Honorine.

"As I came in here a very worried gentleman was being shown into their room." He smiled and leaned forward to kiss her. "I had better go and finish that business."

Angry but muted voices were coming from the Corneilles' room as he passed the door; they interrupted one another in a way that reminded him of an opera. The vehemence seemed too charged to be real.

Out in the courtyard his professional eye estimated the number of cobbles at around forty-five thousand. He walked the length and breadth of the yard slowly, heel and toe, idly checking the guess, biding his time.

Before he had finished, a choleric little man, wrapped tightly in a cloak, came stalking out of the kitchen. He almost bowled John over, muttered a perfunctory "Pardon, M'sieu," and vanished through the archway to the street.

Less than a minute passed before Madame Corneille, in obvious agitation, walked out into the courtyard. She did not see him, standing in the far corner by the coachhouse door.

"Congratulate me, Madame!" he called. "I am the father of a fine new son!"

She came toward him at once, as he had intended. Her congratulations were brisk, but warm. "And Mrs. Stevenson, the deary?" she asked.

"She, too, is well. In fact, I think it is time for me to return to her." He took one step before she sailed in front of him. When he stopped and looked puzzled, he saw the relief on her face.

"Did you see that man?" he asked.

"He came here. He says he is the owner of the inn and he has not been paid."

John looked calmly at her, saying nothing, waiting for her to reveal more of her state of mind.

"When I told him I was Thomas' aunt, he wanted *me* to pay. Me and Corneille!"

John sighed, hinting at reluctant knowledge.

"What do we make of it? Please, Monsieur Stevenson, if you have any notion of these affairs, I implore you to help me."

Her imploring was most professional.

"Madame," he said, even more reluctant, "I barely know or knew Thomas or Sarah Cornelius. I barely know you." She nodded, losing hope. "But," he added quickly, "I am a man of business. I see certain signs."

"What? What signs?" She was so avid he could feel her tremble.

He took her arm and lowered his voice. "If I tell you," he said, "you will please to take credit for the discovery yourself. Mrs. Stevenson, you see, although she does not really know Sarah either, has naturally formed a great sympathy . . ."

"Naturally. Naturally. I understand, m'sieu. Please. Be quick."

Still reluctant but now grimly committed, he began. "In April when I last stayed at the Tabard in London, I find that Thomas Cornelius has suddenly sold out and vanished. No one knows where he is. Some say they *think* he is in the west of England. I think that is odd. Some weeks later, Mrs. Stevenson and I, stopping the night in Boulogne, happen by the merest chance to meet Thomas Cornelius and a former maidservant from the Tabard, whom he introduces as his wife Sarah. That, too, is odd—or unexpected. He is very happy and he tells us that he has bought this inn at Coutances, and it becomes clear that he himself has deliberately spread this false tale of going to the west of England. Later that same evening, he asked me for some help over money. It was little enough he wanted and I was happy to oblige. And now it turns out that even the inn is not paid for." Madame Corneille hung on every word. "Put these facts together, madame, and I ask you—does it not explain, or I should say, does it not *perhaps* explain Mrs. Cornelius' eagerness to be free of the inheritance?" A flinty, cunning smile parted Madame Corneille's lips. John rammed home the keystone. "Remember that she has made her way in the world entirely by her own . . ." He waved his fingers, unwilling to supply the word. "She is no fool."

"Ha!" Madame Corneille sneered. "And nor am I! I said it was a trap. Did I not say so! I was sure of it. A thousand thanks, m'sieu. It was only an instinct with me but I was right. My instinct, and your reason. They make the case certain. Ha!"

"Of course," John added, now beginning to withdraw, "I may be wrong. I may be doing her a great injustice."

"No!" Madame Corneille was scornful, as if she were the clever one and John the simpleton. "Not her. Not that one! Believe me, m'sieu, I know them. Oh, yes! Well, we shall stop that little game. Just you see!"

*   *   *

After breakfast Sarah came downstairs, tired and pale, bearing a note opened in her hand.

"It's very strange," she said to John. "It's almost a legal document. From the Corneilles."

"They have left," he told her. "I saw them go, quite early."

"Yes. They say goodbye here. And they renounce entirely and unconditionally any claim they may have as heirs to Thomas. Why? Don't you find that odd? They didn't even wait for the funeral."

"Not in the least. There was once a man who stood all morning in Lincoln's Inn Fields offering to sell a five-pound banknote for a single golden sovereign—a four hundred per centum profit to the buyer."

"I don't follow you."

"No one bought. People mistrust altruism and generosity. You frightened those Corneilles."

She was shocked. "I hope you are wrong."

"I could *wish* I were. But you remember that. If ever you want to make it easy for someone to accept your help, always stress the benefits the arrangement will bring to yourself."

They went upstairs to Nora, who was suckling baby Clement. "Three weeks early *and* greedy," she said. "He's a Stevenson."

Sarah sat beside her and admired the baby. "You must be very happy," she said.

"I would be happier, Mrs. Cornelius, if you would come back to England and stay with us," Nora began. Then, seeing hesitation in Sarah's face, asked her what was wrong.

Sarah looked shyly from one to the other. "There is no one in the world now to whom I am 'Sarah.' Do you think—would it be too—"

"Of course, my dear!" Nora said. *"Sarah!"*

Sarah beamed at them.

"It would be such a help to us," Nora said, "to have a friend around on whom we may rely. And the children need—oh, you would be so *right*. And you could help me improve my French. What do you say now?"

Sarah, remembering what John had just told her downstairs, smiled complicitly at him; he returned a what-did-I-say smile. Nora almost said "What are you both grinning at?" but, for some reason, thought better of it. And then Sarah happily repeated her acceptance, and the moment for such a question had passed.

Chapter 17

The Protestant burial ground at Coutances was a windswept plot of sand above the town. The afternoon was oppressive. Cloud had steadily thickened all morning as the wind got up off the sea. By midafternoon, when John and Gaston trundled the coffin on its sandcart out to that barren plot, the sky was one grey from east to west. Occasionally a large drop of warm rain fell through the half-gale. The two men and Sarah were the only mourners, the pastor and sexton the only other witnesses.

When they arrived at the graveside, John was shocked to find it barely four feet deep—no deeper than the sand.

"I'm not having that," he said and told the sexton to dig deeper.

The sexton refused; all the graves in the place were like that. The pastor made placatory gestures, more afraid of losing his gravedigger than eager to get a proper job done.

John grabbed a shovel from the sandpile, a long-handled one like the ones in Cornwall and Ireland, and, throwing off his coat and rolling up his sleeves, jumped down into the shallow pit, which came no higher than his waist. Within ten minutes he was in deeper than his own six feet two inches, levelling the floor and trimming the sides to geometrical perfection. It took Gaston on the other end of a rope to get him out.

"Thank you, John," Sarah said.

Later, as they walked slowly back to the inn, he said: "It was hard enough to see Tom go so thinly attended; him who was always the heart and soul of any company. But to see such an excuse of a grave!"

She began to weep then, for the first time in the whole proceedings. He knew he had made her cry, yet he could honestly feel no remorse. "Take my arm if it will help," he told her and was glad when she did so. The wind and the slight rain, too, made her huddle to him.

"I'm glad you are coming to us," he said.

She hugged his arm but did not speak.

"It will be so good for Nora. You will see why. She is—a rare woman. She has rare gifts. They set her apart and make it hard for her to cultivate female society at large."

"I did not like her," Sarah said. "Until we met in Boulogne, I never liked her."

John stopped abruptly. "You astound me. I had no idea."

"Oh, it's all right now," Sarah told him. "I was wrong—very wrong. She is, as you say, rare."

They began to walk again.

"But why your dislike?" he asked.

"I'm not sure I should tell you. Though it was a long time ago. The first time you came to stay at the Tabard."

"Oh! I think I can guess. She borrowed your room to open up some letters she'd intercepted. Or stolen, really. They were stolen, did you know?"

"I guessed it, from her behaviour. I hated her for making me a partner to it."

"Hate?" John said. "That's very strong."

"But true." She laughed grimly. "I was a prig then. And a prude. Hate came easily."

"That was natural."

"You understand," she said, as if it relieved a fear. Her grip tightened on his arm. "There's so much I would permit now that I would have frowned on then."

"It was obvious you had not always been a maidservant. And—or so I guess—you had recently suffered a great drop in fortune. Temptations to—easy money—must have been all around you. I would not call it priggishness nor prudery that armed you to resist."

"Yet it made me think Nora was hard and shameless. I never had the charity to ask what forced her to it. And that made me misjudge her, very badly."

"She has no notion of this, you know."

"To be sure," Sarah said grimly. "Who notes the moods of a servant —until the soup is cold or the mud left on the boots!"

"There's something in that," he said, disagreeing. "But Nora wouldn't notice anyway. She's not sensitive like that. Also, she owes you a big debt."

Now it was Sarah's turn for surprise. "I can't believe that."

"We slept in the Pilgrims' Room, remember? And you told her all about *The Canterbury Tales*. She'd had little acquaintance with books until then. Also she saw all the books in your room. I fancy she envied you. All that summer her nose was never out of a book. You started that. It changed her life."

"I had no idea." She slowed down; they were almost at the gate of the inn. "It's frightening, if you really think of it—the unknown influences we may have on others."

"Aye." He looked up at the inn. "What'll you do about this place?"

*   *   *

That was a question Nora had gone some way toward answering while they had been at the burial.

"Isn't he lovely!" Sarah whispered, admiring the sleeping Clement. "Such tiny, perfect hands they have."

"Don't whisper," Nora said. "The world's not got to put itself out for him. Come and sit here, Sarah dear." She patted the bed at her side. "I have a suggestion to make."

Sarah sat on the bed and John turned a chair around, straddling it and leaning on its back.

"Monsieur Colbert called while you were out," Nora said.

Sarah groaned and buried her face in a hand; Colbert was the vendor of the inn, so impatient for his money.

"Don't fret," Nora told her. "I have made him an offer, which he is now thinking over. And I want you think it over, too. I will buy this inn from him and I will also pay you back your deposit. Count up to one and a half and say yes."

Sarah was delighted. "Oh Nora—you are so *good!* I'll say yes now, with no regret. But *you* must not lose by it."

Nora said nothing. Sarah almost ran to look for the contract, as if she were afraid Nora might change her mind.

"It's done, then," John said when they were alone. "We are over the first hurdle."

"I got it for a good deal less than Tom Cornelius was willing to pay. Mr. Colbert's in a fix and would be glad to settle at any price. We'll rename it: l'Auberge Clément. I like the name Clement."

He watched her come alive as she described how she had done it: "Colbert came in here like Chanticleer on a—"

"You saw him in here?"

"I put *screens* around the bed," she said, as if that had been too obvious to state. "We talked through the screens. He never saw me."

John, picturing the scene, burst into laughter. "Poor devil!"

"I saw *him*, though. In that mirror. I had a gap in the screens there and could see him. But it was too dark behind the screens for him to do the same. You never saw a man less comfortable!"

His laughter brimmed his eyes with tears. "Oh, Nora, Nora! I'm *that* fond o' thee!"

"Shush!" she said, grinning herself. "It's still a house of mourning."

Baby Clement stirred, almost cried, and settled down again. And Nora went on to describe how she had used the certain knowledge she had gained from Gaston to bring Colbert down in price.

"We'll shut the place this winter," she went on, "and Gaston can come over and take a position at the Adelaide. You can order that with the manager, whatsizname, Hurst. He can show Gaston how a proper hotel is managed. And better his English."

John laughed but she pressed on. "When we get the Great Hall contract, you see, I imagine you'll take a suite there. So you can keep an eye on him, too." She settled happily and smoothed her hands over the sheets. "How well it all works out!"

*   *   *

What with visits from Sarah and Sam, and Nora's need for rest, it was evening before he could speak alone with her again.

She wanted to talk of the suggestion she had made to Rodet in the rose garden that morning. She was uncertain now how it might fit into their future. But at least she no longer feared John's anger; it would be a long time before John had the temerity to be angry with her again over any business matter.

"John," she said, "could Rodet become an important supplier to us?"

"It's possible."

"What if we could find out his manufacturing costs?"

John froze. "If it came about through ordinary commerce."

"Yes."

"Not through being a guest of his? Not by underhand means?"

"Through ordinary business."

"Then I wouldn't walk away from the idea."

So she told him of Rodet's proposal to make "Stevenson" rails in France for them to sell out of Southampton. John was not very taken with the notion. "At the very most our profit will be in the low hundreds," he said. "Not very interesting. What did you reply?"

She drew a deep breath. "I said you'd probably go for a fixed-price contract."

"Good God! I would say that's the very last—"

"John. I'm not remotely interested in *his* proposal. As long as we don't make an actual loss. But if we start with a fixed price, and then if we introduce some variations, I will be able to work out very quickly what his real manufacturing costs are."

"What variations?"

"For instance, we'll say we have a glut of pig iron at Stockton and we'll transfer it to him at a nominal cost—since we're going to buy the product back anyway. That and a few other changes—it doesn't matter. They're all legal. The point is, we could soon know his costs. So that when you sit down with him, next year say, to negotiate a really important contract . . ."

"Yes, I see." His eyes held hers in an unblinking gaze. "How many days went by between his proposal and your telling him I'd prefer a fixed price?"

"Oh, I told him that at once."

His look was sheer disbelief.

"I mean within a minute or so. Of course I needed that much time to think it out."

"A *minute* or so!" He laughed flatly. "I'll say it again: Thank God you're on my side."

"Of course," she said, "we must use the knowledge very carefully.

Our 'little frog' must always believe the Stevenson kiss has turned him into a prince, not just a little golden goose."

He gripped her arm, unable to find words to express his relief.

She realized then that a euphoric John was as dangerous to their present state as a John sunk in self-blaming despair. "We must go on absolutely as normal, love," she warned. "No one, not Rodet, not our own people—and certainly not Chambers—must suspect that we are anywhere near insolvent. We may have until November before the bubble bursts. Until then we're well in funds. We must use those funds to go on absolutely as normal. We must even stay on warm terms with Beador! Can you do that?"

"I can!" He grinned.

"I'm not so sure. There's a nasty streak of honesty in you at times."

Chapter 18

Ten days later Nora, Sarah, and the baby were in the Rodets' coach on its delayed return to La Gracieuse; Sam had gone back to the Nelsons a week earlier; John left with him, stopping in Rouen to negotiate a fixed-price contract with Rodet, Maître de Forges. L'Auberge Clément was Nora's, and she left a delighted Gaston in charge. A dignified headstone had been ordered for Cornelius, and it was to be Gaston's most important duty to tend the grave each week.

Now that the bustle incidental to Tom's death had abated, Sarah was beginning to plumb the depth of her bereavement. She did not sigh nor wring her hands, much less weep; but Nora noticed that she would stand for long minutes looking at a view, or a picture, or a stone wall, seeing nothing. And the pages of any book she settled to read would lie long unturned. Lacking John's courage, Nora kept her silence, feeling helpless.

When they arrived at La Gracieuse, Rodie showed, yet again, her extraordinary emotional range, combining intense and sincere compassion with a tactless egotism that left Nora breathless and Sarah bemused. They were hardly through the ill-matched gates when her voice filled the courtyard with *oohoo, ohoo*! and *allo, allo*! And then in one sustained, nonverbal sentence of cries and ohs and tongue clickings and sighs she conveyed her sorrow for Sarah, her muted pleasure at their meeting, her delight at Clement, and her ecstasy at seeing her beloved Stevie once again. Throughout she held in her gloved left hand—totally unaware of the fact—an apple bitten down to its core.

She swept Sarah indoors and up the stairs, talking volubly and much too fast for Nora to make out. But it was clearly no conducted tour of the pictures and ornaments. Nora took Clement from Honorine and followed them more slowly.

Rodet inclined his head toward her and smiled conspiratorially.

"*Ça va bien, m'sieu?*" she asked.

"*Merci, madame. Ça va* très *bien!*"

Sarah was in what had been John's dressing room, next to Nora's room. As Nora passed by the door, Rodie came petulantly out seeking somewhere to put the apple core, which she had at last discovered. When she saw Clement she forgot the core once again. "Oh, but the *bébé* can go with Honorine to the night nursery. *Honorine!*"

Nora looked doubtful. "I must not dry up," she said. "Not until we get to Yorkshire."

"Oh!" The apple core waved inches from her face. "You can feed him at the day. You must sleep undistraught. I have a nourish. You will see."

"Nourish?"

"Wet nurse," Sarah intervened, coming to the door. "*Nourrice, oui?*"

"*Oui,*" Rodie said. "Wet nurse? Oh, it's good." Like a choral conductor, she willed the baby into Honorine's arms. "So, so, oh, the angel! [kiss kiss kiss] Now a little dinner. Just some little crudities. But you will be so fond of them."

Waving the apple core about her like a pennant, she talked them all the way downstairs. Nora felt guilty at abandoning Clement to an unknown night nursery but thought that Rodie might feel slighted if she made an immediate inspection. She went up quickly after dinner and found it, like everything else in the house, elegant, ill thought out, and reassuring. The wet nurse had just finished suckling Clement and was holding him on her shoulder, rocking and singing.

*   *   *

Nora slept "undistraught" that night, but only because she left undisturbed the pile of railway newspapers that had grown during her absence. The following morning, while Rodie took Sarah on the tour of inspection, she went through them, beginning the task with a sinking heart and ending it in the deepest gloom. In the 28 days since she had last checked, 63 new companies had joined the motley, making 377 newly projected lines; and the total capital they now sought was a lunatic £343,010,788. The mad pack was still in full gallop on a drag scent laid by men far less scrupulous even than Hudson. The subscription lists had the names of infants down for thousands, and, beside them, clerks and parsons, servants, sporting men and cooks, dainty ladies and—for all one could tell—their pet dogs. Sir George Beador must indeed be only a small lieutenant in a great legion of numskulls.

Before, she had watched, as it were, from the sidelines, fearing only the backwash when that idiot legion sank below the waters. Now, willy-nilly, she and John were yoked to one of its leaders.

At least she was not now alone in her forebodings. *The Times* was clearing its throat and voicing an ambiguous worry. The railway papers no longer trumpeted the newly announced schemes as if each were the wonder of an age. And even George Hudson was beginning to hint publicly that enough was enough. There was some satisfaction in his belated and cool support for the views she had been laughed at and humoured for expressing; but such comfort in no way matched the deep unease she now felt. If George Hudson, who had once led the pack, was now telling all and sundry that he was winded, things had indeed come to a grim pass.

Perhaps the bubble would now burst within weeks, not months. Certainly she could no longer stay here, so far from the centre of events. She must return at once to London; Sarah could stay or come as she pleased. At least she seemed to have accepted for the moment that John was to be a sort of unofficial trustee of Cornelius' money—*her* money now. As long as that persisted, all they need actually give her was mere pocket money.

Before Nora left, however, there was one more arrangement to make. If she and John ever had to make a run for it, and if they had to start again, they would do it here in Normandy. And they would do it in a line of business she understood—land and property. It would cost them money they could now ill afford, but she would not let that stop her. Never again, she vowed, would she permit John to have an absolute say over their joint affairs.

The land she wanted lay just across the river, westward along the coast from Trouville. The idea of buying it had occurred to her on her very first outing with Rodie, when the britzka had breasted the hill above Trouville and she had seen the great, flat, deserted beach running for more than a mile to the distant headland. Then she had looked at

the fields and coverts that stretched inland along the broad flood-plain
of the river, and she had wondered that it was not already a thriving
resort, a rival to Trouville itself.

And so, in the final week of her visit, she spent the best part of an
afternoon with a man called Pierre Ferrand, a land agent who had
worked for Rodet in the past and who came with Rodie's strong recommendation. Nora already knew, from talking to the farm steward at La
Gracieuse, that good land hereabouts went for about 630 francs per
hectare, or roughly £10 an acre; more marginal land was about half
that. So she was able to come to an arrangement with Ferrand for him
to buy up any land that came on the market within half a mile of the
foreshore and between the river and the headland. But it was not at
all the arrangement she had expected to make.

She had decided to be quite frank with Ferrand and to offer him
some extra percentage on cheap deals to encourage a matching honesty
on his part. But she was hardly through her preamble—painting a rose-
ate view of the future of Deauville, as this undeveloped stretch was
called—when she saw his face fall.

"Is something wrong, m'sieu?" she asked.

He shrugged, eloquently.

"Am I perhaps too late?"

He laughed. "Too early, madame! Five years, ten years too early!"
And he went on to describe how for more than a year now his one silent
obsession had been the potential of this very same stretch of the coast.
Slowly he had assembled thirty hectares—a field here, a paddock there
—but it was too slow. His capital was exhausted. And soon the outsiders
would come. Here, indeed, was the wife of the great John Stevenson.
Soon there must be others.

"Tell me of the Deauville you see, m'sieu," she said, cutting short
his threnody.

And he described the hotels, the spa with its salt-water cures for
everything from extended liver to scrofula, the race course, the casino,
the winter garden, the ballrooms, the theatre, and . . . certain houses
without which no English gentlemen of quality would come—but very
select. He hoped she understood. And there would also be—

"You are talking about a great deal of capital, m'sieu, far more
than I—"

"Yes, yes," he said, still fervent with his dream of Deauville. "It is
important only to own the land. To lease the land. The owner of the
land dictates the lease and so dictates the character of the—of everything. The leases can get taken up by syndicates of initiative—"

"Companies."

"Yes. Also companies. It is not necessary, you see, to gain capital for all buildings. Only for land. It is from more to more important to possess the land."

He needed to say no more; she knew she was face to face with a kindred spirit. "I think, Monsieur Ferrand," she said, "we may join forces. I came here intending to ask you to buy land for me. And my main concern, I'll be blunt, was how to stop you from becoming Deauville's most popular patron at my expense."

He contrived to look shocked and, at the same time, to grin.

"But if we become partners," she went on, "and you are buying for *us*, you have every incentive to get the land as cheap as may be." He nodded but said nothing. "What are we talking about—a hundred and forty, a hundred and fifty hectares?"

"In addition to my thirty. Yes."

"It's my information that seventy to seventy-five thousand francs should secure it?"

"Easily," he said. "I can do it for less."

"Over how long?"

"Three, four years."

It suited her admirably. They talked for a further hour, about the details of the arrangement. No one was to know their purpose; Ferrand would use every trick he knew to disguise the conveyance of so many small parcels of land to one owner. And their bank would be in Caen, beyond the reach of local tongues and conveniently close to Coutances. The money she paid in could be partly concealed as the takings of the Auberge Clément. And he might hint that she had appointed him agent to buy up a small château and some shooting—

"Not shooting," Nora said. "Hunting."

"Oh? You are perhaps fond of hunting, madame?"

She laughed. "Perhaps indeed!"

"Oh, you must come in season. All our French hunts are private, but"—he smirked—"that is no problem. We hunt in the woods. It is very superior to your 'steeplehunting.' "

"Of course!" Nora said, laughing. "Like everything else in France."

Ferrand agreed.

As she drove back over the Touques and then down its right bank to Trouville, she allowed herself a momentary daydream: Deauville! She could already hear the ripe, upper-class voices at work upon that sound: "Goin to Dawvill this summer," "Italy's all vewy well, but a fwightful journey, d'ye know. Thought of twyin' Deoughveel, what!" and "Duv-vle's *the* place nowadays, I heah."

She would finance the dream by selling off some of "her" proper-ties; and she would tell John only when the deed was done.

Chapter 19

Parting with Rodie was, of course, a great wrench—so great, indeed, that having endured the pain of it in the courtyard of La Gracieuse, Rodie decided it was insupportable and, throwing on a cloak and bon-net, jumped into the britzka and came with them to Honfleur. There she played the encore—and came with them to Havre. For one perilous moment it seemed she might even come with them to Southampton, but wisdom triumphed and the tears flowed freely and, this time, in earnest. Even Sarah, who had so short an acquaintance with her, was affected. They waved until the quay was out of sight.

"Unforgettable woman," Sarah said.

"She's so alive."

"I forgot to tell you. We all had strawberries, two or three days ago —when you went to see your Monsieur Ferrand. And you know how here they push them onto the spoon with biscuits?"

"Yes."

"Well, that young boy of hers, Arsène, was just beginning to pass among us with a bowl of biscuits when Rodie screamed, 'No, no, the wedge foot' and she turned to me and said '*your* wedge foot.'" Sarah grinned at the memory. "Can you guess what it was?"

"She said the very same to me once, the night I came. I have no idea."

"Nor had anyone. But Rodie snatched away the biscuits and van-ished into the passage. And then for ages we could hear her opening cupboards, stumping along corridors, clattering up and down stairs. And every so often she'd poke her head in and say 'You will see. Ah, it's so beautiful and so charming,' and vanish again. Meanwhile, of course, everyone was going on with their strawberries—using their little fingers and tilting the plate. Second and third helpings, too. And then finally, when there were about three strawberries left, she came back with— you'll never guess."

Smiling, Nora waited.

"She had all the biscuits in a green Wedgwood bowl. Wedgwood, you see? Wedge foot!"

Nora began to laugh.

"But the cream of it was," Sarah went on, "that the identical bowl, the very identical twin, had been put on the table every day, holding the sugar. You remember it? So, having finished our strawberries, we then ate our mouths dry on biscuits." And when their laughter died, she added: "Still, wasn't it pleasant for her to take all that trouble for me to see the bowl. Because it was English and I was English."

And Nora thought how (quite apart from any other consideration) —how pleasant it would be to have Sarah share their house. Sarah, she was sure, would be a real confidante and friend. Not since Arabella Thornton, Walter's wife, had moved away from the north and gone to settle in Bristol had Nora known the close company of another woman her own age. And Sarah, like herself, had come up through hardship and challenge; she was no goose, as—one had to admit it— Arabella often was.

Sarah had gone over to the port side, from where she could watch the coast of lower Normandy vanish in the evening mists. There was barely a swell on the water, just a lazy network of ripples. Toward the setting sun their bow wave stretched a shimmering line of gold and black as far as the horizon, or so it seemed. To starboard, where night was reaching up into the sky, the wave was a muted green band on the darkling water. The writhing effervescence of their wake turned the ocean as black as stout. But it soon calmed, and only a chain's length behind them the sea was a smooth trough of quicksilver. Their little paddle steamer was the only feature in that vast and silent emptiness. Nora, who had glimpsed some of the perils of a seaman's life on her first sea voyage, now, on her second, felt something of its ineffable magic, too.

She, and everyone else on board, experienced some of its frustrations the following morning when, having steamed past Spithead and through the Solent into Southampton water, they came to dock. Their space at the quayside was taken by a three-masted schooner unable to sail. Half her crew was sick from having taken soured pork, and the other half was in dispute with the master for wishing to sail short-handed. The ferry had to moor alongside her; but the paddlewheel was in the way, so that although the decks of the two ships were level, they were still several yards apart. And across this large gulf, with deep water beneath, the company could find no better bridge than a narrow ladder.

The first man across was a seaman, who, either out of bravado or because he was under orders to make it seem easy, strolled across like a soldier on Sunday. He almost came to grief halfway and finished the journey, slowly and prudently, on all fours. It was in fact the only safe way to cross, especially for the ladies, hampered by their great skirts and shawls. Baby Clement and several young children were swung ashore, like cargo, in a net. It took over an hour for everyone to disembark.

"For the life of me," Nora said when they were all together again, "I can't understand why the sailors didn't at least put their ship out on an anchorage before they began their dispute."

The porter, collecting their trunks, smiled to himself.

"Do you know?" she asked him.

"Ah," he said. "They *say* it's because if they slips moorings, a dispute could be called mutiny. But I says, if you asks me, it's because a master must pay more demurrage fast to a wharf nor fast to an anchorage."

As a particularly English combination of bloody-mindedness, of pig cunning, of official indifference and ill-preparedness, of risk to the innocent public, and of muddling through, it was a fitting welcome to the old country and, though even Nora did not know it, a neat augury of the times that lay ahead.

PART THREE

30° November 1845

Chapter 20

Ruin was inevitable. One of the penalties of keeping immaculate accounts is that they leave no room for hope—there were no errors in Nora's books to offer the firm a surprise salvation.

Only John and Nora could see it, for only they knew of the terrible demand that would sooner or later be made on their resources—and it was going to be well over the hundred thousand that John had estimated. His hope of getting rid of at least half of Beador's worthless debt proved far too sanguine; if they unloaded a quarter, they would count themselves fortunate.

Yet in one way they *were* fortunate. Everyone could feel the abnormal strains that were now racking the monied world. Everyone knew that a breaking point had to come; and everyone who could took extraordinary measures to protect himself. So the measures that John and Nora now took—to disguise their ruin for as long as possible—could be passed off as acts, not of desperation, but of shrewdness.

John's role was to get together as much hard cash as possible. Nora's was to start moving that cash around from bank to bank—and even from country to country—in quite novel and unconventional ways, so that when the time came, and there was no cash left to move around, the fact might go unnoticed for . . . how long? She had no idea. Last year an East India company in the tea trade had gone bankrupt, and the court found it had actually been insolvent for a quarter of a century—which had come as a great surprise even to the directors. Yet in each of those insolvent years they had turned over a good half million.

On such frail straws they floated their hope for their own survival.

All that summer and autumn, John harvested for cash. If there was a contract that might be finished, or brought to a stage payment, by mid-September, he bent heaven and hell to achieve it, even to the extent of moving men from longer-term contracts. For the first time in his career, John deliberately allowed some contracts to drag behind their timetable. The supervising engineers were naturally unhappy and only his promise to catch up—and his reputation to back such a promise—prevented the companies from operating the clauses that allowed them to take over the work and reassign it.

He also tendered low for a host of tiny contracts—sidings, drains, realignments, even routine maintenance—things he would not normally bother with. And these, too, he hastened to finish before Steptember. And every bill dated November or later he got discounted at once and turned into cash. He liquidated all his material stocks and bought everything spot, paying in ninety-day bills, if possible.

As the money flowed in, first in a dribble, then in a torrent, Nora began to move it around according to the strategy they had devised. At first she managed from their home up in Yorkshire; later, as the pace grew more hectic, she moved down to a suite at the Adelaide in London.

There was no word to describe what she was doing. *Swindle* was too crude, for if the plan worked, no one would lose a penny; all that would have happened was that a few banks would inadvertently have lent them money for an undefined period. Most of the other words— *cheat, defraud, shave, pluck, mulct,* and so forth—suggested something too irreversible; in any case, they were too strongly associated with criminal and aristocratic behaviour. Nora's own word for her strategy was "hudsoning," a word fitted in every way to the matter, the manner, and the age. And if she ever used it where it was overheard, the eavesdropper would consider the activity admirable; for George Hudson was still the Railway King.

The first bank she "hudsoned" was right on her (and Hudson's) doorstep: the York City and County. She let a draft go through for wages when Stevenson's had no funds in that particular bank to cover it. The manager, knowing what a big and steady account he had in Stevenson's, wrote a polite, almost obsequious letter, drawing their attention to the deficiency; but he allowed the payment. Nora composed a tart reply for John to sign, pointing out that these were difficult times for everyone and that sound firms and sound bankers would survive them best by staying calm. To underline the point, she kept that bank well in surplus for a good long time after.

"Sound" and "staying calm" were the constant themes of the whole "hudson" campaign. Bank after bank bleated to John about a sudden dearth of cash in the Stevenson account. Each received a variant of Nora's lofty homily on the virtues of *staying calm* and of reposing confidence in firms whose *soundness* was beyond question—plus, to be sure, the gold to back the words and to sugar the message.

Surreptitiously she sold her properties; from her lucrative firstborn at Alderley Edge to her failures at Pendle and Ayr—all went under the hammer. Money was tight that summer and they fetched only two-thirds of what she considered their true value; hoping for sixty thousand, she got a mere forty. But she was too busy then to grieve overmuch; the bitterness was to come later. In return for all this, Sir George handed them the deeds to Maran Hill, still unmortgaged; and he assigned his heavily mortgaged lands around Stockton. None of it was of any immediate benefit, for they could not turn him out. Everything had to go on as normal.

The hudson strategy was not without its problems. The one account she did not meddle with was their permanent one with Chambers. Sooner or later every Stevenson bill came to him for discount; and every foreign transaction went via him. In addition, most of the banks they hudsoned would write to Chambers for reference. Stevenson's had to be able to rely on a good word from him. Even so, the abnormal number of requests for references that poured in from provincial and oversea banks was bound to set him wondering. At last he was driven to ask John whether Mrs. Stevenson was quite well.

"I left him feeling uneasy," John reported back to Nora, "as you asked me to. But I hope he doesn't begin to panic."

"On the contrary," Nora replied. "I hope he does. Begin, I mean. The whole essence of this thing is in the timing. And Chambers is the key to it. He's no little provincial banker—yes sir, no sir, here's three bags full sir. The problem of Chambers demands very particular attention. We want him to *begin* to panic and then, just at the right moment, *we* must appear as the one rock in his own private storm."

From that day, early in the October of 1845, she began drawing on all their outlying accounts and amassing the money with Chambers. But from that day, too, events began to pass out of their hands. Now they had to watch every move in the City, snap up every bit of stray gossip and try to assess its true worth, take daily, even hourly, soundings of the railway intelligence. From that day there was no appeal from the consequences of even one false move.

For John, on his endless round of visits to cuttings and embankments, tunnels and bridges, it was sometimes hard to believe that all this buzz of well-organized industry could be brought to a halt by the movement of bits of paper in the far-off City. He stood, hearing the picks ring on the rock and watching the spoil fly from three hundred shovels, and he would realize that perhaps, even at that very moment, a papermaker in some small East End papermill was drying the very sheet on which Chambers or someone would write the final, damning words, "insufficient funds." Then the workings would fall silent. The navvies and the bricklayers, masons and blacksmiths, would troop off to other masters. The bailiffs would seize the wagons, the stores, Thorpe Manor . . . their very furniture. He knew it could happen for he had seen it, too often now for his own comfort, when other contractors had gone under; indeed, his own business had been founded on the bankruptcy of another contractor.

Still, the activity all around him was reassuring, for every yard was another step nearer a payment to him.

For Nora, whose daily landscape *was* that endless to and fro of paper, there could be no such comfort. The office servants were cheerful, knowing they were in a thriving company at a time when others were tottering; she had to run an endless gauntlet of their cheer. She had to endure the congratulations of Jackson on the steady increase in the firm's wealth. And all the time she knew it in no way matched the reckoning, whose day could not much longer be postponed.

In mid-October the Bank of England raised its discount rate—a belated attempt to stem the flood of credit it had itself created. The rise was a mere token, from 2½ to 3 per cent, but people were so nervous they clutched at straws, assuring each other that *now* all would be well. In case Chambers should catch this new form of laughing sickness Nora decided to pay him a visit.

Chambers was a tall, lithe, powerful man. Something about him, and about his movements, reminded Nora of a leopard—not the leopards in zoos, but those on Egyptian papyruses. Semitic leopards. He had the same flat back to his head and angularity of neck, and his walk was tense and silent. At thirty-eight he was certainly a very handsome man, but there was nothing in that to endear him to her. His eyes, dark and set deep beneath a firm, unfurrowed brow, were sleek and watchful; one's first impression that they twinkled with a friendly mirth soon vanished. His lips, too, seemed to smile; but they were so mobile, even when he was silent—*especially* when he was silent—as to cancel out the cheer and leave instead the impression of a man unwilling to reveal how he might appear if he allowed himself to relax.

His office had changed greatly since John and Nora had first seen it. Six years ago, Chambers had been in a very small way of trade, on the outer fringe of the dozens of banks that belonged to the London Clearing House. He had risen, however, with Stevenson's. As a Jew, he would never penetrate the very inner circles of the City; but, also as a Jew, he knew more European bankers and understood their ways better than any other London bank of his size. This and his link with Stevenson's had served him well over the last few years, and he had become something of an expert in railway funding, especially in European railways. Millions in British capital had gone into overseas lines, and Chambers had managed a greatly disproportionate share of it.

So the delicate gilded furniture and the rococo mirrors had gone from his office; and in their place were desks and chairs that renaissance princes might have sat on in perfect safety, even if they had weighed three hundredweight. His inkwell was a silver replica of Kitson's new long-boiler locomotive *Hector*, the gift of George Hudson and the York & North Midland. The quills stood in its funnel and the lid of the "boiler" hinged up to reveal the ink well.

"Isn't that pretty," he said. "I'm so pleased with it. And how kind of Hudson."

"Hudson is a one-man disaster," she said evenly. "It will take a generation for this country's railways to recover from what he has done in this one year."

This opinion was so absolutely contrary to the general view of the man that Chambers merely laughed, as anyone might laugh at eccentricity.

"You've done well enough," he said. "Stevenson's, I mean."

She looked puzzled. "*What* d'you mean?"

Her sharp tone startled him. "Your account, Mrs. Stevenson. That's what I mean. Your funds. Never better." He spoke as if to placate her.

Now it was she who looked astonished. "You have no idea what it is all about?" she asked.

He shook his head.

"You really don't know why we've done it?"

"I assumed . . ." he faltered.

"That it was an attack of prosperity, plain and simple?"

He laughed. "Nothing to do with you is 'plain and simple,' ma'am."

She did not laugh. "Then I must tell you, Mr. Chambers. In 1836 Sir Charles Knightley, one of the richest men in England, had to ride twenty miles to break open his daughter's money box and borrow a few sovereigns before he could . . ."

"Yes, yes!" Chambers was impatient. It was a well-known story among City men and was often told as an example of what used to happen in the bad old days of ten years ago—and what, by implication, could never happen now.

"Then I tell you, Mr. Chambers, I tell *you* most particularly, the money crisis of 1836 is going to seem like a high feast when people look back on 1845—and '46, *and* '47 . . . and more for aught I know."

He pretended to believe her. He pretended to take her analysis seriously. But he turned the conversation to the actual sum they had amassed. It was far too much for their daily operations, he thought. Why didn't they put it into something solid and endurable? Property, for instance? No doubt he thought the suggestion would please her.

She persisted in saying that the wondrous new banking system was about to collapse and that only those with gold in the hand were going to survive. She could see him growing quite testy beneath that polished urbanity of his. But she kept her best argument to last—until he was driven to assure her that "we people in the City have all these matters perfectly under control now, you know."

"Then consider these facts, Mr. Chambers," she warned. "There are now over twelve hundred would-be companies looking for capital. And the total they seek is now around five hundred and sixty million pounds —of which they must deposit ten per cent by the thirtieth of this month. Fifty-nine million pounds!" she stressed. "Where on earth will they find it?" Even to name the sum brought a sinking feeling to her stomach. She knew only too well where they'd find some of it.

"How can you be certain of these figures?" Chambers asked. "You'd have to comb through a year's issues of about thirty different railway magazines to be—"

"Or keep a running total in your mind," she said. "All year."

He laughed in agreement, thinking she was speaking in irony; then he realized she was not. "You have done that?" he asked.

She stood up, smiling acidly, and bade him good day.

*   *   *

Early in November the Bank of England moved again, another half per cent. But confidence had gone. Government securities, which had started the year at 67 premium, were now down to 19. The trust fund Chambers administered for her and the children was now worth less than half the thousands that had gone into it.

"I doubled the value of what you gave me," Nora told John. "He halved what you gave him."

He looked at her with hunted eyes. "You are pitiless," he said.

She threw her arms around him and buried her head on his huge chest, loving the solidity there. "I'm sorry!" she repeated, several times. "I'm not really pitiless. You've no idea how many times I've willed myself not to say that—and won."

He laughed.

"Tighter!" she said, wriggling deeper into his embrace.

He obeyed. "We're bound to be on edge," he said, speaking into her hair. "I live through each day in a silent terror." Her hair tickled his nose as she nodded. "We must try not to be short with each other."

She remained silent, content to hold him and be held.

"Aren't you terrified?"

"Not yet," she had to admit. "There's still one more action we have to take. We have to move all that money away from Chambers, back to all those little provincial banks. And then we have to start the biggest hudsoning of all. That's when I'll be terrified—when there's nothing more we can do but wait."

"When? When should we begin, d'you think?"

She broke free then, biting her lip. "I don't know," she admitted. "That's what worries me. I don't want to start haunting Chambers' doorstep, yet I want to be absolutely sure that the moment we pick is the right one."

In the event, Chambers saved them the trouble of deciding. He came to them.

*   *   *

It was their habit to take lunch several times a week at Dolly's Chop House, by St. Paul's Churchyard, one of the few places in the financial district that would allow a woman in. On this particular day, the seventeenth of November, they had barely started their lunch when Chambers, who rarely ate there, came in, saw them, and made straight for their end of the table.

"Have you seen this?" he asked, putting a copy of *The Times* before them. He grinned.

They had, of course. The article on the Railway Bubble by Spackman was the talk of the City that day.

"Join us," John said, pointing to the empty seat next to Nora.

Chambers accepted with as little formality as he had shown on coming in. "It's terrible," he said, quite cheerfully.

The main feature of Spackman's article was a set of tables showing railways completed, in course of construction, and projected. There were 47 lines completed, 118 in construction, and 1,263 seeking capital—seeking, to be precise, £566,019,006. "Can we," thundered the leading article, "add one-tenth of this vast remainder? *We cannot*, without the most ruinous, universal, and desperate confusion."

"It's as bad as can be," Chambers said. He rubbed his hands and ordered half a dozen mutton chops.

"When *I* tell you," Nora chided, "you don't believe me. It seems you prefer your news three weeks cold."

He smiled and lowered his head, good-naturedly accepting her rebuke.

"You're cheerful company anyway," John said. "Have you acquired some shares in Disaster?"

"Any man who is banker to the great John Stevenson has a right to be happy at this hour," he said.

Nora felt the pressure of John's foot on hers. She could sense his delight. But something in the way Chambers kept glancing sidelong at her kept her on her guard.

"You're going to need all that confidence in the next few months, Mr. Chambers," she warned. "They will be extraordinary times and we will take extraordinary measures to deal with them."

His hands waved permissive circles before him, like a blessing upon the chops. "Dear lady, you have *carte blanche!* You especially." He turned to John as if introducing Nora. "Do you know what treasure is here?"

Her wariness turned to deepest mistrust. He had never spoken like this.

She told herself to clear all thought of their bankruptcy from her mind, to think like the rich he still believed them to be. That was the thought in Chambers' mind: *These people are rich.* Now where did it lead him?

"I owe you an apology," Chambers was saying to her. Yes—to *her!* "I think it was last March when you first pointed out that a madness in railway dealings was growing." Nora nodded, still watching every move. "March, eh? And it was not until June that *The Times* began to ruffle its feathers and not until today that we get this." He had the paper out again and he tapped Spackman's tables with his spoon. "Well, when it's five hundred million, it's obvious to any fool, even"—he grinned wryly—"to a City banker. But *you* saw the danger when the figure was one-tenth of that. And I'll tell you what I find even more impressive: The figures you gave me accord exactly with Spackman's. And you told me you've kept a running total in your head all the year. Is that really so?"

She nodded, watching him all the while with an unblinking gaze.

He still found it difficult to believe. "But why?"

How do you tell a child *why* two and two make four? "It never occurred to me not to," she said. "I do it as a matter of course. All the time."

Chambers merely stared. Nora, not knowing whether he had taken it in or not, tried another approach. "This man"—she took John's arm —"could shut his eyes and walk yard by yard in his mind down any line he's built. He could tell you the geology underfoot—every hedge—every feature, every boundary. He could date each milepost. Am I right?"

"Near enough," John admitted diffidently. "Give or take."

Nora returned to Chambers. "Well, if you could wander like that behind here"—she ran a finger over her brow—"you'd find it ordered just like that with figures. I can't explain it better than that."

Chambers breathed in and out; at last his eyes left Nora's and he turned to John. "Have you any notion," he said ponderously, "of the value of a mind that works like that?"

"I hope so," John said uncomfortably.

"I doubt it. It's incalculable. You realize that there are probably only half a dozen big firms in this country who could actually laugh at a money panic now. Five of them are in that happy position by chance; *one*, just one, is there by deliberate design, carefully phased and executed over months. And why?" He pointed toward Nora. "Because it never occurred to one person *not* to keep that running total."

"Oh, come, Mr. Chambers," she said, embarrassed.

He turned full face to her. "I don't believe even you know what I'm really talking about."

She became deliberately vapid and girlish. "Indeed? Do tell me." She wanted him to be mocked into silence or at least into changing the subject. The conversation was not taking the line she wanted.

"I have never been more serious," he said. "I freely confess I have often dismissed your opinions as mere intuition. But it was I who was blind. Believe me, I have thought a lot about this since your last visit. I think that you, without fully realizing it, have a way of ordering or arranging that internal landscape of figures that amounts almost to—clairvoyance."

Nora burst into dismissive laughter; she was sure now that Chambers was up to something very subtle.

"I don't mean anything mystical, at all," he went on stolidly. "If you stand in a real landscape and pick out with your eyes a path ahead, then walk the path and find it was a good route to have chosen, why, that is nothing mystical. I think you do that, too, in this mathematical landscape. I'll go further: I think it doesn't even occur to you *not* to do it!"

Nora stared at him, hoping her confusion did not show. It was true! Every word he spoke was true; but she fought with all her will against the impulse to agree to his face. What *was* his game?

John had no such inhibitions. "Eay!" he said. "I'd never thought of it that openly. But there's aught in what Chambers says, love."

It was as if Chambers had been waiting for this admission. "And how often do you use it?" he asked, turning to John. "This extraordinary faculty? One of the biggest assets any business could have? Yet when did you last use this talent?"

Now she was certain he was out to do mischief. Never once in all the years they had known each other had Chambers gone further than a grudging admission that she had a certain flair for bookkeeping. Yet now he was praising her to the skies. It did not fit—not even in these extraordinary times, when the unexpected performed twice daily. She could not guess why or how, but she knew that in some way he was out to drive a wedge between herself and John.

She decided then that the conversation had gone Chambers' way long enough. She saw, too, that they would never get a better moment to start the final, grand hudson. Chambers had freely walked into the trap, now she would spring it. Taking his last rhetorical question to John—"When did you last use this talent?"—she answered: "This very morning, Mr. Chambers. We are not so silent at home as this panegyric of yours has forced us to be here."

He grinned an apology and listened.

"My 'faculty,' such as it is, inclines me to advise that we withdraw all our funds from the centre and spread them in their due proportion among the banks nearest to each contract."

The silence that followed became almost unendurable. This was the keystone-moment in the strategy they had followed all that summer and autumn; if it failed, the entire structure would fall.

Chambers swallowed a morsel of chop he had forgotten to chew. It made his eyes water. "Leave nothing here?" he said. "Nothing with me?"

"Five years of goodwill," Nora reminded him, supremely gracious.

"I don't pretend," John broke in, "to understand all of Mrs. Stevenson's reasoning—not all the time. But, by Jupiter, I understand her here! *If* there is to be a money famine."

"And if there isn't?" Chambers was clutching at straws.

"We'll know that by the new year," John said.

"And come back to you, filled with gold and gratitude," she promised.

Chambers shrugged.

"We'd still want you to discount our bills over that time," John warned, as if it were a mere afterthought.

Chambers shot him a look of astonishment, then turned to include Nora.

Her face and eyes still smiled but there was a new sharpness in her voice as she said: "Who else could we ask so much of? Who else could we trust? Who else would trust us?" Her hand presented him to himself. "Unless what you were saying earlier was just so much ..." She left the idea in the air.

"We shall see," he said miserably.

Inwardly she exulted, for she knew they had won. So far at least.

Chapter 21

Chambers had *seen* the money—had seen how rich they were. Now several dozen provincial and oversea banks saw it, too. And, such is trust, they went on seeing it after it had gone, for by now they were used to the constant and bewildering ebb and flow of Stevenson money. Each banker took it to be part of some grand strategy of which he was privileged to see, and be entrusted with, but a small portion.

They did not notice that there was now more ebb than flow. And they did not know that the portion which ebbed, never to flow again, made its way to an account in Hertford town, where Sir George Beador also banked. As fast as it came in, it went out to clear his debt.

There was a time, at the end of summer, a hopeful time, when it looked as if a lot of would-be railway companies would simply vanish, like the mushrooms they were. Their directors, despairing of raising any money from the cooks and porters and pet dogs who made up the bulk of their subscribers, quietly ceased to badger. But then the lawyers got wind of it—the vultures of the money system. They knew that in every list of a hundred subscribers there were one or two with real money, and on them they descended in their raucous, black-gowned hordes.

A list worth (in theory) fifty thousand could be bought for five hundred. Then for the mere trifling expense of printing a few worthless shares in a company that had no hope of building a line, the owner of the list could issue writs and summonses enforcing payment on the hapless subscribers. Quiet country parsons, who had applied for twenty shares in the hope of being allotted one, now had to buy all twenty, at fifty pounds apiece, or go to debtor's jail—all for a railway that the judge, barrister, company, and jailer knew would never exist. Many thousands of decent people of all classes were made bankrupt in that way. All the resources of the great firm of Stevenson's now were squandered to keep John and Nora from joining them.

The system was a scandal. Everyone knew it was a scandal. Everyone said it was a scandal. The members of Parliament said it was a scandal; they were still debating it long after the last vulture took his last victim. Then it was easy to decide to do nothing. Most of the members were lawyers themselves.

"They're as much use as the bishop who could fart Lilliburlero through a keyhole," John said in disgust.

On the last working day in November, Stevenson's ran out of money.

The firm still had tens of thousands lodged in provincial banks, but every penny was needed to pay out wages between then and the next large foreseeable piece of income. If they dipped into that, they were knowingly making themselves insolvent.

They had dreaded reaching this moment. Yet now it had come, now there was no possible turning back, and no alternative path to take, they found it oddly liberating. So that when John suggested they should spend Sunday "watching the fun" down at the Railway Office, it did not seem at all out of key. In any case, as Nora said, it's exactly what they would be doing if they were still in funds; and now, more than ever, they had to keep up their pretence.

"We'll go up on the roof," John said. "I'll put an awning up there in case it rains, and we can have a coke brazier to roast some chestnuts and heat the chocolate. Sarah can come, too. It'll be a pleasant outing for us all."

It was an easy promise to make, since Stevenson's had the contract to extend the New Treasury Building, which housed the chaotic Railway Office, which, in turn, was a division of the Board of Trade.

The last day of November 1845 was set by the Board of Trade as the day on which all new railway plans had to be lodged if they were to stand any hope of a parliamentary hearing. At the time of the announcement it had occurred to no one that the thirtieth was a Sunday; then, rather than admit the error, the Board had to announce further that it would be open for the reception of plans until noon, sabbath or no sabbath.

This was to be the "fun" that John had promised.

*   *   *

The last fortnight in November was more hectic in railway business than all the other weeks of that mad year put together. Go into the remotest tavern and you would find it filled with tired and perspiring committee men almost buried in survey and legal papers. Go to a printer with some ordinary business and he would refuse you, for he was working double tides—and quadruple rates—on railway maps and prospectuses.

As the end of the month drew near, the roads and rails leading into London provided scenes that lingered for years in local memory. Coaches and four and post chaises went thundering by in a lather of horses, their occupants cheering and whooping as each milestone was passed. Dozens of "specials" were chartered on the railways. One, on the Great Western, broke down at Maidenhead, coaxed beyond its limit. The party behind, in another special, paid their engineer well enough to drive into the rear coach and smash it—they being rivals with the stranded party to serve the same area with a new railway. Some railways refused to carry parties whose projects clashed with their own. One group of speculators thus thwarted overcame the ban by staging an elaborate funeral, complete with coffin (in which lay all the requisite plans and papers) and mourners. The deceased's name was given as Stafford Lawry I.A. (an anagram of Stafford Railway); the I.A., they say, stood for *in aeternum*—the whole thus implying "Stafford Railway forever!"

On any day there was a great advantage in arriving at the Board of Trade early, for people were called up in the order in which they handed in their cards. Often the clerks would accept no more cards after midday, and even then those whose cards were taken in close to that hour were not called up until near midnight. The agents complained fiercely at having to stand twelve hours on Whitehall's pavements in pouring November rain, clutching maps and papers, waiting to be called; but there was no other way to get through the work. One special, coming up very early on the Great Western, with a clear line all the way, made over eighty miles an hour—which even the engineer said was impossible.

When the final Sunday dawned, John, Nora, and Sarah went to the early service at St. Martin's Church in Trafalgar Square and walked down Whitehall to the site, arriving just after eleven. It was a clear day, cloudless and cold, with the overnight rain still glistening on the cobbles. The wintry sun, pale yellow and barely warm, hung above the new towers at Westminster, still with their fuzzy outline of scaffolding and looking more like giant columnar trees than a work of man. At the corner of the Privy Garden some gas engineers were returning a repaired main to service, flaring the gas to make sure no air had entered it during the work. The brilliance of the flame had collected a large crowd of urchins, dancing in the warmth; behind them the cab-men stamped their feet and held forth their hands to the glow.

Each passing minute brought one, two, or even more cabs and post chaises clattering down the street to great cheers and cries of "In time! In time!" from the crowd. And even if the drivers had never visited London, they would have no excuse for mistaking the building; the throng around it was already twenty or thirty deep, spilling far over the pavement and into the street.

John took his party in by a back door, using the yard between the Foreign Office and the new building.

"There'll be murder here before the day is out," the doorman said cheerfully as he let them in.

He looked so extraordinarily like Tom Cornelius that Nora glanced at once at Sarah to see how she responded. But she appeared not to notice the likeness at all.

From the roof they had a splendid view, not only of the proceedings below but also over the houses in King Street and Parliament Street, which forked at the end of Whitehall and led into Parliament Square. They could see the Abbey and the new Parliament, where every finial and crocket on every pointed spire showed sharply in the brilliant noon-day sun. And beyond was the Thames, curving away at Battersea and Vauxhall; a thin miasma rose from its putrid, oily surface, and the smell of drainage—the smell into which all London smells sooner or later merged—hung over all. The strongest smell on the roof, though, was of the coke that sang as it burned in the brazier.

A coach and four came hell-for-leather up King Street and almost collided with a chaise coming down Whitehall. Men poured from both and raced through the cheering crowd, up the steps, to hammer at the door. When it was not immediately opened, one of them began to shout "Too late! I said it!" and set about his colleagues with his fists. Only the doorman's assurance that they were within time reconciled them. In the final quarter of an hour more than forty parties drew up in this same agitation; and the closer they were to the final minute, the wilder their excitement to give in their cards.

"I don't know about murder," Sarah said, remembering the door-keeper's words. "There'll surely be heart failure."

"How many of those gentlemen will be handing out work to us next year?" John wondered aloud. He looked down at their faces—those he could discern in that sea of tall hats and paper, half-lost among the scaffolding: common faces, glowing with common avarice, indulging the common pleasure of gloating at the latecomers' despair.

"Here's some gentlemen who won't," Nora said, pointing at a cab coming down Whitehall like a runaway.

But by a kindly error of the doorman's watch they were just in time. The four gentlemen actually danced a ring-a-rosy when they regained the pavement. They scattered for safety as a coach pulled up; it had begun its final tumultuous dash from Trafalgar Square just as they had hammered at the door. Now the coach party hammered there, too; three of them carried a titanic roll of paper, like a stage battering ram.

When the doorkeeper said "Too late!" a universal cheer went up, from all except the coach party. Now the fun would begin. The leader of the latecomers began a furious argument through the crack in the door, which was now held on its night chain. Odd words carried up clearly to the roof. "Great Missenden time, sir! Great Missenden time!" the man bellowed at the doorkeeper and pointed to his watch.

It was too good for the Cockney punsters in the crowd to ignore. "Great Missin 'em time!" one of them shouted. And there was a ripple of laughter that grew to a delighted roar as the words *Great Missin 'em time* passed from mouth to mouth. Then for an hour, of course, every bemused latecomer—and there were dozens—was greeted with the same ironical cries and laughter.

Many of the latecomers, especially as the afternoon wore on, were furious to find the doors locked, not having heard of the noon closure and so thinking they had all day. Whenever the doorkeeper opened up to let in an applicant who had left his card in time a great throng would press forward, hurling their plans through the door like assegais. But always some clerk would gather them up and shower them back from an upper window. It was not long before someone threw a lump of broken paving through a window; a dozen sets of plans followed it in short order.

John laughed grimly. "Observe," he said, "how the foremost nation in all the world determines the future shape and course of its railroad system! What a model of logic and order!"

"Oh, yes, dear," Nora said. "Now tell us how marvellously the French arrange these things."

He pointed down. "You can't defend *that*."

"Why ever not?"

"Suppose among those late plans—which no one will even look at now—suppose there are schemes so much superior to those already submitted that they would save hundreds of thousands in running costs each year?"

"I don't care if they are all like that," Nora said. "I wouldn't trust them to people who've had a year to get ready and still manage to come two hours late. In fact, I'd reject every plan handed in today—on the grounds that we don't want railways operated by skin-of-the-teeth men."

John shook his head and yawned. "Folly," he said. "If they break any more windows, I think you'd better go. Does anyone want the last hot chestnut?"

Sarah was still watching the latecomers. She was the only one to show any sadness on their behalf. "What happens to them now?" she asked.

"Most of them will be ruined," Nora said. "And their subscribers will lose all their deposits. *That's* the folly."

For brief moments that day she could almost believe she was talking about third parties.

Chapter 22

By the middle of December they had exhausted all their cash—whether it was needed for wages or not. True, with a firm the size of Stevenson's, working on up to fifty contracts for a dozen or so companies, there could never be so dead a reckoning that the final moment could be named with certainty. All Nora could say was that funds in all the banks were exhausted and their known outgoings over the next four weeks exceeded their best estimate of income three-fold. From that moment on they were trading on nothing more substantial than every banker's memory of their "soundness."

Even Sarah's money had gone. They kept it intact to the last but both of them knew, without any discussion, that to keep themselves afloat they'd jump on any passing raft.

On the credit side (if that was the word for it), they had discharged the last of the luckless Beador's debts.

"He wept," John reported back to Nora. "He could hardly sign the final draft."

"He'll do more than weep before we see this out," Nora promised. How she wished they could turn him out at once.

The moment it was free of debt they dissolved the partnership and replaced it by the limited-liability company she had suggested in the first place.

For the whole of the following week they waited daily for the soft, insistent question or the outraged cry that would begin to crack their flimsy structure. None came.

"Too soon, yet," Nora warned.

She thought it would be best then if John found some sudden reason for going to France—or to a small line they were doing in Belgium. "They can't arrest me," she said. "You're the one that's in danger. And I've no power of attorney—so any banker can take that as a good and valid reason for waiting until you return."

Something about this suggestion made him acutely uncomfortable. "It won't do," he said. "If we were in funds, I'd never leave so soon to Christmas unless there was a disaster somewhere. No!" He rallied. "We're safe enough this side Christmas. I'll leave for France on Boxing Day."

She felt he had some other reason for refusing but he would not admit to it. Anyway, he was right. They were almost certainly safe now until after the holiday.

By the third week in December, when Chambers had honoured the fourth weekly wages draft not covered by funds, they both admitted, with some mutual bravado, that they had now grown quite used to skating without ice. Nora said she could sometimes forget their predicament for an hour on end.

They decided to go north to Thorpe Old Manor and spend Christmas as if they had as few cares as they now had pence.

Chapter 23

Christmas that year was dry and cold.

There was a slight hollow in the field beyond the old fortifications to the east of Thorpe Manor where water sometimes collected. This year it froze right through and they all spent the afternoon of Christmas Eve sliding on it. The strip of ice was not broad enough to skate on but you could run over the crackling, frosty grass and leap onto it and slide the best part of thirty yards. John, with his weight, could get up momentum (and courage) enough to go hurtling and somersaulting off the end; but everyone else came to a halt before the end, despite desperate jerks, which added no more than inches to the length of their slide. Sarah would not take a flying run, but with John and Nora running and holding her at each side, just catching the fringes of the grass, she had her stately share, too.

Mrs. Jordan came down in midafternoon with a basket full of hot spiced rolls and honey, all wrapped in white linen; behind her came Mrs. Jarrett with cups and two cans of steaming chocolate. And of course John and the two oldest children wouldn't let them go without taking *their* turn at the slide. Todd and Woolley, two of the girls, came out to watch, and John beckoned *them* down. "And the others!" he called.

Nora and Mrs. Jarrett protested but he would have none of it: Everyone must come. And one by one, as they arrived, he organized competitions and prizes: for girls with names beginning with *C*, and for all cooks, or all housekeepers, and all stablehands under 16 years, and so on—prizes that each was bound to win, being unique to the class. The lad's prize was a silver shilling, the maids got a shilling and a kiss, and Mrs. Jarrett—well, for one terrified minute she thought she was due a kiss, too, but instead she had a stately one-round waltz on the meadow with the master, while everyone else laughed or cheered or sang their own idea of a waltz tune. Cox, the cold automaton, got a waltz and, as it ended, *stole* a kiss, and then ran off giggling up the hill, back to the nursery.

At last, while the shadow of the ramparts reached quickly over the grass, they gathered up the debris of their afternoon and skipped or ran or walked or grumbled up the slopes to home.

"What a pleasant way to give out Christmas boxes," Sarah said.

Sarah had previously suggested that they should try the effect of Queen Caroline's "Christmas trees"—young fir trees set in tubs and put upon the table or in a window seat and then decked with penny candles. They spent the evening trying them in different places and ended with one in the hall and one in the window seat in the winter parlour. John twisted soft iron wire around some thick dowelling, whittled to a taper, to make candleholders.

The trees looked very pretty when they finished. Then they went upstairs and filled the children's stockings with apples and nuts, and sugar pigs with string tails made by Mrs. Jordan. For Winifred there were some hair ribbons too, and a book of tales by Maria Edgeworth; for Young John, a half-dozen new brass buttons and a coloured alphabet book. For Caspar there were crayons wrapped in a roll of drawing paper.

At six next morning they heard the treasure being discovered. At

a quarter past six Young John came in, bearing a candle and his alphabet book. He poked his father's eyelids open. "Happy Christmas," John
said to him in a voice like a death rattle. Nora, without apparently
waking or stirring, said, "Who lit your candle?"

"Winny."

"That's naughty. Happy Christmas. And don't call her Winny."

"I can read," Young John said. He put down the candle and began
to turn the pages of the book. "I can read that. And that. And that ..."

At the fifteenth, John, his eyes still shut, said, "What's that one
then."

"That's the letter orange. And that's the letter pudding. And that's
the letter queen. And that's the letter ... colours."

John opened an eye quickly. "Rainbow."

"Yes, rainbow colours."

Winifred, not to be excluded, began a processional reading from
the door: *But his father caught hold of him by the arm. "I will whip
you now," said he. So Robert was whipped, till he cried so loud with
the pain that the whole neighbourhood could hear him.* She read with
bright-eyed relish. *"There," said his father; "now go without supper.
See how liars are served!"* She closed the book and clutched it to her.
"Aren't they glorious tales, mummy!"

The bed shook with John's silent laughter.

"Happy Christmas, popsie," Nora said wearily.

"And that's the second letter horse. A different horse. A stripey
horse. And that's what I can read."

*   *   *

When the last mince pie had gone and the last slice of plum pudding
had been washed down with the last drop of Madeira, the children were
sent up to recapture the sleep of which Father Christmas' bounty had
robbed them.

The postman came just as the grownups were moving into the
parlour. He rode back up the drive one shilling heavier and two letters
lighter.

"For you—" John handed it to Nora. "From Arabella Thornton."

"I thought so," Nora said. "She never forgets Christmas." And she
explained to Sarah how they and the Thorntons had been married in
the same month in 1839 and had all four spent that Christmas together.

"The GS&W, Dublin, wants us to begin next week," John said,

folding his letter. "Flynn can start without me. I'll go over in the spring."

Nora read rapidly through Arabella's, throwing out her own summaries: "They have a new cook ... very good. ... The road dug up *again*, drains very bad. ... Bristol has plans for roads and great civic works which we should interest ourselves in. ... Scandal at Bedminster parish—but we read all that in the papers. ... Terrible water shortage all year, a *real* scandal, and new waterworks urgently needed. ... Walter offered a tempting salary in the South Wales Union Railway but doesn't think it can ever become profitable. ... Children all well—*oh!* and she's to have another next June ... hopes for another girl as three boys are quite enough for the moment. They must be—five and a half, and four, and just turned three."

"Quite enough for the moment!" Sarah echoed.

"Hello!" John, rooting around near the tree on the window seat, picked up a small package. "For me!"

"I thought that was a good place for them. Let Sarah have hers first."

"Oh!" Sarah said, as if she had never suspected it.

Their present to her was a tortoiseshell brush and comb and mirror, each with her initials engraved on a silver cartouche let into the shell. She was enchanted with the set and thanked them half a dozen times. Then she shyly produced, from behind the sofa, something like a tray wrapped in paper. When they opened it, they found an embroidered firescreen in a mahogany frame with the feet left loose and unglued. "If they'd been on, it would have spoiled the mystery," Sarah explained.

Nora looked closely at the pattern. "You really do the most beautiful needlework, Sarah. But I say—isn't this the embroidery Rodie was doing?"

Sarah was delighted she had recognized it. "The same picture. I saw her doing it and took a copy."

"But it's perfect!"

"I don't suppose it is. But I thought you could look at it here, by your fire, and think of Rodie at La Gracieuse, with hers. You see."

That pleased them even more.

Nora's present from John was a lovely, dainty little diamond brooch. Its beauty awed her so that her thanks were quiet and almost reverent. "I'll wear it now," she said. "No one can object, surely."

"I should think not," Sarah agreed. "It's the very opposite of showy. It's exquisite. Now yours, John."

"Do you know what it is?" he asked, taking out a pocket knife.

"Don't *cut* it!" Nora called. "Look, it pulls undone. Your extravagance!"

He laughed. "Here's me, who condemns miles of rope, each year, most of it probably sound, and now I'm saving string!"

"Open it!" Sarah almost screamed.

It was a hunting watch—one of the new ones with a metal cover over the glass.

"What a splendid idea," he said. "Why didn't anyone think of that before!"

"Push that little thing that sticks out," Nora said.

The watch chimed three for the hour and then three for three-quarters. "That means it's between quarter to and four o'clock," she explained. "It'll do it again, as often as you want."

He pressed and it chimed again. He was about to put it in his pocket when Nora said, "Open the back."

There he found the greatest novelty of all: a twenty-eight-day dial that showed the phases of the moon—at least, it had been the moon when Nora bought the watch but she had got a miniaturist to overpaint it with an enamel portrait of herself.

"I shall take it out and kiss it hourly," John said. "*And* every time I condemn some rope. And if folk ask me why, I sh'll just say, 'Oh, that's my wife—she's a *lunar-tick!*' "

He and Sarah fell about laughing, especially when Nora said she thought it *clever* rather than *funny*.

Later, when they were in their bedroom, preparing for Evensong, John pulled out a long legal envelope from his travelling writing case and said: "Here is my real present to you. I didn't think it appropriate in front of Sarah."

She took it cautiously. "It won't bite," he said.

The enfacement read *Power of Attorney: Stevenson to Nora Stevenson, 3 December 1845.*

"Won't bite!" she said. "It could send me to jail. I see now why you were so evasive when I said I hadn't power of attorney." She looked at the document again. How happy it would have made her at any other time. "Here's a pig's pizzle," she said, using a favourite phrase of his. "What *ever* possessed you?"

"It was prepared in much happier times," he explained. "You know how lawyers can drag things out into the years. I wanted to give you power to deal with . . ."

He could not go on. She realized with shock that he was trying to fight back tears.

"John!" she said gently. "It doesn't matter now."

". . . to deal with . . . your property." He choked on the words.

He fell to his knees in front of her and threw his arms about her waist. "Oh Nora, love! What have I done to you!"

She held his head tight but it was an automatic response; she was too astonished to do anything else. Suddenly she realized she had *loved* these last few months. Not all of it, of course. Seeing her properties go, and then signing away all their money—that had been terrible. But everything else had been alive and splendid in a way it had not been for years. She and John had been together again, as they had in their very first year. The excitement had all come back. Even this new threat of jail was part of it.

And precisely what distressed her about John's outburst was that it once more put that distance between them; it made them opposites— sinner and sinned against, penitent and confessor, worm and angel.

She pulled his shirt away at the back of his neck and dropped the document down inside. "Never mind what you've done, love. You're not getting me in jail with you—who'd arrange the escape? No—you take this to France tomorrow. Lose it for a while."

She held him until his dignity returned and then she broke free.

To get the paper out he had to stand again. "You're better when you're tall," she told him.

He grinned. "You won't let me do an easy penance, then," he said.

"Such rubbish!"

He put the document in his writing case, buried among other as-sorted papers. "Funny thing," he told her. "It was Chambers' idea, really—giving you power of attorney."

"But he's always *hated* me having properties, independently."

"I said: funny thing."

Chapter 24

Nora endured one day at Thorpe after John had left; then she decided that to be without him but surrounded by the children, the house, the land—by all they stood to lose and all that would make the loss hurt most—would be intolerable. She would go hunting.

Better still, she would go to Maran Hill, where, squired by Sir

George Beador, she would hunt with the Puckeridge under their master, Lord Wyatt. Now they had less than nothing to lose she felt an ancient pugnacity stirring within her. She had not felt it since her days of poverty, when she had faced the world alone; it was something different from the polished ruthlessness that money had brought; it was brighter-eyed, more truculent.

At the last moment she decided to take Sarah along, too. It was a decision that almost completed their ruin.

*   *   *

An avenue of limes, dead straight and exactly half a statute mile in length, ran from the gates to the big house at Maran Hill. On either side there was open parkland grazed by a herd of red deer—or, now that it was December and the males were apart, two herds. Gideon's wood and Red wood, two large game coverts, blocked the view to the north of the park; they almost joined with Home wood, a coppice to the immediate north of the house.

But on the south side, looking down and across one of the loveliest valleys in the county, all the views were open. There was no covert there larger than an acre or two and they had been placed as much for their scenic effect as for their game-preserving role. None of their trees had been coppiced, so that knolls of tall beeches and huge, spreading oaks delayed the eye as it swept over rolling pastures and ploughed fields. The winter sun reached through the bare branches of the limes, making bars of startling light and shade that flickered in the carriage like a pyrotechnic display.

Sarah, who had leaned out of the window to see the house, sat down again, smiling and blinking at the water drawn into her eyes by the cold and the wind. "What a beautiful house!" she said.

"How would you like to live in such a place?" Nora asked.

"Oh, I'd prefer a town house. There's the same amount of work and you have more interest for your time off."

Nora laughed. "Silly Milly! I meant as mistress, not as maidservant."

"Oh." Sarah looked out at the park, assessing it now with different eyes.

Nora watched her fondly. "You'll never get used to it, will you. To being independent."

"Not to *that* degree." She pointed at the park to stress the word.

"You could rent a place like this, on a maintaining lease, for less than two hundred pounds a year."

"Nora! It's unthinkable."

Every now and then Nora took such opportunities to remind Sarah of her fortune; she tried not to think of it as a kind of hudsoning.

Shallowness had saved Beador—that very shallowness which had enabled him to engage in such monstrous debts when he had nothing to meet them but his partner's money. His character was as bankrupt as his purse; he had nothing with which to meet his debt of obligation to John and Nora. And, as in business he knew no way of earning by his own labour, so in his relationship with them he knew no means of restoring himself by his own effort.

True, at the start he had been filled with remorse. A broken man, pale and much given to outbursts of weeping, a man trembling on the threshold of self-murder. But it was the remorse of youth—intense, yet so shallow its depth is plumbed at a glance. By the time of Nora's visit he was his old, uncaring self again. It made Nora (who, at 26, was actually his junior by a year) feel vastly older.

For it was she who told herself that nothing was to be gained at this moment by recrimination, that Sir George's land and influence at Stockton were still big assets (though nowhere near worth the price at which they had been bought), and that a moping Sir George—a sackcloth-and-ashes flagellant—could be all it needed to bring the whole structure of confidence tumbling down.

Coldly she watched him pour out his careless charm, telling herself to be thankful he could sustain no deeper soul. Inwardly she longed for some sparkling revenge.

*   *   *

"Pretty woman, your friend," Sir George said, as they rode out into the cold.

"It is her nature," Nora agreed.

"Looks as if she might harbour quite a temper there."

"I wouldn't say that. She certainly has a mind of her own."

"Hm."

He said no more until after the hunt.

There had been a sharp frost overnight and the ground was frozen hard. A poor day for scent. They drew three coverts blank, found at a fourth, but lost the line in less than a mile.

"They'd need one nostril up the fox's arse today," Nora heard a farmer say to the first whipper-in, not knowing she was the other side of the hedge.

She was disappointed. Beador had lent her a magnificent five-year-old mealy bay gelding, called Fontana. She was certain that if only they could get away, he'd go superbly over this country.

Lord Wyatt, the Master, seemed to take every check and every lost line as a personal affront. He was a choleric, self-important little man. The cold wind and his own anger turned parts of his face as scarlet as the hunting "pink" he wore. At one point he grew so angry he failed to blow any kind of a note on his horn; he dashed it to the ground in a fury of petulance.

Nora took care to stay on the fringe of the field. She did not think he noticed her.

When the hounds checked for the fourth time and could not find again no matter how the huntsman held them round, Nora and Sir George withdrew.

"I'm sorry," he said. "It's more what you'd expect of Durham country than Hertfordshire."

"I'm sorry not to have made better use of Fontana here," she answered.

He brightened. "Care for a bit of a swish?" he asked.

She smiled then, for an idea had just occurred to her. "Yes," she said. "Take me through Wyatt's place at Panshanger."

Beador tried to dissuade her but she insisted.

He led her at a good trot through the country lanes, by Bramfield and Tattle Hill, through Thieves Lane to Hertingfordbury. There they turned west, into the grounds of Panshanger, which stretched up the Maran valley for about three miles. It was park and pheasant covert and partridge manor all the way.

"Ready?" he called. "Hold tight."

She increased her grip.

"Now!"

The horses had been waiting for it. They went at once from walk to gallop. Nora felt the blood begin to race. Beador knew the ground well for he led the way unhesitatingly through a maze of rides, some broad and straight, some narrow and zigzag. A brilliant sun shone through the trees. The frosted leaves crackled underhoof. And from somewhere came drifting the lazy smell of woodsmoke. All the fears and stresses of these last weeks deserted her on that gallop.

Here and there the way opened into glades, in one of which the woodmen had left the trunk of a once mighty beech. To her astonishment Nora saw Beador's horse fly at it as if to clear it in one bound— which was impossible, surely. Then she began to feel anxious, for she could sense that Fontana was getting set to make the same impossible leap. In fact, she was on the point of reining in when she saw that Bea-dor had come to rest on the top of the trunk; he stood there, poised like a trick rider in a circus.

Very well, she thought, suddenly daring. *On you go!* and she touched Fontana forward.

She leaned over the crupper, ready for the jump. At the last minute her courage failed. The height, which had before seemed merely daunt-ing, now looked terrifying. No horse could do it, not even this great-muscled giant. But they were both committed and had to go forward. For a moment she thought it shared her doubts; there was a hint of a fumble as it doubled its hind legs under for the leap.

"Haaaa!" she yelled. And she frightened it into the supreme effort that carried it up, soaring and stretching, reaching beyond any achieve-ment it knew of, until, by a hairsbreadth, it gained the crest of the fallen trunk. It did not need the tug of her rein to stop; every ounce of its ability had gone into that leap. There was no momentum left to be checked. Their coming to rest seemed both magic and effortless.

"Heigh!" she gave a cry of relief and delight and turned to Sir George.

He was as pale as the bleached wood on which they were both now perched. "Magnificent!" He merely breathed the word, shaking his head in disbelief. "But mad!"

"Why?" She laughed. "You did it."

"Would you look behind us."

She obeyed. "Oh!" she said.

A ridge, perhaps the roots of an ancient wall, crossed the glade at an angle to the trunk, running under it. Sir George had made his im-pressive leap from the top of it; she had made hers from fully three feet lower. "That was stupid," she added, beginning to tremble at the thought of what she had done. "But what a hunter!" She patted Fon-tana's mane.

"No one's going to believe me," he said, looking around. "Did anyone see?"

Automatically she looked around, too. And there, over the tops of the trees that grew on falling ground to their north, there on the other side of the valley was one of the loveliest country houses she had ever seen.

As big as a cathedral it stood, in red Midland brick and warm Ox-ford limestone, with the noon sun full upon it. The woodland, marching up the hill, vanished before it but reached an arm around to the west, fringing the road, and then ran behind it to the north, forming a long backdrop to the palm house and the terraces. Only the clock tower on the stables showed from behind the trees. With the sun shimmering on the glass of the palm house, and the frost turning every shadow pale blue, the whole place looked like a gem, set perfectly upon the hillside.

"Pretty place, really," Sir George said.

For her it was a citadel.

"Hardly buzzing with activity," she said. Very few chimneys were smoking.

"Only Wyatt himself is here at the moment. He can't stand his wife and children. They're at the family's main estate over Maidenhead way. To them this is just a huntin' lodge. There's only a handful of servants here on board wages."

"Let's go closer then," she said.

They galloped down the rest of the long gentle ride to the river, across a wooden bridge, and then up the grassy slopes to the terraces below the house. It was even lovelier at close quarters. Winter sweet, viburnum, and witch hazel were all in flower; the air was so still that they could hear the distant gurgle of the river from down in the valley. The smoke rose straight from the chimneys.

"Home!" she said suddenly. The display of the Wyatts' wealth, so casually used ("just a huntin' lodge") was more than she could bear.

Beador seemed relieved to be going. They went around the house by the gravel drive to the east. The gravel was a mixture of hard flintstone and sand. The two-mile ridge on which both Panshanger and Maran Hill stood was composed entirely of the same mixture, locally known as "hoggin." It makes an iron-hard road. Today, bound by the frost, it was as good as tarmacadam.

They soon left the estate, crossed the highway, and entered the park around Maran Hill.

"Now there's a happy couple," Sir George said, pointing to the gate lodge. "The Bagots."

The Bagots were nowhere to be seen.

"Yes," Sir George sighed, "I don't think there's a more contented little family anywhere. They adore each other, and the children. They never fight. You never hear the children quarrel. They're all the picture of health. The house and garden's like a new pin. Yet I doubt they have meat more than once a week—and I doubt he thinks about money from one year's end to the other."

Nora kept an amused silence. She remembered the laughter and the happy times they had enjoyed in her father's cottage, where "meat once a week" would have been luxury indeed. No doubt the Duke of Bridgewater's agent had thought them happy when he collected their rent each week. But she knew what a constant and life-deforming worry the money had been.

"Yes," Sir George said, "you could base a book of sermons on the Bagots."

"It would probably sell very well, too," Nora said, unable to resist it.

"We'll have one last gallop down to Lambs Dell and then up to home, what?" he said, his pastoral vision of the Bagots already forgotten.

"I think I could ride to Wales today," she answered.

But they soon found galloping impossible. Fallen branches littered the rides and new growths of whippy little sapling twigs poked down at head-and-shoulder height to a horseman.

They left the woods and went around by the neighbouring fields—"blind" country where the ditches and drains were all concealed in coarse, overgrown grass. They dared not canter there.

"Refresh my memory, now," Nora said. "Which are the farms that belong to Maran Hill?"

They had ridden to the far end of the long gravel ridge. The whole upper valley of the river Maran stretched away from them in a succession of rich pasture, coppice, and deer park. There were a dozen fine estates between them and the distant skyline.

"Since we now own it," Nora prompted, "we ought to know its extent."

Sir George kept silent. He pointed vaguely here and there, scowling, and then let his arm drop.

"I can't follow *that*," Nora said.

He pretended to be busy adjusting his horse's bridle.

"Show me again," she asked.

He spoke to the bridle. "There aren't any bloody farms."

Quickly she thought back to the day that the deeds for Maran Hill had arrived. Quite a pile of them. They hadn't checked them all at the time, and then they had forgotten. *They hadn't checked the farms!*

"I suppose Lord Wyatt won them, too!" she said, thinking it could not possibly be so.

But it was. Four farms, nearly eight hundred acres—Wyatt had taken them in settlement of various wagers.

"I won things off him, too," Sir George said defensively.

"For instance?"

"I won three of them back once."

She stifled her fury. There was no point in being angry with him—

he was nothing, *nothing* but a fool. "Show them to me anyway," she said.

Sullenly he pointed them out. They were good farms with plenty of water meadow along the river banks, all of it drowned in protection against the frosts. Their loss—again to Lord Wyatt—was, at this point, worse than all that had gone before.

"Wyatt is going to have to give them back," she said. "I don't know how, but I'm going to make him."

"You can't. He won them honourably."

"Honour!"

Her scorn stung him at last. "*You* could hardly be expected to understand. There's no honour in the gutters you came from. But a wager is a matter of honour among gentlemen."

She was so angry she dared not trust herself to speak above a whisper. "You say that to me! When we've honoured your debts? *Honoured!*" She found her voice. "And you sneer at me about honour, sir? You? Lecture me?"

He could not look at her.

"I swear to you that your honourable gambling partner is going to restore those farms to this estate. Our estate. And you will do nothing to hinder me."

Still he was silent.

"Do you hear?"

"I hear you."

"And you give me your word you will do nothing to hinder me?"

"I give you my word." He reined about and spurred his horse into a gallop.

"I hope I may trust your honour even that far!" she shouted after him.

But she had no idea how to make her threat come about.

Chapter 25

Next day the frost had gone. A fitful northeast wind blew a dampness over the country, threatening rain that never quite fell.

"There'll be scent enough today," she said as they set off again for the meet. This time one of the grooms came, too. Nora was once more on Fontana.

It was a huge field, more than eighty riders, all as certain as Nora that the scent would burn today. Their excited babble and their laughter carried far—the cacophony that ruined many a good hunt. Nora's spirits sank.

They drew a long covert upwind between Queen Hoo Hall and Bramfield. Nora, seeing its western end thinly attended, went there at first. But as they drew deeper into the coppice, moving farther east all the while, she began to fear they would leave her entirely behind. Slowly, for she could still hear them less than half a mile away, she walked forward into the thick of it.

If Beador's rides had been bad, these were deplorable. Elderberries, whitethorns, sycamores, and other volunteer saplings of every sort barred the way. Soon she was quite alone, and wondering whether or not to go back and make her way around by the fields. Then she heard a commotion in a thicket some way in front and to her left. She urged Fontana carefully ahead. Three loose hounds were in there; one, she was sure when she got a good look, was a bitch, Wrathful, who had impressed her that memorable day last February.

A rider, still out of sight around a bend, came toward her, crashing heavily through the regrowth. As soon as he came to the turn, where the path was open to the sky, she saw it was the Master, Lord Watson Wyatt himself.

"The buggers have found *some*thing," he said.

Nora was too astonished to reply. He peered toward her. "Who in hell's name are you?" he asked amiably, still unable to make her out in the thick shade of an ivy-infested oak.

"Mrs. John Stevenson. I hunted with you in February." She was damned if she'd call him Master, speaking like that.

"One of Beador's." He was not the least embarrassed.

"Yes."

He looked away at the dense thicket where the three hounds were working. "Rioting after a badger," he said, drawing in breath to bellow a discord.

"It's my belief there's an earth in there. Wrathful wouldn't riot."

"Eh?" He paused, uncertain now.

"Unstopped, too."

"Devil!" he said and dismounted so as to approach the thicket more closely. "I was sure I knew every earth here. I'm me own huntsman today."

Wrathful had worked round the downhill side of the thicket until she lost the scent; now she had come back and was working around the uphill side. Nora guessed that if there was a fox in there and if it broke, it would seek first to go downhill. She pulled Fontana around and trotted quickly back the way she had come. When she arrived at the edge of the covert, she made her way cautiously along its downhill fringes. There was a rider standing ten yards out in the fallow.

"You'll head him if he breaks here," she warned.

He looked at her scornfully. "They won't find in *that*!" he said. Then he looked her up and down appraisingly.

But just at that moment came Wrathful's opening challenge, quickly taken up by the other two hounds. The rider spurred for the edge of the covert, immediately in front of Nora, arriving there only just before the fox broke. There was a great deal of crashing behind.

The scornful rider gave the fox no chance to get well away. As soon as it entered the fallow he began an excited scream of *view halloa, halloa!* and flapped his arms.

"No!" Nora shouted, unheard. She could have shot him.

The fox turned at once and went back into the covert, about ten yards from the point where he broke. All the activity around his earth, and the fact that there were a mere three hounds, had combined to make him think the open country might be safer today; now they'd given him proof that it wasn't. He'd go to earth and stay there till dark.

She almost went home then. But it was such perfect weather that if they could not get a fox away, even the most incompetent hunt in England couldn't fail to make *something* of it.

She went back to the overgrown ride where she had left Lord Wyatt. He was just remounting as she reined in. He had obviously decided to be pleasant to her.

"Gone back to earth," he said. "Sorry I swore, by the way. I was sure you were my cousin." He grinned. "I suppose that makes it worse."

"If true," she said. "There's a young fool down there in pink, shrieking like a banshee and windmilling away. That's what headed Charley back to earth."

He nodded sourly. "That's my cousin, Meredith Wyatt."

They trotted in file up the ride, still having to pull this way and that around saplings and brambles. In a little while they came upon the rest of the pack at the upwind end of the covert. Most of them, to judge by the paw marks, had gone straight up the ride, not working the covert on either side at all. Of course they had drawn blank.

"See that small bit of sticks there," the Master asked Nora. "In the hollow, two fields away?"

"Yes."

"I'm going to draw that next. From the upwind side—I don't want to surprise the fox and have the hounds chop him. As I'm short of a huntsman, might I ask you, Mrs. Stevenson, very kindly to go down-wind and watch him away?"

He had the difficult task of taking the field around and beyond the covert and getting them to stand well back before he could attend to his hounds. The gossiping and the cigar smoke carried strongly downwind to Nora, who had chosen a place to the south of the covert, where she could stand unseen in a gateway, her silhouette lost against a spreading oak at her back.

How often as a girl had she and her father and brothers deserted their looms and raced out to watch the hunt! Many a time she had seen the hounds draw such a covert and heard them open and challenge as the fox broke. And then the music as they followed in full cry! And, afterward, the sadness as the pack and the field vanished over the hill, leaving their world silent and dreary once more.

That was the excitement of today: She could follow that music wherever it led.

Lord Wyatt gave one crack of his whip as a signal to his pack to begin drawing the covert. The fox needed nothing more to start him from his kennel. He slipped from the edge nearest Nora as soon as the hounds entered at the farther side. Only she could see him, a gash of red streaking over the pasture. She let him pass her, fifty yards to the east; the temptation to shout was strong but she waited until he was at the hedge. Then "View halloa! halloa!" she screamed, making sure that the pack had started to chase before she spurred Fontana toward the point in the hedge where Charley had threaded through.

But then the fox's behaviour went somehow wrong. He ran a great circle almost passing through the covert where they'd started him.

"A ringer!" people shouted.

Then he ran a short foil along part of his original track and broke abruptly northward, almost dead straight. Through Perrywood he led them, and Watkin's Hall, between Datchworth and Broom Hall, over the Stevenage road, through the park at Frogmore Hall and on up the valley of the Beane. All the while a dark suspicion was growing in Nora's mind: a ringer that broke and ran dead straight for so many miles. It was not right. It was not Charley Fox, not in such country as this.

On top of that there was the slovenly, almost token, way they had drawn the first covert. And when they had accidentally found, the

Master had sworn, and his cousin Meredith had deliberately headed the fox back to earth. Everything about this chase was wrong.

At Frogmore Hall she turned back. Beador was nowhere to be seen, but she did not care. She needed no squire for the kind of hunting she now had to do.

A furlong short of the small covert where the fox had started she slipped from Fontana's back. Quietly she went forward to the edge of the trees.

There was a scuffle, and then a woman's giggle, among the undergrowth toward the centre of the small coppice. Nora tied Fontana to a thorn and walked briskly toward the sound.

The man and the girl were guiltily rearranging their clothing when she reached them. Their movement dislodged a stone beer jar that rolled into a small depression and began glug-glugging its contents into the soil. The man leaned quickly forward, on hands and knees, to right it.

Nora put her foot on the jar. "Your name?" she demanded.

He looked at the beer, gurgling away. He tried to tug it but had no leverage. She stood more firmly on the jar. The girl was hiding her face, pushing her hands up into her hair.

"Bryant," he said. "Charles Bryant."

"And you?" The girl turned completely away from her. The movement exposed the very thing she had come expecting to find: a large jute bag. The couple had been lying on it.

The girl's move revealed something else—a wedding ring upon her finger. It was that, not so much her face, she had been trying to conceal.

"You!" Nora repeated.

"Cory," the girl mumbled.

Swiftly Nora took her foot off the jar and, while Bryant was busy retrieving what was left of his beer, she darted forward and whisked the bag from under the girl.

"Now," she said, "I want the truth of this matter. Or Lord Wyatt and Mr. Cory shall be told."

The bag reeked of fox.

Moments later she was cantering triumphantly back toward High Wood, near the head of the Beane Valley. For High Wood was the true home of their ringer fox—he had no more business in the small covert where they had found him than the man in the moon. That fox was a bagman! And she had the bag concealed beneath a fold of her riding habit.

Honour! she thought exultantly. *Lord Wyatt—a man of honour!*

To introduce a bagman was one of the worst crimes in hunting's social calendar. Rather be caught cheating at cards or forging a friend's signature. Rather go into seven years' voluntary exile!

She rejoined the field on the slope below High Wood. The bagman-fox, now on home ground, had delayed them by running up a long culvert. They had smoked him out and now he had run for home in High Wood. Once again Nora was among the leaders. Sir George was still nowhere to be seen. Cousin Meredith Wyatt was there, though—and looking at her rather impertinently, she thought.

Lord Wyatt did not want the fox to slip out unseen, so he first made sure every side of the wood was watched.

He turned to the remnant of his field. "First ten or dozen," he said, "go around and hold up the northern half of this wood. We'll force him down to Dane End or Watton."

Those he had asked, Nora among them, set off at once to take up conspicuous stations around the northern fringes of the wood. Nora took the lead, determined to go right around so that she would be nearest to the line if Charley broke in the directions the Master had hoped. She heard the numbers falling off and the cries of "Try over-r-r-r!" and "Edawick!" as they took up station, one by one. Then she became aware that the horseman behind was following her very closely indeed. If she fell at a fence he could not avoid trampling her. She snatched a quick glance backward and saw that it was Meredith Wyatt, grinning like a death's-head.

"Hold back!" she shouted at him.

From inside the wood she heard the cries of "Leu-try, leu-try there!" and "Try over, yoi try!" They were working across very quickly; unless she got around soon the fox might break unseen.

Over the next fence she went, with young Wyatt right at her heels. He was laughing! "Stop!" she called, not stopping herself. "You stop here!"

But on he thundered, not a horse's length behind. When she took the last fence it brought her right around the wood, opposite the point where the Master had asked them to fan out. She could hear he was somewhere close now, in the wood nearby.

Again Meredith Wyatt was almost on to her over the fence. She turned hard upon him, doubly enraged—at his folly and at his interference with the joy of the hunt. No doubt he thought himself a national marvel.

"Damn you to hell!" she said, trembling with her anger. "Go back!"

"Where?" he asked, all innocence, walking his horse slowly toward her.

"To your riding nursery. If I fell, you'd trample me to a powder."

"Grind." He spoke the word like a correction; he was alongside her now, still grinning. "If you fell, I'd grind you all right."

She lashed out suddenly with her crop, intending to hit him in the face. But some last-minute impulse lowered her aim so that the blow caught him, hard but not painfully, on his chest.

He was startled, though he did not flinch. "Quite a governess," he said, lingering on the word as if it were especially endowed. "Do you relish . . . whipping?"

She looked angrily past him, into the wood; the cry for the Master was already in her throat. But there *was* the Master, not thirty yards away. He urged his horse into a walk, toward them, all the more ominous for its slowness. Meredith Wyatt followed her gaze. The smile vanished. He pulled his horse back, doubling and trebling the distance between it and Fontana. He might as well not have bothered.

"Meredith!" the Master called. "Leave the field at once!"

Meredith looked quickly around; there was no one else in view. "No, Watson. You can go and shit cinders."

The Master turned away in contempt and put his horn to his lips.

"What are you doing?" Meredith asked quickly.

"Going to lift the hounds. Going to abandon this chase. Going to call the field together. Going to expel you publicly."

"You wouldn't dare!" Meredith spoke as if he had some power over his cousin.

The other held the horn an inch from his lips. "You try, Meredith," he said. "Let me touch one note and you'll see what I dare."

Meredith did not wait. He turned his horse at once and ambled off without a word.

"You'll not hunt with the Puckeridge again until Mrs. Stevenson has accepted a written apology from you," the Master called after him.

Meredith looked back and blew a rasp at them.

"He'll write that letter. Promise you. Matter of honour," Lord Wyatt said. "Honour of the family."

Then he saw what Nora was doing. She was prying open the weave of the bag so that she could work the handle of her riding crop into it.

"What the bloody hell is that?"

She laughed—straight into his white face, so white that the red patches on it seemed like a clown's makeup. Bankruptcy was a thousand

miles away. She turned and spurred Fontana forward, leaning down
and dragging the bag over the ground.

"Hark forrard to!" she called to the hounds, still searching in the
wood.

Obediently the whippers-in urged them toward her with "lope
forrard!" and "try forrard!"

"No!" Lord Wyatt called.

But it was too late. Already several hounds had found the line of
her drag. They challenged and gave tongue in delight—only to stop
in bewilderment as they reached the point where she had lifted the
bag and hidden it again. She spurred close to Lord Wyatt and spoke in
a voice full of soft malice: "They know what the bloody hell it is! And
so do I!"

She spoiled several more chases for him that day by surreptitiously
dragging her fox-reeking bag wherever their quarry held them to a
check. There came a time when she thought that if she did it once
more, he would burst of an apoplexy.

"You bitch!" he spluttered when he was sure they were alone. "I
know you have little cause to like me. But to take your revenge in this
petty . . . vindictive . . ."

"This?" Nora said. "This isn't even a beginning!"

She quit the field then. It was early afternoon and she wanted to
be sure of getting to Panshanger before Wyatt returned. She approached
by the same route she and Beador had taken the previous day. Halfway
along one of the rides a gamekeeper stepped into her path.

She reined in. "I am a guest of Sir George Beador," she said. "I
think we have leave to . . ."

"Ah, ma'am," he allowed. "I i'nt stoppin' you. But I'd beg you not
to go in the rides south o' here, 'tween here and Cole Green."

"If his lordship wishes."

" 'Tis the pheasant, see? I'm very short-handed here. His lordship . . ."

"Quite understood!" Nora smiled. "I'll go around by the highway.
Have no fear."

If she had not met the man at that particular moment, she would
not have gone out to the highway and she would not have met Flynn.
And everything would have taken a different turn.

Flynn was the nearest John had to a right-hand man. He was actually no more than a deputy, but John always used him as a sounding
board for his new ideas and always considered his advice very carefully.
Flynn got all the really difficult contracts, or the ones John was unsure

of being able to visit regularly; Flynn was the one man John would trust to manage an entire contract on his own. For his pains Flynn drew the biggest bonus of all the deputies. He would be a rich man soon enough.

"Mr. Flynn!" Nora called when she saw him on the road just ahead of her.

He turned, saw her, and smiled. "Well now! And well met, ma'am," he said. "I was after looking for ye, so I was."

"Nothing wrong, I hope? Have you news of Mr. Stevenson?"

His face fell. "There's quare things happening in the office, ma'am. And I wish we had news of Mr. Stevenson. Here's me who should already be starting the Great Southern and Western in Dublin, and the chief away. And I daren't go."

She felt the blood draining from her. "What . . . 'queer things'?" she asked.

"I think you should come yourself. Mr. Jackson urgently desires you to."

"But what is wrong?"

"God, I'm sure I don't know. 'Tis all a muddle with letters from the banks and Mr. Jackson threatening murder and Mr. Chambers with his hair dropping out . . ."

She had to make light of it, of course. But things were falling apart much earlier than expected. The firm's next substantial income would not be until February—a month away. If what Flynn said was even half true, they could not possibly spin it out until then.

Breathing in to stop her guts from sinking any deeper, she said, "Really! Mr. Stevenson is not gone a week and you all go to pieces! And now I have to interrupt the first bit of pleasure I've been able to take in I don't know how long and put you all to right. I'm disappointed—especially in you, Mr. Flynn."

His face fell.

"Very well," she said. "You shall stay the night and tomorrow you will carry a letter to Mr. Chambers that will make all well."

Still he looked glum.

"Perhaps you need some pleasure, too?" she said. "Have you a mind for a jape?"

It pricked his curiosity but he shook his head, saying, "Ah—I have to be away to Dublin."

"Believe me," she told him, "you may do more good to the firm if you stay here. You know we are in partnership with Sir George Beador? In *company* with, anyway."

He nodded.

"Well, this is his land." She pointed to the left of the highway. "And his neighbour on this side"—she pointed to the right—"Lord Wyatt, has some threat out against him. I wish to show Lord Wyatt that he may not with impunity threaten any partner of ours. Otherwise, if Sir George is forced to withdraw from our company, a lot of work and even more money will have gone to waste."

"I'm at your entire service, ma'am," he said, eager now to know what she had in mind.

It was an idea she had thought of in a vague way yesterday, when she had seen the extent of the gravel ridge that ran beneath the two estates.

"Well then, Mr. Flynn, I would say this is excellent hoggin we're riding upon?"

"I was after thinking the same meself, before you came." He was puzzled at the apparent change of topic.

"The best."

"Pretty good."

"No, Mr. Flynn. The best. The best in England. And we're going to quarry it! Every last cubic yard on Sir George's side of the road. And we're going to do it in the most slovenly way possible, with a nibble here and a nibble there, leaving great gashes up and down the hillside, as near as you can get to my Lord Wyatt."

Flynn broke into a broad smile.

She grinned back; both were enjoying the picture. "And we'll mire and pothole the highway . . ."

"And fell trees accidentally upon it!" he broke in.

"Yes! Yes—force the traffic around on to his land. Good!"

"Ye don't want Stevenson men," Flynn told her. "It'd spoil them. Ye want any catch-hand rabble. I can scour them from the hedgerows and workhouses."

"Wherever you can, Mr. Flynn. They're to have a liberal allowance of liquor. And we'll waive all our usual requirements on the bivouac and sanitary needs. And fires."

By now Flynn was roaring with laughter. "Mr. Stevenson'll turn grey!" he said. "So he will!"

"Mr. Stevenson will love it. I promise," she answered. "One more thing—you could pass the word that the pheasant manors on Lord Wyatt's land are well stocked. And there's few gamekeepers to bother with. The southern part is the best, I'm told."

Flynn went ahead of her to Maran Hill. Slightly mystified, he took the fox bag with him. Nora turned back to wait for Lord Wyatt, on the road between the Panshanger gate lodge and the stables.

It was almost dark when he came; there were two grooms riding with him. He was barely inside his own grounds before Nora urged Fontana out from behind the cedar. A furlong separated them but he knew her at once. He rode on toward her with no change of pace, getting quite close before he spoke. "I've said all I wanted to say to you."

"I am not yet in that happy position," she answered. "Please send your grooms back to the gate."

"Damned if I will!" he said. But he stopped.

"Very well. It is no concern of mine if they overhear us." She pretended to search in the folds of her habit, where she had previously concealed the fox bag.

The look he shot her was pure hate. "Go back," he told the two grooms.

When they had gone he turned again to her. "What do you want?"

Had she not met Flynn, she would merely have asked for the farms to be restored to Maran Hill; but the news from London made her too bold.

"Do you know what those worthless shares cost us?" she asked.

He shrugged. "Two hundred thou', I presume."

"A hundred and fifty."

"You did well!" She was surprised to hear a note of admiration behind the mask of impatient indifference.

"You lured Beador into it, knowing he was in partnership with us. You knew he could not pay and that we would have to."

"You did not *have to* go into partnership with the fool." He grinned complacently. "I'll take the shares back, if you like."

"You'll buy them."

"Five shillings."

"No. A hundred thousand pounds. *And* the four farms—they are to be restored to Maran Hill."

He breathed in, ready to laugh, but something in her face stopped him. "It is quite clear," he said, "that you are insane."

He obviously intended this remark to conclude their conversation for he half-turned to call his grooms.

"I'll *hunt* you!" she said. She could think of nothing else to say. It sounded fine, though. "I'll hunt you from here to Yorkshire!"

Afterwards she thought that, of course she must already have formulated the plan somewhere at the back of her mind; but at the time it burst upon her with all the excitement of a vision.

"Insane!" he repeated. But she saw that he was intrigued with the words—with the insane idea of it.

"By no means," she said, with a confidence she did not feel. "The Oakley, the Pytchley, Fitzwilliam, Cottesmore, Belvoir, Blankney, Lord Galway's, Badsworth, and my own York and Ainsty!" She listed without hesitation every hunt between here and Yorkshire.

It left him shaken, for the outlines of her plan were taking shape in his mind—exactly as they were in hers. "And I'll take the fox bag, *your* fox bag, and its story with me. Every hunt in England shall know of . . ."

"They won't let you in," he sneered. "You are riff-raff to them. And to me."

"Bet me!" she challenged. "The same stake you lured Beador into making—a hundred thousand pounds."

He licked his lips but refused the challenge.

She smiled. Her heart, in delayed response, began to pound. "Whether you take the challenge or not, my lord, it's there. You *are* gambling. I'm going now. And from this moment on you are gambling that I shall fail." She turned Fontana's head.

"No, ma'am. That's a certainty." His voice was very level.

She did not, at first, take his meaning so she replied, "The price of making it a certainty is a hundred thou' and the four lost farms."

Then she saw how he was staring at her habit, and looking at the two grooms. When he called them and turned smiling to her she realized why he had said it was a certainty.

"They'll find nothing," she said, and she pulled her habit this way and that, exposing every fold. "The bag is safe, many miles from here."

A flaw in her plan then struck her, just as she was about to go. She turned to him again. "I'll give you a sporting chance," she said. "I'll hunt my way to Yorkshire without saying a word. If by then you haven't paid, I'll hunt my way back, chattering like eskimos' teeth."

Her first enthusiasm began to wane on the short ride back to Maran Hill. True, it would suit her very well just now to be darting hither and thither between Hertford and York. The journey and the sport would usefully consume at least three weeks, during all of which she would be beyond the regular or predictable reach of the mails. And it was such a natural thing for her to do if she truly hadn't a care that it would lull any suspicion. Yet there was the one supreme difficulty;

Lord Wyatt had put his finger on it: The hunts wouldn't let her in. To them she was just riff-raff.

Unless . . . it was a small hope . . . unless the idea of hunting from London to York just happened to catch their imagination. Acts that were wild or eccentric—or even plain lunatic—would always intrigue the English upper class. The hope was slim, but it was the only one she had.

She got Beador to write an amused and amusing letter to Mr. Hollingworth Magniac, Master of the Oakley, telling him of Mrs. Stevenson's mad notion and begging his hunt's assistance. Beador's own response was reassuring—he thought it a "ripping good idea" and gladly added Fontana to the travelling stable of two hunters she had brought down from Yorkshire. Since Stevenson's now owned Sir George right down to the buttons on his shirt, she thought that most generous.

He was in very good humour. Later she found out why.

After dinner she wrote a brisk, chatty letter to Chambers, telling him of her notion and in every way (she hoped) putting him at his ease. It was exactly the sort of letter she would have written if they'd had two hundred thousand in the bank instead of less than nothing.

Flynn, she found, had already gone recruiting in Hertford. John certainly picked his men well.

She was about to retire when Sarah knocked at her door. She came in bubbling with excitement; all evening she had brimmed with some secret mirth. Nora had not seen her like that since the day she and Sam had arrived at Coutances.

"You'll never guess," she said. "Sir George has asked me to marry him!"

Nora was thunderstruck.

"Think!" Sarah babbled. "Lady Beador! Me—a Lady! From scullery maid to Lady!"

It was her money, of course. Somehow Beador had got a sniff of it. He must have a nose for money better than any hound for any fox. But if Sarah took her money out now . . . !

"Aren't you pleased, Nora dear?"

Nora made herself smile. "If it's really what you want. If it will really make you happy. But why Sir George?"

Sarah giggled. "Because he asked, I suppose. No one else has."

"And that's all it needs? The ability to put *you, me,* and the verb *to marry* in their proper grammatical relationship?"

"Of course not!" Sarah blushed. "You're a bit sharp, anyway. I thought you liked him. He admires you enormously."

Nora waited. At length she asked, "Am I to be content with that snippet of intelligence: 'Sir George likes me'?"

Sarah blushed again: "What more?"

"Do you *love* him? You goose!"

"I like him."

"What in particular? His frank and open way with money, for instance?"

Sarah actually laughed. "He's told me all about that. I think it's so generous of you to let him stay on here."

Nora's heart missed a beat—and the next beat was a huge thump that shook her whole body—and the bed. "All?" she asked guardedly.

"Well, it was only ten thousand pounds. Or . . . oh, I know one shouldn't say *only* ten thousand pounds. But he has learned his lesson. And when we've repaid you and bought back Maran Hill, we shall live ever so quietly. He's promised that. We shall have to live quietly, because all my money will be gone."

To Nora it was the final blow. After she and John had done so much to guard against the enemy without, the fatal wound was to come from the friend within.

It was not fair. Of all the things they could have foreseen and prevented how could they possibly have foreseen this? Yet now it had happened it looked so inevitable—so predictable, even, given the different natures of Sarah and Sir George.

And why oh why had she asked Sarah to come? It had been the merest afterthought. Anything could have intervened—any distraction. Winifred with a dead bird, Mrs. Jordan wanting her daily orders, even a fit of coughing—if any of these had happened at the right moment, she would never have invited Sarah on this visit.

"What did he say when you accepted his proposal?" Nora asked. She might as well put a date to disaster.

"Oh, I've not told him yet. I'll tell him tomorrow. Or the day after. Soon anyway."

It gave Nora the only hope she had. "Sarah," she said. "I think the very least you can do is not to rush into it."

Sarah drew breath, already shaking her head, smiling radiantly.

"Please listen," Nora went on. "The least you can do is talk to John. After all he is a sort of unofficial guardian to you—a trustee of your fortune. And he was a very good friend to Tom. He would be most . . ."

She stopped as soon as she saw the effect of her words. By chance (chance again!) she had chosen the one thing that would reach, spin-

ning down through all that froth of excited sentiment, right down to
the very core of Sarah's being: the memory of Tom.

She did not let the moment slip. "You didn't say you loved Sir
George," she said.

Sarah did not look up. "I will never love any other man." Now all
the fighting exuberance had gone. "I know that. I'm not such a fool as
to look for love again."

"What then? Liking? Is Sir George really the most *likeable?*"

Sarah looked trapped. "I thought *you* would understand."

"Understand what?"

"I *need* someone. I can't go on being alone." She turned bright
pink. "You must know what I mean."

Now Nora, too, was embarrassed. "I think it's essential you should
talk to John," she said.

"I can't tell him that!"

"I don't think you'll need to."

"Don't *you* tell him!" She was even more alarmed.

"Of course I won't. But there's no man with more understanding—
and you'll find no truer friend."

"I know." She sighed. "You are quite right, of course. Poor George,
he will be so disappointed! How can I face him?"

"You won't have to for long," Nora assured her, and she went on
to explain her idea of hunting all the way home. "Sir George called it
a 'ripping idea,' and he must know I need a chaperone—so he can
hardly object if I take you, since it was I who brought you!"

Chapter 26

When they left the following day, the eastern end of the park had
already begun to fill with tattered bivouacs and shelters of thorn and
tarpaulin. Around and among them lounged villainous men with pocked
faces and broken teeth. There was a handful of verminous women, too,
and even a few sickly children. Rubbish already littered the park and
highway. Mangy cats, and dogs with lice, nosed and fought among it.
Half the people there were drunk; the rest were well on the way. Fires
were lighted everywhere against the cold, and bands of ruffians were

bursting out of the Panshanger woods carrying ripped-off branches and uprooted saplings.

As their carriage went by, Nora smiling, Sarah aghast, Flynn came riding over.

He gave a huge wink. "Sure we'll just let them wet their whistles a bit longer, then we'll start winning this gravel."

"Then we'll start *winning*," Nora said, like a correction. "You can control them?"

"Like the tap on a beer keg." Flynn laughed.

"I'll write and tell you when to stop. Remember—you take your orders from no one but me."

Flynn gave a jaunty military salute and withdrew.

Even Sarah was smiling. "I've never seen you like this, Nora. What is it?" she asked.

"I'm going to do what I haven't done in five years: *please myself.* I think if the world was to end in three weeks, I'd do no different."

She meant it too. Her words were no mere bravado. She was going to live every minute of the next three weeks like a hedonist. No thought of the future, whether it was to be spent in jail or exile or even in restored fortune—no thought of it was to mar those living moments as they were given to her.

It was infectious, of course. Sarah caught it first, being nearest, and she soon forgot to mope for her disconsolate Sir George (who had seen them off with very ill grace). And Mr. Hollingworth Magniac, Master of the Oakley, caught it the moment he read Nora's letter of introduction.

And Nora hunted like a mad Irishman—and in the hunting field none are madder. If a gate was open, she'd jump the fence beside it. If a winding lane led to where she wanted to go, she'd cross two furlongs of field to cut the corner. She fell off all four sides of all three horses. She fell into mires. She was wiped off and left hanging by branches. She half-drowned in ditches. She was dragged backwards and sideways through hedges. Yet when it came to a hulloa and a gallop and a death, she was on terms to the end. She leaped the most fearsome raspers of hedges, where even cavalry ensigns—even Irish cavalry ensigns—turned aside. It was the sort of exhibition she usually despised, but she knew that nothing less would serve her purpose.

The Oakley gave her the brush of the only fox they broke up that day. The Pytchley, under Mr. George Payne, gave her two brushes— and three rousing cheers, for she enjoyed the first day's hunting with them so much she stayed for a second.

And then word began to spread of this dashing, spirited young Yorkshirewoman who was hunting her way home. Lord Fitzwilliam gave an impromptu ball for her at Milton Park and she danced until dawn. Ninety minutes later they were all back in the saddle and drawing their first covert as if the season had just begun.

Sir Richard Sutton said it was the biggest meet the Cottesmore had seen that year. Everyone wanted to see her, shake her hand, watch her fly—or fall.

Invitations arrived from hunts that were off her direct route home—the Quorn, Earl Ferrers, the Meynell . . . even from the Bedale, well to the north of her destination. She took in as many as she could. Only Lord Middleton's, which hunted all around Thorpe and which had turned her down, remained silent—the one hunt, above all others, that she longed to join.

From Lord Galway's hunt the Master, Mr. Richard Lumley, came with an escort of riders to flank her carriage up the Great North Road to Retford. Four days she hunted with them.

Lord Hawke, Master of the Badsworth (her final hunt before her own York and Ainsty), held a presentation dinner with silver-edged invitations and programmes; the presentation was an illuminated map showing her erratic journey through the hunting countries of eastern England. Each of the hunt masters had signed their portion of the map, and each hunt had sent a brush—even those that had broken up no fox while she was in their country. She could hardly thank them for the tears in her eyes.

But best of all was the letter awaiting her at York from Lord Wyatt. "You have won your wager," he wrote. "I do not grudge you your victory. To the contrary: I salute you. As evidence I return the deeds of Framwell, which Beador mortgaged to me. They are now free of any charge upon them. The deeds to the farms will follow in some six weeks."

Framwell was Beador's estate near Stockton.

Wrapped in the folds of the letter was a draft, to *her*, for a hundred thousand pounds.

She was ungrateful enough to regret that the excitement was over—and that she must learn again to be the sort of woman who would find that sort of regret childish and irresponsible.

Chapter 27

When the train drew into York station, bringing John back from his exile, it was not Nora but Sarah who waited to greet him on the platform.

He gave her a brotherly kiss and said, "What's up then?"

Sarah smiled. "I did not understand it either until we arrived here. I felt I would be excessively *de trop*. But, of course, Nora cannot waste a visit to York, and as Mr. Hudson is in the city . . ."

"Ah! Say no more! And we are to wait for her?"

They climbed into the carriage, which was standing outside the Railway Office. An urchin was holding the horses.

"We sent Willet to collect some dress lengths and other things," Sarah explained. "I hope he hurries. It'll soon be dark."

They sat facing each other in the gloom of the carriage while the cold January twilight deepened around them. John stifled a yawn and apologized.

"You must have had a hard month of it," she said.

"It's the irregularity, not the hardness."

"But it must be a great comfort to know that Nora is looking after her end of things. It's a perfect arrangement."

John agreed.

"Even now. When she knows you are in York, after nearly four weeks away. Even so—she is busy at your interests."

He chuckled and tapped the window lightly, three knocks. "What's in thy mind, lass?"

She leaned forward into the fading light and looked at him intently. "I shall never understand people, John."

"Well, which of us ever does? Given a long life, we may come to understand one or two well enough. And learn a trick or ten for coping with t'others—or keeping out their way. What's the particular puzzle?"

She shook her head and retired again into the dark. "Do you think I should accept Sir George Beador's proposal?"

"You needn't worry about Beador," he said. "We're not throwing him out. He can stay on as a sort of pensioner up at Framwell."

"I feel so sorry for him, though."

"That's no substitute for love. In your letter you made it quite clear it would be no love match."

"Love!" she said, almost with mockery. "I came to it so strangely with Tom. Now I think it an accident—intended for some other."

When she added no more he asked: "What do you mean? Came to it so strangely?"

He could not see her face now. She became a voice speaking out from the shadows. "My mother and father were like two cordial strangers sharing an abode for convenience. I believe he overcame his aversion for—for anything—stronger—long enough to beget me. And after that —never again. I wonder now how my mother felt about that. Though she seemed content enough always. And then when he died and she followed him so soon, you see, I was at once cut off from all example of domestic life between the sexes. All I had ever known was that very dull —at least, now I call it dull, *then* it seemed secure and eternal—but life at the vicarage was dull."

"And you went straight from that to the Church Commissioners' girls' orphanage? That was even less preparation."

"Well . . ." she said doubtfully.

He waited.

"I did not tell you all," she said. Her voice was trembling; he could hear the fear in her pushing it from her control.

"Nor do you need to," he said.

"I do. I do." She was past stopping. But as she spoke, the fear seemed to lift from her. The effort had been to start. "May I tell you something, John? I never thought I would tell anyone. I never told Tom. But since he is dead the thought of it keeps coming back."

"If you are sure of never regretting it."

"I'm sure of that. With you it will be safe."

"I don't mean that. I mean it might be better to talk with a complete outsider." Her exasperation cut him short. "Or a woman—Nora? Have you told her?"

She thought hard before she answered. "It's a man's view I need. That's what I don't know."

"Very well. I hope I'm the right person."

She breathed in, steeling herself again. "You and Nora sometimes mention a Reverend Doctor Prendergast, now bishop in Manchester I think."

John sat upright suddenly, startled out of his role of passive sympathizer. "Go on."

She hesitated again. "You will remember that although I was born a vicar's daughter, I have seen quite a different level of life since then. You will not be shocked if I speak of—things a vicar's daughter—"

"That is not the fear," he warned again. "The fear is that, however I respond, you will regret speaking of it at all. What of Prendergast?"

"When I first heard you mention him to Nora, last autumn"—she laughed—"I was so startled! I thought—now you will be ashamed of me—I thought, I suspected . . ." She faltered.

"You suspected that from the little you told me that morning at Coutances I had made investigations and found out something."

She was astounded. "How do you know that! I'm ashamed to have suspected you."

"But why? It would be very human. Tell me about Prendergast. Is it the same man?"

"It must be. He knew my father, I think. Or so he claimed. He came to the orphanage just after I went in there, and they let him take me out to tea. Of course, they would." There was quite a silence before she continued. "He offered to take me away from there. I thought he meant to adopt me, because that's what it sounded like." She giggled nervously. "I was only sixteen then."

"Oh, dear," John said. "You really want to go on?"

"If you'd rather not . . ."

"I can imagine the rest, knowing Prendergast."

She laughed then, harshly. "Oh, you can not! I mean he told me. He made it very clear. He told me *exactly*. Every detail, every step, every . . . move. Everything. And he spoke so—ooh! So drily. Like a—geometry book. No—a dancing master. I don't know what he was like."

"How terrible for you."

"But it *wasn't*. Because, you see, I had no idea what he was talking about. I thought he was—*strange*, of course. But you know how children accept almost anything that grownups tell them. And especially a dignified old clergyman like that. It seemed no more silly than—deportment classes or—physical exercises."

A flesh-curdling thought began to seize John. "And—did you . . . ?" He could not voice it.

She laughed. "I would have. Truly, I was so ignorant, I would have. But he told me to think upon it and he would come back for an answer." She sighed the relief he felt. "He never came. I never saw him again. Do you know," she said in a brisker tone, "I believe he never intended to come back. I think his pleasure was merely to talk about it in that calm way to a completely ignorant young girl. I even think I was not the first. Nor the last."

He thought that was very perceptive of her. "Poor old gentleman," he said.

"Yes. That's all I feel about him now. But when I ran away from the orphanage, I was so nearly trapped again. In London that was. And in a place that would have made Prendergast's—arrangement—seem almost pure."

He stifled the urge to tell her again that he could imagine it—though, of course, he could. She was too intent upon confession.

"The first man they—let into the room—well, I have often wondered about him. I cannot remember him at all, whether he was young or old or fat or thin or short or tall or anything. I must have been partly stupefied by something they gave me. I remember the madam, though—a hard, pretty woman, still quite young. I'll tell you who she was like—Madame Corneille. Just like her."

"I picture her exactly!"

"Anyway, this man. I imagine he had dreamed of doing what he came to do for years before he tightened up his courage."

"You knew by this time? You understood?"

"Half. I had seen things in that place and heard the girls talking. But this man, when the moment arrived, I think it must all have—evaporated for him. And he saw himself left with a ridiculous, dead feeling, and a half-drugged, frightened, tearful, disgusted young girl. That's what I imagine. D'you know what he did to me? He combed my hair! For almost an hour that's all he did. Until I could talk sensibly. Then he asked me if I wanted to go from that place. And I thought he meant with him. I thought it was Prendergast again—the same offer. But, anyway, I said yes, because I thought I could escape from him easier than from madam. So he made me pretend I was in a dead faint. I had to chew soap to froth and so on. Then he ran out in a panic and said he was a doctor and thought I was dying. And she was so terrified she let him take me to—he said—the women's hospital. Or perhaps she thought she could always pretend to be a relative and come and claim me from the hospital. Anyway, the miracle worked."

"It *was* a miracle."

"It's like a moral ballad, isn't it! The man took me straight to the Tabard. I don't know what tale he told Tom—certainly not the true one. But there I stayed. First as scullery maid, then—when he found I was a vicar's daughter—Tom put me upstairs. Why can't I remember that man's face!"

"Did he never come to the Tabard again?"

"He may have. And I wouldn't have recognized him, you see. For a long time I thought of him as 'my saviour' and even—though it was blasphemy—as my Saviour. You know?"

"That wouldn't be blasphemy. To rescue girls in that situation would be His work." Struck by a thought he looked over the street, where the gaslights were being lighted. He moved to the seat by the window on that side. "Look there," he said, pointing to where the "gay" girls of Station Road shivered, stamped their feet, and walked morosely up and down beneath the flaring gas.

She moved across and looked out too. He felt the sudden warmth of her nearness in the dark and withdrew. "How many of them lacked only the good fortune that saved you?"

She shuddered and returned to her former seat. "I often think it."

"Still. A tavern in Southwark is, many would say, only one step up from the place you were spirited from."

"But a very important step, John. A girl couldn't close her eyes and ears to it, but she could keep *herself* pure. And then I fell in love with Tom, years before he even looked at me. And that made it easy. Oh, but wasn't he a marvellous man!"

"He was. He was lucky, too, in you. You were both lucky. I ought to light the carriage lamp."

"Leave it a bit. Nora's a long time."

He wondered why she had told him all this. "A long way from George Beador," he said.

She sighed. In the light that shone feebly from over the street he saw her hands grip and rub one another. "Does it still happen to you, John, that you look back at yourself as you were six months ago and you think what an ignorant, innocent goose you were! How little of life you knew *then* and how wise you are *now!*"

And he had to confess that it was years since he had had such notions.

"It's like that all the time with me. All those years at the Tabard when I was so *prudish*. And then when I went to France with Tom last year I was still like that at first, until . . . He was so patient and gentle. And so I learned it is not *always* shameful and wicked. Does that sound brazen?"

"Of course not." He sat tensely, guarding himself for one false word or gesture that might dry her up.

"Remember, we were not married. Yet even in the depths of my soul, even when I faced God in church and took His Body and Blood at communion, I could feel no shame."

He almost told her that he had once lived for a year with a girl he had married navvy-style, over the anvil, and had got her with child before she ran away from him. But caution checked him before he began to speak.

"You still aren't shocked?" she asked.

"Not at all. That kind of shock is really a sort of timidity."

"I remember how it was to lie with Tom. And I still feel no shame. Those uxorial memories are very strong. Are they equally strong in everyone? We can never gauge that, can we?"

"Do you really think marrying Beador would help?"

"I would have no other reason for marrying him."

"But do you really want to marry him?"

A man was walking past the girls across the street, looking at and talking to them in turn; then he went off with one of them. Sarah drew an enormous breath, let it out, and said: "If you really ask me, I want it to be as easy for me as for that man over there. I will never fall in love again. So what am I to do with—those feelings? You call them uxorial, but we both know what they are. Now I'm sure you are shocked."

He knew exactly what she was offering him then; and he was fairly certain that she knew, too. The moment was exciting and he wanted to prolong it—to think of himself as capable of taking up such an offer— though he knew that in the end he would have to decline it. The conventional response: If only there was some way *I* could help . . . rose to his throat and was half uttered before he realized its implication. He changed it to: "If only there was some way I could . . . illustrate it for you. What you say is not unnatural, not shocking, not even uncommon. The same longings overtake me when I am away from Nora for weeks. So how could I be shocked or surprised? And a few nights ago, in London, I did what that man over there just did."

"Oh, John! I didn't mean *you* to—"

"Wait! Listen to the whole story. I actually went with this girl to a little hotel. But just before we got there I realized how—*tawdry* it was going to be. Unlovely and tawdry." He laughed. "My one thought then was how not to hurt her feelings."

The lamplighter came back and put on the lamps along their side as John spoke.

"How like you," she said. "What did you do?"

"I had some filberts in my pocket. I bit the shell of one and gave the kernel to her, and then bit another and pretended it had broken one of my teeth and I was in too much pain." The incident had actually happened two years ago but to say so would have diluted the force of the tale. "Suppose you suddenly had that feeling—*tawdry*—while you were walking up the aisle with George Beador. Or, even worse, afterward! Toothache would offer no escape."

She nodded glumly. It was cold comfort, all right. To change the mood he returned to the seat opposite her and, daringly, reached a hand across and squeezed her knee. And daringly he grinned a wicked grin as he said: "Find a discreet lover. You'd not be the first young widow to do such a thing."

"John!" She kicked him in mock outrage.

And that was the moment Nora chose to open the carriage door.

Chapter 28

Nora had been prepared for almost any response from John, except the one she got—or thought she had got. She knew it would wound his dignity that he had been forced to skulk abroad while she had saved the firm—never mind that she had done so in the most unbusinesslike and outrageous manner. She had prepared so many ways of telling him how accidental it had been, how only the thought that he was safe in France had made her bold enough. She even thought up ways in which —had he been at home—he might have managed the rescue more easily and with far greater certainty. Even more, she had been quite ready to apologize for the public exhibition she had made of herself, and to ask his forgiveness.

So to catch him taking advantage of Sarah's desperation like that shocked her far too deeply to allow her to tax him with it directly. It was not that she lacked sympathy for Sarah; she had made that plain in her letter to John. She knew, from John's frequent and long absences, what it was to yearn to lie entangled with a man again. She knew how unendurable the lack of that fulfilment, and the lack of any prospect of it, must seem to poor Sarah. But the last thing she had expected was that John would take advantage of it, especially after so long an absence from her, and even more especially after the crisis they had endured and survived together these months past.

She did not blame Sarah in the least. Had she not heard Sarah's cry of outrage the moment before she opened the carriage door and caught John in that position?

She had passed it off at the time, saying, "That's right, Sarah! Keep him in his place!" Which was not the welcome she had prepared and longed to give.

And even when they reached home and she and John were at last alone together, she could not forgo the homecoming she had dreamed of for so many weeks. So she continued to make light of what had happened in York.

"Couldn't wait, eh?" she asked, grinning as she began to undo his shirt buttons.

His bewilderment looked very genuine.

"Our Sarah's proving a bit of a hot lot," she went on, thinking that to blame Sarah might ease his guilt. "A bit of a Fulham virgin, eh?"

"She will be, unless she finds . . . well, someone."

Nora eased his shirt off and began on her own dress and stays. He watched her, frank in his longing. "For God's sake," he said. "Who are we talking about!"

She grinned. Her eyes gleamed in the candlelight. "Mistress Sarah," she whispered.

She kissed him. Only their lips were yet in contact.

His hands went to the buttons of her dress. Lifting his lips a thousandth of an inch from hers, he said, "Forgotten her."

He felt the blood hammering at the pit of her neck, and among the tendons at the back of his skull. "No sleep tonight," he said at the corner of his lips.

She undid his trousers and let them fall. "You dare try!" she said.

A month of unslaked lust bound them, racing their hearts and shivering their breath. Sarah was truly forgotten. When Nora's dress fell to her knees he pulled her swiftly to him, trying to lift her off the ground. But she turned a little to one side. "Don't be hasty now. Savour it." And she turned for him to unlace her corset. And she went on turning, pressed to him, after she stepped from its loosened clutch.

Her slim, nude body, warm in the candlelight, warm by the fire, turning and turning, now this way, now that, against him . . . the curve of her back . . . the firmness of her hips . . . her soft breasts . . . the grace of her neck and the beauty of her, and of her face, and the dark, desperate eyes, begging now, and entranced—these were the images of her he had only half captured in his years of days away from this house.

"Nora!" It was hardly his own voice.

He fell to his knees and buried his face upon her belly, his tongue into her navel. "Oh, love!" Her voice shivered down through the magic air around them; her fingernails were a cap of spikes upon his head. His tongue and lips and breathing rose up her body to her breasts, her neck, her shoulders, her ears, her stifling hair. And his grip tightened as he rose, bearing her aloft, and then, with infinite gentleness, lowering her, lowering, lowering, upon him.

As the cry of her throat tore the air, and the warmth of her closed around him, not death itself could have held him back. Then she fell upon him, leaning out and abandoning herself to his grip, throwing both legs up until she was rammed to the hilt of him, and feeling that marvellous pulse as he squandered his month of continence into her, spending on and on.

When the crackle of the flames, the creak of the floorboard, and the weight of their bodies returned, he lowered her to the carpet before the fire and sat himself beside her, leaning so that his face was only inches above hers. His eyes smiled; hers responded. "I can face anything if *you*'re with me," he said.

She closed her eyes then. "Nothing could take you from me, or put aught between us."

Neither of them had said anything like that to the other for years. Or needed to.

He still had said nothing directly about her rescue of their fortune. He had written, of course—quite warmly. But he had said nothing, and his silence was beginning to hurt her.

                              *   *   *

In the small hours he awoke, feeling ravenous; he slipped quietly from the bed, trying not to awaken her, and tiptoed from the room.

He's hungry, she thought. It could hardly be . . . well, anything else. He often felt hungry when they had made such magnificent love. He often stole down to the kitchen when he felt like that. *Of course he's hungry.*

But for the first time in their life together she rose, slipped on a dressing gown, and went down to join him.

The kitchen clock whirred and struck three—that is, its hammer flailed the air three times, having been bent by Mrs. Jordan, the cook, so that it would fail to strike the chimes. The sound of chimes, she said, made the air stifling.

John was not there, but the light of her candle showed the signs of his visit: the cut pie, the crumbs on the table, the pickle barrel and the sticky wooden ladle beside it.

On her way up the west stair, which led, it so happened, past Sarah's rooms, she saw a light in the business room across the courtyard in the east wing. She took no pains to be silent as she turned back and went that way. She did not want to catch them unawares again.

He was alone—or as alone as the owner of a large enterprise can be when he has a case full of unanswered letters, of contracts awaiting perusal or signature, of complaints, of surveys, of claims, of excuses and explanations, of alarms and false alarms.

He grinned apologetically when he saw her. "Eay love, did I waken thee? I tried being quiet."

Ashamed now of her suspicions, she could only smile shyly.

He was eating the last of the pie with gusto. He pointed at the pile of documents spread before him. "I think we've accidentally hit on one of the cardinal principles of business," he said. "Look!" He passed her a letter. "Tucker to me; Exeter, 28 December: Come at once, the world's falling apart. In eight pages." He gave her another letter. "Tucker again; Exeter, 4 January: Come if you can but it's not so bad as it seemed." Another. "Tucker; 9 January: Ignore all previous letters. All is well." He laughed.

"What's this cardinal principle?" she asked.

"In difficult times the chief's job is to vanish. There's half a dozen similar cases there." He waved his hand over the correspondence. "Half a dozen cries for help that would have had me losing sleep and tearing out my hair. All solved."

His tone was self-dismissive, but to her he seemed, obliquely, to be minimizing all that she had done. "Perhaps I should have joined you," she said.

He winked. "It's only because you stayed—and did what you did— that I can make light of it." He reached out and took her hand.

Suddenly she felt herself close to tears.

"I can't go on and on telling you," he said. "But you *know* it. I owe everything to you now."

The tears came then. She could not stop them. But she did not want to withdraw behind them; feeling every inch a fool she kept her eyes on his, as well as she could, and smiled.

"Thou great softie!" he said, delighted; and he wiped her cheeks with the kerchief on which he had cleaned his fingers after eating the pie. She could smell the pork fat and pastry on her skin.

"Anyway," he said, "the future's not holding back. Look at this." And he passed her the list he had been looking at when she entered.

It was in his own hand and read:

February: Canterbury–Ashford (South Eastern)	14½ miles
March: Worthing–Littlehampton (London & Brighton)	7½
April: Canterbury–Ramsgate (South Eastern)	15¾
May–June: Exeter–Teignmouth (South Devon)	15
Middlesborough–Redcar (M&R)	7½
June: Berwick–Edinburgh (North British)	57½
June–July: Leeds–Bradford plus Hunslet Junction (L&B)	14¾
August(?): Dublin–Carlow (GS&W)	56½
September: Syston–Melton Mowbray (Midland)	10¼
Clifton–Bury–Rawtenstall (E. Lancs)	14
October(?): Hull–Bridlington (York & N. Midland)	31

"These will put up the value of my land," she said.

And then it struck her: *She had no land!* The moment embarrassed them both to silence.

"Or the bit of land where I was born," she added lamely.

He did not look directly at her. "You realize there's the best part of four million pounds in those contracts—most of it still to be paid to us."

"We'll certainly need it," she said.

There was an odd, plaintive note in his voice.

"Perhaps we'd have been all right anyway," he added. Again there was that note—defensive and hesitant.

"Of course, darling!" She took his hand in both of hers. "Of course we would have! All I did was . . ." she thought hurriedly ". . . I merely made it possible for you to come back to me the sooner."

Let him believe it if it helped. He must know it was not true. He must know it was not *how much* they earned that was important—not when they were insolvent—it was *when* they earned it that counted. Still, if it helped to restore his own estimation of himself, let him think otherwise.

With a contented smile he fished deep among his papers, using his free hand. "You can have this now," he said. "It really won't bite."

It was her power of attorney.

She could not stifle a slight truculence as she took it. "And what may I practise on?" she asked.

Now he looked at her steadily. "I'd like to treat the money you won from Wyatt as a loan to the firm," he said. "As all this money comes in"—he pointed to his list of contracts due for completion—"you could progressively withdraw that money and . . . er, 'practise' with it."

She had actually thought of asking for no less than John now proposed; so why did it feel like a slap in the face? John was going to make his comforting fiction—that she had not *really* saved the firm, merely secured it a little earlier than the normal contracts would have saved it anyway—he was going to make it true, by (in effect) doctoring the books. In six months her winnings, which *had* saved the firm, would have degenerated into a mere loan. That is what the books would show: "Per loan to Mrs. J. Stevenson—£100,000." In red ink.

She realized that she had some confusions of her own that needed sorting out. Now that the single overriding goal had been removed from their lives, what did each of them really want? How close were they really, in matters other than their mutual love? Worst of all, would their money once more drive them into a tolerant and easy separation?

He broke into these thoughts with a forgotten piece of news. "It's your brother Daniel," he began.

"I know," she told him. "Sam wrote to me. He's to be pardoned."

"He's *been* pardoned. I've heard he's already back in England." He could not read her face. "What'll you do, love?" he prompted.

"If Daniel knocked on that door now, dying with the cold, I'd not so much as cross the room."

The intensity of her hate made him quail. "By God!" he said. "I hope I may never make an enemy of thee!"

* * *

That morning at breakfast—a rather late breakfast—a messenger came with a letter from Lord Wyatt. He was staying a few miles away, with the Earl of Carlisle at Castle Howard, and he would be hunting that day with the Lord Middleton's. Perhaps, he suggested, she could arrange to go out riding and for her path to cross his? He would have a further communication for her then.

"He's going to humiliate you," John warned. "Why else does he want you and the hunt to cross paths? *That* hunt in particular."

She agreed it was possible but was too intrigued by the note of challenge in the invitation to stay at home. "They're hunting Burythorpe way today," she said—Nora, who claimed to take not the slightest interest in anything the Lord Middleton's did! "We could at least ride that way and see what's what."

"As long as we're back in time for Livings' visit," John said.

Livings was their architect for the iron foundry at Stockton, which John now had ideas of enlarging.

*   *   *

That afternoon they both went riding out along the ridge of the wold toward Burythorpe. John was on Hermes; Nora was trying out a new three-year-old she had just bought—a dun-coloured filly with white stockings, a little undersized but very sturdy and, the dealer said, "a double-tit of great stamina." She had been ridiculously cheap because of a few slight zebra markings.

Some early rain had completely cleared and the higher parts of the road had even started to dry by the time they set off. They rode almost due north, making for Birdsall Brow and facing into a gusty north-westerly breeze. Patches of sun and shade of varying density swept toward them over the fields and hedges. The treetops thrashed violently in a wind that seemed to spend its force before it touched the ground.

"That'll shake out the cobwebs," Nora said, drawing in great lungs-ful of the breeze, until she shivered.

"Let's canter," he said.

And for more than a mile they threaded their way around the stand-ing pools that reached from the verges out into the drying roadway. Hermes cantered slowly but Tessa, Nora's filly, was close to a gallop. Yet when they returned to the trot, Hermes was the more winded of the two.

"You've not hunted him much," John said. "You could at least let the lad take him down and back, even if you don't use him."

"Aye," she said. "I think I will."

At the edge of the brow they turned eastward along the bridle path to Burdale. Almost at once they heard the music of the hunt—the pack and the leaders, running crosswind a furlong or so downhill from the path. Both their horses became restive at once.

"We'd better pull aside," John said. "We can wait for them here on the highway."

Nora squared her shoulders. "I don't see why. We've as much right to ride as they have." And she rode on down the path into the teeth of the arrogant crowd who had blackballed John's and her application for membership.

She pretended a greater surprise than she felt that the leader of those upon the bridle path was Lord Wyatt. He was smiling but with such grimness that she began to regret her rash decision to come. If he were going to humiliate her, he could not have picked a better opportunity. The whole "quality" of the East Riding was behind him.

"Mrs. Stevenson!" he called, with a surprise to match her own. He halted, forcing the rest of the field to bunch up behind him, a captive audience to all they said. "How very well met!"

"Lord Wyatt! How good of you to say so. May I present Mr. Stevenson."

The two men nodded warily at each other.

"Yes," Wyatt went on. "I rode out today of a purpose to meet you. England's foremost huntswoman, what!" He was oblivious of the sounds of well-bred impatience arising from behind. "But they tell me you don't hunt with them."

"That's very true," Nora said. "Ain't it odd! I may hunt with my lords Fitzwilliam and Forester and Hawke, but here in the East Riding they still have standards to maintain."

She heard John draw a sharp breath beside her but she spoke with a bright-eyed defiance, not to Lord Wyatt but at the crowd behind him, noting with pleasure their discomfiture and annoyance. Both reactions intensified when Lord Wyatt looked around, surveying what was to him a motley collection of petty gentry, squires, and baronets.

"Extraordinary!" he said and turned back to her. Then he produced a letter from his tunic. "We have our standards, too, what! From my cousin Meredith. Handsome enough, I hope."

She took it, smiling, and thanked him.

"Jove!" he said. "What a ride you had, eh? What ever put such an idea into your head?"

"I had a sort of wager," she said simply, amused at the alarm that now crept into his face. "A private wager with myself, you understand—that it would turn hostility into friendship."

Her look included the rest of the field.

Wyatt laughed then. "Ye didn't lose," he said to her. "Ye didn't fail. I *for one* will swear to that!" He spurred onward a good few yards before he turned and shouted back over his shoulder: "You're always welcome with the Puckeridge at least!"

Like royalty on a saluting base they watched the rest of the field troop past; not an eye met theirs.

"Now wasn't that kindness itself," Nora said.

John at last breathed out his relief. "You do take chances," he said.

"Oh no, love. As long as we are sitting on God knows how many million cubic yards of best gravel at Maran Hill, I think we shall have a very kindly and attentive neighbour in Lord Wyatt."

Chapter 29

Bernard Livings, architect, with an academy diploma to back the claim, was an ambitious, easygoing, round-faced, sharp-nosed, curly-haired, straight-bearded young thirty-eight-year-old. He was a devout Methodist, a devoted husband and father, and—though John would not believe it —an ardent womanizer.

"You don't understand the word," John would say. "Thornton's a womanizer. This man Livings is altogether different."

"It's you that doesn't understand," she told him. "Thornton's no womanizer. His interest begins eight inches north of the knee; go twenty inches higher and he's already starting to yawn. Faces and names mean naught there. He'll take it any place, any time, free, bought, or bribed. But Livings wants everything—except the details between calling the banns and cutting the wedding cake; he'll forgo them."

John could not really grasp the distinction.

Later, in the business room, with the site maps spread out before them, John explained his new ideas. They would use more land, beyond the first twenty acres, on both sides of the little Billingham Beck. On one side—the side of the twenty acres—they would build the mill, with its attendant wharfs and railways. On the other side they would lay out a little town, using the river as a division. It was to have a small park, with a stand where a German band could play, a church and dissenting chapels, a hospital and dispensary, a school, an evening institute and library, a gasworks, waterworks, and a sewage outfall works. Also almshouses. The gasworks and waterworks would, of course, serve the mill as well. There would be no public houses, but markets and shops would all be in the plan.

As he spoke he deliberately failed to notice Nora's increasing bewilderment and anxiety, until he thought she would burst. Then he turned to her. "We'll not *build* it all at once, but we'll allow space for it. We'll plan it, d'ye see. We'll not be building any more than we intended for this year—well, a house or two more, maybe, but nothing beyond. But we'll be building it in such a way as lets us add without making a pig's breakfast of it. If"—he remembered the architect— "Livings here says it may be done."

Livings, who had come to Thorpe expecting a host of small, annoying revisions, could not believe his luck. But, being a thorough architect, his first instinct was to find an objection to his client's scheme. "It's a splendid idea, sir," he said. "Truly magnificent. The town presents no insuperable difficulty. But"—sigh—"your manufactory. Now that will be a problem. How big might it finally be?"

"Let's say it will cover all twenty acres. It occurred to me that you might plan it as one great central shed with bays let off it on each side. D'ye see? Like a spider. The original works can be one of those bays. A spider's leg. What d'you think?"

He nodded, and his eyes said it was feasible; but his voice said: "It isn't necessarily that easy. The proportions . . ." he began vaguely, and then thought of a better line. "The bays would impede each other's light."

"We want twenty foot between them, for two rail roads. And the overshadowing would matter less if the roof were made of glass."

"Glass!" Nora and Livings exclaimed together.

"Yes." He was amused. "We make a simple flat triangular truss of iron, like a railway station roof, and we glaze it direct. I was looking at Euston the other day and thinking how much lighter it would be if they had glass instead of that wood and flashing. *But*"—he gripped Livings' arm—"these are just crude ideas for you to work on. It's to be *your* design. I want that firmly understood." He smiled. "If you still want to, of course."

The client's coup de grace.

"Indeed. Indeed!" Livings said. "I welcome the challenge, sir. But in the space of a single weekend—I fear—"

"No, no, no, no," John assured him. "This weekend I want you to design three grades of house—for a labourer, for a mechanic, and for an overseer. I want each unit costed before we even start to plan the town."

Nora was relieved at this return of monetary caution; it supplied the motif she had missed in all the previous talk.

"What's this new town to be called?" Nora asked.

"We had a competition for a name in the London office last week. Chambers suggested Learlington, as an anagram of Nora Telling. One of the clerks thought of Middleton, since it's midway between Middlesborough and Stockton. But I won the prize."

"What was your suggestion?"

"Stevenstown. People will find that much easier to remember."

*   *   *

Livings took a bare two hours' sleep that night. By the following morning he had rough-planned all three houses and produced elegant little water colours to show their appearance. "Theme and variations," he said proudly.

It was certainly most elegant. For the labourers he had produced, on a twenty-seven by twenty-four-foot ground plan, a unit containing a lobby, living room, scullery, indoor w.c., and one large and two small bedrooms. These units were grouped in blocks of four, two down and two up, with a central entranceway. And each four-unit block stood on a quarter-acre plot, allowing each family a seventy-five-by-thirty-foot vegetable patch.

The mechanics had basically the same but with an extra hundred-square-foot room at the back.

The overseers had exactly twice the labourers' allowance, having both the upstairs unit and the one downstairs. Their gardens, too, were twice as big as the labourers'.

"You see," Livings said, "they all have part of what is basically the same building. Labourers get a quarter-building; overseers have a half-building; mechanics get a quarter building with an extra room. It's easy to convert any one to any other. For instance, if that's an overseer's house and you extend the town and want to turn it into two labourers' houses, all you do is add a w.c. upstairs, change the stair entry, and remove the coloured-tile decoration from the balcony and cornice."

They were very impressed. John could see some trivial improvements but deferred any mention of them. "Any idea of cost?" he asked.

"About five hundred and sixty pounds per building. That includes builder's profit of fifty. For each labourer's unit it comes to one hundred and fifty with the land."

John rolled his eyes as he did a rough calculation. "Two shillings a week rent. It sounds marvellous."

"Wait wait wait," Nora called. "Sewerage? Water? Repairs? Insurance? Share of civic provisions? Roads?" John drew breath to speak, but she continued: "It's no answer to say the company will bear part of the cost. We've got to know the *size* of the millstone before we hang it around someone's neck."

"It's a good point. I'm convinced."

"It's your visiting manufacturer you have to convince. If you can tell him the whole town pays for itself, that's far more impressive than—"

"I agree. I've said it. Just work it out."

Livings' head went left, right, left, right.

Ten minutes later Nora said: "With two thousand dwellings, the weekly rent would be four shillings for a labourer, four and tenpence for a mechanic, and eight shillings for an overseer."

"Still *very* cheap," Livings said. "What are you allowing on the civic side?"

Nora looked back at her figures. "Roads, park, dispensary, institute, and so on—a hundred and twenty thousand pounds; repairs and upkeep, recurring, four thousand . . ." and so on through all the elements that make for the running of a town, ending with the caution that it was "all very round-figurey."

"It sounds of the right order," John said. "I can't believe the rents are so low."

Nora checked a sample of them again. "Well, they are," she confirmed. She was feeling quite excited now. On her properties she usually thought only of leasehold for the most superior housing, as at Alderley Edge, where the houses had between one and five acres each. She wondered that she had never done the calculations for renting humbler and more close-packed estates. Of course, there was the cost of building and repairing, the cost of collecting rents, bad debts, quick turnover of tenancies, property empty. No, it was not for her. Not yet, anyway.

"How much more would it be," John asked, "if you added a modest profit to us on those outlays?"

Nora smiled sweetly. "It never occurred to me not to do that in the first place," she said. "Three per cent. Already in."

Later he teased her for her character-reading ability. "That man's no lecher," he said of Livings.

"You've found the cure," she said. "Fame and a fat fee."

Chapter 30

Flynn's great progress with the GS&W line astonished even John, who already had the highest opinion of the man. It was not merely that he had the work done quickly but he had done it *thinkingly*. For instance, there was a shortage of surveyors in Ireland at that time; the perennial shortage of all skilled artisans and middle-class professionals had been made worse by the demand for public works to relieve the distress following the potato disease. Trevelyan at the Treasury insisted that every scheme should be properly surveyed and costed, and be personally authorized by him in London, before work began. So surveyors were in great demand all over the country.

Flynn had overcome this shortage by holding a night school for his gangers, where he taught the simple precepts of laying down a line on the ground from a survey map. Then each ganger was taught how to range the first curve he would be working on. If it was a simple curve, he was taught the "ranging by offsets" technique, which needed no theodolite. If it was a complex curve, starting lazy and getting tight, say, Flynn made up a set of templates, each consisting of a plank and three nails to mark the tangent and the offset sighting lines. These planks he marked A, B, C, etc., and all the man had to do was to sight along them in the proper order and he could not help getting the line right. This, in turn, freed his one surveyor to do the really difficult parts —where sight lines were obstructed, for instance—and the parts where errors would be very costly, such as embankments and cuttings.

It is true that there were one or two errors; but they were all on level ground and cost little to rectify. And it is certainly true that the surveying profession was ouraged at the "Flynn system," as it was soon called. For years afterward, whenever a line was accidentally misaligned (as happened, for instance, at Sough Tunnel on the Blackburn & Bolton in 1847), it was always said to have been "laid out on the Flynn principle." But the joke was most unfair, for the Flynn system enabled Stevenson's to lay out the line and start preparing the rail bed from a number of focal points along its path without waiting for survey engineers. By April, track laying had got beyond Lucan, over eight miles from Dublin.

John was confident enough then to leave Flynn to it and to go off himself to look at the proposed routes of the Waterford & Limerick and the Waterford & Kilkenny lines, both of which had been authorized by Parliament last year but neither of which had yet gone to tender. He was making these trips at the suggestion of Lucas, the engineer to the GS&W, who said that if the distress got much worse, the government could hardly resist appeals to include authorized railways in the list of acceptable public works.

Lucas "lent" John a guide whose name sounded very like Mac-Minimum—whose baptismal name, More, made this unusual surname even less likely. John listened hard at each introduction and heard, variously, MacMahanon, MacManamon, MacMarneymum, and—once—MacMillan; he gave up and settled once again for MacMinimum, to which the man invariably answered without so much as the lifting of an eyebrow.

MacMinimum's relationship to the GS&W remained obscure.

"Do you work for the company?" John asked, when they were set out on their journey.

"I *do* work for them," was the reply. "That is, I do *some* work. But also for others."

"For the Waterford & Limerick, for instance?"

"Oh, of course." He spoke as if he were giving elocution lessons in the Irish accent.

"And the Waterford & Kilkenny?"

"Beyond doubt."

Several minutes later he added: "But I would not like to give you the impression I have worked for either of them *yet*."

"Do you have an interest in them?" John asked, meaning, of course, a financial interest.

"Oh, I'm deeply interested in them, and always have been," he drawled. And again, long moments later, he added the qualification: "Though I want to tell you one thing—I know very little about them."

John began to wonder whether More MacMinimum was not, after all, a most apt name for this man; perhaps, indeed, he was the figment of his own name. Half an hour in his company left John feeling that nothing of that sort was impossible.

*   *   *

Most countries that have both mountains and seaboard usually have their highest points somewhere near the middle; they are built on the principle of the pitched roof. But Ireland is like four pitched roofs built around a central depression. As a result, more than three-quarters of its considerable rainfall does not easily run off to the sea. In Ireland, even in high summer they say, never bet on mirages; as you approach ever closer to those distant shimmering patches, they go on shimmering until they force you to detour around them—or get wet.

This accident of geography has created a vast central bog. It extends up and over all but the highest mountains, between whose feet all main roads and railroads must thread their way. There was thus little difficulty for the GS&W in choosing its line from Dublin to Cork. It had

to go south of the Slieve Bloom mountains, on the southern rim of the
central depression, just as it had to go north of the Ballyhoura mountains, seventy miles farther to the southwest. John had ridden this route
the previous year, before he had tendered for the contract. He felt a
superstitious, almost fatalistic reluctance to look too closely now, in
case he discovered some horror he had overlooked on that earlier
journey, for the tender was accepted and the price could not be varied.

So he was pleased enough that MacMinimum was a hard rider and
got them to Tipperary in only two days. John noticed that as they left
the rich pastures of Leinster and rode into Munster the degree of destitution worsened considerably. Even in Queen's County, in the Great
Heath of Maryborough, still technically in Leinster, they saw appalling
signs of starvation—though it moved John far more than it seemed to
move MacMinimum.

"Sure aren't they like that every year," he said.

That evening, at the Royal in Tipperary, John asked MacMinimum
if that was really so—was the distress always as bad as they had seen it
today?

He replied that he knew damn all about it but would swear it was.
They were dining at a common table, and a man sitting opposite to
them begged to differ. Ormond, he said his name was, Captain Cashel
Ormond. Not only was the distress worse, it had been aggravated by interference from Westminster. Would they wait now while he took another slice off the joint?

While he was away at the buffet, MacMinimum said quietly to
John: "For God's sake, say not a word on railways. The quare fella here
is Master of the Tipperary and they hunt all along the valley of the
Suir—the way the line is to go. Sure he'd kill ye."

John began to understand why Lucas had sent MacMinimum along
with him.

Ormond returned. First he tried, not very energetically, to find out
what John's business was. When he failed, he reverted quickly to the
subject of the distress.

"You were blaming the government?" John prompted.

"Indeed, sir. They have no notion of what monster they have
formed. If they had said *no* help would be forthcoming and *no* stock of
food had been set aside and *no* extraordinary public works would be
undertaken, they might have provided all three by stealth and so avoided
a great nuisance. But by God, when governments meddle with labour,
trade, and supply, it's time to look to your shutters and locks."

"Isn't that the truth of it, sir," MacMinimum said.

"It is. It is," Ormond confirmed. "Look at it here. Not a man gone to the English harvest, because the Board of Works had promised work in Ireland."

"Not *promised*," John corrected.

"You explain that to the countryside *here*! Wasn't there three thousand men in Tipperary last Saturday in a riot for work, outside this very building. And the Relief Committee and the Board of Works inspector upstairs—four of them go out on the balcony, and there was a silence would have lifted off your hat. And every man out there, three thousand I say, *goes down on his knees!* In the street! The Board of Works sits at God's right hand." He grinned and beckoned John conspiratorially close. "Now you know, sir, and I know, that the Board of Works comprises four clerks working in a back corridor of Dublin Castle, trying desperately to reduce a mountain of ten thousand schemes to order. And we know that when they're finished, though God knows when that will be, the schemes that survive must all be sent on to Whitehall where Trevelyan, and Trevelyan alone, will pronounce upon them. And another thing we know is that when word finally arrives back to Clonahoe or Ballyeen that they can build their road as a relief work, there'll be no one there fit to supervise it."

"Not the poor law guardians?" John asked. "Surely they are the ideal people?"

"Of course they are, but that has nothing to do with it. The law provides that they may administer *indoor* relief; they may not touch *outdoor* relief! So we shall see hundreds of gangs of idle men, smoking and drinking, and half-building roads that no one needs anyway."

"Why don't they undertake drainage?" John asked, remembering the appalling wetness of much of the land they had splashed across that day. "God knows you could do with it!"

"Sure that's the truth!" MacMinimum said.

"That, too, is forbidden," Ormond explained.

"But why, for God's sake!"

"Because some individuals might benefit more than others; and the rule for public works is that all must benefit indifferently, or none may benefit at all. And meanwhile, next year's potatoes will not be planted because the men who should be doing it are on the public works instead —and they are on the public works because that is the only place they can get money to buy the meal they need to replace the potato that failed."

"And of course," John said, thinking he could see the end of this train of thought, "the price of meal is bound to rise beyond their reach."

But Ormond shook his head. "Would to God that were true! Even though it would go hard with the poor for this year. But Trevelyan has brought in over a hundred thousand pounds' worth of Indian corn from America, all of it held in the Commissariat depots. Vile yellow stuff it is, hard as flintstone. The people call it Peel's brimstone. And the sole purpose of this corn is not to relieve starvation, but to release onto the market whenever the price rises. Their aim is to keep *down* the price of meal!"

John shrugged in resignation and disgust. The lunacy of it! He had seen enough of the country to know that, outside the main towns, there was no mercantile system of any kind. He and MacMinimum had ridden through parish after parish, in one of the more prosperous parts of the country, without seeing a single shop of any description. If the government wanted to encourage a new trade in supplying meal to the populace, the last way to do it was to remove all profit from the enterprise.

"Trevelyan has a thousand eyes, they say," Ormond added. "Well, I'll tell ye—nine hundred and ninety-nine of them are glued to the Holy Writ of Economic Theory; the remaining one, which ought to be fixed on Ireland, is blind."

"And deaf," MacMinimum said.

They talked on for the best part of an hour, ending in agreement that there was no solution to this problem, short of the mass emigration of millions. The potato had been Ireland's ruin. It had encouraged the growth of a vast population who had sprawled over the land, preventing its improvement; and because they needed no money in order to survive —for their sole equipment was a spade—they acted as a monstrous brake on the monied system, a millstone around the necks of those who sought to improve land and trade. If they could be cleared, there was some hope for the country; while they remained, there was none.

It was a long while before John got to sleep that night. Something Flynn had once said to him kept repeating itself in his mind. "Don't you think that if after seven hundred years of London government, you can't do better than *this*, you ought to leave Ireland to govern itself, and get out with the best grace you may?" Flynn, of course, meant that the English government was uncaring and malignant—out to break Ireland and keep her as an inexhaustible well of cheap labour and a fertile nursery for the British army. But John's talk with Ormond had shown him that the danger was far more insidious: The corruption of a kindly, well-intentioned, paternal government could do more harm than the worst of tyrannies. Men who might have gone to England and earned good wages at the harvest now stayed at home and waited for relief work at one-third of those rates. Traders who might have started a line in meal for the populace would not even think of it, knowing that the government was always ready to step in and depress the price. And landlords and people of substance, who might normally offer charitable relief of their own, would certainly guard their purses as long as the government declared itself to be the great provider.

The result of such "government" would be a nation in which all enterprise was stifled, all charity smothered, all industry stagnant, and all self-reliance stultified. It would be the ultimate in the corruption of a people by paternal kindliness—a corruption that had already taken great hold in the country. Its eradication would inevitably be painful and the miseries of the people would be intense; but they would even so be light compared with the miseries of eternal enslavement at the wheel of poverty and relief works.

Perhaps the famine—like the plagues of Egypt of old—was sent by God as a warning to England and Ireland to turn from this course while time still offered. He was glad to hear that their priests were telling the people that the potato murrain was a visitation of the Almighty; he only hoped they went on to draw the full lesson.

These convictions of his were to be tested hard in the days that followed.

*   *   *

The first of those tests came the following afternoon, when they were riding along that stretch of the route, around Carrick-on-Suir, where the rail was to run near the northern bank of the river for the best part of ten miles. It was a bright, breezy day, with plenty of blue sky, now filled with shoals of pale, dove-grey cloud, now empty of all but the merest whisps of white. On every side of them, as they rode down the winding valley of the Suir from Clonmel to Carrick, stretched great rolling hills, rising to the distant mountains—Slievenaman to the north, Comeragh to the south. The green of the spring grass and of the new leaves upon the trees was so intense that even riding through it for hours could not dim John's sense of wonder. In fact, the beauty all around was so breathtaking that, for the first time in his life, he actually caught himself thinking what a shame it would be to put a railway line here, to bring dirt and clamour to this Eden.

And it was at that moment, half a mile before Carrick-on-Suir, that they heard an actual clamour—of angry voices, hundreds of angry voices. John, who had many times heard the distant rioting of armies of drunken, brawling navvies on a payday randy, recognized it at once.

"The route goes north of the town," MacMinimum said with relief. "We'd best stay clear."

"You may," John answered. "I want to see this." And he spurred his hack forward at a canter down the hill and into the town. The noise guided him straight to the wharfs, down on the river side, for this part of the Suir is also an inland navigation up to Clonmel. The centre of the turmoil was a string of ten barges so laden with grain that only inches of freeboard remained. At first John imagined that this was relief food on its way to a Commissariat depot, for it was guarded by a large body of troops, about eighty infantry and fifty cavalry as well as two field guns and their crews—half on one bank, half on the other. But the cry that went up from the angry crowd, kept at bay by the military, was "Ireland starves, England profits!" Clearly this was a normal commercial shipment of grain for export.

John had come to the tow path as the stragglers of the crowd were passing. As soon as he saw their mood he made no attempt to join or follow; and the people, seeing he had not the cut of a government man, passed him by. All were in old, tattered clothes, some in outright rags; many were barefoot and hatless. Starvation gave a gaunt menace to their sullen anger—and they *were* angry, he could not doubt it. He had seen angry mobs in England. It is rare that a large crowd—and there must, he calculated, have been at least two thousand there—is entirely united in any mood. If they are happy, there will always be at least two men fighting, and children crying; if they are annoyed, there will always be at least two swapping jokes, and youngsters will be skipping at the fringe. But here there was none of that. They were angry to the point of erupting into riot. It would need only a charge of the cavalry, or a shot fired over their heads, to set them off.

As the stragglers passed he noticed a man sitting on a tree root, nursing a bloodstained foot. He was ragged and starved, one of the mob.

"Are you hurt?" John asked.

"Ah—I trod on glass beyond."

John got down to look.

" 'T will stop soon enough," the man said.

It was badly cut and needed stitching. "I'll take you to a doctor," he said.

"I have no money."

"Would he refuse you?"

"He'd send me to the dispensary at the workhouse."

"I'll take you there, then."

"It's not open until tomorrow, d'ye understand. It's the same doctor. I thank you now, but it'll be well."

The man took a lot of convincing that it would not be well unless it was stitched; and when John said that he would pay, there was a further argument. In the end the man agreed to take a loan of two shillings, and John's card, and he promised to send repayment when he was next in funds. John got him to sit facing backward in the saddle, resting the foot on the horse's rump.

The man's fastidiousness over money marked him as one not belonging to the mendicant class, and on the way to the doctor's John asked him about himself. He was a small farmer, with three acres and a stone house, plastered walls within. His name was Conroy. His rent was thirty-six pounds a year, which was very hard on him. Some of the landlords had reduced or cancelled the rents this year; but his, a near-bankrupt squireen in a mouldering mansion with half its roof gone, could afford no abatement. Conroy had had to sell his entire grain harvest of last summer, and the family's pig, to raise the money.

"It's on the navigation there this very minute," he said.

If he had eaten the grain instead, he and his family would not now be starving, but they would be homeless and the remains of the grain would have been seized for the debt. They would be beginning to starve; and once they had dropped to the level of homeless, destitute paupers they would never again rise. He had had no choice but to ignore the whimpering of his hungry children and take the grain to market.

"I can bear it all," he said, "but the keening of the little girls is hard . . . hard."

For John it was hard at that moment to remember the calm imperatives of economic law.

* * *

It was even harder the following day when he and MacMinimum rode north out of Waterford along the proposed route of the other railway, the Waterford & Kilkenny. It was only 31¼ miles, with a branch of 6¼ to Kells, so they expected to finish within the day. They covered barely a third of that distance. As he wrote to Nora:

We had gone through Mullinavat and came to a village whose name I do not know—if it ever had one. If it did, it will surely live forever in the annals of infamy; but for the mapmaker it has ceased to exist.

When we came to it, the militia had been there already for about an

hour. They had come in support of the constabulary, who had come in support of the agents of the landlord, a certain Mrs. Pedelty. The village, com-
prising forty-nine houses, solidly built and dry, with plastered walls, was
upon her land and she wished it cleared. The tenants were not in arrears
with their rent and they had, entirely by their own industry, cleared and
reclaimed more than two hundred and fifty acres of bog.

When the landlord's agents and the militia arrived, the tenants offered
the whole of next year's rent in advance if only Mrs. Pedelty would leave
them at peace; it had taken half an hour to get word to her of this offer and
to bring back her refusal. Then they asked for compensation for the land
they had cleared and she sent back to say if they persisted in the claim she
would sue for delapidation and waste. The sergeant of the constabulary said
that any change in land or buildings by a tenant, even an obvious improvement, was, in the eyes of the law, a "waste" and entitled the landlord to
compensation.

The villagers then, seeing they had no defence anywhere, rushed indoors
and put up what pathetic barriers they could. It was at this moment when
MacMinimum and I arrived. He was for going on at once, but I would stay;
so he said he would return to Mullinavat and wait for me in a bar there.

The officer in charge of the militia refused to let his men take part in
the eviction, saying they were there merely to *prevent* disorder. Neither he
nor his men had stomach for such business. The implication that the constabulary were *fomenting* disorder angered the sergeant, but he commanded
his men to assist the bailiff and agents in evicting the tenants. The scenes
that followed were so piteous that even now, two days after, I tremble to
recall them; and the screams of the women and frightened children are with
me day and night. They were dragged, shrieking and weeping from their
homes and hurled like so much old clothing into the middle of the road.
They were not even allowed to take such belongings as they had—pots and
stools and the like.

I saw one young boy, of thirteen I would say, have his leg broken by
one agent—a brute of a man who grinned when the lad cried out. I actually
heard the bone break though I was ten paces away. I went to the sergeant
and told him this, but he ordered me to be on my way. I then said I was a
friend of Sir Randolph Routh and that if the agent was not immediately
taken in charge for assault, I should send in the strongest adverse report on
his conduct of this entire vile business. The agent then walked away with a
constable, ostensibly in arrest, but whether they spent the day over the brow
of the hill twiddling their thumbs I cannot say. At least I have the man's
name and have written to the Inspectorate of Constabulary at Dublin Castle
and to the Sheriff of Kilkenny County.

As soon as they had a family got out, they rushed indoors with poles and burst out the slates near the ridge tree of the roof. Then a man would go up on a ladder outside and put a hook on a chain around the ridge tree. The other end was already harnessed to a team of horses, so it was easy work pulling off the entire roof in one smack. Forty-nine houses they wasted in this way. On some, the roofs were so flimsy they could pull them off with rakes alone.

You may imagine the anguish of the people as this was going on. The men and women were on their knees, begging the agents and constables not to persist with the evictions. And then the wailing that went up and the curses that fell as the roof came off. I confess without shame I was un-manned—choked with dust and tears both. I spoke to many of the soldiers, they were of the 72nd Highland, and they answered to a man that they detested the business. I saw several give money to the people. I gave them all I had, too, which amounted to 5*l*. 2*s*. 4*d*.

Shortly after two, when all the roofs were off, they stopped for a bite and a drink. Then the people were allowed back in to salvage what they could of their possessions. Which was precious little (yet precious to them, for all that). I saw one woman standing at the door of her ruined home, crying and bewildered, with dried blood on her forehead. She had in her hand a broken china plate, and I asked her what it was. "It's my life away," she said.

Yet such is the fortitude of these people (remember they were not desti-tute paupers but were, by Irish standards, in a fair prosperous way) that before evening they had built shelters of furze and stone out along the way-side. And such is the ruthlessness of authority here, that they were hunted out even from these rude shelters and scattered far and wide over the coun-try. Three constables went along with torches, firing the furze. There was one crippled young girl did not get out in time and had her hair and neck and face badly burned. There is no poor law infirmary nearer than Water-ford, so I took her there, and that was the last I saw of that dreadful day. When MacMinimum and I rode through the next day, they were pulling the walls down and even uprooting the foundations.

A little way on we came to another village, where some of the evicted had been taken in and given shelter. The constabulary was hard at work driving them out again and giving out cautions that whoever took in any of the evicted would himself be turned out.

So Mrs. Pedelty (who collects 11,000*l*. in rent and has not subscribed one farthing in relief) has regained several hundred valuable acres, while the British Treasury has acquired two hundred and fifty more mouths that can be fed only through relief. And Ireland has another cause to detest us—

and rightly, I say. The tolerance and friendly hospitality that greets me everywhere baffles my comprehension.

When I told Flynn of this, he said, "Oh, that's been going on for centuries, did you not know?" And when I showed him a list of names I had collected (why, I do not know, I had some notion of an appeal or inquiry), he read: "Lynch, Connally, Egan, Kelly ... etc." and then he looked at me and added, "I was looking at the lists of those who died in the recent great victories of general Gough at Aliwal and Sobraon in India. I'd swear half of it was Lynches, Connallys, Egans, Kellys ... etc. 'Roll of honour,' it said, 'of those who died for *their* country.' "

My dearest, I tell myself—what you will certainly say—that it is a landowner's inalienable right to do what he wishes with his own land. I know all this—yet it does not stifle the cries of terrified children and the weeping of their parents. It does not efface the picture I have of that young cripple I carried ten miles before me on my horse, she mad with pain, blistered from her shoulder to her temple; and the cloying smell of her burns is there now in my nostrils. I am too wounded still to say what *is* right. I know that all I saw was wrong.

Three days later this letter was followed by another, scribbled in great haste:

After sending my last I felt compelled to turn about and go back to Waterford for news of the little burned girl, whose name is Mary Coen. Since I had taken her from her people, I felt in some degree responsible for seeing them together again. I have searched high and low and cannot find them. I have sent others out, two dozen, also seeking, and they cannot find them either. The constabulary have also (they claim) made inquiry, to no avail.

What shall I do? What must I do? I am minded to bring the child, Mary, back to England with me. We may surely find her a place, even though she is crippled. She could no doubt be taught to sew or clean things. She hardly needs the use of a leg for that. Her family were decent folk. I cannot leave her in this bastille. I wish you were here. Could you come and see to the arrangements? I will await you here.

*   *   *

If rage had been a fuel, Nora would have been in Waterford within the hour. As it was, she steamed from Liverpool that night and was with John the following evening. Her way to Liverpool ran through the

Pennines via Summit Tunnel on the Manchester & Leeds—Stevenson's first contract. As the train drew near she looked out for Rough Stones, the house up on the hillside where they had made their first home; but it was night, and all she saw was a glimmer that could as well have been a shepherd's lantern. And then the train swept into the tunnel.

She was glad not to have seen the place. It had held too many of her hopes, too much optimism, to suit her present anger and despair.

She was furious at his neglect of the rest of the business—she told herself. He was behaving in a secretive, high-handed way—the way that had led to their disastrous partnership with Beador. This had all the signs of that same flawed judgement. That was another good reason to be angry. And he was going soft. He was losing his grip on reality. He was even assuming that she was a willing accomplice in all of this . . . this madness. He did not even consider that she might hold the contrary viewpoint. Yet hadn't she been the one who pulled them out of the mess, *his* mess, last time? And she still hadn't got much in the way of new property to recompense her loss—yet here he was behaving in this lofty, inconsiderate way, as if she didn't count at all.

Well, she would show him!

She did not pause to marvel that she had so many reasons for anger—as if the anger grew first, and grew tall, before any reason came along to prop it up.

The ready smile of welcome left John's face the moment he saw her. "Eay, ye look badly," he said.

"I'm fit," she answered curtly. "Fit for what has to be done here."

It had never once crossed his mind that she would take exception to what he had done. Even now, when her anger was plain, he could not at once adjust to the notion. "You're not . . . *vexed*, are you?" he asked incredulously. "Surely not."

She let him see what effort it cost to stay calm. "I am vexed, John. And so would ten thousand others be if they knew of this . . . what can we call it? Escapade? Escape, anyway. Escape from your duty."

"Duty?" The word stung him.

"Plain duty. Duty to a dozen railway companies. Duty to every man who works for us. To every man as trusts you and has tied his fortune to yours. I don't know what sort of weighing scale you've found to make one child heavier than all that."

He smiled at her when she said the word "child" and held out his hand. "Come and see her," he said.

"I'll do no such thing." She saw the hotel porter preparing to carry her bags from the post chaise. "Leave it all there," she said sharply.

Her meaning was not lost on John, but still he held forth his hand. "Come on, love. At least see the child."

She was adamant. "I've come here to restore your judgement," she said. "Not to be swayed out of mine. I'll not see her."

"You must," he said and began walking away down the street. He did not look behind him until he reached the corner. When he saw she still held her ground he had to turn and come back. "Afraid you might, after all, see my side of it?" he taunted.

She had to go with him then. On the way he explained that he'd paid to have the girl moved out of the workhouse into the direct care of a nurse in the parish. "But they'll not let her beyond the parish-union boundary except by way of proper apprenticeship," he added.

Daylight was quickly fading as they walked up the street to the nurse's house. The nurse, a sprightly, middle-aged woman, full of nervous good humour, was set for half an hour's good jawing before she would think of showing them the girl, but John cut her short.

The girl lay stiffly, half sitting on top of her bed, a gaunt little scarecrow in patched and threadbare workhouse reach-me-downs. The room was low, and precious little of the falling day crept in at the one small, grimy window.

"Hello then, Mary," John said. "Here is Mrs. Stevenson come to help us."

The girl's head was swaddled in dressing made from torn sheeting. She kept as still as possible; every slight movement made her whimper. Nora thought she might be dying. The nurse left them alone with her, one on each side of the little bed.

Nora had not needed to see the child in order to understand what had moved John to behave as he did. But to her mind it still did not excuse his neglect of everything else. She looked around the room. "Well," she said. "It's clean. It's dry. It's not cold. Where is the difficulty?"

He stiffened angrily and was about to speak when she cut him short. "See thou—I came through Summit Tunnel last night. It put me in mind of the man I met there, and I'll tell you for free, you're nothing like him. *There* was a man who'd just lived through an explosion underground, who turned round and sawed off Pengilly's injured leg smack smooth, who passed the night forging a banker's letter of credit, and who spent next day drawing wool over the eyes of the Manchester & Leeds directors. That was a man who knew where the main chance was —and how to take it. He'd never have spent a week milksopping around this godforsaken backwater on account of—one little bag of bones." She smiled at Mary, who smiled wanly back.

John pressed his knuckles into his eyesockets, trying to contain his anger in front of the child. "You cannot have read my letters," he began.

"What?" she asked. "About the evictions? They weren't the first. Nor will they be the last, I daresay. Why you had to go and involve yourself—"

"But I *was* involved. I was involved because I was *there*. I was involved because they were people, not animals, that were treated so." He gestured at Mary.

"Well, where do we stop, John? Why don't we shoulder all the burdens of this wretched country? Eh? And what about England? Things every bit as bad happen there, too. Any day of the week."

"At least you agree it's bad."

"Of course I do. I find Mrs. Pedelty despicable. I hope all doors are barred against her. I hope she's denounced from the pulpit."

"And? That's all?"

"Is it not enough?"

"Certainly not. At the very least the law on evictions must be changed."

Nora could not believe it. She began to shiver and she felt her heart hammering in anger. "You must be mad!" she said.

"You did not see what I saw."

"I could see a hundred evictions and still keep a level head on *that* subject. It's a hard fact of life, but a landlord must be free to do as he likes with his own land. If the law were to curtail that right in any way, the value of land would fall. If that happened, then people of enterprise would stop putting their money into land. And agricultural progress would halt. Or even decline. Think of the destitution and misery *that* would cause. Not in one village but in thousands. You can't cure one evil by bringing in another a thousand times more pernicious." *What an absurd discussion*, she thought, *to be having in front of this child!*

He laughed mirthlessly, despairing of her understanding. "You can't expect those who are evicted to see it like that."

"I do," she said stoutly. "I've been evicted too, you know. When our dad died, we were turned out by the Bridgewater agent. I screamed murder at him but I never questioned his right, though I had the rent in my hand."

"It's different here in Ireland. You can have no idea—"

"I believe they must have different water, or different air or something. It seems to rot the backbone out of good men."

If they had been on the same side of the bed, he would have struck her. As it was, he clenched his fist and glared at her across the gulf that divided them.

A whimper from the girl distracted them. Both looked down at her. Large tears brimmed in her eyes as she stared dumbly from one to the other. When she blinked, the tears overflowed and ran back along her cheekbones to her ears, where the swaddling absorbed them. She raised her hands feebly outward, the left to John, the right to Nora. She had nothing else to offer them.

Ashamed, each took one shivering hand. The girl shut her eyes and gripped back for dear life. Neither of them felt able to speak.

"I hope you're satisfied," Nora said, breaking the silence at last. Before John could answer, she sat down at the child's side, took out a lace handkerchief, and, with her free hand, dabbed at the run of the tears. "It isn't you, Mary," she said. "It's not you, popsie. You're going to be all right. You'll be safe here, and we'll go on looking for your mammy and daddy. Have no fear." She spoke in this way until the girl's hand went limp and she seemed to have fallen into a doze.

Nora looked up to see John doing his best to hide a smile of triumph. "I mean we'll pay someone to do it for us," she snapped at him. "Which is what should have been done a week since."

"Shhh!" he whispered, grinning.

Outside in the street, where she could raise her voice again, she almost shouted at him, telling him he was to stop behaving as if he had been right and she wrong—as if he believed she now shared his views and endorsed his ridiculous maunderings. When he refused, and persisted in his lofty, tolerant self-satisfaction, she understood that only some drastic gesture would persuade him of her seriousness. So when he went to take his bath, she hired a fresh chaise, had her luggage transferred to it, and left at once for Dublin.

She was tired enough then to feel a certain caustic amusement that John's infidelity to the firm touched her so much more on the raw than his infidelity to her.

Chapter 31

Nora's abrupt departure had, at first, the desired effect upon John. That very night he saw a lawyer, the priest, the chairman of the poor law guardians, and the nurse, putting in hand all the arrangements necessary to secure Mary's immediate future. Early the following day he, too, set out for Dublin.

The more he thought about it, though, the less pleased he felt. He told himself he had fully intended to make all those arrangements in any case. Nora's virtual command, reinforced by her petulant departure, had no bearing—except that she had taken all the pleasure out of it for him. She had turned an act of his own free will into an act of meek obedience to her. The hurtful things she had said came crowding back in his memory. They became less and less forgivable as time cooled the heat of the moments in which they had been spoken.

She was getting too damned arrogant. Flying across England and Ireland like that to deliver him an angry homily on *his* duty to *his* firm! Well, he'd have a flea or two to put in her ear next time they met. Ever since he'd given her that power of attorney she'd been getting above herself. He ought never to have listened to Chambers' advice on that.

Yet it was comforting, too, when he was alone—especially at night —to say her name to himself and to think of all the good things about her. There were still plenty of them, too.

Business had piled up while he had been "milksopping" around in Waterford. He arrived back in Dublin to find no trace of Nora—and several urgent letters, each making demands on his time. Before he left, he wrote to Routh suggesting that if some of the money now wasted utterly in relief works were instead put into interest-free loans to the Irish railways, a great deal of employment would follow, not only on the lines but in the trade they would stimulate. His anger at the ineptitude of the present government action led him to suggest that "when the loans were repaid and the revenues from new commerce were collected, the Treasury might even be able to soothe Parliament with the claim that it had, after all, turned famine into a going concern." Once the letter was sent he regretted the remark—and he got a frosty reply from Sir Randolph. The lack of judgement that led him to write to Routh in such a vein was Nora's fault. He had not realized how deeply she had disturbed him.

The most urgent of his letters was from Jack Whitaker, his deputy on the Chester & Holyhead line through North Wales. Whitaker had been with him from the very start, a solid, dependable man who knew his own limitations. Chiefly he lacked the flair, or the confidence, for tackling out-of-the-way problems, especially among the men. His trouble this time was that masons, carpenters, and other mechanics were leaving the job almost as soon as they started, because of the outrageous rents being demanded by the people with houses bordering the line, especially in Rhyll, where they wanted ten shillings a week just for a room. John could easily believe it; he remembered how, when he was walking the route of that particular line, he had once asked for a glass of water at a cottage and been charged eightpence for it.

Another letter was from Robert Stephenson, son of the great George, who was the engineer to the Chester & Holyhead; he was eager to advance the Conway tubular bridge, and could John meet him at Conway in the coming week?

*   *   *

The worst of the lodgings in Rhyll consisted of one dirty room with decaying plaster and a leaking roof, over a coal merchant's in the narrow part of the town. Here a carpenter and his wife were lodged. "And it's ten shillings a week?" he asked the man.

"Ten and sixpence," the carpenter said. "He wanted twelve shillings. I said we'd sooner sleep under the hedges. But I shall leave at the end of this week, Lord John. I can't pay a third of the wage in lodgings."

All the while the coal merchant looked on, smiling.

"Why do you charge so much?" John asked him. "You know the room is not worth two shillings, much less ten."

"It's worth what it will fetch, see," the man said, unruffled. "Who says only two shillings? You. I say twelve, and I let it for less because I'm soft-hearted. Rooms is scarce in Rhyll, see. Demand and supply. I do both, see."

One way and another John had had his fill of the theory of price lately, and the last person he wanted to take lessons in economics from was an avaricious north Welsh merchant. "I'll teach you about 'demand and supply,' sir," he said angrily. "You shall learn of the law of avarice —a gluttonous trader makes a glutted market. In ten days no man of mine will seek a single lodging in Rhyll. No, nor anywhere else in this neighbourhood."

He had no idea how he was going to fulfil this promise; he knew only that he was determined to teach these greedy people a lesson.

"What now, guvnor?" Jack Whitaker asked when they were on their way back to the workings.

"That's a good question, Jack. Are you friendly with any farmers locally?" He had an idea of renting barns, putting up partitions, and making some form of acceptable shelter, at least as a temporary expedient.

But on his way to one of the farmers that Jack had forlornly recommended, John hit upon the real answer: a large timber plantation of about twenty acres—ash, sycamore, larch, balsam poplar, noble fir, silver pine—all in just the right condition for his purpose.

"Jack!" he said excitedly. "Where's our nearest timber yard, our own yard, where we could handle trees like yon?"

Whitaker looked at them. They were not so big as to require steam lifting machinery and powered saws. "We could handle those here," he said. "The timber yard's at Mostyn, five miles back."

So John bought all twenty acres of timber as it stood. He took three gangs off the line and within a week not a tree was left standing. A fourth gang had meanwhile laid a narrow bogey line downhill from the woods to the workings and soon a steady flow of timber, all cut to lengths, was arriving at the lower end. There it was quickly turned into log cabins and dormitories—all erected on company ground along the fringes of the cuttings. John had never seen men work so willingly or cheerfully. All had suffered the greed of the local landlords to some extent and the thought of taking this revenge had really fired their spirits. On payday, at the end of the week, most of them refused their wages and John had to be called to the site to intervene.

"We think as you're out o' pocket enough, what wi' buyin' the timber, an' it's to *our* advantage," a carpenter explained—the man who had been cheated by the coal merchant.

All the counterarguments flitted through his mind—the law of price and the business of supply and demand again—and he saw how impossibly incongruous they would sound in these circumstances. They *wanted* to sacrifice the wage so that they could feel they had personally taken part in the humiliation of the local landlords.

"Well, I thank you," he said. "I thank all of you. But you must know that my main interest is in getting men to *stay* on this line. And if it meant the purchase of a hundred acres of timber, I'd count it cash well spent—especially to get men who can work as I've seen you lads work this week!" Ironical groans began at that. "If you put that same elbow grease into finishing this line . . ." He was drowned in laughter and mocking cheers. "But seriously now, lads," he went on, "I'll not be out o' pocket in th' end. I've worked out that a rent of tenpence a week on each log cabin, or sixpence for each bunk in a dormitory, will just pay me back by the end of this contract. Timber *and* wages. So you must take the wage. If ye don't, it'll bugger up all the books."

He had known it would not satisfy them, and he waited for the rumbles to grow before he said: "Very well. You want more? You want the chance to spit in the eye of these landlords?"

"Aye!" a great raucous cheer went up, joyful at the implied promise.

"I'll tell you what, then. Most of them are petty tradesmen. The worst was a coal merchant. There's a way we could hit a lot of them, especially that one. There's enough spare kindling and wood up there, trimmed off the trees, to keep Rhyll warm for a year."

"Burn the bloody place!" called an excited navvy.

"Nay!" John said with relish. "Cleverer nor that! If on *my* time you prepare that waste wood into bundles such as any man could store at home, and if in *your own* time you will carry those bundles around the town and distribute them free, to rich and poor alike—but not to any man who was landlord to any among us—we may together teach them—" The rest of his words were drowned in a universal roar of delight.

"So that's why you wouldn't let them burn the trimmings," Whitaker said. "I wondered."

"Aye. I had that in mind all week, but I couldn't see how I could afford it."

*   *   *

Robert Stephenson, when John met him after the week's delay, was amused at the story of the Triumph of Rhyll.

"You're a lucky man, Stevenson," he said. "Your men will work with a spirit all summer now. They always do after something like that. And *now*"—he made a gesture that cleared the air around them of all such trivia—"I want to show you a machine that's going to put some spirit into *my* work this summer. If I told you I want to install the first tube of the bridge next March or thereabouts, what'd you say?"

"I'd say good luck. And we'll be ready for you."

Stephenson chuckled. "You're good for my digestion," he said. "I'll tell that to Fairburn when he gets back."

The machine was a device for punching rivet holes in flat sheets of wrought iron. The ingenuity of it was that it operated exactly like a Jacquard loom, which is a loom for weaving tapestries without human control no matter how intricate or varied the design. It is very easy to devise a machine that will punch one rivet hole every six inches, but imagine a column of newsprint in which every letter *o* was a hole through the paper, and then imagine that the paper was magnified to a width of two feet and pasted onto a sheet of wrought iron, half an inch thick. It is easy to imagine, then, the labour and skill that would go into making such random—yet precisely required—holes in the metal and punching them out by hand. The machine Robert Stephenson was so proud of could punch such a sheet in less than four minutes, never forgetting a hole, never punching a superfluous one.

They watched it chew its faultless way through several plates. John marvelled at the way it seemed to be thinking for itself.

They left, then, to be able to talk without having to shout over the noise. The tide was ebbing, and they went down on the steeply shelving bed of the Conway. They walked over the firm mud, among the sea-weed, cuttlefish bones, and the jetsam of the sea below and of the mountains above. A pack of stray dogs on the far bank tore at the sodden carcase of a dead sheep.

"Will that machine pay for itself?" John asked.

Stephenson looked at him cannily. "It might, just," he said. "Why?"

"I could make you an offer for it when this is over. It's ideal for boiler plate."

"Ah. When this is over, it will go down the line to Menai. I want this bridge to be in every way a dress rehearsal for that. I'd be obliged, Stevenson, if you'd see to it that as many people as possible, and certainly all your chief people who take part in making this Conway bridge, will be at Menai afterwards. The lessons we learn here will be invaluable."

"I will indeed, sir," John said.

"As to that machine paying for itself, let me tell you that one side of one tube alone has thirty-nine thousand rivets to be inserted. Seventy-eight thousand holes. If you count the holes for nuts and bolts, too, there's not far short of seven hundred thousand in the entire structure. I think it'll pay for itself all right!"

They were approaching the open riverside yard where the giant square tubes were being assembled, on pontoons that floated with each spring tide. The base of one tube, four hundred and twelve feet long, was already complete, and the side panels of wrought iron were being added. It looked huge—far greater than the empty space between the foundations of the towers suggested. When all the plates were riveted together, the structure would form a square tube fourteen feet wide and about twenty-five feet high overall—big enough for a train to pass through. Several much smaller tubes, also square, would run at the top and botton to strengthen it. The whole would, in effect, form a gigantic hollow girder supported only at its ends. Two such girders—one for the up line, one for the down—were to be made here at the riverside and floated on the tide, to be fitted into niches in the masonry piers. Then they would be lifted by hydraulic machinery from above, while masons filled the niches with stone beneath each as it was raised.

"Does it not tie your stomach in knots to look at it?" John asked. "To think of that vast length of tube supported only at its ends and a whole train running through it."

"Think of Menai, then," Stephenson said lightly. "The same tubes, but forty-eight feet longer—and a hundred feet up, not twenty. However, none of the models we built failed, so I don't see why these should."

They watched several rivets being hammered home. Then Stephenson went forward and tried to force thin metal gauges between the plates. None would penetrate, which seemed to satisfy him. He returned to John, and they strolled back toward the castle and the site of the railway bridge. The old road suspension bridge, built by Thomas Telford twenty-four years earlier, spanned the river just downstream of the rail line; its fake medieval towers looked incongruously new against the castle behind it.

"The city fathers are still determined to have battlements and arrow slits on the rail bridge," Stephenson said. "I am composing a poem, which begins: 'Sir Walter Scott, Ought to be shot . . .' and I want to work in something about hits and arrow slits, but I'm not ingenious enough."

John laughed. "Why not, on the opening day, conceal in the tube of the bridge a little band of knights in armour on horseback and long-bowmen and varlets with pikes and that sort of thing. Imagine it! The engine steams slowly in at one end. Everyone's eyes turn to the other to await its reappearance. And—what? what? what I say!—it seemingly flushes out a long-lost medieval army!"

Stephenson roared and howled with laughter, slapping his thigh and stamping in the mud. "How I wish I dared! Oh, would it not be a superb revenge! Stevenson, you're a cure for dull aches, you really are."

*   *   *

Day followed day and no letter, no word-of-mouth message, came from John. Nora's anger, so hot in Ireland, turned cold and hard. She was damned if she was going to make the first conciliatory move; it would blunt the point of all she had done in Waterford. But news was meanwhile piling up, news that she would ordinarily have passed immediately to him. Eventually the accumulation of it forced her to break the silence.

"If your taste for the dull business of railroad contracting has reawakened," she began. Then she tore up the sheet.

Just facts, she told herself, and began again: "(i) We have an invitation from Spain to tender for the line Locke has surveyed between Barcelona and Mataro. (ii) Also several from Italy and Austria, less well advanced. (iii) I assume you know of the English tenders that are invited—including Scotch. (iv) I now know Rodet's true manufacturing costs. (v) We must let them know when we shall visit La Gracieuse this summer. Tentatively I have told them June. (vi) Do you need any further information touching any of the foregoing? (vii) When do you return to Thorpe again? (viii) Maran Hill is now ours for life. Sir George will move back to Co. Durham in May. We shall take up residence in autumn, not later, for I am to have another child close to Christmas, I believe. Dutifully, Nora."

She read it through, added the word "yours," and sent it to him. She liked the way she had not openly offered reconciliation yet had managed to imply that forgiveness would not be unreasonably withheld.

It did not please John at all. Yet he realized it was the best he was likely to get from Nora and that, on balance, he would do well to think of it as "Nora's apology," accept it as such, and hope that these aberrations in her behaviour would die away.

Chapter 32

This year Sam was at La Gracieuse before them. He had, in fact, come over three days earlier and gone straight to Paris. There he spent two days alone before coming back to Normandy, arriving an hour before the Stevensons and Sarah. He stood at Rodie's side while she made the courtyard ring with her eerie yodelling welcome.

Nora closed her eyes on tears of joy. "That noise!" she said. "All the way over I've been trying to remember it. Dear Rodie!"

And then there were long minutes of crying and embracing and mangled French-English before they even moved indoors. In the midst of it, Nora's "Hello, Sam love," and his "Nora luv!" and their warm (but English-warm) embrace seemed like an ice chip.

Only an English eye could have discerned the warmth in the handshake and the "Mrs. Cornelius"—"Mr. Telling" that Sam and Sarah exchanged. Rodie was disappointed. "Oh," she said severely, "you must *kiss* the hand, Monsieur Sam. But you shall tonight, you see." She turned to Sarah. "You are going in a bowl."

"Really?" Sarah was bewildered. Sam's smile showed he knew what was meant.

"Oh, yes! All." She threw wide her arms. "All of we are going in a bowl. But it's for the youngs—the youth." She narrowed her compass to just Sarah and Sam. "The quadrille," she said into the face of Sarah's bewilderment. "Kiss the hand."

"A *ball!*" Sarah said. *"Un bal, hein?"*

"Oui. What I say. *Très grand!"*

"Not," Nora said to Sarah when Rodie was out of earshot, "a wedge-foot bowl, you see."

*   *   *

The ball was a very grand affair at the château of Monsieur Tallien, the man whose name had led John to tell the Rodets that Nora's maiden name was Telling. Someone said they had two thousand candles lighted that evening, and two servants working full time to replenish them. Everything else was on the same scale—an orchestra of sixty players to dance to, eight large buffets with four tiers on each so laden with food that hardly an inch of rosewood or mahogany showed, a winter garden where gentlemen could smoke their cigars, and a long terrace where perspiring dancers could escape the candle fumes and wander in the warm, starlit twilight. But all the wealth and all the lands of the Talliens could not provide the one element that Nora sought: the fragrance of the oaks—the smell of Normandy in spring; for spring was gone for another year.

She danced several dances with John, who then excused himself and went off to talk business with Rodet. She stood watching him, wishing fiercely that she could go too. Then something, a movement to her right, caused her to turn that way. It was only a couple coming in from the terrace, and she was about to look away again when she caught sight of a tall, stooping man standing outside and peering lugubriously at her through the glass. He smiled and came in from the terrace. She smiled back and looked away; she was sure they had not been introduced.

"May I present myself, Mrs. Stevenson, since I am unable to find Madame Rodet to do me the honour?" He was foreign but not French. Dutch or German perhaps. He spoke in English to her.

"You know Madame Rodet?"

"A very dear friend. I am Julius Wolff. Of Hamburg."

The name awakened her interest. "There is a firm of bankers in Hamburg—" she began.

"Gebrüder Wolff," the man said. "The same."

Nora gave him her hand at that. "But, then, we are hardly strangers."

He kissed it and murmured, *"Gnädige Frau."* As he leaned forward she noticed that his lower eyelids, which were loose and wrinkled, fell free of his eyeballs, like loose pockets. He had the face of a starved pug with little pearly beads of fat just under the skin; a whole cluster of them, like a family of yellow ticks, were stuck between his left upper eyelid and his nose. Yet his smile was inviting and friendly, promising more. She thought him to be about sixty. "The family name is Wolff-Dietrich," he added. "It's the old name for the leader of the werewolf pack." He grinned to show that he was joking; the effect was ghastly.

"You act as Chambers' agent in Hamburg," she said.

"And the whole of Holstein."

"Ah. We have bought and sold a lot of paper through you."

He chuckled. "Much. And more in the future, I hope."

She smiled.

"Against—pesetas, perhaps?"

"If the arbitrated rate is good, we will buy and sell against cowrie shells from the Spice Islands."

He laughed. "You give nothing away, Madame." He pulled out a handkerchief and dabbed water from his eyes; the loose lower eyelids kept filling like cisterns.

They danced two dances together—or, rather, one and a half, for in the middle of the second, a waltz, he complained of feeling hot and giddy and she took him to sit out at the side. She asked a footman to get him a brandy, for he was trembling. He smiled at her and apologized. "I did not eat," he said. "Stupid."

The brandy steadied him but now he began to sweat. "Come outside," she said, "where it is cool. I will support you, see."

But he was firm as a rock—so firm that she began to suspect that the whole episode was a ruse.

"You like France, Mrs. Stevenson?" he asked.

"What I know of it, Herr Wolff-Dietrich. Only Normandy. But I have such a good friend here in Madame Rodet."

"I, too, share that good fortune. Please—'Wolff' is enough. In fact, I think we meet there tomorrow."

"I look forward to that—and so, I know, will Mr. Stevenson when I tell him."

Wolff seemed on the point of saying something; he hesitated, looked at her, then looked away and breathed out.

They leaned against the heavy stone balustrade of the terrace, looking down over the gardens, dark and mysterious. The stone harboured the heat of the day's sun. She wondered if Wolff and his brother were *good* bankers; Stevenson's had used them only as agents for buying and selling foreign exchange. Would it be etiquette to talk of his business? Continentals were sometimes very funny about that.

"Do you enjoy banking, Herr Wolff?" she risked asking.

It was as if the question touched a start lever within him. "It is at once the most absorbing and frustrating of professions," he said. "To see inside so many great affairs, sometimes even to help plan them, yet always in the end to be the—you say, third person?"

"Third party. Chambers says it's the trade of sultan's eunuch."

Her frankness, which was deliberate, took him aback. For a moment he did not know what to say, then he composed himself to pretend she had said something else, and then he laughed. She decided that a man of sixty years' experience who, when surprised, let so much of his thoughts show in his face was probably not a very good banker.

"It's good," he said. "He is amusing, Chambers."

"There *is* a funny side to him," Nora agreed. She looked away again, for her gaze seemed to discomfit Wolff, and said: "I imagine there was never a more interesting time to be a banker than the present."

"In London," Wolff agreed. "But on the Continent we meddle with mere currency; we argue of currency unions and common coinage. We are *techniciens*. But in London you are artists."

"Why do you say that?"

"Because of what happened last October and November. The manner in which the extraordinary demand was met." He looked at her. "Did you not find that—exciting?"

She decided to say nothing; instead she smiled, making him smile, too. "On the Continent, it would have been—chaos." He said *Kaos*, the German word; it sounded much more doom-laden than mere "chaos"—which, to her mind, was a fitting description of the everyday state of the London money market.

He became even more lugubrious. "But we can procure *Kaos* without extraordinary demand. You are so comfortable and secure in your little island. But here on the Continent things are terrible."

"Really, Herr Wolff!" She laughed. "What a thing to tell me at the start of a visit here!"

"Truth," he said, with a Germanic intensity that carried no apology. "Do you realize—of course you don't—how close revolution is, here, in France too, also in Germany, also Italy—everywhere?"

She began to feel a little bored with Wolff. Only the suspicion that he had something important to say and could not work around to saying it kept her out there with him. His recovery from "giddiness" was so complete that it could not have been real. "If you are so certain," she prompted, "why do you not close your business and come to London?"

"Oh!" It was a dismissive sound. He shrugged and waved his hands aimlessly, as if ten dozen contrary reasons presented themselves. "Do you know how little a banker can move? Only his fixed capital—his own money. But his loan capital—his good name—how can he move these? Yet they are his real trade."

"You have survived revolutions before," Nora said, preparing to return to the ball.

He did not move. "This one is—will be—completely different. In England you are so clever. Peel repeals the Corn Law, and what happens? The country workers, rural workers, are at once in harness with the aristocracy and proprietors of land, for expensive corn. But the town

workers, they of course are in harness with the factory masters and proprietors of industry, and they want *cheap* corn." He brought down his
hand, like a guillotine blade, on the baluster rail. "*Boomz!* The worker
class is divided."

It was an interesting insight, one she had not heard before; she made
no further effort to disengage. "Here they are not?"

"Here we have *no* rural worker class; only peasants. So the town
worker class has no—no interest together with the *bourgeoisie*, they
say. It is a hard fight. It is revolution like no other before. It is not
ancient against modern, or country against town, it is the modern against
modern, the *bourgeoisie* against—we call it *das Proletariat.*"

"We use the French—*prolétaires.* What are their demands?"

"They wish the state. They wish to be masters, to direct capital, to
appropriate profit. They wish to become the proprietors—the *sole*
proprietors!"

Nora began to laugh. "You mean communists and socialists! But
how can you take them seriously? It is so easy to demolish all their
arguments and pretensions. Their leaders are idealists, their followers
are greedy; and, as always happens, the greedy will swallow the idealists. And then they will choke."

"Of course we take them seriously!" he said. The note of anger
carried to the groups and couples passing by, provoking amusement and
raised eyebrows. But he persisted, unnoticing. "It's easy for England.
You have been so clever. You divide the *prolétaires,* you give them
slow improvement—enough to stop revolution. So you avoid danger—
and you think it is no danger on the Continent, too. But it *is.* And it's
dangerous for you, as well. A hot fire can jump the water! It can jump
the English Channel, even the German Ocean."

"Perhaps we do not see these things as clearly as we should, Herr
Wolff," she said to soothe him. "But you, too, are misled if you think
we have solved the problem in the ways you say. Perhaps we do not face
immediate revolution, but our danger, seen over years, is worse. We are
facing a new kind of leader of our workers. He is not communist. Perhaps he is socialist out of convenience, but certainly not out of conviction. He *thinks*"—she tapped her forehead—"like you and me. He thinks
of supply and demand and price and market. And so he thinks of his
labour as a commodity, like tea or iron. He says if a Baltic trader can
corner the market in Russian tallow and then dictate his price, why
cannot the labourer make a corner in *his* own commodity? How do we
answer that, Herr Wolff? It is our own ideal thrown back at us."

He nodded. "Here, too, in France and Germany, is such an element.

I tell you how we answer it: with guns and soldiers. And then"—he made his fist explode with a flurry of fingers—"revolution!"

"But that is not *your* answer, Herr Wolff?" she asked, certain now that she was close to his purpose in drawing her out here.

"No," he agreed. "We—my brother and myself—because we are bankers, and very cautious, old-fashioned bankers—and also not young —we can have only a little answer. We wish to put some money abroad, in England. Not much, of course, because everything that goes away makes smaller our—fundament, do you say? Our fundament for lending."

"Basis. I can see that."

"Ach so! Basis. It's the same."

"Why do you not speak to Chambers?"

"I did. We did." He looked calmly, almost—as far as she could tell in the light that poured from the house onto the terrace—amusedly at her.

"And? What did he say?"

Wolff lowered his voice. "He says that of all people who would know how to use best this money, it's *you*."

The slight smile on her face did not vanish, but inside she was furious. It was all a joke. This whole charade of Wolff's was the elaborate opening round of some little scheme of theirs to humiliate her. A little Jewish bankers' joke on the gentile lady. Chambers! He was so sure of himself they had even agreed to bring his name into it from the beginning. Her first instinct was to sweep majestically from the terrace, as any affronted heroine would feel impelled to do. But Nora was no longer a woman of first instincts.

Instead she said, quite neutrally, as if reserving the choice of being pleased or angry: "He had no right to say such a thing."

Wolff looked pained. "He did not discuss your business. But he admires you so." He gripped her gloved arm fastidiously in his gloved fingers and said, confidentially, "He told me not to mention his name. He says you unreasonably mistrust him. But I do not like secrets."

It was too amusing—that they would imagine she could be taken along so easily. She decided to play them out at the game they had chosen. "I think, Herr Wolff, that you are a victim of Mr. Chambers' humour. You know him well?"

"Nathan?" he asked. (He pronounced it Nahtan, which Nora did not at once recognize.) "From a child. I used to give him—what do you say?" He gestured the holding of a child on his shoulders.

"A flying angel," Nora said.

"Oh? It's good. A flying angel. I give him many." He chuckled at the memory.

"And now *he* is playing a little game with *you*."

"Oh no!" Wolff was at once serious. "I assure you, no."

"Very well, Herr Wolff. How may I help you?"

"We wish, my brother and I, we wish you to take some of our money and to invest it for us in—in such places where you invest your own." He studied her face closely for the effect of this extraordinary proposal. She could tell from his reaction that he found nothing there.

"In whose name?" she asked. "Understand, I think this is preposterous—a joke of Chambers' in poor taste. But—let us play, let us amuse ourselves. In whose name?"

"You will see it is serious." He pulled out a bill drawn on Chambers in London. It was marked *a vista*, which made it payable at sight. It was drawn in her favour. And it was for ten thousand pounds sterling.

An expensive joke. The first doubt that this proposal might, after all, be genuine occurred to her. She pulled her shawl around her and said: "It has gone far enough. And I wish to dance."

She walked away from him. "Please!" he called after her. His anguish sounded genuine. "I have done it so badly. Nathan has said not to say his name. And I—fool—think I know better. Please, just listen."

She stopped then. She had been walking slowly back to the terrace doors with him jogging at her elbow. "Very well, Herr Wolff. I will listen. And I will try to believe."

He thrust the bill into her hand. "You take. You invest it—anywhere you believe good. You are free, totally free. And you keep ten per cent of its profit. And the other ninety per cent you reinvest on the same conditions as before."

"Fifteen per cent," she said at once. There was one way to scotch this silly idea. But moments later she wished she had said twenty, for, although he looked unhappy and muttered about having to consult his brother, it was clear he was going to agree. Quickly she added: "And there will be management fees. Were you thinking of a trust?"

"No," he said unhappily. "We cannot so certainly revoke a trust. We give power of attorney."

She nodded. "So there will also be a fine for cancellation of the power of attorney. The management fee will be one-half per cent on the investment each year that the profit or yield is not realized on that investment. The cancellation fee will be ten per cent if in the first five years, five per cent between five and ten years, two per cent thereafter."

That will surely kill it, she thought; *at least I come out butter side up*. She wished she could see Chambers' face when Wolff-Dietrich, the werewolf king, carried the tale back.

But Wolff was looking at her with frank and breathless admiration. *"Du liebe Zeit!"* he said. "You must be certain of your power. It's outrageous! Highway robbery!"

She smiled with relief, thinking he was at last calling off his proposal. "Good! I'm glad that's agreed." She forgot to return the bill, though.

"Oh, no! No, no!" he chided playfully, snatching the bill from her. "I still must talk to my brother. I tell you tomorrow. *Adieu, Gnädigste!*" He kissed her hand and was gone.

Only then did the amazing truth dawn. He had not been cancelling his offer! He really intended it. All this "I must consult my brother" was nonsense. He was going to say yes tomorrow. Could she think of any other fees she might impose? No sooner had she asked herself the question than she realized the folly of it—and of the fees she had already demanded. She had simply, and thoughtlessly, intended to kill what she had in any case thought of as an insincere proposal. Now, clearly, it had all along been sincere. And how close she had come to stultifying it! She trembled at the memory.

In the small hours of the next morning, when they were back at La Gracieuse, after dancing her feet raw with Sam, with Rodet, and with half of Normandy, she told John what had happened and how it had come about. He parodied a huge chagrin. "You say *you* trembled!" He laughed despairingly. "You drift into these situations all your life. And how you come out unscathed—let alone with gold in your palm—I'll never understand. You're like the drunken smoker in the gunpowder works."

"What do you mean?" She laughed.

"The *day* I met you, that very first day, you were running away. Running for your life. Why?"

She smirked.

"Because you found your gaffer had his fingers in his employers' till —and you told him you wanted a quarter of whatever he was getting."

She bit her lip and grinned.

"And when you intercepted those letters of Chambers', and you tried to blackmail him—"

"I *did* blackmail him."

"Very well. But, in fact, as I pointed out the minute you told me what the letters said, there wasn't one line there to connect them with Chambers. Your 'blackmail' was pure bluff."

She squirmed with delight.

"And with Wyatt. There was more bluff than real threat in what you did."

"*He* didn't think so. And it's my opinion we both ought to be glad for that."

It was a rebuke and John knew it. She often did that sort of thing these days—repulsing him just when she seemed to be warming again. For the first time in this long climb back to their fortune he began to feel a sort of panic. He and Nora were growing apart, and he could not understand why. In so many little ways she was shutting him out, building a complete life of her own. He wondered whether she was even aware of it. There seemed to be a permanent but suppressed hostility there, cooling everything that had once been so warm. What *did* she want?

He reached a hand across the bed and caressed her. "Come on," he said. "You've got me going now."

She kissed him, affectionately enough, but refused the offer. "I have a lot to do tomorrow." She threw away the explanation, as if she knew he didn't really need it. "I must have a talk with Ferrand before I see Wolff again."

He chuckled, pretending to a lightness he did not feel. "That's my lass! The priorities are right."

She laughed good-naturedly, too.

Chapter 33

Ferrand was very pleased with himself. He had, of course, kept Nora posted on his acquisitions over the year, so she knew he already had more than half the land they were after. But only yesterday he had pulled off the best purchase yet—not the biggest, but a vital strip of land running along the foreshore. He was rubbing a red crayon over this latest addition to his map when Nora arrived.

"*Voila!*" he said proudly, dusting his hands and standing back. "Four more hectares."

"Well done," she said. "That strip of seafront was beginning to worry me."

"It has emptied our account, but I got it for twelve hundred and fifty francs. It was worth five—ten times that to us."

Nora made that about five pounds an acre for the ten acres. "Very good. Its value to us was incalculable. I'll fill our account again. Another —what? Hundred and thirty thousand francs?"

"Excellent." Ferrand smiled and took out a bottle of brandy.

She accepted a thimbleful reluctantly; today had to be clear-head day. "What would my esteemed partner say *must* be on that land before it can become a resort?" she asked.

"Ah!" He flexed his hands like a conjuror and dived into a lower drawer in his desk. "See!"

He spread an artist's folio before her, untied the ribbons with delicate fingers, and invited her to lay it open.

It contained perhaps half a dozen large water-colour sketches of a seaside resort; because of the context she knew it had to be Deauville— his imagined Deauville. Only the distant headland was recognizable. The rest was obliterated by buildings and private and public gardens. Her heart quickened to see it; she had imagined the resort often, of course, but without actually picturing it. Her mind did not run to pictures, only to labels—salt-water spa, theatre, library, gaming club, racecourse, houses, and so on. And here, beautifully realized, were the images to match all those labels.

"It is perfect, Monsieur Ferrand. What a shame it must one day become reality—it will never match these views for charm and elegance. Who is your artist?"

"Myself."

She looked back at the painting with redoubled surprise. "But you have a great talent."

And, with Gallic frankness, he agreed. "I was to have been an architect."

"If this becomes reality, you may yet live to become one."

He shook his head and shrugged. "If it becomes reality, I shall be too busy."

"You must, in that case, have some idea of the cost."

He shrugged again. "Thirteen million francs. Say, half a million pounds."

Nora pursed her lips, breathed slowly in, and nodded. "People will not lay that out all at once." She tapped the drawings. "So what is the first stage? We must make it *very* select." She watched his reaction carefully. "It must be where a few people, of the very highest quality, come to stay." She could see he had not thought of it this way. "Or what do you say?"

"I say we assemble first the land. Then we seek capital, in Paris, in London . . . and *bonjour Deauville!* You are beautiful!"

Nora laughed. "I agree. Entirely. Yet I think you underestimate the difficulties of raising such capital. If you say Deauville now, people will say 'where?' and pull their beards and make long faces. But if we could say, 'You know—where lord so-and-so and the marquess of such-and-such and the dowager duchess of elsewhere have their places.' " She could see he was assimilating the idea. She let it soak while she searched again among the water colours. She quickly found the view she was looking for; in the foreground was a perfect French seafront villa— elegant, sumptuously decorated, a bit overripe, yet full of charm and suggesting an informal but entirely proper gaiety.

"Can you sketch several like this?" she asked. "All different yet all with this character, which is perfect."

He could not resist such a challenge. "Very easily," he said.

"You see! You will be Deauville's first architect after all."

And she went on to explain to him how they would now have to hasten what had previously been a very leisurely, long-term affair, at least in her mind. The longer they had in order to establish this bit of coast as an aristocratic retreat, the easier it would be to turn it into a fashionable resort when time and money offered. She was determined now to do as much of it out of their own resources as possible. And, in the short term, she wanted to put the Wolffs' money to immediate use.

"I think," she went on, "now that we have more than half the land —and most of the best part—you must come out into the open. It cannot remain a secret much longer, in any case."

He nodded glumly. "The price will go up."

"I have always been prepared for that. When I do this sort of thing in England, I tell my agent to go out and say, 'I have been instructed to buy all this land by a woman who is completely mad. Believe it or not, she is prepared to pay . . .'—and then he mentions what is no more than the market value of the land, but he makes it sound like a king's ransom—'. . . per acre. She is very old and a bit soft in the head, you know; my advice is to take this offer before she dies!' And most of them do. For the stubborn ones we go no more than ten per cent over the value and say the offer stands one month only. Very, *very* few resist it. Of course, in France you may be more clever."

He conceded that possibility. "But I'll try," he said.

She refused a further brandy and hastened back to La Gracieuse.

*   *   *

The britzka overhauled Sam and Sarah halfway up the hill from Trouville; Nora made the coachman pull in and let Sarah climb up; he and
Sam walked beside the horses to the top.

"I'm neglecting you this year, Sam. I'm sorry," she called to him.

But Sarah said that Nora's loss was her gain. "I've had ever such an
interesting walk down on the beach with Mr. Telling. And such beautiful shells as we have collected! We could make a grotto if we had a sack
to carry them in." She was fishing in her reticule as she spoke, and from
it she produced a handkerchief tied in a loose bundle. It fell open, spilling out a mass of shells on her lap. She turned them this way and that,
selecting four perfect specimens, which she put on the seat between
herself and Nora.

"Name them!" Sam said, climbing in. "I'll wager you've forgotten."

Sarah smiled a challenge back at him. "*Patella nimbosa*," she said of
a plain limpet shell. Then, of another limpet with a starburst pattern of
ribs and a spiny edge: "*Patella granatina.* Right?"

Sam nodded.

Then came a scallop. "*Ostraea jacoboea.*" The last was a spotted
cowrielike shell. "*Cypraea tigris!*" She got her tongue triumphantly
around the syllables.

"Well done, Mrs. Cornelius. You are a star learner."

"Mr. Telling knows so much about shellfish. And about how the
tides are caused," Sarah said.

Sam laughed, a little shamefacedly. "I do about *those* shellfish, for
I picked up their cousins last year and learned all about them from
Rees's *Cyclopedia* in Mr. Nelson's library."

"Where could we make a grotto, Nora?" Sarah asked.

"Ask Rodie."

"Ah." Sarah and Sam exchanged glances.

"What?" Nora asked.

"There's something else we want to ask Rodie," Sarah said.

"Yes. I want to come and see the Auberge Clément with you and
Mrs. Cornelius."

"But we had arranged not to go until next week. After you go
back."

"I know. Would Madame Rodet be upset if you changed?"

"I should think she would. She's arranged so much this time."

They said no more then, for the coach had pulled up at the main door.

*   *   *

That afternoon Rodie had arranged a grand outdoor tea in honour of the English guests. It was almost exclusively a Protestant gathering—sober, energetic, hard-working, careful people who spoke endlessly of business, land, and alliances. Nora enjoyed the undercurrents and tensions she felt in the light-seeming chatter all around. Even when they bent to sip tea, their sharp eyes, like those of wary creatures at a water hole, flickered this way and that above the teacup rims.

Nora had smiled at and nodded to Wolff several times but the affair was almost over before they found occasion to be casually alone together. They wandered into an elegant little classical temple, with a statue of Hygeia—somewhat marred with birdlime—in the middle. Before he could speak of their business she pulled out of her pocketbook some sheets of notepaper on which, just after lunch, she had dashed down what, if accepted, would become the heads of agreement between them.

In essence it was simpler than what she had suggested the previous night; but the details were far more involved. Basically, it provided that they would be investing in *her* rather than letting her buy this or that security for them. Whatever capital they put into her hands was secured by a mortgage debenture on her property at large. Their income from that capital was a proportionate share of her total net income (and here there was a long schedule of allowable deductions) . . . and so it went on, carefully balancing her interests and theirs.

Wolff was very impressed by it, even at a quick read-through. "In some ways it's even better," he said.

"Not necessarily. You might make more profit with your proposal, but the security is less."

"Of course," he said. "I like the security. And income, for sure. But this has a good balance. We write to you from Hamburg."

"Herr Wolff," she said as he started to leave her, "I hope you and your brother understand that, though I am grateful for your trust, I do not admire your judgement. The risk you are taking is madness."

"Risk?" It worried him.

"Well—what do you really know of me?"

"Nathan has told us much already. Also Rodet."

"Rodet! What does he know?"

Now Wolff looked at her with sardonic amusement. "He knows how you have discovered his manufacturing costs."

Nora stared at him, stony-faced. Her stomach sank. She thought of trying to brazen it out, but realized how futile that would be. "He told you?" she asked.

Wolff nodded. "We work it out together, yes."

"But how dreadful! I am a guest here. I would never have come if— Is he very angry?"

"He says he is amused." Wolff shrugged. "But we say, if the oats are stolen, one must thrash the hay instead. Rodet says Stevenson's is an intelligent firm. You will not starve him. You will look after him. I think so, too."

Of course, Rodet was using Wolff as a messenger.

"It's your idea, yes, *Gnädige Frau?*"

Nora, unable to keep an entirely straight face, nodded.

"We take no risk I think, my brother and I." He kissed her hand and left.

She walked back to the house, thinking over Rodet's strange reaction. She could not imagine any English capitalist taking kindly to the idea that someone out there in the jungle was "looking after" him. Yet that was the situation Rodet was accepting; and Wolff had not sneered at him for it. How different these Continental capitalists were. They all liked the cosy life. Could one call it decadent or effete? Or were they really older and wiser? It was, in any case, a difference to bear in mind if Stevenson's worked more extensively in Europe, as now appeared quite likely.

When she returned to the house, she found Sam skipping on the terrace like a child. "We can go Friday," he said gleefully. "Friday first thing."

"But I thought on Saturday, Rodie had arranged for—"

"She doesn't mind. In fact, between you and me, I think she's relieved. I think she's fallen out with this friend of hers we were going to visit."

And it was true that Rodie was very abstracted throughout dinner. Nora later asked her if anything was the matter.

"I am fearful," she said, not smiling, "of the future."

"Your future? The business—is anything wrong? Could we help?"

At last Rodie smiled. She patted Nora's arm. "It's so generous. No, thank you. *Our* future, thank Providence—and thank Rodet—is secure. But for France—" She pulled a glum face. "And the poor people." She shook her head sadly.

"You've been talking to Wolff!" Nora said.

She nodded. "But also Rodet. He says Wolff is right. He says we must find some way of coming closer with the poor. I think I must begin some charity. Do you? In England?"

Nora shook her head. "I have so little time. We give to certain proper charities, of course—the Invalid Asylum, which is for respectable females, and the Female Refuge, which is for penitent fallen women, and the Yorkshire Boys' School in London, and the Railway Servants' Orphanage. And, of course, the Society for the Suppression of Mendicity. That's a wonderful thing; do you have one here?" And she took out one of the society's cards. She kept several always about her. "You see, if a beggar comes up to you in the street, you give him, or her, this card. They can then go to the society's offices, at the address on the card, see? And the society investigates them, and if they are deserving, either refers them to some appropriate charity or grants them relief or refers them back to us with a note of recommendation."

Nora did not say it but she and John gave between three and four thousand pounds a year to these various causes.

Rodie was delighted with her description of the way the Mendicity Society worked. "That's good," she said. "I can do that here, in Rouen."

"It's a lot of work, Rodie. Why not something simpler? Supply coals and soup and good used clothing. You could do that here in Trouville."

She nodded, glum again. "It will be necessary. The harvest is very bad, they say. The worst in memory."

"They always say things like that in June. Wait till August."

Chapter 34

The following day they had no set plans until after lunch. Nora got up looking forward not only to John's return that evening but to a quiet morning lazing on the sands beneath a big parasol, with Sarah and Sam. But Sam said he had a surprise to show her; and Sarah, obviously put up to it by him, claimed she would prefer to sit in the shade on the terrace and do a water colour of the garden at La Gracieuse. So, excited, and wondering what surprise her brother could conceivably have arranged, she set off with Sam in the britzka for Trouville.

The mystery deepened when, instead of going seaward at the foot of the hill, they turned up the right bank of the Touques as if making for Deauville. Had Sam discovered something there? Did he know of her schemes?

But they stopped before the bridge and Sam told the groom he could go home again and meet them back in the centre of the town in two hours. Nora repeated the instructions in French, just to make sure. Then she turned back to Sam, expecting him to lead her off somewhere at once. But he waited until the carriage was out of sight and then took her in its wake, halfway back into the centre. "We must be careful," he said.

"Why? What of?"

"Not 'of'—*for*. You'll see." He would say nothing more as he led her this way and that through the streets, doubling back often, like a fox laying a foil. When he was certain they were not being followed he darted down a narrow, stinking court and knocked at a door. Almost at once it was opened, not wide, as he obviously expected, but just to a slit—enough to pass out a note. As soon as he had the paper in his hand the door slammed again. Absolute silence reigned. No child, nor even a cat, was at play in the court. No eyes beheld them from any of its windows; no one beat a carpet or scraped a cauldron or swilled out their slops. It was an unbearable, unnatural silence.

Sam read the note, shielding it from her. He smiled. "The artful dodger," he said. "Come on."

And she was so relieved to be out of that place that she ran after and even overtook him. Still offering no explanation, he led her down to the riverbank and then the rest of the way back to the centre.

"Where are you taking me now?" she asked.

"To the beach." He smiled. "Isn't that where you wanted to go today?"

The beach was less than a furlong from the centre. As soon as they arrived she saw, about half a mile away, a tall figure in a cloak, with a wide-brimmed black hat. A poet, she imagined, or a painter. He was the only figure on the beach, apart from two children and a nurse nearby.

"It must be him," Sam said, and began a fast, exhausting walk along the sand. But soon he had to slacken, for Nora made no attempt to match his pace. Her heart sank at the thoughts aroused by the sight

of the romantic poet-painter, and Sam's puppy eagerness to reach him.
What had Sam done? Was this some indigent artist he had picked up
with in Paris? She could just imagine him saying "Oh, but I can help.
I have a sister who's very rich. Come up to Trouville and meet her.
She's bound to be interested. And she's bound to want to help." It would
be just like Sam.

How could she say, politely, that she had better calls on her time
and money than to devote either to mendicant *little* talents? She
couldn't. Sam would be so hurt and humiliated. She'd have to give
this . . . person . . . something or it would spoil Sam's holiday—which
was like saying it would spoil his entire year. For Sam's sake, she would
have to be pleasant to—to—

Daniel! The day suddenly dislocated its joints; the sky went brilliant and black in turn; she lost all sense of movement though she still
moved forward. The person she would have to be nice to, for Sam's
sake, was their brother Daniel. Bearded. Dressed like a Frenchman. He
even managed to stand and walk in a new way. But the flashing grin
and the warm Leeds dialect of "Eay, Nora luv!" were pure Daniel. She
had forgotten how fetching he could be. She had forgotten the compulsion of his confident smile, the total assurance he carried everywhere
he went. For a weak moment she almost relented.

She let that impulse fetch a smile to her drained face. She let it lift
her arms toward him. And she let it force out the delighted cry
"*Daniel!*" and make her hug him and kiss him—even while the darkness and the ice returned within. *How dare he!* she thought. How dare
he imagine he could charm his way back into her life, after the way he
had deserted her and left her destitute with Sam and the two children
to rear.

"Thou looks well, Nora," he said. "Thou 'ast fleshed out."

"Aye," she said. "You're far from starved yourself, I see. Revolution
must pay a good dividend."

He parodied shock, and a hint of accusation. "Sam tells us thou
bears a grudge."

"Aye," she said flatly.

He sighed. "I don't blame thee bein' radgy."

"Radgy!" she cried. "More than bloody radgy, I tell thee! Thou
got my eckle up the day thou left, and it's been sky 'igh over eight
year." Spittle flew from her lips; she was trembling; her breath shivered.
It took Daniel completely aback; and Nora herself was more than a
little surprised at her own sudden vehemence.

"Nay—don't barge now!" Sam called in dismay.

"Thou left me speyed down wi' the family. I were dickey-up in a week." Anger, and the chance to shout it to the wind in the elemental language of their common childhood, fired her. Long years of poverty had filled those words with a special resonance; to use them now brought out again the risk-all abandon of those times, before responsibility had taught her caution. She became once more a woman of first instincts.

"Aye. I grant thee that." Daniel wilted before her.

"And then our Wilfrid an' little Dorrie dead. And Sam and me heart-sluffed. And where was our great lad o' wax? Slammockin' in jail, beyond our ken or ken of us."

"Nay, luv, fair jannocks!" Daniel protested. "It weren't *my* orderin'."

"Eay—don't fratch!" Sam pleaded.

"Nay, Sam," Nora told him. "We sh'll have this now or it's never. Our Daniel were born a shuffletoppin' an' 'e'll die a shuffletoppin'."

Daniel stood at bay, steeling himself not to be afraid of her. "What I were born and what I've since become, the likes o' thee'll never fathom, see thou." Now that the shock of her assault was passing he grew bolder. He turned full face to her.

But Sam, taking advantage of the momentary silence, leaped between them and grabbed a hand of each. "Praya!" he shouted. "Please!"

There was nothing—there never had been, never could be anything—that anyone could say to warm Nora to Daniel once again. Nor did she think he could ever feel anything but shame for the way he treated them; if he was now ready to pretend otherwise, it could only be that he saw some advantage in it. So, not wanting to hurt Sam any more for this ill-thought-out gesture of his, she broke his grip on her wrist and, turning on her heel, walked off in the direction of Trouville.

"Aye," Daniel called after her. "Turn thy back on thy own folk—as thou 'ast turned thy back on thy own class these many years. Traitor!"

She looked around at him, contemptuous beyond anger. "From *thee*," she called, "I sh'll own that name wi' pride! And I'll tell thee for naught, Daniel—never look to me for succour. Do that, an' I sh'll flay thee. An' that's Wilfrid an' Dorrie speakin' an' all."

Daniel drew in breath to reply but Sam's "Nay Dan, leave loose wi' thee!" quieted him. Nora left them and walked back to La Gracieuse on her own.

Sam returned an hour later. She was waiting for him and ran across the entrance court to meet him. He looked most disconsolate. She put an arm around him. "Eay, thou great soft cuddy!" she said. "Why do a thing like that?"

To her dismay Sam burst into tears. "I love the pair of ye," he sobbed. "That *much!*"

She stood beside him, lost, and bereft of comfort for him. "You've heart and stomach," she said. "But no brain nor sense. That man and me can never meet, not on any terms."

Sam ran off across the yard; he did not appear for lunch.

When Rodie heard of what had happened, she went up to Sam's room and comforted him enough to bring him downstairs and sit with them on the terrace. Yet in a curious way it was John who did more to restore Sam than any of them. He returned late that afternoon, eager with the good news that they had been awarded the Rouen–Dieppe contract. But when he heard what had happened that morning his face darkened and he turned angrily on Sam.

"You've no more sense than Old Man Fuzzack," he said. "Did you not know your Daniel is wanted by the French government? There's fifty thousand francs on his capture, alive. Did you know that?"

Nora turned sick to her stomach on hearing this news, and she, too, rounded on Sam. Yet she could see the shutters falling across his eyes, and he became a stoic, much-put-upon servant taking a rating from his master and mistress. Contrition turned from a feeling into a technique. "I'm sorry," he said, "to both of you. I just thought that, being family, like . . ."

She saw Sarah nod agreement out of the corner of her eye.

"Thought! You didn't think at all," John said. "You didn't think of your host, Monsieur Rodet, who depends in part on government work. How many new contracts would he get if it came out that guests of his had held clandestine meetings with wanted men? You didn't think of *us*. We too rely on, if not the direct patronage, at least the goodwill of people in government and high places. You talk of family and you mean one ruthless and callous renegade. We've family enough without that. There's a family of seventeen thousand relies on your sister and me."

As Sam repeated his apology, Nora stood up to leave, offering no polite word of explanation. John followed her. "I'm surprised at you—" he began.

"I'd no idea he was wanted," she said. "I spent less than a minute with him." She was putting on her shawl and bonnet. "I flared up at him right off. And I told him I'd flay him if he ever sought me out again."

"Where are you going?"

"To the prefect," she said calmly. "I know where Daniel's lodged. At least I hope I can find it again."

Even John was a little taken aback by that. "Your own brother," he said.

"You're as bad as Mistress Sarah," she answered. "I've got interests in these parts to look after too, see? The last person I'd let interfere with them would be Daniel. Don't tell Sam."

*   *   *

She returned just before dinner with a new silk cravat for Sam. "Just to show that, though we're vexed with you, we've not lost our fondness," she said. He took it as the closing of the incident. "I'll not involve you and the Rodets with him again," he promised. And so an uneasy, smiling peace was patched up—enough to last to the weekend, and with all the year to mend in.

"Well?" John asked. "Taken?"

"No such luck," she answered. "He'd gone already."

"And the house?"

She grinned. "An ordinary *maison de tolérance*, class C, mainly for sailors. A lot of them leave and collect messages there, so there was nothing to blame the owner for. The prefect was more concerned that we and everyone should keep quiet about Daniel having been here; the last thing he wants is word to get out that a wanted renegade came and went on his demesne without hindrance. I gave solemn word I'd turn Daniel over if ever it was in my power again. So I think we're saved, and all damage repaired. My God, I hope so!"

Chapter 35

Next morning it was a quiet, somewhat chastened party that set out for Coutances. John, his "holiday" over, returned to England. Sam was so quiet that Sarah stopped the coach in Caen and went out to buy him some fine cotton shirts. "It'll cheer you up, I know," she said. "I remember when I was at the Tabard, with a *mountain* of work ahead, nothing helped me face it like the wearing of nice new linen!" And Sam, indeed, was almost his old self after that act of kindness.

Nora's letter changing their arrangements had arrived at the Auberge Clément only the previous afternoon, so Gaston had not had enough notice to rearrange bookings and guests to accommodate all three of them. In fact, only one room was vacant.

"But you, Madame, and Madame Cornelius, may sleep at my sister's. I have arranged it," Gaston said.

It was still midafternoon, on a fine June day. The sky was almost cloudless and a slight breeze blew off the sea, enough to make a pleasant coolness under the blazing sun.

Nothing seemed to have changed. Sea gulls still wheeled above the rooftops of the little town, rapacious for scraps. Under the eaves of the room where Cornelius had died, the bees still built their prototype swarms, never quite managing to emigrate. The dog with the bark of a despairing man still yapped at the passing minutes. Even the same children seemed to laugh and quarrel in the same tones at the same causes. The scrape of the stable door, the slosh of water over the cobbles, the singing and laughter of the maids, the smell—all were just as they had been exactly twelve months ago.

"I think I will go up to the cemetery now," Sarah said. "It would be hard to sleep tonight knowing I could have gone and didn't."

The remark surprised Nora. How quickly, she thought, love had turned to duty! But she was glad to be left alone; she had a whole year's accounts to inspect.

Gaston had made great profit of his time at the Adelaide in London last winter. There were no scraps of food kicked into odd corners. Flowers stood in bowls on the tables and sills of the public rooms. Everything was polished. The exterior had been repainted and white-washed—which made it unique in the whole of Coutances, which observed the French habit of painting exteriors only when the property was new or when it changed hands in a dull market. And there were even cushions on some of the chairs. On the door was a proud notice: *English spoken within.*

The changes, unfortunately, did not reflect in the receipts, which were barely up on previous years. She was disappointed. Having been so enthusiastic last year, she had expected to see the effect of the changes almost immediately. But Gaston, though his relative loss was much greater, was more philosophical. "It must take time," he said. "People cannot know of all these grand changes at once. We have much better *quality* people this year, even at the same quantity. They will spread the word. Next year you will see."

And Nora had to be content with that. At least the accounts were immaculate and the inn had made a modest profit.

That evening, when they had finished several rounds of three-handed whist, Nora hid a yawn and said it was time for bed.

At once Sarah said: "Sam and I have talked it over, Nora dear, and we are adamant you shall not be turned out of your own inn. If Sam and I go to the sister's, there will be no need for Gaston to accompany us. And I know Gaston's sister because Tom and I stayed there last year, before we bought this place."

Nora offered token resistance to this kindness and then gave in, thanking them both and confessing it *had* been a tiring day. *It's their life*, she thought; *no affair of mine.* She felt a century older than both of them.

*　　*　　*

The sister's was only three streets away, in the shadow of the cathedral; but it was not quite as Sarah remembered it, for during the previous year the woman had bought the adjoining cottage in the terrace. With Gaston's help she had refurbished its rooms as guest rooms and they were used, as now, to accommodate the excess from the inn, and as guest rooms for the sister's own business.

Darkness was just falling as she let them in at the neighbouring front door, which butted right against hers. "Next year," she said, pointing to the party wall, "we have an arch here." It was almost an apology for leaving them alone. "I light your candles," she said. Sam told her they would manage.

As soon as they were alone they fell into each other's embrace—as they had done for the first time in the cemetery that afternoon—and kissed and breathed each other's names and kissed again, until all the light had gone. The cathedral clock struck half past eleven. Outside, Gaston's sister, who had watched in vain for the gleam of candlelight at the windows, went quietly back indoors, shaking her head. *These English—they come to France for one thing only*, she thought.

But for Sarah, scandal had ceased to exist. The kiss of a man's lips on hers again, the voice of a man breathing her name reverently in her ear, the press of his strong arms about her, the pressure of *him*—these stirred her ardent spirit beyond the reach of any voice that did not cry out *Enjoy! Live!* She did not think of the night that lay ahead, but the whole of her mind and body rose up to welcome it. She was on the point of saying "Take me to bed," when Sam whispered: "I suppose we had better say good night, Sarah."

The sudden stiffness of her body astonished him; it revealed a dimension to his holiday flirtation which he had not even considered. "Don't you think?" he added.

"Let's not think, Sam," she said. The pressure of her hand was toward the stairs; she withdrew from him a bare inch in that direction.

"Mrs. Cornelius—" he began, confused.

"Sarah, she said. And when he still did not move or speak she added, "You must have thought of this."

"No," he whispered. "Not once. Not in the most—secret moments."

"Oh." She was deflated. "What does that make of *me?*" Then, before he could respond, she said: "Suppose you think of it now, then."

She wished she could see his expression. She pressed herself back into his arms and buried her face on his shoulder. He swallowed audibly.

"You would think so ill of yourself in the morning," he said at last. "And worse of me."

"I promise not to," she said.

Again he was silent.

"Have you thought of it now?" she asked.

"I do not think I could. I respect you too much."

There was a pause before she pulled away and leaned her head up to his for one final chaste kiss. "Good night, Sam. *I* don't think less of you for it." Her tone implied that hundreds would.

She walked quickly into the downstairs bedroom and pushed the door almost shut. She busied herself at once with undressing, struggling with the buttons at her back, struggling, too, not to give way to her tears. They bathed her cheeks as unfeelingly as sweat. *I am hard*, she tried to think.

And then the door opened again and Sam was close behind her. "What do you mean?" he asked. " 'Think less of you'?"

As soon as he touched her she spun around and hugged him. "Don't think!" she said. "Don't think."

His hands discovered that her dress had gone; only a corset, a chemise, and six petticoats separated them. She felt the shiver of his discovery, and she pulled his head down to kiss her. His hands held her neck . . . her shoulders . . . her arms.

"I don't really know," he said. "I've never—"

"Never mind," she soothed. "Just get undressed. We'll manage."

Impatient minutes later they stood naked, two feet apart. In the dark they could each feel the heat of the other's body, each hear the other's shattered breathing through the pounding of their hearts.

And there they stood in thrall to the monstrous power that neither understood; for a moment each was afraid to move, afraid to shatter the little gain they had dared.

She reached out. Her unclothed arm moved silently. Her hand touched his, reaching through the dark for her. His paused, but she swept it on and up to her breast. She spread his hand and fingers on her breast; with her other hand she reached for him—for the heat she felt and the stiffness her nights with Tom had added to her imagination. And there it was.

But it was not still. It throbbed. And it leaped like something demented. And there were sudden stabs of heat on her fingers and arms and stomach and thighs, which turned wet and cool. And sticky.

Then she heard the little puppy noises and gasps he was making. And they turned to sobs as he fell to his knees against her and threw his arms about her hips, saying, "Sorry ... sorry ... sorry ..." like a litany. He kissed her stomach and her thighs as he wept and repeated that one word.

She stood and held his head while the realization stole over her—bringing no understanding in its train—that it was over. "Why did you do it like that?" she said at last. "That wasn't the right thing at all."

He laughed—or was it a sob?—into her flesh.

She withdrew from him then and, taking up a petticoat, wiped the wet patches dry—or at least damp—before she got into bed. He fell in beside her and was at once asleep.

When he woke again, half an hour later, Sarah was almost asleep, having cried herself cold.

His arm, encircling her, stirred nothing within. His hand, curling around her breast again, did not rouse her. But for memory's sake, and for the hope the magic would return, she sighed his name and amazed herself at the realism of the tremble in her voice and breath.

Encouraged, he raised a thigh upon her and began to widen his caressing exploration, while she, unblinded now by any passion, experienced him with a clinical candour. Even her naïvety could not ignore his apish clumsiness.

But the stiffness would not come to him again and after five increasingly hectic minutes he fell limp upon her and laughed silently and in despair. Suddenly it seemed funny to her as well. She gave a little giggle. For a moment he held his breath and then he giggled, too.

It was no more than that. She stroked his naked back and felt his male bulk as if she herself had never known the burdens of sex; and in that same instant she was overcome by a neutered friendship for this stranger. It was so intense as to be a kind of love. "Oh, Sam!" she said. "What *was* it all about?"

He took it as a real question and thought long before he answered timidly, "The triumph of fondness over passion?"

"You're heavy," she whispered.

Later, when she was deep asleep, he managed to complete, alone, what they had so unavailingly begun together. It was a guilty, cold, aching pleasure, with her lying there so soft and warm behind him.

But—as he was to say many times over the years that followed—it helped him off to sleep.

PART FOUR

Maran Hill, 1847

Chapter 36

John paid Flynn the compliment of not being present when the Carlow branch was inspected and—of course—given its clearance. It was the first time he had ever been absent from the inspection of so large a contract. Instead he took Nora, by coach, down the route of the main line, as close to it as the roads permitted. It was very much the route he and MacMinimum had followed that April. Nora had agreed to come only to lay to rest the ghost of their flare-up last May. But she set out from Dublin with great foreboding. This country seemed to bring out the differences between herself and John at their starkest and most disruptive.

Though the distress was still great, the mood of the country was far happier, for a fine, luxuriant potato crop filled the fields. Everyone said it was going to be the heaviest crop in memory; and though the blight had shown in odd patches here and there, it was much less severe than last year.

They had another reason for happiness, too: Peel's Irish Coercion Bill, introduced in February, had been defeated on 25 June by a combination of Lord John Russell's Whigs and a rebel group of Tories, still angry with Peel over his virtual repeal of the Corn Laws—one form of repeal that had *not* been popular in Ireland. Now, with the prospect of a glorious harvest, everyone in England could reasonably hope that only the usual two-to-three million Irish would starve this year and so there would be no need for extraordinary coercion.

For John, too, the promised harvest and the change in government brought fresh hope. The new liberal ministry was far less likely to start doling out government charity and food to the people. The liberals were staunch believers in the virtues of the free market, self-reliance, and initiative. True, when the distress was abnormal, governments had no choice but to offer such palliatives as food and relief works—it was the market price of buying freedom from total insurrection. But now, when the distress would be back to its usual levels, there would be a chance to let a proper mercantile system and an effectual farming system grow, all under the stimulus of competition and profit, and free of Tory paternalism. Bad, bankrupt landlords would no longer have the umbrella of the Corn Laws to raise over their own leaking roofs; they would crash—and newly rich merchants with some idea of business would buy them out. Estates in Ireland were going to be right cheap. It was going to be a long and painful upheaval, but a newer, stronger Ireland would emerge at the end—strong enough, perhaps, to govern itself. Already Trevelyan at the Treasury had turned away cargoes of relief Indian corn. And all relief was to end in mid-August.

He discussed these thoughts with Nora on their way down through Queen's County and County Tipperary.

"Do you think we should buy any estates here?" she asked. "If they are going to be so cheap."

He did not answer at once, and then all he said was: "It's tempting."

"That's not very enthusiastic."

"We'd be at the wrong end of a bad tradition," he said. "Absentee landlords."

"They're not all bad," she pointed out. "Sir George Staunton at Clydagh, everyone praises him as a model; and he's an absentee. And the Duke of Devonshire. It's a case of getting the right stewards and giving firm instructions. What this country needs is *good* landlords, absent or present."

"But that's not *us*, love. You've never bought land merely in order to improve farming. Anyway, we'll think on it. I fear we'll do precious little land buying on any scale these next few years."

                                  *   *   *

Almost the first person they saw in the dining room of the Royal, in Tipperary town, was Captain Cashel Ormond, whom he and Mac-Minimum had met in this same place in April. He greeted John warmly and was then introduced to Nora.

"You and Captain Ormond have something in common," he told her. "He is Master of the Tipperary. And Mrs. Stevenson is an enthusiast for . . ." His voice tailed off as he saw the bewilderment spreading over Ormond's face. "Are you not?" he added.

"Sure I never hunted in me life. Now, if it's fishing ye're seeking . . ."

"How odd, sir. I was told quite categorically that you were Master of the Tipperary."

"By MacMinimum?"

"Yes."

"God, isn't he the quare one! Sure he knows me like his own brother."

"Queer is the word. He told me particularly not to mention the

Waterford & Limerick Railway, which was our business. He said you hunted the Suir valley and would kill us."

Ormond sat down, shaken, lost in thought. Then he looked sharply at John, seeing him in an altogether different light. "Stevenson?" he said again. "*That* Stevenson! Dear God! I'll *kill* MacMinimum, I swear it."

"Are you connected with railways then?" John asked.

"Connected! Aren't I the chairman of the Waterford & Limerick!"

*   *   *

The next day, the second of August, was damp and close. A strong southeasterly wind carried a fine drizzling mist almost horizontal over the fields. It obscured the carriage windows on the south side and cut off their view of much of the proposed route to Waterford. They spent the day wondering why MacMinimum had prevented John from revealing himself and his business to Ormond, and coming to no very tenable conclusions. Also, to be sure, they talked of their business in general. John, only half jokingly, said how strange it was that to find release enough from the everyday press of affairs they had to flee to a remote Irish valley to see a line whose building would occur—as even Ormond had said—the Dear One knows when.

Another thing Ormond had said was that John's evidence before the select committee of Parliament on railway labour, given about two weeks earlier, had been very well received in railway circles. "You said a lot that needed saying," he said firmly. "There's few can command the gratitude of labourers and proprietors. And you, sir, are one of that few."

The praise had delighted Nora. If word of John's evidence had reached these parts of the world so soon, that was surely a mark of the respect he now commanded.

But John was more cautious. "Remember," he said, "that Ormond is Irish, and Irish hospitality has no equal. It's hospitality makes him say that. You'll never hear ill of yourself from Irish lips. Always remember that."

"I don't believe it," she said. "Not that they're *so* different."

"They are," he reaffirmed. "They're as different as the wine that goes in and the water that comes out, as Lucas once told me. Take Ormond and MacMinimum now. You'd never credit that they could be friends again, not after what MacMinimum did to Ormond."

"Certainly not," she said, forgetting Lord Wyatt and herself.

"If they were Englishmen, Ormond would find it hard to speak to MacMinimum. Yet if we turned back to Tipperary now and found the pair of them drinking and laughing this evening away, nothing would surprise me less. Two Englishmen could call themselves friends and sit the whole evening by the fire, the one reading, the other smoking and thinking. Not a drink or a word exchanged. And they could be the best and closest of friends. Now, I think there's not an Irishman born could begin to comprehend that as friendship. Friendship means talk, means laughter, means drink, means slander, means secrets blurted to the world, means a fight, means a grand memory. Loyalty isn't in it. An Irishman is hardly an Englishman at all in my view."

Nora, who wanted to talk about John, not the Irish, said, "All the same, Ormond knew what to say, so he must have heard of your evidence." John could not deny it. "I wish I'd been there to see it," she said.

He smiled at the memory of it. "I thought it was going to be held in Gothic splendour in Barry's new palace."

"Wasn't it?"

"It was held in a draughty wooden shanty in Palace Yard. I've seen navvies better housed."

The day was so overcast it grew dark early. They had to light the carriage lights long before Waterford. When they pulled into the town they noticed a strange, sour, nauseous stench, which filled the whole valley.

They had barely drawn into the hotel yard when the nurse came running across to the coach door. "Your honour!" she called in high excitement. " 'Tis Charles Coen himself come for his own little girl." Breathless she pointed to Char-less (as she pronounced the name), a stocky, curly-haired young man who followed her across the yard with the rolling swagger of a prizefighter. "He was after arriving yesterday," the nurse added. "And stayed on for to see yourself."

Young Mary bobbed behind her father, dodging the pools of dung-mottled water. One side of her head was badly scarred; the skin looked more like the membrane that sheathes an ox kidney than anything human. No hair grew upon it. But her smile was that of a seraph. "Would ye ever look at her!" the nurse said, beaming. "If it wasn't her leg hindered her, sure she'd fly the carriage for joy."

"Mr. Coen, I'm John Stevenson." John shook him by the hand and presented him to Nora.

Coen had intended saying something but now the moment had come he merely stood and smiled, and blinked. And swallowed. John bent down to see Mary more closely. "Well, young lady," he said. "You're a lot better than when last we met."

"God be praised," Coen said above him as Mary retreated once more behind her father. "And your honour, too. God be good to ye!"

"Have you another home now, Mr. Coen?" John asked, standing tall once more.

"I have, sir. I have a brother in Philipstown."

"And work?"

"I . . . ," he began. Then he lowered his eyes. "No, sir."

"Have you tried the railroad?"

"I have that. God, that Flynn! He's the divil. There's no place there."

"Well, before you go back to your brother—tomorrow?" Coen nodded. "Call at the hotel here. There will be a letter for you to carry to the 'divil Flynn.' He will give you work. I promise it."

"Ah, God, sir!" Coen began, his eyes filling with tears.

But John cut him short. "The thing that was done to you and your family, Mr. Coen—and to your neighbours—should never be done by any man, no, nor any woman either, to a fellow creature." He glanced casually at Nora as he spoke. "The world owes you the chance to start again. It's not charity, man. It's a debt discharged. I wish I could find all those who were evicted and give them work."

Coen's eyes brightened in such a way that Nora truly feared he was about to say he had all seven hundred of them waiting just around the corner. But he merely repeated his thanks and left with Mary's hand in his.

*   *   *

Next morning the smell they had noticed on first entering the valley was overpowering. It woke them long before the maid came with hot water. John, unable to bear it, went to the window and threw back the curtain. There was nothing in the street to account for the odour, no refuse tip or dead animal. He looked farther, at the rooftops and spires. There was no fire, nor any wet and steaming remnant of a fire, as far as he could see.

And then, above the rooftops, he noticed the fields. They were black and dark brown, for mile upon mile. It was not wheat and corn that had blighted—their golden acres stood out bright against that terrible darkness—it was the potato. It *had been* the potato.

Not a patch of its bright green leaf remained. No matter where he looked, not a field had been spared. Overnight the entire crop had perished.

"What is it?" Nora asked, still in bed.

He was too shaken to reply at once. "A death warrant," he said at last.

But the devastation they could see from the window was as nothing to the utter ruin they drove among all day, from Waterford up the valley of the Barrow to Carlow. At breakfast the maidservant, subdued like everyone else in the town by the local calamity, had thanked God the crop in the rest of Ireland was so luxuriant. But by that evening they knew that the "local" calamity extended fifty miles at least.

Over all that blighted land lay the cloying stench of decaying potatoes. The earth looked as if a wet fire had passed over it. Everywhere they saw families digging desperately among the wilted plants, seeking a few tubers they might salvage. Several times John stopped the coach and got out to see the blight for himself; it was as if he could not believe the vastness of it and had to remind himself, time and again, of its horror. In all that sombre day they did not see one potato plant left green, nor one potato tuber that would not crush to an evil black slime at the slightest pressure.

The faces of those who alighted from the "celebration" train from Dublin next day told the rest of the story. They, too, had come through mile after mile of black field upon black field. The day was so wintry that the green upon the trees and hedgerows seemed incongruous. Fierce and heavy downpours of cold rain swept down from the Wicklow mountains, drenching the land. Lightning flickered over the wasted fields. And toward evening a dense, chill mist sprang up, seemingly out of the ground, and enveloped them all. The Carlow branch had a very muted opening.

Over the days that followed their return to Dublin the reports from all parts of the country made it clear that the potato failure had been total. Not a parish had been spared.

The anguish of the people was now universal. For months the relief works had kept a bare sufficiency of flesh on their bones; but the hopes that survived with it had all been pinned on the coming bounteous harvest of potatoes. Overnight the crop and those hopes had turned to the colour of despair. Everything that could be pawned had already gone. Every debt they could incur they had already incurred. Every last scrap of food they could find they had long since devoured. They faced the winter with nothing. From the far west, where the deepest poverty lay, the most piteous tales were arriving. Naval boats put ashore where every shellfish had been pried from the rocks and every last strand of seaweed been eaten; there they found whole villages of skeletons, some still with flesh upon them, a few still actually breathing.

When John realized the magnitude of the disaster he was tempted to the same despair as had seized the rest of the country. What could one *do?* The government, encouraged by the prospect of a good harvest, had closed down all relief, had ordered no new supplies of grain to fill commissariat depots that were now empty, and had voted no new money for public works. The European harvest in general was, as Rodie had said back in June, deplorable; prices were already high and the English labourer was feeling the pinch. If the government now went into the market for grain for a starving Ireland, the price would hit the moon and there would be bread riots at home. It was too late. Hundreds of thousands were going to die and all the money in the exchequer could not save them. What could one do?

"We can take away no profit from these Irish contracts, love," he said to Nora.

He expected her opposition but she agreed at once. "The question is," she said, "what do we do with it? Where do we apply it? It will be tens of thousands of pounds. We must not waste it merely to make ourselves feel good."

She was surprised at her agreement. It made her wish they had not come to Ireland. When you saw the misery of so many people and sensed the terrible fear that gripped them, it was hard to think properly and make calm decisions. She hated mixing money and emotion; no good ever came of it. Unreasonably—knowing it to be unreasonable— she turned her annoyance upon John.

"I have no idea what to do yet," he said, unaware of her mood, glad only that she agreed—or appeared to agree. "We must think hard and consult with many people. Certainly it would be folly for us to try anything on our own. The desperation that swamps every government effort would annihilate us entirely."

"And meanwhile," she said, "we have forty-three other contracts, great and small to tend. And fifty to sixty thousand mouths dependent on those efforts."

*   *   *

Their intended return to England was delayed twenty-four hours by the arrival of an urgent message from Lord George Bentinck, saying he was coming to Dublin and particularly asking John to stay and meet with him and advise him on the drafting of a bill requiring the government to support Irish railways.

Bentinck was a strange figure in English politics. The third son of the Duke of Portland, he was now forty-four, having sat in Parliament as member for Lynn Regis for the last twenty years. His love of racing (which he had purged of much corruption) and of field sports had led him to decline several ministries, yet he had had greater influence on Parliament than most who held high office. His liberal opinions on Catholic emancipation and the Reform Bill had led him out of the liberal camp into the Tory, where he had been one of Peel's staunchest supporters. Yet when Peel went over to free trade, Lord George Bentinck had led the protectionist wing of the Tories against him on that crucial defeat over the Irish Coercion Bill. There were many who said he would one day be a great prime minister. Young Disraeli worshipped him.

He and John met in Dublin Castle. Nora had come along too, intending to write some letters. But Bentinck had brought with him the proof slips of John's evidence to the select committee on railway labour; he said he had come upon them by chance at the government printers and, in reading them, had become aware of the true calibre of John Stevenson. "You are just the sort of person, sir, to advise me on this legislation I am preparing. I would deem your help a kindness and an honour."

Nora had borrowed the slips to look at while they conferred in another room. She read:

Veneris, 17° die Julii, 1846.

———————

MEMBERS PRESENT

Sir Thomas Acland   Mr. Hudson
Mr. Lambton   Mr. Rich
Mr. Ewart   Mr. Mangles
Viscount Barrington   Lord Hamilton

The Right Hon. LORD EGERTON, IN THE CHAIR

John Stevenson, Esq. called in; and Examined

———————

3174. *Chairman.*] You are a railway contractor at present residing in Yorkshire?—I am.

3175. And how long have you held that business?—I have been in the business of building railways for twelve years, eight of them as contractor. I began as a navvy and worked up to it.

3176. Sir Thomas Acland.] Do many do that?—Not many stay. I have known one man who had contracts for 50,000*l* in 1841 who was reduced again to a ganger in 1843.

3177. How have you avoided that fate?—By carefulness. Careful estimating before the work, careful accounting on it, and careful use of the subsequent profit. And careful use of men.

3178. Chairman.] How many men do you now employ?—A little more than 19,000. Most are directly contracted to me, about 17,000; but some are subcontracted.

3179. So you are as big as Mr. Peto?—Taller by nine inches, I believe. (Laughter) (Order) I apologize, sir. We are much of a muchness in size, as firms.

3180. You have heard his evidence. He has described a method for dividing a contract among deputies, agents, overseers, timekeepers, and gangers that sounds for all the world like colonels, captains, subalterns, and sergeants in other clothing. Does your practise accord with his?—In effect it does. It accords on almost every detail in practise; though Mr. Peto and I are sharply divided in precept. In practise we both understand that a master with so many thousand men would soon go bankrupt if he failed to exercise that sort of military authority over them. In Mr. Peto's view that is *absolutely* right. His is an autocratic character. I do not mean that critically. He is a most benevolent autocrat and greatly respected by his men. But I look forward to a time when men accept the discipline of the working as a carpenter accepts the discipline of the grain of wood—of their own free will and understanding. So I do nothing to hinder the growth of self-reliance and self-discipline, even at the cost of actual discipline when my trust proves premature. I may say I am greatly hindered by the presence of the poorer and more ruffianly sort of contractor on adjacent workings. They encourage every sort of bad habit and low behaviour as well as low standards of work.

3181. Mr. Lambton.] Some witnesses claim the quality of workman has greatly improved lately.—It has, taken since 1835. But it is too slow for me. The tramp-navvy has almost disappeared. I think it wrong to blame the workman, though. A contractor who cheats his men, paying at two-month intervals and giving endless subscriptions meanwhile in truck, forcing poor beer and scrawny beef on them in place of coin of the realm, such a master reduces his workmen to despair and *makes* them terrors to the countryside.

3182. Mr. Ewart.] And a burden on the parishes.—Yes. I have had such men come to me, who, when paid regularly, properly victualled, and fittingly

housed, have turned into model labourers and even become smallish capitalists on their own account. It has often amazed me that the most dangerous
ruffian under one system of employment becomes the chief ornament of the
other system.

3183. Mr. Lambton.] Of your system?—Yes.

3184. Chairman.] Which is also Peto's system.—Not in every detail.

3185. Where then do you differ?—I have tommy shops on all my larger
workings. I heard a porkbutcher once claim he had made 5,000*l* profit in one
year from navvy trade. That was before I was a contractor. I determined then,
if ever it was in my power, I'd have none of it. My tommy man is the
guarantee of it. But the labourer's liberty to buy where he will is also the
guarantee that my tommy man does not replace one evil by another.
There is a great and abiding sense of fairness in every Englishman
which comes to the fore if you can only clip his avarice. (Laughter)
By controlling the tommy man I also control—indeed prevent—the
sale of intoxicants at a working. It is a point that has not been sufficiently appreciated at this committee, at these inquiries. May I explain? It
may happen that several gangs are working in a cutting, say a hundred men.
The method is to work with three sets of wagons, one set filling, one set
going to be tipped, and one set being tipped and returned. Each man among
that hundred has his proper task. Now I have seen it come on to rain at
ten o'clock and all the men take shelter. Some contractors let their gangers
manage beer supplies at the working, and if the men have worked three
hours they will know they can call on the ganger for at least nine pence—
which they may then settle to consume in beer. After six or seven pints,
many will not resume work but will sit about under the hedges and sing
and fight all day. Six men behaving in that way can so disorder the regular
flow of the sets of wagons that the value of work done at the cutting is
halved for that day. I have seen that more than once.

3186. Mr. Mangles.] Do you think the safety of the railway labourer is
adequately provided for?

Lord Hamilton (intervening): There was a large difference of opinion there between Mr. Peto and Mr. Brunel.—I think, with respect, my lord,
you are misreading Mr. Brunel. His evidence has been wrongly taken to indicate that most railway companies would deprecate the introduction of
liabilities on the French system. In France, as you know, the companies are
responsible for the support of men injured, for the support of widows and
orphans of men killed, and for injury or damage to third parties or property,
regardless of any question of actual blame or negligence. But he was concerned to point out that there are circumstances where to put *absolute*

liability on the company would compel the directors to interfere with day-to-day working much to its detriment. And there I agree. There are certain independent labourers, among them being miners, whose self-reliance would be greatly diminished by that degree of interference.

3187. Mr. Mangles.] Can you exemplify that? We have no experience of the conditions you refer to.—You may imagine a miner who has contracted with me that he and a mate, or two mates, will remove so many yards of face for such and such a fee within so many days. If I, or the company, were to be liable to him or his dependents, we should be ever about his ears, saying, you must use more shoring, you must use better timber, you must not undercut so high a face . . . and so forth. His independence would go.

3188. Mr. Ewart.] As it is, then, what happens? His dependents are cast upon the parish?—As it is, on *my* workings, he takes out insurance through me at 4*d* a week. And so we avoid all inquiry into negligence or liability. And I think that a better answer than throwing liability on the company.

3189. Sir Thomas Acland.] Is this 4*d* a week compulsory to every man? —Only if he wants to work for me. (Laughter) There is a further stoppage of 6*d* for sick club and funeral benefits. That will pay 10*s* a week to any man sick or injured at work. A penny a week per man will go from that 6*d* to pay a doctor to attend. Which the doctors get whether called or no.

3190. Mr. Rich.] Do the men not complain of this stoppage?—They administer the entire fund themselves, by committee. Before I gave them that administration, they complained frequently. But now they are most jealous of the right. All I do is maintain the accounts in proper order.

3191. Mr. Mangles.] Do the doctors always come when called?—Like a genie from a bottle. The capitation, as we call it, may amount to 600*d* a week, or 120*l* a year.

3192. Lord Hamilton.] I have heard of a doctor who left a titled patient to attend a navvy.—If the titled patient owed as much as many are reputed to owe, I find that not impossible. The benefits are great. On workings where there are no medical arrangements I have seen men, still working, so eaten with smallpox that not an inch of fair skin could be found upon them.

3193. Sir Thomas Acland.] What is your practise as to housing your men?—It varies greatly from place to place. On the York to Scarborough there was ample and good lodging to be had in the towns and villages beside the line. In South Devon that is also the case, though in the warmer weather men will sleep under hedges ("skipper it" as they say) to save 2*s* a week on lodging. I do not like it but cannot stop it.

3194. Viscount Barrington.] Is 2*s* average for that class of lodging, taken over England as a whole?—In general it is. But I have had married men and their wives, in North Wales, charged 8*s* and 10*s* for small rooms over shops in Rhyll, in the old and narrow part of the town. To remedy that, I bought trees from a farmer and made cabins on the colonial pattern. But last month I found an excellent builder of wooden houses, made in demountable sections, for colonial use. I believe this committee could profitably question him and see his plans, which would thereby get wide currency among contractors in general. It would alleviate much distress among railway labourers, for this trouble is wide spread.

3195. *Chairman.*] What is his name?—It is Peter Thompson and he lives in Commercial Road here in London.

3196. *Sir Thomas Acland.*] You do a great deal for your men, Mr. Stevenson.—I do. Listening to myself give evidence, it is a great deal more than I had thought. And, as I say, it goes against my true conviction, for in an idealized world all men would be sober, honest, vigilant, thrifty, considerate, careful, and diligent. But as they are not, and as the itinerant nature of the work and the prevalence of bad employers hampers their development that way, I have to do for them what I know they ought to do for themselves. But it is self-interest compels me, and I think I see at least twice the profit per man that a bad master sees—despite the profit he gets on truck and tommy rot and on outright swindling.

3197. *Chairman.*] Is there anything you wish to add to your evidence to this committee?—Yes. I did not explain the system of payment for men subcontracted to me. The largest part of a railroad is simple tracklaying in shallow cuttings and small embankings. When I start a line, I will piece out these with my deputy and we will determine a rate for the work. But these simple pieces I am ready to give out to that class of labourer which prefers to work by the lump, as we say, than by the day. They form themselves into gangs and elect a leader to be their ganger. He will come to me and bargain for a lump of simple work. I will say 300*l* is my price; and he may say I think you are tight with me there; and I will say, well that is the price; and so we agree. (Laughter) I will yield a little if it later proves tight. Then I have no duty but to supervise the quality of the work and pay upon completion.

3198. *Mr. Rich.*] Do they earn more by that way of working?—Very much so. It is worth it to me to be relieved of timekeeping and bookkeeping. If a day labourer takes from 18*s* to 22*s*, a man at the lump will, at the end of his time, take money equivalent to 25*s* to 32*s* weekly. Under my system only the provident man can work this way, for I give no subsistence to them and I permit no truck. So they must fend many weeks for themselves.

3199. *Viscount Barrington.*] That is not so on others' workings?—By no means is it so. A bad contractor will let a lump go to a ganger at a very keen rate, usually much too keen. Then the ganger has to make by truck and by swindling what he cannot make by honest work. It is a pernicious system and very vexatious to those of us who try to live by fairer means.

3200. What remedy do you propose?—As I understand the common law, a magistrate may distrain against goods when a ganger will not pay the agreed sum to his gang, but if the ganger has no goods, there is an end to the matter. I believe the law should be changed so as to allow magistrates to distrain against the person as well as against goods. These defaulting gangers would pay up if the alternative were prison; and they would not then be so reckless in accepting such very low piece rates.

3201. Mr. Peto makes himself responsible for paying where gangers default. He believes all contractors should be made responsible.—I think it would not answer. Of course on my workings I am the same as Mr. Peto. I would pay any men whose ganger levanted and decamped. But he and I are men of enormous capital. And we give out lumps only to men of known good character, men who have been with us for years and have put money by and are on the way to becoming small capitalists themselves. I would think it a scandal if we did not make ourselves responsible. But it would be most burdensome for a smaller contractor who has not our opportunity to know these gangers. Or our resources to underwrite them.

3202. *Chairman.*] In general, then, what is the sum of legislative changes you believe necessary?—I would favour the very minimum of legislative intervention. The law, as I see it, should balance out the advantages and disadvantages of master and servant, making no especial favour for either, nor placing any unnatural bar in the way of either. It should, in short, be neither repressive of the servant nor paternal.

3203. *Mr. Mangles.*] You say nothing of safety.—As to safety I will say this, with some diffidence. The many canals and highways associated with the name of Thomas Telford were built without the loss of a single life. The modest cost of a canal enabled companies to be patient as to completion. But the ruinous capital cost of a railway, which is exacerbated in this country, though not upon the Continent nor in America, by senseless competition and by outrageous payments for land (and lately by fevered speculation), this high cost, I say, enforces an unnatural speed to finish the line and set it to earning its profit. If your learned committee, my lord, can find a way to apply the French or American systems here, you will do more to promote safety among railway labourers than all the obligatory insurance or government inspectors you might muster.

3204. You do not then think, as some have held, that unions if they were formed among the labourers, would encourage safer working?—Unions put a permanent tyranny in place of one that is temporary. They do not suit the nature of railway work nor the spirit of the railway worker.

When Nora had finished reading this evidence she understood exactly what was making her so nervous about John and his behaviour toward Ireland—more than nervous, in fact, angry. There, in every word he had spoken, was all his humanity, all his wisdom, all that deep, unsentimental knowledge of human nature—the very qualities that had brought Lord George over of a purpose to see him. So why did John only have to set foot on Irish soil to abandon even the most obvious, commonsense notions of business and human nature? The country had allowed millions of people to slip beyond the reach of the monied system; they lived without trade, cash was no inducement to them, and lack of it was no discouragement. Until now. They lived on a food—the potato—that could be made almost as available as water. Until now. Their survival had seemed to mock the great natural laws that govern the wealth of nations. Until now.

Now those great laws were taking their delayed but inevitable course, and it could no more be prevented than the onset of winter. To pretend that it could was both arrogant and cruel—arrogant of oneself and cruel to those poor souls whose deaths were now about to show how wide the writ of economic law could run—and how deep. *And damn it*, she thought, remembering the winter before last at Thorpe, *who was it berated myself and the children for feeding all the birds of the air!*

She distrusted Bentinck, too. Governments had no business meddling in trade. Ireland had more than enough private wealth to satisfy her need for railways. If the owners of that wealth preferred to invest it in Spanish or Austrian, or even Indian, railways instead, that was a clear message to the Irish that they were not offering enough of the right security. Let them stop their outrages—and their outrageous demands—and the capital would come falling out of the very thatch. There'd be no need for government subsidies then. The only thing such subsidies did was to prevent the people from ever learning the hard but unavoidable lessons of economic life.

Nora was well in steam by the time John returned. She congratulated him on his evidence to the select committee and asked him how his talk with Bentinck had gone.

"I told him all I knew about the Irish companies, and of the lines that, in my view, could be made profitably if they only had the capital."

"And did you also tell him that in your view the Tories have ruined this country with their protection and patronage? And that the last cure she needs is another dose of the same medicine?"

He laughed.

"I'm serious," she said.

"I know you are."

"Well? Did you?"

"I would have liked to. But we were not talking to that purpose." He could sense the anger in her silence. "However, I told him all the arguments that Russell and Wood and Trevelyan might muster against him, and—"

"And how to rebuff them, I suppose!" She threw up her hands in resigned disgust.

"It will mean money for Irish railroad building—which can certainly do *us* no harm."

She said nothing.

"Or do you think we can manage without?"

She turned to him, trying to stay calm, trying to keep the heat out of her voice. "Give a government a million to invest and their first thought is who do we owe a favour, or who can we bind to us with a favour, or where can we buy support or buy—"

"Or buy the public peace," John interrupted. "That's understood. Support for industries that cannot attract commercial capital is exactly that: buying peace. Like everything else, public order has its market price. No one is pretending otherwise."

"But that's just what they will do—pretend otherwise. They'll pretend it's charity—the soul of a Christian nation expressing itself. Such hypocrisy!"

His tolerant smile angered her even more than his argument. "What would you prefer? Let the ruffians know their disorder has a value in cash?"

"Of course not! But bring them to understand that peace and hard work do have such value. In the long run there can be no benefit to anyone in buying them off by unsound investment. If governments are to start pumping money into unprofitable business or unprofitable corners of the kingdom, they will end by impoverishing all business, impoverishing all the parts of the kingdom, and all the people. I say we should not take one step along that path. And nor should we assist those like Bentinck who want us to."

"Well," he said, stretching his shoulders, "I'm sure this ministry will take your line. Lord George's bill has no more chance than . . . Prosser's Patent Wooden Railway."

"Ooooh!" she fumed. "When you don't want to discuss anything—!"

His attitude changed at once. He appeared to resign himself—painfully—to the necessity of talking with her, which brought all her anger
back to the boil.

"Very well, Nora," he sighed. "What do you want? Let's talk about
our money. The profits we're making on the GS&W. Do you now think
it would be wrong to invest them here?"

It was a question too important for anger; she forced herself to
speak reasonably. "If the government are going to start handing out
money to everyone who waves a begging bowl under their noses, it will
make reasonable business decisions impossible."

"I doubt if the government will do that. I doubt it very much."

"Too much. There is altogether too much doubt. We ought to wait
until it's resolved."

"You twist my words."

"And you don't answer mine."

He began to pace the room restlessly. "But we cannot just hold onto
that money while people are starving to death. We'd never sleep easy
again."

"And I say we cannot lay it out anywhere the government may later
come blundering. We could lose it all."

"Now we have it! There is the exact difference between us. I
would rather lay it out and lose it—knowing at least I did all I could."

"Then you ought to be in politics, not business. Go and vote the
repeal of economic law—and the law of gravity while you're at it."

"How dare you talk to me like that!" His tolerance broke at last.
But then he merely glowered at her, afraid in case he should go too far
as well.

To her surprise his anger calmed her. "What else should I do? Pretend I no longer care for our business?"

"You care for it well enough. You care for it to the exclusion of
everything else."

"But it *is* everything else. It makes everything else possible."

"Things are so terrible here," he said, making one last stab at the
argument. "Distress is so abject. It is not time to observe every scruple
and nicety of economic law."

She buried her face in her hands. "John, oh John!" She looked up
wearily. "There's no two people in all the country who know better
than you and me how to take one pound and turn it into two—or
twenty-two. If there's any faculty Ireland needs desperately at this crisis,

it's *that* faculty. For God's sake—and for Ireland's sake—let us use it. How will it be if we, and all the others who possess it too, if we all resign our responsibilities and contemplate instead turning each pound into—into nothing? How can that ever help this country?"

He sighed. "I wish we'd never come here. Brassey's wise to stay away."

"Amen to that," she said.

Chapter 37

Stevenstown, or its first two hundred houses, and the vast steelworks, or at least the first bay of what might become such a works, was opened just before Christmas that year—twelve months to the day from the turning of the first sod. It was a festive ceremony, with a dinner for the operatives in the works, and a champagne supper for deputies, super-visors, and local bigwigs in Stockton. John spoke at both—a simple message that labour and capital were a partnership, not foes locked in permanent and inevitable combat. They had more in common, he said, than the interests that divided them. Above all they had initiative; the road to the top was open to any man who lived in Stevenstown; thrift, diligence, perseverance, study, daring, and luck were all that was needed.

The message was better received at the mill than among those al-ready well advanced along that road. And there were rumblings from the townsfolk, too. The mayor pressed John especially on the sewerage system he had installed; he was plainly worried it would lead to de-mands in Stockton among the "progressives" for a municipal drainage system there, too. It was all very well to put in a system in a new town; but the cost in a town whose buildings went back over the centuries was ruinous. "D'ye mind," he asked John, "if I put it about that it's mainly for the run-off from your ironworks? The connection to the housing's only incidental?" He was diffident because of Sir George's connection with the firm. Sir George, restored now to modest fortune, was there, ensuring respect.

"Oh," John said, with a wink. "I thought that fact was already perfectly understood." He liked aldermen; he felt at home with their petty-minded venality.

But his spirit was not really in these proceedings. Over two hundred miles away to the south, at Maran Hill, Nora was having a hard time of it with their fifth child. They ought not to have moved; he saw that now. But she had had a succession of minor ailments all autumn and with the baby due and winter coming on, it seemed only sensible to move somewhere milder and less isolated. Their doctor had advised it, as well. And now the child was two weeks late in arriving.

He was on the point of retiring for that night, ready for an early start south next morning, the morning of Christmas Eve, when a lad in a fly came hell-for-leather to the inn. He did not even hammer at the door but stood in the yard and bellowed "Mr. John Stevenson!" over and over.

John flung wide the window. "Aye, lad?" It was a porter from the station.

"You're to come back with me, sir. A train is waiting to take you south."

He wasted no time over questions. Nor did he take anything but his writing case and wallet. The horse, which had been merely winded in the tavern yard, was lathered to a terror by the time it got them back to the station. Mills, the stationmaster, grim-faced, handed him a sheet of paper. "Off the company's telegraph, sir. Twenty minutes ago."

John read: "Stevenson go south at once special waiting at Stockton with priority through to Boxmoor regret grave news from Marran Hall God speed Hudson." He looked again at the misspelling; it definitely read "Marran Hall."

"From Mr. Hudson himself, sir," Mills said. "Thank the powers we had one still fired up." He pointed down the line, where an engine was lurching toward them on skirts of steam. "She'll get you to Stockton."

John nodded, unable to speak. His mind, clutching at any straw, prayed for there really to be a Marran Hall and for that misunderstanding to be the basis of this nightmare.

"I'll wish you God speed too, sir," Mills said.

"And me," the porter added.

"Thank you." John spoke at last as he swung himself in beside the engineer on the still-moving engine. The porter, trotting beside, dropped his writing case onto the footplate.

"I'll fire for you," John said, grabbing the coal shovel from the engineer. The man hesitated. John thrust the shovel back into his hands and opened the steam valve further. "Or I'll drive," he said. The engine, free of any load but its own tender, lurched forward. The engineer gave him back his shovel. "Right!" he said.

They took that engine to its limit over the twenty-six-odd miles between Stockton and the main line at Darlington—the line on which public steam railways had begun, twenty years earlier. On that day a man had walked in front of the engine; tonight a hare could not have run before them. The engine groaned and clanked as it hurtled through the dark over the ringing metal; the fire roared and the water boiled with a muted thunder—the explosive birth of a million steam bubbles.

The night was windless but the air, rushing past them, shrieked over the engine's surfaces and streamed through their hair. It was like a goodish gale. John put his hat on the writing case.

"Must be fifty mile an hour," he shouted to the driver.

"Just the night for sheep on the line!"

"How often does that happen?"

"Never! But it's times like this you think of it."

The man's words were comforting. *Indeed*, John thought, *it's times like this you think the worst—and it doesn't happen.*

At least the sheep didn't happen, and they reached Darlington in just thirty-one minutes. His hat had blown away somewhere on that record dash.

Christmas Eve was thirty minutes old when the special pulled out of Darlington on its long journey south; it was Kitson's long-boilered *Hector*, the very engine of which Hudson had given a silver model replica to Chambers. John wondered if that was an omen. This time there was both an engineer and a fireman; he had a coach to himself. The master at Darlington apologized that it was not a directors' coach.

There was a further telegraph message, also from Hudson: "News is no worse and I will see you at York."

He tried to sleep. His rolling-stone way of life had taught him to catnap in any position at any time of day. But tonight, with the whole padded seat to lie out on, sleep was nowhere near. The unthinkable clamoured at his mind, besieging his wakefulness. To hold it at bay he said, "Nora my love ... Nora my love ... Nora my love ..." like a compulsive prayer, in time with the chatter of the wheels over the rail butts. He pressed his ear to the cloth of the seat and filled his mind with the deep, sonorous rumble of the axles. It was, he said, the coursing of the blood in Nora's veins.

At York they stopped to take on water. While they were still moving, the door opened and Hudson's huge bulk swung up and in. He hung his lantern, momentarily blinding John, and sat shivering, drawing himself inward. His neck, never prominent, vanished into his great chest.

"It's very good of you, this," John said.

"Good! I never felt less adequate."

"Any more news?"

"None from your home. You will be met at Boxmoor. I wish the Great Northern were already built!"

John laughed faintly. "The worst is being so far away," he said. "These things are often better when we're there." He saw from the faintness of Hudson's smile that such hope was, in this case, thin.

A porter opened the door and put in four footwarmers and a number of blankets. Behind him stood the engineer. "Ready, Mr. Hudson, sir," he said. Hudson climbed out as swiftly as he had got in. "How long to Boxmoor?" John asked.

"If we make the same time as we made since Darlington, we'll be there by five. A little earlier."

Hudson gripped his hand. "If prayers count," he said, "there's hundreds praying already. Tomorrow it will be thousands. The day after, tens of thousands."

John nodded, too moved to speak his thanks.

A half mile down the line he blew out the lantern Hudson had left and, wrapping himself in the blankets, sat with two footwarmers by his feet and one on the seat each side of him—a tent of warmth in that icy carriage.

Years ago Nora had said to him, "Why don't they conduct the waste steam back through the coaches?" and he had explained there was no heat in waste steam. But it would surely be warmer than *this*.

He let himself think of Nora now—of all the amazing contradictions she was. How she could think of their business and future with such cold and long-sighted vision; she put more effort into that alone than most people could put into several lives. And yet how impetuous she was at times, and what risks she took! In anyone else it would have seemed both blind and mad; but with Nora you felt that even in the highest flights of her impetuosity that cold, logical part of her mind was still quietly at work. There were times in their discussions (outsiders who did not know them well would say "arguments") when she was pressing some point of view most vehemently and yet he could see a momentary flicker of doubt in her eye, which showed that other possibilities were even then passing through her mind. How did she hold that endless ferment together? It was like a monster class of unruly, brilliant children.

There was an image of her he had carried from the day they had met, that hot August day in 1839, when he had been no more than a navvy ganger. They had supped together and walked out on the banks of spoil from the tunnel he was working on. Then she had gone back to his bed to wait on him while he spoke with Walter Thornton, who was the engineer to the tunnel. He had come back to find her exhausted and asleep. Again in his mind he saw the rough blanket fall from her, saw her underfed naked body in the moonlight, saw her waken and realize where she was, saw the lust and invitation kindle in her eyes. And then his own reluctant voice, saying, "Nay, lass, there's more important work afoot." How she had worked that night! She had costed the operations and materials on that tunnel six ways to Sunday, before dawn, while he had forged his letter of credit on Chambers' bank, and thought of ever more desperate ways to spin his capital out until the payments came in. All next day, while he fought and won his case with the railway company to become their main contractor on the tunnel, she had helped break open a rabbit warren, standing over the holes and hurling great rocks down upon the luckless would-be escapers. When he saw her that evening she had two dozen of them slung over her shoulder.

That was the image he treasured above all: Nora, turned to gold in the evening sun, dusty, barefoot, stained with blood, smiling, and breathless. But the image was coloured too, as it had been then, by the memory of Nora with her pen, making the figures come alive, and Nora in her nakedness in the moonlight, and the parting of her thighs as she smiled that invitation. They could never be separate again, those images. You could not say "lust" and "huntress" and "adept" and say you had described her. But what word was there? There was only . . . only . . . *Nora*. No other word came near it.

Nora. He whispered it and did not hear himself above the furious rattle of the coach and the huffing of the engine. He said it aloud. He shouted it at the darkness. He had the idea that if he could hold the image of her constantly in his mind, it would somehow keep her alive. He pictured himself as a free spirit, soaring and wheeling over the park at Maran Hill, always turned toward the house. He imagined that, though he was so free, his very movement above the house turned the intervening air into a heavy weight upon its roof and walls, imprisoning everything within it. Not imprisoning. *Securing*.

When he could sustain that image no longer, he reached his hands into the blackness before him and sought to form her in the nearby air. If she were there, he would grip her *so*, though it made her cry out; he would hold her *so*, pull her to him *so*, fold her *so*, kiss her *so*, hug her *so*, say Nora Nora Nora Nora in the hollow of her ear, hear the soft richness of her laughter hot in his, Nora, put flesh to flesh . . . *treasure* her. Nora! Golden, bloodstained, smiling girl, do not die, do not leave me.

At the last he was reduced to one word, which he laid upon the darkness like a prayer. "Please . . . please . . . please . . ." It was not in him to pray that night. The words were an invocation to her; *please live* was all they said. Please live.

When he arrived at Boxmoor he could not remember their having stopped to take on more water and coals at Derby. Perhaps, indeed, he had slept.

"Stevenson!"

The voice spun him around on the dark platform. His body was shouting its thanks to the engineer and fireman and taking in the triumphant words: "We averaged over sixty."

"Thornton!"

Walter Thornton was walking up the platform to him, bearing a gig lamp. "Don't be surprised. We're spending Christmas down here with Arabella's father. You made good time! Did he say over sixty?"

"How is she?"

"Have you brought any things?" He answered himself by diving into the carriage and pulling out the writing case, which John had forgotten.

"Thornton!"

Thornton stood up slowly and slowly turned to face him. "I have been here since half past ten, when I sent down the message to York. I left Maran Hill at nine."

"And? There's no point in—in being—"

"Things were not good, Stevenson. She has been in labour two days, and this afternoon she went into some kind of a coma."

"And the baby?"

"No sign. Come on, let's hurry."

John, almost abstractedly, walked behind him to the gig. Walter took the reins and they set off at a smart pace, fast enough for the horses to maintain over the dozen or so remaining miles.

"Who is tending her?"

"Dr. Hales from Hertford. He was talking when I left of getting Professor Liston from University College Hospital." Several moments later he added: "He is professor of surgery at the college."

John, who had been expecting "professor of midwifery," did not at once understand "surgery." Then he did not dare ask why. But Thornton went on: "They think the child may be . . . already dead."

For the rest of the hour's journey they went mostly in silence, until they were racing down the long driveway. There were lights showing in the kitchen basement, in two of the servants' rooms in the attic, and in the Gothic boudoir over the main entrance.

John was out of the gig before it had reached the turning circle. He raced across the grass, up the steps, through the portico, into the hall, on up the great stair, curving around and back upon itself, to the landing outside the boudoir. And there he paused, breathless, with racing heart, suddenly fearful. He stood in the attitude of prayer, still unable to pray.

A man slipped out between the great double doors, a doctor by the cut of him. "Dr. Hales?" John asked.

"Yes. Mr. Stevenson?"

"Yes." He waited, not daring to ask the question he yearned above all to hear answered.

The doctor smiled; it was the merest twitch of the corners of his lips, but it pointed him irrevocably toward hope. "She is a little better," he said. But at once his face was grave again. "Well enough, at least, to operate. We need your consent."

"You and Professor Liston? May I go in?"

The doctor nodded and opened the door for him. He fought down the fear that held him back and strode into the room.

She lay on a high bed in the centre, with a nurse, a midwife, and the professor standing around it. He looked only at her.

At first he could not believe it *was* her. She was so pale and her face was drawn so thin with the pain. He felt weak just to look at her.

"Mr. Stevenson?" The professor's hand poked into view. He shook it.

Nora stirred at the name and opened her eyes. They were red as coals. "John?" Her lips formed the word while a hoarse croak, unlike any word, came out between them.

He took her hand and felt her answering squeeze; it was strong. "All's well," he said. "Never better."

She smiled and closed her eyes again.

The professor moved away. "A word," he said. It was a Scots voice.

Delicately he untwined her fingers from his and clenched her fist. He gave it a squeeze and left her again. Still smiling, she opened her eyes and watched him to the door.

"We believe the baby she was—*is* carrying has died," the professor said. "I want to perform a laparotomy—what, if the child were living, we would call a Caesarean section—to remove it."

"If you do not?"

"The labour has endured so long her muscles are now in a sort of spasm. Like a cramp." He shook his head. "With every minute a normal birth, even a normal stillbirth, becomes less and less likely."

"I see that. Will it be painful?"

The two doctors exchanged glances. "That is the trouble," the surgeon said. "I have a substance here, a new substance, that will render her insensible." He looked to see if John was following. "It is a volatile substance called sulphuric ether. It has been used in America for some years by dentists. I heard of it some time ago and I have used it in London in a number of operations since—with, I may say, great success."

But there was a hesitation in his voice. "Were any like this?" John asked.

"No. They were—amputations, a broken tooth root, a deep gash, an impaling. . . . What I mean, Mr. Stevenson, is that they were all acute cases. There was no history of long, weakening illness previous to the operation."

"I see." John turned from them and went to the landing rail. What a responsibility. If he said no, the pain might kill her. If he said yes, the —whatever he called it—might do it. At least she would feel nothing.

"Does it act quickly?" he asked. "This sulphuric—material."

"Ether. They call it an anesthesiant. It's very quick."

"Minutes or seconds?"

"Seconds."

He took a deep breath. "So it would be possible to give her the very minimum necessary to take her to the shallowest levels of insensibility? And as she grew restless, showing signs of pain, you could . . . do you see?"

Liston nodded and looked at Dr. Hales. "Who would do it?"

"I will," John said.

But Liston would not consider it. "The legal implications make that impossible."

"I'm willing to try," Hales said, "as well as to assist you."

Liston stood square. "Very well. Let's not delay."

John was halfway up the stairs to the servants' attic, intending to lie in the bedroom over the boudoir with his ear to the floor, when he realized what a monstrous form of self-torture that would be. He turned and went back down to the library.

His entrance woke Walter Thornton, stretched out full on the leather sofa.

"Thornton," he said. "You've been damned marvellous. I can't begin to thank you. Letting Hudson know was the master stroke."

"How is she?"

"A little better, they say." And he explained what Liston and Hales had proposed. All the while his ear was straining for a sound from upstairs. Which would be worse—cries of pain, or silence until morning?

"That's marvellous," Walter said. "If they can use this stuff in ordinary childbirth it would be a godsend. Arabella would have given her sight for some of it when she had Lionel last June. I know that." He got up and threw some small logs on the fire; they soon made a cheerful blaze.

John, strolling restlessly around the room, pulled open a shutter. "It's snowing," he said. "Pretty heavy. I hope the two who brought me down get back for Christmas."

"If they really did average more than sixty miles an hour from Darlington, that's quite an achievement for the narrow Stephenson gauge," Walter said. He came over to the window and looked out at the snow. "Oh, that's it," he said. "I'll stop the night. What little is left of it."

"I'll get one of the servants up to make you a bed." John walked to the bell pull.

But Walter ran to it first and held it with his hand. "No such thing," he said. "I wouldn't hear of it. The resources of this house must now be devoted to one thing and one thing only."

John pulled a punch on Walter's chin. "You're a grand fellow," he said.

For the remaining hour of darkness they sat and talked of the works they had done, together and separately, ranging in a desultory way over past and future, England and abroad, north and south, fact and fantasy, triumph and failure—coming to no conclusion and forgetting most of it the moment it was uttered. "Isn't it strange!" Walter said, looking around at the leaden dawn and the snow, still falling heavily. "The last real chat we had was in a snowstorm, too. On the South Devon, remember?"

At that moment they both were brought to a shocked silence. Into it, tearing the air, on and on, rang the cry of a baby.

"Clement?" Walter asked.

John shook his head. "Can't be. The children are all in the north wing."

"Then . . ." He did not finish.

John strode from the room and out into the hall. Still the baby's crying rang on—a lusty, malevolent, egotistic caterwaul. It echoed in that great space and re-echoed from the dome above, a cold sound. He fought to suppress the hate it roused within him—fearing all that it might mean.

Slowly he mounted the stair and sat on the chair below the single lamp that burned. Its light was a hot gold in the pale grey morning, filtering through the drifted snow around the dome above.

God, he was tired. He felt ninety.

For ten murderous minutes the baby yelled, settled, yelled again and yet again. Feet walked over the boudoir floor. Instruments clattered on the slab. But the one sound above all others for which his aching ear was tuned never came. He stood and began to pace the landing. Then he saw Thornton tiptoeing out of the library by the gun-room door. At the foot of the stairs he looked up but failed to see John standing against the alcove immediately above him. He began slowly to mount the stairs.

At that moment the door of the boudoir opened and Dr. Hales came out. Thornton paused.

"Mr. Stevenson," the doctor said. His voice carried no news.

"How is she?"

"You have a fine daughter."

"I care not a fig for her, sir. How is my wife?"

Hales looked down. "We cannot say. It would be as well to send for the vicar, I fear."

John took three shattered breaths before he heard his wavering voice ask, "May I see her?"

"In a moment. She will be insensible."

"I will come back."

With a resolution that was entirely mechanical he sped downstairs and ran for the stables. But there he found Walter already saddling a horse—Fontana, the horse Beador had given Nora for her long hunt from Hertford to York.

"Did you hear?"

"I was on my way up. I'll be back with him in less than half an hour. Reverend Paine is his name. And, you may remember, he is Arabella's father."

Wordless, distraught, John raced back across the snow-filled courtyard and up the main stairs again. This time he was let in to see her. The baby was howling in the next-door bedroom. The smell of ether was strong.

He stopped, not daring to breathe, several paces short of the bed. He thought she had already died, she looked so grey in the strengthening dawn. The lines of pain on her face seemed frozen there. His vision closed in to a funnel; he could see only one thing at a time. If he looked at her eyelids he could not see if she might breathe. Yet he could not tear his eyes from her face.

In some way he had come to be standing beside her. He heard a breath, a shallow, rattling breath. From her.

"Fresh air," he said. "It reeks in here."

He felt the surgeon, at his side, nod to someone, and someone opened wide the double doors onto the hall. The nurse shook more coals onto the fire. Fresh air surrounded him.

"She is very far gone, Mr. Stevenson," Liston said. "We must prepare ourselves for the worst."

John took his hand and shook it. "Thank you . . ." He struggled to say "Professor" but uttered only nonsense.

"There is nothing more I can do for the moment."

A strange voice, which he did not immediately recognize as his own, said: "You will do everything? She is the rarest, most finest woman of this or any other age. You will do everything."

"Of course." That was MacHale. No. Whatsizname. The other.

They put a chair against the back of his knees. His legs folded under him and he sat down heavily.

Still the baby next door kept up her endless routine of crying herself to exhaustion, resting a bare ten seconds, then beginning all over again.

He touched Nora's brow. It was dry, and cold as alabaster. But still she breathed. Her fingers, too, were cold. The sandbag over her stomach made her appear pregnant still.

The door at the side of the hall gallery opened. That could not be the vicar, for it connected only with the upper floor of the house and of the north wing. A moment later Sarah stood, with Winifred and Young John, hand in hand, at the door. The crying of the baby gave them hope, and they were smiling; but the smiles vanished as their eyes took in the scene within the boudoir.

"Come, my dears," John said, standing and holding out his arms. He forced some cheer into his voice.

Liston nodded to Dr. Hales, and they went into the other adjoining bedroom, opposite to where the baby was crying.

"Is Mama very tired?" Young John asked.

"Very tired and still very ill," he answered. "We must all be very careful for her."

He could see Sarah close to tears. He gripped her by the wrist and, darting his eyes at the children, said, "Be strong now." It was a leviathan effort for her but she managed it.

"Poor Mama," Winifred said. He could see she knew how close death had come.

Nora's eyes flickered open, saw nothing, and shut again.

He let the children stand there a minute more and then said casually to Sarah, "Reverend Paine is coming soon." He could see it was a shock, like a physical blow, to her.

"Come on, children," she said. "We'll go back with the vicar and go to church and pray." She stayed behind long enough to whisper, "Poor Winifred hasn't slept. I sat with her all night."

He smiled and patted her arm. "Bless you!"

They heard the vicar, Arabella's father, coughing a raw, winter's cough as he came up the stair. Professor Liston came out at once. "If you have a cough, sir," he said, "I think it most unwise to come in here."

The Reverend Paine nodded patiently. "I can administer it from here," he said, settling upon the landing. John went out to him.

In later years John came to look upon this night, begun in Stockton at midnight, ended in the cold Hertfordshire dawn, as the time when he finally lost what little faith he had. The vicar rattled through the communion of the sick as if he were holding a private auction with God for Nora's soul. And when it was over he threw in an extra prayer—the commendation at the point of departure. At the words "whatsoever defilements her soul may have contracted in the midst of this miserable and naughty world, through the lusts of the flesh, or the wiles of Satan, being purged and done away, it may be presented pure and without spot before Thee . . ." he wanted to stand and shout to the heavens: "No! Take her as she is—spots, lusts of the flesh, and all. If that's not good enough for You, then leave her here with me! With *me*!"

All that day he sat at her side, except when they had to change her sheet and the dressing. Dr. Hales came twice; Professor Liston went back to London. Sarah sent word to Newcastle for Sam to come down. At dusk they brought the baby for John to see but he would not even look at her.

"Go on, sir," the nurse said. "She's a fine, lusty girl. I never knew one so 'earty."

But still he refused. The nurse went out in tears. The baby started to cry again, too.

They tried to give Nora some soup that evening, though she was still unconscious; but she would not take it. He sat by her all that night, waking from his shallow doze every time she moved or changed her rhythm of breathing. Next morning the doctor ordered him to bed, "or you'll be of no use to her when she does come to."

Chapter 38

Three hours was all he could manage. Then he tossed and curled and stretched and turned while the Christmas bells rang out over the snow-bound countryside. He got up, took handsful of snow from the window sill, and rubbed it over his face and neck. For half a minute it left him feeling fresh and rested; but the sight of his slack, bloated face and bulging eyes in the mirror soon confirmed the feeling that crept back out of his bones once the sting of the cold wore off. Only to sit by Nora brought its own kind of peace. It held no hope, but it suspended his despair. She took water, drop by drop, that day. Half a pint. But it did not wake her.

Walter and Arabella came that afternoon. "We are praying for a happy Christmas," she said, offering a cheek for John to kiss. Five children and seven and a half years of marriage had taken far greater toll of her than they had of Nora. She seemed always to be anticipating a pain that never quite took hold of her. She knelt to pray at Nora's bedside as if she herself were only just out of convalescence. But her eye was still sharp and bright and her skin clear and firm. It was the will that was ailing there, John thought, not the body.

He went down to take tea with them in the library, which they were using for all purposes during this crisis. They could talk only of trivialities. Nobody mentioned the baby.

Then the day nurse came running down the stairs. John was out of the room before she reached their foot. "Oh, sir!" she called excitedly. "Do come now. Mrs. Stevenson's awake!"

He left her standing and was breathless at Nora's side before the woman was halfway back. Nora seemed no different from when he had last seen her. The same closed eyes in the same haggard face.

"Nora?" he whispered.

There was no response.

He spoke her name. A terrible urge to punch her, or the pillow, came to him. He noticed he was trembling and he felt a sweat pass over his body.

"She was. She was." The voice of the nurse.

And then Nora's eyes fell open.

"Nora!" he said.

They sought him, first to the wrong side, then, guided by his repeated call, they turned full on him.

And then that most wonderful moment as her face flooded with recognition!

"John!" It was hardly a whisper.

"Aye, love. I'm here."

She smiled and closed her eyes. Her lips said something.

"Water," the nurse said.

They lifted her gingerly to a half-lying position and held a glass to her mouth. She took two gulps and moved her mouth away. The nurse looked triumphant. "We'll try some soup again in an hour or so," she said. They laid her down once more.

Still she was trying to speak.

He put his ear to her mouth. "What is it, love? Whisper it."

"I knew you were there," he thought she said.

"Aye." He squeezed her arm. "I was. And I will be." He turned to the nurse. "Go and tell Mrs. Cornelius, and Mr. and Mrs. Thornton. They'll want to hear."

She was gone only a minute. "Mrs. Thornton says she will come back tomorrow and sit by Mrs. Stevenson," she said. "Or tidy the library."

"Or *what?*"

"That's what I thought she said, sir."

That night Nora took a small cup of beef tea and a spoon of honey. She did not ask for the baby, which was by now in the night nursery in the north wing, beyond earshot.

"She'll sleep easy five, six hours, I shouldn't wonder," the night nurse said. "No point you sittin' aside 'er, sir. Why not rest now?"

They made up a bed in the front part of the boudoir, where there were curtained windows on three sides. He slept right through till breakfast.

During the night the doctor had come and gone. He and the nurse had changed the dressing, and the doctor took some of the sand out of the bag.

"He said she's healin' wonderful, sir," the nurse told John. "He said even if she was still unconscious, it'd be a wonder, the healin' she've done to herself."

Nora sat half upright for fifteen minutes that morning. They spoke little; she was still plainly exhausted and could not keep her eyes open for long. But if he squeezed her hand, she would smile and squeeze back, again with that surprising firmness of grip. Mostly he told her the news —how the opening of Stevenstown had gone, what a marvel Hudson had been, how Arabella and Walter were in the neighbourhood, when Sam would arrive, how glad the children were. . . . He did not yet mention the baby, though he could not say why. To each of these snippets she would nod and smile, and pat his hand. At the end she said, "What of the business?"

He laughed. "Dearest . . . oh, dearest Nora! It is Boxing Day. There is no business."

"Ah," she said, content.

Soon she was asleep.

He had lied about Sam. Word had come back from Newcastle that the Nelsons, and Sam, were at their shooting lodge and snowed in; the servants were trying to get word through.

That afternoon with Arabella it was the same thing. Arabella prattled thirteen-to-the-dozen about home in Bristol and the children and Walter and her father and mother . . . and did Nora know that she and Walter had been married from this house and indeed this boudoir was the very room in which she had changed into that wonderful dress . . . of course she knew, it was the one she had worn to Squire Red-mayne's ball that first Christmas in Todmorden—*no*, it wasn't, but Nora *had* seen it, of that she was sure, and, dear oh dear, wasn't it all such a long time ago and now here they were with *five* children each. . . .

Nora smiled and listened and sighed when sighs were in order.

And Arabella left looking more perky and energetic than she had in years. It was so wonderful, she thought, to be of such great *use* to someone—outside the strict call of family duty. And she went down to tidy the library with ten times the vigour she had felt when she had set herself the task yesterday.

"Did she tire you?" John asked.

"She does . . . chatter so. She said we've *five* children." She opened her eyes and looked at John. "Have we? I've been feared to ask."

He smiled. "I've been feared it would overexcite you. Would you like to see? It's a grand little lass. Lungs like Stentor, solid brass."

She nodded.

The long walk from the north wing quieted the baby so that, although she was bawling blue in the face when John set out, carrying her, she was down to snuffles and hiccoughs by the time they were at the boudoir. He took his first real look at the child on that walk, ashamed now of his previous hatred. She wasn't a bad-looking baby, as babies went; in fact, she looked better than any of the four previous. She had stupendous violet eyes.

"She's the best-looking one you've ever produced," he said, holding the baby vertical in her field of view.

She raised her hand and touched its tear-stained face. "Abigail?" she said. "What about Abigail Stevenson? Bringer of joy."

Abigail began to cry.

Nora closed her eyes and lay back again. "Good," she said.

He wanted to know how it had felt to be so close to death. "What do you remember of the operation?" he asked.

With her eyes still closed she shook her head. "Nothing. I just had a feeling all the time that you were there and all would be well."

*   *   *

At about the same moment Sarah walked into the library to see Arabella standing on the book ladder, holding half a dozen books precariously against her left hip, and reaching for a seventh.

"Mrs. Thornton!" she called. "Be careful, you will fall."

"I'm glad they've only just been moved," she said. "So there is no nasty dust upon them." She came down. "There! I think that is all. I *hope* so." She added the seven books to the fifty or so that lay on the table.

Sarah looked at them: *Home Influence, Sense and Sensibility, Conversations with Lord Byron, The Diary of an Ennuyé, Domestic Manners of the Americans, Sacred History of the World.*

A fearsome thought struck her. "Do you intend trying to read these to Nora?"

Arabella laughed. "No, no! I merely thought it would be—*nicer,* if these had a shelf to themselves. Don't you agree, dear?"

"I suppose so," Sarah said carefully, having no idea what was meant. She helped Arabella carry them to an empty shelf on the other side of the room.

"We'll keep them in alphabetical order still," she said.

"Of course," Sarah agreed.

When they had finished, Arabella said, "There! Isn't that *so* much more—suitable. One's library should reflect one's delicacy."

Exactly what lay behind all this activity did not become clear until John came down that evening to get a travel book by Harriet Martineau, which Nora had asked him to read to her from. He could not find it among the *M*'s, nor anywhere between the *K*'s and the *O*'s, which filled that particular shelf. He went to see if Sarah had borrowed it.

"No," she said. "Perhaps it's among those Arabella sorted out this afternoon. In fact, I'm sure I saw it." She came back with him to the library and took him to the shelf they had filled. "There it is," she said.

But John had burst into laughter, which rapidly got wilder and more hysterical. All the tension of these last days erupted into that mirth.

"John!" Sarah laughed, still mystified. "What is it?"

"Well, look!" he said, pointing at the shelf. "Look at the names."

She did as he told her: Grace Aguilar, Jane Austen, Lady Anne Barnard, Lady Blessington.... Quickly her eye ran ahead: ... Mrs. Hemans, Mary Howitt, Anna Jameson, Harriet Martineau ... right on to Charlotte Smith, Agnes Strickland, Frances Trollope, and Sharon Turner.

Sharon Turner! she thought, now bursting into laughter herself. "John, I had no *idea*," she said. "I actually helped her to carry them over here. And not once did it occur to me."

"What did she say?"

"I didn't understand it. *Then.* She said something about one's library should reflect one's delicacy. Really!"

They had to sit down then; their laughter weakened them so.

"The joke is," Sarah said, "that Sharon Turner is a man. He's a lawyer, isn't he? He published that strange poem on Richard III last year. Shall I move him back?"

"No, no. The ladies should have at least one man to defend their honour. And who better? Look at them! On opposite walls like milkmaids and bumpkins at a harvest dance!"

"What *have* we been condoning, John? All unawares!"

"What? Orgies of paper and leather?"

They giggled helplessly.

"Where can she have got such an idea?" Sarah asked.

"Oh, those *Ladies' Drawing Room Companion* things. They cram them full of rubbish like that."

"Well, she's a tonic."

He sighed, unable to laugh any more. "I'll tell Nora. It'll brighten her up, I know."

*   *   *

Later Sarah wondered what it was like to have a mind that saw the salacious possibilities of everything around it—a goat in every finger. What sort of connubial life did Arabella and Walter have?

She was no longer ashamed that such questions could occur to her. It was a way of letting the fire consume itself, she said, whenever it struck her that she *ought* to feel guilty. The passions that Tom Cornelius had awakened would, she now realized, never slumber again. For good or ill they were *there*, a fact of her history, and she had to come to terms with them.

She could not go back in memory to that source, to her few precious nights with Tom. The pain of reliving any one of her moments with him was still strong. For material memories she was reduced to the imagined shape of Sam, standing away from her in the dark making his little cries—and an even more imaginary Dey of Algiers, who was featured in a story called (for some reason) *The Lustful Turk*, which had once circulated among the kitchen maids at the Tabard.

So she was not ashamed to picture Walter and Arabella, together, like that. Especially not Walter; there was something foxy, gluttonlike about his stocky little body, bearded grin, and glittering eye. She would *do* nothing about it, of course. Sam had been her first, and would be her last, foray into the world of real men. But it was comforting to think of the possibilities—out there. Ready.

Chapter 39

Nora did not maintain the momentum of her recovery. For days she lingered in that half-world between silent, grateful consciousness and complete oblivion. She took some solid food but lived mostly on soup and milk. Often she was not awake above an hour a day. Dr. Hales came often and seemed pleased enough with her lack of progress.

"She'll take months to be well over it," he said. "It was a very close thing. The surgery is healing wonderfully." He said they could send further word to Sam saying the crisis was over.

The children came to see her every day, too. If she was awake she would hear them recite or read to her, and she would tell them to be good to Aunt Sarah.

"Does it distress you to hear us play outside, Mama?" Winifred asked one day.

"I haven't heard you at all," Nora said.

"But would it if you did?" Young John added.

Nora smiled and shook her head, and they left barely able to subdue their excitement, for tomorrow Uncle Walter had promised to bring over his three oldest boys, Nicholas, Thomas, and Albert, and a big sled he had made from some old copper tubing.

When the children had left, John and Nora were once more alone. The silence returned. They smiled at each other, like strangers.

"How is the business?" she asked again.

He laughed gently, more embarrassed than amused that she could ask no other question.

"I remember nothing," she said. "It must have been worse for you."

"I think I was in a kind of fever. The worst things that I—my worst fears seemed real. But real things, like the train, and Thornton waiting, and so on—they seemed to float. You know the way things look after you've banged your head? Immediately after? They were like that." He paused. "It was strange to hold onto one's fears as the only real things." He wanted her to know exactly what it had been like.

"I remember nothing," she repeated.

"That must be the anesthesiant. What a wonderful thing."

"Only the feeling that you were there. I kept feeling that."

"You mean before I really came?"

"I don't remember."

She looked out over the snow-shrouded park. "D'you know what? I'd love to be in a horse-drawn sleigh. All wrapped up in furs. Gliding over that snow."

"Really?" he asked. "Would you like that?"

His earnestness turned the idea from a pretty fancy to a request. She looked back at him, smiling. "I would. But of course it's out of the question."

"Anything you want," he said. "Anything that's possible."

She reached for his hand.

"Strong grip," he told her. "You had a strong grip that night, too. It was the only sign of hope for me."

"It's not like you to despair."

"I didn't exactly despair. I was angered."

"Angered!"

"With meself. With *us*, to be honest. I thought of all the time we had wasted. Chasing business we'd no need for." He felt her hand stiffen. "Time we could have better spent in each other's company. Why do we do it? I sometimes think there's a sort of madness in us."

He spoke to their linked hands but when she did not reply he was forced to look up. Her gaze was steady, her blank face watchful.

He looked back at their hands. "Why don't we take our ease, eh? We could live this whole century out. We could live beyond any dreams we had when we got wed. *And* see the children off with a good competence."

She smiled as mothers smile at the enthusiasms of children.

He wanted to tell her that perhaps they had made their business a substitute for too much in their life. So that happiness at its success had sometimes stood in place of a deeper happiness—in fact, of the happiness he had felt slipping away when he feared she might die. But it was too hard to put all that into words, or into *exact* words; and if he got it wrong, it might only cause her pain.

In an odd way she expressed the same thought, but gave it an opposite colour. "I'm more than content," she said. "Look at Walter Thornton and Arabella. They must spend ten times as many days together as we do—or, I won't say *together* but under one roof. Yet they remain strangers. In fact, think of all the people we know. There isn't one couple doesn't spend more time together than us. Yet even if we were four hundred miles apart, I'd say we get more out of being Mr. and Mrs. Stevenson than all of them get out of their—arrangements." She took her hand from his and smoothed down the counterpane. "No. I can't wait to get back into things."

He looked glum.

"Oh, John!" she chided. "You'd go mad in retirement."

"I'd find things to do."

"Build model cathedrals in fishbone. If that isn't madness."

For a long time he looked out over the snow. She wondered if he had heard her. "So you don't think we make too much of it," he said at last.

She closed her eyes, weary now. "We do what we have to. What we know. What we were put here to do." It was luxurious to sink down into sleep, so slowly.

After another long pause he said, "I sometimes wonder if we've gained so very much."

But all she heard was his voice; and all she felt was the comfort that he was still there.

He stayed for the best part of the afternoon, watching her sleep, glad it was now such an easy sleep. Gradually the sense of all that he had failed to say receded within him.

*   *   *

Walter trudged a path through the virgin snow between the rectory and Lamb Dell. There he joined the shepherds' path through the wood and along the lime avenue to Maran Hill. The boys scampered and snow-balled behind him and tried to steal rides on the sled. Walter pretended not to notice for a dozen or twenty paces; then he would either turn around and chase them in fury, or, still pretending not to notice, he would drop of mock exhaustion and, when they crowded round shouting "Up, Neddy! Giddap!" he would grab the two nearest ankles and up-end their owners in the snow. He was truly exhausted by the time they arrived. John and Sarah came out with Winifred, Young John, and Caspar, running with controlled excitement, reminding themselves with every step not to scream and whoop.

The park was separated from the lower pasture and water meadow by a thorn hedge halfway down the hill. But John and two of the gardeners had been out that morning and not only cleared a twenty-foot gap, cutting the thorns back to ground level, but had packed it after with fresh snow. So now there was an uninterrupted downhill run for over half a mile.

"Who will go first?" he asked, meaning himself or Walter.

"Me, meee, meeee!" chorused six raucous throats.

"You," Walter said. "I'm exhausted."

So John set off on the test run, with six yelling, disappointed, happy children running in his wake, leaving Walter and Sarah stamping and cheering at the hillcrest.

"I meant to finish making a pair of snowshoes from some old tennis racquets," he told Sarah. "That's why I'm worn out."

"Why didn't you?"

"I got discouraged, I suppose. Mrs. Thornton said nothing would in-duce her to walk anywhere but the road."

"Oh, do finish them!" Sarah said. "I have never seen snowshoes and I would so love to try."

He smiled and looked at her so long that she grew embarrassed. "Very well," he said at last. "I'll bring them tomorrow."

"If they're as well made as that sled, I'll need not fear. Look how it has carried Mr. Stevenson."

"You need not fear anyway," he said.

This time it was she who almost started him out. "No. I fancy I wouldn't," she said.

When John came back with the sled, beetroot-faced and breathless, plagued with children, Walter tried to get Sarah to go down with him; but she avoided the move adroitly and, saying "Ladies first, children," took Winifred in front of her and, to a chorus of groans and boos, set off to follow John's tracks to the bottom.

"Who's next? Who's next?" the five boys shouted in an agony of impatience.

"All of you," Walter said, to loud cheers. "But the two eldest—you Nicholas, and you Thomas—go down and bring it back up for the ladies."

"My granddad's gardener says that in America they call a sled a tarbogging," Nicholas said.

"That's stupid," Young John told him. "It's obviously a sled."

Then Caspar said he was cold and Sarah had to take him back indoors.

*   *   *

That night Nora asked John where consols stood. He laughed and patted her and said he had no idea. For the first time he saw her vexed.

"You must tend to the business," she said. "If I fret because I feel it neglected, how can I ever mend?"

And she made him go down and get the paper. "Consols are 93¼ for money, 93⅜ for time. Exchequer bills are 6 premium," he read.

She sighed. "Two years ago, in 1845, they were 67 premium. One year ago, 32 premium. It looks as if we have until August or September."

He sighed. She chuckled and said, "You'll never understand, will you, poor love." He kissed her hand, not taking his eyes from her face. "All that"—she gestured at the newspaper—"is the magnet pulling me on."

Three rooms away, Sarah was dressing for dinner, letting Kitty— the maid who had stayed on from Sir George Beador's day—try a new plait in her hair. She paid little attention to what the girl was doing for she was deep in her own thoughts, wondering whether she was mad for thinking them and even madder for courting the conclusions they tended toward.

It had excited her all day to know that she could get this Mr. Thornton for the merest nod. How different he was from Sam. She could easily have fallen in love with Sam, who was good and kind—and funny, and comforting, and reliable; a sort of unworldly, unambitious version of Tom. But this Thornton was the very opposite. How *anyone* could love him was beyond her imagination. Arabella must be blind. Or perhaps he had become a totally different person at home from the man who roved abroad. He reeked of experience and self-confidence, and not an atom of modesty or shyness to mar it. "Turn your back and you're on it," as one of the bar maids had said of her most lecherous customer; that was Thornton, too.

In the end she forced herself to stop thinking about him until she was alone for the night. Then she would have to ponder, coldly and step by step, exactly what she wanted from Mr. Thornton, and how she could make him comply—whatever notions of his own he might entertain. Over the last eighteen months she had become adept at stopping herself from thinking about anything, and at thinking about that same "anything" coldly, step by step.

Next day Walter came in his snowshoes. He was not nearly so exhausted, even though there had been a fresh fall overnight, making the snow deeper. And he had brought a pair for Sarah. She let him tie them on.

She was surprised that he took no liberties at all, though her skirts were up to her ankles and his hands had to go up *inches* higher to bind the thongs around her riding boots. A bone setter could not have been more chaste or discreet.

But ninety minutes later, when they all came in tired and happy, and the children all ran up to the day nursery to play with Young John's fort until teatime, Walter said, "Let's put this sled in the garden room. There's no need to drag it back and forth each day, is there."

"I'll go and unlock it from inside," Sarah said.

But he caught her arm. "No, no. Come this way. See if it's still there." He would not be drawn further until they were at the door, which was, indeed, locked.

"I told you," she said.

At once he bent down to a ventilator brick in the wall, a foot off the ground but buried in drifted snow. He pushed his little finger in one of the holes, took a grip, and worked the brick from side to side. It was loose and came free with a jerk. "Ice," he said. "It used almost to fall out." He reached a hand inside and pulled out a rusty key. With it he opened the door to the garden room.

When his hands strayed as he untied her snowshoes there was no ambiguity about it; he did not say, "I can't seem to find the thongs," or anything of that sort. He was like a farmer in an auction, absorbed with the quality and firmness of the flesh.

She tapped him on the head. "Good afternoon, Mr. Thornton," she said. "I'm sure you remember me."

He kissed the hem of one of her petticoats. "Forever," he said, and set to finish untying her snowshoes in earnest.

"How did you know of that key?" she asked.

He looked to see if she was joking. "Didn't you know? This house belonged to my uncle. He sold it to George Beador only a few years ago. I grew up here." It was obviously news to her. She was thinking furiously. His heart began to race. She was very pretty and very imperious.

"So you have often—used this room," she said.

He smiled, not trusting his voice.

His wet tongue and gleaming teeth excited her but she fought it down and said aloud, as she had said in her mind three dozen times that day, "Well, let me make it clear, Mr. Thornton, there will be no rushed embraces in cold garden rooms, fearful of discovery and courting disgrace. In fact, there will be no risks of any kind whatsoever."

He blinked at her. He breathed at her; there was the faintest trace of cloves upon his breath. It almost unsettled her. Tom had been fond of chewing cloves.

"Risks," he said, nonplussed.

"Risk of discovery, risk of conceiving, risk of contagion." If she had not said it so often in her mind she could never have been so calm. But it had the most extraordinary effect on him. His eyes darted over her face, shivering in their sockets like loose marbles; she could *see* the blood hammering at the side of his neck. A gasp, with overtones of admiration, escaped his grinning jaws. "God. You are cool."

She was afraid then she might have overplayed, so, with a coy smile, though still preserving that cool edge, she said, "I think you may find me warm enough—when you remove those risks."

"Me!"

"Well, of course *you*. I will go to London tomorrow. In Mr. Stevenson's coach. He is going up, too, I think. You may find some reason to beg to come with us, and upon the journey you may contrive to invite me to see Paddington Station. Which we will do. And when you have shown me Paddington you will accompany me back to Mr. Stevenson's, where I shall see my banker. On the way you may find somewhere discreet"—she shivered and stood up—"and warm."

"It will not be easy," he said. He could not keep his hands still, and he dared not touch her.

"Of course it won't," she said. "That is why I have gone so far to help you. I hope you will be *worth* it." She had not prepared that last sentence, but he seemed to enjoy being commanded and challenged by her.

He caught his breath in his delight. "Oh, Sarah!" he said.

"Mrs. Cornelius," she corrected. "Never call me anything else, Mr. Thornton. I told you—we shall take *no* unnecessary risks."

*   *   *

The plan was almost spoiled when John suggested she ought to take Kitty, or one of the other maids, along, in case she needed to go shopping. She could hardly explain that she would be going to Paddington, since Mr. Thornton had not yet made his "spontaneous" invitation. But she remembered that Chambers, who lived over his own shop, had once offered her one of his maids as chaperone, so that was that hurdle over. Everything else went as she had planned; she thought they carried it off most convincingly.

Mr. Thornton was avuncular calmness itself as he showed her over the station. "In a few years," he said, "we shall build a new one on the other side of the Bishop's Bridge. So this may be your last view of it, Mrs. Cornelius."

"Oh no, Mr. Thornton," she answered. "I hope I may see it often."

Her imagination did not dwell at all on what they would be doing together very soon now, but the notion of it frequently came, like a kind of memory-in-advance, glancing through her mind. It gave her a sense of luxury not to entertain it but to push it out, waste it.

"I have never used this place," he said when they were in the cab. "Not myself, you understand. But I once made an arrangement there for—an important person."

"Is it a hotel?"

"A sort of hotel. It is a house used for this purpose only by people of the highest class. No common women go there."

"Well," she smiled and pulled a thick veil down from her bonnet, "I am in your hands."

"I will go in at the front," he said. "The cab will take you around to the mews. It is arranged there so that you may alight without being seen. He knows. All you do is to wait until I open the door."

When she was alone she felt the first twinge of doubt, a hint of regret, at what she was doing. She remembered John's words for it, tawdry—tawdry and something—unlovely. Was it going to be like that? Perhaps she would be better left with her imaginings unsullied? Still, there was no turning back now.

Perhaps her passions could only be roused now by things that happened in her mind? She remembered how she had lain in bed with Sam after he had—gone off all over the place, leaving her both unsatisfied and unroused, and incapable of being roused. Was it too late to turn back? She could just say to the cabman, "Drive on to Dowgate immediately." She commanded herself to shout it. Not a muscle twitched. But what if the pleasure *was* all in her mind? What if it lay merely in making and planning such arrangements as this? If she went on now and proved the thing itself was—tawdry and unlovely, that would destroy those mental pleasures, too. She would be left with absolutely nothing. Only the memory of a memory.

Her mouth felt dry when Mr. Thornton opened the door and helped her float out of the cab. "Wait," he said to the driver.

"Of course, guvnor," the man replied, the whisky flask already in his hand.

She felt no better prepared than she had been at the age of sixteen, listening to incomprehensible stage directions from that whey-faced clergyman, or later, when they left her alone with the man who had saved her. It was nothing, nothing, nothing like it had been with Tom.

In his unfeeling, monomaniac way, Thornton helped her through these hesitations. A more sensitive man would have noticed her mood and, in trying to comply with the change, have turned doubt into debacle. But if he noticed her coolness at all, he took it for the same as that commanding, mocking promise which rehearsal had enabled her to offer yesterday.

"If madam will inspect the room," he said. "It is our best Oriental-lascivious, otherwise known as Birmingham-aristocratic."

She laughed. It was more French in style than anything else, with heavily draped windows looking out over Portland Place, and lots of gilding and carving on the furniture. The bed was a wide half-tester, the carpet thick and well strewn with cushions. A cheerful fire burned in the grate, with a kettle moaning on the hob. It was warm—too warm to stay long clothed.

"Enough light?" he asked.

There was the fire and eight candles. "Enough light." His crass insensitivity helped her slip back into the role she had chosen yesterday.

"A drink, Mrs. Cornelius."

"No, thank you, Mr. Thornton."

"I agree." He came toward her.

He's going to kiss me, she thought. *It's going to begin.*

But he took both her hands and, like a dancer, so manipulated them that she had to sit back upon the sofa. Her silk dress made little rustling whistles on its satin covering.

"Now the other arrangements," he said. "As your Highness commanded." And from an inside pocket he drew a large condom, a *huge* condom. She recognized it at once, of course, for she had cleared away dozens from the rooms at the Tabard. But never one so great as this; a quart of water would not fill it. *Oh Lord!* she thought.

"The bishop," he said. "I don't know why we call it that, but see!" From inside "the bishop" he pulled a small oilcloth packet. "Unwrap it," he said. "Please."

She obeyed. The sight of her fingers twitching at the cloth excited him. She lingered over it, feeling a sort of borrowed excitement, too. "A present?" she said. "For me?"

"No." He laughed. "You could say it's the very opposite."

Inside was something like a watch case, sealed with wax strips that pulled off with a tearing sound.

"Open it!" he said, trembling now quite eagerly.

Her dainty fingers struggled with the fastening. At last the two halves parted and out fell a salmon-pink sheath of the finest silk. "Woven air!" he said with reverence, taking it gently from her. "And see—it is dipped in a solution of the purest rubber, which dries to make a perfect seal. My own invention. You will catch no—present from me, Mrs. Cornelius."

She took it from him and tried its fineness where she tried all soft materials—on her lower lip.

"Wait!" he said. The emphasis his eyes added to the word made her, for the first time, confused. She handed him the sheath, which he folded carefully back into the tin, without closing the lid. He put it between them on an occasional table behind the sofa. In the candlelight its colour looked raw and almost vicious.

"Is that your monogram?" she asked, looking at the lid of the tin.

"Yes. I send it back to have it refilled. The sealing stops the rubber from perishing." He was closing in upon her, speaking the words like a special endearment.

It struck her then: the mechanics of it—the cabman, knowing exactly what to do, the very existence of such a house. It was an industry. For so long now she had planned some affair like this, thinking it extraordinary and very special. But what they were about to do was no such thing. It was probably the most normal, ordinary, everyday activity in London—in *any*where. And that was the thought which finally unlocked her reserve. It was not special. It was not supposed to be special. It was everyday. It was just—nice.

She leaned back then into the softness of the sofa and let Walter kiss her, and found herself responding, quite warmly. She thought, as she closed her eyes, of all the others who had met in this same room day upon night upon day for years and years. Momentarily she even saw them, rutting men and wriggling girls—here, where they now sat, there, on the hearth rug, there, standing, there, on the bed. The pictures her long-starved fantasy now served up lighted the fires within.

He dropped to his knees and with palsied fingers, struggled to undo her boots. She leaned forward to help him, with fingers no less tremorous. "Try to stay a little calm," she panted. But when he threw up her petticoats and began to kiss her thighs and explore her with his lips, her sexuality swelled and engulfed her mind and body both.

She did not care then what he did. And he, seeing he had the mastery, dropped his queen-and-slave pretence and took command, undressing her in the way and order he preferred, and making her do just the things he wanted. And he was *good*. Even in the extreme of her delight she knew he was a virtuoso, with skills that went far beyond mere technique, up into the realms of art. For the best of an hour he drew her on, now frenzied, now languorous, slow, talking to her of how wonderful she was being, whispering in her ear, thrilling her with wordless noises—on the sofa, on the floor, kneeling, standing, backwards, sideways, on top, crushed . . . stretched, shivering, tense . . . curled up and unmuscled . . . thrashing, heels in the air . . . surrendering into spasm, melting and filling every angle of the room.

Then he finished too, almost as an afterthought. He rolled off her and went to sleep. She watched him go limp, fascinated at the shrivelling of the sheath. The pink colour had run and darkened; the liquid blob at the end was blotched like a carrion crow's egg. She sighed and felt wonderful.

He slept less than a minute and woke up already apologizing. "Always happens," he said. "Wasn't it good?"

"Your—finale seemed a bit . . . ," she said.

He got up, peeling off the sheath. "The older I get, the less important it becomes. When I was fourteen I couldn't sleep without four or five a night. Now, I sometimes don't get there at all, but it doesn't seem to matter. When I'm old I think memory and imagination would be all I need. Memor*ies*, I mean." He laughed.

"It's very important to you, isn't it, Mr. Thornton?"

"Congress?"

She nodded.

"It is the entire joy and meaning of my life. I used to feel ashamed of it, but not now." He went over to the washstand, filling it with the kettle from the hob. His gesture invited her to use it first.

Amazed that she felt no shame she walked across and began to wash her face and neck. He took a cloth, wrung it out, and, kneeling, gently washed her privities from behind. Looking down between her knees she saw him swell again. Carefully she lifted one foot and pressed it down. "Oh no no," she said. The cloth was red with the dye from the sheath.

"It's important to you, too," he said. "And you are not ashamed."

"It's true, though I don't understand it. I like to hear you talking about it. Next time will you tell me about the things you like doing?"

"*Next* time!" he said. "Well, now!"

"Don't be arch," she told him crossly. "Don't spoil it. Of course there'll be a next time—and many more." She began to dress. "What we must do now is settle all the arrangements. Next time, by the way, I shall pay for the room." He protested, but without conviction. "I insist," she said. "We are two free beings who meet freely for our own mutual free enjoyment. If you always pay for the room, that makes me at once merely a—a part-time mistress. No longer free."

"Before you put that on," he warned, "you might like to use this." He opened a cupboard door and took out a medical-looking thing on a mahogany tray. There was a rubber bulb and tube connected to a silver pipe, coiled around a porcelain bowl with some powder in the bottom. "Compliments of the house," he said. "It's a sort of cannula washer— or a *douche*, as they call it in the French houses."

"What for?" she asked, half guessing.

He told her and showed her how to use it. She giggled at the touch of it and at the water. She thought it was blood coming out but it was just the dye again. She lay down and spread herself while he dried her, which he did slowly and tenderly. "Beautiful mother-of-pearly pink," he said.

She watched him, looking down at her with such intensity. "Have you known a lot of women, Mr. Thornton?" she asked.

"Three hundred and eighteen," he said, still half in a dream.

She sat up at once and then laughed, thinking he was joking.

But he was not. "I told you," he said. "It's what I live for."

Still she laughed. "How can you be sure of the number, though?"

"I can be sure it is at least three hundred and eighteen because I keep a diary. Religiously, you might say. These"—he pulled her thighs together, stroking them with the towel as he drew away—"are the pillars of my temple."

The possibility of a diary had not occurred to her. "Please, Mr. Thornton, do not record *this*, today, in it. Oh, if it should be read by—"

But he interrupted, smiling at her fears. "Believe me. It could fall into the hands of my closest friend—into Arabella's even—and there is not a word or detail to connect me with it. Each incident is recorded in loose-leaf and undated. The sequence is constantly shuffled. Places, times, names, everything is altered. I have even taught myself to write in a different hand, with my left hand. My own clerk would not recognize it."

"Where do you keep it?" She was still worried.

"Absolutely safely. I rent a garret room in Bristol. The landlady thinks—I have told her I am writing a history of English everyday life. It will be my own life's work, I say. She is certain I am a harmless fool. I tell you what—you shall choose the name you are to bear in my diary."

Sarah, intrigued now, thought quickly. Silvia Carey was the name of the girl in that book at the Tabard—and, it suddenly struck her, the initials were the same as her own. "Silvia Carey," she said.

His look changed at once to a sort of watchful mistrust. "There are depths to you, Mrs. Cornelius. Are there not?"

"What do you mean? What depths?"

"*The Lustful Turk*. There's depths if ever I plumbed them."

She coloured. "It's the only such book I've ever seen," she said. "One of the maids at the tavern had it."

"Ah." There was half belief in his tone. "I have lots more like it. They help me when I am—ill. Otherwise I don't think much to them." He was trying to repair the mood between them.

She began again to dress. "Call me what you like," she said lightly. "When did you start this diary?"

"About a year after I married Arabella. When I knew for certain that marriage was not going to bring—all that I had hoped."

Sarah sighed. "That is what I fear most. Meeting Mrs. Thornton again."

He turned her then and held her by her arms. In all their time in the room, it was the closest he came to a really loving gesture. "Of all fears," he said, "that is, believe me, the most groundless. What you gave me today it is not in her to give. What you took is something she values less than—house dirt." His intention was humorous but the effect was to fill her with sadness, all the deeper for its suddenness. Once again he did not notice. "I used to feel guilty," he said. "All those girls, taking what was rightfully hers. But not anymore." He buttoned her dress and knelt to help her on with her boots.

"How long before you go back to Bristol?" she asked.

"A month at least. My father-in-law's throat is not mending. Arabella will wish to stay, and I may work as easily at Paddington as at Bristol just at the moment."

"Good," she said briskly. "Then we shall meet here next Wednesday at three in the afternoon. I shall come direct to the back door. And you will let me in. Meanwhile, we must both think about our longer-term needs and arrangements."

"As a matter of fact," he said diffidently, "can you pay for the room today? It was rather more than I expected."

"How much?"

"Five pounds."

She blanched. A half year's wages in the old days! But she handed him the money with a smile, saying: "We *must* make other arrangements."

Later she wondered if Nora knew how much money there was in such houses. She at once regretted the cheapness of the thought. *Come—I must not lose my standards*, she said to herself.

Chapter 40

"John," Sarah said that night after supper, "I was not born or brought up to a life of idleness."

He grinned. "That's why you take to it so well."

"That's just it: I don't. I want to feel of some *use*."

"You teach the children, better than any governess. You've helped Nora's French. You cheer both of us up, just being around us. Do we make you feel useless?"

She took his hand and squeezed it. "Of course not. But—I don't know—going to London today—I thought the world does have an especial need of people with education, time, and money."

"If you want to be useful," he said, "I've some particular work for you. You could do it well, too."

And she, not wanting to appear to have too clear a scheme already formed, acceded gratefully to do whatever it was.

It turned out to be writing letters on his behalf—the more personal sort of business letter, such as a recommendation for a man, an arrangement to meet, a thank you, an acceptance to a public dinner, a covering letter for a donation to a charity, and so on. All John had to do was to write a sentence explaining why the letter was in another hand and craving indulgence, and to sign it.

It was the letter to the Female Refuge, with a donation of four hundred pounds, that gave her the idea. She said she would like to see the people who did such fine work and would take the letter and draft herself.

"You're up to something or other," John accused.

She blushed, and then, to cover that reaction, she agreed she was "up to" something and promised to explain all if it worked. "If it doesn't, then it won't matter, will it?"

When Nora saw Sarah that evening she knew something had happened. She remembered that John had taken her to London that day, and all the suspicions that had died down over the last few months began to grow again.

John repeated his conversation with Sarah to her. "It has something to do with Thornton," he said. "I'm sure there's something going on there."

"Tittle tattle," she said, afraid for him to go on—afraid that something in his voice would betray the lie.

*   *   *

The Female Refuge was a charity of the Female Rescue Society, whose offices overlooked Islington Green. The Refuge itself was out in the country at Hornsey, beyond the city's temptations.

Islington Green was virtually on John's route into London, down the City Road, so he needed make no great detour to let her off at the Society's door. And he even pointed out the cab rank to her and told her how much to pay for the journey to the City—just as if he, rather than she, had lived in London for the best part of eight years.

With a draft for four hundred pounds, she was naturally a most favoured caller, and a comfortable chair and a cup of tea were brought at once. She told the clerk that she had money of her own and had thought of making a donation—perhaps the same, or even more—perhaps five hundred pounds. The chief clerk was beside himself with gratitude.

But, she went on, just giving money was so passive—especially when one had time to *do* things—be more active. What she was really wondering was whether she might serve on their committee—or, indeed, play any role?

The chief clerk could not say—but he was sure—oh, if only Lady Bere were here—perhaps Mrs. Cornelius could come back this afternoon?

No, she would not be in London again until next Wednesday, in the morning.

Well, he was certain that, in those circumstances, Lady Bere would arrange to see her then.

Good, that was settled. Then, feeling she ought somehow to substantiate her interest in the work of the Society, she asked exactly how they went about their task, and what they did under the heading of "rescue."

Lady Bere would explain all that, too. Meanwhile, perhaps she would like to look over the Society's prospectus and its most recent report?

From the prospectus, she learned that Lady Bere spelled her name

Bear. She had wondered why the clerk was so insistent on the "beeer" pronunciation; he must have suffered more than his due of ribaldry about a lady "bare."

*   *   *

That afternoon no doubts assailed her as the cab drew into the mews off Foley Street and pulled up outside the back door. Mr. Thornton opened it at once, and they went along the passage and up the stairs like a master and mistress in their own home. She heard the silken swish of her dress and petticoats and looked down at the swelling of her bosom and realized that her femininity had become exciting to her as well. These things no longer felt like an accident of convention and inheritance. They were *for* something. For giving. For giving to Mr. Thornton. And for giving herself such delight. Already her limbs felt weak at the thought of the pleasures to follow. She could not understand how she had carried the instruments of it around for so long without once appreciating their quality.

They had the same room, with its French opulence, heavy curtains, and glowing fire; but this time there were only two candles, one at each side of the bed. "Make a change," he said.

She was different, too; much more equal to him, more daring, more demanding—to him more lascivious. This time he did not spin matters out so long, but the joy was sweeter and more intense for that. Afterward she lay with her back to him, curled up upon his naked body, on the hearthrug, luxuriating in the heat from the coals.

"Fallen Samson," she said, playing with him.

"Samson?"

"Well," she said archly, "he thrust apart the pillars of the temple."

He chuckled. "You are very good," he said.

"We are both very good—if you mean it like that. We know exactly what we want, and we will not allow complications."

"You don't know how difficult it ought to be," he said, unconvinced. "I've known no other woman I feel so immediately at one with as you—it really is amazing."

"Don't start nurturing romantic illusions," she warned. "Much as I love Samson here, I'd stop seeing you if I even suspected that was happening."

He stroked her back and shoulders. "Do you not want me to tell you that though all women are nice before, few are even tolerable after?"

She lay back on him and purred. "You can tell me *that*." After a pause she said, "How many befores and afters have there been?"

He laughed a long time, until she began to feel isolated. As usual he did not notice. "I'm sorry," he said, mechanically, and still laughing. "I *knew* you would ask me that."

"So you've worked out the answer."

"No." He sighed his laughing to a halt. "I'd need to go back to Bristol to tell you exactly. But very roughly, very round-figurish, I'd say a hundred and eighty times a year—perhaps two hundred—for thirteen years. And before that—you mean with women, not solitary?"

"Yes. With the three hundred and eighteen."

"Before that, before I was twenty, probably not more than two or three a month from when I was sixteen. Thirty a year for five years. That's a hundred and fifty plus two thousand six hundred. I make it two thousand seven hundred and fifty."

She let out her breath in astonishment. "How many do you remember?"

"They are all written down. When I read back I remember them all. Each one."

"And the girls?"

"I remember how they felt to me. Their bodies. And a lot of faces, too, of course. But mostly their—where they were soft or bony or angular or tall or pneumatic, and mobile or still. That sort of thing."

She longed to ask where she ranked in that monstrous galaxy but had too much pride. And he had too little sympathy to tell her without being prompted.

"Did you enjoy them all?" she asked instead.

He pondered that a long time. "There's only one I remember not enjoying. That was an unfinished one on a canal bank, among the reeds, with a girl who was a simpleton, and a bit crippled. I didn't enjoy that because I was interrupted in the middle by another man who claimed he'd seen her first."

Sarah clenched her jaw and eyes tight shut, trying not to laugh at the utter, gargantuan selfishness of this man. Yet even in the moment that it shocked her, she realized, too, that it was precisely the quality that made him right for her purposes. So whose selfishness was top?

"Funny you should ask that," he went on. "Usually I have to— worship at the temple, let's say, at least four times a week, otherwise I get so—impossible. But since last week, just knowing this day was coming, and remembering the last one, I haven't even wanted to. So that shows, doesn't it."

"Shows what?"

"There must be something lacking in those other encounters."

She giggled. "I imagined *I* was obsessed by thoughts of sexual congress. But I see I am still in the nursery."

And then she told him how she was proposing to make one clear day a week in London, so that they could go on meeting. "And we cannot possibly spend twenty to twenty-five pounds a month on this room. We could rent a whole house for that. So you, Mr. Thornton dear, are to look for clean and decent furnished rooms, somewhere quiet and discreet and near the West End and off the paths your friends and mine might tread. And get two sets of keys made. We will share the rent, of course. And we shall be Mr. and Mrs. Carey. Silvia Carey and—Samson Carey."

He laughed. "It will deceive no one."

"It will not have to. It is the form alone that matters. And one more thing. I insist that your—aides-mémoire of these encounters of ours should not lie among two thousand seven hundred and fifty others. You are to leave them in our apartment."

"At once, majesty! May I ask why?"

She almost burst out laughing again; of course he *needed* to ask.

"Because," she said, reaching for the first convenient lie, "if it so happens that you are delayed or unable to visit me—which must happen from time to time—I shall not then be entirely inconsolable."

It pleased him inordinately to hear it.

Chapter 41

The Lady Bear-pronounced-Bere was not at all as Sarah had imagined her—no kindly, distant lady bountiful but a tough, vicious harridan. She wanted it quite clear that she had no time for mere charitable intentions, that she suspected everyone who walked through the doors of prurient curiosity, that *she* ran the committee and was not particularly upset if no one liked her or what she did. And what extraordinary qualities did Mrs. Cornelius imagine she had to offer the Society?

"Understanding," Sarah said without hesitation. And she was gratified to see that despite all the care her ladyship took to conceal it, the word and Sarah's pugnacity had pricked her curiosity. "You do not know," Sarah went on, "that when my father, who was vicar of Coldharbour in Cheshire, died, and my mother followed him soon after, I was left in dire peril of the fate from which we attempt"—she liked that *we*—"to rescue our girls in this Society." An imp of mischief prompted her to lean forward and ask, with intense seriousness: "Have you, Lady Bear, ever lain drugged and barely sensible while your undoing is bargained for upon the stair outside?"

Lady Bear was too astonished to reply coherently, but the word "impertinence" and flecks of saliva escaped her moustachioed lips.

"*That*," Sarah said dramatically, "is understanding."

Her ladyship was curious still, despite herself. "You?" she began.

Sarah nodded. "I was rescued in the very nick of time. And taken and placed in virtuous and honest employment where"—her voice fell to its normal tones and she became sincere—"where I had the fortune to attract the favourable notice of my employer, Mr. Cornelius."

For the first time Lady Bear smiled. "And now you are—"

"His widow," Sarah said quickly, now hating herself for using the story so, and disliking Lady Bear for having provoked it. What did she care whether she had Lady Bear's approval or not? She had only come here because of the Stevensons' letter. She could easily find some other charity with a weekly committee to suit her needs.

But it was not going to be necessary. She had won Lady Bear's grudging approval and, on handing over the donation of four hundred pounds, won her place on the committee, which met every Thursday morning. The trust John had set up with Tom's money yielded eight hundred and fifty pounds a year, which was hers absolutely. And since John and Nora wouldn't take a penny for her keep, most of the twelve hundred it had yielded so far was still intact.

"Come and see the Refuge out at Hornsey," Lady Bear said. "My carriage is outside."

But Sarah explained she had business in town; would tomorrow be as convenient? After the committee meeting.

"Of course, Mrs. Cornelius. I suppose you may have a reference? Since your parents and husband are all passed over? Please do not be offended, it is the commissioners of charity who insist."

"Not at all. It is most proper. The only friend I remember from those days, a friend of my father's, was the Reverend Doctor Prendergast, who is now bishop of Manchester. I'm sure he will speak for me. He will remember me as little Sarah Nevill. In fact"—the imp returned—"when you write to him, do say that it was something he told

me at our last meeting which awakened me to the perils a girl may face
and that has brought me to you, eager to help."

*   *   *

Each week her lust for Thornton grew stronger. Fear had gone completely. So had her simple, ignorant curiosity. The days that led up to
each Wednesday and, later, each Thursday, were filled with bodily
memories of him, of his hands on her hips and breasts, of his teeth and
tongue down her back, of his priapic strength and his glinting, greedy
eyes. She found it odd to like him so much, to like his sexual gluttony,
his towering selfishness, his total insensitivity to anything that was not
part of his finale or of the long and devious road toward it. How could
she like these things so warmly, while the thought that anyone could
love him made her almost bilious?

If one could not answer that question, there was no point in framing
lesser ones. So she asked no questions at all, but accepted the extraordinary things she was doing, the tissue of lies and fantasy she was
weaving, as normal. And what made it normal was that she could face
the thought of John and Nora being in bed (not now, of course, because Nora was still very poorly, but the memory of them, and the
prospect)—she could accept it without envy or self-pity. Now she could
admit that for eighteen months she had felt both those destructive
emotions. And she was not now plagued with stupid, arrested-schoolgirl
fantasies of lustful Turks. And she no longer went around feeling like a
boiler at the point of bursting. Anything that removed such blemishes
could not be utterly wrong. It could not even be very wrong. If Mr.
Thornton were a Musselman, he and she and Mrs. Thornton would
probably be very happy together.

Chapter 42

In the first week of January 1847, Nora had healed well enough for
Dr. Hales to take off the sandbag entirely. "But the fascia will take
some time to knit thoroughly. So you must still treat yourself tenderly.
No Valsalva's manoeuvre—d'you know what I mean?"

Nora, thinking she did, blushed and agreed. The thought of *that*
had, for once, not crossed her mind. But later she looked it up in the

Household Physician and found that it meant no more than straining at stool, straining to cough, or to exhale vigorously. What a strange world doctors lived in, where one did not cough or sneeze but "performed Valsalva's manoeuvre."

Soon she was allowed up, briefly, each day, to walk around the room and sit in a padded chair by the fire and read. John usually stayed part of the mornings and went to London each afternoon and evening. He told her he was delighted at the way those to whom he had delegated parts of their business were coping. She had private doubts—because nothing in her experience ever went that smoothly—but she pretended to accept all he said.

One thing that did please her was the way John now spoke about the wider world beyond their business. Before, he had always behaved as if railways were the prime force of the times; it mattered little what governments and factions and the Treasury planned, the railways, he said, would sweep everything before them. Human wishes were power-less before the greater might of steam and iron. But now he spoke more often of things people had said in Parliament—not in pity at their blindness but with respect for their wisdom. Lord George Bentinck told his friends he had consulted John on the drafting of the bill for the aid of Irish railways. And since railway legislation in general took up more than a quarter of parlimentary time, John was, one way and another, canvassed and consulted by an increasing number of people in both parties and at the Board of Trade.

Near the end of January he came back with the news that a new British Association had been formed for the relief of the distress in re-mote parishes of Ireland and Scotland. There had been serious riots in Scotland, where poor country folk were just as dependent on the potato as were the Irish, and where the failure had been equally universal. In Ireland there had been disturbances and a flood of violent talk but no rioting on any great scale. In fact, where the distress was worst—in the far west of Ireland—whole villages had been quietly dying without a word of protest or the throwing of a single stone. The snows of this winter lay in one unbroken shroud from Cape Clear, right across Ire-land, England, Europe, and Russia to Siberia. It was the hardest winter not just in memory but in written record. People who had half starved for a year and fully starved for another six months were dying in num-bers that stirred even the most antipapist conscience. The new British Association was one response.

"The people organizing it," John told Nora, "are bankers like Rothschild's, Baring, who bought the relief corn in America in forty-five, Abel Smith, and there's Pim from the Society of Friends. They've asked me for advice on feeding large numbers in out-of-doors circumstances—which is one up to us and one in the eye for the army commissariat."

"How much have you promised in money?" Her tone was carefully neutral.

He smiled at her, forcing her to smile too. "That is a problem. We've a little over five thousand waiting to go to the right sort of activity in Ireland. But Rothschild's only given a thousand and the queen's only given two thousand."

"Only!" Nora said.

"Well, I agree, yes, it is generous. But it means we must give eight or nine hundred. To give more would make us look—pushing at it. So what I think, if you agree, is for me to go straight to the Friends and propose to them that I should buy up the first convenient bankrupt estate and lend it to them, free, to remodel. And pay for whatever they do. So we'll look for the worst and try to make it the best."

"It sounds a good idea," she said. "But fancy going out and looking for an estate in the worst possible condition!" She yawned, unconvincingly. It was the nearest she could go toward telling him he had carte blanche with the Irish profits.

"You see, we have the money—some money—but no time; they have the time but no money."

"It fits well," she said, pretending to fall into a doze.

"Trevelyan says we'll need a few more horrifying accounts of the distress before the general English hostility to the Irish is overcome and the subscriptions begin to come in."

"Well," Nora said, almost asleep, "they do make such threats against us." It was a speech of abdication. How little it all seemed to matter now.

*   *   *

All next month the news from Ireland dominated the papers. Tales of the mass deaths of whole villages written with incoherent anger by customs men and returning travellers turned Trevelyan's gallows humour into an accurate prediction: Money was flowing into the British Association's coffers.

The government, too, was looking for money. The new liberal ministry, appalled at the waste and muddle of earlier relief works, had brought in a new scheme making local ratepayers responsible for funding all relief. The Treasury would advance the money, free of interest, against the promise of the ratepayers to repay over a fixed term of years. "Ireland's property must support Ireland's poverty," was the watchword.

But once again a remote government and an even remoter Treasury had not the slightest grasp of Irish reality. No ratepayer who valued his life and the lives of his family *dared* to oppose any scheme that offered employment, no matter how costly or fanciful. Without second thought they put their names to schemes that would bankrupt themselves twenty times over—knowing full well that in the end the Treasury, unable to take the entire country in pawn, would simply have to write off the debt.

And that was why the Treasury was coming into the money market for a loan of eight million pounds, just to cover Irish relief work.

Nora knew none of this; and John, wishing above all to let the wounds of their own private Irish question heal, naturally told her nothing of it. So she sat in the boudoir at Maran Hill reading the newspapers, seeing the gold reserves fall almost by the hour—in one week nearly a million pounds' worth of bullion went to America alone—and wondering if there was one sane man left at the Bank of England. The country was bleeding gold from every seaport.

Now it would begin, she thought. Not just a few rotten apples falling out of the trees, but whole boughs would break. *Why can I not get better quicker?* she fumed. *Now when I am needed most of all!*

If anger and impatience could heal, she would have been well by the end of January. But though her general strength and vigour returned slowly, she constantly anticipated that regeneration by pushing herself beyond their present limit. She would ask to see accounts and would herself make mistakes in checking them; her angry letters of reprimand had to be followed by humble apologies to the clerks or seniors concerned. After three such lapses she came to mistrust herself.

"I've invented a new mathematics," she said to John. "I call it 'elastic adding.' I add up everything three times and take the average of the three different answers." And then, still laughing at her joke, she burst into tears.

"I don't know what's wrong with me," she said when he had soothed her back from her hysteria.

"If only you could forget the business," he said, making a gouging movement, dipping an imaginary spoon into her skull. "How can we remove it for a month or two—all memory of it?"

She sighed.

"Perhaps," he said, looking guardedly at her, "this isn't the thing to tell you, but we *are* managing quite well without you. Nothing like so well as with you, of course. But that's to say we're only twice as good as all our competitors instead of four times as good."

She wished she could respond to this kindliness of his, but her anger at her own feebleness, and at being kept away from life, overwhelmed that impulse to tenderness. She knew he was keeping things back from her and she resented it—even though she understood his intention. He became the only focus for her anger. And all her knowledge and understanding could not stop her from venting it.

He, too, was ashamed to find that something within him resented her illness. He had come to depend on her far more than he realized. In a loose way he had imagined that she represented part of that "delegation of authority and decision" which was so important to the firm's continued expansion. One point of such delegation was that if any delegatee fell ill or was absent, others, including himself, could cover. He had swiftly found that no one could cover for Nora. They could do the mechanical things—the transfer and management of funds and accounts—all the things he had thought formed her real contribution to the firm. But what they could not supply was that uncanny ability to think about the firm as a whole, not as it might be set out in a prospectus, but as a thriving, bustling entity.

Something in her mind was like a little working model of their business and the world—far more intricate and rare than any clockwork or machinery. It was, as Chambers said, priceless. As each week passed he missed that faculty more sorely—and disliked himself for the resentment it bred.

By March she was well enough to go for a few gentle rides around the park with Sarah on their underexercised horses. On one of these trots Fontana put a foot in a "money hole," as Hertfordshire people called the sudden and unpredictable pits that open in deep gravel, and threw her. She was conscious again by the time they carried her indoors, but she was badly concussed and shaken. Dr. Hales said she ought to go abroad.

They thought at once of Rodie and Normandy, and within a week it was arranged for her to go on the first of April and to stay until she was fit.

On the first of April the Bank put up its minimum rate to five per cent.

*   *   *

For most of that spring she sat in the gardens at La Gracieuse or, on the finest days, down on the sands at Trouville. Once or twice, for the extra encouragement it brought, she and Rodie went and sat in royal isolation on the Deauville side. "One day, Rodie," she said . . . and she described the fashionable resort she and Ferrand had planned. There was no harm in it now they had bought all but a couple of acres of the land.

And Rodie, thinking it a charming fantasy but no more, was delighted to see her darling Stevie's strength returning so well. "It is the oaks," she said. "The fragrance of the oaks of Normandie." She had begun her soup kitchen and clothing depot for the poorer workers. *Everyone doing good works suddenly*, Nora thought.

John assumed a quite disproportionate interest in the Dieppe line, though his deputy there was one of his best. Usually, too, there were small things that needed Nora's decision or advice and he would take a fly up from Rouen to Trouville to see her—though never, she noticed, finding time to stay the night. At the end of May she threatened to seduce one of Rodie's young gardeners if John didn't stop with her; they resumed relations in a night of loving that left John in bed "with a spring chill" all next day. She felt that to be a particular triumph. Sarah had never left him so *drained*, she thought. It was also the first time she had ever felt sure, right from the night itself, that she had conceived. Next day she worked forward through the calendar; it might, she realized, be born on leap year's day next year.

That re-establishment of their marriage marked, in her mind, the last stage of her recovery. She wanted to return to England at once and catch up on all that had been left to look after itself: her children, the stable, her own property, the firm. She needed to be back there in London, putting out her roots into that rich soil, soaking in the information and conjecture that had become her life blood. Here she was too dependent on the papers, and the papers were full of gloom. To the journalists the most ominous sign of all was now apparent: The weekly totals of notes and coins issued by the Bank of England's lending department had steadily fallen, week by week, from about forty-two million a week in January to less than thirty-two million by mid-May— a period in which it would normally have risen by an equal amount. Not one week had shown an advance on its predecessor.

But to her mind there was an even more ominous sign, though no one seemed to remark upon it. All kinds of commodities were beginning to show quite unprecedented leaps. Wheat had almost doubled. Iron was rising even though all ironfounding, except for railways, was in decline. Indigo, tea, coffee, sugar, feathers, rice, rum—all were being to some extent run up. She worried for some time at this new evidence of instability but could find no explanation. Perhaps, she thought, there were firms whose basic unsoundness had been concealed by years of cheap money; now that they could no longer borrow to cover their insolvency, perhaps they were, as a last desperate throw of the dice, trying to speculate in commodities to recover their position.

In April there were five bankruptcies she considered abnormal—that is, of firms generally thought to be sound. In May there were six. In June, ten. It was time to go home. The whirlpool was forming.

Chapter 43

The first shock, after her return, was to find that the precautions they had adopted against their own crisis in 1845 were now being applied in the most slovenly way. The firm was now almost half as big again as it had been then, but at the present rate they would be less than half as well prepared to face a general panic.

The preparation of accounts had also got slack, being brought up to date weekly instead of daily. It horrified her. Even the daily accounts were still a week or ten days behind the true state of affairs, because of delays at the workings and in the mails. To add to that delay seemed madness. John did not understand her concern. He preferred the weekly pulling-together of everything, rather than the confusing daily ups and downs.

She began to feel that her return was resented; they'd all been a lot more comfortable in the easier times when she was absent. But she steeled herself to all protest, took a room at the Adelaide for a fortnight, and restored what she considered to be proper discipline and procedure to the London office—supported by a string of blistering memoranda sent out to the clerks on the workings.

John had a lot of ruffled feathers to soothe on his visits to their various lines and other contracts, and he came back to tell Nora that she would have to be a bit more diplomatic. She said the time for diplomacy had passed. With the storm now brewing, only the tightest discipline would get them through.

"I don't manage that kind of a ship," he said patiently. "My lads do things not because someone orders them to it, but because they understand what's right from what's wrong."

"But in a crisis," she said, "there must be command and obedience. There's no time for committees and—"

He laughed. "I'm not turning myself into a water-colour version of Henry Peto and his military men. For one thing, I'd be so bad at it, I'd be bound to bungle it."

In the end she agreed to smooth the rough edge of her tongue and her pen, but only because he virtually made it a command.

At their most heated moments she could see a sort of anger and a desperation in his eyes. It was as if he felt himself trapped. Which, she had to admit, he was. The world, the good, ever-providing world, was closing down all around them. The rules were changing. *We are all trapped by the rules*, she told herself. John must accept it.

Their lovemaking became more tender and more frequent in proportion with these disagreements. It was as if they wished to show that, despite all that external conflict, they were at heart closer and more solidly united than ever. There came a time when she wondered if it was wise to reward their arguments with such pleasures; once or twice she thought she opposed him for the mere sake of provoking his frustration and the release that came when he was in her arms.

In July there were thirteen abnormal bankruptcies, some of them vast. The effect in the City was immediate and drastic. You could see people looking at each other and saying "Who's next?" Merchants of the greatest reputation had difficulty getting their bills discounted. The mischief of suspicion was abroad and the flimsy card-house called confidence was teetering. The reserves, which had been steady or even rising since the rate went to five per cent, once again began to fall. Exchequer bills, despite a doubled rate of interest since January, were now at a discount for the first time in years.

There was no question now of a return to France that year for Nora. The Auberge Clément, not to mention the plans for Deauville, would have to be left to themselves and to chance for another year. Sam wrote from Newcastle to say he would not be able to come to France; he did not say "this year" or put any term to the statement.

The change in Sarah was too profound to escape notice, even in those troubled months. She no longer moped around with unread books and half-written letters; she no longer said how much she envied Nora her full and busy life. Her work with the Female Rescue Society seemed to have transformed her. Everybody remarked on how vigorous and active she was nowadays. She even became quite an adventurous rider and took a couple of fairly nasty falls.

Nora, who knew exactly why Sarah was so radiant, wondered that she could find so little anger in herself against John. It was the fear of the gathering storm, she said (and she meant in the world of business); it would be so great that she and he could not afford to fall out. In fact, she was almost looking forward to it. They were never more united than when they were staving off disaster together.

What did this rather minor affair with Sarah matter in the face of that?

*   *   *

At the end of July she drew up her own accounts, for the benefit of the Wolff brothers, and showed profits for the year of £33,279 14*s.* 10*d.*, or twenty-seven per cent on the total investment, hers and theirs. Of course, these were book values—the notional increase in the value of her land as it was developed. It was not actual, bankable cash. The fall in trade had not affected development yet; so it had proved the best sort of investment for the year. The Wolffs were £2,318 3*s.* 1*d.* better off, even after her commission, which came to a useful £409 2*s.* 3*d. They ought to be delighted with that*, she thought as she drew the final double line under the summary of accounts.

They were so delighted that they came tumbling over the German Ocean as fast as steam could carry them—having first written to Chambers to ask if there was any possibility that the referee he had chosen to audit the accounts might have been bribed by Mrs. Stevenson. They asked to see her the day after their arrival, arranging the meeting in Chambers' office.

They were late. While she waited, impatiently, Chambers watched her with cool amusement.

"I suppose I oughtn't to tell you," he said, "but I will. They are coming here to offer something very big."

She looked at him, undecided. "How big?"

"Very." He would not be drawn further.

And there they were, breathless as a pair of running dogs, on the stair.

Oskar Wolff-Dietrich was a squat version of his brother, but clear skinned and sharper eyed. He made notes of everything on tiny loose sheets about the size of small playing cards. Like a dealer, he kept squaring them up between his fingers when he was not writing. This time he did the talking, so that he could dictate the pace of the dialogue and not lose it while he wrote. And before he started to write, each time, he said "Sorry, excuse" in a flat monotone.

At first the technique unnerved Nora, until she realized why. It was stopping her mind from working at its usual pace. The apparent luxury of having so much thinking time, while he wrote, was a delusion; the mind wandered off along so many permutations of possibility, which it would never have time to notice much less explore in the ordinary cut and thrust of argument, that it ended up confused and irresolute.

As soon as this became clear she took to talking with Chambers in a polite undertone while Oskar Wolff was busy; she spoke of trivial details of their business, or that week's bankruptcies, or other City gossip. She noticed that the notes became much shorter once she started this tactic. Julius Wolff smiled complicitly at her, as if she had done something very clever.

Oskar had wasted his rather good gambit on the generalities; by the time he came to the day's actual business, Nora was level again.

"Our purpose, Mrs. Stevenson, today is to explain to you that we, last year, were the vanguard of a much larger army."

"Army?" she questioned.

He shrugged. "Forgive me. Corps. Group—what do you say for a collection of capitalists?"

"Clutch?" Nora suggested.

Chambers laughed and agreed.

"There are many of us in Holstein, Brandenburg—Schleswig—Braunschweig—and also France who fear revolution this year, next year. . . ."

He went on in this vein for some minutes, sketching a banker's view of the history of socialism and communism in Europe; Nora wondered how they would respond if she just casually let slip that her brother was one of the revolution's leaders.

"Without mentioning your name, Madame Stevenson, we, my brother and I, have allowed it be known, in a very small, very select circle of close acquaintances in banking and the mercantile fraternity, that we have invested part of our capital in a number of English firms and properties."

"I hope you were able to say you were pleased, Herr Wolff."

The brothers smiled at each other. "We had to lie," Oskar said.

"No one will believe twenty-seven per cent," Julius explained.

"We said twelve per cent. As a result we have gold coin to the value of just over one hundred eighty thousand pounds to invest."

She thanked God that Chambers had told her it was big; even so, it was three times what she had expected. She thought rapidly. It was more than her own fixed capital. Fixed capital! Already she was thinking like a banker! The arrangement would have to be different.

"Short- or long-term?" she asked. If it was short she could not, in all honour, touch it.

"Long as you like."

"Really?" She did not believe it.

"For you, not us. We have an arrangement. It's thirty people involved, you see. We agree, each other among, that five per cent of the total can be withdrawn any year. But we manage it among ourselves. We do not touch this sum we bring to England."

"It doesn't affect you, Mrs. Stevenson," Chambers said. "They are assured you have the money securely invested, so they treat it among themselves as any banker treats fixed capital. They can lend on it."

"It's right back to early Lombard days," Julius said excitedly.

When Nora said nothing, Oskar asked what she was thinking about.

"I'm wondering if I'm on the right side of the fence."

"I think," Oskar said casually, "you ought instead to wonder how such a sum may be kept in one identifiable piece."

It was a very oblique reference to one aspect that was worrying Nora. "Her" property was all legally John's, despite his power of attorney, which he (or his executors—and these things had to be faced) could revoke at any time. If Stevenson's got into trouble, she could get the Wolffs' ten thousand (or, now, twelve thousand-odd) out safely for them. But she'd never manage that with this far larger sum.

"I think," she said, "we will go back to the arrangement that Herr Julius Wolff proposed last year. Then there is no dispute over title. And you merely give me power of attorney."

Oskar laughed. "And fifteen per cent? And cancellation fees? And management fees? No, no, Mrs. Stevenson. Not this year."

She had not dared look at Chambers yet. Her proposal, in effect, made all this capital unavailable to Stevenson's—or, at least, available only at her whim. How did he, as Stevenson's banker, feel to be sitting here taking part in such a discussion?

"Listen," she said, directly to Oskar. "When I made those conditions it was only ten thousand pounds. I did not want the trouble. I wanted you to withdraw. Now it's different. Now *I* withdraw. Unreservedly. All those extra conditions."

"All?" Oskar was astonished.

"Except, of course, the cancellation fee, or I have no protection. And the fifteen per cent—or I have no incentive."

Oskar did not laugh. "Ten per cent," he said.

"I never ask for more than I want," Nora said, as if she did this a dozen times a day. "And I never settle for less than I ask. Fifteen per cent."

"Twelve. Fifteen is not reasonable."

"Nothing is reasonable or unreasonable. That just happens to be my price. I am not greedy."

Chambers had stopped breathing. Oskar was furious. "Not *greedy*!"

"Of course not. If I were greedy I would snap at every little morsel you held out. On the contrary, my appetite for money is so sated that if you want to tempt me, you must lay out a very good feast. Fifteen per cent."

"Twelve and a half. We meet halfway."

Nora stood, hoping her nervousness did not show. The two brothers stood, too, and then, prompted by them, Chambers. In this room he had long ago forgotten her sex. "Let us go and see the new Academy exhibition," she said. "There's a young painter called Roxby I'm rather interested in."

"If we agree to fifteen, where do you put the money?" Oskar asked.

"Is that a condition?" Nora did not budge.

Oskar sat down, defeated. "No," he said.

Nora sat down, too. Julius laughed and dug his brother in the back. She realized there had been a competition between the two. Oskar must have called his brother a fool for giving so much away last year; and Julius must have challenged him to do better. She had wondered why, all through the meeting, she had sensed hostility from Oskar but a sort of cheering-on from Julius.

It worried her. She did not want to start with his hostility. She stood again, saying, "Come over this side, Herr Oskar. I will show you something."

Chambers had a street plan of London framed on one of the walls. She took Oskar's arm and led him to it. Chambers and Julius followed.

"Long ago," she said, "hundreds of years ago, before even I was born, London finished here." She ran her finger along Long Acre. "And out here were all fields and a little stream called How Bourne. And there was a merchant, called William Harpur, who bought a farm here, most of these fields, which we now call Holborn." She ran her finger from about Kings Cross to Lincoln's Inn. "He gave it when he died to a charity, called the Harpur Trust, to support the schools of Bedford, which was his town. I don't know what he paid. A few hundred pounds, perhaps. Today? A million. The income alone supports eight schools."

Oskar whistled.

"People nowadays say, 'Oh, if only my forebears had been wise in Harpur's time! How rich I would be now.' Well, I tell you, in the year 1947 there will be people in London saying, 'Thank God for our great-grandfather Oskar Wolff who bought us Chalk Farm—or Notting Hill gravel pits—or Forest Hill.' "

Oskar shook his head and chuckled, knowing what flattery was being so blatantly thrust upon him. He dug her in the ribs, like a colleague, and said, "No, no, dear lady. They say, 'Thank God for great-grandmama and fifteen per cent!' "

She drew back, smiling, eyes twinkling, half-outraged, all charade. Then she put her head to one side, shrugged, and opened her hands, as she had seen Jews do among themselves. "So," she said. "We are both blessed with families who know a good thing when they inherit it!"

Oskar, totally won over by now, nodded at her, nodded at Chambers, nodded at his brother. "You are right," he said to both men. "She is—astonishing."

But that judgement did not stop him driving some very hard conditions through in the two hours of lesser bargaining that followed. They had had weeks to prepare this; she had to think on her feet. All in all, she fancied she had come out of it quite well.

She had absolute control of the money, and there was no guarantee of its security or of any return upon it. At first she had thought they must be fools. But then she realized how great a compliment it was to her and what an enormous responsibility now rested entirely on her shoulders. If one granted that their confidence was not misplaced, then it was a very shrewd move on their part, for she now had to prove that she was not only more secure than a traditional bank but also could show a better yield.

When they had gone she kicked off her shoes and lay back on the leather-covered sofa between the windows. She breathed deeply and closed her eyes.

"Why have you done all this for me, Chambers?" she asked.

"Ah!" He said no more until she opened her eyes and looked at him. "Perhaps," he went on then, "you are just on the point of believing that I really do not mean you ill."

"If you think it's time for candour," she answered, "let me say I am still a mile or two short of that." Exhaustion robbed her of the tension this conversation ought to produce; they were, after all, talking about antagonisms that had tarnished their relations for many years —and there had been times when only fantasies of Chambers' sudden death, or departure for Australia, had helped her to sleep. Now? It did not give her heart a single extra beat. Perhaps he was right. Perhaps all of her, except her conscious mind, was on the point of this new recognition.

"When you first came to this office," he said, "I knew you were clever."

"You hated that."

"Yes—but not—it wasn't so simple. I did not hate *you*. I have never hated you."

"You've resented me. Remember how you taunted me for using red ink for liabilities and blue ink for assets? 'Pretty-pretty!'"

He laughed. "I do it myself now. I was thoughtless. Of course I resented you. I have to admit to that. But what I hated was having to confess that you were my—you see, even now, when I have said it to myself a hundred times—a thousand times—the word sticks in my throat. *Superior*. There! You are my superior." He sighed. "I make it better for myself by saying you are not only *my* superior but everyone's. Your grasp of finance is greater than—"

"I learned most of it from you," she said, feeling very embarrassed now.

"Even Jenny Lind must take singing lessons. But I have watched you. Whenever I tell you something, you not only absorb it at once, you make it fit with everything else you know. I give you an example. One of the most difficult things about banking to explain to people outside is why a country bank with a licence to issue its own money must try to drive all its competitors' banknotes out of circulation. Do you remember when I told you that? I cannot say I explained it, for you needed no explanation. I simply stated the fact. And do you remember what you said"—he snapped his fingers—"like that?"

"No." She shook her head.

"You said, 'I suppose that for the Yorkshire Bank to have one of its fifty-pound notes in my purse is like you having fifty pounds of mine on deposit.'"

"But that's *true*," Nora protested. "They are different aspects of loan capital."

He buried his head in his hands and laughed. "Please!" He waved her to silence. "I do understand it. Forty years of close association with banking in its various forms have at last driven that point home."

She blushed and joined his laughter. "I'm sorry," she said. "I mis-understood."

"Do you not know that whole volumes of books have been written to establish the connection your mind leaped to in that one instant? Do you know there are country bankers who go to their graves not fully understanding it? Not here." He tapped his chest. "They know it for a fact, but they never understand it."

"Then they probably go early to their graves."

"Not at all. It is quite possible to go a lifetime in that sort of banking with a few simple rules to guide you and not one shred of understanding to hold them together."

"Yes!" Nora said excitedly, for Chambers had just illuminated something that had often puzzled her. "Many of them are just like that. In fact"—she grinned, as if giving away a secret—"I prefer dealing with them; they never try to get clever."

Again he laughed. "You see! It is not only the high and abstract principles of this trade that come to you as second nature. Or *first* nature." But when his laughter died he said, "When you talk of 'clever' you mean me."

"I do," she said, made wary again by his sudden change of tone. "And never more so than now. If this is all some clever ruse, Nathaniel, to try to become a sort of junior partner in the management of the Wolff money, think on!" She had never once called him Nathaniel; the intimacy it implied now, coupled with her blunt hands-off, con-fused him.

"Oh, Nora," he said, also using her name for the first time, "for seven years my personal and professional admiration for you have been growing. Two years ago they utterly quashed my stupid resentment. I did hope that today . . . I did hope . . ." He sighed.

Oh dear, she thought. *Not the waterworks.* "Listen," she told him. "I cannot possibly—not after this—regard you as hostile. That would be churlish. More than churlish. It would be wicked of me." She paused a moment. "And, of course, I am grateful. And I will show it, appropriately. But what I said before was true—I do need your critical —not hostility, but you know what I mean. I need to know, when I think 'what-next, what-next,' which I do about twenty times a day, I need to ask, as well, 'What'll that *bugger* Chambers say?' D'ye see?"

He laughed. "I promise you, Nora, my admiration will vanquish only my resentment. All my other faculties, critical and professional, are at your service."

"Then you can take me out to dinner," she said. And on their way downstairs she told him it wouldn't be too difficult. "Criticism is just a habit. Like most things in the end. Did you know I'm having another baby? There's a habit!"

"Good heavens! I hope all goes well this time."

"It's got to. John and I couldn't afford another illness."

*   *   *

After dinner, when the wine had relaxed them both, she took his hand and played with the rings on his fingers and said, "Tell me, Nathaniel, why am I so angry?"

"Angry!" It was not the word he had expected. "You mean now? With me?"

"I mean now. With—everything. Myself."

"It doesn't show."

"A lot of things don't." She got one of the rings off and tried it on each of her fingers. "All too small," she said.

Chambers took it back and looked at it reminiscently. "Onkel Felix," he said. "I wonder." He looked at her. "This was my uncle Felix's ring."

"What do you wonder?"

He looked at her a long time before he answered. "I remember once—it was, I think, the first time the business world ever intruded into my childhood—Uncle Felix was in shipping and he had tried for years to gain a certain contract—this was in Hamburg—to carry Russian furs for a Hamburg merchant. And we children were to meet with my aunt and to have lunch at the menagerie with my uncle. It was a celebration. After years of negotiation, he was going at last to sign this great contract, which would make his fortune." He smiled. "It did, too. But that lunch was terrible. Terrible."

"Why?" She was intrigued, wondering what it could have to do with her. "Did he not sign?"

"Oh, he signed. Oh yes. And for half an hour he was more jovial than any of us ever remembered. He was a moody man. Very unpredictable. But that meal he was marvellous. He joked with us. And teased us about little things. Things he knew about us. And slowly these jokes grew more pointed, more cutting. As if he wanted us to know he knew *everything*. In the end no one was laughing anymore and he was completely insulting. You say 'a cloud comes down' over someone; well, it was exactly like that. I swear he made the whole terrace darker. We were sitting out on a terrace. Then my aunt just touched his arm and said, 'Felix!' in the most mild reproof. *And!* I thought he would throw the table over us all. He stood up. *Shivering.* He was smoking a cigar. He always smoked cigars. And he took it out and mashed it in the jelly! Huge hands! Mash mash mash! You can imagine how such a scene impressed itself in childish minds. Then he walked away and paced around the gardens. In real torment."

"Yes!" Nora said. "I feel a little like that. Not so dramatic. But I can understand the feeling."

"My aunt said he was always like it after he had signed a contract. Always. First elation. Then anger. The contract, she said, became a prison. By evening he was already thinking of ways to break it. Then he would feel free again."

The story had helped her divine her own mood. "That's not it," she said. "I couldn't be so childish. I think I am angry that I shall be doing it all with other people's money. I want it to be my own." She smiled and, taking the ring from him, put it back on his finger. "And now that I know the reason, I don't feel nearly so angry." She squeezed his hand and let go. "I'm glad we are friends at last, Nathaniel. There are some terrible months ahead. At least we are all going to be united in facing them."

"Not 'at least,' " he said. "At last."

Chapter 44

In August, the Bank put its rate up to five and a half per cent. There were eighteen abnormal bankruptcies. The first to go were all corn chandlers who had speculated back in May, when prices were up to 105*s.* a quarter; now, with an abundant harvest and huge grain landings from America, the price was down to 60*s.* and falling. The corn dealers fell with them, many for large amounts. In their wake fell the banks who had discounted their bills, and suppliers who had furnished them with goods that could not now be paid for. The ripples spread.

In September there were thirty-seven bankruptcies. The reserves fell. Issues fell. Commodities fell—with wheat down to 50*s.* Only the Bank's rate rose yet again, now to six per cent. It was not just commercial

firms that went bankrupt; several banks went to the wall, too—among
them the Royal Bank of Liverpool. Most of the Duke of Buckingham's
sixty thousand acres went up for forced sale and the duke himself was
adjudged bankrupt. The Duke of Beaufort and the Earl of Mornington
were both tottering.

To be in London and in commerce in those months was like standing on a large ship and watching the biggest, blackest sky you ever saw
build up over the weather quarter. The solid, reassuringly massive
vessel you went aboard in the calm waters at the quayside, slowly comes
to seem as frail as cheap furniture. No wind is upon you yet; no great
swell pitches you. But you know the storm is inevitable and it is going
to be worse than anything you ever imagined. You cling to the small
incidents and occurrences of normal life as to something precious and
vanishing.

In such a mood Nora looked to the cleaning of her hunting saddles
and equipment, ordered dresses for the winter, listened to the head
gardener's plans for next season's flower beds, and went through the
book list from Hatchard's—all familiar acts made poignant by the
crisis now upon them. Would she be doing any of these things next
year?

In October the crisis came. There were eighty-two bankruptcies that
month. No one would discount bills beyond thirty days, and almost no
business was done apart from railway business. Toward the end of the
month the Bank's reserves, which had stood higher than nine million
pounds at the beginning of the year, were down to a million and a
half. Issues of money, which were tied by law to the reserves, were at an
unprecedented low. Once again it seemed as if cash was going to vanish
from the tills of banks and shops.

Stevenson's had only £240,000 in notes and coin; their outgoings
were now at least £45,000 a week, so they could face less than six
weeks of a money famine.

"It's a good thing you have the Wolffs' money," John said. "It
might be what saves us."

"Oh, no," she said, feeling almost panic-stricken. "That's not its
purpose."

He laughed. "Of course it is. They gave you absolute discretion.
You said so. It is still in cash, I hope."

"At the moment, yes. But I don't feel I have that kind of discretion."

He became angry. "You behave as if you weren't part of the firm."

"I tell you what I will do," she said, not wanting to cross him so directly. "You raise a cash loan from Chambers. Every pound he lets you have, I will match from the Wolff fund."

Next day he came home in an ill temper. "Not a penny," he said. "All the years we've banked there! Not a penny. I *made* that man. The ingratitude!"

"John," she said, trying not to anger him further, "you must know that he wouldn't withhold support gratuitously. We're one of the lucky ones—to get *any* of our bills discounted. You go and stand in the Salisbury Arms, or any tavern, and listen to the grumbles. Even Chambers can't conjure money out of air."

"You talk just like him," John said. "His very words."

"We should have stored up more cash this spring and summer."

"We! You mean I."

She shrugged.

"You may have forgotten that I had to run the firm singlehanded."

"Of course that was my fault."

"No!" He turned his anger on himself, now. "No. You know it wasn't. Oh, darling." He put his arms around her, but it was an effort. "I am so afraid now. The City is terrible. You have never seen such gloom on so many faces."

She was annoyed with him still, though, for making her feel such a traitress in not offering the Wolff fund to the firm.

She felt even worse next day when she went in and told Chambers to buy Exchequer bills with the entire fund. He was to spread the buying and to switch to consols if the rate rose more than twenty points.

He was a bit taken aback. "You know the rate is very low? Thirty-seven under."

She knew the risk well enough, but she shut out all objection, from him as well as from her own thoughts. She did not even wonder why she was courting disaster like this.

That evening she told John what she had done. She had expected him to be angry, but he merely looked at her with a cold malevolence she found ten times more frightening.

"Don't you *see*," she said. "What with the land I have and the way that is going up in value as it's developed, and with my commission on the Wolff fund in time, there's less and less need for you to keep taking off ten per cent of your profits to put into our trust fund, mine and the children's. So Nathan and I are agreed—"

"Oh, it's Nathan now!"

"Listen, will you! Chambers and I are willing to put the trust fund's securities as guarantee to Stevenson's against—"

"No!" he roared. "Never! It's out of the question."

"Why, John?" she asked innocently. "Would it not be safe?"

"Of course it would be safe. But the whole purpose of having such a fund is to secure you and the children against the firm's bankruptcy."

"What a lovely arrangement!" she mocked. "If Stevenson's goes bankrupt, the children and I have a quarter of a million to play with— money that could have saved the firm. How would that make us feel!"

"But you can't use such a fund for such a purpose. It'd be like stand- ing on your own hands and lifting yourself off the ground."

"Well!" She turned from him and flung her hands up in a hopeless gesture. "There's two completely incompatible ways of looking at the same thing. In fact, there's no way of stopping Chambers and me from putting the fund as guarantee. We could guarantee this month's entire crop of bankrupts if the whim took us."

He walked across to her and turned her to face him. He was very calm now. "You'd go against my express wishes?" he asked. His voice was completely neutral.

She thought of many evasions before, equally calmly, she said, "If your wishes were contrary to your best interests—yes. You should have thought of all this before you made me a joint trustee."

"I shall tell Chambers that if ever he does such a thing, he'll never see a penny of mine."

She smiled, trying to rekindle his warmth. "Of course we wouldn't. You provoked me into saying that. I only talked about the trust fund because I knew you'd reject the idea. And I thought you'd understand I had the same reasons for rejecting your use of the Wolffs' fund."

But he would not now be moved. "The two cases are worlds apart. Well"—he smiled thinly—"if I'm not to have your confidence with the German money, I shall have to use the land you've been buying."

"Use it?"

"Sell it. Like we sold it last time."

"You wouldn't!" If he had hit her, the shock could not have been more violent.

"What alternative do you give me?"

"I think it will not be necessary. None of this whole ridiculous con- versation is necessary. We have enough cash. You'll see. They'll suspend the Bank Act this week. Then the Bank can issue more money. The drought will end."

"You have it direct from the governor, I suppose, or the prime minister, perhaps."

"John!"

"All the same I'd be obliged for a list of the properties and their present rents."

"You're bullying me. You've never bullied me in your life."

"I'm doing what I can to protect Stevenson's. Someone in this house has to."

She watched him walk from the room and wondered why she felt not the slightest inclination to burst into tears, or run after him, or plead, or win him back to her. He slept that night in his dressing room —which he often did when he had to leave home very early. But that was not his reason now. He had made too big a rift for a few moments of sexual indulgence to bridge.

*   *   *

She did not furnish him with any list of their property, because the very next day the government suspended the Bank Act and the Bank began to discount bills beyond the limit of its own reserves—but for a monstrous eight per cent on even the best and shortest bills. Money was available once more—but at what a price!

Fortunately Stevenson's could stay out of the market while the most desperate firms took advantage of the issue; and within a month it was possible to reimpose the Bank Act and bring the rate down. From then on, trade picked up steadily. In December there were only twenty-six new bankruptcies (*only!* people said when they passed on the news) and by the end of the month the rate was down to five per cent. In January 1848 it fell to four and even the worst pessimists began to breathe easy.

The Exchequer bills, which she had bought at 37 discount, now went to 39 premium and she was tempted to take her very big profit. The size of it made her feel weak, for it showed what a colossal gamble it had been. However, she took only half of it that month, in the nail-biting hope they might go even higher in February. As, indeed, they did —to 42 premium on the day she sold. She had turned Wolffs' £180,000 into £326,314 5*s*. 2½*d*. after all deductions.

"I think we now have enough for what I want to do," she said calmly to Chambers—much more calmly than she felt. "And I'll never try anything of that sort again!"

"You were more than lucky," he said.

"Well—with everybody losing, *some*body had to benefit. It just happened to be me!"

But she remembered, too, how she had once said to Tom and Sarah Cornelius that currency speculation was something "you and me should never meddle in." She could not find the smallest measure of self-congratulation within—only relief, and a heartfelt resolve never to risk so much again. She wanted to rush at once to John and tell him of her folly and the lesson it had taught her. But he was not at home. He had gone to make arrangements for the start of work on the Great Northern line from London to York, of which they had been awarded the first 78¾ miles—from the temporary terminus at Maiden Lane to Werrington Junction, north of Peterborough.

He had never apologized for his bullying threat to her but behaved as if it had either never been made or had not really been intended seriously. Their general relief over the Bank's tardy but, in the end, well-judged management made it possible to overlook the affair. It lingered, though, in uneasy memory. And Nora could never contemplate "her" land and property now without remembering the threat that had hung over them and might easily do so again. Those few rash words of his marked a permanent new note in their relationship.

He returned, nonetheless, in good time for her confinement at the end of that February, when, on leap year's day, as she had hoped, she was delivered without trouble of a healthy baby girl. They called her Hester, child of starlight.

*　　*　　*

Outwardly, then, nothing of their discord showed. Certainly Sarah noticed no difference, and the few signs of disagreement she had observed the previous October she put down to the extreme worry of that very fraught period. She told Mr. Thornton when she and he met for their by now well-established weekly session together. "Oh, yes," he said. "I've been reading in the papers that traders have been having a thin time of it. I wouldn't have thought it would touch old John Stevenson, though. Railway receipts are down."

The only thing that astonished her now about Mr. Thornton was that she did not tire of him. Every idea he was willing to impart to her he had already imparted—on the progress of steam (which concerned, in fact, the niche now being carved in some future hall of fame and reserved for one W. Thornton Esq.), on the drainage of Bristol (which was a small scrapbook of letters to the Bristol papers by one "Salubritas," alias W. Thornton Esq.), and the need for a rational money system based on fixed values rather than fluctuating market prices. (Sarah had tried some of these notions out on Nora, as if they were her own spontaneous thoughts; Nora had advised her to "wash her mouth out with some Harriet Martineau.")

Sarah sometimes tried to get him to talk about Arabella, but he would not be drawn very far. He said that the notion of enjoying sexual traffic with one's wife was grotesque; how could they face each other at breakfast and sit beside one another at the theatre and go through all the motions of their public life if the very sight and touch of one another would conjure up their craving. Life was wonderfully arranged in this age so that a man could find comforts and security at home, where all was serene and tranquil, and carnal pleasures abroad, where they could not harm his loved ones. And because this usually involved the passage of money from wealthy men to the otherwise unemployable girls of the surplus classes, it also contributed to the levelling down of inequality and to the pacification of the dangerous and deprived masses.

She was, in general, relieved that he was not very interested in her opinions on anything—and that he rarely wanted to communicate more to or with her than his all-consuming passion in his own sexuality. And because his fascination was so genuine and so childlike, it became absorbing to her as well. He was by no means the prodigy of virility he had at first seemed. He did not want to lead her on to greater and ever more desperate feats of performance. But he was minutely obsessed with his and her sensations and reactions, and experimented endlessly to find ways of intensifying their pleasure. "What was that like . . . was it better, was it . . . tell me about that . . . what do you remember best from last week . . . when you imagine us here, what are we doing . . . what's the most exciting way we ever did it?" He made the apartment resound with those questions.

At first she had found it irritating to be constantly talking and thinking while acting, but he was so insistent, and his joy in it was so infectious, that to her surprise she began to share his strange combination of an almost detached curiosity and an obsessive love of his and her own carnality. And in a reverse, feminine way she even understood how he felt about marriage on the one hand and the act of congress on the other. She could not now imagine finding carnal pleasure half so intense with any other man; when she and Mr. Thornton were naked together, whatever they did, she *knew* it was supreme. But the merest thought of being married to him would make her feel sick in her stomach.

PART FIVE

Britannia Bridge, 1850

Chapter 45

That February the promised revolution struck France. A week before Hester was born, a strange alliance of the bourgeoisie, bent on political reform, and the Red republican leaders of the working class, bent on social revolution, began the insurrection that was to lead, three days later, to the abdication of King Louis Philippe and the formation of a provisional republican government in his place. In its own Gallic way it was a repeat of the English revolution of 1832—that is to say, the English revolution was ruthless, quiet, and nasty; its French counterpart was ruthless, raucous, and very bloody—though the bloodshed was still to come. The English middle classes, as soon as they attained the political power for which they had struggled, severed all connection with the working-class allies they had made during the fight. The French bourgeoisie took until June to consolidate their power; only then did they find the confidence to deliver the real downward kick in the teeth.

It was in early July that Nora chose to go to Normandy, not for pleasure—there was little pleasure anywhere in Europe that year—but to see Ferrand and console him for the further, inevitable postponement of any plans for Deauville, and to visit the Auberge Clément and see Gaston.

The line from Dieppe to Rouen was now open so that she could go direct to France from Newhaven. She went over with John, who was keen to show her the new line, and George Acton, a new manservant. She was determined to come back with a French maid, though it was useless asking Rodie to help her there—she dismissed them all so quickly.

The mood at La Gracieuse was very sombre. France was now going through the commercial crisis that had shaken London last year—the same toll of bankruptcies, the same shortage of money, the same crippling interest rates. The ironworks were almost idle and Rodet was very depressed.

"He's all right, really," Rodie explained. "He has been clever and we are secure. But it's not good for a man to walk in empty sheds and see only ten men working and one furnace hot."

There was a mood of economy about the house. No parties this year. And very little riding out. Almost every meal was held in the breakfast room, *en famille.*

"These economies, I don't mind them," Rodie said. "I am from a not so rich family. But Rodet has paid off his mistress and sold his apartment in Rouen." Her tone showed it was the ultimate economy.

"Things must be very bad then," Nora said.

"For *me*! Oh, it's terrible! But I am firm. I say no."

Nora laughed then, and hugged her. "Oh, Rodie! We are so different really."

"Oh, you! You have a dynasty to make. But we are never more than a small patron. It's enough."

Another time she asked Nora if they had communists in England.

"Of course," Nora told her. "They issued a 'manifesto' this last January."

"You have read it?"

"Naturally not. They are no threat to anyone. Enthusiasts and dreamers. One of their leaders in London is called Karl Marx—an impractical Jewish refugee, a dreamer. He looks forward to a world composed entirely of ladies and gentlemen standing around in green fields, wearing morning dress, and writing and reading poetry. I can't understand that he is taken seriously."

"Rodet says they are all very dangerous and must be shot."

"Give them time and they will do it to each other. Look what happened here in May. You actually had a communist government—which fell apart in mutual hatred within three days. The history of all previous revolutions is the history of personal ratfights. Why on earth are you worried?"

"It's not May that worries us. It is June. Cavaignac killed thousands of workers in June and closed the national workshops, everywhere. Already now in our soup kitchen we have many hundreds more apply for food. There is no work for the poor anywhere, now the workshops are shut."

"In times of hardship the poor must look to private charity. It was quite wrong of your government to offer work to everyone who wanted it. We learned that lesson bitterly in Ireland. Now you are learning it, too."

Rodie shook her head admiringly. "To be so—like a judge. You are a strong woman. I can not. I see the children and the women and I say economic law tomorrow; today—charity. Work."

Nora smiled, not really seeking an argument, but thinking it too important to turn aside with a soft answer. "I've starved, Rodie. I've struggled to keep Sam and two small children, my brother and sister, on ten shillings a week—in a filthy little hovel without roof or door. And when the mill was slack, we had nothing. And we starved. I've heard them cry, my own little ones, crying all night with the hunger. Going out and begging for cabbage stalks."

Rodie was looking at her in amazement. "Stevie"—it was almost a whisper—"I did not know. How terrible."

"You ask Sam, when he comes next. All it did for me was to give me the ambition to get up from there and get out. But I wanted to do it by my own effort. I didn't want some jack-in-office coming and telling me what to do and giving me money I'd no right to. The sad fact is that a lot of people aren't like that. When they get kicked to the bottom, they give up and settle to stay there. They are the people who —even Christ said it: For ye have the poor always with you—Matthew, Mark, and John. And that means, if you have the poor, you also have the rich. To try to make it otherwise, except by natural economic law and free trade, is against nature and against God."

"Oooh!" Rodie took refuge in the pretence that it was all beyond her, buzzing her fingertips around her head.

*   *   *

This was hardly a holiday for Nora. So when she had spent a week or so at La Gracieuse, and exchanged all their news, gloomy though much of it was, she left to go to Coutances and to see the maid Gaston had looked out for her. George Acton had gone back with John. She went to the inn with old Honorine and one of the grooms from La Gracieuse.

The Clément had done much better this year. Word of its comfort, food, and cleanliness had spread among the English; and there had been a goodly exodus of the Parisian bourgeoisie to Normandy—conveniently close to England's safer shores—ever since the brief communist government of May. In the two weeks after the "June days" they had been able to treble their usual prices.

She heard all this from a happy Gaston within minutes of her arrival, but she did not then begin to look at the books—though she itched to open them, for she needed some good news. It was then late afternoon but, like Sarah, she made it her first duty to go up to Tom's grave. After a brief, silent prayer she told him aloud how well the inn was doing and what a fine woman Sarah had become—what splendid work she was doing at the Female Rescue Society and how it had made her blossom out. Knowing that the spirits of the dead could read thoughts, she avoided all thoughts of Sarah and John.

All next day she went through the books, finding them flawless. Gaston had been a real discovery of Tom's. She showed him her own private colour code of red ink for debits and blue for credits. "It just makes it easier for me to follow if everyone who works for me uses it," she explained. He agreed to use it in future. The new maid, Nanette Clébert, would come for her interview that evening. She was a very dependable girl, the daughter of the housekeeper to the bishop, so she understood all the arrangements for a grand establishment. They were, of course, most respectable people and she had a good and strict upbringing. She was just beginning to learn English but had only three or four words as yet. Nora thought she sounded admirably suited. "Tell her to come wearing clothes she has made for herself," she said. "Dressmaking's an important part of her work."

The girl was due that evening after the Angelus. About fifteen minutes before that time, one of the maids came to Nora's room to tell her that a gentleman had come to see her. He would not give his name but said to tell her he'd "come to judgement in the hope of mercy." *Daniel*, she thought. The maid's description fitted, as did the fact that he would not come indoors but waited in the stable. Nora went down at once.

There was no doubting this time it was Daniel. The disguised stance and the flamboyant clothes were gone. It was martyr Daniel, last seen in an epic role, *Transportation from Manchester*, who stood with his back to the door and turned only slowly to face her. He was dressed in the borrowed clothes of a French *gentilhomme*, not well fitted; the fact that he had not washed before donning them made them look even more borrowed.

"Nora," he said uneasily when she did not speak. The horses stirred at his voice.

"I suppose that's the dust of the Place de la Bastille on you still," she said.

He wiped a bit of grime from his cheek and looked at it. "Aye," he said proudly.

"It earns you no welcome here," she said. "You'd best be on your way."

"There's no price on my head now, love. That went with Louis Philippe. I'm a free man."

"Then behave like one. Come inside. Register. Take a room. Twenty-five francs."

He laughed, not believing her. "I've no money."

"Then you must pawn something. There's a *mont-de-piété* just up the street."

"No-o-o-ra!" he wheedled, drawing her name out, not knowing what to say.

"I told you everything I ever wanted to tell you last time, two years back. The day you left me with Sam and Wilfrid and Dorrie you stopped being flesh of mine."

"But I was struggling *for* you—and Sam and the bairns. It was to make a better world for folk like us."

"We didn't want a better world, Daniel. A better hovel would have suited us. A *door* would have done for a start. A door would have kept back the boar that ate your brother Wilfrid. Do you know what it was like, Daniel, to come back that evening and find no Wilfrid—just his arm flung up among the branches that served for our roof? Think how that boar must have shook and shook that poor little lad to shake an arm up into the roof!" She felt herself beginning to choke at the remembered outrage, so she fell silent; she was not going to offer him the spectacle of herself in tears.

"My whole life is a struggle for a world in which that cannot happen," he insisted quietly, respecting her anger.

"Then you *have* changed."

"What do'st mean! I were the same then."

"Oh, believe me, Daniel, you were *not*. By deserting us you made sure it would happen. You wanted it to happen. You wanted proof that the world was exactly what your communist friends said it was. You wanted Wilfrid and Dorrie to die. You wanted Sam sold off into service. You wanted me to starve and go on the streets. Because that was the only thing that would mend your conscience for what you'd done."

"I'm allowed a conscience, am I!"

"In those days you still had the remnant. I remember the last night of your freedom, when I asked you to mend that door, and instead you sat with those two Chartists and wrote your appeal—you knew then what you were condemning us to. I saw it in your eyes."

"Huh!" he sneered. "Anyway, going on the streets would have been a step *up* for thee."

"What's that supposed to mean?"

"Sharing our father's bed. After our mam died."

"What if I did? If I helped that poor, lonely man, whose world had flown to pieces all around him, if I helped him find any comfort, I'll answer for it on judgement day. He had no notion of what was happening. And if you've come here to mock his memory, you may piss off now." She gathered up her dress and turned to go.

But he raced across to the stable door ahead of her and stood barring her way. "No, love. I'm sorry. I never meant to bring that up. Thou stung us to it, that were all. Listen. I've no cash. I've eaten naught for two days. I'm on the run—I can't disguise that. All I need is somewhere to rest up and hide for six hours."

"Not here, Daniel. You've no chance of—"

"Listen!" He was beginning to show desperation. "Listen—there's a boat coming to Blainville at three o'clock tomorrow morning. I can reach that in two hours from here, on foot. Then I'll be away to Jersey. I'll be safe there. All I need is to be able to lie here—I'll get in the hay up there. No one will know."

A low whinny from one of the horses drowned his last words, like a stage laugh.

Nora said: "No, Daniel, you'll have to do your lying somewhere else. I'm going to the gendarmes." She waited for him to get out of the way.

"You *can't*," he said, incredulous at her determination. "I'm asking for my life. If I'm taken, I'll rot in Devil's Island until I die. I know we are on opposite sides of the struggle now. And my beliefs threaten your—business. But I'm thy own brother. Blood's thicker than water, love."

"Not in my books, Dan," she said, absolutely unmoved by his appeal. "In my books, red ink is thicker than blood. The most I'll do for you is to promise it will take me fifteen minutes to find the gendarmes and tell them. And don't thank me. I'd do the same for a fox or any other vermin I intended to kill."

"*Thank* you?" he echoed. A hard glint came into his eyes. "No, I won't thank you." He pulled out a pistol.

At that moment the door opened. A young girl, about seventeen, soberly dressed in dark blue with white cuffs and a collar, almost nun-like, stood transfixed in shock as she took in the scene. Daniel was the first to recover. He grabbed the girl and jerked her toward him. She drew breath to scream but he put a hand over her open mouth and then pointed the gun at her neck. The intended scream turned to a strangling noise in her throat.

"Now, Nora," he said, "if you fail to do as I say, I will shoot her. You will go and get me some food and you will tell everyone to keep away from these stables this evening. Here"—he shook the girl—"is my *laisser-passer* to Blainville. *Parlez anglais?*" he asked the girl.

She shook her head inside his grip; only her terrified eyes showed above his hand.

Nora sighed wearily and began to walk toward the door. "You'd best shoot her at once then, Daniel. I've never seen her in my life— she's nothing to me. I'm going to the gendarmes."

"I mean it!" he screamed, cocking the hammer.

"I know you do. I never doubted it. You were born a fool. Kill her and you'll not get out of this town. Run now and you've a chance. But I would never expect you to do the sensible thing."

Daniel flung the girl from him, almost between one of the horse's feet. She rolled quickly out of the way, and then began to vomit. Once again Daniel had the gun pointed straight at Nora.

"I'll kill you if you go," he said. "I will."

She looked steadily at him, frankly puzzled. "Now you *do* surprise me. I'd have thought the death you'd planned for yourself was on a barricade, or leading a charge on the militia. But now it'll be Daniel Telling who had his shaved head guillotined into the sawdust one cold morning for a squalid family murder in a tavern stable. Your comrades will *want* to forget you. Still, you'd best be quick about it because I'm off."

She walked straight to him and, to her own surprise as well as to his, kissed him quickly on the cheek; she felt the gun shaking against her breast. "Goodbye, Daniel. Fifteen minutes."

Outside was the ordinary, everyday, evening world. She looked around, knowing that the gun was now levelled at her back, wondering what in all that ordinariness would be the last thing she happened to see. The cobbles seemed to shimmer. She heard but did not feel her feet upon them. She was halfway over the yard and still no shot had come.

"Nora!" His anguished voice.

She stopped and turned. He had the gun pointing in her direction but it shook like an ill-adjusted machine. "Don't make me do it," he cried.

"Make you!" she sneered. "I couldn't even make you mend a door!" She turned and began again to walk, convinced now that he was going to shoot but thinking he would almost certainly miss her.

Before she had reached the corner, where the carriageway turned under the arch and out into the street, she heard him give a little strangled cry of despair. Then came the sound of his running feet on the cobbles. She walked on without pause.

There was a sudden unbelievable stab of pain in her side as he pistol-whipped her in passing. She had to stop then to fight the flying black oblivion that began to crowd her from all around. She had to fight to breathe—and every breath was agony.

"Monsieur Gaston, Monsieur Gaston? Monsieur Gaston . . . !" the young girl stranger standing in the stable doorway yelled across the yard.

By magic Gaston was at Nora's side and, still racked with the pain, she staggered back indoors, supported by him. He sent the groom from La Gracieuse for the gendarme and one of the maids for Dr. Grimble.

The doctor, being nearer, came first, his wheezing announcing his impending arrival.

"Kicked by a horse?" he asked as soon as he saw the redness and the swelling.

"Someone threw something heavy at me there."

"Well, you can bless your steel stays it's not broken, but there may be a slight fracture. We'll bind you just in case."

The binding was very constricting and left her rattling in her corsets like a ripe nut in its shell. But it seemed to ease the pain—or to spread it and make it less acute. He left her with some opium to ease it further.

Daniel had thirty minutes' start by the time the gendarme could see her. The fact of her injury and the girl's story removed any possible suspicion that she had played a part in furthering her brother's escape. She wondered, then and later, whether he had done it deliberately, as a sort of perverted act of kindness.

It would not have pleased Daniel to find that the authorities were not particularly interested in him as a revolutionary hero on the run. His name was on no list that they had received. Only the fact that he had assaulted her and caused bodily harm made them pursue the case at all. She did not tell them where he was to leave the coast that night; it was the same instinct that would lead her to let any fox get well away from a piece of covert."

"Somewhere Cherbourg way, I expect," the gendarme said. "Good riddance."

How Daniel would have hated that envoi!

When the man had gone, Gaston showed in the young girl in blue.

"Mademoiselle Clébert?" Nora asked. "I felt sure it was you. How are you now?"

"Much better, thank you, Madame Stevenson." She was even paler than she had looked out in the stables, but her hand did not shake and she was composed again.

Nora explained what had happened while the girl nodded solemnly, not showing any surprise. "I cannot promise you such excitements every day, mademoiselle—*if* you are still interested in the position."

"*Mais oui*, madame!" The girl was astonished that that should even be in question. More than anything Nora liked that tough cheerfulness, unflustered and self-possessed.

She described the job to the girl in as much detail as she could. As lady's maid, she would be found in all clothing, bed, and board, would travel with Nora, would have all the privileges of an upper servant, including dining in the housekeeper's parlour. Among the servants, only the housekeeper would be her superior. Nora proposed a six-month trial period. The usual maximum wage for a girl in such a post was twenty-five pounds—six hundred and forty francs—a year, but in view of the girl's youth and inexperience, she would receive only fifteen —three hundred and eighty-four francs. If she proved satisfactory, an increase would not be unreasonably delayed.

"Thank you, Madame Stevenson," the girl said. "That will all be adequate. May my mother come to interview you tomorrow morning?"

For a moment Nora was surprised. Then it struck her that in reversed circumstances she would wish to do exactly the same, and that the mother's concern was an additional recommendation for the daughter. It made her think suddenly of what facilities they could offer the girl.

"How often do you go to Mass?" she asked.

"Never!" the girl said. "I am *protestante!*"

When she had gone, Nora asked Gaston if he had not said that the mother was housekeeper to the bishop—and did he mean the Roman bishop?

"The mother"—Gaston smiled—"is a cook supreme. In France, dogma has its limits!"

Everything was to the mother's satisfaction next morning, so, after an early lunch and with despairing pleas from Dr. Grimble not to go, Nora and the girl set off with Honorine and the groom for the long and this time painful ride back to La Gracieuse. Nanette showed almost no emotion on parting from her mother and the home of all her seventeen years. It did not square true with the way she had vomited in the stables. Nora took the liberty of asking why she had done that.

"Oh," she said, wrinkling her nose in disgust. "It was his hands. The taste. They were so dirty."

Of all the epitaphs she had ever devised for Daniel, that seemed the most fitting.

Chapter 46

Rodie suggested she should stay a further week, not only to help her rib to heal but also to let Danielle, her latest maid, grudgingly admitted to be "quite good," teach Nanette some points of being a lady's maid. It amused Nora to see Rodie standing eavesdropping outside the door, getting more and more annoyed at what she was hearing and eventually thrusting in saying, "No no no. It's not right. Like this. I'll show you!"

On the second day of this extended visit she had a fat letter from home. Winifred explained it in a covering letter.

Dearest Mama,

We your children have decided that, as you and Papa are so frequently at your travels, you will need a newspaper to tell you what has passed at Maran Hill, being unlike most people, who need a newspaper to tell them what is passing in the world. *Therefore and accordingly* [that was done in florid penmanship, as on a legal document] we have determined to provide such a newspaper at a price of a dozen kisses for each contributor from each reader (you and Papa), and a Stamp Duty of a dozen hugs. We will supply you on credit but can in no circumstances extend it beyond twenty-eight (28) days.

Given under our hand and seal this . . . [and then four successive dates in June and July were inserted and stricken, leaving it undated] Winifred, John, Caspar, Clement (assisted), Abigail (forced), Hester (her mark).

Extraordinary Discovery of a Hare at Maran Hill
Hilarious Scenes in East Park

The permanent residents of Maran Hill were at their daily walk in the West Park one day last week when what should they see but a hare, which ran away. All and sundry gave chase but, they being without canine assistance, to wit: *viz* Tip and Puck, the hare was abandoned, pro tem. But what should happen that selfsame afternoon when, lessons being done for the day, the newly formed Maran pack of harehounds (the said Tip and Puck, a fine couple recently entered) under their master Sir John Stevenson, M.H.H., resplendent in his outdoor clothes, and first whipper-in Caspar, likely clad, as ditto second whipper-in Clement, and followers including the vivacious and charming Miss Winifred Stevenson in a glorious white summer dress with wide straw hat and blue silk band to match, driving the pony cart with her troublesome sisters, Abigail and Hester, who do not yet understand the glories of the chase, and sundry other followers, among whom Aunt Sarah in a new summer dress of pale blue with pretty posies and a cream bonnett and shawl in blue foulard stripes and tassels, which occasioned most general approval and acclaim—what should happen, I say, but that the hare was nowhere in evidence and could not be started no matter where the pack drew.

Most masters, faced with such a dire quandary, would have gone home, hiding his disappointment in manly good spirits. But Sir John is made of finer clay. Thinking the morning's surprise might have sent the quarry to the East Park for the day, he cunningly divided his entire pack into two equal halves and sent them around by the southern and northern hedges. He stationed the charming Miss Winifred Stevenson at the gorse patch, between East and West parks to block the doomed creature's return, and himself went to draw from the east. Picture the poor hare's miserable despair! Surrounded from every quarter of the compass, he sees advancing upon him two ferocious hounds bent on his destruction from north and south, while the dashing Master sternly denies him the east. Piteously he looks westward to where the lovely Miss Winifred bars his way. Perhaps there he will find one spark of tender compassion? Alas, it is not so. Her heart of ice is fixed as constant as the polar star.

He is doomed! He is doomed! But no! The pack closes in and the two hounds, misunderstanding the entire nature of their business there, fell to fighting one with the other. While this diversion was in the course of proceeding, the quarry slipped away. Such was its infinite cunning that, throughout the entire chase, the said hare was not once seen by huntsmen, hounds, field, nor following. A worthy opponent for another day!

N.B. The Maran Hunt has taken for its motto: *De nihilo nihil, in nihilum nil posse reverti* (Persius), which, for our dear Mama's sake, we translate: From nothing nothing can proceed, and nothing can be reduced into nothing.

[To this Sarah had added, in pencil:] No prizes are offered for guessing the name of the writer! Caspar is in bed with a cold—the next piece of news tells you where he got it:

Astounding Hydraulic Works near Completion
Transformation of Walled Garden at Maran Hill

We append a sketch by our Artist of the latest state of the ingenious waterworks now under construction in a corner of the walled garden. Following an amazing demonstration of the well-known method of how to "puddle" a canal by the great John Stevenson Senior, the world's foremost contractor, thus rendering it impervious to water, his children have determined that the benefits of hydraulic civilization should be carried to the farthest corners of the walled garden, where there is a new tap installed for the farm stables. Under the direction of Sir John Stevenson, they have devised an ingenious network of sluices, aquifers, spillways, traps, and pounds, which, with Great Labour, they have dug, extending from the wall to the cooking apples.

Early progress was marred by a strike of younger workers, under their wicked ringleader Caspar. But firm action by Sir John quickly brought the miscreants to heel. Sir John's firm action was to grant their demands, which were to be allowed to build soil castles with the spoil from the workings.

The first attempt at "puddling" was a failure and resulted in the wasting of many hundreds of gallons of water. Further attempts to seal the waterways will be made when it stops raining, which it is doing very hard at the moment.

[Here Sarah had added:] (She does not exaggerate about the quantity of water wasted. They emptied the entire tank in the water tower and the gardeners were pumping in relays all afternoon to refill it! They now have orders that only Wikes is to turn on the tap.)

Intelligence from Ireland. By electric telegraph from Holyhead, Friday 23 June. Our Paternal Oversea Correspondent sends word to say that Mr. Flynn, his worthy deputy, has called his unhappy country "The Land of That'll-do" on account of the poor workmanship acceptable to the GS&W. We do not think the well-known firm of Stevenson is capable of poor work and are mystified at this intelligence from that unhappy Isle.

By the new electric telegraph from Dover, Saturday 1 July. News has just arrived that Mrs. Nora Stevenson, celebrated wife of the re-

nowned John Stevenson, has landed safely at Dieppe, France. Her
husband was at hand to conduct her down the railroad he has recently completed to Rouen last year. She declaimed it "very pretty
and smooth." Our paternal and maternal oversea correspondents are
expected to contribute regular news to these columns.

[To this Sarah had added:] Do not imagine this last sentence to be a
mere statement or wish, it is a command. You must be proud of Winifred,
Nora dear. The whole idea for and production of this newspaper is hers; she
has certainly inherited your spirit. You must get a governess this autumn. For
a child of seven, she is quite outstanding, even if she did copy many of the
phrases from the *Illustrated London News* and the *Gazette*.

There followed several drawings by various hands: a pretty water
colour from Winifred showing Sarah's new summer dress; a sketch by
Young John of the "hydraulic works" in the garden; a drawing of a
hare by Caspar, with the grass scribbled painstakingly in by Clement;
and some coloured smudges and fingermarks from Hester. There was
another sheet of paper that had been crumpled and straightened again.
It was a drawing of scribbled spirals. This one had a note not from
Sarah but from Winifred:

This is Abigail's drawing. She screwed it up and threw it away because, she
says, one of her flowers is drawn bigger than the others. She started a drawing of birds instead, but did not finish it, so I rescued this. Fancy screwing it
up after all that work! She howled for an hour. She is mad.

Nora was most heartened by this letter and she and Rodie laughed
over it many times. But it had, for her, one sad aspect. Until recently
her experience and knowledge had, naturally, been greater than any of
her children's: She knew everything that they knew, and a lot more
besides. But now, as Winifred's clever little Latin tag showed (and
Latin was a language she had *asked* to be taught; no one had made
her), their world was, in these and those directions, growing bigger
than hers and escaping from her. One could say it was growing up,
and only natural—but that didn't stop its being sad.

At the end of that week her rib was still painful, though the swelling was down and she could breathe without discomfort if she did not
breathe too deeply. France was settling into its new moderate-republi-
can government and the whole atmosphere was much easier than it
had been only a fortnight earlier. Rodie's old humour began to return

and Nora now regretted the arrangements that forced her to go back to England. But those arrangements could not be broken. Sarah had accepted an invitation to go to Scotland in August with the Thorntons, who had rented a shooting lodge up there and were making a party with Tom Brassey and Joseph Locke, the engineer once so despised by Hudson. The four eldest Thornton children, Nicholas, Thomas, Albert, and Laetitia, were coming to Maran Hill for ten days, then they and the Stevenson brood were all going up to Yorkshire for two weeks. Lionel Thornton, then just two years old and always an ailing child, was to stay in Bristol with his baby sister Araminta, born last December. For the first time since they were married both Arabella and Nora were free of pregnancy; it seemed that both families were taking a rest.

Nora planned to accompany all the children up to London on one of their visits. They could go to the Regents Park zoological garden, and see the half-finished Great Hall at Euston, and John, with all his parliamentary friends, could get tickets to see the new clock tower at the Houses of Parliament, and then they could take a boat down to the Tower of London, where the girls could see the royal jewels and the boys look at the old cannons and walk under the Thames Tunnel, so that they could tell Mr. Brunel they had seen it. It would make an instructive and memorable day if it didn't rain.

She herself had important business in London, too. Back in January, Chambers had hired a young clerk called Bernard Bassett—the sort of greedy, bright-eyed, silver-tongued young cockney who makes a good companion but an atrocious friend. He was smart and ambitious, and much too big for Chambers to manage. Every day he came with five new ways of improving the London banking system. Nora had noticed him from time to time and had listened to Chambers' complaints as they grew. Then in February, when she had turned in such a big profit on the Wolff fund, Chambers said he was going to let the young man go; she persuaded him to hold on to Bassett until after her confinement. In April she had come back to London to find poor Nathaniel at the end of his tether. That was when she had offered the young fellow the job of land agent to the Wolff fund. The salary was only fifteen pounds, but if he was as smart as he said, he could earn ten times that on various commissions and bonuses that she offered. She knew the look and smell of greed, and he had both. He leaped at the chance.

In general Bassett's job was to do in one area of London what Ferrand had done in Deauville—buy up a big parcel of land and prepare it for development; in this case he had to clear part of it of its agricultural tenants, too. The area Nora had chosen was a long marshy strip of land north of Camden Town and west of Kentish Town. Two rivers, the Fleet, flowing down from Hampstead, and the tributary from Caen Wood, flowing down from Highgate, made it unthinkable for housing—to most people. But Nora had asked John to look at the soil and the fall of the land, and they had concluded that, when properly drained, it would support houses as well as any of the more obvious parts of the capital.

Having eliminated that element of gamble, Nora took the real risk. John's first response on seeing the land was "But no one will want to live this far out, surely—I mean, people come out to stay in Kentish Town in the summer to get *out* of London." She hoped that was the general response. Her aim was to buy the entire block of land but to build only on the southern portion, against Camden Town. The northern part might lie as farm land for twenty more years yet without harm—her windfall profit on the Wolff fund gave her the breathing space and the audacity to do that. She had similar plans for the green fields on the other side of Kentish Town, right down to Holloway. Bassett could be busy out there this autumn, buying in all he could get his hands on.

She was remembering the lesson of Alderley Edge, south of Manchester—so far south that when she had bought land out there people had said she was mad. But her instinct had said otherwise. Rich people wanted to live on hills, up in the fresh air, above the marshes and the bad drains and the cholera, where the views were full of distance. Just look at the number of fine country houses called something Hill, like Maran Hill. And where were the hills in London? Hampstead, Highgate, Highbury. . . . That was where the rich would live. But she was sure there was soon going to be a new army of clerks in and around London—men of whom Bernard Bassett was the very type. Thrusting, in awe of money, feeling a cut above the shopkeepers and the tradesmen, knowing a little of how the rich lived and wanting to copy it as closely as possible. It was for that poor, ambitious motley she intended to build. They would be able to say "We live in Hampstead—*South* Hampstead really," or "We're at the *Highgate* end of Kentish Town." They would want to say that.

All one needed to do was to take the grand houses around Grosvenor Square and Berkeley Square and St. James's—all the fashionable squares—and make reproductions of them as small and as cheap as possible. Height was important, she was sure. Give them four floors and a semibasement, even if the area of each floor was ever so mean. Put some imposing decoration on the front, something classical . . . a little private garden at the back, even if it was overlooked by a hundred neighbours . . . an impressive staircase to attract the eye (or, rather, to *distract* it from everything else) as soon as the cheap-but-imposing front door was opened—these were the ingredients of an entirely new kind of house. The people she had in mind would pinch every penny to afford a cook and a maid of all work.

She shuddered briefly to consider the bleakness of life in those tall furnished tombs; but the arithmetic was most compelling. In all, she needed about a thousand acres. They could still be got now for around twenty-five pounds an acre—twenty-five thousand in all. She could cram in, she thought, about thirty-eight houses to an acre at a building cost of about a hundred and fifty pounds each. The rent would be twenty a year. When all possible charges, deductions, and bad debts were included, the *net* return on each developed acre would be four hundred and twenty-five pounds—giving a valuation of ten and a half thousand an acre. The cost would be about six thousand, so the Wolff fund could buy a thousand acres and develop forty-five of them without having to borrow a penny.

In twenty years they could build, entirely without borrowing, a hundred and fifteen more acres, making the estate worth over a million and a half. Of course, they *would* borrow, long before that. Her aim was to have the entire estate built over by 1870. Then it would be worth over ten and a half million. And by 1880, it would be free of all charges. One and a half million would be hers. And she would be fifty-eight years old.

Yes. She was going to have some very grateful, very loving, very respectful grandchildren.

That was why it was important to see cheeky young Mr. Bernard Bassett and—however well he had done—encourage him to do better by Christmas.

Almost his first words were, "Is that true, Mrs. Stevenson, that you was once as poor as wot I am?" And when she said she had been a great deal poorer, he looked amazed and said, "Go on! I 'ad you down for a rich un. You act like you always 'ad money. Honest, you do. . . ." And when her sour skepticism showed in her eye, the torrent of "No, honest . . . God's truth . . . Cut me froat . . . would I lie to you . . ." would begin. He did not bend truth, he cheerfully outraged it. She soon learned to trust nothing but the actual, formal, legal evidence of title, and the certified draft on the bank. But for all his untrustworthiness, he did well. He got over three hundred and twenty acres on the Hampstead side for eight thousand and seventy and, by Christmas, nearly six hundred and twenty acres on the Holloway side for under seventeen and a half. It was close enough to what she had hoped. In the spring they could start to build.

Chapter 47

These successes came at a poor time for John. He had actually or almost completed all his big contracts except the Great Northern and the Dublin–Cork. That had reached Limerick Junction in June and been opened on 3 July. Stevenson's had failed to get the contracts for the Waterford & Limerick, whose line through Limerick Junction had opened in May as far as Tipperary. John was sure the failure had to do with MacMinimum's deliberate misdirection of him at his first meeting with Cashel Ormond.

"I want to tell ye something about that," MacMinimum had said. "I had the whole story heelways. The man who told me Captain Ormond was Master of the Tipperary was a monstrous liar."

"That puts you and me in the same boat," John told him.

Flynn could offer no explanation for it. John concluded that truth in Ireland was like one of her own mountains, part-hidden in mist; and when the mist lifted, and your spirit said, "At last, now I will see it," you found instead that the mist had settled elsewhere, obscuring a region that was previously clear.

The hundred and seven miles from Dublin to Limerick Junction had earned a profit of sixty-four thousand. He had given Flynn a bonus of seven thousand and to others, right down to individual navvies, bonuses making a further four. He had bought, as planned, a bankrupt estate of over two thousand acres in County Galway and had given the Friends five thousand to try to turn it into a model estate of the kind the country would need if it was ever going to prosper. His Dublin acquaintances thought him mad; the only place to buy land was in prosperous Leinster or Ulster, on the English side of the country. No good money ever came out of the west. Privately he thought he was mad, too. He almost steeled himself, despite what he had seen of evictions and distress, to take the rest of his profit—some thirty thousand pounds—back over the water. God knows he needed it. But Lord George Bentinck's bill had failed, and Trevelyan had substituted a much stricter government measure offering limited aid only to companies that had managed to call up half their capital. And with the famine and epidemics and disorders of the last few years—especially the disorders—such capital was not easily found. In the end, against his better judgement, he put the remaining profit into Irish railway stock, knowing there was scant chance of any dividend.

One way and another he was coming to hold a fair bit of railway stock, especially in foreign lines. He was, in 1848–49, building over five hundred miles of line in France, Spain, Italy, Bavaria, and Austria. When he looked at his diary for that period, he found that of 380 days he had spent 274 overseas.

European lines were, he soon learned, built on very different commercial principles from those in England. England was a sink-or-swim country. If you saw a chance, you took your capital and your courage in both hands and leaped at it. If you failed, no one in government would throw you a lifeline—the very idea would have horrified them. And if you succeeded and the profits were vast, no one in government felt obliged to trim them—that was the other side of the same coin. But these foreign capitalists wanted someone to guarantee success before they put down any real money; and if it also meant that their profit would be deliberately limited, they didn't mind. They were happy to live in a cosy little cartel of capital and bureaucracy. Small wonder that it was English money (nearly nine million in 1847 and '48) and English engineers and English contractors who were taking on most of the important foreign work. All those foreign countries had words that meant "enterprise" and "risk" and "self-reliance" but very little use for them.

One result of this was that companies looked to governments for part of their capital, often for most of it. And governments generally were not willing to part with a penny until the line was opened. So the companies had nothing but their own stock to make payments with. Stevenson's went into the year 1849 owning a nominal million and a half pounds' worth of foreign railway stock whose actual cash value, if sold immediately, was no higher than twenty-five thousand—on which the banks were prepared to lend only fifteen. To earn that stock the firm had put in over a year's work; its actual negotiable value would not pay a week's wages. It was no way to stay in business.

So when John came home with the Dresden–Prague line among

his trophies—sixty miles at six hundred and eighty thousand pounds, to be paid in stock—his welcome from Nora was not the warmest.

"It must be the last of these contracts for a long time, love," she told him after she had spent a fraught afternoon on the firm's accounts.

But he was still cock-a-whoop. "Come on, sweet—the commercial crisis is over. There must be the money out there somewhere. You've just got to work harder to find it."

She hid her exasperation. "The commercial crisis is not over. The bankruptcies may have stopped but that's all. Trade is terrible. Everyone's just pulling in their horns and sitting it out."

"That's good, surely! It leaves the field to us. Look—I can build this line for four hundred and eighty thousand. So there's two hundred thousand clear to us in a year's time. That's over forty per cent profit. Now where can we find profits like that in England these days? We can't anymore."

She still kept her temper. There was no sense in antagonizing him; he had to understand the difficulties. He had to stop working on credit.

"You can't get profits like that here because there's no money to pay them. Railway investment has dried up—and you can't blame folk for that when you remember how they got burned. Meanwhile railway income has followed trade down into the pit. But at least you can still get paid in *cash* here."

"Piddling little lines!" he sneered. "Ah, but you should see the Dresden–Prague!"

"Go back, John! Go back and tell them you'll build it for half a million in cash, instead of this worthless stock."

He really thought she had lost her reason. "What!" he laughed. "Settle for four per cent when I can get forty!"

"You'd do more good for Stevenson's, I promise," she insisted.

"Go on! Ye've lost your sense of adventure. No—there's good pickings in Europe. The best. We'll end up worth millions."

She closed her eyes and sighed. What more could she say? How could she put it even more clearly? Explanation seemed of no use. Simply state the fact, then: "One more such contract and you will break the firm," she said.

"Ah!" He dismissed her pessimism with a wave of his hand. "You and Chambers will find the money. Chambers will, anyway. He'd never let us go down. It's not just our business he'd lose. Hudson would withdraw his patronage, too."

"If by this time next year Hudson has enough patronage left to

move a single coal wagon one yard over any English metal, I'll boil
and eat my best riding boots!" When he stared at her, not knowing
how to express his disbelief, she added, "Hudson hasn't yet realized
that *this* railway age is not the one he grew up in. And nor have you.
He'll fall all right. And so will you unless you wake up and face facts.
No one is too big."

But it sobered him only slightly.

Early in 1849 he was sobered properly when Edmund Denison,
chairman of the Great Northern, took a leaf out of the foreigners'
books and said they would have to pay partly in stock rather than cash
for the work Stevenson's was doing. He was only the first of several.
It was just as Nora had forecast two years earlier, but she had not foreseen that it would be so sudden or so universal.

Where, Nora thought with sour satisfaction, were the triumphant
brayings of 1845! Then the railways were ushering in the New Jerusalem and every other child would be born a millionaire! If there was
a law of money to match the law of gravity, it was that any person or
any group who tried to snatch a disproportionate share of the available
wealth impoverished everyone, including themselves. People never
learned that lesson.

She and Chambers did all they could. They realized the fifty thousand Hudson had promised on the 250 Great North of England shares
he had given to John to keep the York–Scarborough line cheap. She
wondered how much of the money came out of Hudson's own pocket.

"He'll not last long now," Nora said. Once, she had made that prediction with relish; but now, as the inevitable day drew on, she began
to feel almost sorry for the "king." It was not a nickname one heard
so often now.

They sold most of the shares John had bought over the years. They
called in loans the firm had made, often giving a good discount for
cash. They brought the stocks of the Stevenstown mill down to the
danger point, where they would have been unable to fulfil any quick
order, even of medium size. And Chambers busied himself around the
City as never before, tapping all possible sources of loan. She even got
her lawyer, Charles Stoddart, to prepare a complete schedule of all her
properties and their values.

There was no point keeping Chambers in the dark this time. This
was no short-term crisis, compounded by the firm's own private difficulties; it was a universal slide toward ruin. No one was safe. Only those
who worked as closely and as frankly as possible with their bankers
stood a chance.

Even so, this squeezing of the sponge yielded much less cash than either she or John had expected.

"It's a good thing you're ready to build at Camden Town," he said with a relieved grin. "Seventeen hundred houses at twenty pounds profit. A good thirty thousand there. And in cash."

His face fell when he saw her response. "Oh, no," she said firmly. "That's going out to tender."

Then he grinned again and nudged her. "Clever! Of course it's got to *look* aboveboard."

"It will *be* aboveboard, John," she said, feeling sick within. "Cubitt, Fox, Brassey, Jackson—they'll all be invited. They'll bring their bids. And they'll all be present when opened. And the winning tender will be declared then. And *only* then."

He was too angry to speak to her. But as he strode from the room —and for a moment she feared he was going to smash his way out through the door—he said to a portrait of his horse Hermes, "*Someone* had better think again and think harder."

She thought hard all right, for the rest of that day. She took out Prometheus, a large black stallion she had hunted most of that season, and went through their own rides and the park and then on through Panshanger to Hertingfordbury before she felt equal to asking herself why she was being so insistent. Then she came back and, though John was still in the house, she wrote him a letter.

Dear Husband,

Your wife (your still- and ever-loving wife) is sad to report, that she finds herself poacher-turned-gamekeeper. You remember that Chambers recently advised you deliberately to fall down on the Austrian and the Italian railroads? When you rejected that advice you did so partly for good business reasons but mostly for your own pride in your reputation and because it is not in you to do a thing badly. I hope you may come to understand that I have identical reasons for my decision touching the building of the Camden Town houses.

It is true, that our business started on a forgery, and that forgery was compounded by a blackmail. It is true, we have often fished downwind of the law. Many of the contracts we have won have depended on our unfair advantage, of knowing the tenders others were going to make. Without bribery we would quickly come to ruin. Knowing and accepting all this foregoing, it is doubly hard to explain my sudden scruple.

Truly, if the money were mine, I would do as you suggest. But it is not. Absolute discretion is not the same as ownership. This is a contract for

1,710 houses. Between now and 1870 we shall let contracts go for nigh 35,000 more. If I cannot show now that all who tender may expect honesty and fair dealing, I am asking to be robbed. Not myself, for I have said I would take that risk, if the money was mine, but those who have trusted me. I would be asking for them to be robbed. I cannot do it.

As witness of my good faith, when I say if it were mine, it were yours, I append a list of the properties I have bought freehold and leased at profit over nine years. You have given me 37,000*l* in that time. The land it has bought is now largely developed and is worth some 220,000*l*, and brings a rental after all proper deductions and expenses of 12,475*l*. Chambers is confident of raising 150,000*l* on these estates at six per cent, which in today's City is most fair.

All these I unreservedly place at your disposal.

                                                                        Nora.

Of course she did not expect him to take this rhetorical gesture literally.

                            *   *   *

He did not come to her that night and next morning there was a note before her place at breakfast. It read: "Thank you. Will you please be good enough to let Chambers have the title deeds. He is to discharge any debt upon them."

She read these terse commands several times through before she could bring herself to believe them. The threat to sell instead of simply to mortgage could not be made more plain. He meanwhile had gone to North Wales, where the Britannia Bridge was now well advanced.

She had expected him to go on to Ireland, where Flynn had now pushed the Cork line almost as far as Mallow, thirty miles beyond Limerick Junction and only another twenty or so from the terminus. So she was more than surprised, when she delivered the deeds to Chambers later that week, to hear that John was with him. She went into Nathaniel's office and put the deeds on his desk.

"With all my worldly goods I thee endow," she said to John.

He treated it as a great joke. She could not tell from his mood whether he was now reconciled to her decision or not. Of course he would not behave in public other than as he had always behaved.

"I've just been telling Stevenson that with any luck we shan't need to touch these properties," Chambers said.

"Aye. I've been getting the riot act on bidding for too much long-term work."

"I don't know why he lost his interest in sewerage systems," Chambers told her. "That's the sort of contract the firm ought to be going after."

"It's not we who've lost interest; it's the municipalities," John grumbled.

"Aye," Nora agreed. "Just let there be a bad cholera epidemic this summer and the interest will come—if you'll pardon the expression—flooding back."

"You've a ready wit today," John said.

"Thank you. You're remarkably cheerful yourself."

The flat normality of their talk was turning brittle.

"I spent the morning at Euston. The Great Hall opening is definitely set for May the seventeenth. And they've promised to pay the entire sum in cash, or draft, but no shares."

"Oh!" Nora wanted to dance on the desk. Her properties were safe!

"Aye. I threatened to demolish the roof if they tried paying in shares. That may have had something to do with it."

It'll save whatever's left between us, Nora thought.

But later she was less sure. John was not exactly cold with her, but he was punctiliously correct—almost a parody of a husband. She began to long for a blistering argument to clear the air. She thought she'd have it when it turned out that Cubitt's had tendered for just over £146 a house at Camden Town—a mere ten shillings below Stevenson's tender. But John took the news in grim silence, saying only that Cubitt would "do her well."

Even when he was warm with her and allowed something of his former tenderness to show, it was as if he were making a special effort —almost as if he were trying to remember how such feelings and behaviour had once come to him quite spontaneously. There was nothing she could *do.* The harder she tried to provoke him to anger, the more apparently forgiving and gentle he became. Even worse, there was nothing she could have done differently. It was not as if *she* had behaved foolishly or wrongly, so that she might now beg his forgiveness. She would do it all again—withhold the Wolff fund and let the houses go to honest tender. It was so unreasonable of him not to understand that. The more she thought about his unreasonableness, the angrier she grew with him—and the less chance did he give her to vent that anger.

Then one day she overheard Flynn and John talking idly about this and that in a neighbouring room. She was paying only scant attention to what they were saying, until she heard the name Bochnia mentioned, followed by a shocked silence. It was actually the silence that focussed her hearing on their talk. Then she distinctly heard Flynn whisper "Sorry!" before their casual chatter resumed.

"Bochnia" rang a bell, but she had to search through several recent railway papers before she came upon it: Annaburg–Bochnia, proposed railway, first 100 miles, tenders invited. Payment likely in stock.

There it was then. A hundred miles in Saxony, conveniently close to the Dresden–Prague line. John hadn't been able to resist it. But he *knew* they could not take on more work for credit. What could he be thinking of?

There was only one thing, she realized with a sinking heart: her property. How foolish she had been to value it for him! A quarter of a million pounds. Already she knew they would have to mortgage some of it—perhaps most of it—over the coming months, just to meet their present commitments. But if he really was going to build this Annaburg–Bochnia line, they would have no alternative but to sell it. *Sell her property!* She began to tremble with fury, until she realized that all this was mere supposition. In fairness, she'd have to find out if there was any truth behind it.

She tackled him directly they were in the carriage and on their way home.

"Aye," he said evenly. "We put in a bid for eighty miles. It's not accepted yet, of course."

"We?" she asked.

"Flynn and my good self. I don't know." He sighed. "Sometimes I think you and I ought to get out of this business. Leave it to men of vision like Flynn. He's the only man left who can still think grand—only one I know, anyway."

"Am I to know the details?" she had to ask.

"If you wish." He yawned. "As a matter of fact, we put in two bids. Eight hundred thousand if they pay in stock; a hundred thousand less for cash—in round figures. And the actual cost—which you were no doubt going to ask next—will be just over five hundred thousand, not a word to a soul."

She kept calm, knowing he was trying hard to provoke her to anger. "Where do we find half a million?"

"Well, of course, we don't have to find it all at once. Some of the earlier lines will be finished soon and we can sell off the stock. Gensendorf–Pesth in Hungaria will finish before we're halfway. That's a sure hundred thousand for a starter. And there's others. We'll manage."

"And completion? I mean on the Annaburg–Bochnia?"

"Eighteen months."

"Then I can tell you, John, we shall fall short by at least two hundred thousand."

She saw the lower part of his face jerk into and out of the light of a gas lamp as they passed. He was grinning as he said, "We shall manage. Never fear. We can sell our property if necessary."

Her mouth went dry. He meant it. He might be grinning, but he meant it. "It's mine," she said. "You gave *me* that money 'to do what I like with' you said. It's me who's turned it into—"

"You've done what you liked with it," he interrupted. "And no doubt you've had great fun. But playtime is over, Nora. We need it now."

"We? Is that Flynn and good self again?"

"No no!" He was testy. "I was teasing then. I'm sorry, I shouldn't have teased. But I'm serious now. We're not a property firm, love. We're railroad builders. We need that money."

"But it's mine!" She still could not believe it.

"Ours, dear. Look, I know how you must feel. Very disappointed. It's only natural. But try and look on the bright side. We lose two–twenty thousand now—or rather, we take it out of property and put it where it belongs—and when the line's finished we get back a clear three hundred thousand. You must see the sense of it. You above all must see that."

It was unarguable—once you accepted his notion that she had merely been "playing" with the money, "having great fun," as he put it. But she knew that she could never face the sale, however compelling his arguments. She still had hopes of reviving their marriage once they had weathered this present crisis. But if she had to face the sale of her properties for the second time in a few years, all such hopes would vanish.

Yet she knew, too, just from the reasoned way John was speaking, that he would never understand her feeling. They would live out their lives yoked together in a hatred he would not understand and she could not control.

There had to be some other way. "Leave it with me, love," she said brightly. "We'll mortgage the land by all means. But it may not come to a sale. We must try to find the rest some other way."

"Oh? How?" He sounded as if he were smiling.

"I don't know. We'll find it somehow."

"See?" he said, settling back to doze the rest of the journey away. "It just needed a little encouragement. I'm sure you'll do it."

*   *   *

That Thursday he left for Berlin to hear about the Annaburg–Bochnia contract. Twenty minutes after seeing him off at London Bridge station she was with Chambers in his renaissance-princely office in Dowgate.

"You look awful," he said.

She smiled wanly. "I hope it's your afternoon for truth on *all* fronts, Nathan."

He became wary at once.

"Did Stevenson tell you why he's gone to Berlin?" she asked.

"The Dresden–Prague line?"

"And the other? Did he tell you about that? The Annaburg–Bochnia line?"

Chambers froze where he sat. "No," he said. "You tell me."

So she told him—exactly what had passed between herself and John that night in the carriage. It left him looking very unhappy. "If he insists on selling your property, Nora, nothing can prevent him, you know."

"Balls," she said flatly. It shocked him. Wearily she closed her eyes. "Listen, Nathan. The time is approaching when you must decide where your real loyalty is. To John Stevenson? Or to the firm that bears his name—the firm that puts the meat under your gravy?"

"Or to you!"

She laughed coldly. "Oh, no. I have no illusions about that. But I tell you this: If he sells my property, I will finish forever with the firm of Stevenson's."

He laughed. "You can't be serious!" She said nothing. "Stevenson's without you? Why, it's . . ." He could find no word strong enough. Then he looked into her eyes and saw she meant it.

"I'd have the trust fund," she said quietly. "And my share of the Wolff fund is already beyond his grasp. I'm younger than he is. I shall outlast him. I can wait."

When Chambers breathed out he seemed to shrivel. "How can you talk like that! You would finish him. Just for a bit of money!"

"It's not a bit of money," she said fiercely. "It's a bit of *me*! You don't understand it, either of you. All this praise you lavish on me—it's meaningless. It's empty. You understand nothing about me."

"I understand you to say you'd wreck your own marriage for the sake of a bit of property."

"Not I. He. He would do that. In any case, he would never believe my departure would finish the firm. He thinks you'll always bail him out. He thinks you've got so much tied up in the firm that you couldn't possibly afford to let him go under."

That made Chambers' eyebrows shoot up. "Little he knows of banking then."

"Yet you would be a heavy loser if he did crash."

"I'd survive."

"But the loss would be immense—especially the loss of future business."

Reluctantly he accepted the truth of that. It was all she had been waiting for. She smiled at last. "Fortunately I have thought of a way around the problem. It will not be necessary to put the properties on the market."

"Ah!" His relief showed how great his misgiving had been, despite his bravado. But she judged that he had not been worried enough to fall in at once with her plan, so all she said was: "I'll tell you if it ever becomes necessary."

He shrugged, disappointed.

"Don't you think he's changed a lot lately?" she asked.

Chambers seemed to weigh her up before he answered. "Has it ever occurred to you that he may be tiring of being a contractor?"

"Never!"

"Perhaps he goes for these bigger and bigger contracts as a way of keeping the glory alive? I only say perhaps?"

She realized it was possible. "Has he hinted as much to you?"

"Well—in a way. He said something to me last year which I thought was just one of his jokes. Or not jokes but oddities. He said, 'When will it happen that we have enough money to say I'm free? Free of all of it?'"

"What did he mean?"

"It's an odd question, isn't it? And the more you think about it, the odder it gets. *Free* of it all. You couldn't think of a less likely word for him to use."

"Yes. But what did he mean?"

"That's what I asked. And he looked at me a long time. You know how sometimes he looks at you as if he's thinking of twenty things to say and which one is he going to select for you?"

"I know that look. Very well, lately."

"He said, 'Chambers, I'd like to go to Scotland or America or somewhere virgin, and take Nora and the children, and an axe and a plough and a shovel and a team of horses and break that land by myself.' Of course I just sat like this." He mimed astonishment. " 'Don't you ever ask yourself,' he said, 'what's the purpose of it all? What am I sitting here for, worrying about the Austrian government's promise and the Aberdeen line and the Board of the Railway Orphans and the bricks for the Welwyn viaduct? And I then think of someone out there where no man ever yet sowed or harvested, who hears nothing but the winds and the rushing waters and the cries of birds and beasts and the voices of his own family. I think of him sitting there at peace with his world, watching the sun set, and then of myself going home in my fine carriage, long after that same sun has set, still churning over those endless questions. And I wonder who is the rich man?' "

Nora laughed. "What did you say?"

"I said why not try. He said, 'Because I know damn well it isn't like that. The pioneer, after two years of spirit-breaking toil, ends up with four hundred tree roots that nothing will burn and no team can plough over. And he can't sit anywhere for the flies. And the water's brackish. And the well runs dry. But that doesn't stop the other picture from coming to me.' "

"Did he mean it? Or was he just talking, the way he often does?"

"I don't think it's exactly what was in his mind at first, or he wouldn't have said '*enough* money to be free,' would he?"

"Do you think he's forgotten what he wants?" she asked.

"It did occur to me. Or perhaps he found what he had sought—and it wasn't enough."

"Wanting, he found it—and found it wanting."

"Is that what you think?"

She could not reply. And then she said, "How odd I cannot tell you that at once. To be married to a man almost ten years, thinking your goals were identical, knowing you were never alone because of that. Whether he was in Ireland or France or Scotland or Spain or . . . downstairs or beside me, we were united. That's what has gone. I can't tell you any longer what it is he really wants."

"What is it that you want, Nora?"

She smiled, and without hesitation said, "More."

He looked puzzled.

"Whatever we have," she explained, "I want more of it."

"Suppose he really meant that foolish romantic dream. Or even the realist picture, tree roots, flies, and all. Suppose that was what he discovered he really wanted?"

"He wouldn't be John, if he wanted that. He wouldn't be the same person."

"We all change. You change. Even two years ago you would not have dreamed of taking on the Wolffs' money the way you did, with so little reference to John. And never, never in your life would you have arranged for an honest tender."

In that moment all her suspicions about him came flooding back. The terrible thought occurred to her that he was telling her these things, in that flat unemotional tone, as his final triumph over her. He was saying that he had brought her and the Wolffs together because he knew it would push this wedge between her and John and cause the split he had for so long desired.

In her innermost heart she knew it was not so. She knew, in fact, that Chambers was not really clever enough to work over that time and distance and on such a well-judged emotional scale. John could have done it. He could use people in that grand manner. And because she knew John so well, she knew, too, that Chambers was not made of such material.

There was no comfort in the realization. It did not ultimately matter now whether or not Chambers had engineered the division between herself and John—the division existed nonetheless. It was a fact. And it cried out for something to heal it.

"Broader horizons," Chambers said. "Encourage him to look outward."

Nora laughed despairingly. "I've tried that for years. I thought ironmaking might do it. Then the foreign work—and look at the sorry state that has brought us to! Then it was to be general building. And the only reason I encouraged him to squander all our Irish profits was that I thought it would get him involved with Pim and the British Association—and Parliament."

"It may yet," Chambers said. "That fuze is still burning."

She made a glum face, not soothed. He looked at her speculatively and licked his lips. "What are you not saying?" she asked when his silence had persisted too long.

"Probably wrong," he said and fell silent again. At length he went on: "Not that it matters; it's all under the bridge now. But it's my belief that if you had falsified the tenders to make sure the job went to

Stevenson's, you would have destroyed all chance of saving your marriage."

She looked at him coldly. "Thank you for telling me in time."

He ignored the implications of her remark. "It's quite clear," he said, "that in all these months you have not once tried to imagine these matters from start to finish as *he* must see them."

"But that is because I know he sees them wrongly."

Chambers shrugged. "If neither the mountain nor Mahomet will budge—we must pin all our hopes on an earthquake."

She left him annoyed with herself for having gone there at all. Whatever else Chambers had become, he also remained their banker. How many tens of thousands had she just subtracted from their credit with him? It was her first serious commercial blunder in years; and she knew she ought to confess it to John and seek his pardon.

She also knew she would do nothing of the kind. Blunder or not, she had had to soften up Chambers to get him ready to accept her plan.

Chapter 48

"When we started this I had no idea things would become so entangled," Walter said.

"Yes," Mrs. Cornelius agreed. "Yours is very much an engineer's approach to life."

"Of course it is."

"Of course!" she echoed. She leaned hard against him, forcing him to lie supine again, then quickly she leaped to straddle him, hanging her breasts onto his face, caressing his face with them as she spoke. It was an aggressive gesture, devoid of all tenderness. "You like to test a thing, as you test a bridge or a tunnel, and give it a certificate, and then use it without thought forever after." Her tone was soft, almost admiring—as if she were about to say "you old devil!"

He had no defence against such mockery. His body mutely adored her attack, especially when she was so lascivious; and he reached his trapped head, his lips, his tongue, into all that warmth and softness hanging like fruit above, craving for it to be still and to fold around him.

"There's maintenance," he said, pretending to play her game.

She stopped moving and giggled. It became a long, long laugh, humourless and low-voiced. A gurgle. A mad noise. She lowered her breasts onto his face then and reached her arms straight behind her; but her spidering fingers could not touch what they sought. She inched herself down, putting her hair and lips to his face. Her eyes gleamed with a mirth she was not sharing as her fingers clawed the air above dead Samson.

"Come on," she challenged, "the rope trick."

He groaned. His tortured eyes begged up at her for the peace his tongue would not demand. But Samson, like an aging king, raddled with all the pains of time, hoisted himself wearily, with limp zest, into the salacious, gentle torment of her clutch. "Do you like that?" she asked. "Or this? Is it better than yesterday's? Do you remember the twenty-third of August, 1848?"

Her tone was loving and warm, as if she really, really were besotted by him still and lived only in the memory of their rutting—of what he called their leching hours. That was what made it so difficult to counter. She was shooing him off territory he had always thought supremely his. Each time they parted he thought, with vast, inexpressible relief, that he would never go back to her again. His spirit would sing all the way home to Bristol; *this* time he meant it, he certainly, decisively meant it. He had done with Mrs. Cornelius for all time. Over his dead body. But the following Thursday would find him with his key in the lock, his besotted craving flesh trampling in over his dead resolve, hungering for her as from three months' continence.

He had tried everything. He made important arrangements in Wales, the wrong way from Bristol. But come the day it was a telegraphic message crossed the Bristol Channel; and he was trembling his way to London. He sought out the best of the hundred Bristol harlots he had known, and spent the evening before with her; but as he recrossed her threshold, back into the street, the images of Mrs. Cornelius, naked and inviting, pressed around him like Furies. For nothing could gainsay the fact that Mrs. Cornelius was supreme.

He had found wonderful joys with the other three hundred and eighty-nine girls and women in his life. If he had never known Mrs. Cornelius, he would have counted himself the luckiest man who ever lived. At his actual moments of ecstasy he had often thought that no one could ever have been so blessed with pleasures. (Indeed, once he had said to the girl he was on at the time, "My cup runneth over." She, being evangelical and thinking he was blaspheming, had struck him violently and made his nose bleed; she had refused payment, too, which he had lost all intention of offering.) True, he always parted from their company with the feeling that something had already escaped him. Some memory had been left behind. And when he wrote about the experience, in his record, that element would not return. Even in the minutest description, where he tried to set down with the utmost fidelity every memory of the event, he could not revive it. Once he wrote rhetorically: "Is that why I keep returning and returning to them—to discover what it is I can never carry away with me, even in memory? When secret flesh warms itself in intimate folds of secret flesh . . ." He never finished the sentence. Its proper ending was his perpetual quest. But the look of the words *secret flesh* so pleased him that he filled the rest of the page with them, repeated and repeated, without punctuation. At the very foot of it he added the word *ejaculate*. In its childish way, he thought, it came closer to the ineffable than all the sheaves of memoir he had compiled.

He did not resent the sense of loss that pervaded his memory when each lech was done. He took it for a fact of existence—just as the happiest day of your life must end in sleep, and so must the saddest, and the fact of sleeping had nothing to do with the quality of the day it closed. So the forgetting was a fact of the body's mechanism, not connected with the quality of delight to which it referred. Or so he had decided.

But all that was before he had met Mrs. Cornelius. She had hungered after him, or after Man, as ardently as he had ever craved for Woman. And she gave *more*. More in every way. Whatever his fantasy might conjure, the fact of Mrs. Cornelius could top it. He left her, in those early encounters, with the memory not of loss but of surfeit. The memory of her flesh in intimate embrace with and around him and his was more than the actual experience, not less. Then he knew what all those other leches had lacked.

Only slowly did he realize—and she, too—that to have your fantasies topped by reality is the true state of hell—where your dreams reach forward into an inexpressibly magic world of fleeting lusts, and you wake to find yourself already far beyond them; where nothing is half-seen, no temptation is withheld, no delights are saved for other days, because half-seen things, and things withheld and other days are limits—and in the hell of more-more-more, on the farther shore of your dreams, there are no limits.

So now when they met, chained to one another by a perfection of erotic skill that a million leches would neither improve nor exhaust,

they ended always with her sweet, gentle, loving aggression and his
mute, adoring abhorrence—as today, and as last week and next, world
without end, an antiprayer with no amen.

She had got him stiff enough now to work into herself again. She
shivered with pleasure and straightened on him, kissing him, dragging
her hair over his face, pulling her breasts outward for his fingernails,
writhing, rising effortlessly into her ecstasy, staying on that plateau
all his pain-filled lifetime—until he rammed and pumped his aching
emptiness into her yet again, yet again, yet again. How it *hurt*.

He reached for the future. What was reality going to be like? And
was it soon? Like a drowning man he clutched the page of the book
where today was going to exist . . . secret fleshsecretfleshhh secrete shhh.
The Ejaculations of Walter, 8vo, silk bound, Privately Produced, En-
riched with Numerous Curious Illustrations. In which our hero . . .
builds a new Inferno. He wanted to laugh.

He laughed—except that to the external world it had all the appearances of weeping.

Mrs. Cornelius was sitting beside him, gleaming like alabaster with
the perspiration. She wiped the tears from his cheeks, hoisting them up
unbroken on cool fingertips to her face, placing them on her own
cheeks, as if trying out an effect. "You have never done that before,"
she said.

He turned suddenly on his stomach, away from her, burying his face
in the sheets.

She struck him hard with her fist on the shoulder blade, hurting herself more than him. "Talk!" she said.

"I thought you didn't want me to talk." His muffled words were
barely intelligible. Then he lifted his face off the bed and said clearly,
"What *do* you want?"

She leaned over and spoke gently an inch from the nape of his
neck. "I want one lech so perfect I need never see you or touch you
again. Nor any other man."

The low, vibrant intensity of her hate made him shiver. He was
afraid of her. "You're mad," he said.

She lay on her back beside him, speaking to the ceiling. "I know
that. I've known it for a long time. I thought it last Sunday at the Female Refuge, listening to the Reverend Wharton giving yet another
variation of his Lusts of the Flesh sermon—what nonsense it was! There
was only one female there it could possibly have any meaning to."

"Why—how can you say that?"

"Oh, Mr. Thornton." She shook her head bitterly. "If I told you, you would hate me for it."

"I never did understand you. From the moment I tried to have you in the old garden room, I thought you were odd."

"Odd," she echoed.

"Go on," he cajoled. "Tell me. You know how it excites me. You know I like to think of you among all those—women."

She laughed without a trace of mirth. "You defeat me every time," she said flatly. "You cannot be vanquished."

"Stop talking in that silly way. Tell me whatever it was you were going to say."

"I *wasn't* going to say."

"Well, tell me what you weren't going to say."

She sighed and obeyed. "In the last few years—centuries—I have spoken, I should think, to as many fallen women as you have clicked."

"I don't like that word."

"I can tell you four hundred others."

"You talk to them about that!"

"And clothes, and cooking and sewing. It's all they know. The one thing they do *not* know is the Lusts of the Flesh. The red-faced Reverend Wharton might as well preach to them on—"

"Do they not talk of lascivious things, then?"

"Constantly. But utterly without feeling. They have not the vaguest notion of the urges that drive men to shower them with silver. Your fine leches are to them a military drill. Their endless chatter is of method and mechanism."

He laughed. "That is how they brazen it out amongst themselves. It is not so when they are with *me*."

"I knew you would say that. I have read your memoirs."

"It was a mistake to show them to you. And it is a mistake to listen to the Reverend Wharton if it occasions these morbid fancies. I think you should stop, my dear."

"I think *we* should stop, 'my dear,'" she echoed.

"Oh, if we but could!" He sighed, heavy with insincerity. "How many times have I made and broken that resolve!"

"Nevertheless, I think we must, Mr. Thornton." She was serious.

"You can't!" he said urgently, feeling almost in a panic. It was one thing to make the resolve yourself, quite another to have it forced upon you. "It'll be different next week, just you see! I'll be ever so much better."

"Better?"

"I know I haven't been much in sorts today. I didn't want to tell you so immediately, but there's a good reason for it." He stood up and reached for his shirt.

"Huh!" She turned on her front, not wanting his eyes on her there.

"It's true," he said. His voice acquired a measured solemnity. "My little son Lionel, you remember, the three-year-old. Last Thursday, while we were here, he died." There was no sound from her. He sat down to pull his stockings on. His back was to her. "It was cholera," he added. "It's been raging in Bristol this summer." Still there was no sound. "Not that I could have done anything if I had been there. He was never a well child. I felt more sorry for Arabella than anyone. . . ."

He stopped then, feeling the bed shake. Could she be laughing? At him? He turned and looked closely at her. She was crying, sobbing in silence. He shouldn't have told her. "Come," he said. "It's past now. We're all learning to get over it. It was a merciful release."

Whatever he said and whichever way he tried to turn her, she would not stop her crying, nor show him her face. He tried to tickle her while he laughed, he tried to caress her sexually while he made lascivious promises for next week, but nothing would shake her out of it. In the end he grew quite worried. But the time for his train was drawing on, so he had to go. When he left her she was still lying naked on the bed, face hidden, sobbing and sobbing. He wondered then if he would ever see her again in that room and state of nature.

But when he came next week, so did she.

Chapter 49

There was no holiday for anyone connected with Stevenson's that summer of 1849. The firm had never worked so hard. It now had between twenty-five and thirty thousand men, engaged on fifty-nine contracts in England and Europe. Just to service them all with the cash that each needed routinely was a double-tide nightmare for a staff of fifteen clerks and a treasurer, quite apart from Nora. She alone had the "extraordinary" demands to cope with, too: the unforeseen expenses that could overturn all their careful budgeting. She alone knew how close to disaster they stood—the disaster of having to sell all her properties.

Yet that moment never quite came. She anticipated it by midsummer at the latest; but autumn arrived and with it the expectation of their seventh child and still, by the skin of its teeth, the business roared ahead. John had more to do with its salvation than Nora. He developed a special knack at bringing a line to completion, and fetching home its profit, just in time to stave off catastrophe. "See?" he would crow. "I knew it would be all right!"

He developed an image for those times; it grew out of a trivial incident that occurred to him on the North Wales line, late that autumn. After work a number of his men were larking around on a two-wheel velocipede one of them had bought. As he passed the group one of the lads dared him to have a try on it.

The night was dark but there was a good moon and he decided to free-wheel down the hill, leaving the machine at the bottom for the men to collect. He had set off in a chorus of cheers and good-natured barracking. But halfway down he had come to a hollow, full of cattle—of fierce-horned cattle—all walking purposefully and silently down the hill under the moon. He was among them, doing a good thirty miles an hour before he realized it. And then there was absolutely nothing he could do but try to steer the best course he could among them, making decisions about a thousand times faster than normal, and praying that none of the beasts ahead would turn toward him. If he hit one of those horns sideways, he would be skewered easier than fillet beef. Somehow he steered among them, suffering not the slightest touch. He was through so quickly he did not even begin to sweat and to tremble until he had skidded to a halt beyond them and got down off the machine. He counted the cattle as they passed: fifty-four. One of the last among them swung her tail across his face, leaving it well shitten and reeking. "I deserve better than that!" he shouted after the herd, laughing. When the men caught up and heard his story, they said it was just one more example of "Lord John's luck."

"Aye," he agreed. "I'm doing it all the time."

The whole year, he thought, had developed that same madcap quality of an existence charmed to survive: "Lord John's luck."

He was away in Italy when the luck finally ran out. It was the Monday of the week before Christmas. Nora was going through the summary of the previous week's credits, wondering why they were so meagre, when she noticed that an expected credit from the Austrian government was missing from the list. It was for over seventy thousand pounds so she remembered it well—an impressive bit of coloured paper festooned with eagles crushing neat bundles of firewood in their talons. The sum had been drawn on a bank in Prague, and there had, as usual, been four signatures. The Hapsburg empire was, as John said, "a paradise for clerks."

At once she sent around to Chambers to inquire why it had not been credited. Back came a terse note: "Can not leave here. Please see me as soon as possible. N.C." She went around at once.

He was not seated at his desk; indeed, he could hardly stand still. She had never seen him so solemn. "Terrible!" he said. He pointed to a note on his desk. "It came five minutes before your inquiry."

Nora touched it and raised her eyebrows at him. He nodded.

It was from the firm of Collins & Wilcox, the London agent of the bank in Prague. Briefly it said: "Herr Schapka is no longer entitled to sign drafts. Please re-present with the signature of Herr Adolf Bauer. The remaining three signatures are in order."

Mystified, Nora let the note fall back on the desk. "But I have seen Schapka's signature on several drafts," she said.

"It seems he has been promoted—my clerk has just run back from Collins with the story. Schapka has been promoted out of the department that authenticates drafts."

Nora laughed tendentiously. "That can't invalidate a draft duly signed before his promotion, surely."

"He was promoted last month. The draft was signed ten days ago."

"Very well." She shrugged. "I can't see it's anything so terrible. The other three signatures are authentic. Surely Collins will advance something on it?"

He breathed in deeply before he said. "Not a penny."

"But they must!"

"There's no must in it, Nora. They won't, and nothing can make them."

Chambers seemed just a little too earnest, as if he were covering up some pleasure in what he had to say.

"We'll see about that!" She walked to the door.

"Careful," he warned. "It would be a pity if they saw how close-hauled the firm is."

Half an hour later she was back, in a towering rage. "They will not discuss a husband's business with his wife, they said. I told them I had power of attorney. In that case, they said, they would consider dealing with me by letter. Never in person. Ooooooh!" She shivered her body in impotent fury.

"Exactly how does this leave the firm?" Chambers asked, now back at his desk.

Nora grew slightly calmer as she thought. "We can meet all the bills due except the big one for the Welwyn viaduct bricks."

He looked up, intensely interested. "How big?"

"Twenty thousand. This Thursday." Her voice grew more hopeful. "Of course, *you* can advance us that much, on the strength of this Austrian draft."

He was shaking his head before she was halfway. "How can I? If their own agent won't?"

"Not a penny? Nothing?"

He was very unhappy. "Sixteen thousand's the highest I dare go."

"Marvellous!" she sneered. "Here we are, drowning twenty yards from the canal bank, and you go and throw us your best-quality sixteen-yard lifeline!"

"I'm already in far deeper than a prudent banker should go."

"We'll give you ten per cent on the loan."

"That isn't the—"

"Twelve per cent, then. There must be a point where greed beats risk. That's what banking is: greed versus risk. *Cupiditas periculumque* —what about that for a motto! The only words of Latin I've learned."

"It won't do, Nora." He was not to be distracted from his solemnity. "I've supported Stevenson's far beyond the point where mere commercial judgement would have said stop. If you go down, it would be touch-and-go with me now. If I advance twenty thousand, on top of it all, and you still go down—"

"But we won't."

"I've heard that sentence all this year, and it doesn't get quieter— only more frequent and more insistent."

"Very well, then. Prague isn't the other side of the globe. What if I went there, with a letter from Collins?"

"We've done better than that. I've already sent a courier to Calais. He's sent a message over the electric telegraph to Paris for relaying on to Munich and Vienna."

"Oh—to think of our whole future in the hands of telegraphists and postmen! Still, we can now be sure of an answer before the month is out."

"You know the Hapsburg empire."

"In Scotland the banks let you overdraw your current account. You don't think?"

"Nora!" At least his laugh was sympathetic. "We have done the same thing here by a different route. I know you've got to try everything, but believe me, you've had more from this bank than you would have got from—"

"What about the Prague bank? If I went out there—surely they would advance us what we need, on the strength of their own guarantee? They could hardly question—" His face was already saying no. "What's wrong? Why not?"

"I don't think it would help," he said reluctantly.

"Nathaniel," she said quietly, "shall I tell you the very first thought that went through my mind when you mentioned about the signatures? I thought, 'How very nice and convenient for our friends in Prague—who keep their hands on our seven hundred and fifty thousand gulden for a further month. It'll earn them at least four thousand gulden more in that time.' I dismissed the thought as *unworthy*."

"There are lots of unworthy people in banking. It's a great deal dirtier than railways, believe me."

She stood up abruptly, unable to sit still any longer. Her whole body was tense with frustration and rage. She walked to the window, having a fantasy of smashing it with her gloved fists; it was the City beyond the panes that invited the attack—Cannon Street, Lombard Street, Cornhill, the Bank of England, and Collins & Wilcox.

"I swear," she said gently, "that when we have come through this period and are rich again, I will spend half our fortune to ruin that bank in Prague."

"When a bank is ruined, it is the innocents who suffer. You can't disentangle them."

"Oh, Nathaniel!" Her breath clouded the pane for an instant. "What a cobweb world!"

There was a long silence before Chambers said, "Well, which of us is going to broach the subject?"

Something in his tone, a slight edge, a nuance, told Nora that Chambers had been waiting all morning for this moment. No! All year—all this decade even. She felt suddenly tense with fear and excitement; but she forced herself to appear morose as she said, "My properties?"

Chambers looked away. "You've done wonders to avoid selling them so far. But . . ." He let the rest of the sentence hang.

Now she was certain of it. He was secretly relishing all this. It made her feel easier about putting her plan into effect. Until now the same latent honesty that had prevented her from using the Wolff fund to bale out John had also stopped her from operating her save-the-property plan. But Chambers' eagerness to wrest it from her removed that doubt. Lots of unworthy people in banking, were there? A great deal dirtier than railways? *Well, watch me, Mr. Chambers!*

"They're heavily mortgaged," she warned as she returned to her seat. All the while she played utter dejection.

"It doesn't matter in this case. They're worth at least another eighty thousand. If you agree to sell, I'll certainly lend against it."

Damn! she thought. That would scotch her plans. She would have to outplay him on that offer. "Wonderful!" she said bleakly.

She left, telling him that she would think it over.

After lunch she was back, nervous, angry, and bitter. "Very well," she said brusquely. "We'll offer them for sale." She flung the schedules that listed her properties onto his desk. "How you must have longed for this moment, Nathan!"

"Nora!" He really did seem hurt at the accusation. "You cannot know how deeply I wish there were another way."

She sniffed. "And here, just so that you know what's coming up next week, are our expected payments and our anticipated receipts."

"Good-good," he said mechanically, pushing the two lists to one side. "All's well now."

Nora's heart missed a beat. If Chambers did not look at the lists, the whole thing would fall apart. "You're suddenly very taciturn," she said in a slightly more conciliatory tone.

"Why?" His bewilderment, at least, was genuine.

"This morning you could lend us no more than sixteen thousand. Yet *now*—" She pointed at the two lists and let the gesture finish her sentence.

Uneasily he glanced at them, then—unbelievably—relaxed again. "You'll be sixty thousand to the good." As he spoke he grew puzzled once more. "But in that case why have you consented to sell your properties?"

God, would he do nothing right! she thought. "It's the other way, Nathan," she said slowly. "We need to *borrow* sixty thou'."

"Impossible!" he spluttered. He looked back at the lists and saw that she was right. "But I can't do that!"

"You said you could. This very morning." She was outraged.

"I meant I could lend *twenty*, the twenty you wanted, for this . . . bricks. The Welwyn viaduct bill. Not—" He waved the list of next week's debts like a pennant. "You know I didn't mean all this."

"You promised!" she spat at him. She stood up. He cowered for a moment as if he feared she might strike him.

"I did not. You know I did not. You know enough about banking to understand I couldn't possibly have meant to lend you so much."

She looked at him as if she thought of a hundred things to say; then she let the futility of it all show in her face. Her shoulders slumped. "Then we must try and sell the property as quickly as possible," she said.

He gnawed his lips. "We'd never do it in time. It's out of the question."

She walked to the window. Sleet was falling in the twilight outside. The City looked filthy. There was a dead mongrel dog in the gutter opposite; as Nora watched, waiting for the worry to grow and engulf Chambers, a ragged woman stooped and caught up the corpse. She carried it off in triumph. Meat for Christmas somewhere. Steadily Nora beat her gloved right fist into her gloved left palm, stretching the purple silk at the base of each finger.

"Oh God!" she heard Chambers say behind her. She searched for his reflection in the glass that covered the framed map of London; in it she saw him raise his fist and bring it down to smash the desk. Then, as if he remembered how much the desk had cost, he pulled the punch at the last minute. "Oh God!" he said again.

She spun angrily around, trembling with cornered fury. "Why can't you lend that much? D'you think the land is worthless?"

He fended off her words with his hands. "Of course not, my dear. Why, they're as good as Treasury stock, these properties—even better in the long term, I'd say." He smiled. He really was trying to be very nice now.

The wonderful man! she thought. She wanted to hug him. After going so wrong earlier, he could not now have gone more right. But none of this delight showed in her face. Instead she looked at him in a sort of hesitant admiration. "Nathan! You genius! You thoroughbred genius!" She spoke very slowly, as if an idea were just at that moment occurring to her.

"What?"

"Well, what did you say? As sound as . . . ?"

"Treasury stock." He tested each syllable for poison.

She waited, hoping he would see the connection for himself. When he did not, she said, "The Stevenson trust fund. How blind we've been! That's practically all in Treasury stock." He was already shaking his head. But she went on, now even daring to give a light laugh. "I used to sneer at you, remember? 'Who wants all that negotiable stock!' I used to say. Now I know: Stevenson's wants it!"

He almost shook his head off. "No, Nora. No, no, no. It will not do."

"What? You yourself said it's as sound as—"

"No! That's an end now."

"Give me one good reason?"

"Stevenson."

She paused and then smiled lightly as she asked, "The man? Or the firm?" But she could see the refusal forming yet again behind his eyes —a refusal even to consider the idea.

She stood quickly, giving him no chance to utter it. "Very well, Chambers." She swiftly gathered her things and moved to the door. "You had better take due notice. I shall go home now. Tomorrow I shall start to prepare our accounts for a hearing in bankruptcy. I tell you this so that you may take what protective action you can." She reached the door. "At least *we* do not desert *you*."

Later she wondered whether she ought to have added that when all the accounts were in they would have enough surplus to settle their debts a hundred times over—and how would that make him look as their banker? But no, she thought; he could work that out for himself.

Next day she arrived at the office to find a note from Chambers: "Another piece of Latin for you, from Horace—*Virtus post nummos* (cash first, virtue afterwards). It is the real motto of banking. I yield to it and to you. Merry Christmas!"

At least he was yielding with good grace. He had plotted to get her properties liquidated and she had outbluffed him. Just to make sure he understood that, she gave orders that no payments of any kind were to be made the following week; she could put it all straight after Christmas. Then he would see that the list she had furnished him with was as false as the letter he had (or so she suspected) persuaded Collins & Wilcox to write.

By the end of that day the Stevenson trust was contracted to buy Nora's properties; the mortgages were being discharged; and the firm's credit was a hundred thousand to the good. Merry Christmas indeed!

To make all straight with John—to show him that they really had scraped the barrel to its bottom splinters—she decided to sell Fontana, her prize horse, and to mortgage Thorpe Old Manor. She went riding the following day and returned limping, saying she had taken a fall in the Home wood. Dr. Hales came and examined her as best he could through her skirts. He looked dubious.

"If I might be permitted to see and palpate the limb?" he suggested timidly.

"Certainly not!" Nora said, outraged. "You may ask Mrs. Cornelius or Mademoiselle Nanette to . . . 'palpate' my limb. They will tell you all you need to know."

So with the doctor on one side of the screen calling directions to Nanette, and Nora on the other wincing and suppressing louder cries of pain, he arrived at a diagnosis of "traumatic hyperplasia of the acetabulum." Nora thought it sounded a good enough reason for getting rid of a valued horse without causing tattle about their financial state.

The following morning she went to York with the deeds of Thorpe Old Manor. She wanted to raise the loan up there rather than in London because Stevenson's had used the York City & County Bank a great deal and had never yet asked a favour; and when she had later to explain these moves to John it would seem the natural thing to have done.

There was only a small staff then at Thorpe, on board wages; all the principal rooms were shrouded in dust sheets and the shutters drawn against the sunlight. She got the maids to open only the business room and to make up the small bed in the room leading off it. The fire soon took the damp off everything. She was pleased to find it all in order, although her arrival was quite unheralded.

She had just finished her supper and was going out for a walk in the last of the evening sun when the maid said that Mr. Hudson was calling.

Her spirits fell. There had recently been one unpleasant railway-company meeting after another, all filled with angry shareholders demanding the dismissal of George Hudson as their chairman. First the Eastern Counties, then the Midland, and on through all the others. Now only his debts connected him to the railway world that had once called him its king. Irregularities amounting to over half a million pounds had been uncovered and he was pledged to pay back every penny—though such losses were a small fraction of the total sustained by his companies in the general decline in trade and business. She and John had written to him expressing their sadness and saying he would always be a welcome guest, and so on; but she knew they ought to have been to see him. If things had been easier this year, they would have done so.

She had no idea what he would be like. There had been such conflicting stories about him. Some said he had all his old arrogance and spirit, others told of how people who had once trembled and walked on tiptoe in his presence had actually spat on him at meetings, and he had behaved ever so meekly in response. "Meek" and "Hudson" had not seemed possible partners, to her way of thinking. He must have heard she'd come off the train at York. What, she wondered, did he want here?

He was certainly his old wary, genial self in his greeting to her. She told him she had been about to walk in the garden, the air being so mild, and suggested they both should go. He said nothing would delight him more.

"Someone told me you had a bad hip," he said.

"Oh it comes and goes. Worst at sunrise, best at sunset. And what a sunset!"

They basked in its glow, and in the retained warmth pouring out of the old brick wall to their left. The December air was alive with it.

"Have you ever been up the old tower?" she asked. "Would you like to see?"

He nodded affably. Despite his ponderous bulk he leaped up the stairs more easily than she could have—even if she had not remembered to limp slightly. At the top, the merest zephyr of a breeze stirred the air.

"A red sky at night is a shepherd's delight, we used to say in the West Riding," she told him.

"Here too," Hudson agreed. "But there's an East Riding sign of good weather, as well. Yon cloud, shaped like a ark." He pointed to a squarish cloud that could charitably be seen as a Noah's ark. "It's going over the Humber. That's a sure sign of fair weather in these parts."

Away to the west, where the sun was gold and huge, the sky around it was a cloudless green. The smell of woodsmoke was strong on the air. The yews and hollies were thick in leaf, like ramparts, their shade already turning black.

"On such an evening," Hudson said, "even the poor may forget their cares."

"Aye. On just such an evening Stevenson and I met first," she said, stretching truth by a few months. "We were poor."

"Imagine!"

"It seems only yesterday, sometimes. Yet think of all that's happened. Look where he's gotten to."

"And you. The credit's yours every bit as much as his."

"Aye. I'd deny that to many, but not to you. You'd not think less of *him* for it."

He smiled bravely. "If I'd had such a partner in my line of business—"

She pushed him in the ribs. "You'd have sacked him in less than a week! He'd never have suited your style." -

She wanted to avoid talking of his troubles except lightly and bravely; otherwise she could not avoid pointing out how foolhardy he had been. Also there was the undeniable fact that Stevenson's present difficulties were entirely due to the low value of railway securities— and that, in turn, was largely because of the disastrous financial management that had been uncovered in all of Hudson's former companies.

But he, perhaps sensing her unwillingness, said bluntly: "What *was* my style, Mrs. Stevenson? I hear and read so much from men who never knew me, and nothing from those who did."

She looked at him steadily; up there on the battlements, with his squat frame and motionless face, he seemed half-man, half-statue. She wondered how people had ever been afraid of him. But they had. She knew men who would leave any building he entered rather than risk an encounter. And though she had never known him in that light, it struck her as sad that such a man should now be standing atop a ruined tower in a remote parish, not a railway in view, asking a mere passing acquaintance for an honest opinion. But, if he asked, he should get—sad or no.

"What I've never been able to explain to myself about you, Mr. Hudson," she said, "is how a man who was such a genius at railway politics—and on your greatest days you were a juggler with a million skittles in the air at once, without a mishap—how such a man with such a mind could have failed to grasp the relationships between capital, income, and dividends."

She thought, once the words were out, they were too harsh, so she added what was also true: "But I must say you had an idea of what railways should be, long before anyone else. When others were merely thinking of individual lines, you had a grand vision of a network, which no one had ever seen before. When all the money's forgotten, that's what folk will remember. But for me it only deepens the mystery."

"When the money's forgotten!" he echoed. "When will that be?"

"Well . . ." Her voice was dubious. "Give it a century."

He laughed then, as if it was a compliment. "Aye," he agreed complacently. "It was very bad. Shall I tell you a secret—as I've told no one?"

Nora waited.

"I never *understood* it."

"Money?"

"Aye. Never understood it."

"I knew that."

He sniffed. "I understood what it *did*, though. If I took some shares and stuffed them in Lord Tomnoddy's back pocket so that he would give my company a wayleave, with no argument—who was I benefiting? Myself? Or my company? Obviously the company; so who should pay for it? Me? I didn't think so. That's why I made the company pay for those shares. They say I paid it out of fresh subscriptions, but that's a lie."

"What did you do?" Nora asked, knowing the truth very well but wanting to hear what possible gloss he could put on it.

"All sorts of things."

"For instance."

"Well, for instance, we would make provision for a hundred thousand in bad debts, and if there were only, in fact, four thousand, I'd take the remaining ninety-six and use it to buy favours—pay for shares—and so on. But the favours were for the company, never for me. Now they say I must pay it all back. Well, so I will, but I'm still mystified why I have to."

She smiled to herself. If he really did not understand it, there was little purpose in pursuing the point. "What I find most disgusting," she said, "is the spectacle of those who cheered you to the echo and who profited so vastly during all the years when you were making such money for them, and now they turn around and revile you as if all the ills of the railway world could be laid at just the one doorstep. Other sins may be morally worse, but, to me, ingratitude is the least edifying of all. You know there's always a Yorkshire welcome for you wherever Stevenson and I may be."

Hudson could not answer. His eyes were moist though not actually brimming with tears. He nodded gratefully and looked rapidly from her to the sunset and back.

"You'll manage, I take it," she said, hoping her tone implied help without actually offering it.

He drew breath and rallied. "I've sold Albert Gate to the French ambassador, and my estates are going up on the market. But I'm far from done. In fact"—he sniffed—"I'm here on a bit of business now. May I?"

"By all means." Intrigued, she turned away from him and began the descent, forgetting to limp until they were halfway down.

"Do you remember the rail we used for the Newcastle & Berwick?"

"Aye. We supplied most of it."

"I heard a whisper that you'd made too much of it."

It was true. They had made, in fact, over ten thousand rails too many, enough to lay fifteen miles of track. It stood on the books at nearly five thousand pounds. Rather than scrap it they had put it into stock to sell when the line needed maintenance. This was not among the stock they had reduced—the Newcastle & Berwick was the only buyer for that shape of rail.

"Ooh, you have gotten out of touch, Mr. Hudson. It's true we put a certain amount by for stock."

"Ah." He seemed to lose interest. "Pity. It's no good then. I need a fair bit. I have a market for thirty miles of it. Twenty-one thousand one hundred and twenty rails. Good price, too, for quick delivery. In Norway, so your mill was ideally placed."

"How quick?" she asked and before he could dictate she added: "We could supply enough for five miles at once. Then three and a half thousand a week—enough for five miles a week. You could have the lot by mid-February. If the price was right."

This rate of production was, in fact, twice their actual capacity, but she wasn't going to tell him they had such a heavy stock. Let him make what he liked of the rust on it when it was delivered. She wondered where his buyer really was.

They haggled on until she got her price—and the promise of a ninety-day bill to be waiting at the York City & County Bank in the morning.

They did not go back indoors but went straight around to the stable yard.

"So," he said as he remounted. "You think they'll remember me?"

"No doubt of it, Mr. Hudson. History might even know you as George Hudson, the great ironmaster who also had something to do with railways—in his youth."

He laughed uproariously at that. "Thou'll do!" he said as he spurred his horse away. "Eay, thou'll do!"

A broken man indeed! she thought, scorning the rumour mongers, as she watched him trotting back up the lane to the highway.

Chapter 50

John spent that Christmas in Italy before going on to Bohemia, Moravia, Hungaria, and then back to southern France, and so home via Spain. Nora expected him to be exhausted but he was leaner and more vigorous than ever. It took years off her just to be beside him again. From the moment he stepped off the train she could feel how strongly he wanted her. As soon as they were in their carriage he began to kiss her and fondle her with an overwhelming fervour.

"Want to risk it?" she asked. They were only just driving onto London Bridge.

He shivered and pulled a little apart. "You'll never meet a man more charged. But we'd better wait a while, eh?" He folded his arms and kept her gently at bay.

"Well I can't," she said. She had her skirts up and was straddling him before he could move. His resistance was a mere token. It was all over before they were fully across the Thames.

"More!" she whispered.

He lifted her bodily and put her in the seat opposite. "Don't you move until—"

"Until we reach where?" she taunted. "Come on. Name it!"

"I'll decide."

They giggled like schoolchildren as they dawdled on through the City. He opened the window to let the chill March air revive him. "Your true home," he said, looking out.

"It has been for the last half year."

"How are we?"

"You mean the firm? Or me and the baby?" She grinned.

"Well, I've just had proof of you and the baby."

"The firm's out of the wood, but I still can't say how far."

"Still not!" He was disappointed.

"We're too big to get a clear picture day by day. I sometimes think there's a sort of square law for businesses. Twice as big is four times harder to manage. Three times as big, nine times harder."

He shut the window to a crack and settled contentedly into the upholstery. "I won't say we could exist in the conditions of last year all the time. That strain. But while it lasted I don't think it was . . . I believe it did us a lot of good."

She beseeched the heavens. "Speak for yourself."

"I do. It put everyone on their mettle. Taught them what they're capable of when they're really stretched. I tell you, we've come out of this with some first-class deputies. Men who know they've won something. They know how to win now. I could take a year off now, and no harm done."

"You!" She was astounded. "Four days off and you start to twitch."

As if to give point to her words he made a stop at Finsbury Park to see the progress on the Great Northern, and again at Wood Green, where they also took tea. Then he made the coachman hurry on so that he would see the Welwyn viaduct before dark. They made love again on that last part of the journey; slowly, luxuriously, exhaustingly. The sun went down before they turned into the Maran valley, where the great viaduct was now nearly complete.

By moonlight it was even more impressive than by day. Its abutments in the hills each side were lost in a mysterious dusk, stretching its forty vast arches to an infinite chain, arriving out of the dark and vanishing back into it. Over the road in the centre of the valley the arches soared to lift the track more than a hundred feet above ground. The brick piers, so delicately light from a distance, were black and massive close to. Just the farther edge of each tight curve was silvered by the moon. It was awesome to drive in the rumbling coach beneath so vast a mass. John kept his head out of the window, looking back, until a network of intervening branches, also silver in the moonlight, obscured the viaduct completely.

He sat back and sighed out his satisfaction.

"A piddling little line!" Nora told him.

He pinched her in the dark. "You waited a year to say that," he said.

She giggled.

*   *   *

A week later, "twitching" as Nora said, he went to North Wales, where his other large bridge, the Britannia, was being prepared to have the third of its great iron tubes lifted into place. Then to the Highland Railway for a week. Then to France . . . and on it went, as busy as ever.

He paid flying visits to Maran Hill between these journeys, and always his question was, "How is the firm now?" And still Nora did not want to tell him exactly how well off they were. Partly she was afraid he would pledge all their profit into even vaster railway schemes —work for all those first-class deputies, but work that would put the firm back into the perils it had faced last year. And partly she wanted to have some really breathtaking profit to distract him—for she was also going to have to confess what she had done with the trust and with her properties. Indeed, she was surprised he had said nothing on the subject yet. He had not even made the most casual inquiry.

By mid-April, though, there was no point in still refusing to be spe-
cific. Many of the lines for which they had been paid in stock had now
been completed. In almost all of them the stock rose to its face value
and soon began trading at a premium. Stevenson's, who had got the
paper at big discounts, now began to make profits out of all proportion
to the work and investment. The change in the market rubbed off on the
unfinished lines, too, and they began to trade at or even above face
value.

When John next asked his eternal question she decided to answer
him specifically.

"How do you want it?" she asked with a broad grin. "We now have
a fortune of sixteen million silver roubles." His brow furrowed. "Or
would you prefer eighteen million American dollars?" He began to
smile. "Or twenty-five million Austrian gulden?" He laughed. "Or . . .
let me see . . . forty-five million Swedish crowns?"

"No!" His laugh was accelerating.

"I've not done yet. You may have fifty-one million German marks."

He advanced upon her, grasped her arms, and shook her lightly,
laughing even harder. "Stop!"

"Very well. Sixty-three million French francs?"

"Stop! Just tell me what it is in real money."

"Oh, that!" She sniffed. "A bit of a let-down I'm afraid. Only two"
—she made a glum face—"and a half million pounds."

He lifted her off the ground and turned her in a gentle half circle.
"Eeee! To me that sounds a great deal more than all that foreign
muck."

In his euphoria he arranged for them to go to Paris for a month.
Nora stuck it out for three days. She had her hair done in a new swept-
back style. They went to the Italian opera and heard Madame Persiani
in *Lucia di Lammermoor*. But the city was so torn and patched, so sad
and rotting, so vicious and mistrustful, that she and John agreed they
would enjoy far more a visit to Normandy.

So they went to Coutances and sat on the beach at Granville and
explored Mont St. Michel and went on excursions to the Calvados hills
and visited Cherbourg and Caen and saw the Bayeux Tapestry—in
short they did nothing at all. The world came to see them. Deputies
came to ask John's advice and left after telling him what they proposed
to do. The London office ran a regular courier service of delighted
clerks who came bearing files, summaries of account, and memoranda.
Mademoiselle Nanette was given the month off to stay with her mother,

but nevertheless came almost every day to help Nora with whatever she was doing. "It's my life now," she said simply.

Toward the end of the month, when the euphoria was dying, John asked her if she wasn't going to make any arrangements about Deauville this year.

"When you've gone back," she told him.

"You—er, still have the land there, then?"

"Me and Ferrand."

"Of course. Ferrand." He cleared his throat. "I've been meaning to ask, love. About your properties. I've felt right bad about it, ever since . . . you remember."

She put her face close to his. "Right bad!" she echoed sarcastically. "You flaming liar! You only did it to encourage me."

He brightened. "You mean you didn't sell them off?"

"Why do you ask?"

"Well . . ." He could not meet her eye. "I thought about it since. How unfair it was. You turning so little into so much and then the firm coming along and taking it all from you. I think you ought to take that money out again and—I don't know—buy back what you can. Or buy something else."

It suddenly struck her that he was talking not about her properties but about *them*, their marriage, their love.

The last time he had made this offer, it had devalued her rescue into a mere loan. She had known it, even at the time, and yet she had accepted the offer; she had connived at the act which had done more than anything to drive the wedge between them. Chambers' cunning, Sarah's charms, the Irish mess—these were trivial compared with what she had done in taking the money back.

These thoughts flashed through her mind as she realized she once again faced an identical choice—except that this time the price of a refusal was a quarter of a million pounds. She knew she was going to refuse the offer, but something within her could not utter an outright *no*. Instead she tried to tell him how she would have felt if her properties had gone on the open market.

He was puzzled now. "I can't make out whether you sold them or not. Give us a straight answer."

She told him the bare facts of what had happened that week before Christmas, omitting her fight with Chambers and her suspicions about the letter from Collins & Wilcox. Instead she threw all the weight of her narrative upon the wisdom of the trust's investment in the property.

"It's taught me something about myself, all this," she added. "The ownership of money is much less important to me than the control of it."

She thought he took the explanation very well.

*   *   *

He thought he took it well, too. True, that night before he dropped off to sleep, he pondered wrily the differences between himself and Nora. He now had, just as she once predicted he would, one of the biggest private fortunes in England—perhaps in the world. To achieve it had cost him more than ten years of unremitting labour; ten years of freezing on remote moors and hillsides, sweltering all summer in high-sided cuttings, walking until the blood squeezed out at his toe-nails, travelling long days and nights through dust or rain, lying in mud to check footings, dangling over ravines to inspect abutments, scrambling over mountainsides to look at routes that were later abandoned, eating foul and dangerous food, sleeping between verminous sheets in rat-infested inns, falling from horses, getting stuck in bogs, being lied to, cheated, misinformed, let down, clogging his mind with railway politics until the stink of it almost raised his scalp, scheming, bribing, conniving, conspiring, cheating, losing—ten years of it.

But Nora—in between the bearing of seven children (or six and three quarters, as she would be quick to point out), the managing of two big houses, the assiduous pursuit of almost a thousand foxes, and the financial oversight of the firm—Nora had managed to accumulate a fortune to rival his, indeed, had pledged it to *save* his.

The realization certainly took a lot of zest out of the work, or out of the prospect of returning to it. Or was that just the exhaustion of the past year speaking? Perhaps when Stevenson's was awarded the contract to erect this building for next year's Great Exhibition the zest would return.

In May he left Nora and Nanette at La Gracieuse and went back to London to nurse his Exhibition tender, which had gone in at a very low hundred and twenty thousand. Stevenson's had guaranteed ten thousand of any losses the Exhibition might sustain. (He had made the guarantee the previous autumn, when they were close to the precipice, because Robert Stephenson, as chairman of the Exhibition's executive committee, had asked it; and because to refuse would have caused the sort of talk they could then least afford.) He was determined to be the contractor who put up the Exhibition building, a dreadful squat shed (Euston station out of St. Paul's, they joked) over eighteen hundred feet long and made of brick. His tender barely covered the cost of materials. He would build the shed and its dome at his own expense. It would be a fitting end to his first decade as a contractor, he thought—to give back something to the country that had given him so much.

All May the committee deliberated over the tenders. The design of the building had been their own, a sort of hybrid from Barry out of Wyatt with help from Brunel, Stephenson, Cubitt, et al.—all of them committee members. It was a child spoiled by a surfeit of great parents. The grumbles began to swell. By the end of the month they were almost deafening. There had always been a strong party against the very idea of the Exhibition. It would allow foreign manufacturers a shop window in the very heart of London for their cheap and nasty foreign wares. Excursion trains were already being planned to bring workingmen from all parts of the kingdom—what would happen to their poor wives and children while they were rushing helter-skelter to London, and what temptations would face the men once they arrived in the great metropolis? What would become of the modesty and chastity of our workingmen! *The Times* retreated into a state of blind panic. "The whole of Hyde Park," it roared, "and the whole of Kensington Gardens will be turned into a bivouac of all the vagabonds of London." Foreigners, it warned, were already renting houses near the park and turning them into brothels. In Parliament Colonel Charles de Laet Waldo Sibthorpe, rabid Protestant and ardent xenophobe, fulminated against the expense of the building while the Irish poor (against whose interests he had consistently voted) were starving; even worse, he said, the building would mean the irrevocable loss of some of Hyde Park's most beautiful elms.

With this last objection the colonel touched a nerve that all other warnings and thunderings had failed to reach. Londoners loved their trees and parks. Roads, railways, buildings—all had to be redesigned to avoid the loss of a tree. Why should the Exhibition building have any special privilege in that respect? It was a question the committee could not answer.

That was a terrible month. A million superficial feet of space had already been booked by British and foreign exhibitors. The opening date was set for May Day next year—less than twelve months away. And now it looked as if the entire project was about to fall in ruins, because the elms could not be spared. Prince Albert, one of the founders and the chief proponent of the entire scheme, was in despair.

*   *   *

The first week in June, John had to go up to North Wales, where the third of the four tubes of the Britannia Bridge over the Menai Strait was now to be lifted into place. The first two had gone up last June, on the down-line side (not without mishap); he had been there then, of course, trying to pretend that his nervousness was all to do with the engineering, nothing to do with finances. Now that the money worries were behind them he was really looking forward to this particular operation, and determined that former mistakes would not be repeated.

The operation was the one they had pioneered on the Conway Bridge, except that the Conway was not an important navigation and so they had been able to take four days over the lifting, building the masonry up in the niches as they went. Here, with a lift over five times as great, and in an important tideway, they had to hoist the great structure within the day.

It was a perfect day for it, sunny and calm with only a light breeze. Nora was now back in England and John wished she might have been there, but the baby's time was too close. Most of the railway world was there, together, it seemed, with the entire population of North Wales and the isle of Anglesey. It was, after all, far and away the biggest engineering undertaking in the whole of human history.

At first light the great tube was floated down the tideway. This phase was also the most hazardous, because of the strong tidal currents in the Strait. There was no hope of rowing or gently drifting or even of towing the floating structure into place. It all had to be done by the gradual tightening of hawsers and pulley-tackle against a tide race of nine knots. Even to the casual onlooker it seemed a wonderful operation; but to those with a knowledge of engineering it was a miracle. Only one or two of the hawsers needed to be tightened or slackened at the wrong rate and the forces would combine to try to bend the tube sideways like a snake.

Small wonder that silence was strictly enforced. Every sound that was voiced had a meaning and resulted in some further action as the inconceivable bulk, stressed by forces unimaginably powerful, inched and nosed its ponderous way into the cavern prepared. Then, when it was fast at that end, all eyes turned to the central pillar, where it was "Haul away!" and "Steady at that" and "Ease a point" and "A mite

more, Billy!" and "Hold! Hold! Hold!" and at the last, the sweet touch
of a post horn as the alignment was made perfect.

At the top of the towers, one at each end, were the two biggest
hydraulic hoists ever made: a water cylinder of twenty inches bore with
a piston and shaft capable of rising vertically through six feet. These
massive hydraulic jacks straddled the tops of the niches up which the
ends of the tube were to travel.

As soon as the great tube was directly beneath the two jacks there
were shouts of "Up" and "Hold" and "Down a touch" and "Up a
touch" and another blast on the post horn as the socket holes at the
bottom of each chain were brought into line with the eyeholes on the
top side of the tube.

When the bolts were all home and tightened, the giant tube and
the long chains became one single continuous mass of metal with the
hydraulic rams a hundred feet above. This was the most nerve-stretching
moment of all. Last year the tube had been lifted through a mere nine
inches when the masonry beneath one of the hydraulic cylinders had
crumbled. The box-tube had then fallen back on its pontoon, buckling
the bottom plates and smashing all the castings; whereupon the cylinder
had come crashing down a hundred feet or more onto the top of the
tube, completing its destruction—a costly and disheartening delay.
Would it be repeated today?

The steam engines above began to thud and clank, turning at a
sedate forty-eight revolutions a minute. They drove the pumps that
supplied water at a pressure of nearly two and a half tons a circular
inch into the hydraulic cylinders. Each stroke of the supplying pumps
lifted the ram only six-hundredths of an inch, so there was no sensation
of jerking as the colossal pistons began to raise themselves and take the
strain. The first evidence of it was an eerie groaning and a series of
cracks, like a repeated whiplash, that filled the air and resounded from
the cliff on the Welsh shore as the four long chains stretched and settled. The hollow mass of the iron tube acted as an enormous sounding
box in which each reverberation took an age to die. A giant was coming alive.

To the watchers on the shore and standing on the top of the
completed line, the tension was as great as that in the chains which
now began to hold the tube. For a while the pontoons continued to
take a part of the load as they rose in the water at just over three
inches a minute. At a signal from Robert Stephenson, the men in the
pontoons began to untie the lashings that secured the tube. Ten minutes
later the first of the pontoons moved on the tide race, free of its burden

but taut on its hawser, swaying this way and that beneath the iron tube; the rest followed in short order. In less than thirty minutes the tube had been raised six feet.

Then the chain was clamped lower down, leaving the ram to fall back to the bottom of its stroke, take a new grip, and raise the whole thing another six feet. And so the lifting went on all through the day, at the rate of thirteen feet an hour. There was no pause for refreshment; men either ate their pies and drank their cordials (no liquor being allowed) as they worked, or like Stephenson and Stevenson, went without. Robert Stephenson directed the entire operation from a point at the centre of the tube. John stayed mainly at the mid-channel end, watching the narrow clearance between the tube and the masonry of the tower, occasionally going to the abutment end to check there, too. It was a strange, uneasy feeling to rise at only three inches a minute. Your eyes told you that you were not moving, but your sense of balance and subtle messages from the soles of your feet and your joints brought a worrying contradiction. All the following day John felt an odd light-headedness—a continuing reaction to that uneasy ride.

The last few stages of the lift brought them close to the tube they had placed last year, on the top of which stood the privileged spectators. Soon they were close enough to talk and exchange congratulations across the gap, and there was a great deal of relieved and good-humoured banter now that it was clear the tube would be placed securely. A lot of it was directed at John, reminding him of the collapse of the masonry last time.

"Put not your trust in stone, sir!" Henry Cole of the Board of Trade shouted down at him. "What? Eh? Put your trust in iron!"

He and the man beside him thought this a huge joke; it obviously referred to something private between them.

"Tell it to Robert Stephenson, too," the man beside Cole shouted.

John was sure he had seen him before—he thought at a Midland Railway meeting. "I feel I know you, sir," he said. "Are you connected with the Midland?"

"Indeed, indeed!" The man beamed.

"Allow me," Cole cut in. "Mr. John Stevenson, Mr. Joseph Paxton, proprietor of the *Daily News*, and this is his editor, Mr. Charles Dickens . . . bless me! Where's the fellow gone?"

"Over there with the artist," Paxton said.

"You're also in charge of the Duke of Devonshire's gardens, are you not, sir?" John asked.

"Indeed, indeed. It must be a proud day for you, Mr. Stevenson."

"Aye!" John laughed. "We may say 'a burden has been lifted'! But, as Mr. Cole knows, I hope for a prouder day ten months from now."

Cole's face fell. "Ah, yes, how true," he said and then, turning to Paxton, he added with unnatural emphasis: "Mr. Stevenson has a very keen bid in on the Exhibition building."

"Oh!" Paxton said; the news obviously had some meaning for him. Had he also an interest in the building? If so, John did not like his being so close with Cole, who was also on the committee.

"How keen, Mr. Cole?" John asked pointedly. "Keen enough, would ye say?"

"Pretty keen, pretty keen," was all he would reply.

Then John had to check some detail of the lifting and when he turned back both Cole and Paxton were walking off quickly toward Dickens. He saw none of them again that day.

The last hour of the lifting took an age, it seemed. John, consumed with worried curiosity over Paxton and Cole, could hardly wait for it to be done. He had to force himself to slow down and check all that had to be checked, with an automaton's thoroughness.

But at last, when the champagne was all consumed and the men all well feasted on the roast sheep that had been prepared against this celebration, John climbed aboard the special for London, taking care to be near Robert Stephenson.

"The fifth, including Conway," Stephenson said. "Didn't it go like clockwork! I wish my father had lived to see it."

They talked about their feat and congratulated each other for many miles before John casually brought up the subject of Cole and Paxton. "Have you co-opted him onto your committee?" he asked.

Stephenson grinned. "Probably shouldn't be telling you," he said. "Paxton's a friend of Cole's, who brought him to us the other day with some mad, monstrous idea of making the Exhibition building entirely of iron and glass—like a giant hothouse. Paxton's gone in with Fox & Henderson to change their tender."

"What do you and Brunel think?" John asked.

"We wouldn't normally look at it—but I must admit it's the only sort of building that would allow us to keep the trees. That would pull the rug out from under the opposition."

"Interesting." John pretended to stifle a yawn. "You know the roof of my ironworks is entirely of wrought iron and glass."

"Really!" Stephenson was suddenly interested. "Your own idea?"

"Based on the roof at Euston. I thought if they took the tiles off and put panes of glass in their place . . . it grew from that."

"Strange. I'd never consider glass a *building* material."

"It's not structural. The wrought iron is the structure."

"That's exactly what Paxton said. He's building a house like it at Chatsworth. Talked a lot of stuff over my head about the 'architecture' of some giant water weed being its inspiration."

*   *   *

The following morning John was standing in a coppice at Chatsworth looking through a telescope at the new iron-and-glass hothouse then being built. That evening in a tour of the local pubs he spotted an ironfounder who had once worked for him—and he fortunately not only recognized the man but remembered his name. An hour later he had all the details he needed.

For the next ten days or so he kept his ear to the ground and heard that Paxton had finished his design and had turned it over to Fox & Henderson to be costed. On the sixth of July a preliminary sketch of Paxton's design appeared in the *Illustrated London News*, together with a list of all the advantages it offered: ease and speed of erection, cheapness, use of standard, interchangeable parts, strength, beauty . . . right up to the preservation of the trees. It was exactly what John had been waiting for.

That evening at home he was in higher spirits than he had been for years. He romped on the lawns with the children until they were almost bilious with the jogging and the laughter. And indoors he tried to waltz with Mademoiselle Nanette in time to a tune Nora was fighting at the piano—accelerating, halting, jerking in a manic ballet to point up her struggles.

"What have you been and gone and done?" Nora asked, wide-eyed, abandoning her battle with Chopin.

"I've put one over foxy Fox & Henderson."

"Oh, yes?" she said guardedly. "It sounds expensive."

"It is." He laughed. "It is—but it will make a second fortune for us."

She smiled. "Tell me from the beginning," she said. "You've been up to something for days."

So he told her everything, from the first exchanges on the bridge at Menai to what he had done that day. "I went to the committee's rooms in Westminster and put in a bid for eighty thousand on the building as shown in the *Illustrated London News*. The 'Glass House' as they call it."

"Is it really so cheap as that?"

"Wait. Listen. I made it a condition that we acquire the materials after the Exhibition closes. One great advantage of this all-iron building is that you can put it up and take it down and put it up again. And that's what we'll do!"

"Where?"

He laughed. "If I told you, you'd go and buy the land ahead of me."

"Don't be silly. I'm about to have a baby. I won't be going anywhere for six weeks."

"I saw just the place to re-erect the Glass House—when we were building the Great Northern. You know the stretch just by Wood Green—quite near the Female Refuge, where we drop Sarah off sometimes? You remember the big hill beside the line. There! On top of that hill. A great, permanent pleasure palace for London—the Colosseum and Wyld's and the Panorama and Cremorne and Vauxhall Gardens and Batty's Hippodrome and Epsom race course all in one: The Wood Green Palace of Glass. What about that!"

"Eay, John!" she said. "I think it's the most exciting idea I've ever heard!"

What else could she say in the face of all that enthusiasm?

"What makes it certain we'll get the contract is my condition about keeping the material after dismantling. No one else will think of that. So no one will get *near* eighty thousand!"

She hid her dismay as best she could, though John's enthusiasm made her want to weep. What on earth could have possessed him? And how could he possibly see himself as a sort of cross between a theatrical impresario, a circus ringmaster, and the proprietor of a pleasure garden! What picture had he come to form of himself that such an enthusiasm could carry him off?

Chapter 51

On the sixteenth of that July, Nora had a small but healthy baby boy, whom they called Mather. On the same day the committee, by word of mouth, conveyed to Fox & Henderson acceptance of their bid of £79,-800, which had been made on condition of their receiving the materials when the building—the "Crystal Palace" as *Punch* had scornfully called it—was dismantled. The news did not come out at once and it was not officially confirmed until ten days later. On the thirtieth Fox & Henderson obtained possession of the site and began their work. They had 274 days until the opening ceremony, and their task was to enclose thirty-three million cubic feet of space in a building of a type that had never before been attempted.

Privately Nora was overjoyed that they had failed. Like John, she was certain that someone on the committee had passed the word to Fox & Henderson. For their bid to come at just two hundred pounds under John's was too narrow a coincidence to afford any different explanation. Nonetheless she thought Fox must be insane. There was no royal charter permitting the building, and its proclamation was unlikely to come until 1851. Before that the committee could issue no contract. So the firm was undertaking at least fifty thousand pounds' worth of expenditure with nothing more than a word and a handshake to go on. She was glad it was their contract, not Stevenson's.

John was at first too shocked and then too deeply hurt to allow it to show in any superficial display of anger. But, as he agreed much later, it knocked the heart out of him. His interest in the business seemed completely lost. He appointed Flynn his general manager and left him the whole running of the firm. He took to walking and reading a great deal. He played with the children, told them stories of his adventures in the contracting business, made toy sailing boats, and once he made a hot-air balloon from tissue paper which soared into the branches of a dead tree, crashed, and set it ablaze. The children loved those weeks and he seemed always happy, too. He sat with Nora a good deal, telling her of the farmers he met on his walks and of their views about the coming harvest.

"We might retire to Ireland," he said. "We could take a hand in the estate there with the Quakers. Very good hunting with the Galway."

Sometimes he went to London to walk about the site of the Crystal Palace, seeming to feel no rancour at what had happened. "They wanted to move a line of young trees last week and couldn't get permission. So they moved them nonetheless and put the carpenters' benches against the former line so that the shavings would cover their traces!" he said once when he came home. He was as wrapped up in the building as if the contract had been his.

Nora could not bear this change in him. Indecision had turned him soft. His aimless days had made him into a shambling, mild-natured child who, at the lift of an eyebrow or any other faint encouragement, would regurgitate the callow nostrums of the yokels whose gates (and whose chewing straws, for all she knew) he shared, as if each rustic word were a distillation of all human wisdom. He was becoming—she could hardly bear to think it—a bore.

Her unease redoubled when he revived, though briefly, his interest in the circus-pleasure garden idea. He came back from London in great excitement. "I've spoken to some of our people and we think we can build an exact replica of the Crystal Palace out at Muswell Hill Park for only a hundred and ten thousand! I think we'll begin ours the day they start to dismantle theirs. Pity there's a Phoenix Park in Dublin. We could call it the Crystal Palace Phoenix otherwise. But it'll still make a fortune."

Nora decided she had to do something, and soon. She had to get him back wholeheartedly into the work of the firm.

One day Flynn came out to Maran Hill. When he was shown briefly in to see her and the baby, she sent John down to the library on some errand and took her chance.

"Flynn," she said, "what work is coming up that two years ago you'd have said only Lord John could manage?"

"Why, ma'am?"

"Don't question. There's no time. I'm worried about him. I want to get him back into—into being himself again, and I need your help."

"There's the Bristol sewerage contract the week after next. Someone must go there and spread the oil of angels around to make sure we get it. I was intending to go."

"I want you to be too ill. Or something. Make it the last minute so there's no time to find another deputy. Make it so he has to go—so it has to be him."

Flynn was singing a lullaby in Irish to baby Mather by the time John came back.

Later that week Sarah came to tell her that Arabella had opened a branch of the Female Rescue Society in Bristol and was planning a Female Refuge there, too. She, Sarah, would soon go to Bristol to assist her.

"She came to our London house last year and is certain she can manage it. Especially if she may rely on my help," Sarah explained.

"How terrible for poor Walter Thornton," Nora said.

Sarah's blushing confusion at the words astounded her. But she went on smoothly: "Surely you know of his—er—predilection? It will be a case of he breaks 'em, she mends 'em!"

At that, Sarah's confusion grew even worse. So Nora changed the subject and spoke instead of their gratitude to Sarah and how they would all—and especially the children, and most especially Winifred—miss her. Mr. Morier Watson, their new tutor, might have a string of M.A.s and Cantabs after his name but he was no substitute for her.

After Sarah had gone, Nora, remembering her deep embarrassment, fell to wondering if John had not, after all, been speaking the simple truth about Sarah and Walter. The more she thought back over the incidents of the past few years, the more likely did it become—and the more awful she felt at the infidelities she had so unjustly held to John's discredit.

She had grown so used to thinking of Sarah as John's occasional mistress, so used to thinking that theirs was an unacknowledged *ménage à trois*, that it took her all the fortnight between then and Sarah's departure for Bristol (accompanied, ironically, by John and Young John) to rehabilitate them both in her mind and to understand that he was hers and hers alone—and always had been so.

PART SIX

1851

PART SIX

Chapter 52

"Thornton! I don't want to worry you but—"

"Stevenson! Ye gods, but how splendid!"

"Spare all that. Leave all your equipment—do as I say now, you and the lad—leave it all and come up here as fast as you may, if you value your lives."

Thornton knew better than to argue. He and the apprentice fairly ran up the slope to where John was standing. "What is it?" he asked.

John pointed sombrely at a crack in the brickwork of the bridge Walter had just been testing. Walter turned pale. "Ye gods!" he whispered. "Right above us."

"Were you testing for deflection?"

"Yes. I can't understand it. We were getting quite normal quantities. What was your side, Whiting?"

"A quarter inch, sir, a bare quarter."

"And I got three-sixteenths—yet there's a great crack like that in it."

"What weight's on top?" John asked.

"Enough to make me shiver." They looked at the two trains, all laden with iron rail, stretching right across the bridge. "It must be a thousand tons. Whiting, take the bosun's chair back aloft and tell them to get those trains off as quick as possible!"

"Wait, wait, wait . . ." John said. "Before we are all too hasty. Let us think now. This bridge, is it one of Brunel's favourites? Cast iron inside, brick out?"

"Yes. He doesn't trust cast iron alone. There's an iron stanchion inside each column of brick."

"What does it bed into?"

"Into the masonry pier."

"But your brick arches don't spring off the masonry. There seem to be two concrete plates at the springing line."

"Four. Two the other side."

John smiled. "Now we're getting there. The stanchion, of course, doesn't rest on the plates?"

"No!" Walter started scornfully but his voice quickly faded to a near-whisper of doubt. "No," he repeated in quite a different tone. "Dear God, no."

"It's easy to misread the drawings."

"But they show quite clearly that the concrete plates are to be trimmed to let the base of the stanchion rest directly on the masonry."

"The old firm of Miss Read and Cocky Up. Why don't you employ a *good* contractor!"

"If the stanchion is bearing down on the corners of the plates, it would lift the brickwork enough to make a crack like that."

"We could put these two arches right for you."

Walter smiled, not accepting the offer. "But all the others were correct. I saw them trim the plates myself." He turned to Whiting. "When was this done? By the way, Mr. Stevenson, this is Mr. John Whiting, one of our engineer apprentices."

"I'm honoured to meet you, Mr. Stevenson."

They shook hands and Whiting checked back through his log. "It was Thursday the eighteenth of July."

"Thursday!" Walter clenched his fist in annoyance. He resigned himself. "Well, at least we know how to take the load off. Whiting: back up in the bosun's chair and tell them to manhandle each train off, two by two, keeping the weight equal about that cracked column."

Whiting ran off but returned a moment later. "Sir, Mr. Stevenson's little boy is fallen asleep in the chair," he said.

"Oh, come on," John said with glee. "We'll serve him a trick."

They went stealthily to the chair and gave the signal rope two well-spaced pulls, meaning haul up. At once the chair began to soar toward the parapet of the bridge. Young John took a second or so to come awake, and then his eyes opened wide in terror as he saw the ground, his father, and the other two men all falling away from him at a dizzying speed. His jaws fell but he did not cry out. At the top he vanished into a forest of knotted, sun-bronzed, tattooed arms as the men hauled him to safety; they cheered him and patted him on the head and shoulders, pleased at his bravery. Then John rang for him to come down again. He was thrilled and laughing as he sped toward the ground, checking at just the right height to leap off onto his father's shoulders. There he took off John's tall hat and waved it in triumph to the navvies above, provoking a rousing cheer in return.

"You see, my boy," John said proudly. "It's courage wins the hearts of men. Never flinch, in pain or danger, and there's nothing you may not venture with men."

"May I draw the crack in the bridge for the *Maran Hill Times*, Papa?" he asked.

They left him sitting on the bank while John and Walter went to look at the other arches.

"They told me at Bath you'd be here today," John said.

"I was expecting Flynn," Walter replied. "Of course, I'm much happier it's you. It'll be better for you to talk direct to Alderman Proctor, rather than through Flynn. You must stay with us. I'll send word now. The boys will be thrilled."

"That's very kind, Thornton. There's three of us actually. I've brought Mrs. Cornelius."

Walter paused and looked at him almost as if he did not believe it. But all he said was, "She's never been to Bristol."

"She wants to talk to Mrs. Thornton about setting up this Bristol branch of the Female Rescue Society."

"Oh, lord!" Walter put a hand dramatically to his brow, the picture of despair. "Mrs. Thornton has written to me about it."

"Written!"

"Yes. It is too indelicate, she maintains, to be a topic of conversation between us. But she feels most strongly and is so *determined*. I have always found her a gentle, obedient, almost complaisant woman. Her insistence—and it is not too strong a word—her insistence is quite astonishing. Ever since little Lionel died."

"It is not ignoble work."

"That makes the decision more, not less, difficult." And when John kept his counsel, Walter added, "Tell me what you think. You'll see her tonight."

"Look, if it's at all difficult putting the three of us up at such short notice, I've taken rooms at the Montague."

"Wouldn't hear of it, old fellow. Say no more. Cancel them. Is that where Mrs. Cornelius is now?"

"No. We came in our own coach all the way from Hertfordshire. Young John says he's tired of going everywhere by train. He said he wanted to go by coach as in the *olden* time! Before the railways kill all the horses. Our dreams are their yawns."

"And their children's nightmares. Is that your coach? I'll wave in case she can see us."

There were no other cracks in the brickwork. John did some rapid calculation before he said, "Give my firm three weeks, and for nine hundred pounds I'll write you a guarantee on that column. I'll guarantee any of the others for five hundred. Each."

Walter looked stunned. "You can't possibly do it for that. It'll cost ten times as much, even reusing the same materials."

"The offer stands."

"Done!" Walter shook his hand hastily, in case he changed his mind. "How can you rebuild in three weeks?"

"Who said rebuild? I'm going to bring a hydraulic injector down here and force in a slurry of roman cement till every brick weeps gray. In my view that should be standard practise with every bridge."

Walter closed his eyes and laughed silently. "I would have thought of that myself, of course. Given time!" Moments later he said, "But then your price is outrageous."

They were back near the bank now where Young John was sketching. John stopped. He took Walter by both shoulders and said to him solemnly: "Take the contract yourself, Thornton. I'll lend you the hydraulics free. And I'll promise you this: Every pound you come out under my estimate I'll match with a pound from my own purse. There! Only remember: *You'll* be writing the guarantee at the end of it."

Walter was almost tempted, but prudence won in the end. "No. We'll each stick to our own trades. I'll just go and pay my respects and extend my invitation to Mrs. Carey."

"Mrs. Who?"

He laughed. "I mean Mrs. Cornelius. Oh—this bridge has upset me." He ran ahead of them to the coach up on the turnpike.

"Why did you make that suggestion to Mr. Thornton, Papa?" Young John asked.

"Because I knew he'd refuse. He's a salaried man, not a free man like me—and like you will be one day. They're a different breed. They don't take risks. All they take is decisions."

"Could I stay here with Mr. Thornton today and come home with him this evening, if we are going to stay with them?"

"We'll ask."

When they reached the coach Walter said he'd be delighted to take care of Young John. He asked to look at the sketch. He passed no comment but went off with the boy's hand in his saying, "Perseverance and dedication are the two keys in life, young fellow. Apply them to any purpose and you cannot fail."

"He's a kindly, good-natured man," John said to Sarah when they were on the move once more.

"He is not being very kindly to poor Arabella at the moment. She is quite desperately determined to begin with the Refuge and he simply will not believe her to be serious."

"Oh, I think he does. He was talking about it only a moment ago."

"What did he say?" Sarah was very eager.

"He asked me to give him my opinion, after seeing Mrs. Thornton."
She was delighted. "So you will be able to tell him to let her."

"I will do no such thing. Never come between man and wife." He was watching Sarah closely. "He's in quite a state about it already in my view. He called you Mrs. Carey!"

She did not even twitch. "Well, Arabella is also in a state. As you will see. She has spent two years collecting money in every conceivable manner. She has the support of her church and of several prominent ladies in St. Paul's parish and the out-parish of St. James's—and you know what high tone their district has. She has done everything a reasonable man could ask of his wife to prove herself in earnest. If he denies her much longer, he will regret it."

"I may make a remark or two in that direction. An unfulfilled wife is—"

"Wife or woman—it has nothing to do with that. It's an unfulfilled person. You'd be the same."

"I know more than a little about lack of fulfilment, Sarah." He was smiling, not to seem to reprimand her.

She sighed and smiled back, reaching across the carriage and patting his arm. "I'm sorry, John. But Walter Thornton's particular brand of arrogance toward Arabella has always made me boil."

"You don't know what part she played in building it."

"Oh!" She parodied a sort of smiling anger at him. "You are so—laisser faire about people."

"Fair, I would prefer."

"I'll give you an example of his arrogance. Despite all she's done to give proof of her seriousness—and she has worked herself to the bone since Corinna was born last year; she's collected nearly two thousand pounds—despite that, he tells her she's just bored with society out there in Kingsdown. He says she just wants to be like Nora. He has an obsession that Nora's way of life is a constant threat to his own domestic comforts."

John was intrigued now, even though he knew that had been Sarah's intention. "What 'way of life'?"

She shook her head, bemused, as if to ask where one could begin. "Well, it's hardly a natural way for a woman to live, is it?"

"It's not unnatural."

"No, no. It's just—Nora. It's unique. Thornton can't begin to comprehend it. Nor, incidentally, can our neighbours at Maran Hill. I've only lately begun to realize it."

"Do go on."

"Well . . ." Now that the topic was no longer so directly concerned with Walter Thornton she relaxed and spoke more calmly. "I came to share your home in such a strange way that I, as it were, grew into the situation, accepting it as normal. And I love Nora now dearer than if she were a sister. But your neighbours *loathe* her—because, of course, they cannot understand her."

"What can they not understand? They've cut her ever since we came there. Except when hunting. They don't mind our four hundred a year subscription, so they'll tolerate her there—just."

"They don't, you know, John. They cut her even there. I used to think she was a saint of forgiveness, or very brave. But actually she just doesn't notice—or is even rather pleased. When she goes hunting, she is interested in only one thing: the sport. The rest of the field might just as well not exist. Of course, it infuriates *them*."

John started to laugh. "I can imagine."

"And it infuriates them even more when they fail to call on her and fail to invite her—and she doesn't notice that either. It's so hard to snub someone who ignores you. Hetty Beador once told me that to watch Nora at a social gathering was a real study. She says nothing, listens to four conversations at once, watches everybody in turn with those sharp eyes of hers—until they feel *ghastly*. And that's it. Thank you for a splendid evening. I don't think it has ever once occurred to Nora that there is a whole way of life, called Society, which is going on around her all the time."

"It would bore her stiff."

"Oh, John!" Sarah laughed. "I think you're as bad as she is. It bores *everyone* stiff. That isn't the point."

"What is the point? I've lost it."

"We've strayed rather. The original point is that Arabella, after ten years of childbearing and Bristol society, wants to do *more*. She wants to stop being bored."

"She wants to be like Nora. So Thornton's right."

Sarah was patiently exasperated. "Not like Nora. Nothing to do with business or money or anything. It's still woman's work. You could say it's the supreme work for a woman—to rescue one's fallen sisters. It's hardly fit work for a man."

John made a noncommittal noise.

"And don't be deceived by her hospitality when we get there. I promise you, John, she is in a very wrought state."

He nodded and looked steadily out of the window.

"When she does begin," Sarah added, "I would take a few thousand of my capital to help start the Refuge with your agreement, of course."

Still looking out of the window, he said, "All this—regardless of Thornton's desires?"

She was silent, forcing him to turn from the window. And when his eyes dwelled in hers, and hers in his, she said, "I'm more interested in Arabella's needs, and my own, than any desires Mr. Thornton may have."

"I am glad," he said, smiling until he made her smile too.

Chapter 53

Arabella asked Young John if he had a special prayer he would like to say. He, in his husky treble, mangling the metre, said: " 'Lord preserve us through this night Keep our souls unsullied white Keep us from the sinful mire Take us safely through the fire To Thy cold eternal light Amen.' "

She said it was beautiful and they must all be sure to learn it by tomorrow. "Now our last prayer," she said. The bowed heads bowed lower still. "Make us ever-mindful, Lord, that ere long our souls must stand in awful judgement. And as when this darkness is o'er Thou wilt unfailingly restore to us the light of day, renew then also Thine abiding grace, for without it we must shrink in dread of Thy wrath and certain fear of eternal damnation. Amen."

Young John kissed his father good night and scampered off with Nicholas to their bed, along the corridor.

"I believe the last thought of the night should always be a solemn one," Arabella said to John. "Will you come and tuck him in?"

"I think I'll go straight below," John said.

"Mama," Nicholas asked, when she had tucked them in, "why do we pray for God not to withhold His grace?"

"Nicholas! You know very well. It's as the prayer says—so that we shall not be eternally damned."

"But if God did withhold His grace and then later damned us, that would be very cruel."

"God is never cruel, dear, only *seemingly* so. Remember Job."

"But if we withheld the servants' wages until they were driven to steal from us, and then we gave them over to the police . . ."

Arabella laughed. "Bless you, child, it's not the same thing at all. Servants are bound to masters by law, but we are bound to God by love—as well as by His law. That is the great thing about our religion. You could spend all your life breaking the Ten Commandments and at judgement day your fate would still be in doubt, because of God's love. If there were only the law, you would know at once that you were damned. But because God is Love, too, you may turn from your wickedness, even after a whole lifetime of sin, and *not* be damned."

Nicholas nodded, disappointed. Young John watched the exchange wide-eyed.

"Are all Jews damned, Mama?" Nicholas asked.

Arabella realized she had to tread very carefully here. The vicar had preached a most uncharitable sermon last Sunday on the mission to convert the Jews. She had agreed with very little of it. To her mind (though, of course, she would never say it aloud) the Jews had a perfect right to worship God—the same God, after all—in their own way. But she must not contradict the vicar to Nicholas.

"Only God can answer that, child," she said. "It certainly seems wicked to know about Jesus and not to believe in him. As the vicar said, they have not the same excuse as poor ignorant heathens. We must hope God's love really is infinite, or they will live in everlasting torment."

When she had drawn the curtains it seemed momentarily dark; but soon the twilight crept back.

"You do ask her questions," Young John said after she had gone.

"You can always make her talk if it's about salvation."

"What are Jews? I thought they were only in olden days. I thought they were extinct."

"Arnold Jacobs is a Jew and I shall tell him he's going to rot in everlasting torment. Listen, d'you know what spunk is?"

"No."

"Well, it's time you did. It's what the mammy gives to the daddy to make the babby grow."

"What does that mean?"

"Johnny Potter, the stable lad at the Montague, told me that."

"Did he tell you what it means?"

"He showed me how to get spunk. I've nearly got some. Shall I show you? It's ever so ticklish."

"No, thank you."

"I'll give you one of those black liquorice straps if you let me."

"All right."

But it tickled too much and they had to stop.

*   *   *

Even without Sarah's warning John could hardly have failed to notice the tension in Arabella.

"Well?" Walter asked when they were on their way to the Philosophical Institute in Park Street, where they were to meet Alderman Proctor.

"One can hear the fuze burning," John said.

"Oh dear. The complications!"

"I would have thought you'd be proud."

"There's no use beating around the bush, Stevenson. I've never flaunted my private life in front of you. But I've never made a great secret of it either. I do, from time to time—as most men, I suppose, do —a great many anyway—"

John laughed, a kindly laugh. "I have observed."

"Then I'll tell you: I shall not be coming directly home tonight after this meeting."

"Don't let me hinder you. But what shall you do about Mrs. Thornton?"

"Every time I think of her and that damned Refuge—full of the scrapings off my plate!"

John suppressed a chuckle.

"You can laugh," Walter said. "My real point, my real objection, is not selfish. I think these religious people, and I include Mrs. Cornelius and all the Female Rescue Society people, these religious have got the whole thing arsy-versy. I blame the vicar as much as anyone. He has a sheep's head—all jaw. He understands nothing."

"That may well be. What point do you think they miss?"

"Well, they do call it 'the oldest profession,' don't they. It certainly exists in every civilization. And I say that the established order always has a function. Nothing survives as long as that without a profound purpose."

"I wonder what it is?"

"I only know it's folly to meddle with the established order. If I and thousands of men like me have the need and the money, and all these girls are surplus, there's a pattern there, plain enough for all to see. And a pattern means a design. And a design shows a purpose."

"Ah."

The cab reached the foot of Montague Hill and turned right toward Maudlin Lane and the centre of Bristol. The smell from the open sewer was very strong at that corner.

"I believe it's a way of distributing wealth, d'ye see. And a lot better than income tax in that it goes straight from rich to poor. Think how much money—*hard* cash, heh heh!—must pass each year. It must be hundreds of thousands of pounds."

"Hah!" John gave a single scornful laugh. "I'll never offer you the job of quantity estimator."

"Why? It must be at least that."

"Heavens, man! The number of girls alone must be in the hundreds of thousands. D'you think they earn but a pound a year each? The actual sum that passes must be at least ten million pounds."

"Ye gods!" Walter's voice was faint.

"I'll tell you your real problem, Thornton. It could also be your best hope: What are Mrs. Thornton and Mrs. Cornelius going to do when they find that virtually all of those hundred thousand girls rescue themselves—and very nicely too. These Female Rescue people, led by Lady Bear, who is a blind and self-opinionated virago, have the delusion that the harlot's progress is as Hogarth drew it. Now neither your wife nor Mrs. Cornelius is blind. Before very long they are going to twig that the only prostitute that really needs rescue is a battered, blowsy, verminous, alcoholic wreck who couldn't even roll a drunken sailor after six months at sea."

"Eh? How will that help me?"

"If I were you, Thornton, I'd encourage them all you can. Help them set up the Refuge. Help them find the girls. Pick them yourself." Walter gasped. "Indeed," John insisted. "Grasp the nettle, man! Pick the proud and pretty ones. The *bright* ones. The ones you know are only in it for the quick money—who are going to come out of it with enough to buy a small shop and a husband. I guarantee, within a fortnight such girls will tire of soap and sermons and hair shifts and being made to feel like vermin. And they'll go back to the streets, which offer them the only real hope they have in life."

"And then?"

"You just continue—fresh crop after fresh crop, all the same kind of girl. It's bound to discourage the rescuers before long. Kill it with your own enthusiasm. That's what I'd do."

"By jove, Stevenson! I believe you've hit it!" He began to giggle excitedly.

"Only one thing," John added.

"What's that?"

"Make sure the house they pick as their Refuge will convert easily into a suitable residence for a rich young widow!"

Walter's laughter shook the cab. They had reached Griffin Lane, where the driver would normally have turned right to go up to Park Street. But Walter leaned out and told him to make a detour via St. Augustine's Place. "I'll make my arrangements for later," he told John.

"Aren't you afraid of being clapped?" John asked. "A terrible thing to take home."

"I go for the youngsters," Walter said. "They're generally free of it. I look for the new ones."

They were soon at St. Augustine's, where Walter made the cab pull up. "There's two," he said eagerly, and, throwing down the window, called. "Hey, sweetmeats!"

John could not believe it; the two girls who came over, dressed in trumpery cast-offs that hung about them, were hardly yet pubescent. "Hello, Charley!" the taller one said with a cheeky little grin. "Are you kind?" She had a bright eye and a strong, pleasant face.

"What are your names, my dears?" Walter asked.

"Becky, sir. And yur's Annie."

"And how old are you, Becky?" Walter was like a kindly uncle.

"Thirteen, sir. And Annie's twelve." Her Bristol accent made her sound a little adenoidal.

"Are you sisters?"

"Yes, sir."

"Does your mother know you're out, Annie?"

Annie, who had not once looked at Walter—indeed, did not once take her eyes off her sister's face—made a snotty, giggly, gurgling sound. Her mouth never closed and her lips never ceased to smile.

"She ain't got no speech, sir. She'm simple," Becky said with a grin.

Walter suddenly leaped from the cab and began running his hands over simple little Annie. "But well made!" he said admiringly. "By harry! A simple little Venus!" He might have forgotten John's presence.

"She do please. All they men do say it," Becky confirmed.

"What about under? Lift your skirts, Annie." He bent down to her and spoke in gentle encouragement. "Skirts. Lift. Goo' gel! Got any hair yet?"

John watched spellbound as Walter, stooping as farmers stoop to feel cows' udders in the auction ring, reached his hand under her lifted skirt. All the while her simple, giggling eyes never left her sister's face, and the simple drooling gurgle poured happily from her lips.

"She ain't got none. An' 'tis a tanner for a feel. I got more'n what she 'ave," Becky was saying.

"My word!" Walter said admiringly. "She's as big as Marble Arch though."

John leaned out of the carriage then. "Just going to stroll around to the quay, Thornton," he said. "Pick me up on Under the Bank."

Walter, not even turning, held up a hand in acknowledgement. "Shan't be a minute. Only making the arrangement now," he said.

The last words he heard from Thornton, as he turned the corner, were to the effect that Becky had "a sweet little mossy bank."

He breathed with relief as he came out of the Place; what an astonishing thing was Thornton's obsession. He did not believe all he had told Walter in the cab on their way down. He had much more faith in Arabella's robustness of spirit and persistence; and he wanted to see what she would make of this chance.

Right at the corner a girl stepped out fearlessly into the full glare of the gas lamp—and he felt his heart quite literally turn over in his chest.

Alice!

It was Alice beyond any doubt. Alice to a T. The same Alice whom he had married over the anvil when he was a navvy. Alice with whom he had shared one delirious year out at Irlam's-o-th'Ights, on the Eccles road out of Manchester. Sixteen—seventeen years ago?

"Are ye kind, Charley?" she asked. Very West Country accent.

But Alice would have been—thirty-eight; and this girl, *this* Alice looked barely eighteen.

"What's your name?" he asked.

"Charity," she said.

"Your full name?"

"Dunno. C'mon then. Fire be warm an' do need a poke!"

It was Alice's voice, too—except for the West Country accent, that almost American burring of the *r*'s. Warrrm, she said. It made his scalp tingle.

"Listen!" he said, turning her back into the light so that he could see her face again and drink it in. "I don't want—what you're offering. But I'll give you a guinea. Look"—he fished it from his change purse—"a golden guinea. I'll give that to you if you'll just answer me some questions. Right?"

The girl nodded, made solemn at the thought of so much for so little.

"Why do you not know your name?"

"I only do know what they did give I when I was a orpheling."

"Where?"

"Orpheling Girls' Asylum, Ashley Hill. But they give I that name in the other place, in the work'ouse."

"Where was that?"

"Egghouse, they did say."

"Egghouse? Could it be Eccles?"

"I s'pose so. Eccles? Could be. I was there wi' my mam."

"What was her name?"

"I think 'twas Alice?"

Something in the girl's face—a hint of cunning—made him doubt this. Had he said the name aloud when the girl had first startled him? He was sure he hadn't; at least, he had been sure until this moment. Now he would never know. He cursed himself. He ought to have gone away and worked out his questions very carefully.

Too late now.

"I aren't sure, mind," the girl said.

"What name did they give you at—Eccles?" he asked.

"Charity Bedfordshire!" The girl smirked. "Next girl was Diligence Berkshire, an' the next was Earliness Buckinamshire." She giggled and then laughed, Alice's laugh, a warm, rich, infectious invitation. A peal of bells.

He was lost. What could he do? He could not leave her here. If she really was Alice's child, she was his child, too. It was ridiculous—preposterous to think it. But it was just possible. *Possible*, he kept telling himself. Yet where could he take her? Not home. A pretty, vulgar little whore off a Bristol quayside? How to explain that! Even if he told Nora everything and she accepted it, the child would be a constant sore between them.

No, no. It was unthinkable. Leave her! It was trouble.

No. He had to find out more about her. "Listen, Charity," he said. "I believe I knew your mother. At least you are the very living image of someone I—once knew. Now, I can leave you here, if you wish it. I do not want to harm you or disturb your—way of life if it contents you." Her lip curled in scorn; or it could be cynical disbelief. "I do not want anything of you, not the favours you are selling. But if you want it—*if* you want it—I can help you. So tell me honestly—and as God is watching you, I want the truth—do you enjoy this work? Do you do it for choice?"

She spat on the cobbles; an answer and yet not an answer. He tried another approach.

"How often do you go with men? Every day?"

"Dunno. When I do lack money, I s'pose."

"And if you could get money any time you wanted without having to go with a man, would you stop going with men?"

"Dunno. S'pose I might."

Her willingness was beginning to fade. The smile was going. He played idly with the guinea, where she could see it. "What goes on—what d'you think about when you are with men?" he asked.

"Dunno. Dresses mostly, I s'pose. An' dancin'."

"Have you a family? Are you married or living with anyone?"

"Dunno."

"I see." He sighed. "You make it very difficult to know whether to help you or not, Charity. Whether you want it."

She smiled, knocking him sideways again. "I'll be thy missy," she said sweetly, making it seem the most natural offer in the world. "Put I in a nice li'l house, out Clifton Hill"—she began to toy with his waistcoat buttons—"wi' a maid, an' a guv'ness cart, an' give I pretty dresses . . ." That smile again!

"Is that all you want?" he asked. "Nothing more in life than that?"

"Dunno. I ain't thought 'bout it, really."

"Suppose," John suggested with a sinking heart, unable to hit upon anything better, "suppose I did all that for you, not here but in London. Suppose I came and saw you once or twice a week—not to lie down with you but just to talk, and read books, and—I don't know—dance . . . whatever you want. Would you prefer that to this?"

" 'Course I would!" she said, finding affirmation at last. "If you was generous." She kissed him quickly on the lips, a flesh-and-blood ghost of a kiss that floored him entirely.

"Well, listen," he said when he had rallied. "I'm stopping here in Bristol with a man called Mr. Thornton, who at this minute is going mad in a cab on Under the Bank, round the corner here, thinking I've vanished. You'll come back with me now and stop the night at his place. I'll take you to London tomorrow. All right?"

"Me guinea?" she said.

He gave it to her.

"An' you must buy I off of Billy." She held up a hand in the gaslight.

Someone came running over the street.

"Don' give he more'n ten pound. Tha's all he bought I for, an' he've 'ad good value since."

The running figure turned into a squat, powerful man, something the cut of a sailor. He had a badly healed scar down his right cheek.

" 'Tisn't trouble, Billy," she said quickly. "He do want to buy I."

Billy smiled. "What for, matey? Pretty un, isn't she?" He winked. "For a French house, is it? What's the offer? I'm reasonable."

"Something of that sort," John said, also smiling.

Unseen by the man, he was reaching his arm around in the shadows, feeling for something heavy that had made the man run lopsidedly, clutching his pocket. He found it. Quicker than thought he gripped it and tweaked it up and out.

A poker. A heavy, stout fire poker, of slightly wrought drawn-iron bar.

The man backed away, still smiling. "Don't be daft, matey," he warned softly. "You'd never get off the quay alive."

But John was not grasping the poker in a menacing attitude. Instead he held it level in front of him, one huge gloved fist around each end. He prayed it had not been too work-hardened. His arms began to tremble. His breath grew strained. Nothing happened.

The man, who had put his fingers to his tongue to make a whistle, now lowered them again and began to laugh. "Oh no, matey!" he said. "Never in a month!"

John's whole body shook. His neck bulged in his collar. His eyes seemed to be extruding from his head. The man was right. The pain from his tortured hands was intense.

Then suddenly the bar gave. It bent a whole ten degrees at once. Quickly, before it could cool and harden, John redoubled his grip and bent it further. Now it went smoothly and easily round. His hands did not even tremble. He brought the two ends into contact. "Enough, Billy?" he asked.

"No, no." Billy said. He'd forgotten Charity completely and was fascinated at this exhibition of strength. "See if you can go right round."

John laughed. To complete the circle was even easier. He handed back the poker, now much shorter and with an *o* in its middle. At the same time he pulled out his wallet and from it drew a ten-pound note. "I wouldn't cheat you, Billy," he said. "But I didn't want any misunderstanding. She's mine now, right?"

"*Too* right!" Billy said. He looked again at the poker. "Gawd help us!"

Charity took his arm and walked proudly round onto the quay. "Here!" she said. "You be some proper man, be'nt ye!"

What have I done? John thought.

The cab was at the far end of Under the Bank, with Walter standing beside it, searching.

"Thornton!" John waved.

Walter climbed back at once and the cab came rattling down the quay toward them.

"Oh, I see!" Walter said when he saw Charity. "I forgive you utterly."

"This is Mr. Walter Thornton," John said. "Miss Charity Bedfordshire. I think I have Mrs. Thornton's first charge."

Walter's face fell at that. "You can't be serious!"

"Serious enough to hand over a tenner to her bully boy. Come on! Strike while the iron's hot!"

"Not in my house!" He was both frightened and angry. "They must buy their Refuge first."

John laughed. "I'm joking, old fellow. I'll take her to the London Refuge tomorrow. Mrs. Cornelius can come, too."

"Oh, that'll be good!" Walter said, unthinkingly relieved.

"So she may stay the night?" It was all John had really wanted to wring out of him.

"Yes, yes, yes," Walter said.

Charity waited outside while Walter took John into the Philosophical Institute to introduce him to Alderman Proctor. They were gone about half an hour. She got down from the cab briefly to look in the workshop window of James Gordon, who carved, among other things, anatomical models in ivory. There was one there in which you could take out muscles and blood vessels and nerves. It made her shiver. "I do know just how you do feel, matey," she joked to it before she returned to the cab.

This meeting with Proctor was in the nature of a preliminary skirmish. Clark's report to the Board of Health had only just been published, and the deplorable state of Bristol's sewers, though for long known to the noses (and the undertakers) of the city, had only now achieved official recognition. It would be some years yet before the first sod of the first new drain was dug; but that was none too soon for the possible main parties to the transaction to get to know one another. That afternoon John had taken the precaution of driving out to the alderman's house between Clifton Down and the Whiteladies nursery garden, so he was able to compliment him on a fine residence with a splendid view.

"But a very muddy drive, if I may say so," he added.

"The bane of my life," the alderman agreed.

"Why not talk to whoever does this sewerage scheme of yours and see if he can't lay you some gravel or hardcore out there while he's working in the city?"

"D'you think he would?" It sounded so innocent.

"I'm sure of it. You'd do him a favour, in fact. In my experience, one always ends up with too much *spoil*. One is always rather glad to have someone willing to relieve one of a bit. As I say, you do him a favour."

So now both men knew where they stood. That was what the whole visit to Bristol had been about. The rest of their half-hour meeting was padding.

Back in the cab Walter seemed a bit glum. "I suppose it's necessary," he sighed. "The world couldn't keep turning without it. But it does leave a nasty taste around. Public life should have its standards."

"Sewers do worse than leave a nasty taste. I tell you, Thornton: If we get this sewerage contract in the end, there's fifty pounds waiting for you by way of a thank you for the introducing."

"Oh, I couldn't think of taking it. I couldn't."

John nudged Charity. "Why not? Why ever not? What's young Becky and Annie going to cost you now?"

"A few bob. I'll give more if they're kind."

"See? Tonight's work would pay for several hundred such romps."

"You don't understand. It's a question of standards, old fellow."

Beckie and Annie were waiting in the church porch and took him at once to the little garret their mother rented for their trade.

John chuckled and Charity joined in.

"I do know he," she said.

His spirits fell. To be sure, it was only to be expected, Bristol being as small as it was and Walter's Irish toothache being so great.

"Do you recognize him? You gave no sign."

She looked pityingly at him, as well as he could tell by the flickering carriage lamp.

"I recognized his voice. He'm one o' they men do talk an' talk."

"What about?"

"Dunno. About everythin'. An' he do fuck funny, too. He do—"

"I don't really want to hear of it." John smiled. "I want to tell you about tonight."

She wriggled excitedly.

"Mrs. Thornton, Mr. Thornton's wife, is intending to open a Refuge for the rescue of fallen women—"

"Yur!" she interrupted. "I be'nt goin' into no place like that."

"Of course not."

"I done fourteen years in the orpheling. I be'nt goin' back."

"There's no question of it, I promise. It's just a story we'll pretend so you can have a room there tonight. I'll tell her—*we'll* tell her—that you are a penitent woman and I'm going to take you to the Refuge in London. All Mrs. Thornton will want to do is to talk with you tomorrow for a little while. She's never talked to a gay woman—and she *ought* to. She ought to know how she may help."

"Help!" Charity said witheringly.

"Well, there are people she could help. You know there are. Poxed old meat-flashers hawking peppered and pickled carrion in doorways at fourpence upright . . ."

"Oh, *they!*"

"Yes, they. They are the ones who really need help. Mrs. Thornton and all these other goodhearted ladies think their task is to take pretty young girls like you off the streets—"

"An' put us back in factories an' the scullery!" She opened out her purse and tipped out a handful of coin. "Seven pound," she said. "That's what I earned today. And that's what I earned in a *year* when I was scullery maid."

"Very good. You tell exactly that to Mrs. Thornton. Show her why she would be wasting her time trying to rescue many girls like you. Then tell her about those others—the fourpenny uprights." She pulled a face. "You do that," he said. "Pretend you are different. Pretend you are willing to try to be rescued and that's why you have agreed to come to the London Refuge with me—but tell her what I've told you. If you do that, you'll soon find yourself in your own pretty little London house and only me to call on you and be nice to."

She stood up suddenly and threw herself onto his lap, putting an arm around his neck and kissing him—only stopping when she found her own cool, observant eyes staring into a pair equally cool and observant. She escaped from them by leaning on his shoulder. "Tell I about that there house," she begged.

And, playing her game for the moment, he told her.

Even as he spoke, he knew how impossible it was. This entire episode was a momentary act of folly that could never be sustained. In the morning he would bring her back to the quayside, give her some money, and turn her back to her way of life. Even if she was his daughter (and the chances against it were pretty astronomical), she was too set in her way, and he too set in his, for there to be any meeting ground between them. In fact, why not release her now? Back onto her pitch. Say it had all been a joke.

Just a minute more, he told himself, holding her to him and enjoying the feeling that she might be his and Alice's own flesh. *Then I'll do the sensible thing.*

But before the minute was out Walter sprang zestfully into the cab and told the driver to head for home. John nudged Charity secretly. "Wake up!" he said aloud, and then, to Thornton: "Poor child—exhausted."

He was pleased at the speed she showed in responding to his stratagem, and at the conviction she put into yawning and resettling herself back in her own corner. She was a grand little actress.

"Oh!" Walter said, in happy recollection. "Tiny lips, tiny teeth, and tiny little fingers."

"Good, was it?"

"Good! That simple one was like a dip into whipped cream!"

When they were back in Montague Parade, Walter took off his cloak and gave it to Charity. "Cover up that gaudy dress," he said.

He was gone rather a long time, explaining it to Arabella, and no doubt to Sarah, too. John meanwhile complimented Charity on her nimbleness of mind and on her acting. She handed him the purseful of coin she had earned. " 'Tis yourn now," she said. "You bought I off of Billy." And he, thinking it would be better for her to be without cash that night, took it, knowing he could return it when he took her back to the town centre tomorrow.

When Walter opened the door and came out into the porch, John helped Charity down and paid off the cab. He watched her closely as she went up the garden path and saw her acquire a penitent stoop. It was an amazing transformation; she seemed actually to shrivel within herself.

Arabella was fearful and a little effusive in her welcome; but she took heart when she saw what a pathetic figure of penitence Charity offered. "My dear child," she said. "You will come to look back on this as the greatest and most wonderful day in your entire life."

"Yes'm."

"This is the day—come into the light. Let's get a good look at you. Take that cloak off." John shut the door and watched. "Good gracious! You're painted up like a ship's figurehead!"

"Yes'm," Charity repeated. There were tears in her voice; she was very good.

"This is the day on which you return once more into that great, warm family of God's love. Do you love God, Charity?"

This time the girl actually did burst into tears. They almost convinced John; they certainly convinced everyone else—even Sarah, up on the landing to prevent any of the servants, or the children if they should awaken, from laying eyes on this sullied creature.

Arabella, now made even bolder, came forward to grasp Charity by the shoulders. "Your name means 'love'—did you know that? Caritas is Charity and is love and caring. And He loves and cares for you, my dear. His love is all around us now, and always has been. All the time you spurned Him—all the days you have spent so deep in sin—His love was there, warm and caring, trying to reach you. Think of it, child!" Arabella was radiant in her own joy. It made John's scalp tingle just to watch her happiness and to hear that firm, powerful contralto ring out such tidings over that little gathering. "Think! Every minute of every hour of every day of your wretched life, He has been stretching out His arms toward you, hoping you will feel His touch. And tonight, tonight! At last He has reached you!"

She clasped the girl to her. Charity collapsed to her knees, howling. "Oh ma'am, oh ma'am!" John realized then that this was no longer a charade; the girl had become possessed by her own acting. Arabella had said something—or some power had flashed unseen from woman to girl—that had transformed her entirely.

For Arabella it was a dream realized. Firm and benign, oblivious to all around except the weeping girl, she said, "Come, child. Let us go upstairs now and take that vile grime off your face and pray together." She lifted Charity up. "Then you may have a good sleep—a godly sleep. And face a bright new dawn tomorrow." She helped her to the stair. "Bear up. You are walking with God now. He is at your right, the strength in my arm. But He is at your left as well. And He goes before you to vanquish the sinner who lies in wait. And He follows behind lest you falter and turn back."

They passed out of sight at the stairhead.

For a moment neither Walter nor John breathed. It was Walter who spoke first. "I cannot believe it," he whispered.

John was inwardly exultant. For ten years and more, since the first day he had met Arabella, he had been convinced there was a power and a fervour in her that would one day sweep her off her feet. But whenever he said so people merely laughed—even Arabella. And now her time had come.

But he gave no hint of his own sense of triumph to Walter. Instead he asked where Charity was to sleep that night.

"There's a box room at the back of the first floor," Walter answered tonelessly. "She's to sleep there, where she cannot pollute the servants. They've set Bickerstaff to cleaning it out."

Bickerstaff was the Thorntons' only manservant.

"Oh, Stevenson," Walter sighed. "What mischief have we set afoot?"

*   *   *

In the small hours of the following morning the sudden crash of a door rang through the silent house, startling everyone awake. Then came Arabella's triumphant: "I thought so! Vile monster of depravity! Beast of beastliness! . . ." and a great deal more in that vein.

John, coming out in his dressing gown, holding a candle shielded before him, was startled to find Young John on the stair, looking as newly wakened and as curious as himself. "Go back," he ordered. "No child is to come down here." Sarah came from her room to join him. And together they walked quickly along the passage to the box room where Charity had been put and where all the noise was coming from. Though neither said it, both were thinking *Surely Thornton can't be such a bloody fool!*

But the man's voice, feebly protesting, was not Walter's; in fact, Walter himself, even more tired than they, joined them as they reached the bend at the end of the passage.

"Bickerstaff," Arabella was saying, "you will leave this night. The minute you are dressed."

"Arabella!" Walter called.

She did not turn. "You will call back tomorrow at noon and collect your things and wages."

All the while Charity was snivelling. "He made I. He made I."

"And don't think you'll be getting a character."

Bickerstaff, being naked, could not get up from the little truckle bed he and the girl were in. " 'Tisn't right!" he said. "What be one slice more off of a cut cake? That's what she'm for. Girl o' that sort."

"I will deal with this now, Mrs. Thornton," Walter said, marching to her side and trying to take her candle from her.

But she would not let go. "Thank you, Mr. Thornton dear. It is already dealt with. Bickerstaff—did you hear me! Out, I say!"

" 'Tis the way o' the world, m'm," Bickerstaff said, trying to appear placatory. "You be flyin' in the face o' nature."

"Out!" Arabella said.

"You ask Mr. Thornton, m'm," he advised.

"Bickerstaff!" Walter cried in anger and alarm. "Get out!"

"I ain't got no clothes on," he mumbled.

"Oh, for goodness' sake!" Arabella shrilled, as if he were inventing trivia. "Go round behind me." She stood with her face to the window, then, seeing Sarah, added: "You, Sarah dear, can go up to the next landing and stop any of the servants and children from coming down."

Still Charity whined on: "He said as he'd tell ye lies about I. He said as he'd tell ye as I come to *he* and forced he to come to I. I didn't want no fuss, missiz."

"You see," Walter began, talking to Arabella's back, then, noticing Bickerstaff standing, clutching his discarded nightshirt to him, said instead, "Go by, man! Go by! . . . You see, my dear?"

"Has he gone?" Arabella turned back to Charity without waiting for Walter's answer.

"I didn't want to be no trouble to ye, ma'am, not when you'd been so kind."

"Trouble!" Arabella gave a despairing laugh.

"You see!" Walter said. "They are beyond salvation."

"Trouble? Is that all you thought of, child? Don't be blasphemous, Walter dear. No one is beyond salvation. 'The long suffering of our Lord *is* salvation'—second epistle of Peter! Child, do you have no inkling? Don't you understand!"

Charity snuffled. "What, ma'am?"

"Damnation, child! Eternal torment! The fires of hell!"

"I were damned at birth, ma'am."

"Stand up!" Arabella said angrily. "Such nonsense!"

"I'll see Bickerstaff doesn't steal anything on his way out," Walter said.

"I be naked, ma'am," Charity said. Then she burst into tears again. "Oh ma'am, I be so *shamed.*"

"Stand up, I said."

There was no resisting that command. Mindless of John, whom both women had by now forgotten, she stood. The sheet fell from her uncertain grasp. John wanted to turn away but could not. It was a beautiful, lissome young body; she even had the same slightly parrot-beaked nipples as Alice.

Arabella went and stood close to her. The child looked transfixed into her eyes, seeing no rejection or condemnation there, only a tender, angry love. "This flesh," Arabella said, touching it gently, "this . . . soft . . . yielding flesh, which feels so warm and comforting to you. This"—suddenly she slapped the girl's body fiercely, on her side.

Charity, though stung, now stood before her, petrified.

"This," Arabella went on in that same low, compelling tone, "is the source of all your sin."

"Yes, ma'am."

"And it is through this flesh that you must learn of the torment that never ceases. Oh, child! If, now that you have found God's love again—if, now that He holds His arms out to you—if you now turn your back on all that great, that abiding, that infinite mercy, then you shall find no hiding place. Not on the highest mountain nor in the deepest deep of the ocean shall you flee His terrible wrath. How can I bring you to see it? Have you any idea of the torments of hell?"

"No, ma'am. I mean, yes, ma'am. Please, ma'am, I be cold." She shivered.

"Cold!" Arabella snorted, barely taking in what the girl had said. "It is not cold there! I will show you. You shall be made to see it. Take up that sheet now and wrap it about you."

Mutely, still shivering, the girl obeyed.

John knew that Arabella was insane—or, at least, possessed beyond the recalling power of reason—when he saw the fixed, intense stare in her eyes as she and the girl swept past him, oblivious of his presence.

At some little distance he followed them downstairs to the basement. They were in the kitchen. Arabella was thrusting a hot poker into the fire, which had been made up to stay overnight. He stood in the passageway and watched.

"I shall show you," Arabella was saying, "what the torments of hell will be like. You have sunk so deep in wickedness—and all about you are sunk so deep, as well—that you have lost all sense of it. You set it all at nothing. You think a minute's carnal pleasure is something very light and small, no doubt. Do you not realize, child"—she pulled the poker out, looked at it, and thrust it back—"even to *think* of doing what you have done tonight, even to imagine it, is a mortal sin. Even to let your mind dwell on it for the smallest part of one fraction of a second is to risk eternal damnation. Eternal agony. The fires of hell for all eternity. A torment stretching into the endings of time, and beyond, and then again for an infinity of times."

Charity stood, quaking.

"We are now engaged in a fight for your soul, my dear. You understand?"

"Yes, ma'am," she said blankly.

"We are trying to save it from that everlasting damnation. And it's a battle we are going to *win*. Because we have the greatest army in the world, in the whole tide of time, fighting beside us. The whole vast company of the righteous. All calling now to your soul. Charity! Oh, do you not hear them! And there at their head—see! That peerless Prince, that most perfect Man. *Your* Saviour! The Christ who died for *you*. Oh child, on your knees! If you have any prayer within you—one word even, one cry of repentance—offer it now. Quick. Now! While that mighty host is turned to you. Just one word. The whole company of heaven is turned to hear. Now!"

Charity had fallen to her knees and the sheet had slipped from her. She stood, kneeling and naked before Arabella, a gold halo from the now fiercely drawn fire down her breast and hip. "Oh, Father . . ." she began, tentatively. Tears welled up and consumed her. "No one ain't cared for I afore!" She wept.

"There is One! There is One!" Arabella intoned. "And only One. No other hope. No other refuge. No other rock. So go on, child. Offer yourself now. Dedicate yourself anew to Him. Shall He who raised the harlot Magdalene to the innermost circle of God's cherishing, shall He scorn you now! Now, when you and He have drawn so close. Oh no, Charity! For shame, for shame. Fetch out all your sin. All your guilt. All that—filth. Lay it all before Him. Offer it to Him. Tell Him it's *all* you have to offer. And who else could understand that but Him? And then offer Him *yourself*. Open yourself to Him, Charity. Open your soul. Let Him enter you. Give yourself now to Him. Let Him fill you with His spirit. Nothing else can wash out all that . . . evil . . . all that . . . human pollution!"

A sweat ran now from Charity's body. She shook like one with palsy and strange grunts came up from deep within her.

"Do you *feel* him?" Arabella called.

"Yes! Yes! Yes!" Charity cried. "Oh, yesss!"

"And can you doubt His love?"

"Oh, Jesus!" she called. "Sweetest Saviour!"

"And now take one last look at the life you leave behind." Her trembling hand pointed at the fire. "Here! See how it glows! Be strong now, Charity!" She withdrew the poker, glowing white with the heat. "Be strong in Christ. Feel now for one brief agony the torment He has saved you from. For here you see approaching you the very fires of hell!" Charity, with glazed eyes, watched the poker as it came near. "Call on His name now, child. Offer Him this mortification of your vile flesh. Now!"

The girl did not cry out, or even move, as the searing iron bit, sizzling, into her flesh.

"God in heaven!" Walter whispered, having crept up unheard even by John.

He could answer nothing as he watched the poker pull away with a jerk from the body it had welded itself to.

"Call on Him!" Arabella urged.

The child gave one long ecstatic cry: "Je-e-e-sus!" and raised her arms to the heavens. Her face was radiant with joy.

Arabella dropped to her knees, too. The iron fell with a clatter at her side. "Dearest Lord," she prayed, "who desireth not the death of a sinner but rather that she may turn from her wickedness and live; and who hast taught us that there is more rejoicing in heaven at the return of one stray lamb than at the nine and ninety who were ever saved, rejoice now with us that this one lamb is returned. Enfold her this night and ever more in Thy tender care. Stay and comfort her when she is like to fall again. O Thou who seest into all our hearts and all their depths and from whom we may have nothing hid." She reached out tenderly and touched the girl's ribs below the burn mark. "And through this wound, O Lord, take out her sin and cleanse her entirely. That she, being now truly penitent and truly Thy daughter, may daily heal and strengthen, as in body so in soul, becoming at last perfect in Thy service. I ask this, dear Lord, knowing well mine own imperfections, knowing that, in Thy perfect sight, what the world may call my virtue and this my dear sister's sin are as close"—she took Charity's hands in hers—"as these our fingers. And thus Thou seest before Thee not one but two sinners, alike in penitence and humility, alike in direst need of Thy love and guidance. Grant both to both, Oh Heavenly Father, for sweet Jesus' sake. Amen."

"Amen. Amen!" Charity said desperately.

She struggled to stand—and fainted.

That and that alone galvanized the two men to action, and they shuffled unwillingly into the kitchen.

Arabella stood again. "God is merciful," she said, fondly looking down at the exhausted and now mutilated girl. "I know that God is always in this house, but has He ever worked such wonders among us as this night!"

"Please cover her, dear," Walter said.

"There is no sin in her now. She is new born. She is a babe. As pure as a babe."

"That burn!" John said, only now coming out of his trance.

"It is where the spear of the centurion entered the side of our Lord. She will bear it as a holy scar."

"Cover her, do," John said. "And let me carry her up."

*   *   *

She did not awaken until almost noon the following day. Her burn had been dressed with boracic crystals and she said she felt no pain. She appeared very weak but entirely at peace. When John went in to see her she said she couldn't go to London with him now. She would stay with Mrs. Thornton—whom she obviously worshipped. She kissed him sweetly goodbye and lay back again to sleep. He left her purse beside the bed.

Chapter 54

His visit to Bristol and his re-engagement with the nuts-and-bolts end of their business brought him back from his former state of lassitude. To all outward appearances he was his old self again. He did the round of all their workings, in England and Europe, usually being away three weeks, back for one. He went after new contracts with all his former zest, enjoying the skirmishing and back-doors dealing they involved.

"All is as it was," he said, a hundred times.

He went to Ireland to see the progress of their "model estate." It had been cleared of about a thousand tenants, not by the old system of evicting and harrying but by offering free passage and five pounds to any family to emigrate to North America, South Africa, or Australia. Some of the stronger men had come to work for Stevenson's in England. The people did not want to move, of course. Like all peasants, their love of the land went deep. But if there was ever to be any profitable development of the country, the landowners had to create a system in which thirty acres was looked upon as a normal size for a farm; there were still places where people petitioned even for five-acre farms to be divided—on the grounds that such "large" farms were oppressive.

As Sarah's trustee, he helped with her move to Bristol and it was he who negotiated the purchase of the Refuge, a secluded gentleman's

residence in spacious, wooded grounds at the end of St. James's Place—
the road parallel to Montague Parade, where the Thorntons lived. By
buying three feet of garden from a neighbour they were able to arrange
a connecting path between the two properties. Sarah when the time
came left Maran Hill in tears, but Nora knew that she was going for
the best of all positive reasons and that she would find the work she and
Arabella had undertaken was completely fulfilling to her. John said he
hoped that would be so. Charity was being trained to be her lady's maid.

When they went north for Christmas he stayed up there and, with
Livings and his mill manager, Paul Jacobs, planned and began the first
big extension of Stevenstown and the works. "There's going to be a
great expansion in manufactures as a result of this Exhibition next
year," he promised. "We shall be ready for it."

Toward the end of that winter, with the feeling but not the evidence of spring in the air, Flynn came once more to Maran Hill, this
time to dine with them. He arrived in midafternoon. Nora was having
her portrait taken by Llewellyn Roxby, a young painter in whose career
she had always shown an interest. Verbally he flattered her outrageously
and without the slightest attempt to make it sound sincere. But he
painted her with consummate honesty—in fact, too much honesty for
Nora: He had included a little skin blemish she had near her left eye,
a sort of small grey mole on a stalk of skin. She had made him paint it
out again.

"Is it all right if I talk?" she asked when Flynn came in.

"Yes." He was always very short when he was painting.

"You must have better manners, Rocks, when you paint the queen.
Well, Flynn, and was I right last year? Didn't Bristol do him good! No
more circuses or talk of retiring."

"It did," Flynn agreed. "And yet . . . I don't know why I say 'and
yet,' but there's just that feeling about the fella."

Nora was silent.

"Do ye not agree, ma'am?"

"I was hoping you wouldn't say it," she answered. "I was hoping it
was only myself had that feeling and that it was just my imagination."

"I don't know what it is. There's a—"

"I do. You can't put your finger on anything and say 'He wouldn't
have done that before' or on anything he would've done and now
doesn't. In a way it's too much like he used to be. Don't you think?"

"Ah!" Flynn shook his head. "You're right, of course, but it's more
than that. You're right, too, when you say you can't put your finger
on it."

"He's hit his head on the ceiling, whoever you're talking about," Roxby said.

"What!" Nora laughed.

"He's grown and grown and grown and now he's hit his head on the ceiling. He can only get fatter now, not taller. Unless he moves to a different room. It happens to me all the time."

Nora laughed. "Help yourself to a drink, Flynn," she said.

"Thank you, not before sundown."

"We have the same rule here," Nora said. "But we break it when Roxby comes. It helps us survive the occasion. I'd introduce you except I know he'd only be rude."

Roxby sprang to life behind his easel and came bounding over to Flynn, the picture of extravagant good manners. "My dear sir! Mr. Flynn! Llewellyn Roxby's the name. And may I say how very delighted I am to meet you."

Flynn laughed in embarrassment and shook hands. He shrugged, bewildered, at Nora while Roxby returned to his place.

"I really thought," Roxby said, talking to Nora's image on the canvas, "that when I came here to paint you, dear Nora"—at which Flynn shot her a look of amazement—"I really and truly believed that I had come into a room with a very high ceiling. Nay, an infinite ceiling. The sky itself. I can paint, I thought, a picture of true honesty. No more corpulent mill owners' wives who want me to pry out the sylph that still lurks somewhere within those oceans of lard."

Nora sighed wearily. She knew just what was coming.

"Thus I painted a picture of supreme honesty. For twenty minutes I laboured to re-create an adorable, sweet, honey-grey mole on you there . . ." He was still talking to his portrait. "And"—he ducked, miming a hard blow on the head—"I hit the ceiling! The infinite sky was no more than a piece of bad Tiepolo. A sham."

"Shut up, Rocks!" she cried. "It's boring."

"You are as bad as all of them," he said, pouting. "Worse. Because you have it in you to be so much better. Look!" He threw down his brushes on his studio palette. "I will show you." He tore three sheets of paper from the heart of his sketchbook, and, with a fine sable brush dipped in a pale, warm grey he placed a tiny mark, off-centre, on two of the sheets. One of these he leaned against the back of her portrait canvas; the other two he brought to her.

"Which is the better portrait of that sheet of paper?" he asked, putting the two into her hands.

Wearily she lowered them into her lap and looked at him as a mother might look at a child grown too big to be scolded.

He took up the challenge in her eyes. "You say to me, 'It's such a *little* thing, Rocks—so little. Paint it out. Just for me.' And now here; this grey paint is a little thing, too. But see what a difference it makes."

Nora chuckled and gave him back the papers. "I swear, Rocks," she said, "I swear. When the portrait is finished I will take it to Professor Liston and say, 'There—make me like that.' The surgeon's blade will force nature to imitate art for once. Does that satisfy you?"

His dejected walk back to his easel was a parody of Napoleon's retreat from Moscow. "I should know better," he said to himself. "After all these years."

"And that's a fact!" Flynn added.

*   *   *

Later it occurred to Nora that Roxby's insincere and self-serving analogy might be closer to the truth than anything she or Flynn had said. It was not that John had hit a ceiling—precisely the opposite. It was the *firm* that could no longer grow upward, only sideways. With the successful completion of the Britannia Bridge it had taken part in the most challenging and difficult engineering feat of all time. There would be others, of course, and they in their turn would also be the most challenging—the most *something*—but, in a sense it would be more of the same. And now that he had trained several people to do all that he could do, he was the one supernumerary person in the business. If he wanted to go on growing, he had to do it outside of Stevenson's. Perhaps her ruse with Flynn, getting John to go to Bristol, had been a blunder. Perhaps he had been on the point of making this discovery for himself. If so, to have driven him back into the firm had been the wrong thing to do.

At her next sitting she asked Roxby why he was so petulant about having to paint out her mole.

"It's not petulant, Nora, it's a matter of honesty." Now that he sensed victory in the offing, he shed his jocularity. "I don't know whether you go through Mrs. Jarrett's housekeeping accounts. Do you?"

"I have been known to."

"I suppose if you find she's got threepence more in the petty cash box than her book shows she ought to have, you ignore it."

Nora saw the trap even before the sentence was finished for Roxby knew her well enough to suppose nothing of the kind. But if she was going to concede the point, she wanted it to be out of greatness of soul, not by a meek submission to logic.

"It really upsets you so much?" she asked.

"Dishonesty of any kind upsets me. Beauty is truth—truth to nature, truth to one's material, truth to one's self. Your wish is my command, but it does force me to violate all three."

"Would it be very difficult to paint it back in again, Rocks?"

He made a complicit little gesture and beckoned her over. She stood and stretched. While she was crossing the room he soaked a rag in white spirit. She loved the smell of his materials—linseed oil, poppy-seed oil, pigments, turpentine, copal varnish.

When she could see the painting—and it was always a shock to find herself staring so laconically back, with eyes that followed her around the room—he rubbed gently at the flesh tones over the offending mole. They came away almost at once, leaving the original painting showing once again.

"Warts and all," he said, vastly satisfied.

"How?" She had by now learned enough about paints and their drying rates to be mystified.

"I thought you might come to regret it," he answered. "The flesh tones I put on top of it were mixed with olive oil." Still she was puzzled. "Olive oil does not dry," he added.

She was angry. She did not like to be anticipated in her caprice. "You are selfish," she said, walking back to her position.

But his smile soon won her over again. "Rocks," she said, "will you take me to the Exhibition in May?"

"Won't you be going with Stevenson?"

"Of course. And again with the girls. And again with the boys. And we're making a big party of friends, too. But I would like especially to have *your* opinion."

Chapter 55

As one of the guarantors of the Great Exhibition, John had certain privileges—free season tickets for himself and his family; the right to a gallery place on the southeast corner of the junction between apse and nave on opening day, looking immediately down on the royal dais; and, at the end, the right to visit and bring any number of friends on the two days between the closing, on the fifteenth of October, and the dismantling of the exhibits. He also assumed the right to walk around any time he liked in order to watch the progress of the building. Charles Fox, and Paxton when he was there, were always very amenable and sometimes even invited his opinion on this or that problem. Very early on John realized that building in cast iron was a specialty beyond him; indeed, no one in the world but Fox could have put up the building in time—and he often said as much to both men. In January, when an acre of the glazing blew off in a gale, he lent them two hundred Stevenson men to get back the time lost. All rancour was gone.

It intrigued him to think that even ten years earlier the building could not have been attempted in that form. The quality and dimensions of the iron would have been too variable; there was no machine then for turning out glass panes of that size and quantity; the railways to transport these materials had not been built; and the electric telegraph for speeding verbal communication between the many parties had then been a toy on a few miles only of the Great Western Railway. Now there were nearly two thousand route miles in Britain alone, and a third-time-lucky cable being laid across to France.

From February onward, when the exhibits began to arrive, there was always something new and interesting to see. He actually played a part in reassembling the biggest of the machinery exhibits—the great hydraulic ram, one of the pair from the Britannia Bridge. That day was memorable in another respect, too, for it was the day that the famous tenor Herr Reichardt had been invited to pit his voice against the supposedly fragile crystal of the palace. Someone had vowed that the music to be played at the opening and at set times of day throughout the Exhibition would shatter the glass, which would shower down and "cut the ladies to mincemeat." Joshua's triumph at Jericho gave the prediction a scriptural authority.

The building resounded with the usual hammering and shouting, whistling and sawing. But as Reichardt began, those nearest him fell silent. He stood at the crossing, between apse and nave, beside Osler's great crystal fountain, which had just been completed; and his rich, powerful tenor rang out in those confines with a most beautiful resonance. As wave after wave of song poured down the aisles and galleries, everyone else fell silent; in the end two thousand workmen stood spellbound, captivated in that eerie and magical vibrancy. It was the most moving moment John could remember, as they stood bathed in the flood of that perfect voice. When Reichardt finished, not a man breathed. They let the very echoes fade to a whisper before they dared burst into applause, and then it rose to a tumult.

Then came the orchestra, and finally Willis' grand organ with all the power of its forty-five thousand pipes. Later inspection revealed that not one of the 900,000 superficial feet of glass, on its 202 miles of sash bar, fixed to their 2,224 trellis girders and 358 trusses, supported on 1,060 iron columns, was in any way affected by this *onslaught acousti- cale.*

As the official opening on May Day drew nearer and all the 100,000 exhibits found their correct places somewhere along the eleven miles of exhibition stand inside the Crystal Palace, John began to grasp the true magnitude of what was happening in England that year.

Only men of the calibre of Brunel and Robert Stephenson would have attempted anything on this scale and have carried it off so per- fectly. Only they, with their long experience of railways and of catering to the needs of thousands, could have visualized exactly what was in- volved. Even what might seem the simplest task—to get each exhibit to its right place both in the Palace and in the catalogue—could have defeated lesser men, especially when those exhibits arrived toward the end at the rate of five thousand a day.

By the end of April, when the sawdust and putty scrapings were swept out and burned, the floors all scrubbed, the matting laid, the bar- riers and turnstiles installed, the royal dais erected and the great canopy suspended above it, and the dust sheets taken off the machines and the statues, models and cases, carpets and tapestries, furniture and stuffed beasts, weapons and minerals, fossils and fans, chandeliers and foun- tains . . . by then John thought he knew the Exhibition as well as any man living. But, as he was slowly to learn, he knew all about it *except* its one most important feature.

Chapter 56

Thursday the first of May was fine and warm—English-warm, which no one could mistake for hot. And to show it was an English summer, a light sprinkling of rain fell, enough to keep down the dust as the queen and Prince Albert left Buckingham Palace in the state coach, accompanied by a troop of the Life Guards and half a dozen other royal carriages. Since early morning the bells of all the churches in London had been ringing; it sounded like a vast beehive in swarm. Since early morning the enterprising had been out, hammering together the timber shoring on which they would rent staging and benches to those who had failed to get a curbside vantage point. Since early morning, too, East Enders had trudged west with their street barrows piled high with ginger beer, fatty cakes, gingerbread, and tins of brandy balls, the girls and women carrying wicker sieves laden with pyramids of oranges. Others carried trays spread with snow-white linen and laden with pigs' trotters, cow heel, and paper-thin sandwiches of ham. Near the park gates every other man seemed to bear a tray filled with bright medallions of the Crystal Palace, and Crystal Palace charms and mementoes.

No one needed to ask the way—simply follow that irresistible tide of carefree lads and gaily dressed lasses, of fathers and wives and jaunty children—skipping and bowling hoops, flouncing shawls, fluttering ribbons, munching apples, cracking nuts, laughing and chattering their ten thousand ways to the park.

On the calm waters of the Serpentine floated the miniature frigate *Prince of Wales*, its cannon ready charged to salute the queen's arrival. The intrepid aeronaut Charles Spencer stood by the basket of his balloon, ready to enter and rise up into the air the moment she declared the Exhibition open. At half past ten John and Nora had descended from their carriage on the north side of the park and walked under the trees, all in new leaf and bright green in the sparkling sun, over the Serpentine Bridge and Rotten Row and in by one of the back entrances —not, of course, the one the queen was to use. People eyed them curiously. Distinguished visitors did not arrive on foot. But at least they had avoided the thousand state coaches and the three and a half thousand broughams, clarences, post chaises, cabs, and other vehicles that stretched in lines back through Knightsbridge, through the toll gate at Hyde Park Corner, along Piccadilly, down Haymarket, through Trafalgar Square, all the way to the Strand.

When they were up in their places, on the balcony overlooking the royal dais, and had a chance to look around, even John, who had seen the building grow from its marker pegs up, was awed. Already about thirty thousand people were there and thousands more were still to come. The murmur that arose from so many was like the distant chatter of a vast colony of birds, or rushing waters heard from afar. It seemed to charge the air with a special kind of iridescence in which distance was both magnified and lost. The elms enclosed within the Palace had

burst early into leaf and now spread luxuriant high-summer branches to
shade the courts below. Along all the galleries that overlooked the nave
grew a profusion of tropical flowers and foliage, their colours set off
perfectly against the gorgeous hues of the carpets and the richly dyed
fabrics—the choice of the finest weavers and producers from the four
corners of the earth. Detail was lost in that infinite variety; in its place
came an almost mystical awareness of the tens of thousands of unseen
hands—of inventors, labourers, proprietors, and managers—whose col-
laboration on this unprecedented work had now, at last, on this great
day, borne fruit.

Greatest of all was the building itself. Intended as no more than a
cheap and ultimately demountable shell against the weather, it gave a
thrill of surprise and delight to everyone who entered it—especially
beneath the great curves of the transept soaring up over a hundred feet,
and made to seem even loftier by the ease and grace with which they
arched over the huge elms, giants of the park. Never before had people
stood in a building of that size where the play of light and air was so
free. To enter and be still and then to lift one's gaze to the skies in-
duced a sense of wonder and mystery that was as close to a religious experience as a secular occasion could get. On this day, with the massed
choirs and organ and the presence of the archbishop of Canterbury, the
two were in any case merging.

About half an hour before the royal party arrived, the court began
to assemble. It was the most gorgeous scene that London had ever beheld. In the magical light that fell from all around, the gold braid and
glittering medals and ornaments were like a coloured fire. The silken
sashes and garters, the turbans and fez caps, the embroidered waistcoats
of white silk and the rich brown court suits of the ambassadors were all
set off against the uniforms of the functionaries—the gentlemen at arms
with long white plumes cascading over golden helmets, the trumpeters
with their silver trumpets held against cloaks of gold, the beefeaters in
their black and scarlet tunics and black velvet caps, the aldermen of the
City in crimson and ermine, the heralds in the blue silk crested with
golden lions and other devices, Garter King-at-Arms sumptuous in red
velvet emblazoned with gold, the archbishop in cope and mitre with full
lawn sleeves, and, ringing them all, the red and yellow uniforms of the
miners and sappers and the dark blue of the police.

At a few minutes to noon the royal carriages and the bright livery
of coachmen and postillions flashed through the entrance court and
passed on around the building. They were swiftly followed by the troop
of Life Guards, their burnished steel helmets and breastplates sparkling

in the sun. An awed hush fell upon the entire assembly as every head craned toward the entrance from Rotten Row.

Moments later the queen and her entourage entered, glimpsed as yet only fleetingly through the bars of the great bronze gates behind the dais. With that flair for dramatic but unflustered ceremonial that is uniquely English, the beefeaters drew wide the gates at the perfect moment to reveal the young queen, in pink satin shimmering with diamonds and silver, wearing a light tiara of diamonds and feathers, on the arm of Prince Albert, resplendent in the full scarlet dress of a field marshal. Hand in hand with them came the Prince of Wales in Highland dress and the princess royal in white lace, with a garland of wild roses in her hair.

Trumpets flourished and the cheers of the thirty-three thousand within mingled with the earth-shaking roar of hundreds of thousands outside—for the park was now one sea of faces as far as the eye could reach. The gunfire of the little frigate on the Serpentine was quite drowned.

When the queen was upon the dais, the great organ struck the opening chord of the national anthem. Suddenly it was both marvellous and incredible simply to be there—at the heart and soul, it seemed, of a world at peace, united in the productive rivalry of industry and endeavour. Not once in the long tide of human history had that world been so drawn together. And there, in the persons of the prince and of the committee ranged behind him, were those who had caused it to happen. It made John and Nora feel both proud and humble to have earned their place at the centre of it all.

A brief ceremony followed, with an address from the prince to the queen and a blessing from the archbishop. Their speeches were swallowed in their own echoes but, like words snatched from a half-heard ritual in a great cathedral, they had a meaning beyond their literal import. Then the organ, an orchestra of two hundred players, and the massed choirs of six hundred voices broke into the Hallelujah Chorus. For such a day in such a place, no other work of the human spirit could have seemed half so sublime. On every side men and women could be seen openly weeping, their faces marked not by sorrow or embarrassment but aglow with joy.

For half an hour the queen and her court walked the full length of the main aisle and the transept, led by Paxton and Fox. As they passed below the point where John and Nora stood, Nora moved her lace-gloved hand over his.

"Aye," he said into her ear, not wishing to shout above the cheers and huzzahs that followed the queen everywhere. "Now I could wish it had been otherwise." But his eyes were looking up at the ribs and arches, wishing he had put all that vast and delicate tracery between earth and sky—not down, wishing it was he who, with Paxton, led the great assembly.

When the procession returned to the dais Lord Breadalbane, as high steward, declared the Exhibition open in the queen's name. And again the cheers echoed and resounded inside and were taken up across the park; and in moments Charles Spencer and his balloon were drifting upward and away over the sea of people, nine hundred thousand some said, thronging the walks and rides and grassy spaces and the streets that led to them. All their lives they would say of that day, "I was there."

And in a sense it was *their* day, more than the Exhibition's, or the queen's. A day that set so many precedents set one which was to endure long after memories of it began to fade. The best part of a million people had swarmed into Hyde Park, Green Park, and the Crystal Palace. The queen walked among thirty thousand of them as if they and she were in a vast drawing room—with the same degree of safety and decorum. She had driven among the rest to cheers that spread before and lingered behind, making her route one brushfire of sound. These were the crowds who ten years earlier had stoned her coach; many of the people within the Exhibition must have been among those who booed and jeered at her at the opera. Those ten years had seen hungry harvests, wicked speculation, disastrous bankruptcies, and trade as depressed as any could remember it. Yet the entire day passed off without a single disorder. The police made few arrests anywhere in London that Thursday; not one had any connection with the Exhibition or its crowds.

You did not have to wait for the later reports and statistics to tell you this. You could see it as you walked among the people in the streets of London that day. There was no Great Cause to bind them, no speeches were made to induce a sense of purpose; but quite spontaneously, to their own surprise as much as anyone else's, people were taken unawares by a sense of suddenly belonging, one to another, and so to all. Men and women and children, too, who came jauntily down to the parks to enjoy a bit of an extra holiday, went homeward weary and contented, each in some degree aware of that new sense of belonging. Their country had that day renewed herself, and they had played their part. The miseries of the hungry forties were behind them; the long-promised future, made bright and splendid by industry and endeavour, was now at hand.

Chapter 57

The following day, the first day on which the Exhibition was open to the public, admission was a pound. So the "public" came almost exclusively from the West End. John and Nora brought Winifred, now ten years old, Young John, two days short of his ninth birthday, and Caspar, who would be eight in November; all came knowing exactly what they wanted to see, having heard their father talk and having read nothing all that week except the Exhibition catalogues.

Fashion had not yet decided whether it was proper to be seen among the machinery exhibits (the queen had not yet visited there and Albert didn't count), so the haute monde stayed safely among the statues and tapestries and tut-tutted at the undisguised papism of Pugin's Medieval Court. The Stevensons had the machinery almost to themselves. On their way up they heard a man staring at the glass roof and saying, "It doesn't look very novel to *me*. Aldriges in St. Martin's Lane have had half an acre of cast iron and glass over the auction ring since 1844— and no one's made any fuss about that."

Nora smiled at John. "So *you* didn't invent it either," she said.

"No," he agreed ruefully. "It was probably the Romans, in fact. It usually is!"

The first thing they wanted to see was the scale model of the tubular bridge and the actual great hydraulic ram. John also showed them the Jacquard punching machine that put the rivet holes in the plates. Caspar had the satisfaction here of saying, "Ours is bigger, isn't it, Papa"—meaning the one John had just installed at Stevenstown. About the Nasmyth's steam forging hammer he was not able to say theirs was bigger; instead he said, "We've got *two*, haven't we, Papa."

After an hour among the heavy machinery and then the moving machinery they went, at Young John's request, to see the Krupp cannon and the Colt firearms, in the German and American sections. That was when Nora and Winifred went off with Mademoiselle Nanette to look at the Oriental sections. They met again for luncheon at the Schweppes' café in the central area. No hot meals were served in the Exhibition, but there was a good selection of sandwiches, pastries, patties, fruit, ices, tea, coffee, chocolate, and—naturally—lemonade, soda water, and seltzer. After luncheon they separated again, the men to the agricultural machinery and the minerals, the ladies to the European section to look at the glass and silver and furniture and porcelain. They met up again at teatime and all went to look at the sculpture and models.

The models were of all kinds, real and projected. There was a model of Niagara by George Catlin, showing every house, bridge, tree, rock, factory, and island in a square mile around the falls. There was a model in cast iron of a date palm got up as a German Christmas tree, which the catalogue claimed was a new custom brought in by Prince Albert. "We've had Christmas trees all our lives, haven't we, Mama," Caspar said. There was a model of a suspension bridge to cross the Dover Strait . . . a model of a ship canal through the Suez isthmus . . . a model in cardboard of Her Majesty's Theatre . . . two models in cardboard of York Minister . . . a model railway that laid its own track before it and took it up again behind . . . Count Dunin's model man made of seven thousand sliding plates and springs and levers and looking like armour, so cunningly arranged that at the turn of a crank the plates slid over one another and the homunculus would expand from the size of a dwarf to that of a giant . . . a model by Mr. Ryles of Cobridge to show that the Earth is a living mollusk whose surface is its shell—the tides being evidence of its heart beat . . . a model of a building system that conducted smoke from the chimneys directly down into the sewers . . . and, best of all, a forty-foot-long model of Liverpool docks at a scale of eight feet to the mile. The sea was of green glass, silvered underneath so that it shimmered like real water. Upon it floated sixteen hundred perfectly detailed, fully rigged ships—the usual number of vessels in and around the port. Everything was there, all three hundred acres of the harbour and about a third of the city, including all three railway stations, correct down to the slates on the roofs.

"It's almost better than being there yourself," Young John said.

The model was in a great glass case, towering eight feet above the floor and approachable on all four sides. It was while they were around the back, peering at the details of the city, that they looked through the case and saw the queen. She was walking around the building with very few attendants, just like any other visitor, and had come upon them completely unawares. The men took off their hats and caps and the ladies and girls made little curtseys. It was a wonderful ending to their visit. On the way out they had their handkerchiefs passed through the

Maria Farina fountain of eau de cologne and they gazed in disappointment at the rather glassy Koh-i-Noor diamond, whose 186 carats refused
to sparkle even though illuminated by a dozen tiny gas jets.

In the train on the way home—John now had his own carriage on
the Great Northern—Winifred sniffed her scented kerchief and said:
"I've been to India, and America and France and Jersey and—"

The boys took her up, gabbling their list at first and then petering
out with New Brunswick and Montserrat and St. Kitts. In all they remembered over forty places between them.

"You're very lucky to be alive at such a time," Nora told them.
"There were no such things when I was your age."

"What did you have instead, Mama?" Winifred asked.

"There was a sailor who used to come to Briggate once a year and
he'd been with Captain Cook. He'd painted about eight scenes of the
South Sea Islands and he would tell their tales for money, like a Punch
and Judy man. That's all I knew about the world until I married your
father. I thought the South Seas were a little way past London!"

And now, she thought, on the days when there was no entrance
charge, even the poorest children in London would be able to see the
wonders of the entire civilized world spread out before them. Was it
making things too easy? *Could* one make enlightenment too easy? John
had once said to her, "There's no learning without bewilderment." She
had come to believe it profoundly.

*   *   *

It was the first of many visits they paid to the Crystal Palace that summer. They came back with the younger children, Clement, now six,
Abigail, four (who was sure there was a *story* attached to each exhibit
and wanted to be told it rather than just look at the object), and
Hester, now three. They even brought young Mather, barely one, just
to touch the glass and be held up to see the building and its gaily
fluttering pennants—so that in later years he could claim he had been
there and done these things.

He also saw—and giggled at—the "pig organ," a sort of fair-
ground sideshow in which a dozen pigs, each chosen for squealing in
a different key, were penned with their tails connected to a simple key-
board. They could squeal "God Save the Queen," "Three Blind Mice,"
and other elementary pieces—if you listened with a charitable ear.

Another time they brought the older children back, too. And once
Walter Thornton brought up his three boys and Letty, now seven, to

make a party with John and Nora and their three eldest. They saw the queen again that day—which was not surprising, for she paid thirteen visits there during May alone—and she smiled at Caspar and patted Letty on the head as she passed, saying, "Such pretty hair, my dear." Letty had inherited Arabella's blond ringlets.

In July, Nora went around with Roxby, chaperoned by Mademoiselle Nanette. She listened attentively but, in the end, with no great conviction, to his doctrine that beauty was truth—to nature, to material, and to self. As far as he was concerned the entire Exhibition revealed man's dreadful slavery to the machine. The machine, he said, has been liberated to wander at its own mad will through the world of the applied arts; the rest of mankind could do nothing to tame or control it. He showed her one carved wooden trophy, intended for a panel on a door. "Look," he said. "That must have been passed back and forth through the carving machine a thousand times. The spirit and soul of the wood has fled before such an onslaught!" Nora thought the result was rather handsome. She also liked, for instance, a silver spoon whose handle was some perfectly copied seaweed and whose bowl was an exact replica of a cockleshell. It was true to nature—incredibly true—and true to the material, being undeniably silver, and true to self, in that it was a useful functioning spoon in every way. He could not explain how she was misapplying his doctrine. In fact, everything she liked, from that spoon up to the gargantuan four-poster bed from Austria with its uplifting carvings representing the Fall and Redemption of man ("More fit to be laid out on than to sleep in," Roxby said), was completely unacceptable to him. Still, he was a stimulating companion and a most forceful guide; she enjoyed the visit despite her falling out with almost everything he said. At least they were both agreed that a small sculpture of three elkhounds bringing down a stag, by San Giovanni of Brighton, was rather fine. Nora was glad, for she intended to buy it whether Roxby approved or no.

But the most memorable visit of all was on the last Friday in August. The Rodets, secure from revolution and with a more prosperous year behind them, were staying at Maran Hill. That weekend they were all going up to Thorpe Old Manor for part of September, and then going on to the Beadors, in County Durham. Rodie had wanted to see Sarah again and so had suggested they make the Exhibition their meeting place. Then Arabella had the idea of taking her penitent women (now numbering eight) up as a treat during the sixpenny days in October, so she thought she ought to come there first and see which would be the most suitable portions to visit. In the end the party included the Rodets, the Stevensons, the Thorntons, Sarah, and the two maids, Mademoiselle Nanette and Charity—out on her first official "trial" as a lady's maid. All children, having been there twice that week already, were to be left behind.

Chapter 58

The moment they were through the turnstile Rodie asked to see the French section, in the gallery on the south side of the nave. Swamped by her enthusiasm, they spent rather longer there than they had intended. The enamels and tapestries, porcelain and glass, the statues and vases and paintings were all scrutinized minutely and enthused over in her rich, piercing soprano. Only Rodet's insistence that they should go and see France's *machinery* prevented them from spending all day among her artistic products.

The French machinery was all to the north of the nave, so they had to come downstairs and go across to it. John knew it would take about five minutes to get Rodie out from among the Gobelins and Aubussons, so he went out to the stairhead to see that no one strayed too far in front, telling Nora to see that no one lingered too far behind.

While waiting there he looked down at the American section, which filled the entire east end of the nave. Suddenly he noticed a violent movement of the drapery around Hiram Powers' by now infamous *Greek Slave*, voted by widespread public disclaim to be the hottest sculpture there. The drapery, around three sides of her, was to prevent any unseemly *fundamental* display. It was as if a pair of dogs were fighting silently to the death behind the crimson velvet. Then the entire drape fell from its hangings, leaving the canopy above dancing wildly in the morning sun, shedding the rich dust of four months.

The crowd pressed forward to help whoever was now trapped beneath those heavy folds. General laughter was growing, for few people were in any doubt as to what had been going on: Someone had been peeking.

"What's happening, John?" Sarah asked, joining him, with Charity at her side.

He pointed down at the heaving mound of drapes but had no time to explain before Walter Thornton, red, hot, and dusty, emerged from under them. He dived back, retrieved his hat, and then vanished below the balcony with an amazing turn of speed.

John and Sarah dared not look at one another, not with Charity there. They stood side by side, rocking with silent mirth, feeling set to burst at any minute. But few people noticed either them or Walter's swift departure. They were taking full advantage of the all-round view his act had temporarily offered them. Word spread up the nave like a Russian vine—you can see the *Slave*'s tra-la-la, her fundamental features, her jutland, her blind cheeks, her saddle leather, her sitting room, her boo-boo, her derrière—hurry, hurry—for a limited season only.

"Anything amiss?" Walter asked, joining them on the balcony, washed and spruce from the lavatory at the foot of the stairs.

"The curtain seems to have fallen down," John said.

Walter laughed pityingly. "See how they run," he sneered. He did not notice John wink at Sarah.

Nor did Arabella, who joined them at that moment, too. She took one look at the scene below and said it was a disgrace. "It exactly vindicates the sculptor's lofty aims in presenting this carving."

"In what way, Mrs. Thornton?" John asked, surprised at this judgement. He had expected Arabella to pretend not even to notice the statue.

"It clearly says in the catalogue," she told him, quoting from memory. " 'The artist has delineated a young girl, deprived of her clothing [you see—she is not voluntarily in that state], standing before the licentious gaze of a wealthy Eastern Barbarian.' "

The Lustful Turk! Sarah thought. *How that image pursues us.*

" 'Her face expresses,' " Arabella continued, " 'shame and disgust at her ignominious position, while about her lips hovers that contemptuous scorn which a woman can so well show her manly oppressor.' " Arabella pointed at the rapidly swelling crowd below. "These . . . *men*, this rabble, are one and the same as that Eastern Barbarian. I hope the drapes fall again when I bring my girls. They would be highly instructed to see the expression on the faces of all these men, and contrast it with the purity of the slave's contemptuous scorn."

"Take Thornton with you," John suggested. "Get him to pull it down."

"I couldn't bring myself to go near it," Walter said firmly. "I have seen her piteous face in the engravings. It is as Mrs. Thornton says. And it is enough for me."

Arabella was proud of Walter's manly rebuff; she did not think

John Stevenson had taken her sentiments quite seriously. Then she had to attend to Sarah, who had breathed a fly into her throat and was now having a fit trying to cough it up.

Nora had at last pried the Rodets from the French section, though they were still in bitter dispute as to whether a piece of Sèvres on display there was or was not identical to one they had at home. Nora was sure that Rodie had begun by saying it was, but by the time they reached the nave and were pressing through the thickening crowd she was saying it was *not*—and Rodet was opposing her with equal vehemence.

Arabella, rather startlingly for her, and certainly rather loudly, said that the crowd was "like flies near bad meat."

"She seems very much more robust than she used to be," John commented to Sarah.

"She is unrecognizable as the same woman. Nora used to chide you, John, for saying she would *do* something one day, but I think she really has the seeds of greatness." She turned to the girl. "Charity, you tell Mr. Stevenson what you told me the other day. What you say about Mrs. Thornton."

"It isn't me alone, Madame," Charity said—they had been at work on her language and accent—" 'tis all the girls."

"Go on."

"Well—" Charity gulped, and smiled at John. "We believe Mrs. Thornton because she never makes you feel she's up there and you're down there. She says there isn't a man or woman born anywhere in all history, excepting Jesus, who had no sin. In God's eyes we're all sinners. Our souls be all in the same pan of His weighing scales. So she makes you feel if there's hope for her, there's hope for you."

"You see, John?" Sarah added. "I worked for years at the Hornsey Refuge never understanding that. But with Arabella, it was obvious from the start."

"Do you not remember?" he asked Charity. "It's exactly what she told you down in the kitchen basement that first night."

"I remember so little of that night, sir. It was a year ago now."

"But isn't that a mark of greatness?" Sarah pressed. "To understand such things without having to be told them. She has a loving command of those girls that is almost mystical."

"And you, Charity," John said, still looking at her. "Are you content?"

Charity smiled at Sarah, the way all *in* people smile at one another when outsiders ask naïve questions. "More than content, sir," she told him. "To walk day and night in Jesus' love is the greatest possible joy."

He smiled back and drew a little apart from them then. Her radiant piety embarrassed him. Also, though he barely admitted it, religious females had always exercized an appeal for him that lewd women could never match. He found himself beginning to *want* Charity and had to remind himself of the remote possibility that she was his daughter, though inquiries at the two orphanages which she remembered produced no evidence to support it.

Nora had not seen Charity before, but she had heard the bare bones of the story as John had told it to her. She watched this exchange between John and Sarah and the girl carefully, as they strolled up the nave and into the foreign machinery section. She trusted John and was inclined to believe his story, but, even so, in any woman's heart when she hears that her husband, for whatever laudable reasons, has picked up a pretty young dockside whore and brought her home, there must remain some element of doubting curiosity. She found Charity almost *too* good.

When they arrived at the French machinery, dominated by the "improved double turbine," Rodet, overcome by patriotic rapture, launched into a voluble explanation of it and its neighbours to Rodie. Even at his million-words-a-minute, it looked set for a good half hour.

Arabella smiled at Nora. "You are radiant, my dear."

"I was about to say the same to you."

"You realize it's eleven years and three days since my Nicholas was born. On that memorable picnic near Summit—at least, memorable to me."

"To all of us. What happy times they were!"

"Oh, I would not go back, Nora dear. I am so happy now. I have my life's true work ahead of me now."

They stood side by side, leaning on the guard rail surrounding the machines, looking at each other only occasionally.

"Stevenson always said it," Nora admitted with chagrin. "Do you remember how we used to laugh at the very idea!"

Arabella smiled. "Not now, Nora. I bless him every day I get up."

"You don't feel—sometimes—that he rather pushed you into it last year?"

"Not at all. Not remotely. Why do you ask?"

"Well—he found Charity and brought her home. It *was* sudden. It did force the issue."

That made Arabella laugh. "The only thing it forced was Thornton.

I had been ready to begin for weeks. Long before Stevenson came to Bristol. It was Thornton's hand on the brake." She sighed. "But to have selected Charity—out of all the thousands he might have selected, and I mean thousands—that *was* a stroke of genius. I believe God must have directed him."

"Strong words." Nora smiled at Rodet, whose eye had accidentally caught hers; he smiled back but did not even hiccup in his narrative.

"I mean it. Without the help and guidance and advice of that girl I would have—made so many—blunders." She did not sound so happy now.

"Dangerous ones?"

"No. Futile ones. I would have wasted so much effort—pursued wrong courses—squandered our resources." She looked at Nora, as if sizing her up. "Did you realize, for instance," she asked, "that most girls who—take up that way of life leave it quite voluntarily within a few years?"

Nora cleared her throat, feeling nothing more was called for.

"Do you know," Arabella went on, "that if they did not go on the streets they would quite literally starve, for there is no other work for them of any description?"

For the barest fleeting moment Nora thought *She knows! She knows I once let Walter have me for money.* But in her heart she knew that Arabella was incapable of that sort of duplicity. She put her head on one side and shook it, hoping she looked puzzled and encouraging enough to draw Arabella on. She wanted to know more about Charity, especially.

"Do you know," the rhetorical catechism unfurled, "that in their traffic with men they are for the most part—however well they may dissemble it—as coldly indifferent as the most chaste woman among us should school herself to become?"

It was a question that offered Nora the profoundest insight into her relations with Walter Thornton—and into his with the female world at large.

"Do you know that their traffic, far from being confined to people of inferior breeding and station, is largely with respectable people of middling wealth—indeed, the sort of people who live all around us! I could not at first believe it until I sat with Charity in a cab on the quay at night and in many very respectable thoroughfares in Bristol. You will not believe it, but I have seen three of our own neighbours, men from Montague Parade and Kingsdown Parade, take up with—such

girls. And two of these men had donated most generously to the
Rescue Society! I thank God my husband is all that a Christian gentleman should be."

"Indeed," Nora agreed. "You could hardly begin your work otherwise."

Again Arabella sighed; by now she almost radiated her gloom.
"That is the present trouble—I *have* hardly begun."

"Everyone says you have made such a wonderful start."

"Everyone indeed." Her agreement was fervent. "Everyone. That is
exactly what is wrong. I must tell you, Nora, if I have learned only
one thing this past year, it is that when everyone, simply *everyone*,
praises you, your work *must* be defective. Especially in this most delicate
and ticklish field. It is impossible to work effectively and please everyone. I shall not begin to feel useful until I hear the voice of protest
from some quarter."

Their talk was getting no nearer to the subject of Charity, which
was all that Nora was really interested in. She tried to steer it back:
"I would have thought that your work over this last twelve months
is—"

"It's the wrong battle," Arabella cut in. "To put it bluntly. If I can
do no more than to rescue eight women—perhaps two dozen in time—
if that is all, in a town where over a thousand nightly ply for hire, then
I have no business raising other people's money and spending it."

"Why?" Nora was interested now, despite herself. "What ought
you to be doing?"

Arabella smiled, the same slightly pitying smile Charity had used
on John. "It took me so long to understand, I cannot blame you for
not seeing it at once. But do you not grasp the implications of what I've
been saying? That girls go into the 'trade' rather than starve. That it is
no pleasure to them, and for the most part they remain undebauched
and often remarkably pious. That most of them leave as soon as they
have acquired a small capital or a husband. That by far the largest
traffic is with respectable men of some wealth and some position in society. That, by my rough estimate, between four and five thousand
pounds is paid each night for this trade in Bristol alone! Is not the
answer plain to you now?"

Nora shook her head. "Things have always been so, I suppose."

Arabella nodded, pulling a sarcastic smile. "*Who* says these girls are
unemployable? *Who* says they may work only in the most menial oc-
cupations and for wages that force them into at least part-time prostitu-

tion? Is it not the very same people who then avail themselves of these girls?"

Nora drew in her breath sharply. But to her surprise all the energy suddenly drained out of Arabella. She slumped on the guard rail, as dejected as Nora had ever seen her. "You are shocked," she said glumly. "And you are right. What do I now do? If I go on rescuing two dozen a year, I do as much good as trying to empty the city cesspit with a thimble. If I do as my conscience dictates, and carry the battle into the enemy's camp . . ." She sighed. "I keep thinking—five thousand pounds a night. It's something like ten million pounds a year over the whole of England."

"You'd be *mad*," Nora said at once. "*That* is industry on the scale of the railways."

"I would be mad," Arabella echoed. Nora just caught the hint of an impish gleam in her eyes, quickly effaced. "I cannot imagine why I am so strongly impelled in that direction. To channel away the money now reserved by men for their vicious pleasure and to apply it directly to improving the lot of womankind in general. To raise a new standard of chastity among men and a new sense of dignity among women. How do I do that!"

"Through the church?" Nora suggested.

Arabella did not answer.

"Or have you tried that already?"

"The church, I fear, is prepared to offer every assistance short of actual help," she replied. Then, after a further pause, she added, "In any case, I have the strongest possible reasons for not approaching the Reverend Wicks."

"Oh. I see."

"Yes, I fear so. You see how wide and deep this corruption is."

"What will you do?"

"Nothing—for the moment. Except to think, and to pray. It is not something to be ventured lightly, is it?" She smiled at last, and the smile turned hard as if she already sensed some gain. "But I know beyond any possibility of doubt that the regulation and abolition of this traffic is not to be gained by the regulation of its female parties. They are its victims, not its causes."

"It is certainly not something to be ventured lightly—nor alone."

"Oh, but I am not alone. Sarah will always be there, managing the Refuge—and in time we may start several. And there is Charity, too."

"Really?"

"I know she is now Sarah's maid, but it is only so she may have an honest calling should the need arise. But that girl has a brain, I tell you. It was she who, by her quiet insistence on the truth—and by her refusal to bow to my prejudices—she who unclouded my eyes. I would not contemplate such a struggle without her." She smiled timidly at Nora. "She has such determination, do you know whom she sometimes reminds me of?"

"Your mirror?" Nora smiled.

"No. Oh, no. She reminds me of Mr. Stevenson. Though with all those differences of modesty and respectfulness that her sex and station demand, nevertheless there is that same unblinking unshakeable determination at the heart of her."

"She must be remarkable."

"She is. She is."

Nora glanced around to see John striding toward them from the nave. "Come on. Come on," he said fussily. "Even the Rodets have done here."

They looked about themselves and found the Rodets had indeed left. "It's going to be hopeless trying all to keep together," Nora said. "I want to show Arabella and Mr. Thornton something—and you, too. Something Roxby and I found."

Then she had to explain to Arabella who Roxby was. And then they found Walter, taking down the address of the Dr. Gray who was exhibiting a hollow walking stick that would, when tipped up, disgorge medicines, bandages, and an enema. "Could be very useful in out-of-the way places, that," he said.

"Oh, come on," Nora said. "I want to show you a sculptured chimney piece carved by Dighton for Preston Hall. I won't give you my opinion until I've heard yours."

"Preston Hall?" John said. "Betts's new place?"

"Yes." Nora explained to Arabella that this was the E. L. Betts who often partnered Henry Morton Peto, the great rival to Stevenson's. He was building a rather dull but substantial and costly mansion in the Elizabethan style down at Aylesford in Kent; and this was a chimney piece for it. Roxby had liked it for its honesty.

"Yes," John said dubiously when he saw it. "The word 'honesty' in Roxby's mouth is what most of us common inartistic folk call plain and clumsy."

The others agreed. Nora felt no inclination to defend Roxby's opinion. Rodie was especially scornful. "*Barbare!*" she said. The chimney piece featured two of Chaucer's heroines, Dorigene and

Griselda (as the carver spelled them). The poet himself stared out through those sightless, featureless eyes so beloved of sculptors. The motto carved behind each lady explained her principal characteristic. "Dorigene is virtuous," declared the left half. "Griselda is patient," answered the right.

"It must cost quite a bit," Walter said. "Handcarving the entire thing like that."

"Aye!" John spoke in oafish imitation of a rural bumpkin, up for the Exhibition. "When I clap me een on yon, I think theer must be money in t'railroads, see thee. More nor what there be in kine, do'st reckon?"

Even the Rodets laughed. "He has *fantasie*, Monsieur Jean!" Rodie said.

"Nora," Sarah asked her as they left, "do you remember who Dorigen and Grisilda were?"

Nora smiled. Ten or so years ago when they had first met at the Tabard, Sarah had been the maid in charge of the Pilgrims' Hall, where John and Nora had slept. Sarah had beguiled away that evening for Nora by retelling some of the *Canterbury Tales*. "Dorigen was the virtuous wife in the Franklin's Tale," Nora said. "And Grisilda was the patient charcoal burner's daughter who married Lord Walter in the Clerk's Tale."

Sarah was very impressed. "Incredible!" she said.

"Not really." Nora laughed. "I was rereading it last month, after I first saw this chimney piece."

John and Walter were last to leave. "They're a bit like Mrs. Cornelius and Mrs. Thornton, aren't they," John said solemnly, taking a final look at the carvings.

Walter made a noncommittal noise, like a man being magnanimous about *not* disagreeing.

On their way out of that section they passed a glass case displaying the anatomical carvings in ivory by James Gordon of Park Street, Bristol. Charity gave a little cry of recognition and called John over.

"When you and Mr. Thornton were in that place seeing that man, sir, while I was waiting in that cab outside, I got out for a stroll. And this very model was in one of the windows. And now here it is here!"

"What do you remember of it?" he asked.

She gave a shy little laugh and looked down. "I remember thinking, looking at *him*"—she nodded at the model—"thinking, 'I know how *you* feel, mister!' "

"And now? Do you feel that now?"

She looked up then, straight at him, with her warm turquoise eyes. "Not a bit of it, sir."

"I am glad." He gripped her arm lightly to reinforce his words, and steered her back toward the others.

The effect she had on him was most disturbing. He was either going to have to stay away entirely from her and Sarah, until this ridiculous feeling died of starvation, or grasp the nettle and see her whenever possible, until familiarity killed it. To be now, in middle age and the prime of his life, such a prisoner of his youthful reflexes was absurd.

At lunchtime a lady walked through the central area wearing bloomers. It caused almost as much sensation as the mysterious collapse of the curtain around the *Greek Slave*. Rodie once again used the word *barbare*.

"Surely," Walter said, "one of the least elegant female costumes in history."

Everyone agreed they were disgraceful, though Arabella privately applauded the fact that bloomers (being a sort of feminine version of a gentleman's inexpressibles) put a barrier between the world and the—the fleshy part of the thigh; they were from that point of view a more *moral* garment.

After lunch the ladies and the gentlemen made their separate ways around the Exhibition, which Nora had by now come to look on almost as a second home. Arabella and Sarah, helped from time to time by suggestions from Charity, made notes of the exhibits that would be most uplifting for the penitent girls to view.

Rodet, guided by John and Walter, spent the afternoon looking at what he had really come to see—the iron- and steel-working machinery: machines for grinding, milling, planing, boring, routing, forming, pressing, tempering, moulding, forging, extruding, edging, chasing, turning, rivetting, welding, sweating, cutting, blooming, drawing, rolling, figuring, lapping, sleeving, bending . . . it was all there, the skill and ingenuity of the world. And Rodet went through it exhaustively, putting one or two or (his equivalent of the grand medal of honour) *three* asterisks against the catalogue listings of the machines he considered the best. John, without referring to notes or catalogue, told him the characteristics of each machine they passed.

They all stayed until the Exhibition closed for the day, at half past seven, and then went back for supper at Maran Hill. As they drove off to the station in their small fleet of cabs, Rodet looked back at the Crystal Palace and nodded judiciously. "It's good," he said. "It's the best."

John looked out of the window, too, knowing he would not go back until the presentations and the closing dinners. Of all the judgements he had heard and read, he thought Rodet's would be hard to excel for its truth and brevity.

In the cab behind, Nora was telling Rodie and Nanette that the Exhibition would make a surplus of a quarter of a million pounds.

In the cab behind that, while Arabella and Sarah compared notes and came to their final conclusions, Walter sat happily back, his eyes closed, recalling a dimly lit but ever-to-be-treasured glimpse of an ample, inviting, supple, youthful female marble bottom.

The Great Exhibition had fulfilled all its promise: something for everyone.

Chapter 59

When Nora awoke at Thorpe Old Manor, that first morning of their visit, she knew, even before she opened her eyes, that John had left their bed. She got up and went over to the window, pulling on her dressing gown as she went; a glance through his dressing room door showed that he had dressed, for his nightshirt lay discarded on the floor. She felt on top of the world. Last night they had made the most miraculous love and she always felt a hundred and ninety-nine per cent next day; but it was unusual for John to rise so early after that. She was puzzled.

She saw him at once, standing among the already fading roses, lost in thought. He was hatless. She knew, despite his apparent concentration, that he was not looking at the flowers—not even at the one he was shredding, petal by petal . . . she loves me . . . she loves me not . . . she loves me. . . .

The sun was stealing up over the old defensive wall, shortening its shadow on the grass, gilding him from the shoulders up. He had developed a bald patch! How seldom she saw the top of his head.

He plucked the last petal and let it drop. He looked blankly at the remnant of the rose in his hand.

She flung wide the casement, making him look up. "Well? Does she or doesn't she?" she called softly.

He grinned. "Come down and tell me," he said.

"Is it warm?"

"I'll make sure of it."

She left the window open and, slipping on her canvas shoes, tripped lightly down the stair, surprising one of the maids at her dusting. When she reached the garden he was nowhere to be seen.

But there was only one possible hiding place—the old watchtower —unless he had run around to the stables. With all the time in the world she stooped to collect the petals he had scattered. When she straightened again she saw him on the very top of the tower, his back to her, looking out over Painslack Dikes and the southern wold.

A thin skein of peach-coloured cirrhus spanned the heavens in a long, broken streak from north to south; there was no other cloud and the sky was already deep azure. She ran up the steps to join him. For a while they stood, side by side, not touching, not looking at each other. It was warm up there in the sun.

The trees and the golden corn, motionless and heavy in the quiet air, said it was summer still. But that very fullness of the woods and fields, their silence, and the nighttime chill that clung about the stones, spoke of a season on the turn; it looked ahead to the autumn and the days drawing in. A sense of loss was there.

"What will we do when there's no Exhibition?" she joked.

He laughed silently, the air whistling in his nostrils. "You always get the *questions* right," he said.

She began dropping the rose petals, one by one, into the field below, watching them shimmer as they spun and turned in the sunlight.

Beside her he drew a deep breath. "We must never sell this place," he said. "We must keep our roots up here. We must keep coming back."

"What about sending Winifred to the Mount School, in York?"

"Aye," he said. "We must be thinking of the boys' schooling, too. Perhaps Uppingham, or Marlborough. Brassey spoke highly of them both."

Nora smiled at a memory. "They're so different," she said. "Young John and Caspar. When I went to say good night to them last night . . ." She paused. "Perhaps they've heard us talking about 'glory' contracts and 'bread-and-butter' contracts. Anyway, Caspar said to me, out of the blue, 'Mama. I think money is preferable by far to fame.' Just like that! And Young John"—she began to laugh—"turned over in disgust and said 'You would!' They are so different."

"Perhaps they *should* go to different schools." He watched a kestrel wheeling and turning over the cornfield. "How easily we decide for *them*," he added.

She was silent, knowing well enough what he meant.

"What did you reply to Caspar?" he asked.

"I said we must try to have both."

"You sometimes get the answers right, too, then."

"Is it the right answer?"

The last rose petal fell. He watched it all the way and then asked: "Does he?"

"I always cheat," she said. "I always say, he loves me . . . he loves me more . . . he loves me . . . he loves me more. . . ."

He turned to her then and took her in his arms "You're not far wrong," he said. He tried to kiss her but she just brushed the tip of his nose with her lips and pushed him off. He had got very good at steering away from subjects lately.

He turned again to the iron railing and the view. A thrush pecked at three of the petals and flew away, disappointed.

"Money and glory," he said. "We never really settled that."

"We never settle anything. How can we? Things keep changing." She spoke without heat. He shook his head, smiling, but said nothing. "What do you want?" she pressed, still speaking as if this were the most abstract of philosophical discussions. "Send for the three musketeers?"

He looked at her, puzzled.

"They'd settle it." She grinned, challenging him. "A flash of the sword. A dashing smile. A few clever words. A lot of clever words. Pages of clever words . . . oh, they'd settle it." She looked away and a hint of bitterness crept into her voice. "Settle like dust. And the first breath of life would puff it right out the door. Life's no romancer."

She looked up to see him staring down at her in astonishment. "That's not news to you," she continued to challenge.

But he ignored it. "How odd. How strange. To live as close to some-one as I've lived to you for twelve years before realizing such a . . ."

"What?"

"You revel in it. You love disorder. You don't want to change it."

She thought before she answered. "I suppose so. But it's a funny thing to say. It's just a fact of life. Of real life. I don't *revel* in the fact that the sky's above us and the earth's below. I just accept it. Although now . . . at this moment . . ." She looked, as a hawk would look, across the cornfields, down into the shadows of the valley, then far out over the awakening world. "Aye. Ye could say I revelled in it now."

"You see, I think we've a purpose here. We're put on this earth to change it."

"That?" She spread her hand over the view.

"We've already done it there. That was all forest once. But I mean everywhere. Everything. I cannot accept disorder as you seem to be able to. I don't want to revel in it. I don't want to use it to my own advantage. I want to change it. And I want the change to benefit everyone."

She was about to reply when he added, "Perhaps it's just as well I shall be easing myself out of the business. Properly this time. A man who can't accept all the to-ing and fro-ing of circumstance—perhaps he shouldn't . . ." He fell into thought.

She said nothing.

"The Exhibition . . . ," he said, and fell back into silence. She waited, watching him intently. "How it opened my eyes!" He hit the rail with his clenched fist as he spoke. "I've been *blind.*" There was a desperation in him. His eyes scanned the landscape as if he feared he would never find the words he needed.

At last he turned to her. "I've decided what to do." He gave a short laugh, almost a snort. "I decided at the opening ceremony back in May. Then I've used one excuse after another to delay."

"Why?" she risked asking.

"Because . . . it fills me with . . . panic." And when she did not prompt him further, he added, "The sheer size of the task!"

Her silence seemed to embolden him. "There's so much to be done. For us. *By* us, I mean. We can't escape it. Whole continents to pacify. And civilize. And cultivate. We must." He grew calmer as he spoke; his voice became almost a monotone. "From the very beginning of civilization men have dreamed of a world of plenty. A world without want, where poverty is a bad memory. And now, for the first time *ever*, thousands of people—not just me—but tens of thousands, hundreds of thousands, have seen that it is at last possible! It is in sight. Perhaps not in our lifetime, but in the children's. A century from now, if we do right, this whole world could be one civilization, one *single* civilization. Think of that, Nora love: a brotherhood of man, where there is no want, no war, no bloodshed, no strife. A world of peace and plenty. And *we* have seen its dawn. This year."

"No rich and no poor?" she said.

"No poor. There must always be the rich—to inspire and encourage the rest, to pay for invention, found schools and libraries—to lead taste. You know."

"Is it possible?" she asked. "Really? D'you think?"

"I have thought about it all summer. With the machines we have now, and with the ones we can already imagine, and with the improvements that will certainly follow, even though we cannot guess what they may be—with all that, and with a world so rich and bounteous, whose surface we have barely scratched, whose wealth we cannot even begin to comprehend—how can it *not* happen! It must. It is inevitable. Only human ignorance and folly and greed can prevent it."

"And *you* mean to help this come about?"

"Not me," he said. "England. That, too, is the lesson of this summer." The monotone relented; his voice became more joyful. "Without really wanting to, England seems to have taken upon herself the mantle of the foremost among the civilized nations of the world. We have given that world a lead this summer. We must not stop now, and slip back into the old ways—petty nations under petty crown princes fighting petty causes for petty gains. The world is looking to us for a lead. We must not be too fearful to respond. We have laid the foundations of a great empire. On them we can raise one that will shine ten times more glorious still. And that empire, in its turn, will be the foundation of the brotherhood of all the world. When others see the wealth and the happiness that begins to flow wherever Pax Britannica reigns, they will surely flock to join. And if they are prevented, by corrupt rulers or ignorance, we must conquer them and teach them. We dare not shirk our task. What England has is too precious now to let her fainthearts squander."

She looked at him and was overwhelmed with a protective love. The sheer size of his vision made him seem both isolated and vulnerable. There were a thousand questions to be asked, but they stuck somewhere short of her throat: practical, awkward questions that stressed his vulnerability.

The fear of it silenced her. But there was also a new, impossible hope. Here was the John she had known years ago. The night they first met. He had fired her spirit and bound her to him for life with just such a vision as this. If he could now recapture all that zest!

"I must make it happen," he said.

He looked anxiously at her, wary . . . for what? Her scorn? Disbelief?

The gesture hurt—doubly, for it was so unintentional. She smiled, trying to tell him she shared his unquestioning faith in that bright vision.

He smiled too. "I must play my part, anyway."

She hugged him, convincing herself that disunity was now behind them. "Both of us must," she said. "Nothing has ever been able to withstand us when we've been united."

She trembled, so fiercely did she cling.

He, thinking she was cold, said, "Come back inside now."

Going down the steps she sniffed her fingers, hoping to find a trace of him. Nothing was there—only the lingering smell of the rose he had taken apart and she had scattered.

Historical Postscript

When the first book in this sequence (*The World From Rough Stones*) appeared, a number of teachers wrote to me saying they would like to use it as parallel reading or enrichment reading in their history classes; but they wanted assurance on the accuracy of the historical references in the story. It occurred to me then that quite a large number of readers might be interested, and even gratified, to learn how much true history there is in these stories.

To be sure, all the historical accuracy in the world has no *literary* value. If the book does not breathe with its own inner life, the historical facts would lie like dung upon the desert sand, fouling what they cannot make fertile. So these notes are a mere afterthought to what I hope was your enjoyment. By no means are they offered in a sense of justification.

All prices quoted are accurate, whether it's the price per mile of a railway line, the price of lodgings in Rhyll, the price of a seat on the French *diligence*, the price of a whore in Bristol, or of dollars and pounds against all the other currencies mentioned.

All the railway lines mentioned in the text were sanctioned or built or opened when the text says they were—right down to the actual day if a day is given. (Of course, John Stevenson, as a railway contractor, is a composite of men like Thomas Brassey, Henry Moreton Peto, and Tom Jackson, who actually built most of the lines mentioned.)

All the engineering and technological details in the text are accurate (and you may thank my editors that they were not finally given at even greater length!). This refers not only to gossip of the day—such as how Nasmyth's steam hammer first came to be built by Schneider in France—but also to the more enduring achievements, such as the numerically controlled (to use current terms) punching machine on page 251 and the hydraulic pistons that raised the Britannia Bridge.

The railway mania and the consequent commercial crisis are accurately followed, though only those parts that were especially germane to the Stevenson's business are dwelt upon. I had to resist quite strongly the temptation to point up the astonishing parallels between that crisis and the oil crisis of our own times. Both begin when one sector of the economy tries to grab a historically disproportionate share of the available cash... and in both cases the resulting depression in trade rebounds on the sector that did the grabbing. But these are points for the teacher rather than the novelist to pursue.

Similarly, the details of banking, the stock market, and the general management of business are true to the period.

Everything I write about the Great Exhibition is also factual, from the politicking that preceded its inception to the pomp that attended its opening. Every exhibit I mentioned really was there. However, the skulduggery between Fox & Henderson (the actual builders of the Crystal Palace) and Stevenson's is invented—although Fox & Henderson's bid really was £79,800.

Now for some specifics that can't be classified under such general heads. I take them in the order in which they appear in the book.

Mrs. Jordan's superstitions are all genuine Yorkshire (East Riding) beliefs of the mid-nineteenth century.

The firms in which Beador is supposed to have invested all existed, and all went bankrupt in 1846.

The Stevenson's income-tax return is typical of its time.

Nora and Sam's tour of Normandy and Mont St. Michel is based on a similar trip made by John Ruskin and his wife in 1847.

"Great Missen'em Day" really was like that.

Panshanger House was pulled down by a gravel company in 1956—so Nora's threat was not as idle as she might have believed.

"Maran Hill" (under another name) survives.

The artisans' houses designed by Livings are almost identical to similar dwellings commissioned by Prince Albert and exhibited at the 1851 Exhibition.

The Irish evictions witnessed by John actually took place on March 13, 1846, in the village of Ballinglass, County Galway, involving the three hundred tenants of a Mrs. Gerrard. All the other public events described as happening in Ireland are authentic.

Nora's supposed caesarian section under general anesthesia: On September 30, 1846, William Morton, a dentist practising in Boston, Massachusetts, first used sulphuric ether as an "anaesthesiant" upon a patient. On December 21, Professor Liston (the one in the text) used it on a patient in London. On January 19, 1847, Sir James Young Simpson used it in his midwifery practice. (In November he switched to chloroform.) So Nora's operation would have been the pioneer operation by a mere three weeks.

John's evidence to the Select Committee is a précis of the evidence of a number of railway contractors. All the members named actually sat on the committee.

George Hudson, too, is a historical character—"The Railway King" of the 1840's. His rise and fall, and the strong element of fraud involved, suited my purpose so well that I could incorporate the whole of it without violating history. His former mansion, Albert Gate, is still the French Embassy in London (see page 404).

History is so rich it affords material for *any* writer's purpose; so it is no great art to have woven in so much. Yet I have to admit it is a double delight to me to find something that exactly suits my purpose and that really happened. I hope that delight is shared.

—*Malcolm Macdonald*

A Note on the Type

The text of this book was set on the Linotype in Garamond No. 3, a modern rendering of the type first cut by Claude Garamond (1510–1561). Garamond was a pupil of Geoffroy Tory and is believed to have based his letters on the Venetian models, although he introduced a number of important differences, and it is to him we owe the letter which we know as old-style. He gave to his letters a certain elegance and a feeling of movement that won for their creator an immediate reputation and the patronage of Francis I of France.

Composed, printed and bound by
The Book Press, Brattleboro, Vermont.
Designed by Gwen Townsend

An Agreement made on the eighteenth day of February, One thousand eight hundred and forty five Between John Stevenson of Dowgate in the City of London and George Hudson Cha[irman] of and acting on behalf of the York and North Midl[and] Railway of Railway Street, York, of the first part, a[nd] same George Hudson Chairman of and ac[ting on] behalf of the Midland Railway Co. Derby, of t[he] part (hereinafter called "the Company") Where[as] Memorandum of Agreement made on the twenty[...] of August One thousand eight hundred and forty[...] between or on behalf of the parties hereto it was agreed that[...] the first part should purchase from the Company deben[tures of the] description therein mentioned together with all property and ri[ghts] conferred for the nominal sum of Six thousand pounds ste[rling]

Dated th[...]
thousand e[...]

Att[...]

John St[...]
to
Nora Ste[...]

En route to Syston
May 8, 184[...]
Dear Flynn:— I write this from my coach. I wi[sh you] to read carefully the inclosed statement relative to the accident that happened to Wilkins. For my pa[rt] I believe it quite immaterial whether the bar of iron was thrown down or fell down by accident, so far as it may affect our liability to compensate Wilkin. If the[...] caused the damage, and it fell from our scaffold on the public highway, I take the view we are liable; and I should recommend the best settlement to be made that can be without the fuss of lawyers. Still you, after reading the statements I have inclos[ed,] let me have your opinion of the matter, or, if yo[u] concur, settle the affair yourself if you can, with[out] farther reference to me.
The fellow sounds plausible to me, but as an hon[est?] yourself you'll make the better Judge!
I am, my dear Sir, yours very truly
John Stevenson
Mr Flynn

CARROLLTON BANK.
New-Orleans, October [...]
No. [...]
To Messrs [...]
Acting as Agents for the New-Orleans and Carrollton Rail-Road Company [...]
This is to Certify, That John Stevenson [...] the Proprietor of Forty [...] the Capital Stock of this Institution, upon which have [...] [...] Dollars on each Share; and [...]